The King Returns

The Brotherhood of the Black Arrow—BOOK 3

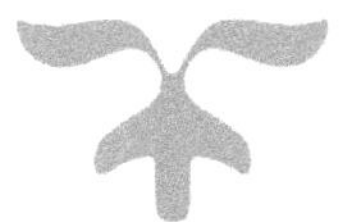

DR. W. PENN WHITE

Kevin G. White, Co-Author

Dr. W. Penn White

FV-8

ISBN: 979-89901221-2-3

For my Grandchildren

A room without books is like a body without a soul.

Marcus Tullius Cicero

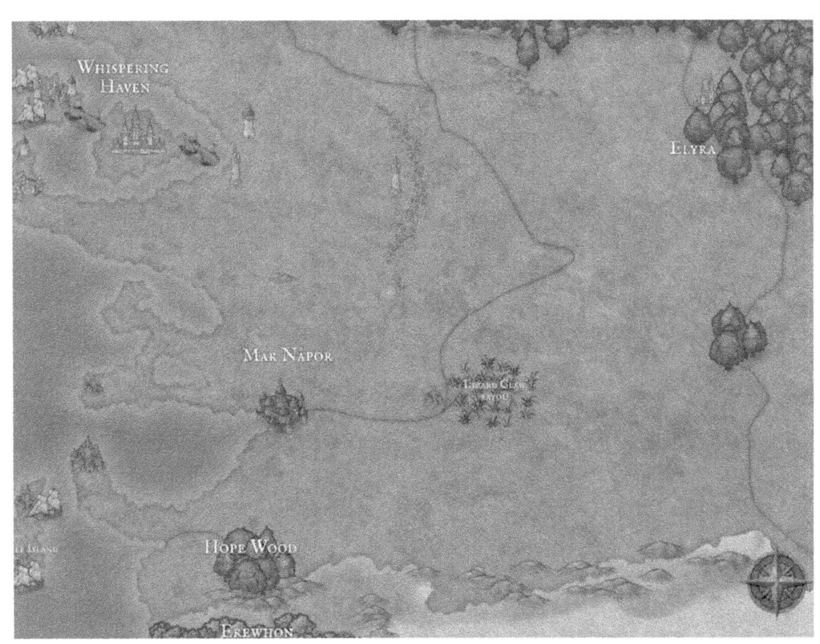

Mar Napor

Brown Dwarves
Plains of Tabor
Oyster Bay
Sacred Wool
City of Spires
Black Hills

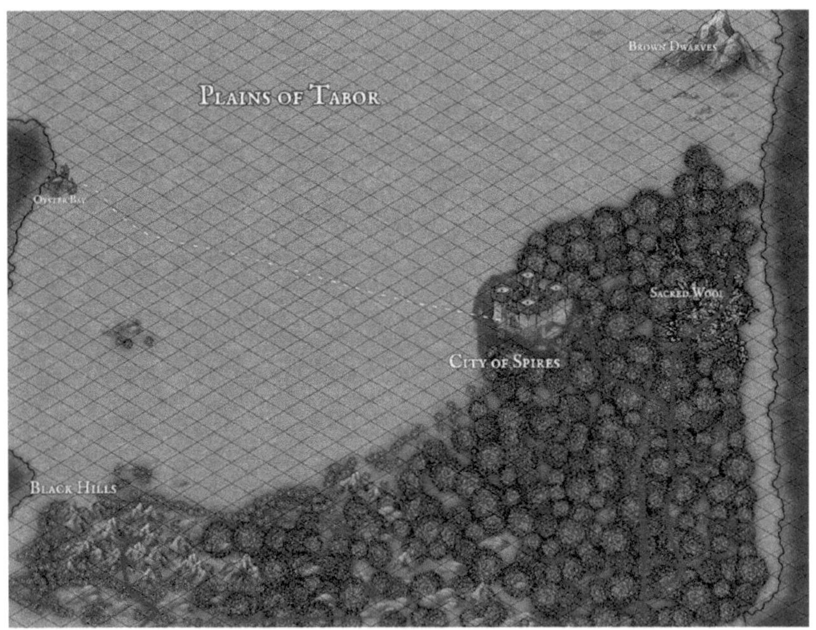

Tabor

Table of Contents

THE KING RETURNS

ONE

She would be a human sacrifice, and she couldn't stop it. The girl had lived her entire fourteen years in the village of Sawtooth on the edge of the Vermin Wood. She foolishly entered the forest in the late afternoon, searching for the many tasty mushrooms and wild berries that grew here. Focused on surprising her mother with her treasure of fresh truffles, the girl never noticed the impending gloom of evening twilight. She rushed home when she realized the late hour, knowing she faced a painful switch from her worried mother.

The dark figure emerged from behind the sycamore, catching her off guard. The girl was clumsy and needed dexterity and speed to evade the club. In the next second, white-hot pain and stars exploded behind her eyes, followed by darkness. Soon, the girl's eyes fluttered open, her wrists and ankles aching almost as much as her head. Where am I? Her head was fuzzy from the blow, leaving her disoriented. The girl tried to take a step but couldn't move, her hands and feet bound tight to each end of a tree trunk on the edge of a forest clearing. Her head lolled to each side, and panic seized her.

In the center of the small clearing was a circle of thirteen candle lanterns on poles, their glow just enough for the girl to make out a hooded figure next to each. In the center was a fire, dry sticks and limbs crackling under the flames and surrounded by a thick ring of salt. A female in a red velvet gown stood over the fire, arms raised, bellowing in an ancient tongue unknown to the child. The other figures chimed in, combining into a symphony of voices.

Sweat dotted the girl's forehead, and she felt the icy vine of terror grow inside, surrounding her heart. A witch's coven! The realization took her breath away, her eyes growing in fear. Mama said they were cannibals. The girl wanted to run, to be home in her loft bed, the straw and covers warm and cozy. She strained and pulled against her bonds; the rope cut into her wrist, and she knew - I'm never going home again. That's when the woman in the circle center materialized at her side; her heart skipped a beat, and she screamed.

The figure was no woman but a hideous monster with wart-marked green skin, a long, crooked nose, and a whiskered chin. Scraggly, unwashed green hair fell over her face, partially obscuring her dark, mismatched eyes, one lower and dragging to one side. The monster whispered through a mouth of sharpened predator's teeth.

"Don't fear, my pretty girl. Mother Crai is here," stroking her brown hair, her icy touch sending chilling goosebumps down the girl's spine. The monster's touch froze her heart, and fat tears spilled down her cheeks.

"Please, let me go. I want my Mama," the child begged.

"Now, my sweet thing, "the witch cooed in her ear, lightly caressing the girl's cheek. "I'll send you home soon. But first, you must honor us with a gift."

"A gift?" the girl whimpered through a flood of tears.

"Oh yes, a wonderful gift. Something essential, our sustenance for the future."

"I don't understand," she said. "Please send me home."

"Soon, my pet."

Crai gazed up as the full moon rose, a ghostly ship sailing on a sea of heavy clouds. The witching hour approached, signaling the completion of all her coven's work. A surge of excitement climbed up her belly as the minutes ticked away, her anticipation climaxing. She walked back to the circle, adding her voice to the chant, her arms raised, encouraging her fellow witches.

The girl hung her head, whimpered, and moaned, "Mother. Oh, Mother. Please help me."

She felt a powerful hand over her mouth and flinched.

A melodic voice whispered in her ear, "Quiet, child."

The girl stopped squirming as the coven chanted louder and louder. The girl felt her wrists release, and her arms fell.

"Now, run like a deer, don't look back, and never return to this wood. Your life depends on it," whispered the voice and the girl felt a shove toward a narrow game trail a few feet away. She felt the urge to look back and thank her rescuer, but survival instinct overcame it, and she gave a hesitant nod and sprinted down the path. Her dryad savior waited several heartbeats to ensure the child was gone, then melted into a massive sycamore nearby.

The chanting stopped, and Crai said, "Father of Darkness. I call forth your minion, the Soul Eater, leader of corpses. Come, oh great one, to lead your undead army under my command to destroy our enemy, Tabor."

The witches waited, but nothing happened. Smoke billowed from the fire after several heartbeats as if someone had added wet leaves. A cloud of black smoke covered the lantern circle, causing the witches to take a step back, choking. An audible burst echoed, revealing a clear view amidst the smoke.

An enormous gargoyle, the size of a bison, squatted on its haunches in the center of the circle. Gray, withered skin covered a muscular reptilian body, which phased in and out of the candlelight. Its head was a barren feline skull, a mouth full of long fangs below a lion-like snout. Two yellowed, crooked horns protruded from its forehead on each side above coal-red malicious eyes. Crai felt sick as she watched the mutant, who was radiating malice.

"You summoned Grine, witch?" The monster growled like scraping asphalt, eyeing Crai like she was his next meal.

But before Crai could answer, she felt a wave of frigid cold wash over her as a second tall figure stepped into the circle, followed by a large orange tabby cat.

The skeletal being, dressed in a black cassock and cloak, stepped beside the witch. Crai's eyes widened with alarm, her heart petrified by icy terror.

Lord Ravenite interrupted Crai's words with a slight flick of his wrist and choked her by tightening an invisible hand around her throat.

"Was I not clear with my command? I was to be present for the conjuring."

She heard a voice in her mind, but no one spoke. Crai wanted to respond but could only nod, the grip around her neck like a vise. "I'll deal with you later."

While the witch squirmed, the gargoyle chuckled but remained immobile. The tall figure removed his hood, revealing the decaying skull of the lich-mage Ravenite.

The monster's eyes narrowed. "What can Grine offer the undead wizard?"

"Your undead soldiers. I will need them in the coming assault against Tabor," Ravenite stated.

Grine ran a long pink tongue over his gleaming white fangs.

"And my reward for such aid?"

Anger sprouted in the lich-mage's gut. He controlled his emotions, knowing he must pay a demon once summoned.

"Feed on every soul you destroy. I will send word when needed across the ethereal plane."

The gargoyle nodded. "Your enemy is my enemy." Then, turning to Crai, growled, "Where is my summoning sacrifice, witch?"

The hold on the witch's neck dissolved, and she fell to her hands and knees, coughing. "Bound to the sapling. There," she rasped and pointed at the wood. All eyes turned to the forest, but the prisoner was gone, leaving only rope coiled at the sapling's base.

Crai's eyes widened, and she said, "She was just there."

Grine's eyes turned fire-red on the astonished witch. Ravenite shook his head and stepped out of the circle. "A pathetic excuse for a coven priestess."

"She must pay the price for her insubordination," said Cas, the tabby cat who had shape-changed to human form by his side.

"Meet your new sacrifice, Grine," the lich-mage called over his shoulder, then he and his black witch lover disappeared into the darkness.

"No, no, Ravenite!" A scream and a tearing noise interrupted the quiet night. The sub-witches ran away in fear.

Jacoby Ironfist sailed his sloop north on the Erewhon River. He docked near the bank where Cor'in, the half-elf Count of Oyster, got off and pulled the boat onto the sand.

"Let's stretch our legs," Jacoby called out to his fellow travelers, and each exited the boat; Allai'nn, princess of the Star Elf realm of Serensith Talem; her husband, a tall halfling named Grullach; Blue Ivy, Timber Elf prince of the Hart Wood; his fiancée, the dryad Rue; Micah, a Moor Elf merchant from the southern elf tribes; Horatio, an Andurian frogman; Nathaniel Aarmon, the heir to the Taborian throne; his girlfriend, Lani Beliel; and Jacoby, the man entrusted by the former queen of Tabor to raise her only son, Nathaniel. The comrades formed a tight bond and called themselves "Brotherhood of the Black Arrow" after fighting against black-blood orcs. Jacoby, Grull, Allai'nn, and Nathaniel had left their home in the quiet hamlet of Streamside months before after a giant had attempted to assassinate the young prince. They journeyed across the continent to escape Crepitus and Ravenite, evil wizards determined to overthrow Tabor, and restore Nathaniel as Tabor's king. The group faced constant life-threatening danger from the winds of war. Along the way, the other members had joined the group, sometimes for adventure and others out of desperation. Their many trials had forged individuals into a fierce brotherhood.

Grull and Allai'nn, with Rue's help, brought their four infants down and let them play on a blanket under the shade from a large Sweetgum. Three of the brood were orphaned elves, they had rescued and adopted, the other their newborn. A squirrel that passed by captivated the children. The squirrel inspected his home's safety, chittering and suspiciously wagging his tail.

Nathaniel pulled out the parchment map given to them by King Acorn of Erewhon and showed it to Jacoby. The king magnanimously offered them a place to stay while they healed from a wolf attack by some vicious lupine rangers. The group narrowly escaped and now had restarted their journey north toward Tabor.

Jacoby stretched his back, erasing the effects of hours hovering over the sloop's tiller as he looked over the map.

"From my guess, we're near where the river splits," said the young prince. "If we continue west, we'll pass under the Hope Wood bridge."

Nathaniel, who Jacoby had raised more as a brother than a ward, had become the de facto leader of their group, a position once held by the latter. Jacoby and Grullach had agreed Nathaniel needed to assert his leadership but remained close advisors. Just shy of his 18th birthday, the prince was still learning as a leader but already exhibited maturity beyond his years. As the only living heir to the throne of the Western power, Tabor, Nathaniel needed all the experience he could glean before accepting his role as future king.

Jacoby studied the map as Grull stepped up beside Nathaniel.

"I agree. We must be close to the split," Jacoby wondered aloud, "but which way is the fastest route to the citadel of Mar Napor?"

"If we take the right cut, we'll end up east of the city and have to travel near Lizard Claw Bayou," commented Grull.

"True, but will that be safer than transiting the Bay of Napor?" asked Nathaniel.

Grullach gave him a questioning look. "What's your worry, lad?"

Jacoby answered for him. "Lizard Claw is full of unsavory beasts and a suitable spot for an ambush. If those relentless lupine rangers are still tracking us, it could be an attack site. But the bay presents its worries."

"How so?"

"The bay is the rumored home of the sea demon, Gyre," Micah said. "Legend tells of a giant maelstrom that opens when the demon feeds. I've not sailed it myself, but few merchants have lived to speak of it."

"What's a maelstrom?" Grull asked.

"A vortex no ship can escape."

Now the entire group listened with rapt attention, worry reflected in their eyes. No one spoke for several heartbeats, fear thick as smoke.

"Old granny tales to scare children," said Cor'in, shattering the silence with a laugh. "Probably spread by the merchants of Mar Napor to intimidate their competition."

The group sighed and chuckled; the tension released like air escaping a balloon.

"Let's hope. King Acorn suggested that route but recommended we hug the coast to limit our exposure to storms or ruffians," said Jacoby.

"What about this forest here?" Grull said, pointing to a small wood on the map. "Wouldn't this also be a trap point?"

"The Hope Wood. Acorn suggested it was a land of benevolent forest spirits," reassured Jacoby.

Nathaniel gave a sidelong glance at the others. Benevolence was in the beholder's eye, meaning anything from supportive allies to neutral antagonists. He weighed the alternatives and decided.

"I think the safest path will be through the Hope Wood. From there, we travel to the Bay of Napor, then follow the coast to the city.
"

"Can the sloop handle the bay's currents?" asked Blue Ivy.

"She's a sturdy vessel. We should be safe if we stay close to shore."

The two elves walked along the forest path, a heavy canopy of Blackthorn and Ash blotting out the starlight from a thousand stars. The two strode purposefully, their Twilight vision allowing them a clear look ahead. After twenty minutes, the two reached the Spicula, a morass of thorn bushes, vines, and wild creepers six stories tall. Carved into the wall of vegetation was an ancient oval door. The elder of the two pounded thrice on the door, hesitated, and followed with a final thunderous knock, the noise echoing across the silent wood. They waited, but after a full minute, the elder elf, not known for his patience, reached to knock again. At that moment, the door latch clicked, the door squeaking open an inch. Vines and brambles blocked the door, so he pushed through with his shoulder.

Someone had carved out a small, empty anteroom from the thorn bushes, making it spacious enough to accommodate a spiral staircase. The two elves ascended round and round until they reached another wooden door. The younger elf took the lead this time, pulling a long dagger from his belt. The door face was absent of a handle, only a tiny slit in its center. He knocked again three quick times, slid the blade inside, and rotated it to the left until, hearing two clicks, he pushed open the door. He entered a dimly lit circular room with a shadowed, domed ceiling. One side held a bed, while a small table and a half-cut deer carcass hung on the back. A thousand flies buzzed noisily along its flesh. The room appeared empty, but the elder elf pretended not to notice this.

"I have a job, Crow."

A rustle came from the shadowed vault above, and a lean Svartalf lowered itself from the rafters.

"Job?"

"A needed disposal."

The younger elf studied the figure attentively. He was unlike any elf he'd encountered. The Svartalf's features were a mask of hideous scars covered in runic tattoos below slate-gray eyes that froze the soul. His scalp had a shaved look, except for the intricately braided mohawk decorated with blood-red beads, which made him look more terrifying. The figure wore only a loincloth, his muscles long bars of tempered steel under his coal-black skin. He fascinated and repulsed the younger elf as if witnessing a grotesque insect species for the first time.

Crow nodded and waited.

"King Gooseberry of Mar Napor, but it must look like the fools from Whispering Haven are responsible."

"Soon?"

The elder elf shrugged his head toward his younger companion. "Colonel Hundmeister will infiltrate the city with an elite force. A Death Raven will be the go sign."

Crow ran a long purple tongue over gleaming white teeth, sharpened like fangs. "It will be done, King Barnabus."

A booming knock echoed through the heavy wooden door. The hobgoblin major waited for several heartbeats, his back muscles tense with anticipation.

"Enter."

He pushed open the door and strode into the dark hall, lit only by rare sconces with torches on each wall. He paused near a table with a tall, bony figure wearing a black robe. The figure's bald head glinted in the torchlight. The lich-mage Ravenite, commander of the evil Western alliance, eyed the officer.

The hobgoblin held out a scroll. "A communication from General Ironback."

The monster handed a parchment to the lich, who read the message. It revealed spies had poisoned and killed Council leader Tyus in the City of Spires. His loss and the death of General Tusk last month have wreaked havoc on the council and army.

"Excellent!" the lich murmured to himself. He hunched over the table, hastily taking quill to paper and scribbled orders. He looked up at the hobgoblin.

"What is your name?"

"Vex, your lordship," stuttered the soldier, his voice cracking with fear. The lich-mage never asked for names unless punishment awaited. The powerful magician was erratic and temperamental, and he had seen guards eviscerated in the past for any slight, real or imagined. Vex closed his eyes, preparing for the worst. But to his surprise, nothing happened.

"Take this message to Ironback, personally. Your life depends on your success."

Vex swallowed the terror rising from his gut, saluted, and took the parchment. "Your will be done, master."

Nathaniel was the last of the group to re-board the sloop. He pushed the vessel off the sandy bank and climbed aboard, taking the tiller as Grullach and Micah unfurled the trapezoidal mainsail. A wind puff hit the canvas, and the boat surged along the wide river surface. Within another half hour, the ship came to a split in the river, the wider cut turning east while the other doglegged west. A change in the wind forced Nathaniel into a tack, slowing their pace, but he maneuvered the ship west. After the turn, the wind died, leaving the boat in irons.

"Reef the sail and pull out oars," he commanded the others. Jacoby and Cor'in slipped the oars into the locks and rowed the boat up the narrow cut while Grull and Micah tied the canvas to the mast.

"Looks like the terrain is changing," said Lani, gazing at the river bank. The endless plains and rare shrubs seen for days were changing. Increasing vegetation and evergreen trees dotted the land, with mountains on the horizon.

"I'm happy to see more forest. I can already feel the Mother's spirit increasing," said Blue Ivy. Like all elves, he had an innate connection with Mother Nature.

"Me too. Hopefully, I'll see some cousins along the way," added Rue.

"I hear the Mother's whisper already," added Allai'nn, smiling.

"In a few hours, we should reach the Hope Wood bridge. But be vigilant; we don't know the inhabitants," suggested Jacoby.

"Agreed," added Nathaniel.

Billowing clouds obscured the sun, cooling the temperature as they drifted north. The cedar aroma and the chirping of birds from the growing evergreens on both sides of the river delighted the elves. However, Nathaniel sensed neither the coolness nor heard the melody. He was lost in thought as he gazed blankly upriver from his position at the tiller. Their journey had taken the brotherhood across the continent's expanse, and now they were closer to Tabor than ever. Did the changing environment signal an omen? What does the next bend in the river hold for us? And what of Tabor? Will they welcome or attack me upon our return home? And with the war raging, what will be left of my ancestral home? I'm no leader of the state; I was merely a stable hand and tavern rat in Streamside just months ago. He shook his head, feeling increasingly uncertain about his future with every mile they traveled. But leaders bore their burdens like hidden, silent yokes, and so would he.

TWO

At the helm that evening, Micah felt the cool breeze as the river split into two separate streams. While drifting leisurely down the river, the boat resonated with the sounds of gentle water lapping against its sides as the brotherhood members and children slept. Hoping to stay awake on first watch, the Moor elf leaned back and felt the cool night air on his skin. Thoughts of an old flame, Ximah, flitted through his mind. As he closed his eyes, memories flooded back, taking him on a journey through time. They had arranged a clandestine meeting in the hay barn of his father's estate. He remembered lying in the soft straw, her body warm against his, the light fragrance of honeysuckle in her dark curls. They had kissed with the passion of youth, her lips as soft as rose petals and her skin smooth as a polished stone. For what seemed like an eternity, they laughed and spoke in hushed tones between kisses, making promises for a future together when he returned. But their fragile storybook affair gave way to her youthful impatience as the months passed while Micah traveled. Upon returning from his first trading expedition with a purse full of gold and thoughts of marriage, he discovered she had already become engaged to someone else. The pain in Micah's heart was so intense that he made a solemn promise never to return to his homeland again.

The sound of water rushing and waves crashing on the rocks suddenly jolted him from his reverie. With his twilight vision, he observed the rapids ahead, where the water clashed against a tall monolith of solid granite before dividing into two streams, one heading east and the other west. Several hundred yards ahead, an enormous roaring bear figure towered over the landscape at a height equivalent to twenty men. The massive beast posed an intimidating figure, the animal's open jaws directed toward the roaring river. Micah scrutinized the structure for an entire minute, attempting to discern whether it was a living creature, a robust rock formation, or even an illusion. As the boat drew near, he recognized the colossal beast as a massive sculpture, with the river current crashing against its gaping stone jaws and dividing on either side.

Frantically, Micah woke up Cor'in and Blue Ivy, instructing them to unfurl the sail. Despite their grumbling, the two warriors obeyed, and the Moor elf deftly guided the sloop past the looming stone bear's jaws, sailing it across the western cut. But the current had the sloop in full grasp, pushing the boat sideways, back toward the open bear's jaws, despite Micah's maneuvers.

"Pull the oars and row on the starboard beam! Hurry!"

Cor'in and Blue strained against the oars, their muscles burning as they fought against the relentless current of the river. The boat seemed paralyzed by the current for a long moment, the two elves unable to push the craft forward. Then, a heartbeat later, the sloop broke free, escaping the killer stone jaws by only yards and catapulting forward with a jolt across the western cut.

The three elves, panting heavily, slumped against the oars, grateful to have escaped another dangerous situation.

"By the gods, that was close!" sputtered Blue Ivy, wiping sweat from his eyes.

"Never a worry," lied Cor'in.

"I'm thankful that you two didn't wake up the entire group, babies included," Micah said with a grin. The two oarsmen shared a light chuckle between them.

"Thanks for the help, but I think we're safe now," Micah added.

"Are you sure you don't need us to stay up to hold your hand? You struggle with navigation," Cor'in said, feigning sympathy.

"I'd rather sacrifice myself to the river god." Micah laughed.

"I will gladly return to my bed, then," remarked Blue, suddenly exhausted and yawning.

"Me too. I was dreaming of a saucy wench I met back in Tajman Sghur," added Cor'in, rubbing his hands excitedly.

"You mean the one who slapped your face?" asked Micah, his face serious.

"Such a comedian. You might find jester work in the court at Mar Napor." Cor'in said, jabbing back.

"Sleep well, Count Red-cheeks!"

With a playful eye roll, Cor'in quietly made his way to his bed in the hold.

The next day, Nathaniel assumed control of the helm, steering the boat into a wide channel that resembled a bay, sparkling with golden sunlight. With the rising temperature, the humidity in the air thickened, clinging to his skin like a warm embrace. Dark clouds loomed on the horizon as a storm sped toward the sloop. Dark clouds streaked across the sky as the wind picked up, bringing heavy rain. As lightning flashed, and the deafening rumble of thunder made it feel like a cacophony of giants roaring all at once. With no cover, the sloop pushed through the building whitecaps and rising swells, each wave crashing against the hull. The sudden gust of wind made the boat sway dangerously, causing Jacoby and Grullach to shift their weight to maintain stability. Inside the hold, Sinbad attempted to calm the distraught children, their terrified cries filling the air. The noise only grated on Nathaniel's nerves as he fought to control his mounting worry the boat might capsize. As six-foot waves pounded against the sloop, he struggled to maintain control of the vessel. All the while, rain poured down in sheets, stinging his face and marring his view.

A sudden wind gust almost capsized the small craft, causing Nathaniel to scramble to right the tiller to keep the boat stable. The wind's force intensified, causing Jacoby and Grullach to lean further out over the hull in an attempt to stabilize the boat's heel angle. To avoid capsizing, Jacoby, who was in charge of the mainsheet, swiftly released the rope, decreasing the drag. As the wind force abruptly weakened, gravity brought the boat's hull back to level with a resounding bang. A crashing wave of spray and rain drenched the two sailors, causing the boat to lurch and nearly throwing Grull overboard. Jacoby's arm shot out and caught the halfling's tunic just in time to prevent him from plunging into the water. In the hold, the other warriors, women and children were crouched together, their voices rising in fervent prayers to the weather goddess, Freyr, for deliverance. Half an hour passed in terror before the wind eased, the waves stilled, and blue skies emerged from behind the storm clouds.

As the sky opened and the rain cleared, Nathaniel found the sloop had crossed the expanse to where the river narrowed and turned north. He maneuvered the craft down the channel and checked on the others.

"Everyone all right?" He called out.

"Soaked, knocked around a bit, but ok," answered Allai'nn, doing her best to calm the infants.

"That was quite a squall," said Horatio, ringing out his tunic.

"When that gust hit, I thought we were flipping," observed Lani.

"You and me both. The waves almost sent me swimming," added Grulloch. "Lucky for me, you have a long reach, Jacoby."

Jacoby chuckled. "Thank Nathaniel. We both might have gone over if he hadn't steered across the next wave."

"I'm just glad it's over. If this is a taste of the Napor Bay, I vote for walking," remarked Rue.

"The bay can be much worse from the sailor's tales," said Micah sagely. "But a far cry better than the evil of the Lizard Claw Swamp. I've heard tales about that devil's den that would curl your beard."

"You and your tales," Cor'in taunted. "Your merchant friends seem to see danger and monsters under every stone."

"Ah, the stories I could tell! Frightening accounts that would send chills down the spines of the bravest," Micah responded.

With an exaggerated gesture, Cor'in rolled his eyes and shook his head.

"Well, let's hope staying close to shore brings safety," Nathaniel interjected, steering the conversation back to the point.

Then, a moment later, Nathaniel rubbed his eyes in disbelief, unsure if what he saw might be an illusion. "What the? Do you see what I see?"

Everyone turned toward the bow, and Rue let out an audible gasp. The terrain on both sides of the river had become more forested, filled with enormous oaks, sycamores, maples, fir, and spruce. Ahead, two massive sculptures stood - one of a unicorn and the other of a stag with antlers. Each statue was several hundred feet tall, the morning rays swallowing them in a supernatural golden glow. A net of crisscrossed ropes blocked the way upriver, stretching from the hoofs of the two figures to below the river surface. Several boats were resting on the eastern riverbank at a small inlet with a sandy beach.

No one spoke for several awe-filed moments.

"I can't believe...," started Cor'in, but he couldn't finish.

"Is that Friend?" blurted Jacoby, his eyes as wide as plates.

"Friend? Who's Friend?" Asked Horatio in a whisper, his eyes fixed in a stare.

"Couldn't be," suggested Blue, but his face told another story.

"By the gods, lad, shore off," called out Grull in alarm as the sloop sailed closer and closer to the net. "We're not going through that."

"Right," murmured Nat, waking from his stupor and turning the boat into the wind, the ship slowing to a stop. "We need a new plan."

"We could land and walk like Rue suggested earlier," quipped Cor'in.

No one laughed, and Nat gave the half-elf a stern look.

"That's great advice. Thanks, Rue." Nat said, his iron gaze lingering on Cor'in another heartbeat. "I suggest we double back and land on the western bank. Maybe there's a trail to the coast where we can pick up another boat."

"Perhaps. I wonder if our best bet is to beach with the other boats," pondered Blue Ivy, a hand over his eyes, gazing at the eastern beach. "I can see a path and sign entering the wood."

"And walk to Mar Nâpor? I was teasing Rue," grunted Cor'in irritably.

"Got a better idea?" Shot back, Blue Ivy.

"I have one," suggested Horatio. "I take a swim to see how deep the net extends. Maybe we can cut through the blockage."

Cor'in rolled his eyes, but Jacoby stepped in. "Good idea, Horatio. That's the first step. Maybe the net is more illusion than obstruction."

Horatio beamed, rapidly removed his tunic, and plunged into the river. After several minutes, the frogman surfaced. Grull and Jacoby pulled him aboard.

"Sorry, folks. The net extends down fifty feet or more. And the ropes are as thick as saplings. It would take weeks to cut through."

"Thanks for trying," said Micah.

"So, what's next? Catch an eagle and fly over it?" said Cor'in grumpily.

Nathaniel ignored the half-elf. "I think we sail downriver and look for a landing spot on the western bank."

"Agreed," said Grull. "It's our closest path to the coast."

The others nodded, except Cor'in and Blue, who crossed their arms, pouting.

Nat took control of the tiller, maneuvering the sloop out of the irons. A light breeze blew from the north, forcing Nat to jibe back and forth across the river's surface. To his chagrin, the mighty river current battled against them, causing no appreciable progress after an hour.

"What now?" Asked Horatio.

"I guess we go to Plan B," suggested Jacoby.

Nat's fists clenched in frustration and announced, "We have no choice but to land on the far side beach. Your advice was spot on, Blue."

The Timber elf smiled and gave a slight nod of acceptance.

The young prince set the boat's vector for the sandy riverbank and, within minutes, had run the sloop onto the soft soil.

The flickering firelight cast shadows on the furry Captain Cinsor and Notch, who sat on opposite sides of the fire. The second watch was already well underway, and the sound of snoring lupine filled the forest. Lost in thought, Cinsor gazed down at his deer flank meal, the smell of fresh blood filling his nostrils.

Notch cleared his throat.

"Sir, what will be the plan moving forward? Do the new orders.... modify our intent?" the Staill mantel wolfman expressed with a careful tone. He knew all too well about his captain's explosive temper and unpredictable behavior. Despite his heroic act of saving Cinsor from a snake-man's venomous bite during a recent battle, his superior's mood continued to be unstable.

"Our intent?" Cinsor growled. He found the order that arrived earlier that evening, delivered by a hawk courier, astonishing.

"Break the hunt and swiftly return to the pack den—Bloodcoat."

The orders from his alpha pack leader were unmistakable. But did Bloodcoat realize how close they were to finding and eradicating the prince of Tabor once and for all?

His squad had fought through months of adversity on their hunt for Nathaniel Aarmon. Despite harsh weather, they tracked him and his group through tundra, mountains, jungle, and desert. Two times, the wolves almost succeeded in seizing the prince in their jaws, but fate had other plans. His platoon dwindled by more than half as they fought through obstacles and battles, but he continued to persevere. Recently, Notch came to his rescue just in time, saving him from the deadly bite of a venomous snake-man. Just as he was on the verge of catching the elusive human, he received a sudden recall. He struggled to understand the rationale behind it. *Why would Pack Leader Bloodcoat recall us on the cusp of catching the elusive human?* Cinsor shook his head, his gray fur swaying with the movement. *Some questions have no answers.*

However, one thing was sure: Pack Leader Bloodcoat did not tolerate failure. And if he disobeyed orders? At best, he faced exile from all lupine packs, shunned by friends and colleagues alike. Alone and friendless, he would face battling to join another pack or die alone. At worst, public execution for himself and his entire family, wife and cubs included. *How in the demons did my journey end here? I can't even blame Notch for our failure, not after what he did to heal me.* Despair flooded his senses like a never-ending storm. He saw no viable path forward. Anxiety bolted through his system at the thought, followed by a wave of nausea crashing over him. Cinsor closed his eyes, willing himself not to vomit.

"Sir?" Broke in Notch, still waiting.

Bile tore at Cinsor's stomach, but he mustered a brave face. "We have orders."

"Orders?"

"The one just received and read aloud," Cinsor growled, confused by the question.

"I wish to keep hunting, sir."

"Are you mad? Bloodcoat's order is crystal clear," he barked incredulously.

Notch had fought at Cinsor's side for years before this mission and knew the wolf's blood lust for success. He predicted how his boss would react to obeying orders, but he also acknowledged the shame that not completing the mission would bring to his community. The lean lupine stroked his chin fur, weighing the two, and took the gamble.

"May I speak freely, Commander?" the Staill Mantel said gently, unsure if Cinsor would listen, or attack and tear him limb from limb.

Cinsor took a deep breath and nodded.

"Perhaps," Notch hesitated a heartbeat before continuing. "The orders found us after we had slain the prey. The others are sleeping, and I witnessed no courier."

Cinsor was speechless. *Are my ears deceiving me?* Notch's insubordination sparked a fiery rage in him, causing his blood to boil with the urge to attack the smaller wolf. Then he realized the opportunity, and the anger drained away like a leaking bucket. *Notch is saving me again! The fool puts his neck out to pull my honor from the fire.*

Cinsor took his time contemplating the offer as Notch anxiously waited, his breath held. He felt a primal instinct urging him to seize the Taborian prince and end him, but he was mindful of the severe repercussions of any error. Failure meant paying dearly, and that included Notch and his unsuspecting troops. He recalled the words of a wise teacher from his past.

"Act and live or die with nothing," the teacher had said, emphasizing the importance of making deliberate, calculated choices.

He grinned, his large canines glistening in the moonlight. "What order?"

After preparing the packs and crafting a carrier for the infants, Nathaniel confidently led the group into the dim, foreboding forest. The decision made his gut twist in knots, but they felt like they had no other option. Despite Grull's reassurance, the discontent with the decision was palpable among everyone except Allai'nn, Rue, and Blue Ivy. The forest trail was a challenging puzzle to navigate, with few markers and unexpected stones and roots lurking on the path. The dense canopy overhead blocked out most of the sunlight, leaving Nathaniel, Jacoby, and Lani struggling to navigate the dimly lit track. They kept tripping and stumbling as they walked. A mountain range bordered the forest, adding to the already thick humidity in the air. While the three humans became increasingly irritable, the elves and Horatio delighted in chatting about the splendor of the wood. As they traveled a half-mile, the trail gradually ascended into switchbacks, leading them up the side of the first peak.

Taking a break for water, Nathaniel could feel the sweat running down his back and chest. Without warning, Rue gasped and dashed towards a sturdy maple tree off the trail.

"Tuar Lenir," she called over her shoulder.

"What?" Asked Nathaniel and Jacoby, looking at each other, confused.

Allai'nn and Blue rushed after her, fighting through the brush to follow the dryad.

Micah's jaw dropped, amazed. "I think they found a sigil."

"A what," asked Grull.

"A sign, silly. Come see," called out Allai'nn.

Nathaniel and the others struggled through brambles to where the others stood smiling. The three were speaking in rapid Elven. All he saw was some irregularity in the bark just below a branch.

"What are you seeing that I don't?" asked the prince irritably, assuming this was more Oread nonsense in praise of another tree. "We need to press on."

"I don't understand either," added Jacoby.

Allai'nn calmly smiled. "Remember when we were in the Serensith Talem forest? I found a signet tree made by my brethren, marking a magical path only elves see?"

Nathaniel thought back. Months ago, early in their adventure, they had traveled to Allai'nn's Sky Elf homeland. They had struggled to find their path through the wood until she found what she called "The Way of the Elves" marked by subtle tree changes pointing the way. She then said that non-elves, whom she called "Dynol", could not see the path.

"I remember. A path for the non-Dynol."

"The paths are rare and require magic to create and hide from outsiders. I'm amazed Rue saw it," said Blue Ivy, placing an admiring arm on his fiancée.

"So, you're saying there's an elven presence here?" asked Grull, still confused.

"Not only elves, but powerful magic. I can sense ancient First-Age spell craft," answered Allai'nn.

"Whoever made this must have close ties with the Mother. I'm sure they will help us," Rue grinned.

Nathaniel gave Jacoby a sidelong glance. The big man nodded subtly. The younger man smiled.

"Lead on Rue."

The brotherhood trudged through the forest following Rue, Blue Ivy, and Allai'nn's lead. The three humans and Grullach walked in the middle of the pack, carrying the infant basket, with Horatio, Micah, and Cor'in behind. We'd never be able to find our way alone, thought Nathaniel. But at least we have a destination now. He had to admit, the further along the sigil trail, the lighter his heart, joy at finding help and potentially a safe refuge sprouting in his heart. They had traveled several miles, ascending over hills and through dells, the copse thick with more giant trees the farther they progressed. The group finally arrived at a massive granite outcropping, stretching hundreds of feet high and just as broad. A wide stream bubbled over painted rust, green, and gray stones at its base, further blocking their path. Rue stopped, unsure where to go next. It appeared as if a giant had placed massive boulders on their path.

"I don't understand. The signet trees pointed this way," she said to Allai'nn, perplexed.

"Maybe we missed a sign," offered Cor'in.

"Are you doubting Rue?" Blue Ivy said, putting a supportive arm around Rue.

"That's not what I said. But your oread led us here," Cor'in sneered.

"How dare you insult Rue!" snarled Blue, his face red with anger, and he stepped toward the half-elf. Nathaniel stepped forward, blocking his path.

"Calm down, Blue," Nathaniel said sternly. "I don't think he meant anything. But we are at an impasse, so we need a plan."

"Perhaps we can go around?" Micah said, intervening.

"Looks like the boulders go on for miles, mate," declared Horatio. The group was silent for a heartbeat.

"I think we should split up and search for more signet trees," Jacoby suggested.

"Excellent idea. Blue and Rue follow the creek west, and Allai'nn and Horatio go east. The rest of us will search the nearby forest for another path," ordered Nathaniel.

"A solid plan," added Grullach.

After the group members separated, Nathaniel leaned down to fill his water skin, dipping a cloth in the cool water to wash the sweat from his face and neck. Out of the corner of his eye, he saw movement. He gazed downstream but saw nothing irregular. Moving on a hunch, he said, "I'm going to look around."

Jacoby observed his brother, who had removed his boots to cool his feet in the stream. Something had piqued his curiosity.

"What is it?"

"Not sure yet."

"Wait for me." The big man replaced his wool socks and boots, then followed him. He found Nathaniel studying a large green boulder covered in cattails and duckweed, a pool of slack water behind.

"What do you see?"

"Shh," Nathaniel whispered, a finger over his mouth, his eyes narrowed. He pointed at the slack water pool.

After several minutes of silence, a line of bubbles stirred the calm surface, and a head popped above the surface. Oily brown fur covered an oval face, overshadowed by black-rimmed spectacles above a broad mouth with bucked rectangular teeth. Before the beast had even breathed, Nathaniel leaped, dagger out. "Got you!" he screamed.

The beaver froze, his eyes growing like saucers under his thick lens'. Just before Nathaniel landed and drove the dagger home, the beaver cried in a sandpaper voice, "NO, MY PRINCE!"

Both men were stunned, Nathaniel enough to slide his dagger over, missing the beast by a hair before landing total weight on the animal. The water splashed with tremendous force. Then Nathaniel rose in knee-high water, holding the beaver in his arm like a furry brown ball, unconscious. He gingerly waded to Jacoby, who slipped off the beaver's spectacles, now severely bent from the crash, and laid the animal on its back. The beast was alive but unmoving. Jacoby rubbed the small animal's chest with his knuckle. The pain sprung the beaver's eyes open, and he cried in the common tongue, "Ouch, that hurts! What if I bit your finger, you beast?"

Jacoby looked at Nathaniel and broke out laughing.

"Sorry," he murmured between laughs.

"You should be!" said the beaver irritably, rubbing his chest with one paw.

"I'm sorry, too. I've never met a talking animal," said Nathaniel, putting out a hand to make peace. The beaver took a hand in his claw and bowed. "An understandable mistake, my prince."

"What's your name?" asked Nathaniel, sitting beside the now upright animal on the creek bank.

"Augustus, your Grace. The Father sent me to welcome you."

Cor'in, Micah, and Grull had heard the commotion and came running. Augustus' terror-filled eyes grew and leaned back into Nathaniel's belly. "Help! Interlopers!"

"Don't be afraid of that lot, Augustus. Their friends." The beaver relaxed, but kept his eyes on Cor'in.

"Let me introduce some of our group. Cor'in, Count of Oyster, Micah of the Moor elves, Grullach Furr, and you met my heavy-handed brother Jacoby."

"Welcome friends of Prince Nathaniel to the Hope Wood," said the beaver, bowing. None of the three responded, their jaws open, unable to take in the revelation.

Just then, Nathaniel heard leaves rustle, and Allai'nn, Horatio, Blue, and Rue broke through the brush.

"More friends?" Asked Augustus, replacing his bent spectacles on his snout.

Nathaniel smiled. "Yes. Augustus of Hope Wood, let me present Lady Allai'nn of Serensith Talem, Blue Ivy of the Hart Wood, Rue, Oread of Tajman Sghur, and Horatio of Anduria."

Augustus' eyes widened with each name, and he bowed again. "The pleasure is mine. Shall we go? The Father awaits."

"The Father?" Allai'nn asked.

"The Father of the Hope Wood, most ancient and wisest of all the animals," Augustus sniggered, rolling his eyes as if the answer was common knowledge.

Augustus turned to slip into the creek, but Nathaniel stopped him. "Wait, is there another entrance? We have infants in tow."

The beaver stopped in his tracks. "Infants?"

"Yes, four Elven children."

"I apologize, your Grace. Follow me." Augustus shuffled over to a part of the granite wall, smooth stone in an almost round configuration. The beaver began speaking in a language none understood, and after several phrases, runes of white light appeared emblazoned in the stone. Augustus waddled forward and placed his paws on the first and last runes. A snapping sound echoed, followed by a dust cloud as a circular door materialized in the stone and screeched open.

"This way, your lordship."

THREE

Augustus waddled beside Nathaniel along the dark corridor within the granite outcrop, chatting as they strolled.

"That was a magical entrance. Did the Father create it or someone else?" Nathaniel asked, holding a torch in one hand. He noticed a few albino insects, centipedes, and tiny spiders crawling over the walls, never having seen sunlight.

"The magic has been here for centuries, some say from the dawn of time. It's a defense against an outside world glad to harvest and extract our forest resources."   "Resources?"

"Yes, the thick trees you noticed growing close to the brook are rare Ironwood trees. They are nourished by the magical waters of the stream."

"I've never heard the name."

Few have, my lord. They only grow in and near magical forests. Few also know their power, but that's a topic for the Father."

Nathaniel decided to change the subject. "So, tell me, what animals and elves live in the Hope Wood?"

"There are a variety of animals and several elven species. We live in peace and protect our home and each other."

"Fascinating. What elven species?"

"Nyads, Oreads, Pixies, Brownies, and other Fae."

"Do all the animals speak?" asked Jacoby, cutting in.

"Yes. It is a gift from the Father." The answer confused Jacoby, but they reached another stone door before he could ask more. Again, the little beaver chanted in an unknown language, and runes appeared in the stone. Augustus placed his paws over the third and eighth rune this time and shoved hard. The door did not move or open, but a blue light appeared in its center. The beaver repeatedly rotated his arm in a circle, the blue spot increasing in size and diameter with every rotation. After several cycles, it grew to a shimmering blue disc, vibrating as if imbued with lightning.

Augustus could see the young prince was confused, and he sensed apprehension.

"Not to worry, my lord. This portal will take you into our land."

Nathaniel didn't move. Jacoby stepped up and said, "I'll go first. He stepped into the portal, more liquid than solid, his body disappearing under the surface of the blue pool. Seconds later, he stepped back through, smiling.

"It's safe and...remarkable," he said, scratching his head. "The sensation is like falling, but through water, so prepare."

Nathaniel nodded and stepped through the disc. It was as if he had fallen through liquid sky. He felt like he had walked through a wet cloud, dropping like a stone, the wind blowing his hair, a chill ran up his spine, and he gasped for air. Then his foot hit solid ground, and he stood on the other side of the massive granite wall, his clothes damp. There was an audible pop, and Jacoby stepped through, followed by the others.

Nathaniel rubbed his eyes, wondering if he had hit his head during the passage. Before him were miles of open land, but not the usual meadows or tundra, this field had light blue grass with scattered black, purple, and orange flowers. The sky was a crystal clear green but for the occasional yellow cloud. He shook his head again, but the colors remained.

"Are you seeing what I'm seeing?" he asked Jacoby.

"If you mean red grass, purple sky, and orange clouds, then yes."

Nathaniel chuckled, "You're pulling my leg. I see other colors; all are quite bizarre."

"Truly, but I wasn't kidding. I think the magic here plays with your mind."

Nathaniel raised an eyebrow. Jacoby was serious, confirming that this land oozed robust and unpredictable magic.

"Wait here," Augustus said and slipped into a flowing river that bisected the field, its waters as pink as cotton candy. Several minutes went by, and the group marveled at the meadow. The grass was dotted with wildflowers of every color of the rainbow, bordered by massive trees the width of four men. Hundreds of animals were across the plain: deer, elk, rabbits, beaver, mink, otter, bear, goats, badgers, and panthers, playing games together, others watching or reading books. Birds of every variety and color sang from the trees, and red and green butterflies flitted from flower to flower.

There was a sudden pop, and Augustus appeared, standing beside an enormous Lamassu. The animal was over forty hands at the shoulder, three times Jacoby's height, with a large head sprouting from a muscular feline body covered in brown fur spotted with gray. Two folded raptor wings of silver, asymmetric pennaceous feathers protruded at the shoulder. The beast's face was circled by a mane of red fur sticking dramatically in all directions; his eyes were a shocking sliver of the sky, bright beacons above a straight nose, and a long graying beard braided into two strands. The beast's unique appearance was so unusual that Allai'nn and Rue gasped, but the Lamassu seemed unperturbed.

The beast never moved or spoke, but Nathaniel could hear a deep baritone voice in his mind. "Welcome, Nathaniel Aarmon, heir to the throne of my homeland, Tabor. Most know me as Father, but you may call me Epsilon."

In turn, the Lamassu welcomed the others in the group and was returned with bows or curtseys.

Then Nathaniel spoke, "Thank you for welcoming us, Epsilon. It is an honor to be in a land of such unique...magic."

Epsilon chuckled. "The colors of our land reflect the individual. The more goodness in your heart, the more vibrant the colors. I find it both enjoyable, and revealing, for our visitors. No one can trick the Mother here. Most minds will correct in time, but the lucky few remain in a world of brightness."

"I hope I'm one of them."

Epsilon said nothing, but Nathaniel hoped he was smiling.

"I would enjoy giving you a tour later. But you must be tired from your journey. Augustus will escort you to your rooms, and I will see you again at dinner."

Before Nathaniel could respond, another pop sounded, and Epsilon disappeared, leaving only the beaver.

"Beings certainly move quickly here," said Rue excitedly, vocalizing what all were thinking. "Is it tied to the magic here?"

"Teleportation within and between sacred forests is an ancient, but little-known, magical asset," Augustus said, wondering how this fact escaped Rue's oread teaching. "Now, if there are no more questions..."

But Allai'nn cut him off, her face red with fury. "I have a question. Who do you think you are addressing, my friend, like some ignorant peasant? This young woman is the daughter of Byrgid the Oread and Gruawane the Healer!"

The beaver's mouth dropped open, and his face crumpled like a used tissue.

"I'm so sorry, Lady Rue and Lady Allai'nn. I apologize for my... dismissiveness," Augustus stuttered.

"I expect more understanding of outside guests, common or royal. Must I speak to the Father about such behavior?"

Augustus's eyes grew to saucers, and he visibly shook. "No, please. This is my first welcoming assignment, and I'm nervous. I meant no harm, my lady." Tears welled in his eyes, his face imploring.

The beaver's look was so pitiful that Allai'nn's anger melted away. Before she could speak, Rue knelt by the animal and placed a loving hand on his shoulder.

"Don't fret, Augustus. No offense taken."

"Thank you, my lady," the beaver choked out, wiping away his tears with a small handkerchief from his pocket.

He took a deep breath, collecting himself, and said, "Please follow me to your lodgings."

The beaver turned and shuffled off toward the center of the glen, where a large copse of trees grew, an island of thriving orange foliage in a sea of blue grass. Augustus stood at the base of an enormous maple and spoke in low tones, his arms wide.

A loud "creak" of splitting wood emitted as the trunk separated, leaving an entrance with open risers climbing into the dark recesses of the tree. Torched sconces on each side magically erupted as he entered and ascended the smooth wooden steps. The group reached the second level landing, which opened into a long hallway. Nathaniel noticed wooden doors of various sizes on each side, ranging from knee-high to giant size.

"Does everyone live in this, um...palace," asked Nathaniel.

"No, not here, sir. This is the visitor's wing."

"You must get a variety of visitors," suggested Grull, noticing the array of doorways.

"Some animals visit from other sacred woods or an occasional royal like yourselves."

They passed a large dining hall, a kitchen, and various storerooms and finally reached a circular wooden door. The beaver twisted a silver handle, and the door eased free, revealing an enormous suite of rooms, twelve in all.

"Everyone has their rooms and bath, which should be hot and waiting. Adjacent to your room, Lady Allai'nn is a nursery with several infant attendants and a wet nurse. The evening meal will be in the banquet hall. If you need anything, think about it, and someone will come." The animal gave a slight bow and waddled out without another word.

After the door closed, Cor'in said, "Did he say "think it?"

"That's what I heard," agreed Horatio.

"What an amazing place. I could get used to life here," said Horatio, sitting on a cushioned high-backed chair.

Nathaniel noticed Allai'nn and Rue whispering by a large picture window overlooking the meadow.

"What are you two conspiring about," he asked, walking beside them.

"I was just thanking Allai'nn and remarking on what a unique forest we've entered.

"I've never felt such strong magic, even in Serensith Talem," murmured Allai'nn.

"And I've never felt so close to the Mother as I do here. These trees must be centuries old, dating back to the First Age," added Rue.

"Can you tell if it's good magic?" Asked Nathaniel, uneasy at how Epsilon seemed to know the brotherhood's history.

"Powerful," whispered Allai'nn. "Magic is neither good nor bad, Nat. Its origin and how it's used is what matters."

"And from where is this magic?"

"If Rue is correct, only one source is that ancient. The Wellspring of Asgard."

He hesitated; the name was strangely familiar but lost in his memory. Where had he read that name? Then the revelation struck him, and his jaw dropped. He had read of the wellspring in a tome from the Meadowland library. According to legend, the Wellspring of Asgard was created by Odin when he, with his two brothers, slew the giant Ymir to make the world. Ymir's blood spilled in such a torrent that all the rivers and seas came from it. But Ymir's heart, though drained, continued to pump, and Odin used it to create an endless spring of magic. Odin gifted each race to drink from the spring, imbuing all future generations with some form of magic, especially strong in the Fae races.

Legend stated that only humans refused the gift, believing their race could thrive on their abilities, separate from the Gods. Odin pitied the foolish humans and, in his compassion, gave them an added dose of courage for what they lacked in wisdom.

Nathaniel had often wondered if the legend was valid and why the first human had rebuffed such a gift.

He shook his head and said, "I hope you're right. Even I can sense the pulse of such a sacred place." Before returning to the others, he added, "And thank you, Rue, for your kind understanding of Augustus. Born in such a powerful place, it might be easy to feel pretentious."

He cleared his throat, quieting the others. "Let's get to those baths and explore this wonderful forest!"

The Staill Mantel lupine ranger padded silently along the timberland floor, stopping to sniff in all directions every few hundred yards. A growing unease stirred in his gut with every step, the source unknown. Notch had traveled through many forests in Curth Talem during his years in the military, some old and some newer, filled with evergreens in the north and broadleaf deciduous hardwoods in the south. Rarely had he ever felt a stirring inside, a faint glimmer of his true wolf ancestry brought on by his surroundings. But this forest was different, and it scared him.

Once, as a cub, he had wandered off from the den chasing rabbits. Foolishly, he had lost track of time or his location during the hunt and realized he was lost when night fell. It was the dead of winter, and the temperature dropped like a stone after dark to near freezing. He wandered, shivering and lonely, howling for help, his winter fur no match for the extreme cold. Finally, exhausted, hoarse, and freezing, he curled up in the root nook of a mighty Ash, closed his eyes, and prepared for the end.

He awoke, sometime deep into the night, his eyes heavy from sleep, snow falling heavily through the trees. Strangely, he felt warm, as if tucked in with his brothers and sisters in his home den. That's when he saw the beast. Standing only feet away was the oddest animal he'd ever seen. He blinked once, then twice, clearing the snowflakes from his eyes. An enormous horse knelt before him, coat white as the falling snow, glowing garnet-blue eyes, and a single horn spiraling from his forehead. Panic rocketed through the cub, terror pulled his ears back, and his hackle fur rose. Then, slowly, as if melting under a blazing fire, his emotions waned, and a calm peace swept over him. Notch realized his fear had vanished and his chill with it. He remembered his skin prickling with magical energy from the beast's aura, enveloping him in restful tranquility.

The horse never moved, but Notch could hear his words in his mind.

"You are safe, Notch. No harm from weather or beast will come to you tonight, little one. Rest now."

His mind grew dreamy, his eyelids heavy, and he was fast asleep moments later. The following day, the weather had cleared, the sun bright and warm. Not long after, one of the pack had found him and guided him back to his den. His alpha father had punished him severely, but somehow, Notch had felt renewed after that night, as if providence had marked him. Knowing how weak it would appear among his wolf brethren, he never spoke of the encounter and had not thought of it in years.

But suddenly, the same serenity he felt as a cub washed over him, increasing with every step into this forest like waves lapping on a beach. The lupine padded through the thicket until reaching a bustling stream bordering a stone buttress blocking his path. He sniffed in all directions but no longer held the human prince's or his friends' scent. Confused, he doubled back the way he came, losing the glow of peace he had felt with every step. Perhaps it was all just a dream, he thought.

Captain Ironhook and his second-in-command, Captain Razor, stepped into the bustling inn; raucous laughter, minstrel music, and the aroma of vomit mixed with stale grog filled the air. Both men wore hooded cloaks to mask their identity, and few noticed when they strolled calmly to the poorly lit back of the tavern, sliding into the last open booth. Along the way, Ironhook had made an imperceptible nod to the heavy-set innkeeper, Torrence. He acknowledged with a wink, and once seated, two foaming meads appeared on their table, and Torrence slid in next to Razor.

"Hello, Captains. Good to see you."

Ironhook gazed across the table at the middle-aged tavern owner, his large balding head covered in beads of sweat from slinging grog and mead to almost every sailor in port; a sleeved tunic under a stained apron hung over his ample belly.

"Looks like every sailor in Clambake is in here," said Ironhook.

"It's the minstrel, Orin. Sings like a nightingale but gets a little handsy with the waitresses after a grog or three, if you understand."

Ironhook nodded. He knew this was one of the few taverns along the western coast that supported minstrels, although most were sorry lushes with a crow's voice. Torrence wisely paid most in lodging, food, and alcohol, leaving a minority he paid in coin. The added crowds more than paid the cost, filling the innkeeper's coffers with profits. Ironhook mused that's why the two got on well, both cunning and driven by greed.

"What news, Torrence?"

"Big changes, Captain. Chief Council member Tyus was poisoned last week, leaving the city leaderless. With the loss of General Tusk in battle, the army is reeling as well."

"What of the Taborian navy?"

"Every man between sixteen and sixty has been conscripted for duty in the army to hold off the northern horde. No navy for Tabor."

"Then who are these patrons?" Ironhook said, waving his arm to cover the room.

"Merchant sailors, dock workers, and those hiding from service."

"Interesting."

"There's more," Torrence said, grabbing a mug of grog from a passing waitress and taking a long draught.

Ironhook patiently waited, running over the news in his mind. The war may have finally broken Tabor, meaning famine and refugees heading south. But that was not his concern. The coastal cities would be undefended and ripe for looting now that every able-bodied man would be sent east to defend the city of spires.

"Well?"

Torrence wiped his mouth with his sleeve and leaned in close. The tavern owner's rancid breath made Ironhook nauseous, but he swallowed the impulse.

"They're rumors from Mar Napor. They are building up their defenses, preparing for when Tabor topples."

"As I expected."

"But the fear ain't just from Tabor. Rumor there's another force coming from the south, more deadly than the Horde."

"Rumors?"

Torrence shrugged. "It's an odd story. A sailor friend, usually reliable when sober, spoke of a ragged wanderer who stumbled into one of the southern coastal taverns, hysterical and begging for food."

"And?"

"The poor chap died soon after but rambled about monsters and dark magic."

"What kind of monsters?" Razor asked skeptically, narrowing his eyes at the bartender.

"Svartalfs."

The pirates were silent for several heartbeats, then began laughing. "You almost had me, Torrence! Svartalfs!" Snorted Ironhook. "Monsters created by graying women to scare children."

"Maybe."

"You can't seriously believe the delusion of a dying man?"

Torrence looked serious. "It's a whale of a tale to swallow, for sure, Captain. But I've served the man here for years, and he's mostly truthful. He swore he held the dying man for his final breaths and believed him."

"And where did this dying wanderer come from?"

"That's the thing, Captain. My friend says he wore an Alfheim uniform."

"He was an elf?" Blurted out Ironhook incredulously.

"True. True. Them elve's land borders the Stygian Wilds, you know. Ain't that the ancestral home of the Svartalf devils?"

The pirates stopped laughing. Ironhook stroked his chin and took on a more serious tone.

"Good information to have. Let me know if you hear more." The pirate spilled ten gold sentochniks onto the table. "For your trouble."

"Always available, Captain." The stout barman scooped up the coins, and they disappeared in his apron pocket. He slid out of the booth, bowed, and said, "Enjoy your drinks, Gents. I'm needed at the bar."

The two pirates were silent for a full minute. Then Razor, in the deep voice of a half-goblin, said, "Thoughts?"

"Tabor's dying. It would take King Aarmon, raised from the dead, to rally their forces."

"A nice opportunity to pillage every coastal town."

"Strike while the iron is hot?"

Razor nodded. "And the other?"

Ironhook felt an uneasy knot forming in his gut. He closed his eyes and remembered his only exposure to the dark elves. As a much younger leader of three smaller sloops, he had stumbled upon a dark schooner off the coast of the Stygian Wilds. The ship appeared ripe for the taking, his greed blinding him to the waiting trap. Preparing to attack the vessel, his ships were unexpectedly boarded and overrun by bloodthirsty dark elves. Although his pirates outnumbered the monsters 2:1, the demon elves fought maniacally, slaughtering anyone who moved. He had learned a harsh lesson that day: escaping with a single ship, a handful of sailors, and his life. He never entered the waters off the Stygian Wilds again in the years since, constantly circumventing the area during his pirating forays south. Thank the Gods, he'd heard nothing of the Svartalfs until now.

"Probably a drunken sailor's fantasy," he murmured, looking away from the half-goblin.

"Ignore it, then?"

Ironhook tapped his index finger over his lips, mentally weighing the risks, doing his best to control the fear rising in his gut.

Razor eyed his superior closely, detecting a hint of deflection he'd rarely seen in his mentor. He narrowed his gaze, wondering what was behind the mask. Disbelief? Concern? Or was it fear?

Ironhook released a heavy breath.

"There could be a grain of truth," he said calmly. "Send a ship south to scout the Alfheim coast, but be discrete. Maybe we'll learn something."

Horatio tiptoed in stocking feet out of the suite, holding his boots in one hand, doing his best not to wake the others. The brotherhood members were sleeping, finally succumbing to the rigors of constant travel over the last weeks. He opened the door enough to slip into the hallway, replaced his boots, and headed toward the stairs. Once outside the giant Ash, he found the pink sun waning, the afternoon rays shining over yellow grass between lavender clouds. The meadow was empty, so he strolled among the many flowering plants and trees until he came to the river. A sturdy wooden bridge arched over bubbling translucent green water. He walked to the zenith of the wooden planks and peered down at the churning water below. The water danced over multicolored stones while orange, red, and blue trout lazily meandered in the shallows.

"What a beautiful and unique place!" He said to himself as he crossed the bridge to the opposite lea. He hadn't gone far when he heard a woman's angelic voice lilting from near the wood. He walked over to where the river snaked by, a thin rivulet branching and entering the forest. He followed the bank for a hundred yards, where the water culminated in a lilied pond abutting a small log cabin. Horatio snuck silently to the pond edge, peering between emerald-green bullrush fronds dancing in the light breeze, searching for the melody's source. A female satyr sang sweetly while sweeping the home's front porch, her twig-tied broom whisking dust clouds to each side with every stroke. She was dressed in a simple summer dress of swirling yellows, greens, and reds held fast by a broad dark-brown leather belt, contrasting oddly with her light blue fur and hoofs. Two dainty horns circled backward over long, pointed ears bordering a round, freckled face; her skin was creamy-white below ice-blue eyes and hip-length auburn hair. Like her voice, her graceful, almost sensual, movement was stunning, melting Horatio to jelly. She was the most desirable creature he'd ever seen, and he had to meet her.

"Hello." He called out, stepping from behind the screen of bulrushes. "That's a beautiful tune."

The noise made the satyr jump, dropping her broom and crying, "Oh, My!"

"I'm so sorry."

She twisted, taking in the frogman, her eyes fierce. "Are you trying to scare me to death? And who are you anyway?"

"I said I was sorry."

"You didn't answer my question," glaring over folded arms.

"I told you; I didn't mean to scare you," holding his hands up defensively.

"I'm Horatio, from Anuria. I'm visiting with my friends. Who are you?"

"I heard visitors had entered the meadow but never expected such an intrusion," ignoring his question. Her eyes narrowed. "What in the Gods are you?"

Horatio's face flushed scarlet. "I'm an Aurian," he mumbled, looking away.

"Speak up."

"A frogman."

"A what?"

"A FROGMAN," he half-shouted, louder than he intended.

The satyr giggled. "I heard you the first time. I'm just teasing you. My form of payback." She smiled at him, leaning her broom against the wall. "Would you like to come in, Horatio?"

The frogman's eyes sparkled. She knows my name and wants my company!

"That sounds wonderful."

"Ruby." She said, sticking out her hand. Horatio smiled and shook, impressed by her firm grip. She waved him inside the house and strode to the kitchen. The house was small but quaint, with one large room sectioned into a living space, a root cupboard and counter, and a straw bed in one corner. Two wooden chairs opposed a river stone fireplace. A fire crackled in the hearth, the warmth mixing with the aroma of lavender and rosemary drying on wall hooks.

"Sit."

"Thanks," Horatio murmured, sliding into one chair, she in the other.

"So, what ails you, frogman?"

"Huh?"

"Tummy ache? Cold or cough? What hurts? I can help." Ruby pulled her chair closer and began poking and prodding the Anuran.

Horatio stared at the satyr, her forehead bunched in concentration. Had he mistakenly entered the home of a witch? Or had she lost her senses? He tensed, brushing away her hands. "Are you mad? Stop poking me!"

"Mad?" She said, raising an eyebrow. "You are sick, aren't you?"

"Huh?"

"I'm the wood's healer."

"You misunderstand. I heard your singing while walking. I'm quite well, thank you."

Ruby fell back into her chair, convulsed in laughter. Horatio waited silently, perplexed.

The fawn wiped her eyes and grew serious. "Are all Anurian's wound so tight?"

"What?"

She shook her head. "I watched you sneak into the yard and guessed you might be visiting, but I couldn't resist pulling your leg a little."

Horatio was speechless.

"I apologize, Horatio. Can we start again over hot tea?"

Horatio relaxed and smiled. "Yes, but no more jokes."

"Promise."

Ruby filled her kettle with water and herbs, slid the mixture over the crane hook, and rotated it over the fire.

"So, Horatio from Anuria, what brings you to the Hope Wood?"

When Jacoby exited his room from his refreshing nap, he found Horatio alone, gazing out the picture window and admiring the forest beyond.

"Hey. Good nap?"

"I didn't nap."

Jacoby tilted his head quizzically.

Horatio turned to him, his chest inflated and his head high, excitement etched over his face. "I met someone."

Jacoby had never seen the frogman so giddy. "Good for you."

"She's special."

"Yes?"

"Full of a joyful energy and fun-loving humor. She sings like a nightingale and is as beautiful as the morning sun."

"Mmm."

"But her eyes...her eyes are like glacial ice, penetrating yet captivating at once. I couldn't stop gazing into those lovely eyes."

"I think you got it bad, brother."

"Got what?" Asked Horatio innocently.

"The sickness."

"Did I tell you she was a healer?"

"Maybe she can cure what ails you."

"I don't feel sick. I feel...energized. Like I could climb ten mountains!"

Jacoby chuckled and slapped Horatio on the back. "I meant lovesick."

The frogman smiled broadly, his face infusing with vermillion.

Jacoby returned the smile, overjoyed to see the sparkle in his friend's eye. "May you never be cured of your disease, my friend."

Captain Cinsor loped across the forest floor and slid to a halt at the feet of other lupine rangers. Corporal Notch and the other three warriors came to attention.

"Well?"

"I found an opening, sir," Notch said, sweeping his arm toward a narrow corner of the gray-white stone, the one area within ten miles where the magical brook ran under rather than around the base.

Cinsor gazed at the corner of the wall and immediately knew Notch spoke the truth. It was the only access to unprotected granite for miles. He grinned, his pink tongue running over his dripping fangs in delight.

He threw his paws up and said, "Climb! Climb!"

FOUR

The setting sun, a blazing ball of fire, hung precariously above the jagged peaks, its warmth radiating across the landscape. The animals had placed two rows of tables in the meadow's center, forming a horseshoe pattern with enough settings for the entire forest's population. Nathaniel and the other Brotherhood, dressed in fine silk robes left in their rooms, followed Augustus as he led them to the main table of honor. Nathaniel sat to Epislon's left, Allai'nn to his right, the air thick with anticipation. They seated Jacoby at the end of the table next to Horatio, who couldn't take his eyes off the satyr at another table. She returned his gaze with a mischievous grin. Jacoby became frustrated at his insignificant seat, his envy growing as he watched Nathaniel and Allai'nn engage in a fascinating conversation with the legendary Lamassu. He suppressed the rising emotion and took a deep breath, using the moment to study the forest for the first time, its unusual creatures, and its rich tapestry of life. Talking animals of every size and shape, from slithering snakes to towering moose, crammed around the tables to his right, their voices a cacophony of chatter. He watched in amazement as a deer and panther, normally fierce rivals, shared a lighthearted moment, their laughter blending together like music. A tortoise, his top hat perched jauntily on his head, chuckled as he exchanged witty banter with a badger sporting a bright pink bowtie, while a lavender porcupine, its quills dusted with a delicate purple hue, erupted in laughter at a joke told by a yellow lynx with piercing maroon eyes. The smell of sweet berries and the aroma of earth hung in the air as fae, pixies, sprites, brownies, oreads, and leprechauns chatted and munched to his left, creating a festive atmosphere. Lutes and horns filled the air with a lively melody as satyrs and centaurs, their hooves tapping to the beat, gathered around a gowned otter, who sang with a voice as smooth as honey.

Jacoby took in the scene, the vibrant colors and sweet scents of the surroundings filling him with a deep sense of appreciation. The gentle breeze rustling through the leaves and the scent of wildflowers made for a truly pleasant bucolic evening. Leinsaplings, animated young trees, brought dishes of hot vegetables and fresh fruit to the event, their roots shuffling across the grass. The aroma was mouth-watering, and Jacoby's stomach grumbled in anticipation.

A lively melody filled the air as the wine flowed freely, the entire forest reveling in the feast. After everyone finished their meal, a deafening roar erupted from Epsilon, the sound silencing the group.

"I wish to welcome Prince Nathaniel and his friends to Hope Wood. May he fulfill his destiny during his quest to return to Tabor." He raised his goblet. "To our guests."

The crowd roared with cheers, their hands clapping in unison, then raised their glasses and drank to the toast. Epsilon's words left Jacoby uneasy, a knot of anxiety tightening in his stomach. He glanced at Grullach, and their eyebrows raised in unison, mirroring the same silent question. What did Epsilon mean by "fulfill his destiny?" Did his destiny include regaining the Taborian crown? Or did his future lie elsewhere? He felt both irritated and confused by the Lamassu's statement. Maybe I'm being overly sensitive. Jacoby hated riddles, especially coming from ancient magical beings.

A guttural howl, sharp and primal, cut through the laughter and music of the meadow, silencing the revelers. All eyes, fixated on the granite peak, searched for the source of the sound, finally settling on an enormous Lupine ranger standing tall at the summit. As the sun sank behind the beast, its fiery light painted the wolf's silhouette in a menacing red-orange hue, casting long, ominous shadows across the landscape. The tension was so thick you could cut it with a knife; no one dared move a muscle, their breaths held tight, until four more wolf men scrambled onto the rocks. Then, a bloodcurdling scream ripped through the forest, a deer's cry of terror, and the gathering erupted into panicked chaos. The forest floor thrummed with the panicked rush of animals and fae, each creature scrambling for safety from the approaching threat. While everyone else panicked, the Brotherhood and Epsilon stood unflinching, their composure a stark contrast to the pandemonium.

The panic was palpable as Cinsor barked his orders to attack. At that moment, the thunderous sound of the Lamassu's paws hitting the ground reverberated through the meadow, magic spreading like a carpet over the lea. Every creature, from the smallest vole to the largest deer, froze in place. Epsilon watched as the lupines leaped down the rocky cliff, only to be repelled by an invisible force field, bouncing back to the ridge top. Each lupine attacked persistently, but the invisible force field repulsed them. Finally, Cinsor ordered his warriors to scamper along the wall in both directions to test and find an opening in the magical barrier.

Nathaniel unsheathed his sword, the metal singing as it slid out of its scabbard, and cried, "Epsilon, how can we help? Each brotherhood member was on high alert, their swords drawn and held tight, their eyes scanning the surroundings. As the warriors prepared for battle, Epsilon stepped forward, eyes closed, his hand outstretched towards the stone escarpment. The meadow vibrated, the earth trembling beneath his feet, as a deafening thunderous boom echoed through the air, like a giant's war hammer pounding relentlessly. A wave of vibrations caused by the increasing tempo swept through the meadow, making everyone and everything unsteady. Then, the shock wave struck the granite wall with an explosive crash, rocking the escarpment like a wet dog shaking his coat. The vibrations blasted the wolves off the wall, falling hundreds of feet to the forest floor.

The lamassu dropped his paws, his massive head slumping with the weight of exhaustion.

"It is done," he whispered, a faint smile playing on his lips.

The ground rumbled and cracked, sending Nathaniel sprawling, but he quickly got to his feet and placed an arm of support on the massive beast.

"Epsilon," he said, his voice thick with gratitude, "Thank you for saving us. We owe you our lives."

Epsilon lifted his head, beads of sweat clinging to his brow like tiny diamonds, and several drops trickled down his mane, leaving damp trails. A tired voice, like a whisper on the wind, drifted into Nathaniel's mind. "The evil is gone, my prince," he announced, his eyes sparkling with triumph. "But there are more dangers ahead. The wood's magic is ancient and powerful, but not impenetrable. It cannot hold off future assaults so easily."

"To protect everyone, we have no choice but to leave. Is there another route north open to us?" Nathaniel asked.

The beast nodded. "Collect your possessions and rendezvous with me at the meadow's northern edge in one hour." Then, with a "pop," he disappeared.

A tense silence hung in the air as the warriors locked eyes, waiting to learn more from the prince. Nathaniel broke the silence, saying, "Our presence here puts the animals at risk of further attack. It's time we restart our journey. "Time to pack up and head to the north end of the meadow. We need to be there in an hour, so let's move it!"

Their footsteps heavy with fatigue, the brotherhood members shuffled toward their dwelling, still struggling to comprehend the events and their implications.

"How in the demons did they track us?" asked Cor'in, scratching his beard.

"God's know," answered Blue Ivy. "We were on the water for days."

"Maybe they had help," Allai'nn interjected.

"What do you mean?" asked Corin.

"It's unlikely they had sentries posted along the river. Which leaves few possibilities," the elf princess suggested.

"I noticed condors circling over the river a couple of days ago. Could they be lookouts?" asked Micah.

"Only if they're some type of conjured beast," Blue said.

"Unlikely, although nothing the northern necromancer produced would surprise me," commented Rue.

"I have detected no traces of dark magic, but I agree we must stay vigilant against Ravenite's cunning," said Allai'nn.

"Wolf bloodlust," added Grull. "I've seen wolf packs track wounded prey for miles, even over streams in the north."

"I guess it doesn't matter, only that they found us," Cor'in said, ending the speculation.

Jacoby spoke up for the first time. "I believe it does, Cor'in. No being could track or catch us after days on the water, especially once the river split. Those condors you mentioned, Micah. How did they fly?"

"I don't understand, Jacoby. What do you mean?" Micah said as the group entered the enormous maple and climbed the stairs.

"Did they fly over one spot in a circular pattern, or more elliptical and irregular, leaving, then returning?"

Micah stroked his chin, his brows together in thought. "I remember seeing them in the morning, then they returned."

"Right," he said, the word sharp and clipped. "Carrion birds, known for their scavenging habits, were lucky enough to find two meals in one day, each in a separate location that followed our route. Absolutely not!"

"What are you saying?" Nathaniel asked.

"The only being who can fly in a pattern like that is a witch. Our blue-sailed boat is easy to follow. And from that height, it is easy to mask their identity," Jacoby stated.

"That would explain how the lupine rangers found us."

"I wonder how they found an opening in the magic?" asked Rue.

"Only magic users can detect weaknesses in another's magic," Allai'nn said.

"So, the witches and the Lupine rangers are in league together?" Grull said, one brow raised skeptically.

"In a way, yes. If Ravenite controls both," Jacoby suggested.

"I don't think a witch has the power to find a weakness in the wall's ancient magic without help," added Allai'nn.

"I agree," Jacoby said. "The enemy has just upped the ante."

"I must be slow. Is our group that important?" asked Horatio as he stuffed extra clothes in his pack.

"Crepitus or Ravenite would never notice us if it weren't for Nathaniel," Jacoby said. "The idea of him returning to Tabor has put the fear of the gods in them."

Is there anything I can do to thwart their plans? Nathaniel's stomach churned with a mix of fear, excitement, and hope. The burning anger inside him, a hot, churning mass, made him feel physically sick. Why do they relentlessly pursue me, putting everyone I encounter in danger? The weight of this responsibility feels crushing. I'm not sure I can carry it alone. The injustice of it all made Nathaniel want to scream. This isn't right! I don't deserve this! Why did this have to happen to me?

His self-pity grew until it swallowed him. Then, just as quickly, the emotions left him, replaced by intense shame. I've put the kind inhabitants of the Hope Wood at significant risk. How could I be so foolish? I let down my guard, believing I was free of the devilish minions of Ravenite. His eyes misted, and regret stabbed at him. No matter where he traveled or with whom, the danger was just a few strides behind him. What can I do now?

As if reading his thoughts, Grull placed a comforting hand on Nathaniel's shoulder. "You can do more than you know, lad. And we're here, every step."

"Every step together. Right," Nathaniel said with finality. "We need to get moving. Epsilon will be waiting."

The witch's cloak billowed behind her as she flew high and slowly in an oval pattern above the Hope Wood, the forest canopy stretching out beneath her like a green tapestry. Lazelle wasn't born of a woman, but rather a creation of the lich-mage Ravenite, a chilling gift bestowed upon the black witch coven. However, this was no gift to Lazelle, filling her with dread, not joy. Since she could walk, she was bound to servitude, tending to every demand of the coven. She endured a brutal regimen of physical and mental torture, the coven members relentless in their efforts to break her spirit and shape her into a subservient copy. Although she had learned from many witches, her heart truly belonged to the one who had brought her into the world. The lich-mage had chosen her for this mission: to tail the prince and his companions, conveying updates to the watchful Lupine. She felt the urge to do more, but Ravenite's violent temper deterred her. So, she banked left in a slow arc, her identity cloaked by a vulture spell, and returned for another pass over the forest. The ancient magic cloaked the wood, but her sharp, hawk-like vision pierced through the veil, allowing her to easily spot any sign of the fleeing cohort. For over a day, her prey had remained inactive, even after she'd carefully guided the Lupine toward the magical fortress's singular vulnerability. She couldn't be sure if the prince was alive or dead without landing and confirming the Wolfmen's success with her own eyes. She bit her lip, resisting the urge to act. Her mission was to observe and report, not to intervene. So, she continued her slow glide below the clouds, waiting.

Epsilon and another figure waited for the brotherhood at the northern end of the meadow in front of a wooden storage hut. The Lamassu sat resolutely on his haunches, wearing the fatigue from the last few hours like a winter coat. His once vibrant blue eyes were a stormy gray, circled by dark rings below and worry-lines above. Next to him was an older satyr, his graying fur mostly covered by a white dinner jacket marked by red wine stains cascading over one side, and sunflower yellow shorts. His face was narrow, and he wore thick-lens spectacles above a hooked nose, magnifying his almond-brown eyes. So bizarre were the animal's features that Nathaniel bit his tongue to stifle a laugh. For several heartbeats, the warriors waited, expecting Epsilon to speak first.

"Wait. Wait for me," came a cry from behind. The group turned as Augustus waddled up, his fur askew and red vest buttoned in the wrong holes.

"Sorry for the delay, Father. I'm here now."

The Lamassu showed no sign of irritation at the beaver's entrance. But the satyr rolled his eyes, his hands on his hips.

"Gussie, why can't you ever be on time?"

"I just got the word, Cornelius. And who made you emperor, anyway?"

"Tardiness is your middle name," rebuked the satyr.

"And yours must be obnoxious," Augustus retorted.

"Funny. Try being less of a nuisance and more value, will you?" the elder satyr said dismissively.

"I'll have you know the Father trusted me to escort these wonderful visitors."

"Trust has to be earned."

"Did you say RUST? Because you're coated in it. Try bringing your bloated head in from the rain!" Augustus sneered.

"Enough!" Epsilon's voice boomed in everyone's mind. "Stop your bickering."

Both creatures hung their heads, answering in unison, "Sorry, Father."

Epsilon sighed away his exasperation. He had the fatigue in his eyes of a parent reprimanding young children.

A silent pause followed, broken by the satyr.

"Hello, Princes and Ladies. I am Cornelius, chief botanist and keeper of the grounds." He stuck out his hand but wavered, not knowing whose to shake first.

Nathaniel stepped forward and grasped the hand in a firm grip.

"Hello. I'm Nathaniel." The prince introduced the other brotherhood.

"Nice to meet you," Cornelius said, smiling.

Another awkward silence followed until Epsilon said, "Be on your way now, Cornelius. And thank you for the use of your tool shed."

"Of course," he murmured, bowing uncomfortably to the group. Then he arrogantly raised his nose, sniffed, and added, "My work is never done.".

The beaver murmured, "Mule," and stuck out his tongue at the back of the retreating animal. Epsilon let out a menacing growl, and Augustus snapped to attention.

Nathaniel, stifling a chuckle, cleared his throat and said, "Epsilon, thank you for your hospitality and your kindness. I feel awful. We somehow led the Lupine Rangers to your doorstep. I'm so sorry."

"No need to apologize, my prince. Evil invariably remains tenacious."

"Well, thank you for protecting us," Nathaniel said. "I wonder..."

"You wonder what's next?" boomed the Lamassu.

"I'm confident you have a plan," Nathaniel responded, smiling.

"Few know that the ancient protectors of this wood created a magical path of escape in times of great peril."

"What kind of path?" Jacoby asked.

"No one knows, for it has never been necessary to use."

"What?" Blurted out Grullach.

"No worries, halfling. The magic always provides."

Jacoby gave Nathaniel a sideways glance, one skeptical brow raised.

"Come." Epsilon turned and entered the tool shed, followed by Augustus and the others.

The shed was so vast, spanning more than a hundred feet, that it felt like a barn, its wooden frame creaking in the breeze. Mallets, hoes, shovels, scythes, and other tools, some worn and some shiny new, lay on wooden tables lining both walls. The corner of the shed was a jumble of forgotten pottery, each pot a different shape and color, while carts and wheelbarrows lined one side, their wooden frames worn with use. A wall of thick vines, their stems as thick as a human thigh dominated the back wall of the room, forming an impenetrable barrier. Epsilon marched confidently to the back wall, his chest puffed out, and spread his arms wide, closing his eyes as he inhaled deeply. His voice, rough and powerful, broke the silence in the cavernous room, filling it with a resonating, guttural sound.

"Great Mother, I call on you to help these warriors. Open a path to fulfill their destiny and shield them from the ever-present specter of darkness."

At that moment, the earth began to shift and rumble, followed by splintering wood as the massive vines separated. Grull grabbed Allai'nn's arm to steady her and two of the children while Blue hugged Rue close to keep from falling.

"Hold on to something," shouted Jacoby, leaning against a side table as the ground shifted. Micah grabbed Horatio, who held another child, and Nathaniel pulled Lani into a bear hug. Cor'in, the odd man out, fell under the shifting soil, landing hard on his side. Augustus yipped as he lost his footing, the vibrating floor rolling him under a workbench in a heap.

"Demons," spat an infuriated Cor'in, but the uproar drowned out his words. The terrified babies clung to their guardians, crying and screaming because of the loud noise, making the chaotic noise even more deafening.

Jacoby's eyes widened as he watched the wall transform, inch by inch, into an opening. Methodically, the wall of vines separated, clearing a path through the brush. As each shrub or sapling moved aside, its upper branches grew together, forming a thick canopied tunnel into darkness. Minutes passed, cracking sounds slowed, and the shifting earth stilled, leaving only the cries of terrified infants.

"By the gods!" exclaimed an angry Grullach, still holding a shaking Allai'nn and babies. "Are you helping or killing us?"

The Lamassu ignored him, turned, and whispered a single word, "Tuan."

Nothing visible happened, but Grull felt his anxiety replaced by warm serenity, like putting on a fur-lined parka in a snowstorm. Each child's eyes grew heavy, their whimpers stopped, and they fell asleep.

No one spoke for several heartbeats, accepting the peace.

Nathaniel released a long-held breath and stepped to Epsilon. The Lamassu appeared exhausted, aging before his eyes.

"Are you alright, Epsilon?"

"My time draws near, my prince."

"What? No."

"All things return to the Mother."

"Have I caused this?"

"Only the Norns weave life and death. But not to worry. They have not yet weaved my end yet."

Nathaniel's shoulders relaxed, and he changed course. "Where does the path lead?"

"To your destiny."

"Could you be more specific?" the prince asked.

A smile creased the Lamassu's lips. "This tunnel will lead north to the river. Augustus will act as your guide."

"And from there?"

"Your path from there is up to you. Use wisdom and compassion in your choice. Farewell, my prince."

Before he could ask more, the beast disappeared with a "pop."

Augustus waddled up, using his paws to dust off his red vest, removing a twig from his fur. He straightened and said, "This way, my prince."

Nat hesitated, then turned to the others. "Let's go."

Micah led the group down the cocoon-like path, his Twilight vision allowing him to see and warn those behind of irregularities on the forest floor. The infants, oblivious to the unsteady journey, slept soundly in a wooden cart found in the shed, lulled by the rhythmic rocking and the hushed sounds of nature. Augustus waddled next to Micah, a small lantern in one paw.

"So, where does this path lead?" Micah asked.

"It winds through the northern edge of the Hope Wood, ending at a branch of the Erewhon River."

"Won't we be seen?" asked the Moor elf.

"The canopy should mask our movements," said the beaver, brushing through a spiderweb crossing the detritus.

"I hope no witches are circling above keeping watch."

"Witches?" Augustus asked, one brow elevated skeptically. "The ancient forest magic will stymie such scrutiny."

"Will the magic keep the Lupine away too?" Blue Ivy asked, from behind.

"I don't know," Augustus said honestly. "But the Father cleverly had a plan for them."

"A plan?"

The beaver looked away, pulled a handkerchief from one pocket, and dabbed at the sweat on his brow before answering.

"What are you not telling us?" said Nathaniel, overhearing the conversation.

"He asked our swiftest volunteers to travel in the opposite direction wearing identical cloaks to yours."

"What?" cried Nathaniel.

Augustus timidly lifted his gaze. "Sorry. You weren't to know, per the Father's orders."

Blood drained from the young prince's face.

"We have to turn back."

"It's too late, my prince."

Nausea rose in Nathaniel's gut. *If the Lupine overtake the animals, what will happen then? More sacrifices to keep me safe? What was Epsilon thinking?*

"No, we MUST turn back. We have to do something!"

"But..."

Nathaniel turned, but Jacoby blocked his path.

"Nat, we've been walking for hours. There's no way to intervene directly."

"Get out of my way; I'm going back."

Jacoby held the younger man by both shoulders.

"No. Our path is forward," Jacoby said sternly.

"I said I'm going back!" growled Nathaniel, twisting to break free from his brother's iron grip.

Grull stepped up next to Jacoby. "Lad, Jacoby's right. Whatever happens is in the hands of the Norns. Our only choice is to keep going."

"I have to help..."

But a soft hand slipped into his and squeezed. Lani gazed into his eyes. "Epsilon said to use wisdom. Listen to Jacoby."

Heat rose in Nathaniel's face, and Lani expected more arguing. But the heat turned to tears that ran down his cheek. For a heartbeat, he looked like a lost child, empty of anything but sadness. But the moment passed, and the leader returned.

"Forward to the river," he whispered.

Lani gave his hand a last squeeze before the group turned again up the path.

The trail twisted and turned for another half-hour, ending at the bank of a narrow river.

"Wait here while I scout ahead," Augustus said.

The bank edge sloped about ten feet, meeting the water at a short, flat beach. The beaver slid down the bank and entered the ice-blue water. He crossed the fifty feet to the opposite side, then returned, swimming on his back and searching the sky for any sign of an enemy. He climbed up the bank, rivulets of water running off his fur.

"The coast is clear. Micah, check that brush downstream."

The Moor elf did as the beaver asked, combing the underbrush. In moments, he uncovered a weathered outrigger hidden under several limbs. Blue Ivy slid down the bank, wading into the river to help free up the bi-hulled boat and pull it over to the beach. One hull comfortably stored all the packs. On the floor sat a rolled sail and mast. Once everyone boarded, Nathaniel leaned over and shook the beaver's paw.

"Thank you for your help, Augustus. And thank the brave souls who sacrificed for our escape, including Epsilon. I promise I won't waste that gift."

FIVE

Jacoby hunched over the outrigger's tiller, directing the craft along a starboard beam with the dark river current. This branch of the Erewhon River was narrow, with submerged rocks and eddies along both banks. Navigating the branch required vigilance to avoid running aground or, worse, damaging the boat's hull. His back ached from hours of sitting on the stern thwart, his long legs unable to fully stretch beyond the aft beam. But his attention was neither on guiding the boat nor his sore back, focusing instead on the depressed figure slumped forward. Nathaniel leaned against the port boat frame; his head hung in despair.

What can I do to help him? Jacoby's mind drifted back to when he was a young, green officer in the Taborian guard. He remembered his first command: track and capture bandits in the Narnian hills. Jacoby had paid a local informant, a nasty, disheveled man named Rotbush, for the location of the bandit's hideout. In his zeal to succeed, Jacoby never wondered why the information came so easily. Rotbush led his company to the site, inspecting the area before the attack. He remembered the dirty, unwashed scoundrel, his greasy hair hung over a hook nose and a mouth of rotting teeth.

"Dun't see no guards, Cap'n," reported Rotbush. "I'se tink dey sleepin."

Foolishly, Jacoby believed the man and charged to attack. But Rotbush had double-crossed the green officer, and the bandits ambushed the platoon. The ensuing attack turned into an utter bloodbath. Jacoby, unsure and panicked, hesitated momentarily before leading a counterattack. The short delay cost lives; a fifth of his force was dead or wounded in the opening minutes. Witnessing the loss galvanized the young lieutenant, and he charged forward like a possessed madman. His heroics rallied his men, and they eventually overcame the bandits. By day's end, Jacoby and his men had routed the bandit horde, sacked their enclave, and taken prisoners. But the toll on his squad was horrific, with two-thirds of his men lost. A sword thrust had wounded Jacoby during the melee, slicing down his forearm. The scar reminded him of his misjudgment, a guilt he would carry forever.

Jacoby ran his fingers over the jagged scar on his arm and understood his brother's despair. The burden of command sits like a leaden cloak, weighing down every decision and action. Nathaniel is up to the task, but his face already reflects the strain. At what cost?

A tap on his shoulder woke Jacoby from his thoughts.

"I'm ready to take over the tiller," Grull said, eyeing the scar. He knew the story all too well. He had been a recruit on his first mission after training and one of the few surviving the bandit ambush under Jacoby's command. In his mind, Jacoby's heroics had saved them, but he knew the memory still haunted his friend. He added, "The lad will be okay."

"I hope you're right." The big man stood and stretched, then shuffled toward the bow, laying a comforting hand on Nathaniel's shoulder as he passed.

Lazelle gazed down at the figures on board the sailing vessel gliding over the river below. Her vulture sight identified the figures from their cloaks as the brotherhood members; she smiled and chuckled.

"Got you!"

She pulled an object from her bag and held it close to her mouth. The item was not food, drink, or a powerful amulet, but an egg the size of a small ball. She loathed magic that required both hands while broom-bound, but had no time to land. She cursed for not remembering her wand to ease the chore, leaving it at her cave dwelling in her haste to accept this mission. The mistake was foolish, but she would adapt.

Lazelle flexed her thigh muscles with practiced skill, securing her tightly on her broom. Then she held the tiny egg and chanted with fetid breath, blowing on the egg between words. The egg momentarily glowed red and cracked open, revealing a small black bird. Lazelle continued to chant, and with each phrase, the bird enlarged until it reached the size of a pigeon. The animal's beak elongated in a curve, and the breast feathers turned blood red, morphing into a juvenile Gore Parrot.

Lazelle placed the bird on one arm and sliced a long gash into her forearm using her claw-like fingernails of the other hand. Black blood pooled in the wound like a miniature pond.

"Feed."

The bird's eyes brightened, and it leaned in, sucking the pooling blood from the wound until it had consumed its fill.

The parrot raised a blood-soaked beak and said, "Thank you, mistress. What wish may I fulfill?"

"Find the Lupine leader. Tell him his prey sails east on the river toward Mar Napor."

"Your will is my will."

Cinsor, bruised and scraped from tumbling down the granite wall, gazed over the remnants of his troop. He had lost one of his wolves to a broken neck, and two others, including Notch, nursed broken arms or legs. He cursed himself for underestimating the magic of the wood and for his continued luck. What can I do? He lamented. My squad is depleted, with my best tracker injured and the rest bruised and battered. How can I limp back to the den after such failure?

Notch limped up, his left arm in a sling.

"Sir, a message," producing a red-breasted gore parrot.

He accepted the bird in his paw and growled, "Yes?"

"My master offers news. Your prey sails north on the eastern branch of the Erewhon River toward Mar Napor."

Cinsor's face turned beat red, and his mind swirled as a torrent of impotent rage surged inside. After chasing them across Curth Talem, his prey had escaped again. The news overwhelmed him. He panted to catch his breath, and his head pounded. How could they have evaded me again? He wanted to howl with every fiber of his being, to lash out at the injustice of his defeat, but he couldn't speak. For a brief moment, the surge of emotions within him was so profound that he felt a sickening wave of dizziness. He leaned against a sapling trunk, its rough bark digging into his back, sliding down to sit before he lost control and vomited. A low moan escaped from his clenched jaws. What am I to do now? His emotions slowly drained away, leaving him hollow with despair. His battered and exhausted wolves struggled to survive, much less travel. He had ignored a direct order to return to the den in his lust to kill his prey. His leadership had almost destroyed them, and his enemy had again escaped. What now? Execution waited with the Lupine command. They accepted no excuse for failure. He had dreamed of slaying the prince, feeding on his blood, and gnawing on his bones. Now, his dream had dissolved into a horrible reality.

Suddenly, an idea sprouted in his mind's eye, flourishing until the swirling dark clouds cleared. Cinsor raised his head, relief entering his face.

"Notch."

"Yes, commander," answered the lean Staill mantel, hobbling to face him.

"Send the uninjured to search for healing herbs and wolfnip. Make sure they start along the bank of the magical stream."

"Yes, sir. I'm well enough to help as well."

Cinsor smiled at his corporal's tenacity and nodded. He turned back to the gore parrot, calmly awaiting his reply. "Ask your master to follow the prey. Once healed, we will continue the hunt."

"As you command," the bird said, flying off in the wind.

Blue Ivy guided the outrigger to the hamlet's dock two days later. Conchshell, a coastal fishing village and port for smaller merchant craft bringing trade goods to Mar Napor, rested between the breakwater between ocean and river. Nathaniel and Cor'in bounded out onto the jetty and strode toward a group of fishermen mending nets. Within minutes, they returned with the information needed.

"The consensus among the locals is that we have two options. First, skirt the coast in the outrigger until we reach the city, about a week's journey. The other option is to ferry out to Elf Island," he said, pointing to a landmass visible on the horizon. "Larger, more secure vessels allow work for transport to the city."

"Thoughts?' asked Grull.

"The outrigger has been a tight squeeze with the children," said Allai'nn.

"And we need milk and other supplies," added Rue.

"How're our funds?" asked Jacoby, looking at Blue Ivy, the unofficial treasurer.

"Not good. We may have enough for a night's lodging and supplies."

"The locals warned of pirates patrolling along the coast," added Cor'in.

"Pirates?" exclaimed Lani, remembering the bandit capture the women had endured previously in the Fossil Wood.

Nathaniel rubbed his chin. "A lot to consider. First, we get supplies. Then we decide on how we get to Mar Napor."

The group nodded and began securing the boat to enter the township. But Horatio intervened.

"I'll stay with the boat. Village folk rarely understand Anurans."

"You're one of us, Horatio. Gawkers be damned," growled Jacoby.

Horatio smiled. "Thanks, but we need to keep a low profile."

"I'll stay behind," said Micah, clapping Horatio on the shoulder. "I hate shopping anyway."

Nathaniel hesitated, not wanting to give in to Horatio's fears. Then shrugged, saying, "I'm with Jacoby, but if you're comfortable here, so be it."

After returning with supplies, feeding and changing the infants, and mending a small tear in the sail, the group was prepared for travel. Nathaniel had decided.

"I believe our safest route is by a defended merchant ship. We'll have to work our way across but it should be safer and have more room. Set sail for Elf Island," Nathaniel said, gesturing with his arm toward a dark rim of land on the horizon.

When the boat docked, a stocky halfling wearing a vested suit waited with an enormous warrior at the Sand Flea pier, the principal port of Elf Island.

"Welcome, travelers! I am Mayor Tolar," the mayor said, smiling. The other man stood stone-faced, arms crossed. "What brings you to our fair city?"

"We are looking for a passage to Mar Napor."

Tolar rubbed his chin. "I see you have little ones. I recommend Captain Spitz of the Seamist. You'll find him at the Dancing Porpoise Tavern."

"Thank you," said Nathaniel, shaking his hand. "And a place to stay?"

"The best place in town is...." The mayor noticed Nathaniel frown and look down. "One can find more affordable inns on K street."

Nathaniel smiled. "We've traveled a long way to reach Mar Napor."

"Southerners, eh?"

"Not exactly. Fleeing the war."

"I see. Like so many others," said the mayor, shaking his head as he turned back to the town. "Enjoy your brief stay." He turned to the uniformed warrior, and added, "Sergeant Pincher, please discuss our city rules with our new friends."

"My pleasure, mayor," the muscle-bound soldier said with a sly grin.

"I don't understand," said Nathaniel.

The brawny soldier blocked Nathaniel's path. "Isn't it obvious? No one wants more riffraff here," he said, his voice dripping with consternation.

"What did you say?" Nat growled, anger beginning to take root.

"We don't accept newcomers here," the officer said, enunciating each word as if speaking to a child. "Transients have twenty-four hours to make plans and leave the city, or I'll have your hide," he spat, stepping closer to the prince. "Register at the gate or return to the canoe."

Nathaniel's face reddened, and his hand drifted to his sword pommel. Who did this guy think he was? But a firm hand on his shoulder calmed him.

"No worries, Sergeant. We will abide as requested," Jacoby said.

"Smart decision," his narrowed eyes still assessing the prince. "Now move along."

Jacoby nodded, and the group hurriedly approached the city gates.

Another husky soldier sat at a broad table surrounded by two other armed men. The soldiers wore poorly equipped, ill-fitting leather chest plates of various sizes and wielded swords that looked like they had been scavenged from a battlefield. These are simple militia, Nathaniel thought, waiting in a short line until he faced the seated soldier.

"Write the number in your party and make your mark," the man said, shoving a parchment forward without looking up. Nathaniel wrote what they needed, and the group moved into the city.

"They have a lot of security for such a tiny hamlet, despite the poor quality of their armor," Cor'in noticed, gazing up at other stern-looking guards on the ramparts as he walked through the city gates.

"Pirates may be a bigger threat than they'll admit," Blue whispered beside him.

Ten intersecting streets comprised the commercial section of Sand Flea. The main street intersected on each end of the city with a coastal beach road on one side and a road into the island interior on the other. A log palisade surrounded the town, with mirrored guideposts abutting iron-reenforced doors at the entrance of the main road.

"Let's split up. Jacoby, Cor'in, and I will search for Captain Spitz; the rest will find lodging on K Street," Nathaniel said. He handed a small coin pouch over to Blue Ivy.

"There should be plenty of coin from selling the outrigger for food and rooms."

Blue mock saluted. "Yes, commander."

Nathaniel rolled his eyes, and the group divided. A short time later, Cor'in eyed a painted blue sign with two green dolphins dancing. "This must be it."

They entered a dingy tavern full of grizzled sailors speaking and laughing over mugs of grog. Several buxom servers carried platters of ale, weaving away from the patrons' roaming hands.

Jacoby strode up to the packed bar, squeezing in between drunken patrons. A stout barkeep, his ample belly covered in a stained apron, approached. "Whadya have, Mate?"

"What's the cheapest?"

"Naporian gin. Rotgut for the poor."

"Three."

The bartender poured three measures on the bar. "Journeyman?"

"Yes."

"Heading to the Citadel?"

Jacoby nodded.

The barman eyed the tall warrior, then said, "Let me warn you. There are rumors King Linus may limit entrance. The capital is overflowing with refugees. But I'd not worry. An experienced warrior like yourself should find work plentiful."

Jacoby wondered how the man assessed his experience. He wore no insignia and appeared weathered from days of travel. "The mayor suggested signing on with Captain Spitz," he said.

"Oh, Spitz, is it?" The barkeep chuckled. "Old Tolar's a crafty one."

Jacoby's eyebrows raised, not understanding.

The bartender leaned in, his voice hushed, "Spitz's reputation is that of a tough commander, and traveling can be expensive, especially after the mayor takes his share. Beware a headwind, mate."

"Any other options?"

"Not since pirates sank the last three ships from port. Spitz is the sole captain who dares to make the run."

"Pirates?"

"Crimson Pirates have been feasting on ships since the news of Tabor's struggles."

"What?"

"Ya ain't heard? The City of Spires has mobilized all men to fight, leaving the coastal ports unprotected."

Jacoby gawked at the man, stunned. The situation in Tabor was worse than he had imagined. "I don't have a choice. Can you point out Captain Spitz?"

The barkeep pointed to the back. "He be the one."

Jacoby turned to see a hulking man sitting alone in a faintly lit corner. He paid for the drinks, bringing them to the others.

"Let's step outside to talk," Jacoby said, looking discouraged.

"What news?" asked Nathaniel.

"Mostly bad. The Crimson Pirates have sunk most transports. Captain Spitz is the only one bold enough to sail."

Nathaniel's shoulders sagged, but he could see more in Jacoby's eyes. "And?"

"He's a rough one, and expensive."

"Cuddly as a grizzly sitting on a tack. My kind of guy," said Cor'in, lightening the conversation.

"In addition, Tabor is facing difficulties, with rumors that its downfall is imminent. We cannot delay our quest to return," Jacoby said.

"Demons!" spat Cor'in, shaking his head.

Nathaniel ignored the outburst. "What's the plan?"

"You and Cor'in do the negotiating. I'll act as a guard."

"Right."

The three downed their drinks and confidently strode into the poorly lit tavern. Cor'in and Nat pretended to be leaving, then abruptly slid into the booth across from Spitz. Jacoby loitered behind, prepared to act if necessary.

"Hello, Captain. Mind if we have a word?"

Spitz responded by spitting on the tavern floor. Two muscular sailors abruptly materialized at the table, grabbing the interlopers.

"Not so fast, gents," said Jacoby, pricking the pirates with a dagger in each back. "Back away, or I'll gut you like a deer."

The men released Nathaniel and Cor'in and stepped back. "Let's step out back," Jacoby whispered, leading them out the back door.

The captain remained silent, ignoring the incident. He wore a white tunic under a black rain slicker, greasy gray straggles falling across his face. Spitz's eyes narrowed. "Well?"

"We need passage to Mar Napor for fourteen, including four infants."

Spitz erupted in deep, hollow laughter. "Infants? The Seamist ain't no nursery, boy."

Cor'in ignored the jab. "Our group comprises eight seasoned warriors, all veteran fighters. I offer our services as mercenaries in exchange for passage."

The captain's brow raised skeptically. "What suggests I need hired protection?"

Nathaniel spoke up, a quick nod toward Jacoby's approaching form. "Your security is noticeably lacking. Pirates would love scuttling the last trade ship."

Spitz rubbed his hand over his three-day stubble. He glanced at Jacoby, who now sat at a nearby table. "I want five sentochniks for each brat and woman."

"One silver each and our services," Nathaniel negotiated. "Or, chance that the Seamist crew feeds the Kraken."

Spitz sighed and frowned. "Have your sea rats at the dock before daybreak. We leave with the next tide."

The following day before dawn, the brotherhood was about to board the Seamist when a husky sailor wearing white linen trousers held up with a red sash blocked the entrance to the gangway.

"I'm Gnarls, the first mate. Stow your gear and the sea mites in rooms under the foredeck. Warriors split up, four on each side."

The group trudged up the incline onto the Seamist as directed. Rue and Allai'nn stayed with the children below while the others split to port or starboard.

The initial day was uneventful, strong winds propelling the two-masted sloop at a heady pace. Late afternoon, Gnarls approached Cor'in.

"Scamper up the topgallant shrouds to the crow's nest."

"Pardon?"

"Bloody landlubber! Go aloft and keep your eyes peeled for pirates."

Cor'in didn't move, his secret of acrophobia freezing him in place. "I...."

His face red with fury, Gnarls grabbed the half-elf by the neck. "I said..."

But before the burly first-mate could force Cor'in, Horatio interjected. "I got this, sir." Before Gnarls could move, the frogman leaped onto the shroud and scampered up the mast.

Gnarls, eyes wide, let go of Cor'in and watched the Anduran spider up to the crow"s nest.

"By the sea gods, he dresses like a fop but can climb like a seasoned hand!" He turned to Cor'in and frowned. "You're a crew member now, mate. When I give an order, hop to it."

"Right," Cor'in said, nodding his head.

Gnarls eyed him a heartbeat more, then returned to the quarterdeck.

The sunny skies began to darken, transitioning to a deep purple as the afternoon progressed, foreshadowing the storm that was rolling in across the Napor Sound. As the sky darkened, the wind whipped up, sending the ship into a violent dance as it pitched and rolled over growing whitecaps. The warriors, battered by the storm, clung desperately to the deck rail, their bodies straining to stay upright against the unrelenting waves. As the waves crashed over the deck, Horatio felt himself tossed about, and in a moment of chaos, he saw a dark figure lurking at the edge of his vision before the ship pitched down again into a wave gully. He waited until the ship crested the next wave, but the thick, gray clouds and impending rain obscured his view. Minutes later, he caught another glimpse of a ghostly form through the mist and rain. What in demons is that? A ship? A sea monster?

A momentary break in the clouds revealed a three-masted schooner, its silhouette sharp against the sky, and an iron ballista, heavy and menacing, sat loaded on the foredeck.

Horatio screamed, "Pirates," just as the enormous iron weapon discharged. An eerie whistling sound broke the air, followed by a massive crash as the iron arrow smashed into the sloop's side. The weapon's impact sent shockwaves through the deck, flinging every brotherhood on guard off their feet, sending them skidding across the polished wood. Horatio, with a yell, somersaulted out of the crow's nest, his fingers desperately grasping for the shroud line, narrowly avoiding a plunge into the churning sea below. As the warriors struggled to their feet, the ship lurched violently again, the jarring impact sending shudders through the deck. A monstrous boarding hook, groaning with the weight of the enemy, had ripped into the ship's railing. With a sickening lurch, the Seamist listed further, water pouring into its hold as the pirate schooner hauled it in, the salty air thick with the smell of desperation.

"Cut that rope, or we'll all perish!" Gnarls shouted at Jacoby. The big man furiously swung his sword at the thick rope holding the smaller vessel until it finally gave way, flinging him again off his feet as the little ship righted. But the big ship had pulled close enough for pirates to leap the gap between and onto the Seamist's deck.

"Prepare to repel boarders!" yelled Spitz, sliding down to the main deck, sword in hand. The Seamist sailors charged with their captain, cutting down most of the first wave of attackers. But wave after wave of howling pirates swung from the schooner onto the deck of the smaller ship, joining the battle. Nathaniel cut down four pirates before another gave a blood-curdling cry, landing on his back. With a jarring thud, the prince crashed to the deck, the air knocked from his lungs, leaving him gasping for breath. With a guttural growl, the pirate whipped out a blade, the cold steel catching the light as it flashed above Nathaniel's head. Nathaniel's attacker let out a piercing scream, his voice filled with agony as Jacoby's sword plunged into his stomach. The pirate fell to one side, allowing Nat a few much-needed seconds to catch his breath.

Jacoby winked, a playful glint in his eye before facing another adversary as the prince, bruised but determined, regained his feet.

Despite their valiant efforts, the brotherhood was being pushed back, outnumbered and outmatched by their adversaries. After what seemed like hours, the battle had claimed all but Spitz, Gnarls, and the brotherhood, who stood amidst the carnage. Pirate bodies lay piled waist-high on the deck, creating a macabre tableau of death, the blood staining the wood crimson.

"STOP!" A hoarse and gravelly voice cut through the chaos of the battle, bringing the fighters to a stunned silence. The half-goblin towered over Allai'nn, a stark figure in his incongruous attire: a ruffled shirt, a blue velvet coat, and deerskin pants. The gleam of his knife against her throat was a stark contrast to the fabric softness surrounding him. "Drop your weapons, or the elf dies."

No one moved, each brotherhood member calculating the risk of crossing the deck and cutting the beast down. After a heartbeat, Nathaniel said, "Let the woman go. We'll drop our weapons."

"You first."

Nathaniel re-sheathed his sword, unbuckled his sword belt, and dropped it to the deck. The other brotherhood followed except for Grullach.

"Touch one hair on her head, and there won't be a place for you to hide in all of Curth Talem," the halfling said menacingly.

"Drop it, or I'll cut more than her hair," responded the half-goblin, inching the knife closer to Allai'nn's neck.

Grull glared at the goblin, his face contorted in anger, but then he noticed Allai'nn's barely perceptible nod, a silent message that flickered across her face.

"All right, all right," he muttered, frustration in his voice. Feeling the pressure lessen, Allai'nn seized the moment, clamping her teeth down on the goblin's hand with a painful bite. With a swift movement, she drove her elbow into his gut, causing him to stagger and lose his footing.

Grull, quick as a viper, spun around in a single fluid movement, hurling a dagger at the startled goblin. The blade found its mark on the goblin's shoulder with a sickening thud, sending the surprised creature sprawling backward.

Pandemonium erupted as Grull reached Allai'nn in two bounds. As he ran, he picked up his sword, the steel cold against his hand, and thrust it towards the goblin's throat. With a roar of defiance, the other Brotherhood drew their swords and surged forward, their attack catching the pirates off guard and leaving them scrambling to defend themselves. Gnarls and Spitz joined the fray, their barks adding to the chaotic din. The pirates, seeing their leader captured, scattered in a frenzy, their panicked shouts and the clattering boot steps sounding like a swarm of fleeing rats. The attack was swift and brutal, sending pirates scrambling over the sides of the ship in a desperate attempt to escape. Many of the remaining raiders fell to the attack, while others were quickly subdued and taken prisoner.

"Everyone okay?" Nathaniel said, checking on each group member.

"Okay," said Cor'in, Blue, and Jacoby in unison.

"We're all right," said Rue, Allai'nn, and Micah.

"Help!" called out Horatio, leaning over Lani. Allai'nn and Nathaniel rushed over, finding Lani in a pool of blood.

"Demons! Lani, where are you hurt?" Nathaniel cried, the fear in his voice clear. The girl was pale white with a penetrating gash in her left thigh.

"Wrap your belt around her leg to control the bleeding while I grab my healer's kit from below," ordered Allai'nn. The elf sprinted off down the hold steps as Nathaniel complied. He stroked her hair, whispering, "You'll be okay, my love."

Allai'nn rushed back up with a leather pouch and cleaned the wound with a damp cloth. Lani's face contorted in agony, the pain so sharp it blurred her vision before everything went black. With Lani unconscious, Allai'nn pinched the opposing wound sides and pulled the needle and thread through, stitching the wound in layers. Then, the healer applied a bandage infused with bacteriostatic turmeric and juniper oil. Throughout the procedure, Nathaniel caressed the girl's head and held her hand.

"You're going to be all right, love," he whispered in her ear, gazing at Allai'nn for confirmation.

"If we can keep infection controlled," Allai'nn answered. "Carry her downstairs to our rooms. I'll monitor her."

Nathaniel cradled Lani gently in his arms, the warmth of her body radiating against his chest, and whispered, "Thanks, Allai'nn." He turned to Jacoby and asked, "Can you interrogate the prisoners? You can fill me in later."

"Gladly." Jacoby turned to Horatio. "Will you, Blue, and Micah clear the other ship of the remaining crew?

Horatio nodded and said, "You heard the man." The three leaped over to the larger ship, swords out.

The smell of the damp, salt-laced air of the hold clung to his brother as he descended, fueling the rage that simmered inside Jacoby. His heart pounded, a storm of emotions raging within him as he sensed his brother's fear and despair. The weight of responsibility pressed down on him like a suffocating blanket. He felt helpless, a bitter taste on his tongue, as he watched the Brotherhood, knowing he could not protect them from the inevitable. He stared at the bound half-goblin, his bloodstained jacket and shallow breaths a stark reminder of the fight, then turned his gaze to the sea, its salty tang a welcome respite from the stench of blood and fear. With a mix of curiosity and apprehension, he wondered what the next chapter of this unfolding story would bring.

SIX

Jacoby's face was as pale as the sea foam cresting the waves as he stared beyond the seated goblin leader at the whitecaps rolling to the horizon.

"Jacoby?" Grull said, his brows crossed in confusion.

The big warrior stood silently; his muscles taut with anticipation.

"What is it?" asked the halfling, his concern beginning to rise.

"More black sails," he said, his voice tight with dread as the ominous shadows of the approaching ships filled the horizon.

"What?" Grull gasped, his breath catching in his throat. A tense silence fell over the sloop as Grull and the half-goblin turned to see three ships, their black sails billowing in the wind, closing in on them.

"Prepare to repel borders," yelled Jacoby, alerting the others and drawing his sword. He gazed about the ship. Everywhere he looked, he saw the bodies of sailors and pirates, their faces contorted in death. The brotherhood members remained calm, their practiced movements a stark contrast to the surrounding chaos. Jacoby's mind raced as he calculated the odds, each number whispering the grim truth - three ships meant there was no chance of success.

Spitz strode up. "By the gods!" he wailed, his eyes bugging at the sight of more pirates. "Quick, cut those hooks away from the other ship." He turned to his first mate, Gnarls, and ordered, "Hard to port and make for the shore with all sail. It's our only chance to escape!" Everyone moved simultaneously, cutting the boarding lines away as the sloop turned and the sails filled. The ship rotated and picked up speed. For several minutes, the ship flew across the waves, the mainland becoming more in focus every second. A smile crossed Spitz's face as the ship catapulted towards the shore, leaving the abandoned pirate vessel bobbing in the surf.

"We foiled the bloody raiders," he said, grinning.

Jacoby looked behind to see the three dark ships following, the largest gaining on their tail. The other two smaller boats veered right and left as if breaking away from the chase. Jacoby brightened, assuming their chances of escape had just increased.

"They're still coming", Jacoby reported, watching as the ships separated. Spitz ignored him, yelling orders, "Tighten those sails. Even a sliver's increase in wind might save us."

The first mate's experienced hands felt a momentary resistance in the steering column, like the vessel had snagged a piece of debris on the bottom of the sea. Gnarls had spent years at the ship's helm, his hands knowing the rhythm of the wheel and his ears tuned to the ship's every creak and groan. A shiver ran down his spine as he instantly realized something had changed.

"Something's wrong, captain. Helm is stiffening."

Spitz strode over, feeling a slight tug to port. "Blast! She's taking on water. You there, Corn, Corny, or whatever. Get below and man the bilge pump."

"Cor'in."

"I said, move, or we'll all be in chains before dark."

Cor'in rushed down the steps, entering the dark hull. Half a foot of water sloshed over his feet as he landed on the hull floor. Where and what was "the bilge pump?" He scrambled along the inside of the hull, dodging crates of textiles and other stores beginning to float in the rising water. At the ship's bow, he found a box with dual clay pipes entering and exiting on one side. A wooden lever arm protruded from the apparatus.

"This must be it," he said aloud. He pulled the lever and heard a whooshing noise of water rushing inside the box. He pushed the lever down, again hearing water rushing through the pipes. Cor'in swiftly got in a rhythm, pumping the lever back and forth. Sweat spilled down the half-elf's brow as he worked the lever. His arms burned from the effort, but he continued, switching from arm to arm as one tired. Despite his work, Cor'in felt the water level gradually rise up his leg.

The other brotherhood pulled sail sheets tight and cleared ropes on the top deck per Spitz's orders. But the trailing dark ship continued to close on the sloop.

"Dump those bodies overboard," Spitz screamed. "We must lighten the ship."

Jacoby and Grull began flipping corpses over the deck rail to speed the ship. Despite these efforts, the ship took on water and struggled toward shore.

"Help them, Gnarls. The demons are catching up!" roared Spitz, shoving his first mate toward the foredeck steps and taking the wheel. As the ship descended a swell, the captain turned his head to watch the approaching schooner. He turned forward just as the sloop peaked the next wave, and his face fell. Hundreds of feet ahead, blocking the sloop's path to the nearing beach, waited the two smaller pirate vessels.

Spitz spun the sloop's steering wheel, hoping he might slide by the blockade. But the ships skillfully sailed to block the maneuver. The captain had hoped to scuttle the ship, preventing the buccaneers from salvaging the boat. Now he realized the pirates had sealed their fate, and he maneuvered the sinking ship into the wind.

"Why are we slowing?" Jacoby called out, then understood. The cats had trapped the mouse, ending the chase. Escape was impossible; only confrontation remained, and even the brotherhood couldn't conquer three bloodthirsty pirate ships.

"Better get Nathaniel, Allai'nn, and the children above deck," Jacoby said to Grull. The halfling disappeared into the hold as the sound of boarding hooks bit into the deck rail.

Fifty pirates, led by a Lizardman dressed in linen pants and a tunic with a blue sash belt, scattered over the sloop. They swiftly disarmed the brotherhood and placed them in chains.

"Who is in charge here?" asked the Lizardman in cultured common tongue. His voice was firm with a slight southern accent.

Spitz lifted his chin and strode forward. "I am Captain Spitz, you pirate scum. How dare you attack a simple merchant ship?"

The Lizardman chuckled and, in one quick movement, drove his sword deep into Spitz's belly. The captain's eyes bulged, his shackled hands drawn to the wound, then fell over.

"I loathe lies and insults," said the reptile, wiping his sword clean on Spitz's corpse.

"Barbarian! Give me a sword, and I'll make you pay," shouted Gnarls, fighting against two pirates who restrained him.

The Lizardman grinned, wagging a clawed finger at the first mate. "Behave, or you'll join your captain."

The Lizardman heard boot steps behind him, and he came to attention, saying, "Captain on deck."

The pirates watched expectantly as a tall, muscular figure approached, the clink of his high jackboots echoing on the wooden planks, the gleam of gold buttons on his surcoat catching the light beneath his claret velvet topcoat. A vibrant red mustache and goatee, like flames on his face, sprouted beneath a straight nose and bright green eyes. He cocked his black tricorn hat rakishly over his head, revealing a mop of fiery red curls that seemed to demand attention. With a determined glint in its eyes, the man advanced towards the Lizardman, unfazed by the Lizardman's menacing presence.

"Flycatcher, I see the captain was uncooperative. Have you secured the booty?"

"Not yet, sir," said the Lizardman, nodding to Jacoby and the others. "I wanted to interrogate the prisoners first."

The captain nodded. "Scour the ship for anything sellable and transfer it to the Reaver. I'll speak with the prisoners."

"Right. Move, you sea dogs! You heard Captain Ironhook! Everything of value carry to the Reaver!" bellowed Flycatcher.

The sailors swarmed the ship, their bodies a teeming mass like ants on a hill. Flycatcher herded most of the pirates below, leaving a small group to comb the upper deck for any remaining threats. A half-goblin stood near the prisoners, watching as Ironhook turned to face him, "What's your assessment, Razor?"

"I underestimated the security, Ironhook," he said, his voice tight with frustration. "These mercenaries are not like the others, they're hardened and dangerous."

Ironhook hesitated, his brows raised. "Interesting. "

The half-goblin obeyed without a word. Ironhook watched his friend climb over to the larger ship, his left arm useless and dangling. He'd known Razor for over ten years and knew he was brave and intelligent. No one had skillfully ambushed the goblin captain until now. He scanned the deck, taking in the many pools of dried blood and the remaining pirate corpses. Who were these warriors? How could so few decimate Razor's crew? A shiver of anxiety ran down his spine, sending a tingle to the base of his neck. He shook his head, the incomprehensible situation leaving him baffled. Whatever happened, he would do whatever he could to not repeat the mistake.

"Double shackle these captives and bring them to the Reaver," he commanded. At that moment, Flycatcher poked his head above deck, beckoning Ironhook to come over.

"What is it?"

"I released fifteen of our men held down below. I discovered a group of four people—a man and three women, and one woman suffered a sword wound. There's no doubt in my mind," he said, "they're part of the mercenary group."

Ironhook waited, expecting more. "What else? "

"The women were tending to four healthy Elven infants."

Ironhook's shoulders slumped. "Wonderful!" He exclaimed, pounding his fist against the deck rail. He had become a ruthless man over the years, pillaging towns without mercy, allowing his pirates unrestricted reign over the populace, and killing anyone between them and valuable booty. But he never allowed or engaged in rape or child abduction.

"Chain the women's legs but not wrists and transport them and the infants to my cabin until I make a plan. Dump the mercenaries in the brig." He changed tack and said, "What else did you find?"

"Plenty of textiles and other sellables, including three weapons cases."

Ironhook smiled. Finally, some profitable news. "How about the hull damage?"

"I can have the carpenter patch the hole and tow the sloop to port."

"Okay. Signal the captains of the Firefly and the Shark Tooth. They can tow the sloop to Pipeweed. I'll message our contact to meet us at the Rusty Anchor."

Besides losing twenty pirates, Ironhook assessed the day as a success. He whistled his favorite shanty as he continued to oversee the transport of crates to his ship, the Reaver.

The Brotherhood sat in the gloomy schooner brig, ten by ten-foot jail cells lined on three sides by stone ballast. A crepuscular glow of lamp light filtered through the hold planks above, giving the dingy prison its only refrain from pitch black. Jacoby stirred to life, his head pounding from a blow from his captors. He could see nothing and blinked his eyes to ensure they were open. He heard heavy breathing nearby, identifying others in his cell, but being free of Twilight vision as a human, he was blind.

"Hello? Nathaniel? Grull?"

"Here, Jacoby," the young man said, rubbing his temples to ease his headache. "What happened?"

"They gave us a beating before dumping us in the brig," said Micah. "The others are still out cold."

"And the women?" asked Nathaniel.

"Don't know."

"Argh! My head," growled Cor'in, beginning to stir. "Where are we?"

"I'd guess at the lowest level of the ship. I can see large ballast stones all around," Blue Ivy said.

"Demons, my head," said a waking Grullach. "If I get my hands on that pirate captain, I'll wring his neck."

"I can't see anything. Micah, can you describe the cell?" asked Nathaniel.

"Except for the ship's hull and the padlocked door, thick iron bars make up the walls."

Nathaniel rubbed his hand over his face, frustration boiling inside. "Bloody hell. What next?"

Everyone was silent. Even Jacoby felt disheartened. Hours passed. Or was it days? Time became an amorphous monster hovering in the darkness but remaining just out of sight. No one came with food or water. The only constant was the movement of the rolling ship with the waves and the endless darkness.

Jacoby squinted against the flickering torchlight as the rough, heavy boots of the pirates echoed on the wooden keelson, their approach to the brig door growing louder with each step.

"Git up, you mangy dawgs!" called out one pirate, opening the door. Jacoby was slow to move, so the man kicked him in the ribs. "I said, git up!"

"Where are we?" Horatio asked.

"Nun o' yo beeswax, toady," said another man, chuckling through decaying teeth.

The guards pushed and prodded the group up the stairs to the main hold, then up two more flights until they stood on the top deck. The morning sun burned into their eyes, and every prisoner cringed, blocking the painful rays with a shackled arm until they became used to the glare.

Nathaniel realized the ship had anchored back at the port of Sand Flea where they had met Captain Spitz to start this horrendous journey. He watched as dozens of pirates offloaded their booty onto the pier. Captain Ironhook approached with Flycatcher at his side.

"I trust you had a pleasant voyage."

"Hardly," croaked Grull, wanting to spit, but his throat was dry as dust.

Ironhook ignored the halfling.

"Take them ashore," he said to the Lizardman. "They can wait in the holding pens until the market opens."

"Where're my wife and children?" Grull screamed, fighting against his chains. "If you've done something to them, I'll...."

A punch from Flycatcher cut his words short, knocking the halfling out cold.

Jacoby and Nathaniel both fought against their bonds, faces red with fury.

"Anyone else have a question?" growled the Lizardman. No one spoke. Two buccaneers, their faces hardened by the sun and sea, hoisted the unconscious Grull onto their shoulders, his limp form dragging against the rough planks as they marched him down the gangplank. Other pirates, their cutlasses glinting menacingly, forced the group ahead with threats and the occasional prod.

"Get mov'in, scum," one pirate said, kicking out as motivation.

Once ashore, the buccaneers herded the prisoners to a circular fenced receiving pen, mixing them with another forty captives.

"What the demons is this place?" Blue Ivy asked.

"Devil's belly," said a raspy voice.

Everyone turned to see a wiry older man, naked above tattered linen pants, leaning against the fence. His unwashed gray hair hung over his face, mixing with a long, dirty gray beard.

"The Devil's belly, you say?" asked Horatio, walking over and sitting beside the man.

The man only grunted.

"What's your name, friend?" Horatio prodded.

"Ain't never seen no talking frog."

"I'm Anuran, from the south," said the frog man cheerfully. "Call me Horatio."

No response. The pause lasted so long that Horatio wondered if the man had fallen asleep. He was turning away when the man said, "Gumz. Ben Gumz."

"Good to meet you," Horatio said, sticking out his hand to shake, but he ignored it. "Ben, have you been here long?"

"Ben's here to stay, two moons. No one cares or sees old Ben."

"Why are they keeping us here?"

"Wait'in for the sale. Sale. Sale."

"The sale?"

"Slavers visit on the full moon. Not for Ben, no siree. Not for old Ben."

Horatio's shoulders slumped, and his eyes closed. He'd experienced the effect of slavery before growing up in Anuria. He remembered a corrupt official had brokered a deal with northern slavers, kidnapping and selling citizens for profit until Horatio's father had put an end to it. As a local militia captain, his father smashed the slave ring, culminating in a brutal battle where the majority of the slavers perished and his father sustained serious injuries. The corrupt official slipped away, but his father's fate was sealed by a festering wound that quickly developed into gangrene, leading to a painful two-week struggle before succumbing to the infection. The memory haunted Horatio, a black cloud of despair that brought back the sights, sounds, and smells of that unbearable day. Time had attempted to mend the gaping hole in his heart left by his father's passing, but the scar remained, a constant reminder of the pain that had once torn him apart. A sharp, searing pain erupted in his chest, making it impossible to breathe. Before he realized it, he fell to his side, moaning. Then he felt powerful hands lifting him to a sitting position, both Cor'in and Jacoby at his side.

"Horatio? What happened?" Jacoby asked, worried.

"What did you do to him?" Cor'in demanded, his voice granite. Before the disheveled older man could speak, an arm shot out, an iron grip on the man's throat.

"Wait," croaked the man, eyes wide in fear.

"Let him go, Cor'in," said Jacoby, placing his hand on the half-elf's forearm. He released the tension, and the elderly man coughed and choked in air.

"Don't hurt ol' Ben. No siree, the ox keeps away from Ben," he wheezed, rubbing his neck.

"Wonderful, locked in a cage with a madman," Cor'in scoffed, tending to Horatio.

Jacoby gazed at the reed-thin prisoner, who had scrunched himself into a ball, arms over his head for protection. "We won't harm you, old-timer," he said, sighing. "Can you tell me what happened to our friend?"

"Panic hit him, says old Ben. Ben seen it. Fraid a slavers, he is. That's what old Ben says."

"Slavers? I don't understand. Is that how they dispose of prisoners?" Jacoby asked, confused.

"Slav'in ain't for ole Ben. No siree. Nobody wants old Ben. Not old Ben," he said, cackling as if he'd told an outrageous joke.

Jacoby shook his head. Even the strongest minds break under strain.

He needed information, so he decided to take a different tack. "Ben, I saw you talking to my friend here. Know what set him off?"

"Froggy ain't right. Froggy ain't right," he chanted incessantly, rocking back and forth.

"Ben," Jacoby whispered kindly, placing a hand on his leg to calm the man. "You did nothing wrong. Just tell me what you said."

"Froggie asked about the pen. Ain't gonna help him though. Ol' Ben knows. Yes siree."

"What do you mean?"

"Slavers dun't play! Slavers dun't play!" he sang, still rocking.

"How often is the market?"

"Full moon gives the light! Ol' Ben seen 'em. Not for Ben, no siree."

Jacoby reached into a pocket and pulled a short strip of jerky, broke it off and gave it to the older man. "Thanks, Ben."

The older man's eyes sparkled, and he took in a surprised breath, tearing the jerky from the big man's hand and stuffing it in his mouth in one movement.

Jacoby turned back to Cor'in, now sitting next to a pale Horatio.

"How you doing?" Jacoby asked.

"I'm all right." The Anuran's eyes were red and puffy. "Slavers killed my father."

Jacoby laid a hand on the Anuran's shoulder.

"Worse, the demon who brokered with the brigands escaped during a battle with the militia."

"Sorry, mate."

The next morning, the guards opened the gate to the enclosure and armed pirates entered. They re-shackled each man, then herded the prisoners out onto a raised wooden deck in the center of the village green. They took everyone but the brotherhood and Ben Gumz.

"Hey, what's happening? Where are you taking the others?" Nathaniel said to the guards, but the words died in his throat when a tough guard backhanded the prince.

"Shut up, scum. You'll be taken soon enough."

Anyone foolish enough to resist forming a line on the platform received a beating or the tip of a cutlass. In front of the captives, a group of half a dozen men dressed in expensive tunics and robes huddled together, talking. Several men strode up to the platform and assessed each prisoner, poking and prodding to gauge muscle strength and overall health. A turbaned man stood at the end of the platform, two suited halflings on each side.

"Is that Mayor Tolar?" whispered Nathaniel to Cor'in, standing beside him. Cor'in eyed the two halflings. They flawlessly mirrored each other, and their familial relations were clear.

"Look like brothers. What is he doing here?" asked Grull.

"Mayor brothers, sister towns!" cackled Ben Gumz from the other side of the pen. "Gettin' their pie and ettin' it too."

Nathaniel watched the turbaned man step forward and speak in a deep, loud voice with an Eastern accent.

"Welcome, buyers. Captain Ironhook has brought in a fine catch. Yes, a fine catch indeed," he said in accented common tongue.

"Be it working in the salt mines, cutting lumber, or working the fields, we offer the best and strongest enslaved for sale." He stepped next to the first prisoner, an average-sized man with long, greasy hair covering his features. He pulled open a parchment and said, "First animal for sale. A tinker by trade. What do you offer?"

"Two silver," came a hefty patron's voice.

"Three," came another. The two dickered back and forth, finally settling on a bid of four silver and three copper.

"Sold!"

The pirate guards pulled the prisoner away, and the turbaned man continued with the next victim. Nathaniel watched in horror as they sold each man like cattle. He felt bile rise in his throat but swallowed it down.

"In what kind of barbaric place have we landed?" Nathaniel said and turned away. "What are we going to do?" he asked Cor'in.

Cor'in shook his head. "I don't know. Overpower the guards?"

"Too many, like bees protectin' hunny," came a voice, followed by a cackle.

"Shut up, you crazy old man," Cor'in bellowed.

"Crazy is as crazy duz. Ole Ben knows. Yes, siree. Ben watches. He knows."

"Did you not hear me?" Cor'in said, his face beginning to pink with anger.

"Don't listen to him, Ben. He's riding with a constant burr under his saddle," remarked Horatio.

"Froggy knows! Froggie knows!" the older man cackled.

"Shut him up, or I will," Cor'in said threateningly.

"Calm down. He's just a bit touched." Horatio turned to Ben. "Be calm, friend."

"Friend! Froggy's ole Ben's friend. Friend, Friend, Friend!"

"That's right, friend," Horatio said soothingly, patting the prisoner gently on the back. "We must be calm, Ben." Ben relaxed, leaning back against the enclosure wall.

"We need to think of a way out and find the women," said Jacoby.

"Elves and babies, elves and babies. Women, women, women," cackled Ben. "Ol' Ben seen women."

"What did you say?" said Grull incredulously. The brotherhood froze, unsure if the captive's words were true or the ravings of a madman.

Ben said nothing, rocking back and forth.

"Ben? Did you see the women?" asked Horatio in a gentle voice.

"They took'em into town. Ben seen 'em. March'in like soldiers, says Ben"

"In town? Where?" Horatio asked, his voice laced with worry.

"Ben don't tell no secrets. No, no, Ben's no snitch."

"Ben, do you know about sharing? Friends share and help each other," whispered Horatio as the other group members encircled the man. "Those women are our friends, and you're my friend. That makes us all friends, right? If you know something, share."

"Froggy's Ben's friend. Ben's friend."

"Right. Ben's friend."

He looked up at Horatio, who placed a hand on his shoulder. Through Ben's gray tassels, brown eyes sparkled with life.

"Not right to snitch. Ol' Ben can show Froggy. That ain't snitchin'."

"What can you show me, Ben?"

The older man hesitated, looking side to side as if being overheard. He lowered his voice to a whisper. "Ben got a secret. He got a secret. He got a secret!"

"A secret? What secret?" Horatio coaxed.

"Mama told Ben never to tell secrets, she did. O'le Ben knows. Don't spill no secrets," The older said, and threw his head back in a fit of cackling.

Everyone released a deflated sigh, followed by an irate Grullach who leaped at the prisoner, reaching out an arm to strangle the man.

"Tell me where they are or I'll choke it out of you!" Grull screamed, fire in his eyes. Jacoby tackled his friend a second before he throttled the man.

"Stop!" Jacoby said, holding down the fighting halfling. "He's out of his mind, Grull!"

The halfling squirmed and punched at his friend. "Get off!"

Grull's last punch knocked the wind from Jacoby, and he rolled over just as Blue and Cor'in landed on Grullach, pinning him down.

"Nooo!" he bellowed, fighting his retainers while the others watched in shock.

Ben's eyes widened, and he curled into a ball, shaking and mumbling, "Secrets, secrets, secret holes," under his breath.

Horatio rubbed his hands over Ben's back. "It's all right, Ben. We won't let him hurt you. Where's the hole, Ben?"

"Nine north, two east. Nine north, two east." The older man sobbed into his hands, shivering with fear. "Don't hurt old Ben! Not old Ben."

Horatio rubbed his chin for a heartbeat. Had Ben ever moved from his spot inside the pen? What could he mean? Then an idea sprouted in his mind. "Ben, do you like to hop like me?"

Ben fixed his eyes on Horatio. "Hop, hop, froggy goes hop. Ben likes froggy. Yes, siree."

Horatio smiled and jumped to his feet, ignoring the three friends wrestling on the prison dirt floor. He looked out at the sun, now just beyond overhead. He lined himself directly with the sun, and turned to face north, hopping nine times. Then, he turned eastward and took two more. He found himself in a dimly lit portion of the prison and leaned down to examine the sandy soil meticulously. He did not realize that this portion of the cage abutted the outside wall of a tool shed. Someone had pried the board up enough to dig under the wall where the cage wire had once bolted to the shed wall. The board leaned against the shed, making it difficult for passersby to notice any change.

"Pull those two apart," ordered Nathaniel. Then, realizing Horatio had discovered a clue, added, "Blue, watch the sale to ensure no one's watching us."

"He knows something about the women," spat Grull, still angry and rubbing his side where Cor'in had held him down.

"Calm down, Grull," said Jacoby, dusting himself off.

Nathaniel walked over to the Anuran, observing from over his shoulder. After several heartbeats, he understood and gathered the men together.

"Our friend Ben has created an opening in the back. With some effort, we can enlarge it and escape and, once free, find the women and steal a boat."

"Nat!" whispered Blue, warning the group that pirates approached. They dispersed, Horatio moving to Ben's side to console his new friend.

Captain Ironhook and Mayor Tolar came to the fence surrounded by several armed guards.

"I see you caught up with the Sea Mist," said Tolar.

"Not before these mercenaries killed twenty of my raiders and captured Captain Razor and the Black Gull."

"I warned you the trading vessel was armed," Tolar said, shrugging his shoulders.

"You could have provided more information," said Ironhook, his tone laced with frustration. "This lot almost cost me two ships."

"I can't hold your hand at sea, captain."

Ironhook's eyes narrowed. "Be careful, Tolar. Our arrangement profits us both, but there is a limit to what I'll tolerate."

The mayor smiled. "Spoken like a true pirate. I wonder if the authorities in Mar Napor would agree."

"Is that a threat?"

"Let's call it a treaty based on mutual distrust. We both benefit despite our disagreements." Tolar hesitated, seeing the anger leave the buccaneer's eyes. "So, how do we dispose of these ruffians?"

"Don't you have a contact with the southern salt mines?"

"Yes. That will take the fight out of them. And the women and children?" asked the mayor.

"Feisty, but controllable. They should work well for one of the Mar Napor elite as household staff. The witches' council may have use for the children."

"What? Human sacrifice? I draw the line at that!" said Mayor Tolar, gesturing with his hand to stop.

"Do you? Fifty sentochniks each should blur that line," suggested Ironhook.

"What line?" the Mayor said, a sly grin on his face.

Ironhook chuckled. "That's what I thought."

"I'll contact the salt mine master by carrier bird," said Tolar. "Can you arrange the women's and children's sale?"

Ironhook nodded. "We should be ready to sail on the morning's tide."

"And the Sea Mist?"

"Repairs will take a few weeks."

"The sooner she's seaworthy, the sooner we change her name and sell her."

"Why rush? Running low on funds, Tolar?"

"I worry one of the townsfolk will recognize Captain Spitz's vessel. What happened to him, anyway?"

"Kraken food."

"And his first mate?"

"Tied him to a yardarm as an example. The vultures will be on him soon enough."

"You think of everything." Both men erupted in laughter as they strolled away from the fence.

"Those Demons!" Nathaniel swore under his breath.

"What's our next move?" asked Blue.

"You heard them talking. We only have tonight to free ourselves and the ladies," said Horatio.

"Let's dig out now," suggested Grull.

"Too many guards," responded Micah glumly.

Jacoby's eyes met Nathaniel's. The young prince stroked the side of his face, a nervous habit when thinking. "Then we wait until dusk, expand the hole, and escape.

SEVEN

Nathaniel looked out from the fenced cage and counted himself lucky. A storm had blown in from the east, carrying pregnant gray clouds and gusting winds. By evening, the heavens had opened and poured pelting rain for the last hour. Visibility was nonexistent giving the group's escape plan a needed boost. Micah and Blue Ivy had dug at the shed edge and created a path under the fence, with the rain softening the soil.

"Are we ready to go?" he asked Micah.

"Ready. What about the guards?"

Nathaniel knew the pirates would check less frequently on their prisoners in this downpour. How long did the brotherhood have before the pirates noticed their escape? The gods knew, but now was the time to act.

""Go. I'll stay and keep watch. Horatio, do your best to use Ben as a guide."

"The demons, you will," Jacoby demanded. "Your presence in Tabor is essential, so you're going first. "I WILL be last."

"I'm in charge," said Nathaniel.

"I agree, and we'll need you to lead. I'm expendable and leaving last."

Nathaniel hesitated until Grull grabbed his arm and said, "He's right, lad. We must get moving." He pulled Nathaniel forward and pushed him down the hole. Grull followed, then Horatio with his arm around a shuffling Ben Gumz. The old man's wild eyes flashed at Jacoby as Horatio pushed him into the escape hole, mumbling, "Ole Ben ain't no snitch."

One after another, each warrior squirmed through the opening. "Demons!" Cor'in exclaimed, biting his tongue as the fence ripped a long gouge in his chest. When Jacoby's turn came, he found the exit too small.

"Don't wait for me," he called, using both hands to shovel the soft soil to enlarge the hole.

He had worked for several minutes, expanding the hole wide enough to squeeze through, when he heard guards approaching. I only have seconds, he thought. He doubled his efforts, squeezed through the tunnel, and pulled the fence back in place. He scrambled to his feet and turned to the edge of the shed, seeing movement ahead that could only be his friends in the mist-shrouded rain. Jacoby sprinted up a narrow avenue, skidding to a stop behind Grull.

"Hurry, the guards were coming as I left," he panted.

"We need some weapons," added Grull. Nathaniel gazed at the two, delighted his brother had arrived.

"Check the doors along the alleyway. Maybe one leads to safety," the prince suggested.

The group dispersed and tested all the door handles, but only one small door opened at the end of the alley. As several pirates shouted, "Alarm!" the group piled through.

"The prisoners have escaped! Spread out and drag them back," called the gruff voice of Razor, the half-goblin captain.

Nathaniel and the others found themselves in a narrow corridor leading to a storeroom filled with mule and horse tack. Saddles, reins, bits, and girths hung on wooden pegs along each side wall, ending in a paneled door. Nathaniel listened before opening but heard nothing. He opened the door and exited into a larger warehouse. Wooden crates scattered the area, several stacked in twos and threes, loose ropes draped from unused ceiling block and tackle.

"Look what I found," called Micah, opening a cabinet holding shovels, picks, and rakes.

Cor'in walked over, hefting a pick-ax in his hands, and said, "Now we're talking!" Micah handed out all the equipment, amounting to two shovels, a hoe, and the pick.

"Better than nothing," commented Nathaniel.

"Let me see one of those," solicited Grull, who used a shovel to open one crate. Ears of corn filled the inside, but one board making up the crate side splintered off.

"We can use this as a weapon, too," Grull suggested, smiling. He kept working until everyone had a tool or club.

Nathaniel placed a finger over his mouth, quieting the men.

Muffled voices were coming down the corridor toward the doorway. Unexpectedly, the door burst open, and four pirates wielding cutlasses charged into the room. Cor'in attacked loudly, "Yaha!" bringing down his pickax on a stunned raider. Micah swung his shovel at another, connecting with the man's temple with a loud "crack." Blue Ivy and Jacoby ambushed two others from behind the door, their wooden clubs colliding with their backs. One fell belly first to the floor, the other knocked off balance, stumbled but swiftly regained his footing. He faced Jacoby, an enormous, muscled man, saber at the ready. He slashed right and left in a whirlwind of steel, keeping a retreating Jacoby on the defensive. The mesomorphic raider hacked at Jacoby's head; he felt the metal woosh by his ear as he ducked. But his assailant pressed harder, backing him against the warehouse wall. A final powerful stroke shattered Jacoby's plank into kindling, leaving the big man defenseless. The pirate feinted right, then slashed left, preparing to open Jacoby's chest. Cornered, he saw the blow coming and winced, tensing at the reality of the sword slicing through him. But the blow never came. Jacoby opened his eyes to witness Micah holding a bloodied shovel and the pirate in a heap.

"Thanks, Micah."

"Glad to be of service," the Moor elf said, smiling.

Nathaniel studied the four prone buccaneers, none moving. "Tie them up, and let's continue. Where's Ben?"

Ben Gumz was curled in a ball, shaking like a leaf in the wind, Horatio at his side.

Nathaniel kneeled in front of the older man. "Ben, I know you're scared, but the pirates can't hurt you," he said softly. "Ben, where are the women?"

Ben opened his closed eyes and whispered, "Women work in the galley. That's what ole Ben says. Yes, siree. The galley."

Nathaniel's shoulders drooped. The old sailor's brain was as soft as mud after a hard rain. What was he thinking, bringing him along as a guide? Nathaniel felt every brotherhood eye on him, waiting for leadership---his leadership. Yet, he did not know what to do or where to search next. He shook his head, a growing sense of self-doubt in his chest.

"Are we leaving or what?" asked Cor'in sarcastically.

The words were like a tonic, replacing Nathaniel's insecurity with a surge of resolute anger. Cor'in is crass and irritating, but he has a point. The prince stood, his lips a line of iron determination. "I'm going to find the women and get off this island. Who's with me?"

"I am," said Horatio.

"And me," added Grull and Jacoby in unison. The others nodded.

"Then grab a weapon."

The prince strode to the warehouse door and peeked out. The rain had stopped, but the dark clouds remained, the air thick with humidity. Five armed pirates checked doors on the opposite sidewalk from the warehouse. He waited until the group of raiders passed around a corner, then waved the brotherhood to follow.

"Wait," hissed Horatio. Nathaniel turned back to see Ben still in the fetal position.

"What about Ben?"

"Leave him."

"But, he's helpless."

Nathaniel sighed. "He can come if he walks unaided. But, he's your responsibility."

"Right." Horatio bodily lifted the older man to wobbly legs.

Nathaniel stepped out the door and hurried half-bent to the next building, hoping to avoid running into more enemies. He hesitated but saw no movement and continued, stopping at each door he came to. He twisted each doorknob, but all were locked. At the third building, he heard voices, lowering his left hand in the universal signal to stop.

He lifted his head at the closest window, glancing inside. Four raiders, each with a colored bandana over their greasy hair, sat at a table talking. The rectangular room had several tables and chairs and a bar counter at one end, lit only by the afternoon sun from the open window.

"Where'd those sea rats run to?" one asked in a raspy voice, a long scar zig-zagging down one arm.

"I'd wager they made for the jungle," said a thin man with pocked cheeks.

Another pirate with one false leg hobbled over with three tankards from the bar. He said over his shoulder, "What'd you think, Clem?"

An older man came from behind the bar, an entire bottle of Taborian brandy in his hand. "Found the good stuff." He said before tipping the bottle and taking a long draught. "I think they'd never leave der women. The vermin's hide'in somewhere close; I can feel it. Best be on your guards, mates."

"I hope they had left 'um. More for us to share!" said the pocked raider, igniting the group in laughter. He grabbed the bottle, took a drink, then passed it to the next sailor.

"If they be near, Cap'n will end 'em," said Scar Arm.

"Best hope so," said Pegleg seriously. "I seen them cut down most of Razor's crew. Beasts, they are."

The conversation paused for several heartbeats, and Nat thought perhaps they had separated. Then he heard chair legs screech against the wooden floor.

"I better check on the lasses. Don't finish that bottle without me, mates."

Nathaniel had heard enough and hurried back to the group.

"Who's in that building?" Grull asked. "Did you see the women?"

"No, but I heard three or four pirates inside talk about guarding them. They're probably in the back."

"I'm going in," said Grull, stepping forward before Jacoby grabbed him from behind.

"Hold on, Grull. We need a plan."

"Allai'nn's inside!"

"I know, but rushing it might get her killed."

"Let's split up," interrupted Nathaniel. "Grull, take Blue, Cor'in, and Micah around the back. Jacoby, Horatio, and I will create a diversion. We'll meet at the far end of town, closest to the jungle."

"You heard the man. Come with me," Grull growled, setting off for the back of the building.

Nat gazed at Jacoby and said, "Ready?"

Before his brother answered, the younger man found a brick-sized stone in the road and threw it through the open window of the eatery. He heard one pirate yelp in pain and another cry, "What in the Kraken's beak?"

The prince stood in the road, sword in hand, and yelled, "Come out, you yellow dogs, and catch me if you have the will."

There was the shuffling of footsteps, then the door opened, and Pocked-Face and Scar-Arm rushed out. Each had a cutlass in one hand, their eyes gleaming at Nathaniel.

"Cap'n will pay dearly for you, sea slug," rasped Scar-Arm as he charged Nathaniel.

But Jacoby and Horatio intervened, clocking the raiders over the head with shovels as they passed. Both men collapsed like felled timber as Nathaniel confiscated their swords.

The three warriors rushed inside just as Peg-Leg hobbled to the door. His eyes widened at the sight of Jacoby in the doorway, and he twisted to run, but his drunkenness slowed him, and his leg tangled in the table leg. He stumbled awkwardly and fell face-first on the dirt floor, his momentum knocking him out cold.

"A cry of "Help!" from the back room inspired Nat, Jacoby, and Horatio to blast into the room, ready to fight. Nathaniel gasped and stopped dead at what they saw—the final raider holding a knife to a struggling Allai'nn's neck from behind. Grullach crouched nearby his sword ready, blood streaming from a nasty head wound. The other warriors blocked the exit, weapons out.

"Get back, vermin, or the lady dies," said the older pirate, his gaze shifting back and forth between the groups.

Nathaniel held up his sword, saying, "Hold on, mate. Don't do anything you'll regret."

"Regret?" the buccaneer spat. "You'll regret you killed her less ya drop them weapons and let me go free."

"All right." Nathaniel said, lowering his sword to the ground and raising his hands. "Drop your weapons, men."

The older pirate hugged the wall, one hand holding Allai'nn by the hair, the other with the dagger at her neck. The others moved out of his way; Grull hesitated, his face a fit of rage. Then he threw down his sword in disgust.

As the raider scooted along the wall to the open door, his eyes darted back and forth, sweat beaded on his forehead. "All you git on the floor. I dun't want no one after me."

The brotherhood members began kneeling on the ground except Nathaniel, who stepped forward and said, "We only want the woman."

The older man finally felt the open doorway and grinned, believing freedom was at hand. At that moment, the he loosened his grip around Allai'nn and reflexively glanced behind him. It was the opening Nathaniel needed, launching himself and tackling the duo. The force blasted Allai'nn and the pirate off their feet, the dagger flying as Nathaniel's weight drove them to the dirt. Allai'nn rolled over to her side; the air knocked out of her from the fall. In a flash, Nathaniel was on top of the stunned pirate, hands around the grizzled man's throat, choking his life away. Suddenly, strong hands pulled Nathaniel off the older man, and he heard Grull's voice, "He's not worth it, lad."

Nathaniel stood, his chest heaving as the pirate whimpered in pain.

"Ya broke me nose, ya sea demon! I wouldn't hurt the lass," he said, staunching the bleeding from his nose.

"Tie and gag him and the others. We're running out of time," Nathaniel hissed, spitting dirt from his mouth. "Allai'nn and the other women ok?"

"They had locked Rue, Lani and the children in the root cellar," Micah said. Nathaniel heard the unmistakable cries of infants.

The next moment, Lani rushed up, swarming him in a bear hug.

"I knew you'd save us," she whispered. Nathaniel smiled and gently kissed her on the head, but he knew the danger wasn't over. He pulled free of the embrace and said, "We need to keep moving before we're spotted again." Then he looked at the group. Someone was missing. Then he realized. "Where's Horatio?"

"He went to get Ben," stated Micah.

Horatio came rushing around the corner and skidded to a stop. "Ben's gone, and I heard more pirates are coming."

"How many? "Asked Jacoby.

"Don't know, but several voices."

"What do we do?" asked Rue, her eyes wide with terror.

"I have an idea, said Jacoby. He whispered something in the ears of Cor'in and Micah and handed a square stone to the elf. They tore off back into the kitchen. Moments later, Cor'in pushed the prisoners out the door, followed by Micah, as dark smoke wafted from inside the bar.

"Follow me," yelled Jacoby, running down an alleyway, the others rushing after him. Cor'in came last, dragging the prisoners.

"Cut them loose," Nathaniel said. "They're slowing us down."

Cor'in cut the pirates free, and they continued running. Jacoby zig-zagged up and down streets. Upon hearing raider voices, he promptly changed course, taking a side street in the opposite direction. Finally, he reached the jungle edge and dove into the foliage. The group waded through the heavy brush, dodging briars, vines, and low-lying branches of elders, cedarwoods, and live oaks. Jacoby finally slid to a stop in a small clearing, his chest heaving from exertion. The others came crashing beside him, hands on knees, gulping the dense air. The jostling trek had frightened the babies, who now screamed and wailed miserably.

"Where are we?" asked Nathaniel between breaths.

"Away from immediate danger." He turned to Cor'in, who held two infants wrapped in blankets under each arm like packages. "Any way to comfort them? That racket will draw raiders like bears to honey."

"I'm doing my best. Allai'nn, can you help?"

The elf princess took one infant and gently rocked it over one shoulder, soothingly rubbing his back. Cor'in tried to mimic the move, as did Blue and Rue with the other children.

Nathaniel straightened, his air still coming in rapid breaths. "I sense Ironhook isn't a man to quit easily. We need miles between us and this town to remain safe. Follow me."

The group lifted their weary heads and trudged after Nathaniel, using his saber as a machete to clear a path through the dense underbrush. After hours of battling sticker bushes, thorn vines, and a blizzard of biting mosquitos, the brotherhood reached a glade where the jungle separated. Nathaniel listened carefully for any sign of the enemy, eyes scanning the sparsely forested area with suspicion. He heard and saw no movement, but focused on a structure at the end of the glen. A wooden observation tower rose above the trees, the height of several men, its wooden plank walls grayed by heat and weather. What was a tower doing in the middle of a dense jungle? And who controlled this? Pirates, the local officials, or someone else? He watched for several heartbeats, but saw no one manning the tower.

"What's going on?" Jacoby whispered from behind. Nat gestured with one arm at the tower, and his eyebrows raised in understanding.

"Strange," Jacoby grunted.

Before Nathaniel could agree, Horatio was at his side, asking, "What's the holdup? The woman and children are being eaten alive by mosquitoes." Then he gazed across the clearing at the tower, nodding his head.

"Looks like the observation towers we had in Andura. You can see for miles from that vantage point."

"We can use it for our advantage," Nathaniel said. "I'll check it out."

"I'm faster," Horatio said. "I'm used to this terrain, anyway."

The frogman sprang forward, hopping in enormous leaps, crisscrossing one side of the glen to another until he reached the building. Horatio flattened his back to the wall, skirting along until reaching the tower door. He placed his ear to the door, heard nothing, and entered. Inside the structure was a hollow shell, a rickety wooden ladder rising from the sandy center to a trapdoor fifty feet above. Horatio clambered up the ladder, but halfway, a cross-rail shattered, and his body gave way. Only his finger pads saved him from falling, sticking perilously to the side rail. Sweat beaded on his brow as he pulled his body back onto the frame and continued climbing, reaching the trap door and pushing his way through. At the top, he found a square observation deck, the weathered floor planks dotted with darkened rot. He tiptoed to the edge, avoiding the weak spots, and beheld the entire island stretching before him. They were now at the island's northern end, the jungle expanding like a vegetative blanket over the white sands. With an arm wave, he signaled the "All

Clear" to Nathaniel, turning his attention to the pirate town. The frogman gasped, then began feverishly signaling the brotherhood, now crossing the glen to the tower. Groups of searching raiders spread along jungle trails, their colored bandanas contrasting with the deep green jungle hues.

"Run, run!" he yelled, terror gripping his chest.

Jacoby saw rather than heard the warning over the infant's continued crying, rushing the group along until everyone arrived at the structure.

"Are we being followed?" Nat said, anticipating the answer.

"Marauders are everywhere!" he yelled as he clambered off the deck and down the ladder.

Once reaching the ground, Horatio rushed to the group.

"How many are searching for us?" asked Nathaniel.

"Too many. But I saw a trail leading toward the coast. Follow me."

Horatio tore off along the edge of the glen, then turned down an opening in the brambles as the others followed. The trail was narrow and overgrown from disuse, but he pushed through waxy glasswort and cordgrass, ignoring the painful sting of the many cactuses populating the sandy soil. The trail abruptly ended after several hundred yards in the overgrown yard of a large house. He stopped short, Grullach and Nathaniel sliding next to him. Horatio hadn't seen the building from the tower, and he realized the answer lay in the moss-covered roof, flawlessly blending with the jungle.

"What the demons?" uttered Grull, mouth open.

"I couldn't see this from the tower," Horatio murmured as an explanation.

At that moment, the warriors heard voices over the fussy children.

"I hears babes, Cap'n. Dis way," said a voice somewhere behind them.

"No time to worry about the inhabitants. Hurry!" Nathaniel urged, running toward the home, taking the lead. When he reached the back door, he kicked it open and scampered in, followed by the others. The home was two stories, the bottom saturated with stale air, empty but for covered furniture covered in an inch of dust. A door to one side emptied into a desolate kitchen and root cellar, reeking of decayed foodstuffs. On the other, a library and office lay untouched for years.

"I'll check upstairs," Jacoby said, taking the steps three at a time. The stairs ended in a windowed landing, with bedrooms on each side. The first two were vacant, but in the last, Jacoby found a mummified corpse, the decayed skeletal remains forever resting in bed. He closed the door and walked back to the stairway, wondering what had killed the poor soul. As he passed the landing window, colors splashed in his peripheral vision. Ten armed raiders warily crossed the lawn, scanning the area for an ambush.

Jacoby rushed down the stairs, yelling, "Pirates coming this way!"

"Odin's beard! Do we ever get a break?" Grullach groaned, picking up his shovel.

A weary Nathaniel turned to Allai'nn. "Can you, with Rue, hide the children in the root cellar until this is over?"

Exhaustion covered the elf princess like a shawl, but she straightened to her full height and said, "I'm tired of running. I'm ready to fight with my family."

He smiled at her courage but said, "I need to know the children are safe."

She begrudgingly nodded, and the two women carried the children to safety. Lani stood at his side. "And me?"

"You're as good a fighter as anyone," he said, squeezing her hand.

She smiled and said, "I'm staying."

Nathaniel turned to see Jacoby whispering to Horatio and Blue Ivy, who nodded and strode upstairs.

"What was that about?' "

"Just a little surprise for our buccaneer friends."

A heartbeat later, a rough voice called from outside. "Cum out, ya sea rats, and we'll be merciful. If we have to root ya out, it won't be pretty fer ya."

Captain Ironhook's first mate, the brawny Lizardman named Flycatcher, waited outside the front door with nine pirates.

Nathaniel gazed at Jacoby, who held a hand to quiet his brother. The big man shouted, "Come in and get us, reptile breath!"

Flycatcher chuckled and pulled the saber hanging at his waist. "Time for some sport, mates. Make the scum pay."

As a group, the raiders let out an ear-splitting war cry, charging the house with cutlasses raised. They leaped through the door, fanning out to meet the waiting brotherhood. Two raiders fell at the door, a shovel strike knocking them out cold. The other eight surged to attack, the sight of their fallen comrades fueling a wildfire of fury in the pirates. They attacked with vigor, driving the brotherhood armed with shovels and picks back to the wall.

Cor'in faced off with Flycatcher, dodging blows from the lightning-like slashes from the Lizardman until the beast slashed so hard his pick handle snapped, and he felt the cutlass slice through his biceps. He fell helpless, blood oozing from the deep gash. Flycatcher smirked, ready to end the half-elf, but turned his attention to Horatio and Blue Ivy charging through the doorway. The Lizardman parried a blow from Blue, twisted into a "passata sotto" slide, stabbing Horatio through the thigh.

"Argh!" screamed the frogman, dropping his sword and crumbling to the floor. Now, Flycatcher focused all his attention on Blue Ivy, pressing his attack with alternating jabs and hacks. Blue expertly parried blow for blow, but the beast aggressively intensified his attacks, his blade becoming a torrent of lightning strikes the elf skillfully dodged. Flycatcher unexpectedly feinted left, then struck his second intention, so forcefully Blue's sword flew from his grip. But as the Lizardman pulled back for a kill strike, Jacoby slammed into the beast, knocking him sideways off his feet. Both bodies rolled, but Flycatcher was quicker to his feet. The beast kicked Jacoby violently in the ribs, stunning the big man. With Jacoby down, he searched the room for his next opponent, only to realize the battle had shifted.

Nathaniel, Lani, and Grull had dispatched three pirates, and were in a fierce battle with three more. Two other raiders had fallen back, trying to bandage various wounds. With five of his pirates out of the fight, Flycatcher instantly read the room, realizing his advantage was disappearing. The two men who fell to the shovels had vanished, running like scared children. Jacoby was rising from the floor, and Cor'in, despite the gash in his left arm, blocked the exit, sword in hand. One thought shot into Flycatcher's mind: Time to cut bait.

He called out, "Back to the ship, mates." The Lizardman feigned a step toward Cor'in, adding, "I'll see you again," then, in a meteoric leap, flew through the window, landing with a jolt on the turf. He rolled to his feet and sprinted toward the jungle, followed by his remaining raiders.

Nathaniel let out a relieved sigh and felt Lani lean into him. He pulled her into his embrace, whispering, "You okay?"

"Ok," she sighed, squeezing him tightly. He pulled her to arm's length, smiled, and gazed around the room. Allai'nn had heard the pirates evacuating through the floorboards and was now bandaging Cor'in's arm. Blue Ivy was doing the same to Horatio's thigh. Jacoby had painfully staggered to his feet, one arm gingerly holding his bruised ribs. Hearing the babies' cries, Micah had trudged down the cellar steps to collect Rue and the infants. The wounded pirates had long since run into the brush to safety.

"Everyone whole?" he asked.

Grullach sat in one corner, sweat mixing with blood from a laceration across his cheek. He half-saluted, messaging his adequate health as others assented they were alive.

"What next?" Asked Blue.

"We may not have much time before that demon Lizardman finds reinforcements. I'm going outside to find an escape route."

"I'll come with you."

The two warriors strode out the open door to the yard, turning left around the house where the jungle gave way to marsh grass covered pluff mud and subsequent white dunes. Nathaniel scanned the brush, but no game trail or path was apparent. On the far side of the home was another overgrown lawn patched with scraggly wax myrtles, tufts of switchgrass, dog fennel, and cacti. The remnants of a path weaved between bushes, phragmites, and scrub oaks opened to a white sandy beach. An overturned catboat lay half submerged in the milky sand, pulled from the surf months prior.

"Help me flip this," he said to Blue Ivy, unable to lift the boat alone. But together, they were unsuccessful.

"Wait," Blue said, wading into the brush and returning with a thick branch. He dug out sand from the lip of the boat and jammed the branch under, then, together, they used their weight as a force on the lever. A "pop-whoosh" sounded as the boat broke free from the shore's grasp, the previous occupant, sand crabs scattering. Nathaniel searched inside, finding a rolled sail, mast, centerboard, and tiller.

"She looks seaworthy enough," commented Blue, running his palm over the weathered hull.

"Beggars can't be choosy. Let's get the others before the raider's return."

The friends jogged back to the house, climbing the front steps in twos. Nathaniel noticed a bronze door plaque, green from oxidation. The prince could still read the letters: "Chillbone Estate."

He shoved open the door and said, "We found a boat. Let's go."

The group shuffled down the path to the beach, Micah supporting a limping Horatio. Upon reaching the catboat, Blue threaded the mast into the mast partner, unfurled the sailcloth, and slid the daggerboard in part way. Then he shoved the rudder pintles into the stern gudgeons, working the rusted connection back and forth until they snapped.

Grull, Micah, Blue, and Nathaniel pushed the catboat into the surf to knee depth, steadying the craft against the crashing waves. Nathaniel prioritized helping the women, infants, and injured, leaving little space for the men. But each climbed in, squeezing into the open cockpit like sardines. Nathaniel was the final person to enter at the stern. A strong breeze filled the sail, and the small craft sped up across the shimmering green water.

"Which way?' Nathaniel asked.

"We need a bigger boat," Lani said, pushing Blue's elbow out of her ribs.

"Agreed, "added Jacoby, his arms pinned between Cor'in and Horatio. But before Nathaniel had navigated the boat a quarter mile to sea, Rue felt the icy touch of water sloshing against her feet. "By the Gods, we're sinking," she screamed, pointing to the water in the hull well.

"We're not sinking. It's only a bit of water," Jacoby said calmly. "We need to bail."

However, the confining space in the catboat left little room to bend and bail.

"The water's rising," Rue screeched, her eyes filling with tears and wide in terror. "I can feel it on my ankles."

"It's all right, Rue," Blue comforted. "The boat is seaworthy."

But the water inside the boat rose gradually, validating the Oread's worries. In addition, ocean pitch agitated the already over-stimulated infants, causing an eruption of wails.

"Thor's hammer!" Nathaniel shouted irritably, a headache blossoming in his temples. "I'm heading for shore."

He slid the tiller wide to come about, the vessel reacting sluggishly despite a healthy breeze. Demons! Rue could be right, Nathaniel thought.

That's when it happened. An unexpected rogue wave, taller than most, slammed into the catboat halfway into the turn toward shore, drenching the tiny craft. The violent force knocked occupants off their seats, Micah and Grull catapulting across the boat. Nathaniel reacted like lightning, pushing the tiller toward the boat's heel and righting the craft, saving the two from splashing into the sea.

"Bail! Bail!" Jacoby urged, pulling his arms free and scooping overboard. But every swell fed the leaking vessel with more water until Nathaniel was unsure if they'd make it to shore. Luckily, the wave current pushed the top-heavy craft into shallower water.

Nathaniel swiftly realized there was just one choice to evade drowning. He tugged his brother by the arm and dove into the surf, lightening the load. The brothers half-swam and half-pulled the craft toward land using the mainsheet as a tow rope. The two brothers fought to keep their legs under them, straining against the tide's current and staggering under the weight of the swamped boat. With each thundering wave, the craft pitched and rolled, terrifying the infants and adults alike. Finally, the men reached beyond the wave break, and the boat glided to shore. They both fell to the creamy soft sand, chests heaving and exhausted from the battle. The others followed, looking half-drowned and trying to console the crying children.

"Well, that was a failure," spat a waterlogged Cor'in, his arm rebleeding from being tossed about.

"I thought we were fish food," added Grull, ringing water from his shirt.

Rue shivered, tears running down her cheeks. "As an Oread, I'm not used to the sea. When I felt the water coming in the boat, I panicked."

Blue Ivy swallowed her in a hug. "We all panicked when that wave hit us!"

Jacoby rolled over in the sand. "All that matters is we survived."

"So, what's next? We can't seem to escape Elf Island!" cried Lani.

"We need food, water, milk, and dry diapers," said Allai'nn, counting off the list on her fingers.

Nathaniel pushed himself to his feet, caked wet sand cascading off his chest and belly like a miniature avalanche. "I know where to find them."

"Where?"

"Trust me. I see lights coming from just above Sand Flea port. We can make our way there."

EIGHT

As they crab-crawled across the dune face, Lani and Micah peered through a clump of cord grass and sea oats, getting a glimpse of the northern end of Sand Flea port. Lani's eyes scanned the wharf, where she observed several small vessels docked and secured by a rotating group of pirates. She longed to use the spyglass in her pack to get a closer look at the militia's weaponry, but had to make do with what she had available.

"I see several pirates guarding the wharf," Lani whispered.

Micah lifted his gaze to the setting sun, its vibrant hues of orange, pink, and gold painting the western sky. "We'll know more at sundown when they change shifts. With the buccaneers firmly on his side, Mayor Tolar is confident that he is safe from any threats. I don't expect many night guards."

"I'll tell the others," she said, scooting backward down the dune until she reached a level where she couldn't be detected. She heard infants crying from beyond the next dune and followed the noise until she reached the group.

"What did you learn?" Jacoby asked as she strode up.

"Guards patrolling the city docks, but none around the town perimeter."

"Good," said Nathaniel. "That makes sneaking into town less risky."

Cor'in asked the obvious question. "How are we to find what we need without getting caught?"

"I have a three-pronged plan," taking a reed and scribbling in the sand. "I remember noticing a dry goods store on the waterfront when we arrived from the mainland. Allai'nn, Rue, and Grull will get the supplies we need. Cor'in, Blue, Lani, and Micah must help Horatio to the pier, then find and steal a boat big enough to travel. Preferably, a boat with a low enough draft to skirt along the coast would be ideal to avoid more pirate attacks. Jacoby and I will cause a distraction so we can escape." He hesitated. "Questions?"

"Why don't we all go to the wharf, take what we want from the dry goods, and leave?" Horatio asked, confused by the ruse.

"I'm worried the buccaneers will be on alert, patrolling just outside the harbor. Ironhook knows we haven't left the island, and this is our one chance before they close in."

"If your guess is accurate, what diversion could draw them in? Wouldn't that alert them to our presence?" Lani said, her brow furrowed in thought.

The young leader had realized the truth of her words, but what else could they do? "If anyone has a better plan, I'm all ears," Nathaniel said, gesturing with his open hands.

"I have a crazy idea," blurted Rue.

"What?"

"We could set fire to one of the pirate ships as the diversion!"

"I remember seeing some smaller craft at the harbor. Maybe one of those sleek ships that blocked our escape," added Grullach, warming to the idea.

"Mmm," Nathaniel murmured, stroking his chin. "It may be too dangerous to steal a ship when one close by is burning. I think setting a fire in the warehouse may be better and draw the pirates away from the harbor. "

Jacoby chimed in, "Some of us get supplies while the others cause the diversion. That will draw the pirates like bears to honey. While they're busy, we can steal a ship for us."

"Right!" exclaimed Rue excitedly.

Crow, the Svartalf assassin, calmly waited in the bows of a hickory tree growing in the courtyard outside King Gooseberry's palace apartment. He wore face paint above a black tunic and pants stained with camouflage red, orange, and brown splotches, seamlessly integrating with the tree bark and autumn colors. He ran his long fingers over the pouch he carried at his side, a nervous habit rather than reassurance. The poison extract he had distilled from boiling Fools Parsley leaves and a Whispering Haven cloak clasp remained where he'd placed them, waiting to be used.

Poison was not his favorite method of assassination. He no longer experienced the excitement of looking victims in the eye as they died from a drug. Crow's favorite method was torture, both for extracting information and the methodical pain produced. He had developed his technique over the years, like an artist perfecting each brush stroke of a masterpiece, wringing maximal pain from victims while keeping them alive to the bitter end. But tonight, he would not feel that joy. Once asleep, King Gooseberry would accept the poison without waking, becoming paralyzed within minutes, eventually choking on his secretions. Tomorrow, his servant would find him, cold and rigid as a tombstone, the clasp left from neighboring Whispering Harbor left as evidence of their treachery. He smiled at the idea that he could so easily manipulate the fools. War often started with a needle prick rather than with a bang. He relished the thought that HE drew first blood.

"Where in the demons are they?" demanded the skeletal figure. The lich-mage gazed at the face of Lazelle in a giant glass orb, his rotting features seething with rage.

"I believe they have left the continent, master," the black witch rasped over the howling wind, crisscrossing the land north of the Hope Wood. "There's no trace since the ruse by the animals. The confederates paid a high price for the trickery."

"I hope so," he said through clenched teeth, barely holding in the explosion of anger inside. How could a group of humans and elves disappear? No, someone was hiding them. But who had the power to evade his scrutiny? No one alive could match his power and abilities except Crepitus. And the eastern war occupied him at present. "And the Lupine?"

"Searching."

Ravenite grasped the goblet on the table before him and threw it clattering across the floor. Where are they? Where? He stroked his chin, ideas churning through his mind.

"You said 'off continent'. Where?" demanded the mage.

"There are many islands, many coves, many sea raiders along the coast. They could be anywhere, but my guess would be a coastal town to find passage to Mar Nâpor."

The battle for Tabor proved to be more difficult than Ravenite had expected, necessitating additional time for victory. The prince's successful return home was a threat that he could not afford to ignore.

"Head along the coast south. Fly over every island and cove until you find them. Have the Lupine proceed to Mar Napor in case they've escaped our net."

"Your will is my will."

The orb went dark, and Ravenite sat back in his plush chair, his frustration surging. In that moment, he felt loving arms encircle his neck, bringing him a sense of calm. His anxiety, which had been building, dissipated like pulling the plug from a water-filled sink. Cas, the fiery red witch queen, gently stroked her lover's neck, showcasing the love and affection they shared.

"What stresses you, my lord? Your neck muscles are as tight as lute strings."

"Just a minor inconvenience, my love," he said, closing his eyes and relaxing. She had heard that lie many times before, so it did not affect her. Ravenite would keep the bad news secret until, with her gentle touch, she could relax him enough for him to let go of his physical tension and finally speak freely.

Jacoby and Nathaniel tiptoed along the alleyway, keeping to the shadows. The byway, squeezed between two large warehouses, was dingy and filled with piles of refuse, used clothes, and broken pallets. The waning sunlight combined with the natural gloom masked the two men's sojourn in the city until Jacoby heard talking coming their way. He shot his arm out, pinning the prince against the wall, both holding their breath. Two fishermen walked by discussing the tide table, oblivious to the hiding figures. They let out a united sigh and continued to the corner. Jacoby peered out, but saw no movement along the road. He waved Nathaniel forward, and the two scurried over to the warehouse door, and slipped inside. A single oil lamp's glow lit the room, revealing several wooden crates stacked on each other.

"This will do," Jacoby said, grabbing the lamp. "Push that other crate over closer."

Nathaniel leaned into the box, driving his shoulder into the side, shoving it closer. "That's heavy."

Jacoby spied some refuse in one corner and piled it next to the crates. Then he took the lamp and smashed it against the crates, exploding in a mini fireball. The flames swiftly engulfed the refuse and wood, black smoke billowing to the rafters.

"Let's get out of here," Jacoby shouted as the two sprinted nonstop out the door and down the alley.

Meanwhile, Grull, Allai'nn and Rue stood next to the locked glass door of the darkened dry goods, searching for any movement. The halfling had found an overturned cart behind the store and wheeled it just outside the entrance. Grull looked both ways before shattering the glass with one powerful pendulum strike with his elbow. The glass exploded, spraying shards in all directions, Grull shielding the women with his body before entering. In minutes, they had piled the cart full of needed items and slunk down a side street to meet the others.

The group didn't wait long before Jacoby and Nathaniel sprinted up, breathing hard.

"Gambit's set. Let's move," Nathaniel said between breaths. After a harsh look from Allai'nn, added, "We can feed the infants on board the ship."

They raced toward the end of the wharf where Micah and Blue were securing a vessel.

Jacoby gazed back, the night sky alight with orange flames and billowing smoke. "That should keep them busy."

Crow slid from the hickory branches, landing noiselessly on the garden lawn. He slithered across the grass and melted into the shadows of the ivy-covered tower. In one leap, he was ten feet up, climbing along the ivy lattice toward the king's bedchamber. Just below the window apron, he waited, listening. Snores emanated across the night air, assuring the king was deeply asleep. The elf pulled himself through the open window, worming his way to the bedside. He watched the middle-aged monarch slumbering. How peaceful he appeared. The assassin wondered what final dreams he had before his last turned nightmarish. The thought was fleeting, and he refocused on his mission. Quietly, the elf pulled the small vial from his pouch, removing the cork. In one fluid movement, he poured the poison into the king's mouth, tightly holding his nose closed with the other hand. The man's eyes fluttered open, and terror registered for a heartbeat. He squirmed and writhed for a moment, fighting the poison, then relaxed as the paralysis took over. Finally, white foam spilled from the king's mouth, and his breathing ceased.

Crow crossed to the window and straddled the sill, assessing his work. Life was fleeting. How easy for me to change the course of history. In several brief minutes, I snuffed out a life and started a regional conflict. Not bad for a night's work! The Svartalf grinned, his sharpened teeth gleamed white against the shadows. Then, he swung out to the ivy lattice and disappeared.

"Look," said Horatio, pointing to the fence prison as they ran toward the ship. Several poor souls paced inside the cell, head drooping with despair. In his usual spot, Ben Gumz rocked back and forth, moaning. Purple bruises littered his face, one eye red and swollen shut.

"Ben deserves his freedom after that beating, "said Nathaniel. "Agreed?"

"Agreed," echoed Horatio.

"Meet me at the waterfront," Nathaniel whispered to Jacoby and sprinted to the cage. The prince snuck around to the back of the pen and peeled back the wire abutting the shed. "Anyone who wants freedom, come with me."

The men seemed confused until Nathaniel squeezed through the opening inside the jail, repeating his words in a whisper. "I said, who wants freedom? Follow me." He rushed over to Ben, now staring at him with wide, vacant eyes.

He delicately grabbed the older man by one arm and lifted him, whispering, "Time to leave, Ben." Ben seemed confused but didn't resist as Nathaniel shuffled him to the escape tunnel and outside.

"You're free now. Gods speed," Nathaniel said to each prisoner as they sped away. Only one remained, a short, younger fellow with broad shoulders wearing a soiled tunic and leather britches. He had the muscular build and calloused hands of an artisan, and was a half-foot shorter than his rescuer. He stuck out his hand, saying, "Thank you."

Nathaniel shook it brusquely, then turned and shuffled Ben toward the pier. But the man followed him, catching up and taking Ben's other arm for support.

"I said you're free," Nathaniel stated flatly.

"I know. I thought you might need help with the old man."

At that moment, Nathaniel heard voices, followed by groans. The three turned a corner to see Jacoby and Grull standing over two unconscious guards.

"Hurry," Jacoby waved, leading them to a sloop bobbing in a slip at the end of the jetty. At forty feet, with a sleek black color, pointed bow, and low draft, the ship had a sinister appearance, like a breaching shark ready to strike. Nathaniel remembered the craft, one of the two which had cornered them on the open sea. Micah and Blue had made sure no one was on the ship and waved them on board.

"Let's get on board and underway. Gods know how long our trickery will last."

Horatio, Allai'nn and the others loaded the children and supplies while Nathaniel walked Ben on board. The other man stood passively by, his head down in embarrassment.

Nathaniel noticed him and frowned. "Are you still here? I said you were free."

"But.." the young man murmured.

"But what? I don't have time for small talk," he said irritably, turning away.

"I thought I might go with you," stammered the man, looking away.

Nathaniel stopped short. All eyes tracked to the man, his face blushing crimson, then to Nathaniel. The prince let out a long sigh, recognizing the young being as a dwarf.

"What's your name, stranger?" Nathaniel asked, his arms crossed. "And what tribe do you hail from?"

"Felix Elmwood. But most call me Elm," the dwarf said. "I'm from a small clan near the Hydra's Teeth," he added, rubbing his toe in the harbor's sandy soil.

Nathaniel assessed the man. Maybe he could work his passage off as a sail hand? "I have friends in the Hydra's Teeth. He hesitated, a strange voice inside telling him to beware. He needed to question the lad in more detail, but time was short. "All right, Elm. You can work your passage to Mar Nâpor, then we part ways."

Ironhook stood behind the bucket-brigade line, his hands on his hips in frustration. Orange-yellow flames engulfed three main warehouses, and a fourth's charred frame smoldered like an overdone steak. Hundreds of sailors toted water from the city well, but the fire raged despite the effort.

Mayor Tolar stepped beside him, wringing his hands in worry. "What are we going to do? This fire may consume the entire town!"

"Did you order the trenches cut two streets over?"

"Your men are digging the firebreak now."

"That's the town's only hope," Ironhook said, his voice thick with frustration.

"How could this have happened?" Tolar challenged. "There have been no lightning storms, and there are enough sailors and militia here to field an army."

Ironhook balled his hands into fists and squinched his eyes tight, realizing his mistake. Why had he missed it before? Am I getting old or more foolish with age? Nothing is ever as it appears! Anger rose through his chest, his eyes burning as bright as the flames. He screamed over the clatter of moving buckets at the large Lizardman returning with twenty dust-covered sailors carrying shovels.

"Bloody escaped prisoners! This is a ruse to keep us occupied. Fly Catcher, get the men back aboard! Now!"

The reptile hesitated, confused. "But captain, the fire?"

"I said, now!" Iron hook spat, shaking with rage. "Or I'll keel-haul the lot of you!"

"You heard the Captain," Fly Catcher dropped his shovel, and yelled over the fire's noise. "Drop everything and head back to the ship!"

Ironhook turned and began striding toward the city harbor, with Mayor Tolar rushing behind him. "Wait, wait," he implored. "You can't leave! The town will be cinders by morning."

"That's your problem."

"I don't understand! Where are you going?" pleaded Tolar.

Ironhook turned on the mayor, his face a mask of fury. "It's a diversion, you fool. Those sea demon prisoners set the place on fire to escape!"

With the calm emerald waters of the Elf Island sound stretching out before them, Blue Ivy guided the ship while Grullach and Micah, working in tandem, adjusted the sail sheets to catch the wind. He smiled, feeling warmth spread through him as Rue nestled close, her body radiating heat that chased away the chill of the night. She was the person he loved more than anything else in the world. The realization that she shared his feelings filled him with a joy that was almost too much for an elf to bear.

As the ship sailed on, Nathaniel found himself looking across at the other passengers and studying them closely. Horatio lay beside Ben Gumz, who slept soundly with his injured leg propped up on the keel hump. Elm's gaze swept across the surroundings, his eyes gleaming with anticipation and excitement.

"Ever been on a ship before?" asked Nathaniel.

"Not until I was a prisoner, and the view we had was of the brig," Elm exclaimed, eager for the new adventure.

Nathaniel appreciated the excitement. He had felt the same when the group had first traveled over water. "So, Elm, tell me your story."

"Not much to it. My father, a brownie merchant, met my red dwarf mother while trading in the Hydra's Teeth mountains. They fell in love, but dwarven law forbade her union with a 'Dajhe'."

"A Dajhe?"

"Sorry, it's nasty dwarven slang for Fae, or non-dwarf," Elm replied bitterly.

Nathaniel frowned, saddened that there remained so many closed societies. Would he have felt the same way if Jacoby hadn't hired Allai'nn and the dwarf, Bluebeard, to work as a server and cook at the Sleeping Dragon Inn? It took months of patience and kindness from the elf and dwarf for him to overcome his bias towards them.

"Sorry. Continue," refocusing his attention.

"They fled, setting up a home in the coastal town of Green Turtle, on the western border of the Five Brother Mountains and south of Erewhon. I learned from my father the art of smelting and ironwork, eventually taking over his trade route to Mar Nâpor."

"How were you captured?"

Elm's cheeks colored, embarrassed. "I was a fool."

Nathaniel patiently waited for more.

"I had a rigorous journey and stopped into a roadside tavern for refreshment. The bartender offered me a free ale. The bartender must have drugged the ale because I awoke in the pirate brig."

Nathaniel shook his head. He narrowly escaped falling victim to the same ruse himself months before in the town of Arcane. "That's more common than you know. He must have been on Ironhook's payroll."

"And what about your group? What led to your escape from Sand Fly?" asked Elm.

Nathaniel considered the younger man for several heartbeats. Though he was roughly Nathaniel's age, he gave the impression of being significantly less mature. The brotherhood, of course, had been tested repeatedly, facing numerous threats, including assassins, various forms of evil, and even continental war, but they had emerged victorious each time. The past months had been a trial by fire, marked by the loss of dear friends, the pain of combat wounds, and a series of near-death experiences. Yet they had picked up lifelong companions with whom he had fought side by side and survived. How could he expect this lad to even have an inkling of his experiences?

"It's a long story. We're traveling to the City of Spires in Tabor. Our ship fell into the hands of buccaneers before we reached Mar Nâpor. By dumb luck, we discovered Ben had tunneled a path to freedom."

"Well, thanks for accepting me as a passenger," Elm said, smiling.

"Don't thank me yet. The pirates will come after us. Do you have any weapons training?"

"Weapons? My father taught me the basics, and I hunted growing up."

"It may have to do. What do you carry?"

"Normally just a knife. But I lost it."

Nathaniel handed the younger man a scaling knife. "I took this off one of the pirate guards. If we're boarded, protect the children."

Elm took the knife and nodded. Nathaniel got to his feet, squeezed the younger man's shoulder, and returned to the stern to relieve Jacoby on the mainsheet.

The horned owl perched high on a hardwood branch at the edge of an open meadow many leagues north of Tabor. The ancient Maple's rich brown bark-covered trunk and limbs, and thick canopy blended effortlessly with the owl's black and gray feathers. Combined with the moonless night and his statue-like repose, and the bird became completely invisible.

The predator listened and observed the witch's coven ritual below, his keen sight and hearing absorbing every detail. Low moans and chants crackled the area with magical electricity, making the bird shiver with dread. Over a hundred witches surrounded a central figure, a tall, skeletal being draped in a dark robe. He held a bucket and ladle in one hand and held up the other for quiet. Immediately the chanting ended, and the lea was silent as a church mouse.

Ravenite, the undead lich-mage dipped the ladle into a dark red mixture and poured scoop by scoop in the geometric pattern of a pentagram. The owl swallowed down nausea as the aroma of fresh human blood filled his beak. The wizard stepped outside the shape and pulled a small pouch from his robe pocket. He sprinkled white powder on the earth, encircling the entire pentagram.

"That should do, eh, Cas?" Ravenite whispered to an enormous tabby cat, rubbing his leg.

He studied his work for another moment, then raised both arms and recited the incantation. A low rumble shook the earth, and the ground cracked and opened within the pentagram. Red flames erupted from the pit, licking the night sky, as all the witches uneasily stepped back. After several heartbeats, two clawed hands reached out from the hole, followed by a horned head. The monster glowed a dull orange-red, tendrils of smoke rising from the liquified lava skin. It had a lean, muscular build, reaching the same height as the wizard, with three spiral horns protruding from an eyeless face. A salamander? The owl had only heard of such hell-dwellers.

"My lord awaits your commands," it said in a raspy, high-pitched voice.

"Let your lord know the time for his undead minions to rise has come."

The monster bowed, turned and disappeared into the pit without a word. With a wave of Ravenite's hand, the ground shook, and the pit closed. An old, hunched-over witch limped toward the wizard.

"And what of us?" asked the coven high priestess.

"Spread the word among your ilk and prepare, black mother," Ravenite said, reassuring the older witch. "The grave-stalkers are coming."

The sloop, guided by Grullach's skilled hand, arced along the mainland coastline in a broad reach, its sails catching the wind. As the larger, faster pirate frigate pursued them, executing the maneuver seemed his only hope for the small vessel's survival. Except for the few who were on sail duty, every able-bodied member of the Brotherhood had drawn their weapons in preparation for the expected boarding. The halfling, however, had different plans, noticing a subtle wave break a few hundred yards from the shore, suggesting an underwater reef.

He smiled to himself, anticipating the pirate captain had not yet seen the change from his vantage point. As he drove the boat closer to land, it became obvious the break held a sturdy reef just a few feet below the surface. If their luck held, which was a misnomer since the group rarely had any fortune at all, their shallow-hulled craft would slip over the shoal and make land. By baiting their pursuers, he hoped the frigate might wreck on the reef.

"Hold on to something," he warned the others as they sped toward the break. With a jarring jolt, the boat was thrown off course, and a deafening scraping noise reverberated as its keel collided with the unforgiving reef. With a sickening lurch, the boat tilted, time seeming to stall as it hung precariously before the impact of the next wave. The boat leaned heavily to one side, throwing Grull and the others off their feet. As Jacoby shot forward into the turbulent surf, Blue held on tightly to the rail, clinging to it for survival. As the boat pitched violently backward, the main boom swung with tremendous force to the opposite side. Another wave slammed into the boat, shifting it to the right once more, then causing it to sway back and forth like a pendulum. The boat stuck once again and jolted violently, causing Blue to lose his grip, and sending Micah tumbling overboard. As the next wave crashed down, it forcefully shoved the boat over the reef, sending it bobbing and floating toward the shore.

Grull, drenched in seawater and disoriented from the pounding waves, glanced back over his shoulder, a wave of disappointment washing over him as he saw the larger ship lowering its sails and veering into the wind.

Nathaniel was the first to react, springing up and shouting, "Jacoby?" Micah? Blue?" with a note of panic in his voice. He searched the water frantically, his eyes scanning the surface, but there was nothing to be seen. His brother's head emerged from the water, one arm wrapped protectively around an injured Micah, as they both kicked toward the shore. A short distance ahead, Blue met them, and they together pulled Micah toward the ship, now grounded on a limb of the coral shelf by the persistent tide.

The prince turned his attention to the others. "Everybody all right?" he asked over the wailing of the terrified children.

"We're all intact," said Allia'nn, her hair askew and consoling her children.

He cradled Lani, holding her tenderly by the shoulders and looking her in the eye. "Are you okay, my heart?"

"I'm all right," whispered Lani, rubbing her shoulder where the boom swung into her, almost sweeping her overboard. "But I'm ready to be off water for a spell."

He chuckled. "Me too." Then his attention flew to the frigate several hundred yards away, and his eyes bulged.

"Demons! The pirates are lowering longboats. Grab anything we might need. We need to get to shore."

Everyone scampered to load the supplies, Allai'nn, Rue, and the children in to the lone dinghy tied to the boat side. When full,

Nathaniel and Grull lowered the boat into the water with pulleys, Allai'nn working the oars into the locks and pushing free.

"Everyone in the water," Nat said, climbing over the side rail and dropping into the surf. Cor'in, Horatio and Grull followed. Only Elm remained planted on the deck, his eyes filled with fear.

"What's the matter, Elm? The pirates are on their way," the prince called out, dolphin kicking in place.

"I...can't...swim," the half-dwarf mumbled, terror lacing his voice.

"Odin's beard! Jump, and I'll help you."

But the poor sod became paralyzed. He knew he should leap overboard; confident Nathaniel would help him to shore. But his muscles rebelled against his thoughts and he couldn't move. Then a loud "thwack" sounded behind him as an arrow struck the hull. He saw several pirates with crossbows bobbing in long boats in the surf only a few hundred yards away.

He closed his eyes and willed his muscles to contract, jumping into the waves. He sank like a rock, and he thrashed in panic, reaching the surface. Abruptly a powerful hand pulled him up, and he broke the surface, taking in a gasping breath. Nathaniel wrapped a hand over his chest, saying, "I've got you." scissor kicking to shore. The half-dwarf struggled, but Nathaniel's arm was like a vice, kicking until his feet touched the sandy bottom, where Jacoby and Blue helped pull in an exhausted Elm.

Once ashore, Nathaniel said, "Let's move. The pirates are right behind us."

Each member collected what supplies they could hold and, with Nat leading the way, pushed into the underbrush. Only Elm lay on the sand, breathing hard.

Cor'in jerked the younger man to his feet and angrily said, "Come now or die."

"But I can't. I'm too tired to move."

"You're with us, or with the pirates. Your choice." He turned and jogged after the group, who were already wading into the dunes.

Elm looked out at the surf. The first pirate boat had boarded their scuttled ship, but the next was far behind. "Wait. I'm coming," he whimpered, staggering to follow.

NINE

"The prisoners are long gone, Cap'n," Fly Catcher admitted to Ironhook over the howling wind. "We found their trail, but with the squall coming, thought it was better to return."

Ironhook studied the dark purple clouds sweeping across the eastern sky. He had expected the news. His first mate was a brave and loyal subordinate with a cunning intellect. He would never risk losing the ship over a few prisoners despite the significant damage they had inflicted on his raider organization. Damnable sea snakes! The fire inflicted considerable damage on the Sand Flea township alone, setting back his operations for weeks, and the damage to the ship only compounded the problem. Doggedly, he pushed aside his thoughts about the past and turned his focus to the present.

"What of our stolen ship? Is it salvageable?" he asked the Lizardman.

"The ship's carpenter has patched the reef-damaged hull enough to sail. I've ordered a skeletal crew to sail her back," replied Fly Catcher.

"Excellent," Ironhook murmured, happy something had gone his way. "Make full sail. If we're lucky, we can outrun the coming storm."

He turned and climbed up the quarterdeck ladder to the helm, but his thoughts slipped back to the escapees. He ran through a list of the prisoners' accomplishments since their capture: escaped from their cell, acquired weapons, evaded recapture, burned a large portion of Sand Flea as a diversion, stole a ship after overpowering guards, released more prisoners, and finally, escaped his pursuit. The prisoners must have had some training in strategy and tactics to pull off so many successes. He hated to admit it, but he was glad to be rid of the lot. Good riddance!

The brotherhood trudged through the sawgrass, oleander, scrub pines, and Adam's needle that covered the half-sand, half-pluff mud soil bordering Mar Nâpor Bay. As the day progressed, so did the temperature and humidity, forcing the clan to stop frequently for water. Although Elm seemed to fall behind, he would always catch up just as Nathaniel was about to continue their journey. Acting as leader, the prince noticed Elm's difficulties and, with an understanding heart, granted an extension of the rest period, giving Elm a few more minutes to recover.

"How are you holding up?" He asked his younger companion.

"All right, if I were a jackrabbit!" he huffed, sweat cascading down his face and chest like a waterfall. "Why are you running like an army is chasing us?"

Nathaniel put a hand on the half-dwarf's shoulder.

"If you stick with us, you'll learn that our enemies always pursue us, and we carry danger with us like a sack," Nathaniel said, putting a hand on the half-dwarf's shoulder. "Sorry."

Elm's anger dissolved into a sheepish realization. His focus had been to survive in a tough world. Being of mixed heritage, he experienced shunning from his dwarf community and complete distrust from humans. Often an outcast because of his smaller stature, he had grown into a loner, unaccepted except as an artisan. Was he being treated as one of the group?

He wanted to ask but feared the answer, so he mumbled, "I'm not used to this pace."

"You get used to it," the prince said with a half-smile. "Ready?" But he didn't wait for an answer, turned and said, "We need to keep moving."

Elm grunted but didn't move.

Jacoby and Micah sat nearby resting, watching the interaction. A surge of pride trickled into Jacoby's chest, but Micah vocalized his thoughts.

"Nat's growing into a fine leader," he said, smiling. "Apple doesn't fall far."

"Ha," Jacoby scoffed. "He's benefitted from being surrounded by some of the best and most honorable men and women for months."

"Right," Micah said, a flicker of amusement dancing in his eyes. Jacoby was reluctant to accept praise for his role in raising the prince. But he spoke the truth. Micah was fortunate to have stumbled into this brotherhood a few months ago, and since then he has grown to admire and accept his comrades, feeling grateful for the opportunity to be part of this group. Because of his own experiences as an outcast and a lone merchant, he was keenly aware of the difficulties associated with learning to trust and be trusted.

He walked confidently towards the younger man, his hand outstretched in a gesture of welcome. "We can do this together, let's go."

With a deep frown, Elm stared at him, then released a resigned sigh and took his hand, his expression revealing a mixture of annoyance and reluctant acceptance. Micah grasped his arm and pulled him to his feet.

"I'm Micah, from Tuath de Rydh," the Moor elf said in an introduction.

"Elm. Tua what?"

"Moor elf lands far to the south." He paused a heartbeat, then asked, "A tinker, right?" I'm a merchant myself."

Interest sparked in the dwarves' eyes. "What did you sell?"

"Moorschreken skins." Before the younger man could ask, he added, "A marsh reptile with tough, smooth scales. Excellent for boots, trousers or jerkins. "

The dwarf nodded. "I make household items. Pots, pans, kettles, and such."

"New to the trade?"

"Is it that obvious? This is my first route alone to Mar Nâpor. So far, it's been a disaster. I lost everything in the attack."

Listening to the dwarf's story, Micah felt his old wounds reopening as he remembered the attack on Tajman Sghar months before that had taken everything from him. But, thanks to Jacoby and the welcoming Brotherhood, he had survived the ordeal. Suddenly, the same feelings of sorrow and despair that he had experienced during his loss resurfaced. He knew just how alone and defeated one could feel, yet over time, his pain gradually subsided and his wound healed. New friends and thrilling adventures had combined to help push the memory far away. He was glad to be a member of the Brotherhood, and he was sure they would welcome Elm, too.

"You might not believe it now, but things are going to change for the better, my friend," Micah said with a smile.

It took the group a whole day to cross the base of what locals called "the finger", a thin peninsula jutting into the mouth of the bay. Food was scarce, other than a few wild apple trees and blackberries, but fresh water was plentiful. The group crossed several freshwater streams that cut across the land, runoff from the melting snows of the nearby hills. They reached the hamlet of Not Far by evening, a small fishing village wedged into a nook of an Erewhon river remnant. The terrain had changed from a sandy scrub along the coast to terra firma with scattered mature live oaks and grasslands.

"We're penniless, so our quickest option is to borrow more supplies from a grocer in town, and keep moving," Nat said to Jacoby and Grull.

"I'm not happy with stealing. We need to find gainful employment," Jacoby said.

"I'm not as straight an arrow, but I see your point," remarked Grull. "For my children, I'll do anything to keep them alive."

"Do you have a better plan, brother?"

Jacoby stroked his chin for several heartbeats. He didn't want his brother to devolve into a hapless cutthroat, always searching for the easiest route to meet his needs, no matter the consequences. However, they were in a time crunch to reach Tabor and rally the kingdom against Ravenite's army.

"We can work our way to Mar Napor like we planned with Captain Spitz?"

Nathaniel considered the idea. Working as a deckhand or mercenary would raise money and expedite the journey. But they still had to worry about Ironhook and his greedy band of buccaneers.

"Traveling by sea again might be risky. Will you enter the town and assess our options? Then we weigh the risks," said Nathaniel with finality.

"Agreed. I'll take Cor'in with me."

The two warriors traversed the path that ran beside the river, eventually arriving at the village where they entered the only tavern, a worn-down building with a faded sign that read, "The Spotted Cowrie." They concealed cutlasses and daggers under their tunics and linen pants for security. In the bustling rectangular inn, boisterous sailors and anglers laughed, swapped stories, and enjoyed cheap grog. Old fishnets and crab buoys hung on the walls as decoration, and the air was thick with pipe smoke and stale beer.

As they entered the bar, Jacoby and Cor'in made their way to the counter. A husky bartender with a thick gray beard and salt and pepper curls covered by a watch cap, arrived after a few moments.

"What can I offer you, strangers?"

Cor'in spoke up, pulling his dagger from his belt. "A trade. The knife for grog."

The bartender studied the blade, realizing it held nothing of value. "

"Umph," he grunted, then studied the two men. Their gaunt faces and dark-ringed eyes divulged a rough past. "Broke, are ye?" The older man shook his head. "This it'll get ya a pint and a bowl of stew each. I'm Cowden, by the way, owner and barman," he said over his shoulder, striding through a hinged door and returning with two steaming bowls of stew and tankards.

"Thank you, Cowden," Jacoby said, attacking the stew like it was his last meal.

"So, what brings ya to Not Far?"

"Making our way to the capital," Cor'in said between bites. "But we ran into some trouble."

"Pirates or bandits?"

"Pirates. But we escaped."

Cowden leaned in, his eyes darting from side to side with suspicion. "Keep ya voice down. I favor they're spies about." Both men went silent.

"Meet me out back in five minutes," he whispered, then turned away.

The two warriors devoured their stew and strolled outside, avoiding eye contact. They rushed around to the back of the building, clearing their swords in case of trouble.

A whispered voice from the shadows said, "Here."

Cor'in could see a figure in the gloom, but little else. They stepped forward, hands on the pommel of their weapons.

"Cowden?"

Emerging from the building shadows, the bartender materialized like an apparition. He extended a small, crumpled piece of parchment to Jacoby.

"Ya find Cap'n Pike at tis house. He's a fair man, and look'in for honest men. Thor's luck be on ya." He disappeared before Jacoby could thank him.

Jacoby scanned the paper. In simple block letters, it read: "Rid Lost Gul." He showed the script to Cor'in, who frowned.

"What does it mean?"

"Not sure. Let's walk the alleys and see what we find?"

For the next quarter hour, Jacoby and Cor'in walked the town avenues, searching. The hamlet was larger than expected, ten streets by eight, with few signposts. Jacoby and Cor'in were close to giving up when the big man noticed a sign reading "Lost Gull Lane."

"This must be it," Jacoby said excitedly.

"About time," Cor'in responded grumpily. "But what about the other parchment word?"

"Let's find out,"

The road was unnervingly quiet, blanketed with a foreboding darkness that made Jacoby's neck hairs rise on end. Being human, it limited his visibility to eight feet, and he relied on Cor'in's "Twilight Vision" to discern a trap.

"See anything?"

"Only colored row houses," Cor'in responded.

"Huh?"

"They're painted different colors: blue, green, orange, red."

"That's it! "Red, not rid!" Jacoby exclaimed; his voice filled with excitement.

"Of course," said the half-elf, shaking his head at his denseness. "Follow me."

He strode up to the only home painted crimson, noticing a single candle glowing in the window. He knocked twice, heard thumping footsteps, and stepped back.

An enormous human with shaggy hair covering his arms, legs, and face opened the door. He was over eight feet tall, wearing a simple tunic under a weathered slicker and leather pants. His eyes were a terrifying bloodshot orange-gold and his skin flushed from alcohol.

"What do you want?" he demanded.

"Captain Pike?"

"Who wants to know?"

"My name is Jacoby Ironfist. This is Cor'in. Cowden sent us."

"What do you want?"

"We need passage to the capital."

"Course you do. I ought to skin that noey barkeep. Got any money?"

'No, but my group has several trained warriors. We can work for passage."

"Work, eh? What experience?"

"I was once a captain in the Taborian army. As a group, we've fought our way from the Lea Lands across to Tajman Sghar and west here."

"Interesting," the beast said, rubbing his beard, leaning heavily on the doorjamb. He studied Jacoby for a long moment. "What Taborian regiment?"

"I captained the First Squad before moving to Palace Guards."

The man's eyes widened, then he shook his head once and said, "Come in, then."

Jacoby and Cor'in walked along a dark corridor, which opened into a rectangular living room. Maps and nautical devices covered the walls, and an enormous bookcase straddled a stone fireplace on one end. Two enormous cushioned chairs, large enough to fit both visitors in one, faced a roaring fire. A wooden table buffered the chairs, a model frigate in the center, and a half-empty rum bottle on one end. Pike slid into one chair, Jacoby and Cor'in the other.

"So, what's so urgent in reaching the capital I had to be bothered?", Captain Pike said, taking a swig from the rum bottle.

Jacoby hesitated, weighing whether to tell the truth or only part. The beast-man's familiarity was perplexing, leaving him struggling to understand why it felt so familiar. "Have we met before?"

"Unlikely, but I grew up near Tabor."

Jacoby's eyes widened, realization rocking him back like an uppercut to the jaw. "Thor's beard! Could it be? Not the mongrel boy?" Jacoby murmured, his eyes wide in shock and fear. He grew silent, the memory from decades before appearing like a hazy specter in his mind's eye.

"What's going on here?" Cor'in asked, confused.

"So you remember?" growled Pike, his voice flinty. He leaned in, his blazing orange-red eyes burning into Jacoby.

"Remember what? Jacoby?" Cor'in demanded.

"Tell him," said Pike with disgust.

A jumble of distant memories, swirling together like smoke in a blurry collage, clouded Jacoby's mind. Long suppressed guilt squeezed his chest, and he gasped for air. He forced down the rising bile in his throat and tried to slow his rapid heartbeat pounding in his chest and head. The big man inhaled several deep breaths, willing his body to calm. Bit by bit, his heart rate slowed, and his mind fog cleared. He visualized that fateful day, the one leading to his transfer to the palace. Jacoby cleared his throat and began.

"I led a patrol to the northern woods, rooting out bandits who wreaked havoc on the surrounding countryside. Our scouts located the marauder's stronghold, and we attacked at dawn. The battle was a slaughter, the bandits poorly armed, until a pack of "Feral Ones" ambushed from our flank."

"What's a Feral One?" asked Cor'in.

"Wild humans inhabiting the forest, mating and living with the animals. Dangerous enemies."

"Tell him more," demanded Pike.

"The entire clan, men, women, and children, fought with berserker rage, rapidly overwhelming my troops. I still carry the scar from a teen who knifed me," Jacoby said, pointing to a jagged scar on his forearm. "Fortunately, I disarmed the teen, taking him prisoner and ending the struggle."

"How?"

Jacoby looked over at Pike, who tensed his balled fists, his face a twisted scowl.

"The lad turned out to be the clan chief's son. Once captured, the Feral Ones surrendered."

"That's not all. Continue", demanded Pike.

Jacoby looked away, then admitted the truth. "We placed the surviving wildlings and bandits in chains and marched them back to the City of Spires. King Aarmon later executed most of the prisoners as a lesson to any opposition. "

"Liar! You ordered them killed!"

"No. I brought them to Tabor as ordered. I had no sway with the king," Jacoby said flatly.

Pike twisted away, pounding his hand on his chair in frustration. "Then how did you end up captain of the palace guard?"

A moment of uncertainty flickered across Jacoby's face as he lingered on his response. By recognizing the prisoners as a political tool, King Aarmon aimed to quell any dissent in the kingdom and thus improve his popularity. Aarmon calculated that publicly praising and transferring Jacoby would generate positive public sentiment. Jacoby saw the transfer as a long-awaited break from the last ten exhausting years of leading First Squad, the most elite unit of the Taborian forces.

"The act of taking the lives of innocent people was an abomination that went against everything I believed in. To escape the absurdity of it all, I transferred," Jacoby stated quietly. "King Aarmon saw the opportunity to use the move to improve his political standing amongst the military, understanding the political influence of the move within the ranks."

Pike sat back and sighed, the anger draining from his face and replaced by sad resignation.

"And the teen?" asked Cor'in, anticipating the answer.

"He escaped and disappeared," said Jacoby, staring into space. "Some believe he fled to the nearby Sacred Wood, a sister haven for magical animals to the Hope Wood. Such a nonjudgmental refuge might allow a feral one to thrive. At least, one hopes."

Jacoby stared at Pike, his head tilted, sadness in his eyes, but the captain wouldn't take his gaze.

Silence enveloped the room, lingering for several long minutes as each individual reflected on Jacoby's story.

Finally, Pike growled, "Merry Mermaid's my ship. We cast off at tide change. See yourselves out."

He exhaustedly rose and left the room without even a glance.

Cor'in closed the front door, and the warriors stepped out into the damp, silent streets. The half-elf waited for Jacoby to speak, but silence lingered. Finally, he said, "I've seen the dungeons of Serensith Talem. If Tabor is similar, it was lucky the feral boy escaped, especially without help."

"It's nearly impossible without help," Jacoby said quietly. "Fortunate."

Cinsor, the pack leader, inhaled the night air, picking up the scents of burnt campfire wood, smoked meats, herbs, and human sweat from the city below, but nothing close. Hidden in the wooded hill bordering the city gates, he and his lupine rangers studied the city entrances for vulnerabilities. To Cinsor's annoyance, he realized they had powerful defenses. A full company of soldiers stood watch at each city gate, examining every person entering and exiting. There has to be a way in. But in what manner? He contemplated climbing the hundred-foot walls, but the stone was too slippery, and attacking the gate directly would be pointless. The lupine leader tapped his paw to his muzzle. Could the human prince and his allies already be inside the city? All we can do is wait.

As if his thoughts were spoken, Lieutenant Notch cleared his throat from behind. "I bring news, sir. I may have found an entrance."

"Entrance? Where?"

Notch's muzzle puckered as if biting a sour lemon. "May I show you?"

In a short lope, Notch escorted Cinsor and the other lupine rangers down a rocky slope to the base of the bayside embankment. The city's foundation rested on an elevated plateau overlooking the sea. As the city grew, they constructed massive ceramic drainpipes to handle the ever-increasing flow of city waste. During low tide, the water receded from the coast, leaving the pipe opening above the waterline and in the lupine's full view. The scent of rotting fish carcasses, refuse, and trash hung over the area like a fog. Mixed with decaying marsh grass and oyster beds, the aroma struck Cinsor like an unexpected punch. His head jerked back, and a wave of nausea washed over him.

"What in the wolf'sbane!" he gagged, swallowing down his rising breakfast.

"Humans are fowl creatures," Notch growled, covering his nose with a paw. "But those pipes lead directly into the capital."

Anger and disgust consumed the pack leader's mind as he stood at the edge of the city's putrid dump, his paw raised in a moment of fury. His subordinate had suggested a plan so foolish and disrespectful that it made him question his sanity. Had Notch gone raving mad? But then doubt crept in. Could there be a shred of truth in his suggestion? Was there a better path, or any entrance into the citadel? The answer echoed through his mind, loud and clear - there was no other path. Notch, as always, had provided an answer, albeit a revolting one. Cinsor slowly dropped his paw, releasing the tension that had gripped him. He took in deep breaths of the fetid air, willing himself to calm down. His anger dissipated, replaced by a steely resolve. He refocused on their aim - to trap and kill the prince. The disgust that had consumed him melted away, leaving behind only determination. This is our road in to trap and kill the prince!

"Well done, Notch."

Golden sunlight broke above the eastern horizon as the Merry Mermaid set sail for Mar Nâpor. Pike and Jacoby kept to opposite ends of the deck, the brotherhood working with the other sailors to raise the sails and release the mooring ropes on the ninety-foot ketch. Work always abounded on board. Managing the sails, tying down loose cargo, and preparing and distributing meals consumed most of their time. When idle, Pike pushed the newcomers to scrub the deck, polish the brass fittings, or clear the deck of unneeded ropes. Instead of the week of travel by foot, the speedy vessel hoped to reach the southern citadel wharf in two days, hugging the shallows of the coast to prevent a pirate encounter. The wind held strong from the north, rocketing the ship over the glassy ocean surface as if tethered to an invisible flock of pelicans.

Even with the demanding schedule, Captain Pike insisted the brotherhood give the crew a break from night watch.

"Why do we have to cover the night watch?" Cor'in complained.

"We work for our passage, remember?" Nathaniel stated, reminding the half-elf for the umpteenth time that day.

"I'm worn out," Lani said. "I've never scrubbed and cleaned so much in my life."

"Get some rest. Jacoby and I will take the first watch. Grull and Micah can relieve us at first bell," said the prince, ignoring the moans of discontent.

"I'm well enough to help," said Horatio.

"All that scrubbing and chores didn't open up your leg wound?"

"No. "It's healed, anyway," Horatio said, averting his gaze to conceal the painful grimace on his face.

Nat looked at the Anuran with suspicion. He doubted Horatio's story, especially after hours of backbreaking labor on his hands and knees. But he appreciated the frog man's positivity.

"Sure. We need the help," he responded. "The dawn watch is yours and Cor'in's."

Darkness pushed twilight into velvet night, the sky illuminated by a blanket of twinkling stars and a glowing half-moon. The evening progressed with no excitement, short of passing several flying fish that danced across the sea's moonlit surface. Nathaniel kept awake by counting stars and conversing with his brother.

"Thanks for finding us passage on the Mermaid. It would take a week by foot to reach Mar Nâpor," Nathaniel said.

"Thank Pike. He agreed to this," Jacoby said, spitting the words.

"I've observed that there's some tension between you two. Not a very likable fellow, our captain."

Jacoby grunted, looking out to sea.

"He's a taskmaster and appears driven to extract every ounce of work as payment," Nathaniel continued.

Silence settled over the moment, enveloping it like a weighty, oppressive curtain.

"Odd appearing. Did you see those eyes? They can bore through you like a hot knife through lard," he added, his voice filled with a mixture of awe and unease.

"Predatory. Like a wild animal," Jacoby murmured, his gaze fixed on the distant horizon. "A hard life molds a man."

"What do you mean?" Nathaniel asked, fueled by curiosity and guessing his brother held some secret he refused to share.

"Nothing," Jacoby said and strode away aft without another word.

Morning broke on the weary group, the sunlight dragging them from their hammocks half-awake for another busy day at sea. Captain Pike paced over the quarterdeck, his face a mask of intensity.

"Get to work, you sea dogs. This ain't no free trip!" He growled at the group, who scattered to change sail and continue chores. The work drove the day along, and by the afternoon, the Merry Mermaid looked polished and clean. After an inspection by Pike, where he criticized every aspect of the crew's work, he finally allowed for some much-needed rest. Not long after falling into their hammocks from exhaustion, the Brotherhood awakened to a shout from the crow's nest.

"Citadel on the starboard bow!"

Exhausted from their duties, the crewmates ascended the hold ladder, one by one, their eyes scanning the deck as they searched for the source of the disturbance. A nasty grin bloomed across Pike's face. "No time for rest," he chuckled. "Prepare for landing,"

The walled city of Mar Nâpor rested on a high bluff and appeared even larger than Tajman Sghur from the water. The sprawling metropolis extended for miles, protected by high stone walls and an enormous round citadel in its center. Like the capital above, the harbor spanned the mouth of the bay, with over thirty jetties encompassing the entire base of the cliff. Boat traffic of all sizes congested the city harbor, from smaller fishing craft to immense naval frigates.

Captain Pike found a slip on the northern end, along the final jetty farthest from the bay's mouth. Sailors leaped off, tying off mooring lines, then jogging to carry several crates waiting on the dock. Pike shouted down to the passengers, "Best be disembarking in a hurry! I'm taking on a light cargo load and setting sail within the hour."

Nathaniel waved, and with the others, began helping unload the women and children. Jacoby was last in line to leave, when a powerful hand spun him around. Fire orange-red eyes stared over the hairy mustache and beard of Captain Pike, boring into Jacoby like two hot pokers. Jacoby held his breath, placing his hand on the pommel of his sword, not sure of Pike's intent. Silence reigned for several heartbeats, then Pike handed Jacoby a jingling pouch and said, "This pays my debt, Taborian."

Jacoby exhaled a long sigh and put out a hand to shake.

"No debt owed. And thank you."

Pike sneered and spat. In one movement, he turned away, leaving Jacoby's untouched hand in the breeze.

At the port-side city gate, a full complement of soldiers inspected the cargo and registered every newcomer. Nathaniel led the group in a crawling line of visitors, gradually reaching a wooden desk with several seated guards. He noticed that, unlike Tajman Sghur, every soldier wore chain mail under a coral-colored tunic, the insignia of an emerald green anchor across their chest.

"Name?" the guard demanded.

"Nathaniel."

"What's your business in the citadel?" a bearded young man asked without looking up.

"Laborers."

"How many in your group?" the soldier asked, noticing the women with four crying infants between them.

"Ten, with the children."

"Write your names or make your marks. Jobs are scarce here, so you have a week to find and report work, or they will expel you, as per the late king's decree."

Nathaniel nodded, and the group moved into the throng entering the city. He pushed and shoved his way forward, eventually reaching the street.

"Odin's breath, the crowds are thick as molasses," Grull complained.

"I've never seen so many people in one place!" added Rue.

"This makes Tajman Sghur look like a small town, and Arcane a village," added Allai'nn.

"For safety, hold tight to the belt of the person ahead of you. I'm going to shovel a path through this crowd and find an inn," Nathaniel howled over the loud din of the shoving masses.

He lowered his head and wormed his way along the storefronts of the main street until he reached the first major boulevard. Humanoids of all species, size and shapes pushed their way amoeba-like, one false-foot at a time. Elves, humans, dwarves, half-giants, brownies, gnomes, goat men, and rare turtle men comprised the city's population. A variety of shops and warehouses lined the wide avenue, scarcely thinning after a half mile of shuffling forward.

"I don't see any inns. Let's try a side street," suggested Allai'nn.

"Sound idea. Fewer people," Nathaniel said, cutting down a side street to a parallel avenue with reduced traffic.

Nat walked past an aging clapperboard building, sandwiched between a livery and hardware, a painted sign swinging over the door.

Above the otherwise nondescript hotel, a faded sign depicted a woman dancing, the letters "Dancing Siren Inn" barely discernible. Navigating through the crowd of patrons, Nat made his way to the bar.

"Have any rooms available?" he asked the barkeeper.

"Full," an overweight, sweaty bald man grunted, turning away.

The group moved on. Over the hours, they passed by three more inns, all without vacancies. Finally, exhausted and hungry, arms full of crying infants, the group stopped to rest.

"We've been walking for miles. My feet are killing me," Rue said.

"And we need food for the children," added Allai'nn.

"Don't forget the adults," Blue said.

"Maybe we could get a stall at the livery we passed," suggested Horatio.

"We could split up. It's a massive city. I'm sure we'll find something," said Grull.

"Let's go a bit farther, and if we cannot find lodging, we split up," Nat said.

"Agreed," supported Jacoby.

The group shuffled into a less dense city street, Nathaniel glimpsing a white sign with a cawing black crow. "I found something," he said, walking down the alleyway to a two-story building next to a small livery. Letters over the red door said, "Howling Crow." Nat and Jacoby stepped into a wide common room full of old chairs and tables, with a bar and kitchen on one side. A few patrons despondently hovered over tankards at the bar or sat talking across tabletops.

A high-pitched voice rang out from the kitchen, "Be right with you, friend."

Jacoby and Nathaniel waited. Shortly, the kitchen door swung open, and both men's jaws dropped wide. Features of an Otter head, complete with a flint-nosed snout, beady black eyes and wire-like bristled whiskers, sat on the round sheep's body. A red sailor's cap tilted over red, shoulder-length curls, framed the round face of an otter. Close-set eyes sparkled with amusement behind round spectacles. His whiskered snout opened in a wide smile of tiny sharp teeth, completed by a long pink tongue and emerald green beard. A rotund, fur-covered body covered by a stained apron ended in thick, hoofed legs.

"Mistletoe's the name. Owner of the Howling Crow," he said, extending his hand.

Nathaniel gawked a heartbeat longer, then took the hand and smiled. "Nathaniel. This is my brother, Jacoby."

"Welcome. Haven't met too many Draskhok, eh?"

Nathaniel's face colored. "No, I haven't. Sorry, I didn't mean to stare."

Mistletoe let out a rumbling chuckle. "Happens all too often. No offense taken. What can I do for you?"

"I need rooms for a group of ten, and food and milk for four infants." Mistletoe stroked his beard, considering, when a more petite version of Mistletoe came squawking from the kitchen. "Did I hear, infants? We had a brood of our own, all grown with their mates now," she said, looking away as if reminiscing. "I'm Mabel, his better half," jutting an extended thumb at Mistletoe. "I adore babies."

Before her husband could speak, the women stepped from around the counter. For a heartbeat, she gazed up into the prince's eyes. Then looped her arm through Nathaniel's and continued, "We have a few goats and a Jersey next door. Let me give you a tour."

Nathaniel stumbled along with the woman out the door, giving Jacoby an astonished glance. They heard Mabel's shrill voice speaking in rapid elvish to Allai'nn outside.

"Well, I guess that's settled," Mistletoe chuckled. "Mabel's from a family of empaths. She can assess one's character in a blink."

Jacoby was speechless, processing the last five minutes. So far, his experience at the Howling Crow had been surreal. He gave his head a shake and stuck out his hand to Mistletoe. "Jacoby Ironfist."

The drashok took it, clasping firmly. At that moment, the rest of the haggard group entered, led by a non-stop chatting Mabel. She gave Allai'nn a mother pat on the arm. She passed Mistletoe with a word, grabbed three keys from a hooked board behind the counter and handed them to Allai'nn.

"Here you go, sweety. Mist will bring up some hot water for baths."

"Please don't go to trouble. We can help you," offered Jacoby.

"Absolutely not!" She crooned, stamping her hoof for emphasis. "I'll be up shortly with food and warm milk for the tikes."

Mistletoe's eyes raised in surprise. She gave him a stern look and strode into the kitchen. Her husband shook his head and started up the stairs.

"Follow me."

TEN

Chamberlain Masters stood motionless outside the king's bedroom as Court Healer Musgrave rushed down the hallway, his cap askew and nightshirt billowing behind him. Sergeant Decker of the Imperial Guard snapped to attention, saluting, as the healer arrived. Masters opened the door, letting Musgrave enter, and looked hard at the guard before following.

"Let no one in, Decker. No one."

"On my life, Chamberlain."

Masters, with a single nod of acknowledgment, shut the door behind them and observed as the elderly physician bent over to scrutinize the lifeless body of King Gooseberry. The weight of his fifteen years of service to the monarch pressed heavily upon him, choking back tears as he turned away, his throat tight with emotion. He had discovered the king's body less than an hour prior, and he had assumed that his friend and king had died from overindulging in drink. Gooseberry lay on the bed, his head lolling to one side, his hair tousled from the bedsheet, and his body twisted as if caught in a nightmare. As he looked closer, he saw the pillowcase stained with dried vomit, his liege's eyes glazed and fixed on something unseen, and his skin had taken on an unnatural green-gray hue, a sickly shade that sent a chill down his spine. Overwhelmed with grief, Masters wept uncontrollably for five minutes, resembling a heartbroken child, before regaining composure enough to summon Decker and Musgrave. The silence stretched on for several minutes before Musgrave, in a low voice, asked, "Masters, I need your kerchief and dagger."

The chamberlain, his brow creased in puzzlement, hesitated momentarily before handing over the items as requested. As the man watched, Musgrave gently scraped the area around the king's lips, stood, and presented the cloth to the chamberlain. Small, sugar-like crystals speckled the fabric, creating a delicate and sparkling effect.

"What is it?" asked Masters.

"Poison. I'll know more once I analyze it."

"Painful?" he asked, his voice breaking.

Overwhelmed with sadness, the healer looked away. The sheer agony Gooseberry experienced must have been unbearable, his body wracked with convulsions, gasping for breath in a desperate struggle for life, before finally succumbing to his fate. The doctor, his face etched with sadness, wiped away the tears that streamed down his face and continued the examination.

He contorted his body, craning his neck upward to look at the silhouette of the roof. Masters understood and dropped his head in despair. How in Thor's name had this happened? He had eaten with the king earlier that evening, each course taste-tested as protocol with no ill effects. Two guards, positioned at each end of the hallway, effectively blocked any attempt by an assailant to enter. So, what had transpired? He made his way towards the window, his eyes fixed on the tower wall, which was adorned with a thick, verdant tapestry of ivy. He observed several vague, uneven features in the vine, suggesting that something, possibly a foot or a hand, had momentarily lost its hold. Even with guards patrolling the area below, the tower stood as a formidable structure, rising five hundred feet from the ground. It seemed utterly unimaginable that someone could climb the delicate ivy to such a height unseen. But was it possible? He twisted to look up at the roof line. A gap of thirty feet existed between the window and the roof. Even the most skilled climber couldn't make that leap. But how else could they have entered the king's bedchamber? What manner of killer could accomplish such a feat? An icy chill worked its way down Masters' spine. What type of assassin, indeed?

Turning toward the healer, the chamberlain found him still leaning over the lifeless body. "Anything else, Musgrave?"

"Yes. The king has bruising on his hand, and the bedside water tankard is half full."

Masters shook his head, his mind clouded by a storm of thoughts and emotions. "I don't understand."

Musgrove leaned back, stretching his back. Dried tears stained his drawn, weary face. "I'm saying someone drank from the cup and clenched his majesty's hand. The monster stayed with the king, watching him die."

Masters' face twisted into a grimace of stunned horror, his features contorting in a display of utter disbelief. Abruptly feeling faint, he reached for the chair arm, his hand finding purchase as the room spun. As the realization hit him, he struggled to speak, his mouth unable to form words. He moaned in anguish, exclaiming, " 'By the Gods'."

Mar Nâpor had lost a capable monarch, and the sword of pure evil had stabbed the kingdom's heart. He had underestimated the magnitude of the danger. No one, including himself, was safe. Tendrils of dread and terror wrapped around his chest, constricting his heart with a suffocating chill, as if frozen solid. The blood coursed through his head with the intensity of a sledgehammer, each beat a jarring, echoing thud.

"What now?" asked Musgrove, snapping the chamberlain out of panic.

Masters took several deep breaths, trying to slow his rapidly beating heart before he answered. As if a switch flipped in his mind, the chamberlain's thoughts became clear, and he knew the answer.

"Two things. First, we must relate the true events to Queen Nira and Prince Caron and keep them safe. As they cope with their grief, the royal family will remain secluded in a secure, undisclosed location under the watchful eye of heavily armed guards. Secondly, we must inform the kingdom that their beloved King Gooseberry has died peacefully. His funeral and burial ceremony will be private, as he wished."

"And?" Musgrove asked, hoping for more.

"I will use your scientific knowledge to help discover who killed our friend."

Elm strolled along the storefronts of Julien Street, another wide thoroughfare crossing the length of Mar Napor from west to east. Sunlight filtered through the nearby hills, warming his face. He had his hand in the pocket of his new trousers, jingling the few coins he had accumulated after working at the Howling Crow as a dishwasher and busboy. Elm whistled an old dwarven song he remembered from his youth as he wandered by shop fronts, admiring the myriad wares and fabrics displayed. Alone for the first time in two weeks, he relished the serenity of the moment. Meeting the brotherhood had saved his life, and now he found himself at his original destination of Mar Nâpor, prepared to reignite his merchant life. Intending to secure a job, he planned to establish connections with the tin and blacksmiths who knew his father, utilizing those relationships to his advantage. They would understand the reality of a bandit attack and losing his family's wares. Capitalizing on his father's established reputation, he could convince potential employers of his abilities, effectively securing a job. Elm's father taught him about sales from a young age, which helped him develop his skills and knowledge. He wasn't just crafting durable pots and pans; he was also upholding his family's long-standing reputation as skilled dwarven artisans. Full of anticipation for the new opportunities, he rubbed his hands together, only to be interrupted by the sound of a girl's voice coming from the alleyway he had just passed.

"Help! Help!" the female voice screamed from the shadowed alley.

Ignoring any potential danger, he brought himself to a standstill before barreling down the dimly lit path towards the source of the mysterious voice. The half-dwarf's journey was short-lived, as he stumbled over a discarded wooden crate and crashed forward, his head the first to contact the ground. The impact of his landing sent a sharp pain shooting up his left shoulder, his head cracking against the unforgiving earth. Dazed and disoriented, he sat up, his vision clouded and swirling, struggling to recall the events that had just transpired. A brutal kick connected with his chest, forcing the air from his lungs as the impact caused his chest to buckle inwards. His breath hitched in his throat, and for a moment, he could not get any air into his lungs. The intense pain from his bruises made it difficult for him to sit up, so he remained lying down. Slivers of blue sky pierced the shadows of the alley, revealing the silhouettes of Elm's tormentors. Two large, husky figures stood in front of him, while a smaller figure stayed close behind. Is that the girl who feigned crying wolf? I must get to my feet and escape. He tried to move, but before he could, he felt another brutal boot connect with his side, the excruciating pain shooting up his spine.

"Stop," he moaned, his belly wracked with nausea.

But the beating continued. A heavy punch to his gut sent bile surging to the back of his throat.

"Ahhhh," he screamed, a boot stomping on his knee, sending agony rocketing down his leg. He tried to roll away, but the other man's foot blasted into his back, paralyzing him with stabbing electrical waves down his legs. Then his vision exploded into a burst of fireworks as a boot struck his chin. His jaw audibly cracked, and his head violently snapped back, the powerful kick driving his head against the street. Time itself seemed to warp and twist as his world spun violently for a brief, disorienting moment. Then the light dimmed and disappeared like a shade being pulled shut.

Elm's eyes shot open, revealing only the oppressive darkness. He felt a searing pain in his left leg, trapped and contorted beneath his weight. Strong arms, powerful and unwavering, scooped him up and carried him away, leaving him with a sense of bewilderment and helplessness. He wanted to question his savior, to ask his name and where they were going. But the agony that pervaded his very being consumed his thoughts so completely that he couldn't focus on anything else. Pain radiated from every part of his body, his flesh inflamed and marked with the deep purple of bruises. His eyelids fluttered shut, and he slipped away, surrendering to the darkness of the night.

Prince Caron was ill-equipped to lead a bustling maritime city with over seventy-five thousand residents, let alone the numerous villages and vast territory within Mar Nâpor's realm. Even at the young age of sixteen, his imposing stature, muscular build, and striking combination of intelligent hazel eyes and sandy hair made him a captivating figure. With little in the way of restrictions, Caron spent most of his time engaged in pursuits of excitement, whether it be the thrill of the hunt, the joy of riding, or charming the many beautiful ladies of the court. Although his father continuously urged him to learn the skills of a ruler, the young prince exhibited little interest in developing the abilities necessary for governing a nation.

He stroked his blond curls thoughtfully, his mind racing as he considered what to do next. The news of his father's death had hit him hard, and he sat alone in his room, grappling with the immense grief. The king's death wasn't a natural passing; a brutal murder extinguished his life. The people adored his father, a ruler known for his kindness and fairness. However, an enemy had stealthily entered, ending his life while he slept. Fearful for his safety and the tremendous responsibility thrust upon him, he thought, "What am I to do? I'm no ruler!" His mother, a former court sycophant known for her beauty but lacking intelligence, was of no help. He ran his hand through his blond curls, deciding on his next step. He considered the possibility of stepping down from his position as ruler and disappearing, perhaps seeking a new life far away from the pressures of his throne. Then, he realized his only source of income was the crown. Without it, he was just another lost noble with empty pockets. A surge of sorrow brought tears to his eyes, and he sobbed. Why did I not listen and learn from my father? Why?

A knock at his door interrupted his recriminations. Chamberlain Masters stuck his head in the room. "May I come in, Your Majesty?"

Caron nodded, sniffing and wiping his red eyes. Masters strode in and sat in a chair across from the prince. The older man was pale, with rings under his eyes from lack of sleep. They sat quietly for several heartbeats.

"How are you holding up?" Masters asked.

"Okay, I guess."

But Masters could see the fear in the prince's eyes. Nothing prepares one for action like a catastrophe, he thought. "I hate to discuss this so soon after losing your father, Your Majesty, but...."

"Stop saying that."

Masters' eyes rose. "Sir?"

"Your Majesty. I'm not king. I can't be king; I'm not ready," the young man said, the words choking in his throat. The young man felt tears welling in his eyes and instinctively dropped his gaze, his hands trembling slightly as he fought to regain control. Masters, understanding the lad's fear, observed him with compassion, silently sharing his anxieties. His mind replayed his father's death, the gaping wound of grief it had left, and the gnawing worry about the uncharted path that lay ahead. His years in the royal court had been a constant struggle against the backstabbing and political machinations, demanding that he rely on his intelligence and manipulative skills to stay alive. Through a stroke of luck, the late king had recognized some untapped potential within him. Call it guts, courage, or practical discernment, King Gooseberry had seen something special in him and nurtured that seed until it matured. Over time, he had grown into an unwavering advisor and friend. The time had come for him to repay his friend and mentor for the generous gift he had received by becoming the lad's mentor. He placed a reassuring hand on the prince's thigh.

"Caron, the gods, in their wisdom, have chosen you to replace your father as king. I offer myself as a guide to smooth your transition to the throne and help advise you for the years to come."

The boy wiped the tears running down his cheeks. "But I don't know how to be king."

"I won't lie. Your path will not be easy. The burdens of leadership can weigh heavily on the broadest of shoulders. Success requires sacrifice, discipline, and a daily intention to improve the lives of the people of Mar Nâpor. But the rewards can be immeasurable. I have complete confidence you'll grow into a successful future king. And I will be at your side every day if you'll have me."

Caron let out a heavy sigh and half-smiled. "Thank you."

Masters hesitated for several breaths. "I must address two issues. First, it would be best for you and the Queen Regent to announce your father's loss by natural causes. News of an assassination might bring unwanted panic."

"I don't understand. You want me to lie?" Caron questioned.

"Not lie. The north is in chaos, and daily more refugees pour into the city than ever before. Mar Nâpor's role has changed to a safe refuge and a bastion of strength against the West's enemies. Withholding full transparency to the populace will give them needed reassurance."

"Are we really strong?" asked Caron.

Masters hesitated, unsure of the correct response. He weighed his options and decided on the truth. "Not yet. Your father worked tirelessly to prepare for the coming war. I suspect that led to his demise."

"War?"

"Our informants suggest Tabor has suffered unbearable leadership losses. They could surrender within months."

The words struck the young man like a kick to the groin. Caron gasped as icy tendrils of fear slithered up his spine. *War's looming? Why didn't father tell me?* He squeezed his eyes together, rubbing his forehead with one hand. *Of course! That's why he persistently encouraged me to spend time in court. I've been such a fool!*

"And the second issue?" he said through gritted teeth, convinced he might not survive another blow.

"Your leadership as future king is imperative. So, I ask you and your mother to remain hidden during your time of mourning, protected by Captain Decker and his guards. That will give me time to root out the scoundrel who poisoned your father."

Caron stared open-mouthed at Masters. *As if losing his father and facing impending war wasn't enough! Now, he must sacrifice his freedom. His entire identity. Never!*

"No way!"

"Your Majesty, the assassin may still be within the city. Another attempt at the crown is possible."

His ears seemed filled with cotton. Did he hear Masters correctly? "What did you say?"

"Losing you or the Queen would be an unrecoverable blow, leading to mass chaos in the land. Please understand this small sacrifice is essential."

The lad sat back, stunned, unable to process everything he'd been told. Masters saw the "deer in torchlight" look and shook his head. The boy's loss of his father and his subsequent responsibility to learn the role of leading Mar Nâpor "on the job" filled him with pity, as this task seemed akin to climbing a treacherous mountain without any safety equipment. It would be a dramatic and emotionally charged journey to witness Caron's shift from a self-indulgent playboy to a mature and dedicated king. In the boy's eyes, he saw a reflection of his father's unyielding spirit, a hint of the same steely resolve that had always characterized his father. Standing up, he bowed respectfully.

"I will give you time for reflection, Your Majesty," he said and walked to the door. To his relief, Queen Nira proved to be understanding and readily accepted the idea without hesitation. But his plan to draw the assassin out and into the open depended on her and Prince Caron's support.

Cinsor used a linen drape to wipe the blood and sewer stench from his leather-studded breastplate. He and his wolves had entered the city through the sewer tunnels hours before, hungry, wet, and irritable. But the wolf gods had smiled on his platoon, allowing one of the first buildings they crossed to be an active tavern. His wolves had ravaged the inhabitants, killing and feeding at will. Passersby confused their shrill cries as the usual raucous noises of drunkards. He shrewdly ordered the wolves to take the victim's clothing for disguises and closed and bolted the bar. The clothes were mostly too tight, but the group would manage until they found and killed the prince.

"This will be our command center. Drag the bodies into the basement after your fill," he commanded the wolves. "No need for nosey passersby to become suspicious from the smell."

The wolfman reflexively scratched his neck fur as he ran over the plan in his mind. Cinsor pictured the rudimentary map he had sketched from his vantage point in the wood overlooking the metropolis days before. Because of the city's enormity, he had broken the town into search quadrants, each wolf responsible for searching two. Using the darkness to shadow their movements, his wolves would explore the city by night.

Cinsor spat, already feeling claustrophobic at being confined in the tavern. As a wild creature, he loathed cities, preferring to battle in open spaces, and Mar Napor was the largest he had ever visited. But the prey's trail led here, so he and his wolves would adapt. He hoped to locate and kill their quarry within a few days but knew from experience the group might be here longer. The wolfman stared through the darkened window at the few stars twinkling above. He closed his eyes and prayed to Badh and Lycaon, the wolf gods of his tribe.

"Let me kill and feed on the human that has, so far, eluded me."

Far away from Mar Nâpor, General Pryus waited inside the haunting Fossil Wood while his human Tajman Sghur soldiers stood five feet apart, with their bows pointed towards the center of a clearing. An owl, unheard of in the dead branches of the ancient forest, hooted three times. Pryus turned to his subordinate, Lieutenant Twist, and held up three fingers. The officer nodded without a word, cupped his hands, and vocalized three short hoots. Several heartbeats passed, and tiny vines of apprehension began climbing up Pryus' spine. Was this a trap? Had the enemy somehow found out about my plans? Beads of sweat popped out on his forehead as seconds dragged on to minutes, and he wiped it away. I'll wait no longer, he thought and turned to signal Twist to retreat. At that moment, a cautious elf appeared in the clearing. Pryus let out a sigh of relief and trudged through the underbrush. He faced the elf and bowed. "General Pryus."

The elf nodded but still scanned the wood's edge with shifty green eyes for enemies. The elf came only to Pryus' shoulder and was reed thin. But the general noticed lean muscle roped his arms and chest. He wore a green-brown tunic over deerskin leggings and carried two short swords over his back. He offered his hand, "Emissary Jarvis from Serensith Talem. Are you sure they did not follow you?"

"No, but I hope not," replied Pryus. "We came through the tunnels at night and blindly made our way to the wood."

Jarvis nodded, cupped his hands, and whistled three times. Two elves of similar dress pushed tarp-covered carts from behind the surrounding foliage. He once more scanned the wood edge, and announced, "Our spies confirm the Rogdye will reinforce Crepitus' army."

"Rogdye?"

Jarvis' face twisted as if searching for the word, then his eyes brightened. "Undead."

Pryus' eyes bugged, unable to comprehend the news. "Undead? Are you sure?" choking out the words. "Impossible."

Jarvis said nothing but turned to the first cart and pulled back a corner of the canvas.

Pryus couldn't believe his eyes. The cart overflowed with hundreds of weapons, the polished metal gleaming in the sunlight.

Spears, swords, daggers and cutlasses made of half-silver. "A gift from King Polaris," said Jarvis.

Pryus stared vacantly, unable to speak. The enemy intends to bolster their ranks with the most challenging creatures to defeat. Then, without reciprocity, the elf had delivered the only weapons in Curth Talem able to defeat the threat.

"I don't know what to say," he mumbled.

Jarvis smiled. "Thank you is fine."

As Elm blinked his eyes open, he stared into the grizzled, scarred features of a dogman. A dirty tunic and cotton pants completely hid the beast's light brown fur, except for one arm, which was covered in healed linear scars and ended in a three-toed paw. The beast stared intently at him with sallow eyes, which were set above a thick, monstrous scar that pulled his face into a perpetual frown.

With a shudder, Elm squeezed his eyes shut, shook his head in disbelief, and then reopened them, certain that he was caught in a strange and terrifying dream. Although he tried to ignore its presence, the monster lingered, its eyes never leaving his. For the first time, Elm took in the surroundings of the room. Faint streaks of sunlight pierced through the dirty windowpane, casting thin lines of light across the shadowed room. Fishing nets and a few floats decorated three walls, while a stone, soot-covered fireplace occupied the other wall. In the center of the room sat a small table with two sea trunks on either side that served as makeshift chairs.

"Whats'er name, mate?" he growled.

"Ah... Elm. Who are you, and where am I?"

"Pedros, at your service," said the dogman, ignoring the question. "Found ye in the gutter."

"Thank you for your kindness, but I should head home." He sat up, the pounding in his head making him swoon. He slid back onto the bed, a jolt of nausea cramping his stomach. "I'm gonna be sick," he murmured, turning on his side to vomit. Pedros kicked a bucket over just in time to catch the bilious mess.

"No need ta rush off, lad, tils ya betta." He handed the half-dwarf a dirty rag and waited. Elm wiped the chudder from his chin and leaned back on the straw pillow. "Where might be home anyways?" asked the dogman.

Elm's eyes narrowed. "Why?"

"Jes wundrin", Pedros said with an uncaring hunch of his shoulders.

Elm lay motionless, his skin pallid like a sheet, and his closed eyes gave the impression of lifelessness. He desperately hoped that his throbbing headache and agonizing stomach cramps would subside soon. But they didn't, and he wretched again.

After a moment, the dog-man shook his head disapprovingly and pulled a dusty cup off a nearby shelf. He walked over to a kettle hanging near the fire. After removing a small package from his pocket, he dumped the contents into the cup, doused the mixture with hot water, and handed it to the half-dwarf.

"What is it?" Elm asked, concern reflecting in his eyes.

"Herbs and such. Fix yo tum," he stated gruffly, filling his own cup with dark liquid from a bottle on the shelf. The dog-man eyed the younger man, then said, "Got a thorough beatin', you did. Rest might do yas good."

Elm sniffed the concoction, then took a sip. The bitter-tasting liquid burned as it went down, leaving Elm with a relaxing heat in his knotted stomach.

Pedros savored his drink for several minutes, studying the younger man. Elm's eyes turned glassy and his head swayed slightly like hearing a song in his head. Warmth hugged his insides like a soft shawl, his thoughts mushy.

Pedros began again. "Wheres ya hail from, Elm?"

Elm swallowed down more tea and said, "Far south. I'm a tinker, or was until raiders got me."

"Raiders, ya say? How'd ya end up in tha city?"

"Long story. I escaped and worked for passage here."

"And then ya fall victim to mo scoundrels. Bad luck follows ya, po lad." Pedros stroked his chin for a moment, then asked, "I's never met one who 'scaped the pirates. How'd ya do it?"

The tea relaxed his belly, wrapping Elm's whole body in the feeling of a warm, peaceful blanket. He felt so much better! Despite his horrifying look, Pedros is a kind and generous being, he thought.

Who rescues a stranger from certain demise and offers them his home? My new friend, Pedros, does!

"Ahem," the dogman cleared his throat, snapping Elm back to the conversation.

"What did you ask?"

"Yer 'scape."

"I was just lucky. Other prisoners set me free. They traveled here, and I tagged along."

"Mus' be powerful friends."

Elm leaned forward and whispered, "You bet. Real royals."

"Royals? Dun't say," said Pedros, giving Elm a suspicious glance. "Ya yankin' me leg, lad?"

"No. Humans and elves. Even the prince of Tabor."

Pedros raised his brows in surprise. "Ain't no such ting. You tellin' ol' Pedros a wopper!"

"Nathaniel and the others are real nobility. He's traveling to Tabor to regain his throne. Promise!"

Somewhere in Elm's mind he heard a suspicious voice asking, Why? Why did Pedros want to know? So many questions, he thought. But his mind had trouble focusing, eerily fogged like mist rising from the ocean surf.

"Whys dos yous...?" Elm slurred each word like after too many grogs. What was happening to him? He couldn't string words together. Something was wrong!

A knock at the door splintered the air at that moment, ending the conversation. The dogman pulled a filet knife from his belt and tiptoed to the door.

"Who's it?" whispered Pedros, standing to one side of the wooden door, knife in his paw ready to strike.

"Aze," answered a gruff voice.

"Cum in den."

An enormous brute leaned through the door, followed by a gust of cold air, closing it behind. The newcomer had the flat, triangular head of a badger topped with a dirty blue bandana pulled over one eye. A weathered gray slicker and boots covered his tall, muscular frame. He stepped in and sat on the nearest chest without a word.

Pedros replaced the knife in his belt and moved closer to the fire.

"Dis 'im?" growled the newcomer.

"Elm, meet me partner, Aze," Pedros said, waving his arm back at the table. "Nows where wers we? Ah, yes. Yous gonna tell mes whar to find yo frindz."

Elm stared at Pedros, not grasping the words. Cotton seemed to fill his head and he felt weak as a kitten. "I'm sos tired. Les me sleep."

"Should I rough him sum?" asked the newcomer.

"Give a moment. Tea ain't fully act yet."

Pedros waited several heartbeats, then tried again.

"Wheres might I find yer friends, mate? Time to git you home."

Elm smiled, remembering the brotherhood members and their kindness. "At the Inns," he said drowsily. "The ones with thes black bird."

Pedros grinned and winked at the newcomer. "Drift off, lad. Time for more 'scussion later," he said soothingly as Elm nodded off again. When the dogman heard the deep breaths of sleep from the younger man, he tiptoed to the door. "Les go tell da guild. Der's gold to be made," he whispered, waving his enormous friend out the door and locking it behind him.

Colonel Kristopher Hundmeister held fast to the top branches of a tall sycamore, gazing out at the city below. Dusk carried a biting chill and brisk gales, which swayed the canopy like a pendulum. But the elf felt neither the icy burn on his cheeks nor the movement of the tree, focusing only on his mission. The city lights sparkled, one after another, but he waited for a particular light to shine. After several minutes, he glimpsed a red glow from the western city, once then repeated. He nodded subtly and pulled a stone the size of a goose egg from his pocket. When kissed by sunlight, the signaling stone, a rare find in the Svartalflands, had a crystalline structure that glowed. Hundmeister arranged the stone so the waning sunlight struck the crystal, waking it to life. He waited ten breaths, then pocketed the stone and began climbing down.

A half-hour later, a lean figure slipped unseen into the Svartalf camp. Hundmeister knew the assassin loved to play games, and sneaking past sentries was his favorite. The colonel studied his drawn city map, not looking at the newcomer. "Welcome, honored Crow. What news?"

When the assassin said nothing, Hundmeister continued. "King Barnabus is concerned. According to our informants, no one has announced Gooseberry's death."

Crow's eyes narrowed. "He's dead as a stone."

Hundmeister nodded. "What game is the crown playing, I wonder?" he said as if speaking to himself. "They can't hide his loss for much longer."

"Not my concern. My gold?" demanded the assassin flatly.

The colonel's hand disappeared into his pocket, emerging moments later clutching a hefty leather pouch. The coins within clinked and clattered as he shifted them around in his palm. A moment of hesitation passed, as he felt the heavy weight of the gold in his hand, before he tossed it to Crow. The agile elf, his movements like a whisper of wind, intercepted the falling gold, securing it in a pocket with a single, fluid gesture before disappearing into the dense woodland without uttering a sound.

Elm awoke alone and cold, the fire in the hearth down to ash. At first, he did not know where he was, but then the image of his grotesque savior came to mind. Elm gazed about, inhaling the scent of smoke mixed with sweaty, moldy clothes, but Pedros was gone. He climbed out of bed, every muscle aching, and his stomach lurched as he grabbed for his clothes. His head swirled as he swallowed down rising bile and stepped into his clothes.

"Gods! The rat must have drugged me. I've got to get free," he murmured, staggering to the wooden door and peering out. Pedros' room led to a side alley that eerily resembled the one where he was attacked. Was it the same one? Elm neither knew nor cared. His only concern was escape. He had reached the alley entrance when his stomach lurched again, and he bent over at the waist to empty his gut. He wiped the foulness with his sleeve and staggered on. By a miracle, after two blocks, Elm reached the city's main street and walked toward the Howling Crow, leaning on storefronts for support. The day had melted into a star-filled night, the crisp air acting as a tonic to clear his focus. He struggled for an eternity to locate the correct street before realizing he was lost. Elm pulled himself into a mercantile doorway and fought the cold by pulling his knees to his chest. With closed eyes, he prayed to Morak, the God of Dwarves, seeking his help and drifted off to sleep.

An explosion of pain ripped through Elm's side, forcing the air from his lungs and jolting him awake with a start. What the…?" What was happening? His eyes opened to see the behemoth, Aze.

The monster reared his leg back for another kick and bellowed, "Git up, scum!"

Elm closed his eyes and prepared for another jarring boot strike, but nothing happened. The half-dwarf opened one eye, his face contorted, ready for the worst. A muscular, dark-skinned elf loomed over an unconscious Aze. Elm's eyes widened with alarm, and he hastily scooted back against the shop door, seeking refuge and a sense of security. His heart pounded with terror, making it hard to breathe, and he struggled to maintain consciousness.

With a swift movement, the interloper pulled back his hood, revealing Micah's cheerful grin.

"Come on, lad," he said, reaching to lift the younger man to his feet. "We've been scouring the city looking for you!"

Micah threw an arm around his shoulder and supported the half-dwarf down the avenue.

"How'd you find me?" Elm rasped, wincing with each step.

"A ghastly Gnoll came to the inn looking for ransom. Nathaniel snapped, and attacked the beast. Even after the creature gave up your general location, it took three of us to keep Nat from beating it to death. Poor sap had no clue who he dealt with."

"Pedros," he whispered.

"He'll have lots of time to consider redirecting his life after a prolonged healing."

"I was attacked and thought he'd rescued me," Elm said, a wave of guilt washing over him. But the feeling rapidly receded, leaving only anger and embarrassment at his poor judgment. "Then he drugged me and pried for information," Elm said, hanging his head. "I told him where we stayed."

Micah stopped in his tracks, his eyes narrowing at the younger man's sheepish expression. "What else?"

Elm tried to remember, but his thoughts were ethereal, like glass reflections disappearing in the waning light. "My mind's sort of jumbled."

"Think. It may be important," Micah commanded harshly.

"Okay," Elm stammered, holding up his hands in surrender. His head pounded like miniature sledge hammers to his temples. "I might have mentioned about royals in the group. And Nat."

Micah's eyes widened in shock and an icy shiver ran down his spine. Not uttering a single word, he seized Elm's arm with a forceful grip and marched resolutely towards the Howling Crow Inn.

ELEVEN

"You told them what?" bellowed Grull, furious at the half-dwarf's stupidity.

"I may have told the dogman about Nathaniel and the others being royalty," mumbled Elm, looking away sheepishly. "They drugged me."

"What exactly did you say about Nat?" asked Blue Ivy.

"Just that he was a prince," said Elm, his voice cracking.

"What else?"

Elm averted their gaze, unable to face the men. If he told the truth, who knows what they'd do? If he lied, he might live to regain his life as a merchant. Unless they discovered the truth. He weighed his options for a split second, then told a partial truth.

"Only that we had escaped from pirates."

"You didn't tell them our plans to reach Tabor?" demanded Grull.

"He never asked about your plans," Elm said, evading the question.

Grull glared but said nothing.

Jacoby signaled to Nathaniel with a nod to leave the room. He shut the door after Nathaniel entered and asked, "Do you trust him?"

Nat scratched at his beard as he often did when thinking. "He's lucky to still be breathing after such a beating. I'd like to believe I'd hold my tongue, despite being drugged. Unfortunately, that's an unreasonable expectation for anyone. What do you think?"

"Doesn't matter. Pedros' information is circulating from the local pub and spreading across the city. We must leave tonight."

Nathaniel's face fell, disappointed at having to end their respite. But Jacoby was correct. Everyone in the city would know his identity by morning, including the King and court of Mar Napor. Reaching Tabor as soon as possible was crucial. He stepped out into the common space where the Brotherhood sat, eyeing the half-dwarf with equal measures of pity and disdain.

"Get packed up. We leave on the hour." Then, as the others sighed and moved to their rooms, he spoke to Elm. "No hard feelings, Elm."

"I'm sorry, Nat. I didn't mean any harm."

The prince gazed at Elm, a spark of pity in his eyes. "You're still welcome to travel with us, but if you've got a mind to rekindle your merchant business, then good luck and Odinspeed." He dropped a small pouch of coins on the table and shook Elm's hand before turning to get his pack. The young half-dwarf hung his head, not speaking, but pocketing the coins as he exited the room.

That afternoon, Commander Hundmeister knocked three times at an ivy-covered door on the western city wall. Hundmeister learned of the door from a traveling minstrel who had used the exit to escape the Mar Napor authorities. The opening served as an entrance to the city slums, where countless urchins lived, hidden from regular society. A despicable older man, face covered in sores and shadowed by stringy, greasy hair, opened the door a crack.

Dressed in a vibrantly colored wool tunic and leggings of red, purple, and gold, the elves appeared as common merchants. With wool caps covering their ears, the group passed for any independent group of human traders.

"Wast 'dis then?" the man said, voice whistling through rotted teeth.

Hundmeister forcefully pushed his way in, knocking the man off balance, landing with a thump on his rump.

"Whatsa meaning a dis?" the man bellowed, regaining his feet.

The elf commander ignored the question. He pulled a small pouch from his shirt and handed the jingling coins to the diseased man.

"Disappear."

"Tanks, Guv," the man said, giving the elf a sham salute before scuttling away.

"Cretin," Hundmeister spat in disgust, turning to his second in command. Lieutenant Pater Hopkins was tall and lean, with tassels of blond curls spilling from under his cap. His green eyes reigned over a subtly raised nose and broad smile, considered attractive by most women.

"Pater, break the squad into teams of two. Give each two flasks of oil, a spark stone, and a torch."

The commander unrolled a map of the city he had drawn and separated into ten sections. "Disperse each team to a section. You and

I will take the section closest. One hour after dusk, set fire to anything that burns and meet back here by midnight. Understood?"

"Of course, commander," Hopkins said, saluting. He barked orders to the platoon, and the pairs scattered.

Hours later, Pater Hopkins and Kristopher Hundmeister slithered along a dark alley leading to the Mar Napor warehouse district. They reached a corner, and Hundmeister signaled to separate. He kept to the shadows, and at the first door he came to, he pushed the door open. He found himself in a warehouse stacked from floor to ceiling with crates. The commander pried up the top of the nearest crates with his knife and looked inside.

"Demons," he said under his breath. "Nothing but clay jars." He pulled one free from the straw covering and held it close. The top was closed with wax, but Hundmeister could detect a chemical smell from the bottle. The jar wasn't empty but filled with a green gelatinous mixture.

He broke the seal and sniffed the contents. "Whew." Hundmeister reared his head away, the chemical smell burning his nose. Whatever the jar contained smelled awful. But, he realized, the straw in the crate would be perfect fuel. He removed some straw and made a pile next to the crate. Next, he knelt down and ran his blade over his spark stone, lighting the straw. He gingerly dumped the burning straw into the container and slipped out the door.

Hundmeister was a block away when a loud "boom" lifted him off his feet, crashing him against a warehouse door.

"What in the..." Hundmeister's shoulder ached, and his head spun. What just happened? He regained his feet and witnessed the unthinkable. An explosion tore apart the warehouse he just visited, leaving a raging husk of a burning, charred frame. Burning debris from the explosion covered the street, causing the adjoining structures to catch fire.

By the Gods, I'm a lucky elf, he thought. He whistled at his good fortune. He had set a single fire, unexpectedly destroyed a whole building, and caused a chain reaction that caused more to catch ablaze. The elf smiled as he ran down an alley, making his way back to the secret wall door. Job well done, Kris.

On the other side of the city, the brotherhood members felt the ground shift and heard the low rumble of an explosion.

Jacoby, Grull, and Blue Ivy had just finished loading supplies into a wagon loaned by the innkeeper, Mistletoe, when the earth jolted.

"What was that?" a confused Blue Ivy said.

"Earthquake?" suggested Grull.

"An explosion. Look," Jacoby said, pointing to a rising black cloud from the western city. The trio watched as dark smoke swelled over the western sky, hovering above the orange glow of fires. City bells cracked the air, warning everyone that the city was burning.

Mistletoe, wearing his stained apron and carrying a butcher knife, ran out of the inn backdoor, breathing hard.

"What in the Gods is happening?" he said between breaths.

"An explosion. "The city is engulfed in flames," responded Jacoby while still gesturing towards the west.

"Thor's beard! That's the old city and warehouse district."

"Look," said Grull urgently, pointing away from the dark cloud. "More fires to the east and north."

"What in the demons going on?" Allai'nn said, holding two fussy children, worry written in her eyes.

Jacoby stroked his beard. "I don't know." What could cause an explosion at one end of the city yet cause fires in other parts? He couldn't wrap his mind around the problem.

Nathaniel strode up to Jacoby, putting a hand on his shoulder. "I have a bad feeling about this. I'd like to leave, but we must help those people." He turned to Mistletoe. "How many live in that area?"

"Hundreds."

"Wait a minute. Your identity may be all over the city by now. This isn't our problem," Cor'in interjected.

The young prince understood his meaning. Only Odin knew if or who might be searching for them at that moment. "Take a look, Cor'in," Nathaniel said, gesturing with his arm in a broad sweep. "No one is running toward the area."

Citizens stood mingling in the street, filled with concern, but none moved toward the western fire.

"I agree with him, Nat. For all we know, a pirate mob could be hunting for you."

Nathaniel cut him off, dismissing the issue outright. "I'm going to help them if I can. Cor'in, will you and Blue stay behind to finish preparations to leave?" Without waiting for a reply, he turned and began jogging down the street. Jacoby and Grull gave Cor'in a withering stare, then ran followed by Micah and Horatio.

Cor'in kicked the dirt road in frustration and said, "Be a fool, then."

As they ran toward the plume of smoke and fire, Jacoby noted the change in the city. Like a wave rippling toward a beach, the beautifully attended stores and homes progressively changed to warehouses and, finally, shanty tenements and shacks. Garbage littered the streets. Fowl-smelling squalor ran along open gutters guarded by bristle-back rats the size of dogs. Who could live in such filth, he wondered Terrified, screaming peasants scattered in all directions like frightened cats, carrying their meager possessions in their arms to escape the spreading inferno. Smoke choked the air in a heavy mist, and the heat from burning buildings blocks away consumed the men like a stifling August day.

The warriors reached a row of three-story tenement buildings not yet afire. The wooden walls were old and dried, with straw insulation between boards. Nat knew the dwelling was ripe tinder for combustion.

"I can barely see," coughed Grull, his shirt covering his mouth.

"Me too," added Horatio.

"Jacoby, take Horatio and Grull down that alley, and I'll take Micah and Lani down there," Nathaniel choked, pointing. "Save anyone in these apartments that you can."

Jacoby gave a thumbs up and disappeared in the haze.

"Follow me and stay close," Nat said to Lani and Micah and rushed to the tenement door. He reared his leg and kicked in the door, splintering the opening into pieces. A stairway to the right of the door ascended into the smokey gloom. The group charged up the stairs, frantically kicking in doors and shouting, "Anyone here?"

They found none on the second floor and swiftly climbed to the next floor. At the end of the hallway, he heard a cry, "Help me!"

Micah found a soot-covered woman lying on the floor, a baby wrapped in her arms. He tore the child from her arms and in one move, tossed her over his shoulder and carried both outside. Nathaniel and Lani staggered on through the smoke but couldn't find anyone else and followed Micah outside. He found Micah staggering away from the coming flames and ran to help. Once the women and child were safe, they turned the corner to the next building.

Out of his eyes' corner, Nat glimpsed a shadow in the haze, his outline highlighted by a burning torch and stopped short.

"What the devil?" he said aloud. "Did you see that?"

"See what?" asked Lani.

"A maniac with a torch," said Nathaniel angrily.

"Let's follow him," suggested Micah.

Nat, Lani, and Micah charged after the figure, uncertain what or who they were chasing. Thick smoke fogged and burned their eyes as the three arrived at the intersection of another alleyway. Nathaniel looked in both directions but saw nothing.

Where the demons did he go? Is the smoke playing tricks on my mind? Nat took a few more steps down the cloudy alley and peered into the gloom. Nothing. My imagination got the best of me, he thought, shaking his head. As he turned around, he heard the faint shuffle of boot steps ahead. Maybe not, he thought. Micah and Lani stepped up next to him. All three quietly waited. The shuffling stopped.

"He's down there," whispered Lani.

"Be on your toes," whispered Nathaniel, pulling a kitchen knife he had borrowed from the inn kitchen from his belt. Micah and Lani were weaponless, each reaching for a loose stone or broken wood as weapons.

The three warriors tiptoed down the dark alley, back muscles tensed for an ambush. The scent of charred wood and refuse assaulted their noses as they crept down the alley. They had only gone half a dozen steps when the alley doglegged left, but still no sign of the shadow man. Lani fought to breathe the dense smokey air, coughing. From nowhere, Lani caught the flash of movement but was too late to react.

"Ugh!" she moaned as pain exploded in her head. Darkness swallowed her, and she crumpled into a heap.

Nathaniel turned toward her, and his heart froze. A dark figure hovered over the Lani, a massive lead pipe raised over its head. His heart froze in panic, and he screamed, "Lani!" before recklessly launching himself, tackling the man.

The scent of soot, oil, and sweat wafted off the assaulter as both men rolled over the cobbled street. The lead pipe clattered away into the fog, each man's hands reaching for the other's throat as they fought to control the other. Momentum slammed them into the far building's wall, blasting them apart. The dark figure sprang feline-like to his feet and charged before Nat was fully upright. Hidden by dark clothes and a face covering except for golden eyes, the attacker was muscular and agile, striking the prince with a fist to the midsection. Caught off guard, the prince staggered back; his attacker saw his advantage and charged again with a windmill of pounding punches. Nathaniel's natural strength and agility nearly matched his enemy, and he surprised the man by side-stepping, then striking with an uppercut. The blow stunned the attacker, driving him back against the alley wall. For the next several heartbeats, each rained punches and kicks at the other, the yellow-eyed man matching Nathaniel blow for blow. Neither warrior seemed able to take advantage, each circling the other in the smoke-filled haze.

"Enough," said the yellow-eyed man in guttural Elvish, wiping blood from a split lip. He held his right hand up in surrender long enough for Nathaniel's tense muscles to relax. Then his left hand drifted down, pulling a thin jeweled needle-dagger the size of his palm from his boot, and charged. Nathaniel met him in stride but tripped, losing his balance for a half-second. That was all the time the elf needed, diving the blade towards Nathaniel's chest.

At that moment, a streaking figure slammed into the enemy, clattering the needle free and driving both bodies to the ground with a crunch. Micah rolled with the attacking elf, clawing at his face and trying to reach his neck for a chokehold. But the masked enemy drove a knee hard into Micah's groin, sending a rocket of white-hot pain shooting through the Moor elf. Micah screamed, "Arrgh!" and loosened his grip.

The dark elf pushed Micah off him and rolled away, feeling something firm under him. The dagger! The enemy elf almost laughed at his good fortune. In one movement, he grabbed the knife and blindly slashed out at Micah. Micah yelped as the knife sliced a long gash through his thigh. But the dark figure wasn't finished, and he raised the blade above Micah for a kill strike.

"Now you die, Pigyhr," the elf said menacingly, spitting in Micah's face. The Moor elf's eyes widened, frozen in shock at the name.

"Micah, watch out!" screamed Nathaniel, now on his feet, charging the enemy.

The enemy's speed was uncanny, changing course in a heartbeat and slinging the blade side-arm at the prince. Nathaniel wrenched his body, the speeding blade just missing his chest. But when he reached his friend, the dark figure had disappeared, melting into the haze like a ghost.

"Thor's beard," Nathaniel groaned, focusing on his friend's wound. The gash was not only deep but sprayed blood with each of Micah's heartbeats. Nathaniel knelt beside him, quickly pulled off his tunic, and wrapped it around the upper thigh as a tourniquet, slowing the blood loss.

"Demons! That blade cut me like a prized hen," the elf moaned, his face pale. Nat pulled Micah to a sitting position against the alley wall, tearing a strip off Micah's shirt and pressing down hard on the wound.

"Arggh!" Micah screamed, his eyes rolling back in his head.

"Just hang on, Micah."

"What did we just walk into?" the elf whispered before losing consciousness.

Nathaniel didn't answer. What or who? Thought Nathaniel. An assassin? Why would a killer be starting fires? Nothing made sense. The chaotic thoughts made his burgeoning headache worse. He sat up, letting his mind clear, but felt something under him. He swiveled and pulled an object from under his hip. Nat held an oval stone in his hand.

"What in the demons?" he said under his breath. The prince pocketed the stone without studying it and groaned as he got to his feet. He had to find help for Micah before it was too late. That's when he remembered Lani. "Oh lord, where's Lani?"

Panic gripped Nathaniel's heart as tendrils of fear wrapped around it. He needed to locate Lani! Yet, he couldn't abandon Micah, who was bleeding out. "Great Odin, what do I do?"

He lifted his bloody hands from the leg wound. Although the gash still oozed, the blood flow had slowed. He thought it would have to do for now and staggered to his feet. Driven only by his will to find his true love, he ignored his swimming head. He lurched forward several steps through the smoke, his boot catching on Lani's prone form. He knelt next to her, caressing her face. Blood caked the back of her head, and some pooled beneath. A jolt of pure terror sliced through him as he knelt, gathering her lifeless body into his embrace.

"Lani, my heart," he crooned, patting her cheek gently. "Wake up."

Lani's eyes fluttered open. Throbbing spasms shot from her head down her back.

"Ugh. What happened?" she groaned. In a sudden motion, she jerked her head as vomit gushed out from her twisted gut. An immense pressure, as if a boulder were crushing her head, caused her to vomit relentlessly until her stomach emptied and only bile remained.

Nat held her head delicately, stroking back her hair. "You're all right, thank Odin," Nathaniel said, releasing his breath. "I.... I was afraid..." But his voice caught in his throat as tears stung his eyes. He held her close for a long moment, relishing her rhythmic breathing, before helping her stand up.

She felt brutal, agonizing pain spreading through her body, a pain mirrored in the violent, jarring rhythm of her head as if two immense rocks were crashing against each other inside her skull. I may wish I were dead, she thought. She gazed about through the haze, but her world seemed twisted. Where am I? How did I get here? She couldn't remember anything before the pain. Lani felt lost, like floating on a turbulent sea far from land. Feeling Nathaniel's comforting warmth and strength, she surrendered to him, melting into his embrace. He would be her life raft, and he would carry her home.

The sound of running boot steps broke the silence as Jacoby, Grull, and Horatio arrived.

"We heard you call out and came running," Jacoby panted, catching his breath. "What happened?"

"We saw someone with a torch and followed them. They ambushed us but escaped," Nathaniel said. "The demon brained Lani and slashed Micah in the thigh."

"I'll be okay," Micah said, his voice wilting as he fell back unconscious.

"Loki! He's lost a bit of blood," offered Horatio, removing his belt and exchanging it for Nathaniel's tunic around the leg. "We need to get him back to Allai'nn right now."

"I'll help," said Grullach, taking one of Micah's arms over his shoulder while Horatio did the same.

"Let's get out of here before we all burn to a cinder," added Jacoby. "I'll carry Lani."

"I have her," barked Nathaniel defensively, lifting Lani in his arms.

Jacoby's brow raised. "Right."

Back at the Howling Crow, Allai'nn tended to the injured. Micah, skin pale and face drawn, slumbered on the shared space couch, his left leg newly stitched and bandaged. In the suite's shared space, Lani sat with eyes closed next to Nathaniel on the sofa, ice-wrapped in a kitchen towel against her head.

"So, tell us what happened," said Cor'in, starting the conversation.

"We cleared some of the burning huts and tenements," began Nathaniel. "I glimpsed a figure in the smoke holding a lighted torch. We followed, and he ambushed us in the alley."

"What did he look like?" asked Blue Ivy.

"He wore a mask, with only his yellow eyes visible. He had cat-like quickness and enormous power and fought like a seasoned warrior."

"Mmm," murmured Grullach. "What kind of warrior lights the city on fire?"

Nathaniel shook his head. "What kind of warrior, indeed? The strange thing was he spoke Elven, but in a dialect I didn't recognize."

Micah's ears perked, and his eyes opened. "Did you notice any defining marks or tattoos?" the Moor elf asked, sitting forward.

"That's an odd question," Nathaniel said, giving Micah a quizzical look. "I was too busy trying to stay alive to notice. There was one thing." He pulled out the stone from his pocket and tossed it to Grull. "I found this after our battle. Maybe he dropped it during our struggle."

Grull studied the stone and said, "Looks like a spark stone."

He passed it to Jacoby. The stone felt smooth, like a river stone on one side but rough on the other, as if scratched by time. He inspected the markings thoroughly, realizing the pattern appeared intentional. He grabbed his canteen and dripped water over the stone. Rubbing revealed the tiny figure of a bird above a single word: Mran.

Jacoby heard a gasp from next to him. Rue was staring at the stone, hand over her open mouth. "What?"

"I know that name. But, it's impossible."

"What do you mean?" Jacoby said, all eyes on Rue.

"It's a term from an ancient Oread legend I was told as a child. My grandmother spoke of an elven branch led by a ruthless and diabolical elf wizard named Rhodite. He magically put the Elf Gods to sleep by adding a potion to their wine and stole some of their most powerful weapons. As punishment, the Gods cursed his clan and chained his followers underground. Their skin and eyes turned black from eating the soil, except for their yellow sclera."

"Interesting. The warrior I fought had yellow eyes," said Nathanial, leaning forward, intrigued.

No one seemed to notice Micah tense; his fists balled. "May I have a look?" he growled.

"Go on, "Jacoby said to Rue, anticipating more.

He absentmindedly handed the stone to the Moor elf, who studied it intently. Micah's eyes widened, and his breath caught. Was it possible? He knew this symbol, and he understood the type of killers who would possess it. But why? After years in the shadows? And why Mar Napor? His heart was beating like a sledgehammer in his ears, thoughts skyrocketing across his mind. Micah struggled to make sense of the stone's meaning. He took in a deep breath to calm his nerves. Luckily, no one seemed to notice his reaction. At least, he thought no one. But Allai'nn had detected the change from her eye's corner and now stared with a questioning expression. He looked away, pretending not to notice.

Rue continued, her expression grave. "Rhodite's magic gradually grew, and he and his clan escaped. The clan thrived in all things wicked. They earned the name "Terror-bringers," or in Oread: "the Mran."

"Sounds like a tale to frighten children," laughed Cor'in. "I've never heard the name."

"Nor I," added Blue. "Probably just a legend to keep children obedient."

"I don't think so," said Rue seriously.

"Why not?" Asked Horatio.

"Because they murdered my grandmother."

Hundmeister waited at the western city gate door, tapping the flat of his sword in his hand. He accounted for every trooper except for his second in command, Pater Hopkins. Where in the demons was he? I can't wait much longer. Burning acid seeped into his gut as Hundmeister watched the horizon where the pink crown of the sun touched the sky. As the sun neared the horizon, Hopkins was nowhere to be found. Hundmeister speculated on what could have delayed his lieutenant. Was he wounded? Dead? Was he captured and imprisoned? Hopkins was more than a loyal officer. He was as close to a friend as the commander had.

Absentmindedly, he rubbed the raised scar on his neck, returning his mind to his youth. He could still feel the sting of the goblin arrow that made the mark. A war party had murdered his farmer parents and left him for dead that night. An old Elven trapper, as large as the mountains he traveled, had stumbled on the attack and carried him to the closest outpost. He still remembered the words his savior spoke that night.

"Boy, yer a scrawny tike. You're gonna need to use your brains to survive what's ahead of ya."

By fortune, the outpost commander placed him in the local military school. Hundmeister remembered the trapper's advice and devoted himself to reading and studying. By sixteen, he was at the top of his class and recommended to the capital city officers' school, where he excelled at every task, physical and mental. But his devotion to books left little time for friends, and despite leaving first-in-class, he kept few relationships.

As an officer, he was hard-nosed and regimented. His battlefield strategic ability had provided him with respect but little else. Until he met Pater Hopkins. Funny, good-humored, and prone to practical jokes, Hopkins was the antithesis of Kristopher Hundmeister in every way. Strangely, the opposites attracted, and the two elves developed a trusted bond over the years. Pater Hopkins was one of the few elves Hundmeister could count on.

Hundmeister had a policy he lived by: Never leave an elf behind.

So, he sighed and closed his eyes, counting to ten in his mind. He squinted his eyes open, hoping Hopkins would stand there with a silly grin and a wild tale to tell.

But he saw nothing but the early sun's rays reflecting off the smokey haze.

"That's it then," he murmured to himself. Kristopher Hundmeister closed the gate and jogged back into the smokey ruins of Mar Napor from which he'd just come.

"Murdered your grandmother?" howled Cor'in. "How?"

Rue took in a deep breath, sadness in her eyes. "Sora was my Nana's name," Rue said. A silence covered the room for several heartbeats.

"THE Sora?" croaked Horatio, his jaw agape.

Allai'nn's eyes bugged, and she gasped. "Sora was your Nana?"

"Heavens," uttered an astonished Blue Ivy. "You never told me that."

"I don't understand," said Cor'in, perturbed at missing the significance. "Why is your Nana so special?"

"Are you kidding? Every Anuran is told of the legendary sorcerer," said Horatio.

"What? How am I supposed to know about every witch born?" responded the half-elf.

"She wasn't a witch!" yelled Rue, charging toward Cor'in, fists clenched. Blue pulled her back. "Whoa there, Rue."

Cor'in snickered. "Guess I touched a nerve. What was she then?"

Allai'nn cut in, placing a reassuring hand on Rue's shoulder before the red-faced Oread could charge again. "Your ignorance doesn't give you the right to be disrespectful, Cor'in.," she scolded. "Sora was the greatest Elven magical seer in an age. Beautiful, intelligent, headstrong, and unimaginably gifted, she rose to become the premier counsel to many of the Elven kings, educating and advising. Sora was so revered that she was unanimously elected the first female leader of the Elven Council."

"That still doesn't explain what happened to her," Cor'in pouted, ignoring his need to apologize.

"I'm not done," she stated firmly. She hesitated a heartbeat, then said, "Sora unified the Elven nations, lifting the Fae out of the shadows and dissolving old grievances between realms. But not without fostering the jealousy of many power-hungry Elven leaders."

"What happened?" asked Horatio, mesmerized by the tale.

"At her peak, she survived an assassination attempt. Someone slipped poison into her wine cup, but a lazy waiter placed it at the wrong setting. The king of Renemark died in seconds. After that, she resigned from the council, fearing more attacks on her family. She spent her remaining years traveling Curth Talem, developing relationships between elves and other nations, and studying magic. My father greatly admired Sora and even studied under her in his youth. He told me that even after leaving politics, several evil-hearted Elven leaders despised her."

"She did wonders for my people," said Horatio. "She was the first to acknowledge us as a distant Elven branch, bringing us into the light of acceptance."

"And fostered equality between races, elevating forest elves as equals, and instituted free trade among kingdoms," added Blue Ivy.

"She sounds amazing," admired Nathaniel. "Who wouldn't support such a visionary?"

"There are always some who covet other's power. They will do anything to take it. Even murder," said Jacoby sagely.

"So, again, what does this have to do with the Mran?" asked Cor'in irritably.

"A month before her death," Rue explained, "Nana's actions took on a strange quality, prompting concern from those who knew her well. I overheard her telling my mother she thought she was being followed by a dark shadowy figure. Nana warned her to be especially protective of me." Tears welled in her eyes. "A few days later, my father found her, hung from her a tree limb like a gutted deer. Carved into her belly was the mark of the Mran—a black raven."

Nathaniel squeezed Rue's shoulder. "I'm so sorry, Rue."

A doleful silence covered the room. Even Cor'in replaced his arrogant sneer with solace.

Grull shattered the air, saying, "Am I wrong, or do the Mran sound like those Svartalf assassins we tangled with last year?"

Jacoby rubbed his beard and gave Nathaniel a nervous look. He would never forget the battle with the two Svartalfs who had kidnapped Allai'nn months before. In a fierce and perilous hand-to-hand battle, he grappled with a powerful Svartalf warrior whose poisoned dagger narrowly missed his neck as the warrior fought relentlessly. He'd been a hair's breadth from death before reinforcements forced the black elf to disengage and escape. The enemy's yellow eyes and hot breath forever left an imprint in his mind. Yellow eyes.

"Worrisome. But we haven't seen a trace of the Svartalfs in months," Jacoby said.

"True, but...".

"Does anyone here know the word, "Pigyhr"?" Micah interrupted. Suddenly, all eyes were on the Moor elf, wondering his intent.

"I've heard the term," responded Allai'nn. Blue nodded in agreement; his brows furrowed.

"What does it mean?" asked Horatio.

"It's nasty elven slang used to demean someone you know. It's meant to be hurtful and personally insulting," said Blue Ivy seriously. "To call someone Pigyhr is ...well, the worst thing an elf can say to another. Basically, calling them scum."

Micah hesitated, collecting his thoughts. "The dark figure in the alley used the term just before spitting in my face."

Allai'nn gasped. She knew the act only intensified the insult.

Cor'in said what everyone was thinking. "Did he know you?"

Micah didn't answer, looking away. His mind remembered the last and only elf ever to call him that. A foreboding silence fell over the room as the implication struck each member. Nathaniel looked at Jacoby, who nodded.

Jacoby cleared his throat. "Whoever he was, one thing's clear. It's no longer safe for us in Mar Nâpor. I suggest we pack up and distance ourselves from the city."

Hundmeister had not traveled far when he saw a figure hobbling toward him. His second in command appeared careworn, with a torn tunic, cut lip, and ash on his face and pants. The younger elf slumped against the building side and saluted, his face a mask.

"Pater Hopkins, reporting, sir."

"What in the demons happened to you?" asked Hundmeister, throwing the younger elf's arm over his shoulder.

"Long story. On my way back, I realized that someone was following me. Three people, two humans, and an elf."

"An elf?"

Pater nodded. "Not townsfolk, but warriors. I was fortunate that they didn't have weapons."

"Militia?"

"No. They wore no insignia but fought with ferocious skill. I was lucky to escape."

Lucky to escape? Hopkins was one of his best soldiers, coming close to beating him in practice combat. What kind of warriors had that ability? And humans and elves fighting together? An abomination! Anger leaked into Hundmeister's consciousness. Could it be just chance? A feeling of uncertainty tickled the back of his mind.

Hundmeister noticed his friend looking away. Was there something Pater had not reported?

"What else?"

"The elf. I thought I recognized....no, it couldn't be."

"Yes? You know him?"

"He looked like our old enemy, the Moor elf prince, Micah."

Hundmeister inadvertently reared his head as if struck, and his heart skipped a beat.

"That's impossible," he exclaimed. "King Barnabus exiled the Moor clan after King Midras led an uprising. His entire family was executed for treason."

Pater looked away. "I remember."

An uncomfortable silence blanketed the two as they trudged to the wall gate. Finally reaching the wooden door, Hundmeister opened it wide, allowing Hopkins to exit. The sunlight crept through a dark cloud of billowing smoke, casting the countryside to the west in an eerie glow. They would circle the city until reaching the wood-covered hills southwest and meet the rest of the squad.

As the two elves hobbled across the dew-covered prairie, something needled at the back of Hundmeister's mind. Could the smoke have been so dense Pater Hopkins misidentified his adversaries? What was Hopkins not telling him? He had known Pater Hopkins for years, eaten and fought with him, but never once had Pater lied to him. But a Moor elf? The idea was madness. Maybe during the battle, Pater hit his head? Perhaps he dreamed it? Or did he witness a ghost? Unlikely. Hundmeister bit his tongue, wincing at the next thought. What if Pater Hopkins had seen Prince Micah alive? That revelation made his gut churn.

Fires raged throughout the city despite the efforts of bucket brigades stretching out like wheel spokes from city wells. Citizens moved through the smoke-filled streets in every direction, some rushing to help fight the fires, others trying to escape the destruction. Prince Caron personally led one fire brigade with several other royal ministers, yet his presence did little to stop the city-wide panic. Strangely, King Gooseberry remained absent, adding to speculation and innuendo growing through the city like kudzu.

Black smoke drifted over the town, carrying with it serpents of uncertainty that slithered down streets and avenues, biting at the psyche of every inhabitant. Some people had decided the fires were an attack by invaders; others said the fires were accidental, caused by a restless cow kicking over a lantern. No one knew the truth, but the earlier explosion that rocked the town suggested to Jacoby it was sabotage.

Whatever the source, the fires lit more than buildings, fanning a spark of madness that did not stop with ordinary citizens. With most of the city's militia fighting to control the fire, there was a vacuum of authority. Bandit-led groups roamed the streets, looting and pillaging. Others randomly attacked and robbed anyone they met, leaving victims in their wake.

Nathaniel and the others had pitched in to fight the flames for several hours, holding the mammoth fire from consuming the southern sector. But flames ate through the north and western city, leaving a charred wood and ash trail in its wake. Eventually, giving in to their exhaustion, the brotherhood had returned to the inn to rest.

Despite his weariness, Nathaniel had discussed his plan for the Brotherhood with Jacoby.

"I'd like to help more, but with Micah and Lani injured, I think it best we leave."

"I already told you my thoughts," Jacoby said grumpily.

"Look, I know you wanted to leave earlier, but I just couldn't leave without helping."

"You're a fine man, Nat. I'm proud of you. But as the leader, you're responsible for the whole group. Was it wise to put more of us in danger not knowing if more Svartalfs were here?"

Nathaniel sighed. "What kind of king would I become if I refused to help others in need? Didn't you teach me to have a servant's heart?"

Jacoby shook his head. "Forget it. What do we do now?"

Nat pulled himself to a standing position. "We pack up first thing. I'll see if Mistletoe can sell us a wagon."

Nat clomped down the steps and met Mistletoe coming from the kitchen with two over-stuffed suitcases. Seeing Nathaniel, the portly innkeeper dropped the bags, his face crimson in embarrassment.

"Leaving?" asked Nathaniel inquisitively.

"Uh..yes. The wife and I are leaving town until this madness dissipates."

"So are we. Any chance you have an extra wagon and some horses for sale?"

Mistletoe looked at him and sighed. "No, but let's go next door and see what we can arrange."

The two men walked to the livery adjacent to the inn. A wagon was waiting with a team of mules harnessed. Mabel was bent at the waist inside the wagon, packing boxes and dry goods. She called out over her shoulder, "Hurry up with the bags, Mist."

Mistletoe coughed, and Mabel turned in surprise. Upon seeing Nathaniel, she frowned. "I'm sorry, Nathaniel. We were going to speak with you before leaving."

"No need to explain, Mabel."

There was a heartbeat of awkward silence, and then Mistletoe turned and said, "I don't have another wagon. But there's an old ox cart in the back I'll sell you."

"Give him one of the goats, Mist. For milk," Mabel said, bending to make room for the suitcases.

"Thank you both. I'll tell the others, and we'll be right on your heels."

"Don't tarry," warned the innkeeper. "The grocer across the road told me he'd seen monsters about."

"Monsters?"

"Wolfmen," whispered Mistletoe as if saying the word aloud might draw one there. "He witnessed several folks get murdered before the beasts bounded away."

Nathaniel's face turned white with concern. First the Svartalfs, and now Lupine Rangers? He sprinted through the door to the inn, calling, "Thanks" over his shoulder.

He relayed the whole encounter to the others when he got to his room. Jacoby's brow furrowed at the mention of wolfmen, and Rue gasped.

"Quickly pack up while I hitch the cart." Everyone moved at once, and in a half hour, the packs were ready and brought to the stable. Nat had harnessed two oxen and placed some blankets for the children on the floor of the cart bed. Horatio supported Micah down the steps to the stable, lifting Micah inside. Next to him were placed the four infants, who began a chorus of tears, sensing the anxiety in the air.

Grull and Blue packed in as many dry goods, filled canteens, and dried jerky left by Mistletoe. When the cart was stuffed, Nathaniel hitched the tailgate.

For their part, Mistletoe and Mabel had bolted the inn doors and then helped the brotherhood load the cart. When all was ready, Nathaniel offered the older man all his coins the group had left. "You'll need that," he said, smiling, putting up his hand in a sign of refusal. Then he reached his hand to shake. "Gods speed, young prince."

"And to you and Mabel. I hope someday I can repay your kindness."

Mistletoe turned suddenly serious. "I saw you today, doing everything you could to save the city like a citizen. That act was payment enough."

Mistletoe turned and climbed into his wagon, Mabel waiting on the baseboard. "Good luck!" he waved and steered the wagon into the crowd of refugees.

Nathaniel waved and led the oxen out of the stable, locking the door.

"Let's make for the closest gate," he called up to Grull and Allai'nn, guiding the cart.

"Right," Grull said, slapping the reins on the oxen into a walk.

The river of fleeing humans was thick as honey, and the pace against the tide of people escaping the city was incremental. Added to the difficulty, the oxen bucked and resisted, frightened by the avalanche of people, sounds, and smoke. Jacoby and Nathaniel covered the animal's eyes with a cloth and then hand-walked the beasts forward. Pushing and shoving against the river of humans, they coaxed the oxen around the next corner and into a darkened alley. The evening dusk, mixed with smoke, made it difficult to proceed without Twilight vision, so Blue Ivy and Horatio took over leading the oxen while Nat and Jacoby fell back to help Lani and the others. The team traveled down one alley and up others, working their way past the charred skeletal remains of buildings toward the south gate.

After what seemed like hours, the group turned a last corner and, to everyone's relief, saw the south gate ahead. But as they rushed forward, an enormous figure leaped out from the adjoining ruins, snarling and barking. Commander Cinsor blocked the exit, his red eyes glowing like coals in the smoke-filled air.

The Lupine yipped rapidly, and three more wolf figures materialized from the mist behind, right, and left of the group.

"Now, you're mine!" Cinsor growled with a triumphant grin.

TWELVE

The air cleared of both the wolves' menacing snarls and the thick, smoky haze, and in that moment, time seemed to stretch and slow. As the lupine commander, Cinsor, charged towards him, Nathaniel swiftly drew his sword from his belt, his gaze fixed intently on his approaching opponent. With a ferocious wolfman galloping toward him, beads of sweat appeared on his brow, and his heart began to race as he braced himself for impact. In his mind's eye, a vague image formed of Jacoby's cry of alarm, a sound barely registered amongst the cacophony of the other lupine rangers attacking their company. He remained unaware of the screams piercing the air from Rue and Allai'nn or the profane outburst from Grull as his hand connected with the oxen's backs to urge them forward. All that registered in his mind as the monstrous creature hurtled toward him was its immense size, its slavering jaws lined with razor-sharp fangs dripping saliva, and its eyes blazing with an insane, furious rage.

With a seamless transition, Nathaniel engaged his analytical right brain, calculating the beast's stride and anticipating when the lupine predator would unleash its attack upon its unsuspecting prey. He steeled himself and yanked his sword back, ready to slash the beast. But the attack never came.

Just as the beast's muscles tensed to spring, Grull drove the bull oxen full bore into Cinsor's side. With eyes solely fixed on his quarry, the lupine failed to notice the large oxen charging towards him, and by the time he registered their presence, it was far too late for him to react. With a mighty crash, they plowed into the wolfman, their horns goring him as they drove him from his paws, sending him sprawling. Despite Cinsor's desperate attempts to twist and claw his way free from the oxen's grasp, their powerful front hooves ensnared his lower body, pulling him beneath the heavy weight of the lumbering wagon. Nathaniel witnessed a moment of panic in the lupine commander's yellow eyes; then, he disappeared under the trampling oxen's hooves. Cinsor let out a piercing "YELP," followed by a crunching noise, then the "lump, thump" of the cart's wheels. The result was devastating. Cinsor lay in a pool of dark blood, his body contorted to one side. Nathaniel cautiously approached the lupine's bloody, inert form, his sword still at the ready. Two open chest wounds where the fur had been torn apart oozed blood, and Cinsor's jaw hung slack and broken. Nathaniel nudged the beast with his boot, and its eyes fluttered open for a heartbeat. Cinsor's yellow eyes registered disbelief as if asking, "How was I bested?" Then, the lupine released a final moaning howl before going still.

At that moment, the clattering sounds of the battle registered in Nathaniel's mind. He gazed up to see his friends fighting the remaining lupine and, without hesitating, charged into the fray. The prince attacked the closest wolfman, its raised paw descending to strike a fallen Blue Ivy at its feet. Nat roared, "Hold on, Blue," he roared, hacking at the wolfman's side and gashing the black fur.

With a guttural cry of "Arggrh," the lupine staggered backward a single step, the dark fabric of its uniform blossoming with a stain of crimson.

"Now you die, human," the enraged beast roared, swinging wildly at Nathaniel.

The prince side-stepped, but not swiftly enough. With a blow so decisive it sent Nathaniel reeling, razor-sharp talons tore across his left shoulder, causing him to lose his balance completely. Slicing through the muscle and bone, the claws carved three bloody gouges into Nathaniel's body, causing him to scream out in pain. As he fell backward, he felt a searing burn shooting up his neck and into his back.

The lupine realized his advantage and raised both paws for a final death blow. But Nathaniel sensed the lupine's intent and plunged forward, stabbing at the blurry black belly. Both figures crashed together and toppled onto the dusty street. Neither moved for a heartbeat. Then the prince rolled to his knees, blood running down his arm and soaking his tunic. The lupine lay dead on his side, Nat's sword driven deep into his chest. Nathaniel's breaths raced, his mind blurring as he pulled the sword free and staggered to his feet. He gazed over as the battle raged, seeing another enormous lupine, bleeding from several wounds, strike at Jacoby with a paw the size of a small tree stump.

Nat screamed, "Watch out!"

But his warning was too late. Jacoby twisted, avoiding the mighty paw but not the beast's four-inch, curved claws. They raked across his chest, slicing through his leather armor like a hot knife through butter. Blood splattered in an arc, painting the deep brown road in streaks of crimson. Jacoby wailed, his knees buckled, and he crumpled to the dirt.

Nathaniel's eyes widened, and let out a gut-wrenching scream, "No!!

At that moment, the tectonic plates of his soul unexpectedly shifted and cracked. Like volcanic lava bubbling under pressure, long-suppressed emotions burst free, and an unrelenting rage poured out, filling every cell with renewed energy. Forgotten were his wounds, his weariness, all other concerns. White-hot fury replaced his meditative mind. Without realizing it, he charged the monster, catapulting his body into the monster's side and slamming it to the ground. Weaponless, Nathaniel hammered with his fists, briefly dazing the wolfman. They rolled together for several feet, finally separating. Cat-like, the lupine leaped to his feet, ready for combat as the rabid prince readied for another charge. But without warning, the oxcart, filled with wailing children, slammed into the lupine, somersaulting the wolfman across the road.

Grull jumped off the cart, pausing at the craze-eyed prince. The older halfling stared into his eyes, shaking him by the shoulder, blood saturating Nathaniel's left sleeve.

"Nathaniel! Laddy!"

Nathaniel felt his rage dissipating, replaced by a profound weakness. His head swirled, and he crumpled to his knees. Panting, he could only murmur, "Check on Jacoby." But Grull threw one arm over his shoulder and laid Nathaniel against the cart.

"Allai'nn," he shrieked, "help!"

The elf princess poked her head out from inside the wagon, where she'd tried to comfort the children during Grull's mad ride.

"Oh, Lord," she cried and slipped out of the cart with a fist full of bandages. She applied pressure using a clean cloth to Nathaniel's shoulder wound, slowing the bleeding. After a minute, she pulled away and gasped. White bone peeked from under mangled muscles and clotted blood. Allai'nn swallowed hard, pushing down the bile rising from her gut. This is an ugly wound, she thought. She began cleaning the wounds as Grull turned and sprinted to another crumpled figure.

Jacoby lay on his side in a pool of claret scarlet. He rolled the big man onto his back, applying pressure to the deep lacerations across his friend's chest.

"Allai'nn, Jacoby's hurt bad," he barked, terror welling in his eyes. Emotions raged inside like a tropical storm. He'd seen and experienced many wounds over his years in the Taborian army and could gauge the seriousness of the injury. From the blood loss alone, he worried his friend, the friend who had saved his life more than once, might be beyond help. "Hurry!"

"Coming," she cried, sprinting to Jacoby, hands full of bandages. She pulled a dagger from her belt and cut away Jacoby's armor. Fortunately, the leather had reduced the damage, but four deep gouges crisscrossed the muscular chest, bleeding heavily. Allai'nn acknowledged the cuts' infection risk despite no signs of entry to the ribs or chest cavity. Gods know what dirt the lupines had on their claws, she thought.

"I'll need some potent herbs to suppress infection," she said, pressing down hard, stanching the bleeding.

Jacoby grimaced and let out a grunt.

"He's alive, thank Odin," Grull exclaimed with relief.

"Yes, but he's lost a lot of blood. Help me drag him to the cart."

They each grabbed a muscular arm, but Jacoby was too heavy for Allai'nn. Micah, hobbling on his injured leg, arrived, and the three dragged the unconscious man to the wagon.

"I'll get started on Nathaniel, while Micah, you keep pressure on Jacoby's wounds," the elf princess ordered.

A few meters away, lupine Lieutenant Notch stabbed at the pesky Anduran facing him. Having previously inflicted a skillful slice to the forearm of the more formidable half-elf warrior, forcing a retreat to tend to the wound, the seasoned lupine now faced the frogman.

He instinctively recognized that the lean amphibian lacked skill but compensated with his quickness and rocket-like prehensile tongue. Whenever Notch made a lunge at the frog, his sword would come dangerously close to inflicting serious injury, only for the frog's tongue to dart out at the last moment, forcing Notch to cease his attack. But not this time. Notch feinted left and stabbed right, dancing away from a tongue shot to his chest and catching the frogman deep in the calf. The warrior stumbled backward, knocking into the bandaging half-elf, both falling to the road in a tangled mass.

Before killing them, he surveyed the battleground in a flash. He had heard Cinsor's scream and the crunch of the oxcart as it rolled over his commander and suspected he was dead. One of the three Gual Mantel warriors lay motionless to his left, struck down by the same oxen that had trampled Cinsor. Another lay in a pool of blood, cut down by the large human now wounded near the cart. The final black-coated Gaul Mantel battled two warriors to his right, an elf and a female human. He wanted revenge for the death of his leader and felt a powerful impulse to kill every enemy he could until they were defeated. Was he capable of doing so? The enemy had sustained several casualties but still outnumbered the lupine. What were his chances of success? He knew in his gut the answer. Success in slaying the prince or surviving the battle remained uncertain. Gnashing his teeth in frustration, he recognized that the moment for swift action had arrived. He barked the retreat.

In two lightning-like bounds, he leaped over his wounded adversaries and landed next to the crumpled body of Commander Cinsor. He tossed the enormous lupine over his shoulder and loped away. The other lupine followed, carrying his unconscious confederate, and the two melted into the smoky haze.

Lani rushed up to Nathaniel but stopped at the sight of his bloody arm and shoulder. Her heart pounded in her chest, and she felt like she couldn't breathe. Nathaniel sat propped against the cart, pale as linen, his eyes closed, head lolled to one side. Dried blood covered his shoulder and saturated his sleeve. She felt dizzy, like the world was spinning off its axis, and she half knelt, half-collapsed next to him.

Tears filled her eyes and ran in streams down her face. "Oh, Gods. No," she moaned, reaching a tentative hand to caress his face. Nathaniel's eyes opened, and he smiled. "

"You're okay?" he whispered.

She stroked his face. Joy flooded her face with tears at knowing he was alive. "Are you?" she choked out.

"I'll make it."

"Let me see." She leaned over to peel back the temporary bandage when she heard Allai'nn's voice. "Don't look!"

It was too late. Gray-white scapula stared out from mangled tissue and clot, and Lani's eyes bugged. Her stomach lurched, and she turned to vomit.

"That bad?' Nathaniel asked, knowing the truth.

"Sorry. I...uh...I've seen worse," Lani lied, wiping her mouth with her sleeve. She tried to put on a hopeful smile and held his hand in hers. "You're going to be fine. Allai'nn can fix anything."

Lani met Allai'nn's tired gaze and saw the uncertainty. The princess healer, covered in Jacoby's blood, placed a comforting hand on Lani. Allai'nn leaned close to Lani and whispered, "Nathaniel needs your strength now. Hold his hand and keep him still while I fix his wound. This will take time and hurt like a thousand bee stings."

The elf princess turned to Micah and handed him her dagger. "See if you can find some smoldering coals at the fire's edge. I need that blade as hot as you can carry."

He nodded and hobbled off just as Blue Ivy stumbled in, leaning on Rue for support. Blood congealed over a laceration to his thigh, but he was otherwise unharmed.

"I'll get to you soon," she said over her shoulder. "Grull, bring me some water and the Taborian brandy."

Her husband knelt beside her, handing her a flask and a water bowl. She lifted the flask to Nathaniel's lips. "Drink this," she ordered.

The prince opened his eyes and took several swigs, coughing as the liquid burned his throat. At that moment, Micah returned, the dagger glowing a dull orange at the tip.

Allai'nn spoke loud and clear for everyone to hear. "Nathaniel, I must get started now. The pain will be worse than anything you've endured. But know I'm not leaving you until I've done everything I can do." She hesitated. "Micah and I will work while Grull and Lani support you. Are you ready?"

Nathaniel's drowsy eyes blinked open, and he smiled. "Ready," he whispered.

"Hold him," Allai'nn commanded, motioning for Lani and Grull.

Allai'nn dowsed the wound with brandy. The liquor sent a poker of fiery pain shooting through Nat's chest, and he tensed for several heartbeats, his teeth gritted but then relaxed. The healer hesitated several heartbeats, waiting for Nathaniel's respirations to slow. When the prince's muscles relaxed, she took the glowing blade from Micah, inhaled a deep breath, and pushed the blade into the bloody wound. Nathaniel convulsed in pain as if struck by a lightning bolt and screamed. With open and wild eyes, he kicked out like a trapped animal, as if drowning in an agonizing sea.

"Hold his legs, Grull!" Allai'nn barked, leaning her weight into Nathaniel, forcing him down. The trio battled a squirming Nathaniel for several moments until, finally, he relaxed and fell back unconscious, succumbing to the pain.

Allai'nn wiped the sweat from her brow and said, "Good. Roll him on his side." Once in place, she cleaned the wound with water. Allai'nn took in a deep breath and said, "Hold him in case he awakens. This will take time because of the deep gash. I must sew the wound in layers."

Lani nodded, her eyes red and fat tears running down her face. She had seen lots of injuries in her life and experienced a few herself. But gazing down at Nathaniel's bloody, irregular flesh made her heart flip and her stomach twist. She winced as Allai'nn stabbed Nat's tissue, feeling every punch through the thick muscle and pull of the thread as if the healer were approximating her own tissue. Lani's chest ached from holding her breath and exhaling with each completed stitch.

Sometime later, Allai'nn, hands stained crimson with blood, meticulously cleaned the prince's wound using a damp cloth; the resulting stitches resembled a complex network of twisting ladders cascading across the prince's skin. From the herbs that were carefully stored in her cart, she created an herbal poultice, which she applied, followed by a clean bandage. She sat gazing at her work for a heartbeat, sighed, and called, "Jacoby next."

Captain Hundmeister squinted in the fading light of sunset to see the raven hovering in the swaying branches at his head. The bird screeched and flapped its wings impatiently. He pulled at the note tied to the bird's clay-colored leg, dodging the half-inch claws, and unraveled it. He read and re-read the message. The dispatch arrived from King Barnabus. It read:

"Use the chaos you've created to kill Prince Caran."

The Svartalf commander cursed and handed the message to Pater Hopkins, who scanned the message with a frown.

"How will we find the prince's location?"

"Search, like always," Hundmeister said.

Hopkins gave his friend a skeptical look.

Hundmeister frowned, then added, "An order is an order."

Pater Hopkins nodded and turned to the other Svartalfs waiting nearby, his face enigmatic.

"Attention!" barked Hopkins, and the elves snapped to attention.

Hundmeister stepped forward, his dark face painted with a severe expression. He cleared his throat and spoke in a stern voice. "New orders. We will re-enter the city in groups of five. Our target is to locate and eliminate Prince Carron. Lieutenant Hopkins will set the teams. Five minutes."

The Svartalfs secreted their way across the open green between the wood and the city wall, re-entering the same secret southern door. Hopkins assigned four groups of five to an unfamiliar city area, leaving the palace grounds for him and Hundmeister. The city reeked of burned wood and ash; thick smoke hung in a gauze-like haze despite the light breeze.

"Daylight is in 7 hours. Meet back here before dawn. You have your orders."

Each elf crossed their chest with a fist in a silent salute and disappeared.

"Let's get moving," Hundmeister said, and the two officers jogged into the smoky gloom toward the palace grounds.

Prince Caron, dust-covered and soot-marked, sat leaning on a charred wall. Next to him, Chamberlain Masters gazed through weary eyes. Masters groaned as he leaned against the wall and closed his eyes, looking older than his middle age.

"I'm as tired as an old dog," he said.

Caron understood, feeling bone tired from hours directing and participating in the central bucket brigade. He had ordered, at Masters' urging, members of the royal court to follow him to help fight the fire. With a heavy heart, he led the men towards the fire, but the ever-growing density of the smoke and heat, burning his lungs with each step, fueled his growing apprehension. As the intense, raging fire blazed before him, a wave of icy fear washed over him, sending a shiver down his spine, and gripping his mind with a paralyzing chill that held him rooted to the spot. He couldn't move. As surging panic overwhelmed his initial fear, he instinctively turned to run, only to find a firm hand clamping down on his shoulder, halting his escape.

"Your majesty," Masters said. "We must save the city from destruction before the fire consumes it completely."

Terror reflected in Caron's eyes, and his throat was as dry as dust. He shivered and stammered, "But I..."

"Now is the time for action. Be the leader you were meant to be," Masters implored.

Caron hesitated, his fear receding like a wave off a beach, leaving only the weight of shame.

"Our people need you," Masters emphasized, each word impacting his mind like a hammer to anvil.

Caron felt like he'd plunged into an icy lake, the weight of the words shattering his emotions, leaving only his core resolve. The lion inside, the one he'd never known existed, sprang forth. Suddenly, the skin of youth peeled away, and a new man appeared.

"For the people," he stated, nodding. "Follow me." The young prince sprinted forward through the choking haze. After another block, he reached a central courtyard where a bucket line had formed.

Burning buildings shone through the dark smoke, like orange lighthouses in a fog. He strode to the end of the line, where several men were tossing water randomly, doing little to stem the blaze. A burly militia sergeant danced about directing the efforts. Caron clasped a firm grip on the man's shoulders, startling him.

"What the demons..," he bellowed, whirling to punch his assailant. But when he recognized the prince's face, his eyes widened, and he dropped to his knees. "I'm sorry, Your Majesty."

"No time for that," snapped Caron. He scanned the area, taking in the fire's enormity. He had to control it. But how? Then he remembered something his father once told him. "When you're not sure, dig in."

"Take five men and start digging a firebreak. There, and over there," he shouted, pointing twenty feet from the flames. He turned to Masters.

"We need more help. Can you send word for half the palace guard?"

Masters nodded with a grin and called out, "Yes, my lord."

Caron then jogged to the well side. A lone woman bent over the stone circular wall wide enough for three people, hauling a single bucket of spring water. He stopped two militia just now arriving, both half-dressed and still wearing sleeping caps.

"Get two more buckets and start pulling more water for the line. We can't stop the blaze from spreading without it," Caron ordered.

"Yes, my lord." Both men nodded, then rushed into the haze, returning with two wooden buckets each.

"Good," he said to the sergeant following him. "Now rotate the buckets so there's no delay while I address the front line."

Yes, my lord."

The fire was like a living animal, relentlessly searching for wooden sustenance, devouring everything in its path. But the firebreaks stymied the fire beast. Over the following hours, Caron and the citizens battled the flames to an uneasy truce. After controlling the fires in one area of Mar Nâpor, Prince Caron and some palace guards moved to the next battlefront. They coordinated citizens, dug fire trenches, and maximized the bucket brigade. Minutes turned into hours, and by midnight, Prince Caron, the palace guards, and the citizens had saved a third of the city from the fire monster's attack.

Prince Caron scanned a map Masters provided upon returning for the next well location closest to the flames.

"Come with me," he ordered, and his guards followed him to the next well. As before, he organized and directed the firefighters like a general on a battlefront. Masters observed with pride and shock as the prince assumed complete command, frequently diving in to assist wherever needed. One thought crossed the chamberlain's mind: This is the leader, the king, that the city craves!

An hour later, Commander Hundmeister, Pater Hopkins, and three elf soldiers watched the grime-marked humans pass bucket after bucket of cool well-water down the line to the fire edge. The last human, his tunic stained with ash and sweat, handed each bucket to several firefighters, directed by a tall youth. Prince Caron, well-muscled for a teen, grabbed the next bucket in soot-covered hands and tossed the water over a firebreak ditch at the encroaching blaze. His blond locks were spotted black with gray ash, giving him the appearance of an older man. His shirt was off, his skin reddened from the heat and streaked with grime and rivulets of sweat.

"Hit that area, men," ordered the prince, pointing to a section of timbers engulfed in flames.

"Right," a burly man said, his word muffled by a bandana tied across his mouth and nose. He grabbed the next sloshing bucket and launched it at the fire. The other men followed individually as if in a choreographed dance with the flames. Caron stepped in at the end of the rotation, adding to the attack. The blaze appeared alive to him, like a relentless beast, consuming everything before it. They had splashed the monster with gallons of water, but the fire continued unabated. The fire's hunger seemed insatiable; its thirst unquenchable.

Caron felt every bucket he carried, his back muscles screaming. He wanted to quit, to give up, but something inside refused to be defeated. The prince glanced at the townspeople in the bucket line, their eyes weary but lit by a light of hope. They watched him, continuing to fight because he fought. So, he took a deep breath and pressed on.

Dark smoke billowed from the smoldering building remains, saturating the air with a mask of smog. He turned to see ten royal guards materialize from the smoky haze from the north. A barrel-chested leader jogged to face the prince. He was as wide as an oak's trunk, with curls over a granite brow and dark brown eyes like coal.

"Sir, we have controlled the fire in the northern section," he saluted.

"What's your name?"

"Sergeant Jaromir, sir."

"Jaromir, rotate five men to relieve the firefighters and have one man carry drinking water to those in the line."

"Yes, sir. May I ask the prince to rest while I take over in front?"

Caron smiled and clamped the man on the shoulder. He was as solid as a tree stump. "Soon."

Hundmeister studied the prince from the shadowed alleyway and now understood the gravity of his orders. Although only a teen, Prince Caron barked orders, galvanizing the firefighters into action and pitching in wherever needed to keep the fire at bay. Physically, the young man was sapling tall and had a well-muscled physique. Calm, intelligent eyes scanned the fire, searching for a weakness to exploit. This was no sniveling, pampered royal teen but a natural leader with a commanding presence. The elf commander found he admired the youth, seeing the solid leadership qualities his mentor had seen in him. A trickle of sadness inched across Hundmeister's heart. The prince would have become a fine ruler under the right mentor. But orders are orders. And he obeyed King Barnabus without fail, lest he face the consequences.

Like a praying mantis, Hundmeister patiently bided his time, waiting for the perfect moment to strike his prey. He counted the minutes in his mind. Another rotation of firefighters was imminent, creating a vulnerable moment when the prince's guards would least expect an attack.

He whispered to Hopkins on his right, "Spread the men over the adjoining street. Watch for my signal to attack." His trusted lieutenant nodded, signaled the other elves with a hand gesture, and melted into the dark.

Hundmeister smiled. He loved the surge of adrenalin he felt before every battle. It had been too long since his last encounter. As he advanced up the Svartalf military ladder, he experienced fewer and fewer forays. Of course, like all military-age Svartalfs, he had trained regularly. But nothing energized him more than actual combat. He licked his lips, anticipating the kill.

"I hope there's resistance," he murmured. "I need the sword practice."

Hundmeister took a deep breath, noticing Prince Caron place a hand on the shoulder of a shirtless, sweat-covered soldier. He uttered inaudible words, but the soldier's eyes conveyed relief, leading to a shout to the other firefighters.

"Time to rotate. Break for water and food," the soldier called out.

This was the moment! Hundmeister fought the urge to rush forward, patiently counting in his mind to twenty to allow the exchange of workers. Wait for it. The workers passed their replacements, leaving Caron briefly alone. The commander signaled for the attack, drew his sword, and charged.

At that same moment, Grullach coaxed the oxen through the smog a hundred yards west, his skin sensing the increasing heat around the next corner. Jacoby dozed inside the cart next to Rue and the sleeping children. Nathaniel walked unsteadily under the aid of the tincture of poppy and holding the oxen reins for stability. Horatio and Micah hobbled behind the wagon while Lani, Blue Ivy, and Cor'in trudged alongside, rags wrapped across their mouths to filter the choking air like common bandits.

"Which way? The heat ahead is stifling," Grull called down from the cart seat.

"Turn south at the corner. Hopefully, we can slip by the active fire," Nathaniel said.

At that moment, shrill screams sliced through the gloom ahead like an ax cutting kindling. Grullach reined the oxen to a stop. "Did you hear that?"

"Someone needs help!" Nathaniel exclaimed.

He and Lani pushed through the murky smoke, but Blue Ivy and Cor'in had already started jogging to the corner, swords ready.

Blue peeked around the corner, and his jaw went slack. Five dark figures, silhouetted by the orange flames, materialized from the gloom like alien gods. They brandished black swords and, as if choreographed, cut down anyone in their path. Three firefighters fell next to their still-full buckets. In contrast, two others stared, paralyzed by the interloper's appearance. Time seemed to stop for a heartbeat as everyone watched the sable-skinned elves, unable to process what they saw. Amidst the haze, a woman's scream erupted, plunging everything into chaos. Citizens scattered like frightened rats in all directions. The elves charged, cutting down anyone in their path. Shirtless guardsmen lept for their weapons. Prince Caron unsheathed his sword, but Masters forcibly jerked him back and shouted, "Protect the prince!"

"The people are under attack!" Screamed Nathaniel, charging past a stunned Blue Ivy and Cor'in on pure adrenalin. Nat met the first elf, hacking at the husky, bearded soldier from the side. But the elf disengaged from his opponent and, in one fluid move, swung his leg in a roundhouse kick. His boot caught the unsuspecting prince in the belly. Nat's air left him in a whoosh, and he dropped his sword, crumpling into a gasping heap.

But Lani, Blue, and Cor'in joined the fight, each attacking a different elf. Lani stabbed at the side of Nat's adversary, but the enemy somehow expected the blow, dodging to one side. In a lightning move, the elf slashed down at Lani's neck, but she ducked at the last second, feeling the blade slice over her scalp. Lani took a half step back to regain her balance but had no time. The elf charged, swinging his sword at her left leg. Lani's feet remained fixed in an awkward position, leaving her unable to dodge the attack. The blade sliced through her thigh like a razor. Blood sprayed like a geyser from the deep cut, and she fell in a heap, moaning in pain. The elf chuckled, driving his blade at Lani's chest for a death blow. But inches from the mark, a loud clang rang out as Nathaniel blocked the kill shot and pushed the dark elf back.

"You'll pay now, human," growled the elf warrior, anger in his eyes slitted eyes.

The two warriors circled each other for several heartbeats, each searching for an advantage. Then the enemy lunged, slicing and stabbing with a whirlwind of steel Nathaniel had never faced. He dodged most, but felt the sting of cuts and slices on every limb. Nat lacked time to retaliate, with mere seconds to counter the next assault. He dodged a jab at his belly, then ducked as the elf swept his sword sideways to decapitate the young prince. Finally, Nat lunged forward, but his opponent skillfully parried each deadly cut. The two warriors danced a macabre waltz of death, neither able to finish the other. Nat breathed in rapid gasps. His heart galloped, and sweat trickled down his chin. He was weakening, his body succumbing to the drain from his previous wounds. He studied his opponent, who remained focused and unwavering. The sable-skinned elf reminded Nathaniel of an undulating snake, sinuously swaying before striking with the quickness of a mamba.

I can't keep this up. What do I do? I need help. Lani? No, not Lani. She lay in her blood, unable to stand. Who else? He scanned the battlefield but saw only vague forms fighting through the smokey haze.

As if reading his mind, the dark elf said in accented common tongue, "You fight well, human, but you can't win. Drop your weapon, and I'll end you quickly."

The elf's arrogance triggered an explosion of white-hot anger in Nat's mind. Bursting with energy, he charged, yelling, "The demons you will!"

Nathaniel struck right and left, but the elf's cat-like dexterity parried every blow. Suddenly, an old memory sprung to mind, a lesson Jacoby taught him as a lad. When nothing else works, switch to your other hand.

Nat smiled and struck the enemy from the right. The dark elf adeptly blocked the blow. Instead of striking again, Nathaniel dropped the sword and swiftly drove it up with his left hand. The unexpected move caught the elf unaware, and he bellowed in pain as the blade sliced through his left side. The Svartalf stared, wide-eyed, as blood dripped from a gash along his ribs.

Without warning, the earth shook, and a loud shout echoed behind the warriors, urging them to jump clear.

Nat sprang to one side, his body connecting with Lani and driving both in a roll. Like a supernatural juggernaut, the oxcart emerged from the smoke as Grull drove the muscular oxen at full gallop, intending to run down the black elf. The enemy, slowed by his wound, rolled to his right, but not before the lead ox struck his lower body, blasting him like a rag doll into the gauze-like haze.

"Hold tight!" Grull chirped as he pulled back on the reins, and the wagon skidded to a stop. Allai'nn and Rue, in the seat next to Grull, both screamed as the shift in momentum lifted them off the seat in the air. With a pale face, the elf princess desperately clutched onto Rue and the cart. The move saved them both from jettisoning over the oxen backs. They landed with a plop back on the seat amid a chorus of Jacoby's moans mixed with infant wails from inside. They gazed at each other for a heartbeat, breathing hard, then Rue's face clouded, and she burst into tears.

"Thank you," the Oread murmured.

But Grull wasn't done. He slapped the reins, spurring the beasts toward another shadowy figure just about to impale a wounded Masters with his sword. The sudden momentum shift caught the women off guard, flipping them into the dirt. Grullach registered little notice, so intent on inflicting more damage on the enemy. The horned ox cantered forward, striking the ebony elf in the back, catapulting him like a spinning top into the mist.

Grull dropped onto the ground, sword drawn, searching for additional enemies. Allai'nn, bruised and angry, pulled Rue to her feet. She approached Grull and, cobra-like, clouted her husband on the back of the head with her open palm.

"What the? That hurt," he said, rubbing his crown.

"That's for throwing us off the cart like useless property, battle or no battle!" She bellowed with anger.

"Sorry. Are you okay?" he said, looking down.

She ignored him and leaned down next to Masters. Blood stained the chamberlain's arm and chest.

"Not too bad," whispered Allai'nn after examining the wound. "You'll survive, friend."

Grull hesitated, then turned to enter the fray.

"Wait," Masters murmured. "Save the prince."

Grull's expression changed from annoyance to confusion. Prince? Nathaniel? How does this man know Nat's identity?

Masters said, "Prince Caron, man. He's here."

The puzzle pieces clicked in the halfling's mind and said, "Where?"

Masters pointed to a tall, blond young man, his clothes covered in ash and sweat. He held his sword in a trembling hand, his face pale under smudges of soot. His back rested against the remnants of a smoldering brick structure behind two imperial guardsmen in life-or-death struggles with two sable-skinned elves.

On impulse, Grull charged, his sword arm ready to stab the closest elf in the back. But he never got the chance. With uncanny perception, the elf expertly blocked Grull's attack and landed a powerful punch to his temple. The halfling's head snapped sideways, exploding with stars before he crumpled into darkness. Deer-like, the sable-skinned elf re-engaged his opponent without missing a beat and, in a heartbeat, stabbed the guard through the gut. The defender crumpled, leaving only the prince to vanquish.

Lieutenant Pater Hopkins pulled back his sword to end the lad. In an instant, the elf caught sight of a blurry figure heading his way. He turned, but too late. The form slammed into his side, lifting him off his feet and driving him into the two fighters next to him. Both elves' swords flew into the smokey air, and all four bodies landed hard in the dirt. Hopkins's air left him in a whoosh, but he reflexively reached for his dagger. He gasped for air, but none came as his assailant leaped on top of him, driving a forearm into his chest. Hopkins lifted his knife to stab the attacker, but the man knocked it free with the other forearm. In an instant, he felt choking hands around his neck. He gazed into familiar emerald green eyes. The warrior, who had almost killed him yesterday, glared back. Hopkins squirmed and kicked, gouged and punched, his yearning lungs on fire for air. But nothing dislodged the green-eyed demon. Slowly, darkness crept from his periphery, his muscles relaxed from lack of oxygen, and he knew his end was near.

At that moment, he heard a thump, and the pressure on his chest disappeared. Strong arms pulled him to his feet, and sweet air surged into his lungs, restoring his vision. Hundmeister stood over him, weaponless except for a heavy board in one hand.

Stunned from the blow to the back, Nathaniel shook the stars from his head and pulled himself to all fours. Hundmeister raised the club to finish him, then uttered a loud grunt and dropped the club. Blood cascaded down his arm from a sword slice through his right forearm. He whirled to face a tall man on unsteady legs, holding a bloodied sword. Jacoby, pale and weak, blood blooming across his tunic like red carnations, rasped, "Not my brother. Not today."

For a tense heartbeat, Hundmeister and Jacoby studied the other. He sensed the big human struggling to stand and considered rushing the man. But then he heard the clomp of iron-toed boots coming from the next alley. The elf calculated the reinforcements from the palace were seconds away. Hundmeister shook his head in frustration, then pursed his lips and whistled a long note, followed by two shorter notes.

Pater coughed between gasps of air, unsure if he could trust his ears, and asked, "Are you sounding the retreat?"

"Half our elves are dead, and we will be too if we don't regroup."

Then the ebony elf threw his arm around Hopkin's shoulder, and each supporting the other, disappeared into the smokey haze.

Jacoby watched them vanish, collapsing next to his brother, exhausted.

Sometime later, Masters leaned against the stone wall of the well, gritting his teeth as Allai'nn sutured a deep gash in his biceps. She finished the final threading, tied it off, and covered the wound with a clean bandage.

"Thank you, my lady. I still can't believe our good fortune at your group's opportune arrival. Saving the prince is a debt the crown can never repay."

Allai'nn gazed across the city courtyard. Bodies littered the area like silent statues, and the wounded moaned on makeshift stretchers in all directions. Dried tears dotted her cheeks, and her eyes were bloodshot. She counted twenty dead, civilians and guardsmen, and another twenty or more wounded. Most of the brotherhood suffered wounds, many severe, including Micah, who barely clung to life. The Svartalf casualties remained unknown; every elf's body had been carried away in their retreat. Was it worth it? What did the Svartalfs mean to gain by killing Prince Caron? Were they after Nathaniel, too? Answers were nonexistent—only the pain of loss.

"I'm not sure anyone had fortune today," she responded.

Masters nodded, acknowledging that many members of her group had suffered injuries. "I've ordered rooms prepared for you in the palace. You and your friends need time to heal and rest before you continue your journey. If you agree, I'd like our healers to help in any way possible."

Allai'nn experienced a sudden wave of fatigue. The physical and emotional injuries to the brotherhood were severe. Gods knew the recovery length and toll were uncertain.

"That's most kind, sir. Thank you."

THIRTEEN

Masters, his left arm in a sling, knocked on the heavy wooden door. "

Enter."

He pushed the door open and stepped into a large room ablaze with multiple torches. Massive colored tapestries depicting historic Mar Nâpor battles covered the space between sconces on two walls; large open windows filled one side while the other wall remained covered in lamps and smaller decorations. The apartments had been the late king's rooms, and Masters could still smell his friend's familiar scent. Prince Caron perched over a parchment at a walnut desk against the windows.

"Your Majesty," Masters said.

The prince looked up, and for a split second, Masters envisioned the late king at the same desk. Caron's sour frown dispelled the vision.

"I can't stand another moment of this ridiculous paperwork," the young prince grumbled, rubbing his tired eyes. "How are our friends?"

"The two healers labor valiantly to save the many wounded. I took the initiative in your name, My Lord, and had all the wounded, soldiers, and civilians transported to the palace courtyard. Thank the gods for Ladies Allia'nn and Rue. They've saved many with their Elven healing."

"Wonderful news," Caron said, rising and rounding the desk. "Walk with me. I must visit the casualties."

The two men walked down the hallway, followed by Major Tarn, the Prince's newest personal guard. Caron ran through the last twenty-four hours in his mind, reliving the Svartalf attack. Who were these dark elves? Why were they after him? And who were these unlikely defenders who saved his life? He needed answers.

"Masters, does the crown employ... uh," he searched for the right word.

The chamberlain stopped and raised a questioning eyebrow.

"Uh, trustworthy informants?" the prince said and continued walking. "I need more information about this new Elven enemy."

"Spies, Your Grace?" Masters said, now understanding. "In our peaceful past, your father found no need."

"Our need has changed," stated Caron authoritatively. "Scour the ranks. I want a short list of loyal candidates to lead a new service, answerable only to you and me."

"Excuse me, Your Majesty. May I throw my name in the ring?" asked Tarn.

Caron smiled, "I need you close, Tarn."

Tarn nodded, disappointed. "Yes, Your Grace."

"Perhaps Major Tarn and I can work together, My Lord?" Masters suggested.

"Wise as ever," the prince answered with a half-smile. "Begin today."

The three men stepped into the radiant courtyard, the morning sun dancing off the azure water in the central fountain, sending sparkles of light across the lawn. But wounded bodies covering the manicured grass overshadowed such beauty. Attendants in blood-splattered blue aprons crisscrossed the greenway, carrying bandages and refuse. Caron eyed a weary Lady Allai'nn and strode to her side. The prince stood next to the elf princess, but she was so engrossed in bandaging a wounded peasant that she didn't notice him.

"Ahem," Caron cleared his throat. "Lady Allai'nn?"

Allai'nn ignored the intrusion, saying over her shoulder, "Empty that bucket of soiled bandages, then return with more herbs. I am running low on Devil's Claw, Calendula, and Snakeroot."

Prince Caron stared for a heartbeat, then grabbed the bucket full of bloody bandages and said, "Yes, ma'am."

When he returned, Allai'nn's face was marred with dark rings, her hair unwashed and tied back with twine.

"Gods give me strength," she murmured, her back and neck muscles feeling as tight as a coiled wire.

Caron laid the empty bucket down and handed the elf a bag of herbs. "What else can I do, Lady Allai'nn?"

Recognizing the young man, Allai'nn's brow rose, and scarlet covered her cheeks. "I'm so sorry, Prince Caron. I did not know you were here."

"I came to thank you and your friends for coming to my aid," the prince responded, ignoring her embarrassment. "And now I'm in your debt again for healing the city's wounded."

"Not at all, sir. The number of casualties overwhelmed Healers Grist and Minca, so Rue and I were happy to pitch in."

"Thank you for your kind hearts. Would you escort me to look in on your friends?" Caron said.

"Of course," Allai'nn responded, weaving a path between the wounded to a shaded courtyard corner.

At that moment a gruff voice screeched, "Allai'nn! Hurry!"

The elf took off at a sprint, leaving Caron, Masters, and Major Tarn behind. She headed to a small rise near the far enclosure wall, secreted below an enormous Camelia bush on one side and azaleas on the other. A rotund brownie pushed through a wall of concerned brotherhood members and beckoned her over with one arm. "Quickly! Quickly!"

"What's happened?" Allai'nn said between breaths, sliding to a stop.

Healer Grist gazed up at her with concerned, bloodshot eyes. The Brownie healer enjoyed a stocky build under a canvas apron, with wild, gray hair thatched under a red cap and wire spectacles hovering over a thin, hooked nose.

"He's worsening, Allai'nn, but I'm unsure why! What do you think?" the healer said, worry reflecting in his eyes.

Allai'nn knelt next to a semi-conscious Micah and brushed a hand through his dark, wavy hair. Micah's eyes flickered open, his pale skin burning with moist perspiration.

"Hello, Allai'nn," the Moor elf whispered hoarsely. "My belly...."

She gave him a comforting smile, squeezing his hand before gently palpating his abdomen.

"Let me know if this hurts," she said before applying soft pressure to all four abdominal quadrants, avoiding the long, sutured incision down his flank. Micah tensed as Allai'nn gently pressed but moaned in pain when she released her hands.

Allai'nn peered up at Grist. The brownie frowned, his arms folded across his chest, face scrunched into lines of deep concern.

"We have no choice but to open his abdomen to release the destructive humors," he stated with authority.

For a long heartbeat no one spoke. Then Allai'nn faced the older brownie, her previous anxiety replaced with stark resolve. She leaned in and whispered in the Brownie's ear as the other brotherhood, Prince Caron, Masters, and Tarn watched.

The brownie's head snapped up, losing his cap and his gray hair flying as if hit by a wind gust. "Are you mad?" stuttered the healer, his eyes wide. "That hasn't been attempted in decades."

"It might buy him some time."

"Or the potency may kill him," rebutted the healer.

"Do we have a choice?" Allai'nn shot back.

The healer cursed and felt Micah's wrist. The Moor elf's skin was clammy despite his flushed face, with beads of hot sweat pooling across his forehead. His heart pounded in a wild, rapid beat as frightening as jungle drums. Grist closed his eyes, cursing again. He had seen these same signs many times over the years, a wound to the gut that rapidly festered until it consumed the whole body with fever and disease. Sadly, he'd never had a patient survive such toxicity.

"There's no hope, girl," he said matter-of-factly. "We need to look to the other patients."

"No!" shouted Allai'nn, painfully grasping the brownie's forearm and preventing his escape. "Together, we have a chance. Please!"

The weary healer took a resigned breath. *Perhaps the princess is right. This poor Moor elf will never survive the surgery without help.*

"All right, but we must act in haste. Who else can we recruit?"

Allai'nn turned to Rue and Blue Ivy, hovering nearby.

"Blue. Rue. Micah needs you."

"Of course," they said together, and Rue continued. "How can we help?"

"Infection has clawed its way inside Micah's belly. We need to open his abdomen and drain the corruption," Allai'nn said as if explaining the procedure to a sick child's worried parents. "But he's too weak to withstand the operation without our help. I know how to strengthen him before we begin, but it requires a personal sacrifice."

Blue's eyes narrowed. "What sacrifice?" he asked cautiously.

"Daenostré Cáto."

Rue gasped, and Blue said, "Daenostré Cáto? Are you mad, Allai'nn? That's dangerous, ancient magic. Giving one's vitality to another pushes the limit of light-born magic, not to mention the ire of the Elven Council."

"Damn the rules. I'll take full responsibility with the Elven Council should they become aware," Allai'nn said defiantly. "But Micah is our brother."

"What is Dayno-caty, or whatever?" Grull whispered in Nathaniel's ear.

"Daenostré Cáto. Powerful Elven healing magic, I gather," he whispered back, half-holding his breath while listening.

Grull bit his lip, wondering if his wife, in her zeal to save Micah, had placed herself in danger.

"It's Micah's only hope," Allai'nn said, her eyes begging.

Rue glanced at Blue, pale as a sheet with fear. "We'll do it," she said, her voice cracking with uncertainty. She squeezed his hand and pulled him next to the two healers.

Allai'nn nodded and slipped one hand into Rue's and the other into Grist's weathered palm. Blue, quivering with anxiety, took Grist's palm in his. The four encircled the dying elf, and Allai'nn closed her eyes and began chanting. Her words began softly at first, a whisper difficult to hear, but with each repetition her voice grew louder and deeper.

"Talmar etu futrtus mar, execular beatrix garto. Relquem daenostré cáto est."

"Talmar etu futrtus mar, execular beatrix garto. Relquem daenostré cáto est."

"Talmar etu futrtus mar, execular beatrix garto. Relquem daenostré cáto est."

Over and over she repeated the words while the four bodies swayed to the rhythm. Nathaniel watched transfixed as the chant volume increased, and with it, a pinprick of green light formed over Micah's body. The tiny ball of light grew with every chorus, finally becoming as large as a melon and dazzlingly bright. The observers shielded their eyes with their arms as the chant and the intensity grew. Suddenly the chorus crescendoed into a final, gut-wrenching scream.

"Talmar etu futrtus mar, execular beatrix garto. Relquem daenostré cáto est!"

Then, in one quick movement, Allai'nn leaped over Micah, palmed the green orb, and slammed it into the ailing elf's body. A supernova of light exploded over his inert form, blinding the observers and chanters alike. When Nat opened his eyes, the force of the explosion had blown Rue, Blue Ivy, Grist, and Allai'nn off their feet where they'd stood.

"What in the demons just happened?" shouted Grullach, rushing over to Allai'nn's side. Nat knelt by each participant and asked, "Is everyone all right?"

Blue stared, unseeing, while Rue swayed drowsily. Grist, his gray hair blown back off his face like sitting in a strong wind, shook the cobwebs from his mind.

"Damnable elf!" the brownie complained, staggering to his feet. "Princess or not, I'm too old for such shenanigans."

Jacoby put out an arm of support, but Grist knocked it away. "If you want to help, get these elves some water. They need hydration.

And you," pointing to Cor'in, "get a full wineskin. And bring a coal pot as well."

"Water, Horatio," ordered Jacoby. The Anuran hopped away and returned in a moment with a full waterskin.

Grist knelt by Micah, studying his condition. To Nathaniel's eye, nothing had changed. But the brownie felt his friend's forehead and pulled down one eyelid, assessing the sclera. "Mmm," he murmured.

"Is he better?" asked Nat.

"Hardly. If anything, he's worse."

"I don't understand. Why the magic?" asked Caron, confused.

The brownie glared up at him. "To give him strength, lad. We each shared a slice of our vitality in hopes he might survive the next stage."

Allai'nn crawled to Micah's other side, her head swimming.

"It's now or never," Grist said gravely. Then, gazing at the elf, added, "Are you ready?"

Allai'nn shook her head and took a long drink of water from a canteen offered by Horatio.

"Ready." She pulled her healer's bag close to her, removed the bag of herbs Caron had given her, and pulled free a clean towel.

Cor'in arrived with the wineskin and the hot coals. Grist pulled his dagger and jammed it deep into the coals. Then he tore open Micah's tunic, exposing his belly.

"Oh, gods," Prince Caron whispered, turning his head and swallowing down the bile rising from his gut. The elf's abdomen protruded like he carried twins. Red and purple streaks veined across his skin, giving the unnatural appearance of quarried marble.

Healer Grist noticed his reaction and said, "Everybody back. We need room to work." Then added, "You there. Hold the lantern; we need light." Nathaniel held a lantern high over Micah while the other observers stepped back. Grist motioned to Cor'in.

"Wine holder, make yourself useful and dowse our hands," he said gruffly. Cor'in frowned but stepped forward and poured the maroon mixture as Grist and Allai'nn washed their hands under the stream.

"Now, pour the rest over the elf's belly."

Cor'in said nothing as he emptied the remaining wine over Micah's abdomen, leaving his distended belly dyed with a pink hue.

The older brownie turned to Allai'nn. "Keep the field clean of blood and suppuration while I search for the source of the corruption," he said, pulling the red-hot dagger from the coals. He took a deep breath and sliced into Micah's belly. A horrific stench saturated the air as bloody, foul-smelling pus poured from the six-inch incision, Allai'nn doing her best to mop up the purulence for Grist to see. Several observers, including Prince Caron, bolted away to empty their guts, overwhelmed by the acrid, nauseating fumes. Unperturbed by the retching, the brownie stuck his small hands inside of Micah's open abdomen, feeling organs and bowel in all directions. After several tense minutes, his face lit with excitement.

"I found it! There's a perforation in the bowel," he exclaimed, victorious.

He pulled the loop out, exposing the damaged intestine. Then, he approximated the sides and sutured the defect, closing it with a needle and thread. Once finished, he stuffed the bowel inside and continued checking the organs.

"I need honey, vinegar, and more wine," the grizzled healer called out over his shoulder. Lani, who had studied the surgery with rapt interest, ran off and returned, juggling two clay jars and another wineskin. She laid the jars and wine within Grist's reach and stepped back to observe.

Once the brownie had completed his exam, he withdrew his hands from inside Micah and emptied half the wineskin inside the belly, followed by the vinegar. Then he motioned for Allai'nn to close the elf's incision, handing her needle and thread.

"Be sure to soak your bandage in honey after you place the herbal poultice," he reminded her, stretching to his feet. He gazed at the other brotherhood members, each face wearing a mask of concern.

"I've done all I can. If he survives, you can thank your friends," he said, pointing down to Rue, Blue, and finally Allai'nn.

"Thank you, sir," came a chorus of voices.

Healer Grist nodded and walked away, searching for the next needy person.

Lieutenant Notch rested next to Private Lox, the only remaining lupine ranger. He tore a thigh off the freshly killed deer with an audible rip.

"Hey, that's my leg," said Lox.

"My kill, my choice," Notch growled, baring his fangs menacingly. The black-furred Grau Mantel backed away but eyed the thigh with envy. Notch bit into the meat, letting warm blood dribble down his chest, and sighed. Nothing satisfies like fresh meat. After eating his fill, he belched and gazed up at the star-filled night sky, wondering how things had gone so disastrously wrong. He and Lox, the last black-furred Gaul Mantel in the troop, had buried the other slain lupine in shallow woodland graves. All except Commander Cinsor, whose rigid, lifeless body lay wrapped in his cloak by his side.

At first Notch had felt his superior deserved more than a shallow grave in some forgotten wood. After all, he was an esteemed Lupine officer slain in battle. But as the night wore on, he reconsidered. To bring Cinsor's body home would be to risk certain death. Clan leader Bloodcoat did not accept excuses, especially after Cinsor had defied his orders by not returning to the Canis Steppes. There was also the small matter of confronting their prey three times and allowing him to escape each time. Originally, he had made up his mind to accept the obvious course of action. Cinsor deserves an honorable burial, and I will accept full responsibility in his place for our failure.

Notch laughed out loud at the thought, provoking a curious look from his companion. He had followed his commander for months, accepting the leader's crazed bloodlust and need to fulfill a successful hunt, no matter the cost. Most lupines in the company had perished over time in the folly, but Cinsor would not give up. Finally, Cinsor had also perished following his maniacal blood trail. Had it been worth it? Of course not, but orders were orders. However, now things had changed.

Notch pondered his responsibility, considering Cinsor's death. What do I owe him? Will I prioritize my survival or Cinsor's honor? He favored the former. What had Cinsor done other than destroy the troop, killing most, including himself, while failing at his mission? And treating me like a common serf the entire journey. No, I won't sacrifice my life for Cinsor's madness. Notch scratched the thick fur under his snout, reflecting on his next move.

"What say we leave this body for the maggots and head back for the Steppes, eh, Lox?"

Lox narrowed his eyes, wondering if this was some test by his lieutenant. "You mean to return home? Won't they reprimand us?"

"Not if we weave a tale of heroism in which we risk our lives to save our wounded commander, only to have him succumb to his wounds later. Realizing that two lupines against hundreds of Mar Nâpor soldiers would be futile, we returned for further orders."

"How will our pack leaders know we didn't murder Cinsor?"

"That's a fine question. His shredded uniform will be our proof." He looked at the other soldier. "But what option do we have? Exile for life?"

The Grau Mantel, not known for his wisdom, considered the words for a heartbeat, then responded, "Agreed."

Notch grinned and motioned for the soldier to start first. But, as he passed the officer, Notch drove his dagger deep into the side of the black-fur's neck. Blood sprayed, and the soldier grasped at the knife, his eyes wild, and crumpled to the ground. The Grau Mantel convulsed, gurgled with a resounding roar, and fell still.

"Sorry, mate, but I can't have any witnesses. It's time for a fresh start."

He left the bodies, lifted his pack, and started the long journey east, whistling as he walked. My destiny lies in the eastern forests, with a new identity and a new life. Sounds excellent to me!

In an abandoned warehouse, Hundmeister studied the lifeless bodies of eight dead Svartalfs before slamming his fist through a grimy windowpane. The elf commander ignored the blood running down from a gashed hand and swore. How had this happened? The mission started conventionally enough, dividing into teams until they located Prince Caron and then launched a vigorous attack. What he hadn't expected was the interlopers. Who in the gods were these warriors, appearing out of the smoke like fire demons? Throughout his long career, he had seldom witnessed such speed and determination in the fighters, which, regrettably, had hindered the advantage he assumed he would have until reinforcements from the palace arrived. Eight excellent warriors were now lost to him, a devastating blow that was compounded by the looming threat of the king's fierce anger and retribution.

Pater Hopkins interrupted his thoughts. "Have you received word from King Barnabus?"

"Not yet."

Pater gazed at the dead elves and shook his head. "I can't believe the same human I encountered yesterday miraculously shows up again to thwart our attack."

"What? Did you recognize one of the enemies?"

"Yes, the green-eyed human who almost ended me. Thank you, by the way, for saving my life."

Hundmeister dismissed the gratitude with a wave of his hand, but his face showed concern. "The same human? How do you explain it?"

"Chance. The Fates seem to think our meetings are entertaining."

Hundmeister sighed. He did not believe in fate or coincidence. One creates his own fortune, and entering a small city twice in twenty-four hours, pushed the envelope too far. The time had come to depart and await the larger force promised by the king.

"Evacuate the troops to the Gnarl Forest, then torch the building," he ordered Hopkins.

Pater gazed down at the dead elves, hesitating for a heartbeat. He knew the Svartalf code: Never leave evidence of your identity behind, but he deeply hated leaving Svartalfen in a foreign land.

"As you wish, commander," he said with a bow.

Three men rose as Prince Caron entered the room and settled into a plush high-back chair at the head of the sturdy mahogany table.

"Sit," he said.

The prince gazed across at his closest advisors, Masters on his right and Tarn on his left. Another man, dressed in street clothes of a simple tunic and vest over deerskin pants, quietly watched the young prince from two seats down from Tarn. To Caron, the man appeared entirely unremarkable. A peasant one might pass in the city market and never register the encounter. Greasy, brown, curly hair cut long at the neck cascaded above intelligent brown eyes and a clean-shaven, pointed chin. He was neither muscular nor thin; his height and weight were average. Caron would have considered him a simple serf or tradesman and wondered the reason for his presence.

"May I begin, Your Grace?" asked Masters, giving the young man a respectful bow.

"Proceed."

"Let me start with your request about intelligence. Tarn and I have found someone who is both loyal and reliable."

He signaled Tarn to continue. The officer cleared his throat. "Your Grace, may I introduce Sir Torrance, better known on the street as "Feliau.""

"The legendary highwayman?" Caron exclaimed, rising out of his chair. "That is your answer to our problem? Are my advisors mad?"

Masters placed a calming hand on the prince's forearm. "Hear us out, please, Your Grace, before you decide."

Caron, wide-eyed and flushed, stared at the man at the table, who seemed unaffected by Caron's reaction. The young man eased back in his chair. "Explain."

"Sir Torrance and I grew up together, Your Grace. After your father's assassination, I asked Torrance to develop contacts throughout the city to better inform the crown on any... unknown anomalies," Masters said, his tone serious.

"What? Why am I learning of this now?" Caron said, his voice frustrated, his eyes burning holes through the chamberlain.

"My apologies, Your Grace. I felt you and the Queen Mother's safety might be at risk. I planned on discussing the matter with you, but the attack, well, honestly, displaced the thought."

Caron relaxed somewhat, readjusting in his chair. He inhaled deeply, sighed, and uttered, "What's done is done."

"I'm so sorry, Your Grace. Never again," said Masters, unable to keep the Prince's gaze.

Caron turned his attention to Torrance, who remained muted. "Under the circumstances, Master's endorsement, Sir Torrence, does not warrant my trust. I'll allow you five minutes to convince me you're free of suspicion."

Torrance bowed and spoke in a level tone. "Your Grace, first accept my condolences on the loss of your father." He hesitated, but the prince remained silent. He continued, "Perhaps unknown to you, King Gooseberry and my father were close friends. In fact, my father died saving the king in a bandit attack."

"I remember hearing the tale. A valiant knight dove before an arrow that would have killed my father," said Caron, steepling his fingers. "So, tell me more about your discussions with Masters."

"First, Your Grace, Masters and I realized that to create a network of loyal informants, we needed two things: patriots loyal to the crown and a way to infiltrate all parts of the city," Torrance said, counting them on his fingers.

"Go on."

"We started by recruiting from the militia ranks, common, unmarried men only."

"Why unmarried and not officers?" asked the prince.

"Common soldiers blend in, Your Grace. No spouse means less risk of accidental leaks. Luckily, many revered your father and gladly joined. But for the idea to succeed, a ruse was necessary."

"A ruse?" questioned Caron, confused.

"We developed the highwayman persona, Your Grace, to shadow our true intent."

"We?"

"Really, it was Masters' idea. The rumor of a bandit commoner who stole from the wealthy but shared with the poor opened doors throughout the city's underbelly. And fortune blessed us, for we now have informant tentacles throughout."

"Excellent," Caron said, giving Masters an affirming nod. "What have you learned?"

"My men detected a wall breach. I interrogated a scoundrel who confessed to taking payment for opening the southern gate to the black elves. Another civilian witnessed them starting the city fires hours before the attack at the well."

Caron shook his head, stunned by the treachery. "What do we know about these elves?"

"Not much," Torrance admitted. "The traitor related they came from the south but knew little else. Clearly, their intent was chaos to mask your assassination. Why, we haven't deduced."

"What is our plan moving forward?" asked the prince.

The room remained silent.

The prince balled his fists in anger. "We need to know more!"

"Agreed, Your Grace," said Masters. "But this is uncharted territory for the realm."

Caron closed his eyes, the stress of the last few days draining his energy like a leech. What would my father do? He pondered the words until a clear path formed.

"Masters, begin by developing a plan for greater royal security. Tarn, your job will be to start a new training protocol for our troops.

"That subject has been on my mind as well, Your Grace," Tarn said, hesitancy in his voice.

Caron stopped and studied the officer. "You have reservations? Speak freely, Tarn."

Tarn's face flushed and he swallowed the lump forming in his throat. He looked at Masters, who nodded.

"Sire, May I be blunt?"

Caron's brow furrowed, and tilted his head.

"I don't think I am being dishonest to say our troops have failed miserably in preventing or stopping two assassination attempts. For that, I take some responsibility." Tarn wavered before continuing, looking down.

"Yes?"

"Our many years of peace allowed us to become complacent. Not a single officer has received any new training in years. If I may be so bold, our visitors have more knowledge than we."

"What are you saying?"

Chamberlain Masters interjected. "Sire, the warriors that came to your aid against the dark elves have better training than our soldiers. May I suggest we ask Nathaniel and Jacoby for help?"

"Excellent idea," Caron said, rubbing his chin.

"But we hardly know these warriors," blurted Torrence.

"That's a fair point, Torrence. But anyone willing to risk their life for me, an unknown royal, has both my respect and my undying thanks," Caron said. "And they bested the assassins, which only adds to my confidence. Tarn, speak to our friends today."

"Of course, Your Grace."

Caron turned and continued walking. His gaze fell on Torrence, and he said, "Torrence, I have a special job for you."

"How may I be of service, Your Grace?" asked Torrance.

"Sir Torrance, it's imperative we develop a system to research these dark elves and any other of our adversaries. I want you to take charge of the task, reporting to the council regularly. The crown's resources will be at your disposal," the prince said, his eyes serious. "Additionally, I expect the southern gate walled over by evening and the scoundrel who aided the elves in chains."

"Of course, Your Grace."

"And one more thing," Caron said, giving Torrance a wry smile. "Welcome to the royal council."

Over the next week, the brotherhood members recuperated from their wounds. Resting, eating healthy food, and sleeping were the magical ingredients to mending. Micah had been the one exception. His course had been rocky; two days improved, followed by three in decline. Healer Grist scoured ancient medical tomes, looking for anything he felt would help but found nothing helpful. Allai'nn had sent word to her father, King Polaris of Serensith

Talem, for guidance but had not received a response. Finally, the day came when Micah summoned Jacoby, Nathaniel, and Allai'nn to his bedside.

The trio found the once sturdy elf skeletal and too frail to sit up. His abdominal wound had never healed, and corruption soaked several bandages per day. He lay with his eyes closed, his pale brown skin hanging on his bones like chicken skin.

Jacoby's eyes welled with tears at the sight of his friend, but he fought to put on a false smile as he grasped Micah's hand.

Micah awakened at Jacoby's touch and half-smiled. "Hello," he rasped.

"How are you holding up, old friend?"

"Not well," Micah whispered, his throat like burning sand. "Water?"

Jacoby took a glass from a bedside table and lifted it for the elf to drink. Micah sipped the liquid, then coughed aggressively, then moaned in pain as the hacking increased his abdominal pressure and caused more corruption to bleed out of his wound.

"I'm glad you came," he said, gazing at a tearful Allai'nn and Grullach.

"We're here for you, mate," Grull said awkwardly, still stunned by the elf's appearance.

"It looks like my journey ends here, friends," rasped the elf, tears running down his hollowed cheeks.

"A tough old Moor elf like you? Why, you'll be on your feet in no time," said Jacoby, squeezing his hand.

"Remember when we left Tajman Sghur? I never thanked you for saving my life when the Owlbear attacked us," Micah whispered, then violently coughed blood-tinged phlegm onto his chin. Jacoby ignored the sign, wiping it away with a rag.

"I remember. But you saved me after the attack in the desert, remember?" Jacoby responded. "And I need you healthy if I get in trouble again."

Micah smiled. "They beat you like a dirty rug." He chuckled, but the laugh turned into a severe coughing fit. More bloody sputum spilled down his chin, and his copper skin turned blue. Jacoby and Allai'nn lifted his head for more air. After several heartbeats, he sucked in a deep breath, followed by several more until he relaxed and regained his color.

Then Micah's jaw clenched, and his eyes turned serious. "The gods blessed me when I joined the Brotherhood. You three have done more for me than anyone ever has, more than I can repay. Thank you.

Tell Nat I'm sorry I missed his corona...." At that moment, the Moor elf's eyes rolled back in his head, his body shuddered a last time, and he went still.

"No!" Allai'nn wailed, tears running in rivulets down her cheeks. And the three friends held onto their companion and wept softly.

"Anything else?" asked Jacoby, placing the last box of dry goods into the wagon provided by the crown as a reward for their bravery.

"Just the children," Nathaniel said, his mind elsewhere. He had spent two glorious weeks in Lani's company, healing and enjoying time together. The two young lovers strolled the gardens, held hands, talked, and when alone, he showered her with kisses. The joy she brought him, a bright, buoyant force, counteracted the heavy weight of grief and sadness that pressed upon his heart following the loss of his dear friend. Within the Brotherhood, many were still healing from the attack, their mending slowed by the grief of Micah's death.

On a cloudless morning, as the sunrise painted the indigo sky with vibrant hues of gold, orange, and pink, Nathaniel happened upon Cor'in during a stroll through the palace gardens.

"Hello. Early for a stroll, isn't it?" Nathaniel said by greeting.

The half-elf glanced up and murmured, "Oh, hello." Nat noticed deep rings sagging below Cor'in's bloodshot eyes, his face swollen and splotched from crying.

"It's been a rough few weeks. How are you holding up?"

"Not sleeping much. Nightmares."

"Mmm. Me too," confided the prince. "I keep running the battle through my mind, searching for a way to save Micah. But I fought across the courtyard, and I never saw him," Nathaniel admitted.

"I was nearby but had my hands full. Those bloody elves were uncanny combatants," said Cor'in, his voice rising with anger.

"That they were. As disciplined and well trained as any we've battled," agreed Nat, placing a calming hand on his friend's shoulder. He hesitated a heartbeat, then added, "I'm happy we didn't lose more."

"Why do I feel so guilty?" Cor'in whispered, looking down with tear-filled eyes.

"Losing a brother leaves an unhealing wound. Our mind looks for explanations, but there are none. Thank the gods, time and distance help."

"You're pretty wise for a human," Cor'in responded, feeling more hope.

Nat chuckled. "Not me. Grull and Jacoby told me the same thing an hour ago."

The two sat in silence, feeling the sun's warmth and listening to the sweet song of a Yellow Warbler. After several minutes, Nathaniel rose and said, "I'll wake the others. It's time to pack and leave some of the pain behind."

But as Nathaniel entered the palace, he collided with Major Tarn, and both stumbled back.

"Sorry. I didn't see you coming," Nat said in surprise.

"Nor I, sir," responded a befuddled Tarn. "However, I need to speak to both you and Jacoby."

Nat led the officer to their chambers, where he found Jacoby and Grull talking in low tones on the apartment balcony.

"Hello. Major Tarn needs a word," Nat said by announcement. Both warriors turned and stood.

"How may we be of service, Major?" Grull asked.

"Prince Caron tasked me with asking for a special favor. As you're aware, the dark elf attack was a complete surprise. Frankly, our soldiers were ill-equipped for the viciousness and discipline displayed by the enemy warriors. Your group was better matched to handle the threat. So, he asked that, as a favor to the crown, you'd aid me in training our troops in case of further conflict."

The three paused, glancing at each other. Nathaniel finally spoke. "Please thank the prince for the honor. But Micah's death has inspired us to continue our journey north."

"Please," implored Tarn. "I recognize seasoned warriors when I see them. My troops aren't capable of deflecting another assassination attempt. Gods forbid if an elf army attacks; they'd overrun us in hours."

Nathaniel looked away and considered the man's request. In every town, the group received the identical request, a consistent message delivered throughout their travels. A long period of peace, lasting for decades, had lulled the Western countries into a state of unpreparedness, a consequence of their complacency. Monarchs only improved their defenses when compelled by a crisis. Sadly, the implemented changes often came too late, resulting in an avoidable and significant loss of life.

"Major Tarn, let us discuss your proposal privately for a moment."

"Of course," Tarn said, bowing and stepping into the next room.

"What do you think?" asked Nat, his arms crossed, irritation masking his face.

"We've been through a lot," Grull said, scratching his beard. "And Tabor remains weeks away."

"True," Jacoby said, pursing his lips in thought. "I have a strong feeling that, while likely annoyed and embarrassed, Tarn spoke the truth. They need help."

"They fought poorly at the well. If that's the best they have, I doubt they'd last a day," Grull stated. "Though once engaged, they showed grit."

"Training Mar Nâpor troops for a week may improve their morale and ours. Forging new allies wouldn't hurt Tabor either," Nat said.

Jacoby and Grull nodded in agreement. Nat stepped in and informed Tarn to have all officers waiting in the courtyard by mid-day to train.

After an intensive three days of training with the entire Brotherhood, Nathaniel felt the Mar Nâpor officers were prepared to train the enlisted militia. Phase two required oversight of the officers' training of the men. By the end of two weeks, Nathaniel felt the entire army had improved.

"Keep a daily training schedule for you and your soldiers," Nathaniel said to Tarn and the other officers. "Positive progress can be slow, but with perseverance it is attainable."

Prince Caron made a surprise appearance daily, training as one of the militia until midday and then relieving himself to attend to other duties. The young noble attentively soaked up knowledge from Jacoby, Grull, Cor'in, and Nathaniel, becoming close to the latter. The two future monarchs bonded easily, as if raised together as brothers.

Finally, the day arrived for the Brotherhood to move on. The group had spent the morning loading a wagon to the brim with supplies, then driving it onto a flatbed barge tied to the Gharial River city docks. Masters and Tarn said their goodbyes and stepped back, allowing Prince Caron to walk Nathaniel out to the pier end.

"Thank you, my friend. Godspeed and smooth travel to the City of Spires," he said, shaking Nat's hand vigorously.

Nat bowed. "Thank you, Your Grace, for the hospitality. I look forward to our next visit," the young man said, smiling. He leaped on board, and they cast off. Jacoby and Horatio poled the barge over the glassy blue water as the others rested. Lani snuggled against Nat, burrowing her head in his shoulder.

"I'm exhausted. I could sleep until..." Lani's voice trailed off, her breaths slow and deep.

"Me too," Nathaniel said, caressing Lani's brown hair. He closed his eyes, drifting into a dream-filled sleep. But unlike in past nights, he did not dream of the dark elves or his friend Micah.

Nathaniel found himself in a woodland clearing; a cabin rested on one edge backed by thick evergreens. Smoke curled from a gray riverstone chimney above a dirt roof and stone walls. A thin blond waif sat on the front porch and beckoned him over. He strode across a carpet of wildflowers growing among trimmed, emerald grass. At the base of the steps, he discovered the girl was a tall child, her thin frame adorned in a glowing lace dress. Her cherub face was powder white, framed with golden locks flowing to her thin shoulders. The girl's nose was small, framed with eyes of different colors, purple and gold.

"Welcome, Prince of Tabor," the child said in a sing-song voice. "Mother awaits your visit," she added, gesturing to enter.

Nathaniel tiptoed into a living space dominated by an enormous hearth and roaring fire. The room was bare except for a single empty chair facing the flames.

"Sit, warrior," came a voice behind him as the door slammed shut. Nathaniel shivered, remembering he was chilled. He sat down and put his hands out to absorb the fire's warmth. At that moment, the fire burned bright, blinding the young prince so much that he covered his eyes with his arm. After a moment he dropped his arm and found he had been transported to another location.

Now, he sat next to the same child by a gurgling brook. A cool breeze blew across the glistening silver water. The child dipped her bare feet in and smiled.

"Where are we?" Nathaniel asked.

"This is my special place," whispered the child. "Mother was called away, so I must relay her message."

"Message?" asked Nathanael, his mind swirling from the venue change.

The child nodded. "Beware the future, Nathaniel. Much adversity lines the path to Tabor. But your greatest challenge awaits in the City of Spires. Your enemies work diligently, plotting against your reign. Make haste before it's too late."

And then the world melted like ice in the sun, and Nathaniel jerked awake. A worried Lani was shaking him.
"Wake up, Nat. Jacoby needs you."

FOURTEEN

"Where are we, and where is Horatio?" Nathaniel asked, stepping up beside Jacoby. The tall human strained against the pole on the port skiff, pushing the barge bow toward the calmer water at the river's edge.

"I sent him to scout ahead. Get the other pole and help me punt the barge out of the current," Jacoby said through gritted teeth. Nathaniel grasped the other pole and struggled to push from the starboard side to inch the boat forward. Once as placid as a docile pond, the river swelled with a strong current. Nathaniel realized the river depth had also increased, making his punting more arduous.

"It's so deep here I can't reach the bottom," he called out to Jacoby.

"I can't control it from my side either. I wish we had oars," Jacoby said, fighting against the current. But the undercurrent increased with every minute they traveled.

Two green hands flopped over the boat rail, and Horatio slithered onboard, out of breath. "The current gets worse ahead," he panted between breaths.

Jacoby saw the worry reflected in the Anuran's eyes. "What else?"

"I felt tremendous turbulence ahead," said Horatio, his green torso streaming with water.

"Turbulence?" Jacoby asked, raising one eyebrow.

"Boils and riffles," the frogman said with professor-like authority.

"Speak common, lad," Grull said, striding up, handing Horatio a towel.

"Choppy water flows around underwater obstacles. Boils are just bubbles created by a vortex beneath the surface. It can suck a craft down in a heartbeat," Horatio warned.

"Demons! What do we do?" Cor'in asked, hobbling up.

"We're too deep for the poles," Jacoby said. "No way to steer the barge."

"Lash the wagon to the barge and get ready for a bumpy ride," shouted Nathaniel as he ran to the wagon for rope. He handed the cord to Grull, who began securing the buckboard to the deck, while Blue alerted Allai'nn, Rue, and Lani.

Soon, the choppy current rolled and pitched the flatboat, the velocity tossing it like a toy boat in a stream.

Jacoby yelled, "Hold on tight!", clutching a loose lanyard to keep his balance.

With one arm around Lani, Nathaniel braced himself by threading his other arm through the wagon wheel spokes, the rough wood scratching against his elbow. Inside the jostling wagon, Allai'nn did her best to comfort the frightened infants, their cries blending with the sound of the rushing water.

The boat's bow abruptly dipped into a trough, cracked against a boulder, and raked over the stone. But instead of slowing through a muted eddy, the flatboat shot forward and banged against another sarsen, sending the craft spinning like a top. Jacoby clawed forward until he reached the bow and peered at the river ahead.

"Odin's breath," he said, and his eyes widened. The churning waterway downstream resembled an intricate obstacle course filled with boulders, stones, and fallen trees. Deep cuts and troughs carved through the underwater terrain, leading to a sudden and steep drop-off. The flatboat slammed into the next rock, catapulting Jacoby into the water. Cor'in witnessed the loss and struggled to his feet as the boat violently shifted again, flinging the half-elf over the rail like a lifeless rag doll. The splash reached Grull's ears, but the turbulent rocking of the ship prevented him from exploring its source.

An earsplitting "crack" shattered the air, followed by a jolting slam as the flatboat collided with a massive stone hidden beneath the surface. The ship split in two, sending Grull, Blue, and Rue tumbling into the turbulent river below. The untethered wagon lurched to the right and disappeared into the frothing tempest. As the wagon crashed into the surf, Nathaniel and Lani found themselves swallowed by the churning water, pulling them below where only the weak sunlight penetrating the surface water above offered any light. Driven by a desperate need to survive, he gripped Lani's hand, summoning every ounce of his strength to thrust them both upward toward the water's surface. The powerful current, however, tore at him with such immense force that he could not maintain his grip. I've got to kick to the surface for air and find Lani. Nathaniel inhaled a desperate gulp as he broke the surface, then dove back into the churning water, but Lani had vanished. Once again, the unrelenting undertow dragged him down, and he fought to stay afloat. He scissor-kicked to the surface and gulped in a moist breath before the swirling current shot him between half-submerged boulders. As he fought to the surface again, he noticed a shadowy figure gliding past him. The wagon tilted on its side and half underwater, raced past. Nat attempted to reach out but couldn't, wrestling to stay afloat in the forceful current.

"Help!" Allai'nn screamed, her heart pounding as she instinctively reached for the children. A jarring jolt and twist of the wagon caused her world to spin off its axis, and she bounced against the wagon's side. A cascade of dry goods fell from the shelves, one clouting her in the temple with a sharp, stabbing pain. For a heartbeat, her eyes blurred, and she fought to remain conscious. Allai'nn's stomach lurched as the wagon rotated again, adding to her disorientation. But her motherly instincts took over, gathering the frightened infants into a loving bear hug to shield them from potential harm. With each moment, the icy river water filled the cockpit of the wagon, rising over the elf's ankles and shins. The frigid river helped clear Allai'nn's cobwebbed mind, and with fierce determination, she battled the strong current to keep the four infants safely above the water. Escape was her primary thought; however, a massive and impassable barricade of boxes and barrels blocked the exit. What do I do? There's no way out!

"Grull! Grull, help me!" she screamed, panic gripping her each second the level of frigid river water around her inched higher. In place of her loving husband, a shadowy figure emerged from the depths, slithering between submerged boxes and into the wagon. "Ahh," Allai'nn shrieked, kicking away from the monster. It's a croc! It's a croc! The words flashed like bright torches in her mind. Her back to the sideboard, she watched, frozen by fear, as the monster kept swimming toward her. Out of nowhere, the monstrous creature lunged at her, wrapping its webbed hand around her leg.

"Help! Help!" she screamed, kicking and twisting against the beast's icy grip. It's going to pull us under! The unbearable, terrifying blend of her panicked thoughts and the children's cries threatened her sanity. Then Horatio's face, as green as an emerald, appeared, his wide grin lighting up the dark space. Allai'nn's eyes widened, and on impulse, she kissed Horatio on the cheek.

"My hero," she said, her relief palpable. "Can you get us out of here?"

"I hope so," he said with a grin, carefully lifting the drenched elf and her infants out of the icy water and onto the submerged wagon seat. "That should offer a brief respite."

Allai'nn's heartbeat slowed, and she hugged the Anuran with one arm. "Thank you, Horatio, for helping us."

"My pleasure," he responded, his voice tinged with caution, "but there are more rapids ahead." The frogman's brow furrowed. "Hold tight while I swim to the wagon harness. The mules broke free when the barge split. I might be able to direct the wagon off the channel."

Horatio's emerald head disappeared beneath the water, and moments later, Allai'nn felt a tug, followed by a sudden jolt that sent shivers down her spine. He reappeared and said, "I wedged the wagon between rocks, but we're at least fifty yards from shore. Can you swim for it?"

"I can't swim with four infants."

"Of course," the Anuran said, feeling stupid for forgetting the crying infants. He considered the situation and said, "I might have a solution. What if I transport each child, one by one, to the safety of the shore?"

Allai'nn frowned, wondering if Horatio's words stemmed from his usual tendency toward exaggerated bravado. "I don't know... What about the others? Could they help?"

"Jacoby made it to shore, but I can't say about the others," he answered honestly. "The current is picking up. I don't think there's a choice."

The elf princess gritted her teeth and said a silent prayer to Rán, goddess of the water, before handing a plump infant to the frogman. "Start with Ivy Oak,"

Horatio accepted the child, placing it on his back.

"Wait," Allai'nn ordered, tearing off a strip from her tunic. She wrapped the cloth around Ivy Oak and tied it around Horatio's chest. As if by instinct, the child's arms wrapped around his neck.

Horatio winked and torpedoed below the water's surface, propelling towards the shore but keeping the child's head above water.

With a sudden burst, he emerged from the water, catching Jacoby off guard. He handed him the babe within seconds and disappeared into the depths. "Three more coming," he said over his shoulder. The Anuran repeated the process three times, noticing each visit another drenched brotherhood member on the riverbank next to Jacoby.

As he arrived to ferry Allai'nn to shore, the wagon shifted; the surging current swallowed the wagon, its powerful force enough to dislodge the fragile anchoring from the stone face and drive it front-first into a hole. Water surged inside, steadily filling the wagon with water.

Horatio yelled, "Quick, grab my hand before we're swept under!"

As Allai'nn reached out her arm towards Horatio, a sudden, powerful undercurrent swept her away from him, pulling her under the water just as the wagon plunged into the watery depths. Horatio dove after her, but the chaotic somersaulting wagon disoriented him. After what felt like an eternity, a flash of yellow caught his attention in his peripheral vision, ten feet below. With a powerful kick, he reached Allai'nn, his heart pounding as he saw blood trickling from a cut on her head. The elf's eyes were closed, and her face was deathly pale. He shook her, but there were no bubbles or signs of consciousness. Grasping Allai'nn under the arms, he kicked with all his strength against the undertow, desperate to reach the surface. Foot by foot, his powerful legs propelled them upward, and breaking the surface, he took in a gasping breath. "HELP!" he screamed.

He dragged her to the shore, placing her on the riverbank as the Brotherhood rushed to help.

"By the Gods, what happened?" Grull asked in a panic.

"She must have hit her head when the wagon broke free," Horatio said, his voice filled with worry.

Jacoby placed an ear to Allai'nn's mouth. "She's not breathing," he said, her face a frightening shade of blue.

"Roll her on her side," ordered Rue, just arriving. She struck the elf several times on the back with a flat hand, but there was no response.

"Lean her over this stone. Quickly!" the oread ordered, taking charge. Grull and Jacoby laid her pale form prone over a giant tortoise-sized rock, Rue pushed hard on her back, messaging from her kidneys to the scapula over and over. On the third attempt, water spilled out of Allai'nn's mouth, followed by coughing and choking. The elf's eyes fluttered open, and she struggled to breathe.

"Help me sit her up," Rue instructed. With Grull's help, they lifted the elf to a sitting position.

Allai'nn blushed while inhaling long gasps of air, mixed with teeth-rattling coughs. After several tense moments, her respirations slowed.

"How are you, my love?" Grull said, his eyes glistening with tears. He stroked her hair tenderly, wet and colored with clotted blood, as he struggled to console her.

"Better, thanks to Horatio and Rue." she wheezed. Fear abruptly masked her face, and she started to rise. "Where are the children?"

"Rest easy, my pet; they are all right," Grull assured. "Cor'in and Blue are looking after them."

"Thank you, everyone," Allai'nn said with a grateful smile. She looked directly at Horatio. "You, in particular. You're a genuine hero, Horatio," she exclaimed, tears of gratitude welling up in her eyes. "And so are you, Rue."

The Anuran bowed, his emerald face flushing a deep crimson, while Rue's face flashed relief. Grull stood and wrapped the frogman and Rue in a group bear hug. "I can never repay you both," he said, tears traveling down his cheeks.

"Ah... that's what brothers do," responded Horatio after an awkward hesitation.

"And sisters. But she's a long way from recovery," Rue said, her eyes concerned. "Keep breathing deeply, Allai'nn, to dispel any trace of water. I'll search for some elfdock and goldenseal to boil. She'll need to breathe in the vapor to prevent pneumonia."

"Thank you, Rue," Allai'nn wheezed, squeezing her friend's hand.

"Cor'in and I will find wood for a fire," Blue suggested.

"Smart idea. We need to change and warm the kids and dry our clothes," Nathaniel said.

"Agreed," Jacoby said. "I'll see what washed up from the wagon to boil water in."

An hour later, the elves had accumulated several armfuls of limbs and driftwood for a large fire. Jacoby had located the wrecked wagon corpse downstream and rescued an iron pot for water. As the sun descended toward the horizon, the group had dried out, and Allai'nn, still hacking and coughing, tilted her head over a boiling herb cocktail. With her face hidden beneath a towel, she inhaled deeply, triggering a short coughing fit, then repeated under Rue's direction.

"I did not know Rue could be such a taskmaster," observed Cor'in, never having witnessed the meek oread take charge.

"She's tough, when necessary," Blue stated.

"I'm thankful she's keeping Allai'nn focused," Grull said. My wife can be a tad stubborn and not used to receiving care herself. Rue will have her on her feet in no time."

"Let's hope so," Jacoby said. Then, turning to Nathaniel, asked, "Where do we head from here?"

The young prince let out a deep sigh. "Tomorrow, we start upriver and, with any luck, find more of our stores washed up on the bank."

On the eastern side of the continent, a hooded figure dismounted and approached the Tajman Sghur's northern gate. The humanoid's leather-gloved hand knocked thrice, pausing briefly before knocking again. A soldier answered the knock with a similar cadence. The hooded figure released a series of whistles, alternating between long and short bursts, and the door swung open. As tall as the color sergeant who opened the door, the slim humanoid's horse was guided through the doorway by the halter. The muscular soldier nodded to the figure before firmly closing and bolting the gate. Without speaking, the cloaked humanoid mounted the horse, urging it onward with a sharp dig of the spurs, and rode at full speed towards the majestic royal palace. A cloud of dust swirled as the rider brought the horse to a sliding stop at the palace entrance, gracefully leaping to the ground. The figure rushed down the marble hallway, footfalls echoing off the stone walls. At the entrance to the Great Hall, the figure halted, confronted by two armed sentries who barred the way.

"What's your business?" one demanded. The figure remained silent but slowly revealed her identity as she pulled back her hood. With her light brown hair braided and circling her head, the female elf scowled at the sentry, her eyes narrowing in frustration.

"Lady Daire," he said, his tone filled with unexpected astonishment. "I wasn't aware that you would be here."

"I have urgent news for the King."

"News?"

In response, the women pushed past the guard and entered the hall. King Michel and General Yow stood at his war table, studying the intricately detailed maps and strategically positioning the colored figurines. As soon as the door creaked open, both men glanced in its direction, and the King's face lit up with a smile.

"Lady Daire, good to see you. What news?"

With a frown, Daire said, "Nothing good, Your Grace."

King Michel glanced at Yow, who gave a disapproving frown.

Daire began. "As you know, our unexpected attacks have thinned our enemy's forces and kept the enemy commanders guessing over the last months. But, our fortune has changed. I intercepted a message from Lord Crepitus to his eastern front officers detailing his strategic plans. As we speak, he is gathering an army of the undead, their moans echoing across the Faire Wing River. The troops are preparing to march on Tajman Sghar soon."

Michel's heart sank, but he concealed his disappointment with a feigned sense of expectation.

"With the weapons from King Polaris," Michel said, as the tension in the air became palpable. "Our dedicated smiths have toiled day and night, fashioning weapons from a blend of silver and other metals. But..."

But. The word lingered in the air, permeating the atmosphere like the lingering scent of smoke from a blocked chimney. Daire broke the tension after a few heartbeats, her voice breaking through the silence. "But what?" she wondered aloud, her mind racing to make sense of the situation.

"This secret remains confidential between us. The shortage of silver has left our smiths unable to produce enough weapons," Michel answered, disappointment clear in his expression.

Daire's eyes locked onto General Yow, who averted his gaze and sadly offered a subtle nod of agreement.

"What about Polaris?" Daire asked, her eyes pleading.

Michael shook his head. "Even if we stumbled on a silver mine tomorrow, we couldn't mine enough ore in time."

Daire looked down and sighed. Her eyes drifted to the candelabra lighting the table.

"Your Grace, what about this!" she exclaimed, pointing to the candle holder.

Michel and Yow glanced at each other, and then the king chuckled. "What idiots we've been! We have plenty of silver in the palace to melt down."

General Yow grabbed the candelabra and studied it. "Not pure, Your Grace, but certainly of help. With your permission, I'll scour the palace for any unused silver items and deliver them to the smiths."

"Excellent," Michel said.

He turned his attention to Daire. The king's eyes lingered on the elf, her once dazzling beauty now overshadowed by unmistakable fatigue, her eyes marked by dark circles after weeks of covert operations for the crown. He placed his hands on the elf's shoulders and half-smiled.

"Thank you, Daire. You continue to amaze me. Your help remains invaluable to the crown. Now, try to get some rest. There will be a need for more sacrifices in the coming days."

Daire bowed and turned to leave; her face lit with the praise from the king. Would it be enough? In her heart, she suspected not. As she understood the truth, her shoulders slumped as the weight of reality settled upon her like a heavy blanket.

The skeletal figure commanded attention as he sat at the head of the meeting table, surrounded by two figures on each side. Ravenite, the lich-mage, could not hide his boredom as General Vulga droned on, his fingers absentmindedly drumming on the polished mahogany tabletop.

"Cut to the chase, General!" Ravenite snapped, his eyes blazing with a brilliant orange-red intensity.

"Yes, master," mumbled the muscular Hobgoblin, his deep voice barely audible. "At the River Narn, our forces have come to a standstill, unable to advance further. Because of the heavy rains, the river has swollen to the point of being impassable. Months ago, the enemy destroyed the only bridge that connected both sides of the water."

"What about the giants?" Ravenite asked.

The Frost giants' king, Icebeard, broke the silence with his commanding voice.

"Da vater too deep and rush too fast. I lost two membas of my clan," boomed the giant, his deep, guttural voice echoing through the air.

"And I lost several lupines to the Crocs," Bloodcoat growled, his voice dripping with bitterness as he clenched his fists, his long talons retracting.

Ravenite tented his finger for a long moment in silence. Who were these blubbering children at his table? Trusted military leaders or crying toddlers lamenting the loss of a few toys? Neither I, nor they, show any genuine sympathy for the losses.

"Very well," the mage said at last. "What say our new, silent friend?" He directed his attention towards the chair beside Icebeard, its emptiness giving off an intriguing aura. A tiny form climbed onto the tabletop. More reptilian than human, the figure raised itself on two legs and sneered. The beast's diamond-shaped head had a wrinkled texture, its skin resembling the dull gray color of a dying man, and its mouth curved like a crescent, filled with needle-like teeth. Icebeard and Bloodcoat recognized the demon as an Incubus and recoiled.

The beast's eyes locked onto Ravenite, and its voice, high-pitched and chittering like a squirrel, said, "Lich-wizard, my master sends his regards. How may he be of service?"

"What do I call Grine's familiar?"

"My name is irrelevant. I am but my master's mouthpiece," said the Incubus.

"So be it," whispered the mage, feeling the room temperature decrease. Ravenite cleared his throat. "How many undead await my call?"

The temperature in the room turned frigid as the tiny lizard's voice changed and, in a deep, haunting tone, said, "Upon payment, five hundred undead soldiers await your command."

"And the cost?" Ravenite said, focused on the Incubus's dead eyes.

"One hundred souls."

Ravenite made a show of considering the number, stroking the decaying flesh of his chin. "I propose a bid of seventy-five, and in return, your undead may feast for an entire hour once I conquer the City of Spires."

For several moments, the group waited in silence, as no one dared to breathe. The room temperature fell, and the familiar transformed into a statue-like figure, its body frozen and unyielding, except for the quick movements of its purple forked tongue. As seconds became minutes, the wall torches dimmed, casting the room into a muted winter twilight. General Vulga's heart pounded in his temples as he stared at the creature, waiting for some response. He glanced at Icebeard, who had leaned back so far in his chair away from the beast he thought the back might shatter. Even Bloodcoat tensed, his eyes narrowed, and his claws cutting deep gouges into his chair arms. Only Ravenite seemed unconcerned with the monster, as if he were at a spring picnic, not bargaining with the emissary of a powerful demon.

After several heartbeats, the creature spoke, "Agreed. My undead will arrive through the ancient pit by the end of the week."

Ravenite gave a respectful nod, and with a flash of red light, the Incubus disappeared.

The lich turned his attention to Vulga. "General, send word to the black dwarf king. We need his engineers to build a bridge over the River Narn. And make haste. Our undead will be hungry."

After searching the northern river bank, the brotherhood members collected enough dry goods to fill a single pack. Nathaniel led the group through a dense thicket of high pickerelweed, their footsteps muffled by the squishy ground. While traveling up a gentle slope, a village appeared in the far distance, capturing Nat's attention. Its empty streets lacked any signs of life, and no chimney smoke filled the air. He scratched his beard, his rough fingertips grazing the wiry hairs. Where are the people?

He turned to the others and suggested, "There's a village ahead, but it might be deserted."

"Deserted?" asked Jacoby.

With a nod from Nat, the group pressed on towards the town, but a sense of unease settled with each step he took. Upon entering the hamlet, Nat noticed the closed doors and cold cooking fires, which were nothing but ash. The young prince's neck hair rose at the eerie absence of life, leaving him curious about the fate of the populace.

"Let's see if there's anyone in the buildings," Nathaniel recommended. "But be on your guard."

With anticipation, the group spread out, entering each cottage. But they found no one. Moments passed, then Blue Ivy called out, "Look at this!"

The others rushed over and Blue gestured at a sign crudely etched onto the side of a hut's wall. The words looked smeared, as though someone had finger-painted them in a vibrant shade of red.

Cor'in read the message aloud. "RUN."

"What the demons?" Grull exclaimed.

"Is that...blood?" asked Horatio.

"Whatever it is, the message is a warning," suggested Jacoby.

Nathaniel's gaze turned upwards, fixated on the darkening sky where heavy purple clouds loomed ominously.

"A storm is approaching," Nat said as the heavy purple clouds loomed menacingly overhead. "Let's continue scouring for food," he suggested doggedly. "These huts will provide shelter until morning."

"But what about the warning?" Rue asked, her voice trembling.

Nathaniel hesitated, feeling the weight of everyone's gaze upon him. "Whatever happened," he said, his confidence erasing the anxiety provoked by the sign. "It must have occurred a long time ago. But to ensure our safety, we'll take turns keeping a two-hour watch. I'll start."

As evening turned into night, raindrops fell sporadically, gradually building up to a torrential downpour. The brotherhood wisely sought refuge in the most oversized bungalow, finding safety within its walls. As the rest of the group slept soundly, Jacoby and Nathaniel huddled together, their voices barely above a whisper.

"What do you think happened here?" Jacoby asked.

"I'm not sure, but I sense an evil presence here," Nat responded, his hand sliding nervously over his sword pommel.

"Mmm. Have you spoken to Allai'nn? Out of all of us, she possesses the keenest sensitivity to magic."

"Not yet, but she has mentioned no peculiar sensations," Nathaniel said, kicking the soil with the toe of his boot. "Perhaps I'm way off, but there's something strange about this village."

"You mean other than the unsettling absence of any sign of life and the ominous message scrawled in blood?"

A mischievous smile played on Nathaniel's lips as he chuckled. "Okay, I may be overreacting."

Jacoby placed a hand on Nathaniel's shoulders. "Go with your gut. Nine times out of ten, you'll be fine."

At that moment, Grullach tapped the young prince on the shoulder. "I hate to break up the party, but it's my watch."

A warm smile spread across Nathaniel's face. "I think it's time to get some beauty sleep."

An hour into his watch, Grull's eyes snapped open with a start, scanning the surrounding darkness. No matter how hard he fought to stay awake, the soothing sound of the steady rain had won, lulling him into a peaceful slumber. Over the next hour, the heavy rain ceased, leaving only a sporadic drizzle when the halfling awoke again. He sought respite from the stifling indoors and determined it was time to venture outside. He opened and closed the hut door with a soft touch, emerging into the all-encompassing darkness that awaited him. After stepping outside, the suffocating humidity smacked him in the face, leaving him regretting his decision. He turned to reenter the hut when movement at the tree line at the edge of the village caught his eye. He stared out into the gloom for several heartbeats, his eyes adjusting over time to the night. Nothing moved, and nothing seemed amiss. A question arose in his mind: "I don't remember that boulder across the green." But before he could dwell on the idea, a tired yawn escaped him, diverting his attention. As he reached to open the hut door, the ground beneath him began trembling, resembling an earthquake. With little time to process what was happening, a sudden, mighty blow sent him crashing against the next hut's wall. The impact was horrific, and he crumpled to the turf, breathless and disoriented. His unfocused eyes locked onto a towering figure, draped in a thick bear hide, and carrying an enormous club.

"Help," he cried, trying to stand.

Jacoby and Cor'in were the first to hear Grull and, with quick reflexes, rolled to the side as a massive club crashed through the hut's ceiling. Nathaniel and Lani awoke with a start, half buried by remnants of thatch and splintered support beams, stifling their escape. With a swift motion, Rue and Allai'nn threw themselves over the screaming children, using their bodies as a shield. Amidst the chaos, only Blue Ivy and Horatio stood untouched, ready to face the onslaught with their drawn swords.

Peering over the collapsed wall into the hut, four pairs of dark eyes scanned the room, taking in every detail. Blue pulled Horatio back into the shadows as the monster rose to its full height of twenty-five feet. Blue noticed a thick muscular torso connecting to two heads, each with a terrifying display of gnarled teeth.

"Thor's hammer, it's an Ettin!" he exclaimed, his eyes wide.

"I smell food," One head bellowed while the other searched inside.

Blue Ivy dodged a meaty hand the size of a wagon, then struck at the monster's forearm, opening a long gash. A yelp of pain erupted from one head, followed by a resounding "Arggh!" from the other, reverberating through the air. The Ettin's arm, comparable in thickness to a grown oak tree, crashed down upon Blue and Horatio, shattering the hut and propelling the defending warriors into the air.

"Run for the woods," Jacoby yelled to Allai'nn and Rue, still covering the infants with their bodies. In a synchronized attack, he and Cor'in charged from the other side, their swords slicing through the air as they aimed for the Ettin's wrist. The monster foresaw the attack and, with a forceful sweep of its arm, reduced the remaining structure into a pile of rubble. Jacoby dove underneath the arm; rushing air filled his ears with a sharp whistle. Cor'in, unable to react in time, caught the full force of the mighty limb, lifting him through the air like a toy and crashing onto the roof of a nearby hut. Both women, carrying crying infants in their arms, slipped alongside the adjoining house and tiptoed in the shadows, hiding until they could run for the trees.

Frustrated and desperate, the monster shrieked as it scanned the village buildings, unable to catch sight of its prey. The beast honed in on Cor'in's unconscious form on the next roof, picked him up in his meaty hand, and shoved the half-elf into a burlap sack at its side. Both sets of eyes continued to scan for movement, but most of the brotherhood were injured or hiding.

As Nathaniel and Lani emerged from the wreckage, their bodies covered in dust and Lani's head bleeding, they took in the surrounding destruction. They never saw the sweeping mitt that scooped them up and dumped them into the Ettin's bag.

Rue and Allai'nn hid in the shadows nearby with the wailing children, terrified the beast might hear and find them soon. The elf princess peered around a corner of the hut and watched as the Ettin, frustrated with not seeing more to eat, began smashing his knobbed club into buildings, one at a time.

"Come out, food," the Ettin roared, destroying one home after another.

Allai'nn looked into her friend's terror-stricken eyes, her heart sinking. It's only a matter of time before the monster finds us. Her heart pounding, the elf princess steeled herself and made the hard decision.

She cupped her friend's cheek and said, "We need a diversion. When you hear the Ettin moving, run for the forest."

"Wait, no!" Rue argued.

But Allai'nn shoved the two infants she held into Rue's arms and rose, saying, "Stay hidden until it's moving away." Then, the elf sprinted to the center of the village green, waving her arms and yelling, "Here! Here!"

Allai'nn's voice diverted the Ettin's attention, the monster lumbering toward her. Without hesitation, she sprinted away in the direction opposite Rue and the children. The monster charged after her, the ground rumbling with each step.

Rue closed her eyes, feeling the children's slight bodies pressed against her; her whole body quivering with fear. The loud sound of breaking branches and fallen trees filled her mind until it came to an abrupt halt, followed by a shrill scream.

"Gotcha!" came the rumbling monster's voice, followed by more thundering steps receding in the distance.

Rue sat frozen in terror, only the infant's cries and the sound of her pounding heartbeat in her ears.

Then she heard Jacoby's voice over the babies' cries.

"Rue? Allai'nn? Where are you?" Jacoby called out, but the oread couldn't answer, her voice trapped in her throat.

The tall human searched the surrounding buildings and debris, locating Grull, Blue Ivy, and Horatio. Jacoby supported Grull, wincing in pain from cracked ribs, while Blue Ivy and Horatio hobbled together, one with a broken arm, the other a twisted ankle.

Jacoby sat Grull next to Horatio and Blue and continued the search for the others. He found Rue, her eyes closed and trembling, desperately holding onto the four infants. The tall warrior kneeled, wincing, and lightly touched Rue on the shoulder.

"Rue, it's me, Jacoby."

The oread stared, eyes wild with terror. He paused, then reached out to take one child. Rue's grip tightened around the infant, her eyes welling up with tears. Jacoby applied steady force, and the oread's grip loosened as he swept the child into one arm. He rubbed the crying child's back, trying to comfort the tike.

"It's ok, little one. Uncle Jacoby has you."

Rue whimpered, reaching out an arm for the child.

"I've got him, Rue," he said, his tone filled with reassurance. "The Ettin's gone. You and the kids are safe."

A strangled sob burst from Rue's lips as tears flooded down her cheeks.

"Allai'nn, she…" she choked, her tears running like streams. "She saved us."

"Allai'nn?" Jacoby's eyes grew large, confused. He didn't hear Grull arrive behind him.

"What do you mean, she saved you?" the halfling demanded, his heart racing. "Where is Allai'nn?"

The oread erupted in shaking sobs, unable to speak.

"Calm down, Rue," Jacoby said, handing the child to Grull so he could stroke the distraught oread's back. "Take some deep breaths and tell us what happened."

Rue coughed and wiped her running nose with her sleeve. "She ran to the woods as a diversion. The Ettin followed her."

"What?" Grull's face turned ghostly pale as he shot a piercing stare at Jacoby. In a panic, he screamed, "Allai'nn! Allai'nn!" Grull tried to sprint toward the woods, but he faltered after a few steps, paralyzed by the pain rocketing through his chest. He stumbled, losing his balance and falling to the muddy ground.

"Ahh," he moaned, unable to move.

With a grunt of effort, Jacoby hauled his friend upright. "We'll find her," he reassured his old friend, determination shining in his eyes. "And the others, too."

FIFTEEN

After checking the children and Rue for injuries, Jacoby set about the tasks of setting Horatio's broken arm and wrapping Grull's ribs and Blue Ivy's ankle. After a quick search of the remaining village structures, he found a used hand cart he repurposed to carry the infants. Within a few hours, they set off, tracing the path carved by the Ettin through the mysterious woods. Jacoby's senses heightened as they advanced along the monster's route, their surroundings transforming with every step. The forest of hardwoods gave way to towering, slender pines, clusters of palmettos, and pickerel grass swaying in the breeze. But along the Ettin's path, the monster broke hundreds of trees like matchsticks and imprinted enormous, wagon-sized footprints in the dirt. The group's path shifted from common bracken to a dense mix of prickly brambles, sharp Spanish daggers, and gentle reeds. Shallow creeks, streams, and brooks engorged by the recent storm turned the terrain into muddy bogs, making the travel slow and difficult. Black flies feasted on the group's bare skin, while mosquitoes formed menacing swarms that assailed them from all directions.

"Where the demons could he have taken them?" Grull asked, his frustration mounting.

"Who knows?" Blue said, his voice laced with fatigue, swatting at an attacking fly. Jacoby halted the group, taking a moment to quench his thirst with a sip from a wineskin filled with cool water from the village well. The midday sun blazed overhead, scorching like searing coal, and Jacoby realized the imminent threat of dehydration, even with the brackish waters all around.

He shared the skin with Grull and scanned the surrounding delta. "A fine place for an ambush," he said.

"I don't care," Grull retorted, his words cutting through the air. "We just need to find the others."

Jacoby's silence spoke volumes, confirming the truth in the halfling's words. "Let's go," he said, his eyes scanning the surroundings for any sign of the returning monster.

The Ettin's path continued for another five hundred yards before veering to the right, revealing a sprawling delta of narrow rivers and streams.

The swamp was a maze of islands blanketed in swamp grass and cypress knees, with deep rivulets cutting a meandering path through them. Tendrils of moss dangled from tree limbs, almost touching the ground, lending a haunting ambiance to the surroundings. The monster's path came to a halt at a narrow point of the nearest river, leaving behind enormous footprints on the opposite bank.

Jacoby stopped at the edge of the brown water, the bank broken by fallen limbs and debris. Downstream, several crocodiles basked in the hot sun along the shore, their knobby dorsal osteoderms resembling studded armor.

"What now?" Blue Ivy asked.

"You, Rue, Horatio, and the children remain here," Jacoby responded. "Grull, ready for a swim?"

Grull hesitated, looking away. Consumed by panic, he was determined to cross the river, rescue Allai'nn, and tear the Ettin apart. But his damaged ribs made it difficult for him to raise his arms, let alone swim. He gritted his teeth and said, "Ready."

Jacoby studied his friend's expression and recognized the unmistakable signs of suffering. Despite the discomfort, pride and necessity took precedence. He gave a brief nod before wading into the foul-smelling water. With each step he took as he crossed, the water in the river climbed higher, reaching his chest before receding again.

"Just like old times," Jacoby said with a half-smile, water sloshing in his boots and dripping off his trousers.

"Like old times," Grull said, both stopping on the far shore to remove the water from their boots. Their soaked clothes reminded Grull of their adventures in the Taborian army. Throughout their campaign in northern Tabor, they crossed rivers infested with loathsome reptiles many times, wading or swimming, and lost a number from their unit to the beasts.

Continuing for another hundred paces, the two warriors arrived at a cluster of water oaks, their branches draped with a dense curtain of hanging moss. Jacoby took the lead, pushing through the heavy curtain of foliage and entering an open lea. Nestled at the heart of the area, a limestone cave lurked, its opening camouflaged by a tangle of coarse rock formations. Jacoby halted, motioning for Grull to remain quiet. A woman's voice reached Jacoby's ears, so faint that it seemed to be whispered by the wind.

"Hear that?"

"That's not Allai'nn," Grull said, the disbelief evident in his voice. "Is it possible more people are being held captive?"

Jacoby whispered, "Gods know," his words hushed as he crept towards the cave opening, careful not to make a sound. Peeking into the entrance, the tall human could make out stone steps leading deeper into the dark abyss. He motioned for Grull to take the lead, relying on the halfling's Twilight vision to navigate the path. The two warriors descended the steps with stealth, anticipation building with each step as they drew nearer to the sound of a female voice. At last, the stairs dissolved into a circular antechamber, unveiling an immense cavern the size of a manor house. Vaulted ceilings studded with craggy stalactites, half masked by shadow, hung over an enormous open chamber lined with cages on each side and a throne at one end. Another tunnel with a wide mouth broke off to the left.

Grull motioned Jacoby to peek into the chamber. Torches hung in sconces on each wall, allowing Jacoby to visualize the room. A thin female humanoid relaxed on a stone throne, her upper body covered in an elegant brown gown. At the waist, her body changed, coiling into a snake's brown and green scales. On each side of the throne stood a guard, dark-skinned creatures with large triangular heads, thin arms, and torso ending in clawed feet. The beings' faces were wide, with thick, wrinkled foreheads and a wide, upturned nose above a jack-o'-lantern mouth of needle-sharp fangs. Chained next to the throne, a beautiful human sat, her pale skin covered only across her chest and groin with clothes.

The serpent leader said in a hissing voice, "I favor a tune, Druzilda."

Without uttering a sound, the chained girl rose. "Your request, Great Murt?"

"Today is the feast day for my pets, the Katavi," she announced. "Our prisoners will become a tasty meal for them."

The girl waited without speaking.

"Let's sing a song of thanks because Titus brought a new quarry from the village, and our cages will be refilled.

However, before the girl could utter a single note, the chamber was filled with the unmistakable sound of heavy boot steps echoing through it.

Jacoby and Grull watched four Katavi guards emerge from the far opening, pulling an enormous chain connected to a heavy iron collar around the Ettin's neck.

"Ah, here is Titus now," hissed Murt, her tail writhing to lift her off the throne. Then, addressing the monster said, "What gifts do you bring the Swamp Queen?"

"Food," the Ettin rumbled, his voice causing the entire chamber to tremble. Titus lifted a burlap sack from his pocket, dropping it on the chamber floor with a thud.

"Ouch," exclaimed a furious voice from inside the sack. "Let us out of here!"

Grull's heart dropped as he watched Allai'nn, Cor'in, Nathaniel, and Lani.

"Take the new prisoners to their cages," ordered the queen. "And line up the others for our feast."

Two of the Katavi broke away and took the four prisoners to an open cage near Jacoby and Grull.

Jacoby signaled to Grull, and the two warriors crab-walked on all fours behind the closest cell. At that moment, Murt said, "Release ten humans for the feast."

As the warriors knelt there, they could hear the unmistakable noise of boots shuffling and doors being flung open. Screams and wails filled the cavern, but one voice rang out.

"Unhand me, you vile creature! Don't you know I am the mayor of Fleabite?"

A gray-haired man yanked his arm from the guard and stomped up to the throne. "I demand to know why you are holding us prisoner," the mayor said, his face flushed with palpable anger.

"You demand?" Murt hissed; her eyes narrowed. "My Katavi says otherwise." Then, turning to Druzilda added, "Call them."

The girl cleared her throat and whistled a long, high-pitched note, followed by another shorter note. Initially, the two warriors heard nothing, but then a sound broke the silence - the unmistakable flapping of wings from somewhere above him. From the darkness above, enormous bats swooped down from the hanging stalactites, aiming for the humans gathered alongside the mayor. The mayor's heart raced as he turned to run, but his escape was cut short when a bat swooped down and latched onto his back, its claws tearing into his flesh.

"Help me! Help!" the mayor screamed, his voice echoing through the chamber as the bat carried him upward into the darkness. Murt gleefully watched as more bats tore into the remaining humans, their screams filling the air. Jacoby called out to Grull, "Follow me."

Using the chaos as cover, the two scurried around to the front of their friend's cell.

With tears stinging his eyes, Nathaniel's voice cracked with emotion as he called, "Jacoby!" his fingers stretched out through the unforgiving iron bars. But Jacoby cut his brother short. He placed a finger across his lips in a hushing gesture, then he clasped his brother's hand.

"Is anyone hurt?" Jacoby whispered. "We have to leave before we're discovered."

Nathaniel whispered, "All of us. Allai'nn is the worst and still unconscious."

"Can you walk?"

"I'll make it," Nat responded, wincing as he felt the pain radiating from his broken ribs.

Jacoby nodded and pulled his dagger to saw through the leather cord used to lock the door. When he had the cord removed, Jacoby motioned for Grull to lead the group to the cave exit. Rising to their feet, Lani and Cor'in winced in pain—Lani nursing a dislocated shoulder while the half-elf supported a broken right forearm. He opened the cage door, and Grull led the injured to the exit. Then, Jacoby lifted Allai'nn over his shoulder and scurried, bent at the waist, to follow the others. The group had just reached the antechamber at the base of the steps when Jacoby became aware the wailing had stopped.

The rumbling voice of the Ettin rang out over the cavern. "Where my fud?"

Jacoby glanced back over his shoulder at the stone chamber. Body parts and blood created a gruesome scene in front of Murt's throne. Ten Katavi knelt nearby, feasting on what remained of the village citizens, and to one side, the enormous Ettin pointed at the empty cages. With a quick heartbeat, Murt's eyes swept across the cavern until they locked onto the antechamber.

"Intruders! Seize them and bring them back to me in one piece!"

The sound of boot steps filled the chamber behind them, growing louder and more frantic as they echoed up the stairwell. Jacoby's voice cut through the chaos, "RUN!"

The group, guided by Grullach, stumbled up the stairs, their progress hindered by the injured Lani and Cor'in. At the tail end, Jacoby could feel the vibrations of approaching soldiers as he struggled to climb the stairwell, his tired body weighed down from carrying Allai'nn. After minutes, the exhausted group tumbled out of the cave mouth into the dazzling midday sunlight as if vomited by an enormous stone giant with a sore tummy. The dark soldiers close on Jacoby's heels came to a screeching halt at the cave door, their arms shielding their wide eyes from the brilliance. One took a tentative step out, then screeched in pain as the sunlight burned his legs.

Jacoby watched, sucking down gulps of air as the enemy pulled back one by one. His shoulders slumped in relief at the withdrawal. He turned to the others and panted, "They're sensitive to the sun. Keep moving. We have a chance if we can lose ourselves in the woods."

"Did you forget about the river?" Grull called over his shoulder as the group pushed down the path. They reached the curtain of moss, Grull holding back one side of the heavy vegetation for all to pass.

Then, the world changed, and the earth shook like a windswept tree in spring, followed by the "galumph, galumph" of Titus the Ettin's footsteps.

The group rushed to the riverbank, and as they approached, Grull suddenly halted, causing Jacoby to nearly collide with the others at the water's edge.

"Why'd you stop?" Jacoby spat in frustration, sweat running down his face in streams.

Grull answered by gesturing towards the riverside. At first glance, all Jacoby could see was a thick layer of emerald-green moss blanketing the sandy shore. He watched in awe as the moss shifted, revealing a gathering of over fifty crocodiles, some as large as canoes, sunning themselves together. As the beasts jostled for space, their movements created a domino effect, forcing the entire group to shift.

"We can't wait! Titus is right behind us!" Jacoby said, wading into the tannin stained water. The others followed, doing their best to limit any significant splashing.

As they reached the deeper, chest-high water, a sudden splash startled them, followed by others as several of the alpha crocs slid into the water. At that moment, Titus' muscular form burst through the moss curtain, his face contorted into an angry mask.

Jacoby understood they had seconds to reach safety, and said, "Swim for it!"

With Grullach's help, the other three tumbled onto the shore just as Horatio and Blue arrived with the cart. Jacoby, with Allai'nn in his arms, struggled behind the others through the dark, viscous river water, his feet slipping and sliding in the muddy river towards the shore. Grull stepped into the water to help Jacoby but froze, his eyes as wide as saucers. Jacoby heard a crashing splash behind him and felt the putrid breath of the enraged Ettin on his back. "My fud!" Titus bellowed, his voice so powerful it caused Jacoby to cringe and stumble.

Oddly, a peculiar sense of calm blossomed in Jacoby's mind, extending over his entire body. This is the end. I can't make it, he thought. The big human had the wherewithal to shove Allai'nn's inert form toward Grull as he landed face-first in the shallow water.

Jacoby twisted just as Titis lifted his war club above his head, preparing to flatten the human. But the Ettin never got the chance. First one, then another, and another of the ancient crocodiles clamped down on the legs of the Ettin.

""OWWW!" Titus bellowed, his face turning scarlet, his jaw clenched. With each swing of its mighty fists, the monster unleashed a thunderous force upon the reptiles. The chaotic dance continued as one reptile fell, only to be replaced by another, enticed by the irresistible scent of Ettin's blood in the water.

Grull used the chaos to pull Jacoby to shore, saying, "Come on. This is our chance to escape."

Jacoby struggled to his feet, his legs trembling with relief. "Run for the forest, it's our only chance."

Grull led the group toward the trees, their footsteps heavy and unsteady as they crossed the marshland. Jacoby, who had picked up Allai'nn again over his shoulder, trudged behind them. After some time shuffling through the forest, they reached a small clearing deep in the woods. The exhausted, injured group spread out and collapsed on the soft grass.

Grullach lay beside Allia'nn, caressing her hair and whispering, "Wake up, my love. Please, wake up."

Allai'nn's eyes fluttered open at his call, and seeing Grullach's familiar face, a smile warmed her lips. "Hi."

"Thank the Mother!" he exclaimed, his heart overflowing with relief. Grull embraced her, and in that moment, all the noise and chaos disappeared. He showered her with kisses, tears rolling down his cheeks.

Grull turned to Jacoby, his face marred by smudges of mud. "Do you think we're safe?"

Jacoby considered the notion. "I think the Ettin had his hands full with the crocodiles. I doubt he'll feel up to chasing us soon." Then added with a smile, "Allai'nn okay?"

"She will be."

Jacoby nodded as Grull lay down beside his wife. Within a minute, he heard his friend's snores and chuckled. He took one look at the others, all fast asleep, and sighed.

"I guess I'll take the first watch."

Fifty leagues to the northwest, an unassuming elf hovered at the gate of the king's garden. With a 'pop', the elf transformed into a garter snake and slithered through a crevice in the rock wall. He transformed again to his Elven form and, keeping to the shadows, snuck close to the king's tower. From three stories below, Nari Mudpucker strained his ears to catch the faint sounds drifting out of the open window of King Topper of Whispering Haven's royal suite. Despite the windy night, he strained his ears to catch any sounds beyond the occasional wails of one of the king's many distraught family members. Frustration etched his face as he tightened his cloak against the forceful gusts of the coming storm, making it difficult to hear any valuable data. Nari shook his head, disappointed he must change shape once again.

He had been Nari, an everyday handyman from an outlying Elven community looking for work in the city for only a few days. He had picked the form of a "nobody" on purpose. The persona had worked well; the anonymity allowed him to reach the King's Garden unnoticed. But now, Nari must change, and with a "Pop," Nari became a gray squirrel. Ah, how freeing! I can easily travel wherever I wish with no actual notice.

The squirrel gazed up at the ivy-covered tower, three stories high, that led to the royal bedchambers. With a playful grin, Nari leaped onto the sturdy vine, his nimble fingers finding firm holds as he ascended toward King Topper's room. Once there, he nestled comfortably amidst the fragrant ivy, attuned to every sound as he waited patiently. The king had been suffering from an illness for some time, his vitality diminishing daily. Now facing imminent death, he recognized the urgent need to address all the royal matters that he had overlooked in recent weeks. So, over the next few hours, one minister after another arrived to speak to the king. Finally, the endless trivialities of the court gave way to more crucial issues.

Prince Astor, the heir apparent, entered with Chamberlain Knotweed and, with a stern look, dismissed everyone from the apartment.

Astor sat on Topper's bed, clasping the monarch's hands in his. Lean and fair-skinned, Astor's iceberg-blue eyes gazed down at his elderly father with deep concern.

"Father, you called for me?"

Topper appeared to the prince paler than usual, his once rosy cheeks now pale and translucent. His once vibrant eyes had lost their sparkle and were now dull and clouded.

"Son, we have matters..." The king coughed violently, his face turning blue, leaving Astor fearing for his father's life. But with a deep gasp, Topper continued. "We have matters to discuss. Especially Tabor."

"Tabor? Tell me."

Topper waved a frail hand at Knotweed to continue.

"My Lord," the chamberlain whispered, "our spies report Tabor is on the brink of collapse. Ever since General Tusk's death, chaos has consumed both the army and council. With supply chain flow diminished and the government in chaos, their survival hangs by a thread. I expect Ravenite's army to overpower them within the month."

"By the Gods!" the prince exclaimed, shaking his head. "I did not know the situation there was so dire."

Knotweed nodded sadly.

Astor considered the situation. On the one hand, Tabor's demise was irrelevant to issues in Whispering Haven. As the major Elven port along the western coast of Curth Talem, the community prided itself on its unwavering independence and preparedness to protect its borders. However, the elves had relied on Tabor to defend the north for many decades. With Tabor falling, Whispering Haven would be next.

"So, do you have a plan, father?"

Knotweed answered. "His majesty has long feared this day might come. His plan is two-tiered. First, you must ride east to the Sylph capital. Meet with King Goldbriar to discuss plans for an Elven defense of our lands."

"And the second?"

"We must vigilantly perceive any threats to our land and remain neutral in this war. Let the humans deal with the threat," rasped Topper, cutting in.

"But father, what if the rumors of an Aarmon heir are true? We must show support."

"No! No! No!" King Topper's voice echoed through the room. Gradually, his voice faded into a feeble whisper as a persistent cough and wheeze took over, leaving him struggling for breath. In several heartbeats, the old king's face changed from a dusky blue to a pale ashen, and his breathing slowed. "Can't you grasp that my time is limited?" he exclaimed, frustration clear. "You possess a compassionate and giving nature, my son, which will make you an exceptional king. But now is the time to focus on the survival of Whispering Haven and the Elven community at large."

"How?" Astor asked with a hint of defensiveness. "Tabor is a neighbor, be they human or otherwise."

The old king shook his head, and Knotweed took over. "Whispering Haven, the sole Elven port in the west, stands as the last refuge for all Elven races in case the malevolent forces in the north and east triumph. As a beacon of hope for all our kind in Curth Talem, we have no choice but to prioritize our safety."

Astor's shoulders slumped. "I understand."

King Topper gave his son's hand an affirming squeeze. "Leave for Clobryn Nyth, the Sylph capital, as soon as possible. Our welfare depends on it."

Nari Mudpucker had heard enough and chittered through the ivy to the base of the tower and, with a "pop," regained the shape of the docile Elven handyperson. I must warn my master of the news that the elves believe they can remain neutral in the coming conflict. That will surely please him. Fools! My master, Ravenite, will leave no stone undisturbed, no enemy unvanquished in his path to conquer western Curth Talem.

Mudpucker was so focused on his thoughts that he almost stumbled into a coming patrol. As the palace guards turned the corner, a sudden "pop" and Nari transformed into a frightened chipmunk, scurrying into the nearby shrubs. The guards continued their patrol, unaware that the shape-changing bogie Nari Mudpucker had slipped past them, scurrying down the avenue. Eventually, Mudpucker reached a dark byway, slipped down undetected, and shape-changed into his usual form of squat, hairy humanoid. The monster's head was too large for his body, and his legs were too short, which caused him to waddle. The alley ended in a thick brick wall with no obvious exit. Using his clawed fingers, he scraped the nails over the brick until he found a hidden latch, pushed on the spring-loaded clasp, opening a secret door. He fit his significant girth through the door and crawled on hands and knees through a dingy tunnel. After several minutes, he reached a rusty gate, the corroded bars meshed across the exit. Outside, the sounds of hungry seagulls and crashing waves filled the air.

As if opening a door, he pushed on the gate, popping it free from the stone wall, and watched as it spun like a top into the afternoon sun. The ocean lapped at the castle walls a hundred feet below, and he heard a splash. Mudpucker hesitated, enjoying the warm sunlight on his sallow skin. He chuckled and whispered to himself, "A beautiful day for a swim." He squeezed himself out of the tunnel opening and allowed himself to free-fall to the aquamarine water below. Just before striking the surface, he changed again into a dull gray hammerhead shark and, with a flip of its tail, swam north toward Tabor.

Seven hundred leagues north, an army of undead creatures, a terrifying mix of zombies, vampires, mummies, skeletons, ghouls, gargoyles, and draugr, stood motionless on the northern shore of the River Narn, patiently awaiting their next command. At the river's edge, a massive skeleton mounted on a colossal skeletal wyvern emerged from the forest, its heavy footsteps reverberating through the ground. The monster, naked save for a tarnished gold chain worn as a necklace, sat atop the fearsome, fiery-eyed behemoth, its saddle a horrifying arrangement of human skulls. The stench of decay hung heavy in the air. An ivory wand adorned his hand, its jewel pulsating with a mesmerizing glow. With a single, commanding gesture, he motioned the troops forward, and the sound of their boots hitting the ground echoed through the air. As the zombies leaped into the river, their cold, lifeless bodies piled against each other, creating a macabre bridge across the turbulent waters.

"Shykza," the mounted skeleton, known as General Sin, screamed in the evil tongue.

The undead army moved in a chaotic line, akin to a grotesque microorganism, as they made their way over the river bridge to the Taborian side. A collection of goblins, orcs, giants, and Lupine rangers followed at a safe distance, led by Bloodcoat and Icebeard.

The ground trembled beneath the weight of the giant skeleton as it rode to the front of the army, where the soldiers massed into a dense group.

"Talak," commanded Sin, a lesser lich whose true identity remained a mystery, pointing ahead with his wand. Slowly, like a moving amoeba, the army advanced south toward the Taborian capital.

In the distant southeast, Lyzelle, a black witch, led a similar undead army marching silently along a road carved through the dense woods of Drom Scarhis. She rode atop a giant black arachnid, their presence casting a shadow over the land. Following at a safe distance, a battalion of newly recruited orcs, goblins, and Khandarian mercenaries filled the air with the scent of sweat and leather. The humid, rocky hills challenged the humans, accustomed to the arid desert of Khandar. Sweating profusely and mumbling complaints about their surroundings, they dragged behind their leader, Count Taziz.

As the army halted near the bank of the Faire Wing River, the soldiers could feel the cool breeze and hear the gentle flow of the water. Count Taziz and his men were miserable, their faces covered in sweat and dirt, their parched throats yearning for a drop of water. Filled with frustration and annoyance, Taziz guided his gray Arabian horse forward, keeping a safe distance from the undead. Lazelle's eyes, void of any spark of life, darted across the opposite shoreline with urgency as if she were searching for a friend who had gone missing. Far in the distance, the lights of Tajman Sghur shone like a hundred fireflies in the evening twilight from the other side of the river.

"Excuse me, Lady," Taziz said, his words thick with eastern dialect common tongue.

The witch ignored the intrusion, swatting it away like an annoying mosquito.

"Ahem," Taziz murmured, clearing his throat.

"What is it, cretin?"

"What? How dare you! I am a Count!" Taziz said defensively.

"You are an insect, a parasite, feeding on my lord's generosity," The witch hissed, her eyes burning red. "Why bother me?"

"I, ahh...we need water." Taziz stammered, trembling.

Lyzelle watched as dozens of black barges appeared, crossing the green river's surface. A satisfied smile crossed the witch's face. "Shortly, human, water will be the least of your worries."

SIXTEEN

From his perch atop the tall elm, Nathaniel smiled as he took in the vast expanse of the open plains. The valley below was a vibrant scene, with elk herds peacefully grazing on the lush spring grass. He estimated it would take the brotherhood approximately four hours to traverse to the entrance of the Horn Wood, on the far side of the valley. The group had spent the last two weeks crossing the hilly grasslands between Whispering Haven and the Lost Lake, their weary bodies still healing from their intense battle with the Ettin. Despite their severe injuries from the attack, Nathaniel believed that the sight of the Horn Wood, the unofficial Taborian southern border, would bring solace to the warriors. He climbed down from his perch and strode back to camp. The others, tired and worn out, took a much-needed break by reclining on their packs or finding comfort against their makeshift pillows made of cloaks.

"I have some news!" Nathaniel's voice echoed with excitement as he hollered, "We're close to the edge of the Horn Wood!"

"I can't believe it," responded Grull, looking up.

"Fabulous!" echoed Cor'in.

"I've been sensing the Mother was near," Blue Ivy said.

"We're finally close to Tabor," Jacoby said, his voice filled with relief as he let out a long sigh.

"Not only that, but a herd of elk graze just beyond the trees," Nathaniel said with a smile. "Fresh venison for our bellies."

"Another day of seeds and berries, and I'd give up," Cor'in said, chuckling.

"Don't forget the insects," Horatio said, grinning.

"Ugh!" Rue said, her face contorting in disapproval.

"What? I'll have you know we Anurans find centipede pie a delicacy," he responded with mock outrage.

Everyone laughed, and Cor'in rolled his eyes.

But Jacoby's smile wilted to disappointment, murmuring, "I wish Micah were here to see it."

Allai'nn placed a reassuring hand on the tall man's back. "Me too."

Nathaniel, sensing the heaviness in the air because of their friend's loss, urged everyone, "Come on, let's get going. We can both hunt and cross the valley by nightfall if we hurry."

The group picked up their belongings and secured the infants snugly into homemade papooses on their backs. They embarked on their journey, their footsteps echoing as they made their way towards the valley beyond the forest.

The hunting, skinning, and securing of meat took longer than expected. As a result, Nathaniel decided the group should spend the remaining hours of the day cutting the meat into strips and smoking it over a blazing fire in the warm afternoon sun. That evening, the brotherhood gathered around the crackling fire, their bellies satisfied and content. Horatio led the others in song, and soon, they became captivated by the frogman's melodious voice. He sang joyful melodies about Whitestar, the legendary hero of the First Age, who vanquished the colossal Giant army and established Tabor's dominance in western Curth Talem. But as the evening progressed, he sang melancholic tunes that echoed with the ache of unrequited love and profound loss. The evening ended with his tribute to their fallen comrade, Micah. As he spoke solemnly, sharing memories of his friend, he offered the others the chance to tell their favorite story about the Moor elf. Some spoke of his valiant fighting, others of his easy friendliness. Nathaniel spoke of his loyalty, and Jacoby of his goodness and humor. But at the evening's end, grief engulfed the group. The camp descended into a hushed silence as every member became consumed by their memories of loved ones lost in the months since the war started. Suddenly, the sound of barking and howling broke the silence. Nat jumped to his feet, pulling his sword, followed by Jacoby.

"Wolves?" Nathaniel asked.

"Sounds different. Maybe they're wild dogs?" the tall man asked.

The closer the beast came, the more intense the barking became, filling the camp with a palpable tension. Abruptly, the barking ended, leaving an eerie silence in the air. Peering into the darkness, each warrior strained their eyes, swords at the ready, searching for the elusive source. Several heartbeats passed, and the warriors let out a collective sigh of relief, figuring that whatever had caused the sound must have found its intended target.

Then a flash of brown shot through the camp, striking Jacoby and knocking him off his feet. Nathaniel whirled, his sword high and ready to attack the enemy. But instead of watching his brother grapple with a monster out for the kill, he witnessed a large mud-covered hound licking Jacoby's face.

"Sinbad!" the entire group shouted in unison, and everyone rushed forward, extending their hands eagerly to stroke the beloved hellhound. The group had lost the hound weeks ago during the pirate raid on their journey to Mar Napor. Despite his showing ribs suggesting severe malnutrition, the hound affectionately licked each member. The loving reunion brought an end to the gloom of the previous hour, and a wave of joy washed over everyone.

Jacoby laughed as he stroked the canine and said, "I can't believe it! How did he find us?"

"I've read that hellhounds never leave their masters," Blue Ivy said sagely.

"Maybe he just missed us. Didn't you, boy," Allai'nn responded, rubbing the hound's coat.

"I know the children will be overjoyed," Rue said, her smile showing her confidence.

After several minutes, Nathaniel said, "After we feed Sinbad, let's turn in." He gazed over the open plain and added, "we're safe without guards tonight."

Jacoby looked up in surprise. "Are you sure?"

"Not really. But we are on the border of the Whispering Haven elf territory. What could happen?"

"I can take first watch," Grull said grumpily. "The lad just jinxed us!"

Nat chuckled. "Okay. Wake me in four hours and I'll relieve you."

"Not tonight, my friend. You and Lani have been on watch each night for a week. I'll take the second watch," said Horatio.

Nat nodded. "Thanks."

As the night grew darker, Horatio took his turn during the second watch, making his way around the encampment, his steps heavy and deliberate. He felt as though the fatigue from the last few weeks had wrapped around him like a thick blanket, making his eyelids as heavy as granite. "Horatio, keep moving! It's the only way you'll stay awake," a voice in his head said. But not his voice. Micah's voice echoed in his mind, and he couldn't help but flash a smile.

"What are you doing in my head?" he said, confused.

"I wanted to visit my friend."

"I don't understand," Horatio whispered, his voice trembling as he struggled to comprehend hearing his dead friend's voice. "How could you be here?"

"Here? Where else would I be?" Micah replied with a mischievous tone.

"Impossible," Horatio said. "We left you in the Mar Nâpor royal crypts. You're dead."

"Oh, that? Only my bodily form. My spirit resides in a new realm where radiant light and unimaginable beauty abound. It's on another plane, but I've been given the gift to see my friends again."

"I'm glad to hear it," Horatio said with a smile. "We really feel your absence. But why are you here?"

Before his friend answered, Horatio felt a sharp pain in his arm. He looked down and saw two red puncture marks and felt an unexpected warmth climb up his arm.

"What in the demons?" The frogman said, confused.

Micah's voice whispered, "Don't fear. It will help you rest, friend."

"Rest? I can't rest, Micah. I'm on watch," Horatio said, but his eyelids felt heavier than lead.

As he attempted to take another step, his foot faltered, causing him to lose his balance and collapse. Just before his eyes closed, the frogman realized he hadn't been talking to Micah in his mind, but to the real Micah beside him. How is this possible? Before his eyes, Micah transformed into a massive snake, its scales glistening in the moonlight, and slithered away toward the encampment. I'm hallucinating, he thought as the night swallowed him.

Back at the camp, two muscular arms grabbed Jacoby from each side, yanking him awake from a deep sleep.

"Thor's beard!" he exclaimed, still drowsy from sleep. Without warning, someone bound his arms tightly behind him and dragged him to join the rest of the already bound and helpless group.

"What do you want?" Jacoby demanded, anger blazing in his veins.

A group of armed bandits, a motley crew comprising men, orcs, and goblins, all wearing tattered shirts and loose linen pants, surrounded the campsite. Despite the chaos, the infants remained in a deep slumber, undisturbed. Sinbad was nowhere to be seen.

In the center of the camp stood an enormous ape, its light skin bronzed by weeks of outdoor excursions. The sight of a red bandana covering its neck caught their attention, but it was the wide protruding nose and startling blue eyes that truly stood out. His attire mirrored that of the other bandit, with one notable difference - a vibrant blood red sash cinched at his waist. He raised one of his long muscular arms, motioning for quiet.

"I am Cypress, clan leader of the Changelings. You are now the enslaved property of my master, the Goblin king, Gyn."

Before the other man could finish, Nathaniel interrupted, stepping forward and saying, "We're simple peasants possessing nothing." What do you..."

In a flash of lightning, the ape delivered a devastating punch to Nathaniel's jaw, launching the prince high into the air. He crashed to the ground several feet away, unconscious and motionless.

"By the Gods," Jacoby and Grull exploded together, both attempting to charge the ape but held back by bandit captors.

"Quiet!" roared Cypress. "Or I'll have the women's throats cut to prove my point."

The weight of his threat hung in the air, and a palpable silence prevailed for several moments.

"Accept your fate," the commander's voice echoed in the air, "and follow orders or face the consequences." Again, he hesitated a heartbeat, letting the message sink in.

"But we have infants with us," Allai'nn said, stepping forward, head held high.

"We have no time for children. Leave them for the wolves," he ordered.

"Wait! I'll trade for their lives."

Cypress raised one brow; his curiosity peeked. "You are a saucy wench. But you have nothing to trade."

"But I do. My friend and I are experienced healers who would be a valuable asset to your group. In addition, our cooking and sewing skills are exceptional."

"Convenient and needed skills," the ape said, "but lacking in equal value." He eyed Allai'nn closely, suspecting more. "What else?"

With pride in her voice, she proclaimed, "I am an elven royal, a valuable captive in any ransom negotiation. Rest assured, any requested price will be promptly and fully paid. But only if the infants are healthy and thriving."

"Interesting," Cypress said, rubbing his chin. "I will let my master decide. Until then, your bonds will be severed, allowing you to carry and care for the children. But fall behind, and my men will gut the lot of you."

"What about him?" A muscular goblin asked, pointing down at Nathaniel's inert form.

"Leave him for the predators."

Cypress whirled, and in a split second, a rugged, muscular man replaced the ape.

"Move out," he said, and as they securely wrapped the infants in swaddling slings, the prisoners began their march toward the wood, walking in a single file.

Sinbad lay hidden in the tall grass several hundred yards away, biding his time like a predator ready to strike.

SEVENTEEN

Nathaniel dreamed he was strolling along the bank of a gentle brook, the gurgling water caressing colorful river stones. After a short distance, the unmistakable rushing sound of a waterfall filled the air, marking the brook's end as it cascaded down a small ledge and settled into a serene, vast pond. He followed a path that stair-stepped down the edge of a twenty-foot cliff, arriving at a tranquil pond adorned with drifting lily pads bordered by cattails. In the afternoon sunlight, the vegetation in the pond glowed with a warm, golden-orange hue, casting a serene ambiance and making the many pads on the water resemble polished bronze discs.

On the most oversized pad, a few feet offshore, sat an enormous bullfrog, as big as a sow and pure white, perched unmoving on a miniature throne.

"Welcome, young prince," rumbled the frog in a deep, melodic tone.

"Ah.. thank you...sir," Nathaniel mumbled, rubbing his eyes in disbelief.

"I see you've encountered the changelings. Did you know you're bleeding from that clout on the head?"

Out of nowhere, Nathaniel suddenly noticed crimson blood slowly trickling onto the calm pond's surface.

Nathaniel touched his forehead, only to be met with a sharp sting and the sight of fresh blood smeared across his palm. "I must have hit my head," he murmured, growing concerned.

"Don't worry," said the frog. "I have just the cure."

With lightning-fast speed, the bullfrog shot out his long, sticky tongue and started licking his head wound.

"What the demons?" Nathaniel murmured, swatting away the beast's tongue. When he knocked it away, the frog wasted no time shooting it back towards his wound, scolding him with a firm "Now, now."

Nathaniel's eyes fluttered open at that moment, startled by the wet sensation of Sinbad's tongue on his face. His head throbbed with a pounding ache reminiscent of a brass drum, and his hair clumped together with dried blood.

"Okay, boy. Okay," he said to the hound, who continued to nuzzle him.

He attempted to rise, only to discover his bonds remained. He twisted and turned, fighting against the ropes, but could not free himself. With a grunt, he shifted his weight to rise to his knees, his eyes inspecting the vast plain before him. Where were the others? He surveyed the meadow, spotting only Sinbad. The prince vaguely remembered his last encounter with the bandit ape before all went dark. Where had the bandits taken the others? He listened for signs of the group's direction, boot steps, or chatter, but only heard Sinbad's moans drifting from his side. He gazed at the hound, his eyes yearning and his dirty chestnut head pointing toward the forested horizon.

"Sinbad, ole boy. It looks like it's just you and me," he said to the dog.

An idea meandered through his mind. Sinbad! Of course!

He thumped his forehead, gazed at the hound, and said, "Do you know where they went, boy?"

With understanding in his dark eyes, Sinbad barked once, his head swiftly swiveling toward the woods.

"Good boy!" Nathaniel exclaimed with a grin. Now I must get free from these bonds, he thought.

"If only Sinbad understood the common tongue beyond the simple word," he mumbled. "Perhaps he could burn the rope or bite into the fiber and chew them apart."

The prince chuckled at his foolishness and scanned the campsite for something sharp to help him escape. But he found nothing useful. Nathaniel's heart sank, and he curled up in the soft grass, feeling utterly dejected. He lay uncomfortably for a moment, both hands and feet bound tight, and twisted to his back, hoping to reduce the pressure from the rope. He felt something prick his mid-back and rolled again to find the source. Hidden in the grass, a thin metal tip twinkled in the sunlight. He leaned in, nipping at the surrounding weeds and grass until he found a partially hidden dagger, like the ones Allai'nn carried. Is it possible that it got displaced when she and the kids were captured? Or was dropping it intentional?

Regardless of the cause, he rotated until his back was towards the blade, used his fingertips to rotate the knife vertically, and started sawing the rope. Over a tedious hour, Nathaniel worked to fray the rope, despite his sweaty palms losing his grip on the thin blade more than once from the awkward position. Finally, with a "pop," the cord broke free. He massaged his wrists, trying to avoid the sensitive raw ligature marks and hoping the increased blood flow might dissolve the numbness. Then he removed the rope from his ankles and repeated the process. It took some time for his feet to regain feeling so he could walk without stumbling. With the leftover rope, he quickly made a leash. Following Sinbad's keen nose, he and his dog ran toward the forest as dusk settled.

Upon entering the forest, following the northerly game trail, they slowed to a walking pace. The dimly lit path, filled with hidden roots beneath the ancient hardwood canopy, presented a challenging terrain for Nathaniel. Unable to see in the dim light, he tripped repeatedly over roots and rocks, clinging to Sinbad's leash for support.

After a few hours, the wood became too dark to continue, so Nathaniel spent the next twenty minutes gathering leaves from the forest floor to make a nest away from the trail for the night. He gazed down at the pile he'd accumulated and said, "I think that will do." He curled into the leaves, with Sinbad nuzzling beside him, hoping that with rest, a plan would come to him.

Just past midnight, Nathaniel startled awake, unsure of what noise awoke him. The half-moon above illuminated the forest with a ghostly white glow, setting an eerie scene along the trail. Nathaniel lay motionless, listening for any sign of an assailant, but heard nothing. He glanced at Sinbad, who crouched low in a defensive posture, his muscles tense and ready, resembling a coiled viper about to strike. He strained his ears, but the only sound he could hear was the gentle rustling of leaves and the endless reel of crickets.

"What is it, boy?" Nathaniel whispered.

From a distance of ten feet, Nathaniel heard a branch snap, and the eerie sound of scraping filled his senses, as if something with clawed hands was unearthing grubs, accompanied by a chittering purr. What could create that sound? The prince's neck hair raised as he scanned the brush for anything he might use as a weapon, but he found nothing. Motionless, Sinbad patiently waited, his ears attuned to the slightest sound. The scratching sound momentarily ceased, only to start again a few feet nearer before abruptly coming to a halt. Nat's heart raced as he estimated the beast to be mere feet away, hidden behind a tangle of thick underbrush. Suddenly, the crickets fell silent, leaving behind an unnatural, eerie stillness.

Nathaniel's heart pounded in his ears, unsure what might happen next. From the undergrowth, a deep, rumbling growl echoed, immediately followed by a menacing hiss. The prince's eyes locked onto Sinbad, his body tense and prepared for battle. In an instant, a ferocious creature emerged from the underbrush, its black-and-white fur bristling, and sprinted towards Nathaniel with bared teeth. With a sudden burst of speed, the hellhound shot forward, closing the distance between itself and the unaware monster. The two bodies collided in mid-air, creating a loud and jarring impact before plummeting downward together. In a panic, Nathaniel jumped up, his eyes darting around, searching for a weapon, as Sinbad and the ferocious beast clashed in a savage fight. The two titans rolled, biting and tearing, each trying to get the upper hand. Nat's hand closed around a hefty branch, its rough bark scratching against his palm, but he hesitated, afraid if he struck, the impact might harm the hellhound. As Sinbad and the monster momentarily separated, the prince's heart skipped a beat as he recognized the creature before him—a gargantuan badger, its claws and teeth resembling deadly daggers.

In a blur, the two animals re-engaged, their growls and snarls filling the air as Nathaniel swung the heavy wood with all his might. The club struck the badger on its side, eliciting a painful twist and a howl of agony. The distraction proved exactly what Sinbad needed, allowing him to gain the advantage. With a single, ruthless movement, the hound seized the beast's neck, its jaws clenching with ferocity. With a mighty force, Sinbad shook the beast until the snapping of its vertebrae filled the air, causing the lifeless body to collapse onto the turf. Panting and with blood staining its fur, the hound triumphantly placed a powerful paw on the lifeless body of the badger. To Nathaniel's astonishment, Sinbad underwent a remarkable transformation, growing to the size of a colossal Warg. He then emitted a spine-chilling howl that echoed through the woods, serving as a foreboding message to all living beings.

Nathaniel, overcome with emotion, wrapped his arms around the hound in a bear hug, conveying his intense gratitude. "Thank you, Sinbad. Thank you for saving us."

The hound's wet tongue licked the prince's face, and Nathaniel laughed, feeling the slobber on his cheek. "Good dog!"

The prince turned to examine the beast, and his eyes widened in disbelief. A disturbing sight greeted his eyes - the badger, now lay lifeless, transformed into a hairy goblin, its neck brutally ripped apart.

In the inky blackness of a cell, less than a league away, Cor'in, Grull, Horatio, and Blue hung shackled to the cold, damp stone wall.

"I wonder what happened to Jacoby," Blue Ivy said.

"The devils took him while you were out," remarked Grull. He jerked his hands to test the shackles, but they remained secure.

"I remember nothing after the beatings started," he responded with a heavy sigh.

"They roughed us up a bit," Cor'in said, rubbing his bruised arm. "Just for the fun of it."

"And what about the women?" Asked Horatio.

Cor'in answered morosely, "Before I got a boot to my ribs, I saw Allai'nn and the others being taken down the hall."

Grull barely contained his fury as he threatened, "If they touch a hair on any of their heads, I'll gut them like a spring deer and feed them to the crows."

A few minutes later, the sound of footsteps reverberated through the cell, growing louder and more intense as the group approached the heavy iron door. As a key grated in the door and the latch turned, two large, powerful apes stood in the doorway. With elongated, muscular arms, they dragged a bleeding, unconscious Jacoby into the cell and shackled him to the wall next to Grullach.

"What'd you do to him, you overgrown simians!" Grull screamed, struggling against his chains.

The two guards stopped abruptly, and the larger one, with shaggy brown hair covering his body, smirked with malice.

"Let me show you, halfling," he growled, his massive fist connecting with Grull's abdomen, causing him to double over in pain.

Both apes let out a hearty laugh before turning to depart, but Cor'in extended his leg and delivered a swift kick, connecting with the shaggy simian's knee.

"Argh!" he bellowed, crumpling in pain, holding his knee. Covered in silky blond fur, the other ape rushed towards Cor'in, howling, "Now you're going to pay, elf."

The ape pummeled Cor'in with a barrage of lightning punches to his face and body. After what seemed like an eternity, the ape stepped back, assessing his handiwork. Cor'in hung unconscious, blood streaming down his face from a cut over his eye, his lip split and swollen. A loose, blood-stained tooth rested where it fell on the cold, hard floor of the cell.

The ape eyed the other inmates. "Try something foolish like your cellmate here, and you'll get the same treatment."

"You bloody demon! Do you think you're tough striking a defenseless captive? Remove these shackles and I'll give you the beating of your life, monkey man!" Horatio spat, struggling against his shackles to reach the ape.

The ape bent over, laughing. "Keep that up, Toadie, and I might grant your wish." Then the ape gave Horatio a sinister glare. "More's coming, tough guy." He draped an arm over his friend's shoulder and the two guards left the cell.

"That went well," Blue Ivy remarked, shaking his head in the darkness.

"Give me thirty seconds with that ape alone, and he'd be the hurting one," Horatio said, his fury still boiling.

"At least Cor'in got one kick in," mumbled Grull.

"We need a plan to escape," Blue said, his voice filled with urgency.

"Right," Grull said, his frustration palpable. "We got no chance to break these chains. Nat's gone. They've locked the women up, and even on my best day, I couldn't beat those thugs."

"Don't...give...up," Jacoby rasped, bloody drool running down his chin.

Grull leaned his head to wipe away the tears welling in his eyes, his loud sniff echoing through the room. "Okay, mate," he replied, his voice filled with a touch of exhaustion. "You should rest now."

The group had endured their fair share of hardships, their bond forged through trials and tribulations. However, even in the darkest of times, the group had fought their way to freedom. In Grull's mind, things were different this time. Without Nathaniel, the Brotherhood was leaderless, unarmed, and utterly alone, the weight of their predicament like a heavy stone around their necks.

Grull's thoughts drifted to Nathaniel's brutal end—the image of his body, torn and scattered, a feast for the wolves—and his heart was heavy with sorrow. He loved the lad like his younger brother, and his loss felt like a knife thrust in his heart. And what of his beloved Allai'nn and the children? What did these tyrants do with them? The pain of Nathaniel's death and losing family tore at his heart, leaving him feeling hollow and broken. In the name of Odin, what options do we have? In sheer despair, he hung his head and whispered a prayer to Thor, desperately seeking strength to continue.

Hours after their fight with the badger changeling, Nathaniel and Sinbad followed a goblin up a hill. Instead of continuing along the game trail, the goblin veered off down a hidden, overgrown path up the rocky slope. Thick bushes and large elephant ears obscured the trail, creating a mysterious tropical atmosphere. Peering through the foliage of a dense mountain laurel, they watched as the goblin reached the trail's end. It stood in front of an overhang, completely engulfed in kudzu, giving it the appearance of a towering green wall. With a suspicious glance over both shoulders, the goblin extended one hand into the lush greenery. The vine mass magically eased open, revealing a hidden dark wedge in stark contrast to the vibrant green of the lush vine leaves. The beast stepped through the opening and vanished. As Nathaniel watched, the mass of black vines seamlessly merged back into its original form.

"A hidden door, Sinbad?" Nathaniel whispered, his curiosity piqued. The beast let out a low, sorrowful moan, its eyes meeting the princes with a deep understanding.

"Let's stick close behind," he suggested, determined to stay on the goblin's trail.

After waiting for five minutes to make sure they were alone, Nathaniel and Sinbad cautiously moved ahead. The human carefully examined the tangled vines, searching for a hidden latch to open the secret door. In a matter of minutes, he discovered a fist-sized rock under the vines and gave it a push. With an audible "click", the stone wall swung open, revealing a mysterious hallway.

"You take the lead," Nathaniel said to Sinbad, encouraging the hound forward using the rope leash. "Find the others."

Cautiously, the two interlopers advanced along a tunnel of tangled roots, the damp earth heavy in the air. The hallway felt endless, extending for a hundred yards until it abruptly ended in a descending staircase that vanished into an ominous blackness. The scent of dampness filled the air as water rhythmically dripped from the ceiling, creating a potential hazard with each slippery step. Carefully, the two descended the stairs and found themselves in a narrow corridor. Nathaniel strained his ears and caught faint voices drifting from a distant room, prompting him to signal Sinbad to be quiet as they moved forward.

Imposing iron doors divided each side of the corridor, and Sinbad strained his ears to catch any hint of movement or activity beyond each door. The hound sniffed at each door but continued until they reached the third door. Out of nowhere, excruciating screams echoed through the corridor, then just as quickly as they began, faded into silence. No sound broke the silence, short of Nathaniel's rapid, nervous breathing. As if on cue, the screams echoed through the air once again, causing Sinbad to emit a quiet moan. Nathaniel's heart pounded in his chest as he heard the unmistakable sounds of agony, sending shivers down his spine. By the Gods, could that be one of the brotherhood? Maybe it's Jacoby or Grull? But where are they originating? Despite closing his eyes, the screams appeared to be coming from all around him. He couldn't escape the horrifying vision of his loved ones suffering merciless beatings and torture. Finally, the wails ceased, but his ears were now filled with the relentless thumping of his heartbeat. He inhaled deeply, feeling the rush of air fill his lungs, and relaxed his clenched fists, their nails leaving imprints on his palms. He had to find his friends, and hurry.

"We need to speed up," he whispered in Sinbad's ear and led the dog to the next door. Finally, the hound's ears perked up, and he gently tapped his paw against the door. Nathaniel could feel his heart race as he leaned in, the heavy breathing echoing in his ears. He tried the latch, and to his surprise, the door swung open.

The room held a chilling sight - an unfamiliar human and an elf, both barely conscious, chained to one wall, their bodies bearing the marks of a brutal beating. On the adjacent wall, a powerful orc stood bound by shackles, his piercing gaze analyzing the intruder. Nathaniel considered shutting the door and continuing to the next cell but ultimately stepped inside.

He approached the elf, who was groaning softly and unable to utter a word, then turned his attention to the human, who lay in a daze, unable to communicate. Facing the formidable orc, his pulse quickened. The orc, who stood almost as tall as the prince, wore a surcoat adorned with a black mountain insignia. He studied the prince intently, his eyes never leaving him.

"Do you speak the common tongue?" Nathaniel asked in a hushed tone.

The orc paused before eloquently stating, "I am proficient in several languages, human."

After a moment of silence, Nathaniel finally spoke up and said, "That's excellent. What's your name?"

"Torque."

"My name is Nathaniel," he stated confidently. "I need your help, "Torque.""

One brow of the orc lifted in an expression of curiosity.

"My family's held captive, and I'm desperate to aid their escape. If I grant you freedom, will you help me?"

The orc eyed the prince, then said, "Set me free."

Nathaniel, uncertain of what the orc meant, took matters into his own hands and used a dagger he had gained from the deceased badger-goblin to release Torque from the restraints. Following that, he turned around and performed the same action on both the human and the elf, resulting in them falling to the ground.

Nathaniel left them where they fell and led Sinbad to the next door. He listened and thought he faintly heard sobbing. He opened and saw the door to another hallway leading deeper into the mountain.

Sinbad and the prince moved on, unsure if the orc had followed. Sinbad approached the next door, sniffing and nudging it, revealing another corridor. Silently, they made their way down the hallway until they reached a T-intersection. Nathaniel listened attentively and glanced in both directions. One pathway concluded with a set of stairs descending, while the other led to multiple doors.

"Tell me, boy, which way should we go?" he whispered to Sinbad, and the hound promptly descended the stairs, sniffing with his nose lowered. At the bottom was another hallway lined with doors. Sinbad came to a halt at the second door. Nathaniel could make out the soft sound of someone sobbing.

Then he heard, "Shut yer yap, woman! Speed up feeding and changing those brats, or I cook one for supper."

Nat looked down at Sinbad, whose eyes had turned fiery red, baring his sharp teeth in a snarl. The hellhound raced across the stone floor before Nathaniel could fully open the door. In pursuit of the hound, he found himself in a grand dining hall protected by a snapping turtle and a moorschrecken who was obviously in charge. Connected to a wall by a long chain, Allai'nn held one of the fussy infants. Lani and Rue were shackled nearby, their heads drooping with despair.

Before Nathaniel had even reached the halfway point of the room, the scene unfolded before his eyes. With his voice oozing malice, the Changeling leader hissed out the command, "Kill him, Tice." While the others stood in stunned shock, Sinbad vanished, leaving the defenders frantically searching in every direction. Instantly, he appeared behind the turtle, casting a larger and more menacing shadow. Sinbad's open jaws unleashed a stream of orange flames, engulfing the snapping turtle and reducing it to a charred hulk.

Consumed by rage, the Moorshrecken bared its fangs, hissing menacingly at the sight of its fallen comrade, vowing, "Now it's your turn to die, hound!" Sinbad dodged the monster's charge with a quick blink, leaving it snapping at space. Determined to catch the hound unaware, it spun again, preparing for another charge. But what awaited him was an even more formidable hound, its muscular frame and razor-sharp canines instilling pure terror. Like a speeding rocket, Sinbad blasted toward the reptile, causing it to tumble and become trapped beneath him. He clenched his jaws tightly around the Moorshrecken's neck, then spun around, launching the beast across the room. The monster struck the metal door with a resounding thud, causing it to buckle and collapse into a twisted heap.

In one leap, the hound bounded to Allai'nn, smothering her in affectionate dog licks.

"Sinbad!" she cried, almost stumbling from the dog's enthusiastic devotion. She hugged him close and then turned to Nathaniel, tears running down her face. The prince gathered her in his arms, holding her for a long moment, then pulled apart.

"I thought you were dead," she wept, but grinned ear to ear.

"I've never felt better, thanks to Sinbad rescuing me," Nat said, breaking her shackle with this knife. He turned to Lani, gently freeing her from captivity, and pulled her into a tight embrace. She snuggled against him, shivering from the cold. Her sobs filled the room as he ran his fingers through her hair, trying to console her. Finally, she lifted her head and choked between tears, her voice filled with relief, "You're alive! I can't believe it!"

"Not even death can separate us, my love," he whispered in her ear, stroking her hair. He cradled her delicately, treating her like a rare and fragile flower, until Rue's interruption broke the moment.

"What about me?" she whispered, her words barely audible but filled with desperation.

With a wide grin, Nathaniel swiftly broke Rue's shackles, his voice filled with remorse as he whispered, "Sorry, Rue. I'm so glad to see you." He hugged her warmly when a voice behind him said, "If we're to escape, we need to press on."

Nat looked up to see the muscular orc he had rescued earlier standing in the doorway.

"Right. I have more friends to rescue."

Frowning, the orc responded, "Lead on."

The women bundled the children and followed Nathaniel to the doorway.

"Everyone, this is Torque," the prince said, introducing the massive orc as he strode into the corridor. Following Torque, the rest stayed close.

"Does anyone know where the others are being held?" he asked.

The women shook their heads. Nathaniel knelt by Sinbad, rubbing his back, and said, "Find Jacoby, Sinbad."

The hound shot down the hallway, his nose to the stone floor, sniffing in all directions. At the next corner, Nathaniel slowed, hearing voices. He peeked around the edge but saw no one in the hallway. They tiptoed forward until he reached a door, where he heard several voices.

"I don't like your face, halfling," said a gruff voice, followed by a cry of pain from a punch.

"Don't hurt him too badly, Abel. He must be healthy enough to fight in the arena," said another.

Abel laughed heartily and quipped, "Just softening the rough edges."

With each punch, the sound of impact echoed through the room, followed by another anguished moan. With Sinbad by his side, Nathaniel charged into the fray, the determination evident on his face. A horrifying scene unfolded before his eyes - four massive bears towering over a helpless halfling, blood seeping from his wounds. Chained next to him were several others, each representing a different race: an elf, a rugged dwarf, a broad half-elf, a towering human, and a green-skinned Anuran.

With a burst of strength, Nathaniel threw his weight onto the back of the abusing Kodiak, causing them both to tumble to the ground. Sinbad launched at the others, his swift movements catching them off guard. With a burst of energy, Torque charged in from behind and delivered a powerful kidney punch to the nearest bear. In an instant, chaos consumed the scene as the carnivores retaliated with lightning speed. Nathaniel rolled on the ground, feeling the monster's powerful claws whistle by his head as he lunged forward with his dagger, slicing the beast across the forearm. Simultaneously, the bear facing Torque collapsed under the weight of the hellhound, but the fourth ape swung a sledgehammer punch that rocked the orc back on his heels. The air resonated with a cacophony of grunts from the fighters, mixed with the cries of both women and prisoners.

Sinbad found his adversary to be a formidable opponent, not only stronger and more agile than the other changelings he'd fought, but also skilled in wielding a dagger. The bear slashed, but the hound disappeared, materializing behind and clamping powerful jaws on the beast's leg. "Argh!" wailed the monster, unable to free himself.

Sinbad used his incredible strength to sling the bear across the cell like a top, smashing against the far wall.

In that very instant, Nathaniel found himself locked in a fierce battle for survival. Using his heavier weight, the adversary had successfully pinned the prince on his back, his muscular hands tightening around his throat. Just as darkness closed in on Nathaniel's vision, the sudden force of Sinbad's form blasted the carnivore free. The bear rolled and danced to his feet, only to face a much larger hound. Sinbad, assuming his full, enormous size, snarled. Dwarfing the bear, he pounced, knocking the Kodiak back and landing his massive paws on the beast's chest. Blood splattered across the room as the hellhound finished the changeling with a ripping bite to the upper chest.

Despite his immense strength, the relentless barrage of punches from his opponent overpowered Torque. At the moment he believed his life was about to end, the bear's agonized scream echoed through the air. With wide, bug-like eyes, the monster fell to one side and went silent, Nathaniel's dagger driven to the hilt in his back.

"Thanks," Torque mumbled amidst his heavy breathing.

With a nod, Nathaniel gripped the hilt of his blade and extracted it from the ape's lifeless body. As he did, the once bestial form started to shift and contort, morphing into the shape of a powerful, muscular human. With swift movements, Nathaniel freed the others, including the mysterious dwarf.

Nat gave Jacoby a bear hug, feeling the older man's body flinch from the pain of multiple cuts and contusions. Through misting eyes, the big man whispered, "I knew you'd survive and come for us," his voice filled with emotion. Nathaniel smiled and hugged each of the others before offering his hand to the dwarf.

"Nathaniel."

The dwarf eyed him suspiciously, then took his hand. "Henry, Henry Oakshield."

Nathaniel shook firmly and said, "I'd love to speak more, but if we need to hurry, we're getting out of here."

He turned to the others and said, "Grab their weapons and follow me. With the noise, more changelings will arrive at any moment."

The group followed Sinbad as he navigated the maze-like hallways, the sound of their footsteps echoing through the empty corridors. Nathaniel had the hound pause at each corner, ensuring no guards were lurking before proceeding. Finally, after only two brief encounters with the enemy, both dispatched by Sinbad, they reached the hidden iron door.

Nathaniel pushed the latch open, and as the group made their way through the vines, they felt the invigorating breeze of a crisp, clear evening. Despite his initial desire to rest, Nathaniel understood the enemy would soon track them down, so he led the group for another hour toward the west until they finally gave in to exhaustion.

While most of the group slept, Torque, Henry, and Nathaniel huddled around a small fire. The three gazed into the flames, lost in their thoughts.

Nathaniel broke the silence and asked, "Torque, where do you hail from?"

The orc lifted his head and said, "I come from the Black Hills."

When the prince looked at him quizzically, he stated, "To the west, on the southern Taborian border."

"Interesting," Nathaniel said. "How about you, Henry?"

The dwarf contorted his face into a sour expression. "Not your business."

Nathaniel, having some history with dwarves, ignored the response and asked another question. "How does a dwarf and an orc find themselves the guests of the changelings?"

Oakshield looked away, his face coloring. "They attacked my caravan."

"And you Torque?"

"Hunting party ambush. You?"

"Captured traveling to Tabor."

"Tabor?" both beings exclaimed together.

"I was born there," Nathaniel explained, "although I grew up in the Halfling lands east."

"A dangerous journey," Torque said, his eyes fixed on the flickering flames as he absentmindedly poked the fire with a stick. "Why embark on a perilous journey toward a war-torn land?"

Nathaniel could feel the intense gaze of all four eyes fixed on him, curious and intrigued. "My mission in the capital holds immense significance, as its success or failure could tip the scales of the war."

Both beings exchanged amused, doubtful glances and let out a chuckle. "Only a fool or a madman would enter Tabor now," Oakshield declared, his voice filled with warning. "There have been rumors circulating about an undead army marching towards the City of Spires, ready to unleash chaos."

"What? Undead?" Nathaniel said, his eyes widening in alarm.

"Only rumors. Why does it matter? Is your mission that imperative?" asked Torque.

"We've traveled for almost a year to reach Tabor. Nothing is more important," Nathaniel said confidently.

For what felt like an eternity, Torque and Oakshield stood in complete silence, their unwavering stares fixed upon the prince. Nathaniel forced a smile onto his face, feeling uneasy inside, and stood up to say, "I've genuinely enjoyed meeting both of you, and you're welcome to travel with us. Good night."

As Nathaniel strode toward Lani, he could feel the intense gaze of the two beings on him, analyzing his every move. Who were these two stoics? An orc warrior and a mysterious dwarf from parts unknown. What in the Gods would tomorrow bring?

EIGHTEEN

The following morning, Nathaniel and Lani rose before sunrise, the sky still dark, only faintly showing the coming dawn. The morning chill and the dying campfire spurred Nathaniel in a search for more kindling to enrich the fire.

"Want to help me?" Nathaniel asked Lani with an encouraging tone. After so much group travel, he hungered for some time alone with Lani.

"Okay. Allai'nn mentioned she needed to replenish her store of medicinal herbs. Maybe I can search for them while you get the wood."

A half hour's search yielded several fallen branches for Nathaniel, their weight heavy in his arms. He broke the wood into pieces as kindling and coaxed the fire back to life. Lani also returned with an armful of Calendula, Arnica, Lavender, and ginger root for Allai'nn's healer bag.

"This is wonderful," Allai'nn said, taking the plants. "I was running low after our most recent misadventure."

"Happy to do it. What else can I do to help?"

"Well," the elf said, rubbing her chin, thinking. "Anything you can find for our breakfast?"

"I'll help you," Nathaniel said, smiling. He took her hand, and they disappeared into the foliage together. After a short time, the two stumbled on another game trail and began strolling along the root-covered path.

When he felt they were far enough from camp, he pulled Lani to him and gave her a long, deep kiss. When their lips parted, Lani whispered, "I wish you'd greet me that way every morning." She pulled him back into another deep kiss.

"I'll gladly do so," he said, flushed with desire. "Every morning, afternoon, and evening."

She squeezed his hand, blushing, and pulled him down the trail. "We need to find breakfast; if you're good, I'll reward you."

Nat chuckled and swore, "On my honor, I'll be good."

Over the next half hour, the two young sweethearts scanned the surrounding area, finding a host of bunchberries, wild blackberries, and Fairy Cap. Unknowingly, their search took them up a steep hill and down a winding path through a dense copse of ancient Linden trees until it abruptly ended at the edge of a small meadow. In the center, a creek flowed from the West, revealing a broad, shining pond.

"Let's get in," Nat said, gazing through the crystal-clear water to the pebbled bottom. The shore glistened as a school of trout minnows swam along, their scales reflecting the morning sun. Beads of sweat formed on his forehead as the morning temperature rose during their food search.

"We need to get this food back for the others," she said hesitantly, prioritizing returning the food, despite the water's allure.

"We won't be in long, and the cool water will feel good.".

"But more bandits might come," she warned.

"Don't be silly," Nathaniel said, pulling off his tunic and boots and wading into the water. As he waded in, the pebbled bottom and icy water sent a jolt of discomfort through his feet. But as he reached the midpoint, he couldn't resist the temptation to dive forward, fully immersing himself under the glistening, crystal-clear water. The cool bite of the water dissipated quickly, leaving him floating on his back, relishing in the tranquility he hadn't experienced in days. According to Nathaniel's estimation, the pond was just slightly deeper than his height, except for the rocky outcrop on the far side. He could see the water cascading down, creating a mesmerizing display as it dropped another ten feet to a smooth stone bottom.

"How is the water?" Lani's voice sounded from behind a bush as she, too, undressed to the waist.

"Fantastic!" the prince said with a smile.

"Turn your head," she called out, and as soon as Nathaniel complied, she swiftly disappeared beneath the surface.

"This water is as frigid as a mountaintop!" she cried before dunking under. In a few minutes, she acclimated and stroked over to the prince. She melted into his arms as he scissored to stay afloat.

"Your skin is full of goosebumps. Hold tight, and I'll warm you," Nathaniel whispered, holding her tight. As she lifted her glacier-blue eyes to meet his gaze, he felt a connection unlike anything he had experienced. Her unparalleled beauty left him speechless, unable to tear his eyes away. As he leaned in and kissed her deeply, the world around them faded away, consumed by their overwhelming passion, until a gentle tickle on his foot brought them back to reality. After their lips separated, he looked down, only to find the empty bottom stones staring back at him. A minnow nipping at my toes, he thought. At that moment, Lani smiled and said, "We earned this, but we really should get back to camp before Jacoby sends a search party."

"Must we?" Nathaniel said with a slight pitiful whine.

"Hungry for more? Maybe after breakfast, we can take a stroll," she said, pulling free from him and stroking toward the shore.

Nathaniel frowned, unprepared to face the rigors of travel, when he felt another tickle on the bottom of his foot. He looked down and realized he had drifted over the deeper pond portion. At the bottom, something shiny twinkled from the center of the rocky bottom.

"Hey, you coming?" Lani called to Nathaniel, now fully clothed and wringing water from her hair. Nathaniel waved, then looked down again.

"Be right there."

With a deep breath, he plunged into the water, feeling the coolness envelop his body as he stroked his way to the bottom. As he inspected the stone, he discovered an algae-covered silver ring nestled within it. As he pulled on the ring, he felt the stone beneath shift slightly, but it stubbornly refused to come free. Nat kicked his way to the surface, gasping for air as he took in several deep breaths.

Lani called out again, "What are you doing?"

"I found something. Head back, and I'll meet you shortly."

Hesitation washed over Lani as a shadow of concern clouded her features. She gazed at the tranquil pond, noting sunlight dancing on the water. Noticing the absence of harmful elements reassured her. I think it's safe to leave and return to camp. With a wave goodbye, she started her ascent up the incline, holding the ripe berries wrapped in a cloth.

Nathaniel returned the wave, then plunged into the water, feeling the chill embrace as he swam towards the ring. His feet planted firmly on the stoney bottom, he exerted all his strength as he pulled. Suddenly, the ring attached to a circular stone portion gave way, revealing a hole underneath. Like a ghostly chorus of water nymphs, otherworldly music filled Nathaniel's mind as it emanated from the opening. Like a lover in need, the tone whispered to him, its ethereal quality creating a calming yet yearning atmosphere. "Nathaniel. Nathaniel. Take me, Nathaniel. I am yours."

The melody caressed him, evoking a desire that surpassed his wildest imagination. At that precise moment, he felt a sharp pain in his chest, realizing with panic that he needed air. Kicking hard, he surged towards the surface, feeling the wild strokes propel him forward while the enchanting song beckoned him to return. A moment later, his head emerged from the water, and he gulped in breaths, coughing and sputtering. What in the world of darkness and chaos? Something magical lives here, casting a spell on all who enter.

Nathaniel calmed, wondering if he should abandon whatever rested below. But something deep inside demanded he return to the bottom.

Inhaling deeply, he braced himself and plunged into the water. As he swam towards the ring, the cool water against his skin added to the moment's thrill. With a firm grip, he pulled the ring back and cautiously inserted his hand into the mysterious hole. As the chorus started again, he focused on the sensation of the rough, gritty bottom of the hole. He half expected his arm to be snatched, condemning him to an eternity as prey for the lake's underwater creatures. The Gods seemed to favor him as his searching hand stumbled upon a fist-sized stone that felt warm and comforting to the touch. With a powerful pull, he freed the stone and propelled himself towards the surface. Once he had made it to shore, he took a moment to catch his breath and then studied the stone he had found.

At first glance, the fist-sized stone resembled a handful of algae, its surface covered in a solid green hue. Leaning into the water, Nathaniel used his hands to clear away the debris. As his hand brushed against it, he felt the cool surface of the stone, only to discover it was not a stone but a remarkable, uneven, purple crystalline gem. Crystal shards covered the mass, jutting out in various directions and creating a rough and unpolished surface. On one side, someone had etched runes into the hard surface. Nathaniel couldn't decipher the words, so he carefully tucked the stone into his pocket. He ascended the incline towards the camp with his tunic casually draped over one shoulder, wondering the meaning of the enchanted stone.

Back at camp, the others were awake and sitting around the fire, eating the paltry breakfast Lani and Nathaniel had provided.

Grull, eyebrow arched, asked, "Where've you been, boy?"

"Didn't Lani tell you? We collected the berries and stumbled upon a hidden gem of a lake, enticing us to jump in for a relaxing dip."

"She did, but that was a half hour ago. Been exploring?"

Before Nathaniel could reveal his secret gem, Blue Ivy cut in.

"I think we could all use a good rinsing after those dungeons. Can you show us the way after you eat?' asked Blue Ivy.

"Of course," he agreed, a smile forming as he spoke. "The water was refreshing and crystal clear."

"Sounds lovely. We could all use a wash before we head north," Jacoby added.

"Here, here!" Added Horatio. "I'm certain my fragrance could be detected at ten paces."

"Your fragrance?" laughed Cor'in. "Perfume de la Skunk, your worship!"

"Funny, coming from one whose odor could wilt a flower."

"I think we're all in need of a cleaning," said Allai'nn. "The children too."

"It's settled then," said Jacoby, standing. "Any sign of our guests? They probably want to come, too."

Nathaniel frowned. He realized neither Torque nor Oakshield were around, something he hadn't noticed before. He made his way towards a small clearing hidden behind a cluster of towering trees, only to find it abandoned.

"I guess they left during the night," he told the others.

"Well, just as well. They were an unusual pair," Grull observed.

Nathaniel shook his head, feeling an odd sense of loss despite not knowing the two beings well. He dismissed the feeling, then he guided them through the woods to the pool.

After the women bathed, then the men and infants, the group experienced a significant boost in their well-being, feeling as though they had cast off days of exhaustion. As they moved up the incline toward the camp, Nathaniel smelled the smoky, savory scent of burning meat, a tantalizing aroma that mixed with the crisp mountain air.

"Do you smell what I smell?" Nathaniel asked Jacoby.

"Smells like fresh cooked meat. Could the bandits be nearby?"

Nathaniel made a hushing gesture, signaling the group to halt and remain quiet. He waited in silence, counting the beats of his own heart, but heard nothing. Grull and Cor'in crept forward silently, careful not to make a sound.

"That aroma is coming from the direction of the camp," Grull whispered. "Bandits?"

Instead of answering directly, Nathaniel proposed a plan. "Let's divide into two groups," he said, gesturing towards the left, "You and Cor'in go left, and Jacoby and I will go right. Horatio and Blue stay here and protect the others." He turned to Horatio and signaled to remain with the women and children with a hand gesture.

The group separated, each finding a heavy branch to wield as a weapon. They silently crept to the edge of the camp, and Nathaniel carefully parted the leaves to reveal a deer carcass roasting on a spit over the crackling fire. The sight initially puzzled the prince, but then he spotted Torque and Oakshield hauling more wood for the fire.

He and Jacoby dropped their weapons and came into the open.

"You must learn the ways of the forest, my friends. I could smell your scent even before I heard your clumsy approach," Torque said, his back turned, placing wood on the fire.

The statement caught Jacoby and Nathaniel off guard, causing them to exchange a perplexed glance before Nathaniel spoke up. "I'm confused. What's going on here?"

"Breakfast," Oakshield grunted, adding another log to the fire.

"Uh.. thank you," Nathaniel said, still confused.

"In return for our escape, it was the least we could do to show our gratitude," Torque said. "Feel free to alert the others, especially the two bulls stampeding on our flank."

"You can hear them?" uttered a stunned Jacoby.

As Torque gazed at him, a brief moment of confusion washed over him, but it quickly faded into a warm smile. "I grew up learning the ways of the forest. To survive, you will need help. Don't you agree, Henry?"

The dwarf grunted, a sour expression on his face. "Good luck with that," he spat. "My smithery awaits my return."

"Smithery?" Nathaniel asked.

Torque answered for the dwarf. "Being an outsider, you wouldn't know, but Henry is an elite weapons artisan."

Nathaniel's brow raised. "Amazing. And what about you, Torque?"

"No one special."

"No one special, why..." the dwarf erupted, but a harsh look from Torque cut the words short. A moment of uncomfortable silence blanketed the air. Then Jacoby touched Nathaniel's arm, his eyes giving a "find out more" expression, and said, "I'll get the others."

Torque changed the subject, asking, "You mentioned a mission to the City of Spires last night. That's a mad endeavor."

Nathaniel looked away; his voice filled with concern. "It's a time of chaos in Curth Talem," he said. "A moment that requires bravery."

Instead of replying, Torque tilted his head and studied the prince curiously, his silence speaking louder than words.

"Any idea where we are?" Nathaniel asked, breaking the silence.

Torque took a stick and drew a rudimentary map in the dirt. "By the sun's position, I suspect we traveled southeast during our escape. However, this is the farthest east I've ever been in the Horn Wood," the orc mentioned, pointing to a specific area on the map.

"What do you think, Henry?" Nathaniel asked the dwarf.

"Human," the dwarf exploded, his words dripping with disdain. "It's Mister Oakshield to you! We aren't friends," he said icily, his words laced with contempt, "and your idiotic quest means nothing to me. Leave me out of your plans." He stalked away after cutting a slab of venison off the roasted deer.

Nathaniel watched the dwarf, puzzled by his unusual reaction. Was this how one repaid being rescued from certain death?

"He's an eccentric loner with a chip on his shoulder. Completely mercenary by my experience," Torque said, as if that explained the outburst. "But a gifted arms maker. For enough gold, he'll make you quality weapons."

Torque changed directions with a question. "May I ask you a favor?"

"If it's in my power," Nathaniel said.

"I would like to return to my home. A branch of the Horn River runs east to west. It can't be far. If you'll aid me in reaching the river, you'll hit the main branch that will take you to the City of Spires."

Before Nathaniel could answer, the rest of the group appeared eager to dig into the succulent venison.

"I can practically taste how good that looks," Cor'in said, his stomach growling audibly.

"Me too. I could eat an entire leg," added Blue Ivy.

"Thank you for providing us the food, Torque," Nathaniel said, putting out his hand to shake. Torque eyed the young prince for a heartbeat, then took the hand firmly.

"As I said, it's the least I could do. Please consider my request," the words rumbled from the mouth of the muscular orc as he nodded and walked away toward his sleeping area.

"What did that involve?" Jacoby asked, coming to Nathaniel's side.

"He wants our help to go home," Nathaniel answered, wondering if he could trust the orc despite his repayment with food. The faint melody from the pond reached his ears, causing his mind to wander to the mysterious object rubbing against the fabric of his pocket. He looked at Jacoby and said, "Do you hear that?"

"Hear what?" Jacoby asked, his face questioning.

"Nothing," Nathaniel said, shaking his head and smiling. "I must have water in my ears."

Jacoby hesitated, suspecting his brother was hiding something, but smiled before returning to the fire and said, "No worries."

But the melody played incessantly in his mind, the notes weaving together to form a haunting tune with the whispered words, "Nathaniel. King Nathaniel, free me. I am yours."

Nat shook his head, but the tune continued. What in the Gods is happening? What kind of stone is this, and why does it call to me? Fumbling with the rough stone in his pocket, he hoped that its touch could silence the yearning within him. Allai'nn is the most magical person I know, and this is pure magic. Perhaps she can tell me its meaning and if it could be harmful.

He searched and found the elf just finishing feeding the children small bits of venison crushed and mixed with water.

"Hey, would you have time for a walk? I have something important to discuss."

With a questioning gaze, the elf smiled and replied, "Absolutely."

She turned to Sinbad, who rested beside the now sleeping children, gnawing on a deer leg bone.

"Watch over the children, Sinbad," she said, rubbing the hellhound's copper fur, and then she and Nathaniel slipped away down the path.

When Nathaniel thought they were out of earshot, he pulled the stone from his pocket and said, "I found this in the lake. It...seems to call to me. Is it enchanted?"

She carefully lifted the stone and cradled it in her hand, marveling at its weight and texture. Immediately, she could feel an electric surge of ancient magic coursing through her veins. Suddenly, dizziness washed over her, causing her eyes to widen and her breath to come in rapid gasps. As she dropped the stone, her legs gave out, and she stumbled, only to be caught by Nathaniel before she hit the ground.

"What's the matter? Are you alright, Allai'nn?" Nathaniel asked as he lowered her to sit on a fallen log.

Allai'nn took a moment for her head to stop swirling, trying to steady herself and suppress the wave of nausea threatening to overwhelm her. She nodded, her voice barely audible as she whispered, "That stone is pulsating with ancient, powerful magic. I would be very cautious wielding such power. However, if it beckons to you specifically, it indicates a mystical bond."

"What kind of mystical bond? Can you read the runes on the bottom of the rock?"

"Runes?" she asked, her brow knitted in a questioning furrow.

"The stone doesn't seem to bother me, so I'll hold it," Nathaniel said, picking up the stone, brushing away any dust, and lifting it for Allai'nn to read the runes.

Allai'nn studied the runes for several moments, then gasped.

"It can't be," she exclaimed, her eyes bulging like apples.

"What is it?" Nathaniel asked, his voice urgent.

At that moment, Grull and Jacoby arrived.

"So, there you are. I was worrying," Grull said, stopping short when he saw the look on Allai'nn's face.

"What's happening here?" asked Jacoby, crossing his arms as if catching two teens kissing.

"I found this gem at the bottom of the pond this morning," Nathaniel said, extending his hand to show Jacoby and Grull the rough yet captivating crystalline stone. "Allai'nn was helping me decipher its magical origin."

"Magical origin?" asked Grull, one brow raised and reaching for the stone.

Like the strike of a viper, Allai'nn knocked Grull's hand away. "Don't touch it! It's imbued with violent ancient magic."

"Then why can Nathaniel handle it?" questioned Jacoby.

"All I know is it knocked me off my feet," Allai'nn said.

"Are you all right, my love?" Grull asked, putting an arm around his wife.

"Yes, but..."

Nathaniel took over. "But... she was just unraveling the mysterious runes etched on the back, shedding light on their hidden meaning."

"What does it say, Allai'nn?" asked Jacoby, intrigued by the situation.

"The runes are in ancient Elven, in a dialect unknown to me. The tangled letters, twisted together haphazardly, create a nonsensical jumble," offered the elf princess.

As Nathaniel looked down at the gem, the once-static runes came alive, shifting and rearranging before his eyes. Rubbing his eyes, he exclaimed, "Did you see that?!"

"Huh? See what?" Grull asked.

"The letters moved!"

Nathaniel copied the rearranged rune in the dirt using a stick. He looked up from his work and noticed Blue Ivy, Cor'in, Horatio, and Rue now watching.

"We were wondering what the secret meeting was all about," said Cor'in. "Now I understand, but why keep Nat's rune illiteracy a secret?"

Jacoby rolled his eyes. "Funny."

Nathaniel studied his work, ignoring the new onlookers, making sure every rune was correct. "There. This is what I see on the stone."

"I still can't understand it," offered Allai'nn, her brow furrowed in frustration.

"That looks like an ancient Sylvan tongue," Rue interjected, her eyes widening with recognition.

"I can't believe it," said Blue Ivy in astonishment. "How did you know that?"

Rue's face turned a deep shade of crimson as she confessed, "Mother made me learn many of the Elven languages growing up."

Blue smiled. "I'm constantly discovering new things about you."

"I have a slice of venison that's getting cold," Cor'in mumbled irritably. "What does it mean?"

With authority in his voice, Horatio shut down the oaf's whining with a stern command. "Even the most clueless person can see," he exclaimed, "that this stone is infused with magic and must hold special significance for Nathaniel alone."

"Unless it will fill my empty stomach, it's less important than my meat. My last decent meal was days ago." Cor'in said, shuffling off to retrieve his supper.

"Good riddance," Horatio whispered under his breath.

Grull put a hand on his shoulder. "Ignore him, brother."

Nathaniel sensed the tension in the air left by Cor'in's departure. He would have to address the row between the Half-Elf and the Anuran later before things worsened. He turned back to the Oread and said, "So, Rue, can you read this?"

Rue scrunched her face and studied the runes. "Only one word. Elyra."

A sudden, deep, gravely voice boomed from behind the group, catching everyone off guard. "By my calculations, Elyra can't be far, somewhere southeast."

Standing rigidly, Torque's crossed arms, his expression inscrutable under his dark, suspicious eyes. The group stood frozen for several uncomfortable heartbeats; their eyes locked on the imposing figure of the muscular orc.

Finally, Nathaniel spoke, his voice firm. "Torque, you're a quiet one, for sure. But I don't appreciate being spied on."

The orc hesitated, taking a deep breath before apologizing, "I'm sorry, Nathaniel. Cor'in mentioned that you and the others were discussing a plan. I couldn't help but feel intrigued and curious."

"Apology accepted," Nathaniel said with a wave of his hand while pocketing the gem and using his foot to wipe away his marks in the soil. "Let's finish eating and start on our way toward Elyra. You and Henry are free to join us."

"What about our discussion?" asked Torque, still unmoving.

"I haven't forgotten your request. But Elyra is our new destination. I believe a branch of the Horn River flows near there. My hope is we can both find transportation there."

The orc pondered the offer a moment longer and said, "Very well, I'll come with you to Elyra."

"What about Henry?"

"Henry disappeared an hour ago," growled the orc.

Nathaniel felt oddly disappointed by the news. Something about the dwarf captivated him, other than his rude and uncouth personality. A voice in the far reaches of his mind suggested Henry Oakshield played a pivotal role in his destiny. But in what way? Only Odin knew the secret, and Nathaniel believed the truth would eventually come to light.

"That's unfortunate. I liked Henry despite his bristling personality," he said and followed the others up the path to the camp.

NINETEEN

Several hundred miles north of the Brotherhood's location, an elderly human rapped a gavel on the Taborian council chamber's walnut table, bringing the meeting to order. With a protruding belly and flushed cheeks, the older man had used his position to remain well-fed despite months of food rationing suffered by the capital citizens. His well-trimmed beard and twinkling eyes added to his overall appearance of health. When he stood up, he gazed at the other rotund figures at the table, nodding to each. Large trays of sandwiches and fresh fruit rested on the table beside several pitchers of wine. None of the council members seemed phased by the opulent spread and dug into the food like ravenous dogs.

"As acting regent," he said in a pleasant tone. "I call this meeting to order. I suggest we begin with an update on the success of the war. The chair recognizes General Thorn."

A uniformed man with a blood-stained bandage circling his head stood and saluted. "Thank you, Regent Mossbrook."

The forty-something officer hesitated; his brow furrowed as if grappling with a complex puzzle. He decided and unfurled a rolled deer-skin map across the table for everyone to see.

"Gentleman, I have grave news," he began, pointing to a blue line that stretched across the map. "As of yesterday, our advanced scouts report the enemy has advanced south of the River Narn and is advancing toward the capital."

Several members shot to their feet, and a cacophony of "By the Gods!" echoed across the room. A short man with scraggly red hair and mustache blurted, "How is that possible? General Tusk destroyed every river bridge months ago."

Thorn sighed at the mention of his mentor, who had died in battle weeks before.

The room fell silent as Mossbrook rapped his gavel loudly on the table, commanding everyone's attention. "Order! Order!"

As the councilmen begrudgingly took their seats, Thorne pressed on with his report.

"Despite destroying the bridges, the enemy devised a clever solution for crossing."

"What solution?" asked another councilman.

"That brings me to my second set of disagreeable news," he said, his mind racing about whether he should deceive the board to maintain calm. He settled on a vague half-truth. "The enemy has received...highly specialized...reinforcements over the last month that provide them with a distinct advantage."

"What kind of advantage?" said red hair, his eyes narrowed, leaning forward.

Thorne ignored the question and said, "The army marching on the City of Spires, if undeterred, will arrive within eight weeks."

The council let out an audible gasp as one, their eyes wide in panic. Mossbrook slumped in his chair, his hands over his head. Red hair also slumped, seeming to deflate like a leaking balloon.

"Eight weeks!" another councilman with a long white beard hissed in resignation. "Can you stop them?"

Thorne straightened. "Every man in my army will give their life defending the nation they love."

Abruptly, the man with vibrant red hair shifted in his seat, leaning forward as his eyes narrowed. "General, you avoided answering the question," he remarked. "We need to know the truth. Is it a matter of being overwhelmed by sheer numbers, lacking sufficient supplies, or facing superior tactics?"

With a heavy heart, Thorn realized he couldn't soften the truth. "Several hundred undead have reinforced the enemy army, making their numbers even more formidable. To be honest, we are completely powerless to stop them."

"Powerless?" Screamed red hair, his eyes bulging.

"Only a few wealthy officers have silver weapons," Thorne said, throwing his hands up in frustration.

An eerie silence filled the room, so heavy that you could almost hear a pin drop as each council member absorbed the horrifying news.

Finally, Mossbrook stood and said, "Considering this news, I suggest the council members consider sending their families south to Mar Nâpor. In the meantime, I recommend we scour the royal weapons cache for silver weapons and contact our neighboring countries for aid." No one moved, the group still reeling from the recent news.

Mossbrook sighed and added, "Meeting adjourned."

From the bank, Nathaniel saw the River Horn's rushing current, its waters churning and swirling. The expansive water stretched out for a quarter mile, flanked by dense forest on either side. His brow furrowed as he considered using the current to expedite their passage to the Sylph lands. *It's the ideal time, Nathaniel, to scout for a sturdy dory.* He chuckled to himself. Of course, they were in the wilderness with no such options, so he turned and said to the resting brotherhood, "We can follow the river south, and we should run into Elyra, the sylph lands."

"Right. Let's keep moving," Jacoby added in a weary tone to several moans.

"Must we? I barely slept because of the children," said Blue Ivy.

"Me too," added Horatio, yawning.

The group had traveled for several days, living on berries scrounged from the forest and the last of the dried venison. The infants had developed diaper rash and cried nonstop during the last few days despite Allai'nn's use of medicinal herbs.

"I know we're all tired, but if we reach Elyra, we may learn more about the gem and why it's important."

The group continued walking for several hours along the winding river edge. As the orange sun melted into a breathtaking display of gold, orange, and magenta over the treetops, Nathaniel halted the troop and set up camp in a small riverside clearing. The clearing came alive with the gentle movement of the weeping willows, their branches swaying in harmony with the evening breeze.

"Let's camp here for the night," announced Nathaniel.

"Gladly," whined Cor'in, plopping down in an exhausted heap.

"Grull and I will collect firewood while you all eat and rest," Jacoby said, gesturing for the exhausted halfling to follow, Sinbad at their heels.

"I'll help you," added Torque, who seemed to be the only one in the group immune to the children's wailing. The stoic orc trudged off into the brush behind Jacoby and Grullach.

"Cor'in, would you divide what's left of the dried meat?" Nathaniel asked.

Cor'in gave him a sour look at having to move and sighed without answering. He divided up the last dried meat and berries, handing shares to each person and leaving some for the three searching for wood.

Lani and Rue added water to the berries to make a fruity mush for the children, while Allai'nn created an herbal paste for their sore bottoms. An hour later, the cool night air had set in, and the fire started by Horatio and Grull helped lift everyone's spirits.

"I'm as worn out as an old shoe," Horatio commented, lying by the fire.

"It's been a tough few days," added Grull.

"Shh," whispered Allai'nn. "The children have fallen asleep."

Grull's gaze wandered across the small clearing, taking in the sight of the infants nestled peacefully in Sinbad's warm and protective embrace.

"That's what I need as well," whispered Grull. "And I know you're worn out."

Allai'nn nodded and settled into Grull's loving embrace, dozing off moments later. The camp fell into silence as everyone closed their eyes in surrender. Only Nathaniel and Torque remained awake, both quiet.

After several moments, Torque broke the silence. "You know, I've been studying your group, this Brotherhood, as you call it."

"And what do you see?" asked Nathaniel.

"A clan with deep bonds. Even the disagreeable half-elf would never turn his back on anyone in the group. How do you do it?"

Nathaniel considered the question for several heartbeats before saying, "I think it starts with Jacoby. He's the soul of the group. His strength, compassion, and respect for every person bonds us. But each person brings something special. Allai'nn is truly the group's heart, caring for all of us yet setting clear boundaries."

"What do you bring?"

"Me? I don't know. I'm feeling my way along, trying to learn the best qualities of everyone around me."

The stoic orc cracked a smile. "I think not."

Nathaniel gave Torque a curious sideways glance. "I don't understand."

"You bring much more to the leadership than you know, Nathaniel. Or should I call you Your Majesty?"

Nathaniel recoiled as if the orc's words had landed a powerful punch. How did he figure it out? And more importantly, could he trust Torque with our deepest secret?

"I.. don't know what you mean."

"The day you swam in the pond, I glimpsed the clover birthmark on your neck. The unmistakable sign of the Aarmon family. But do not worry; there is no cause for fear. I will keep your secret safe."

Nathaniel eyed the orc for a moment more, then relaxed. *If he were a spy or an assassin, he could have killed me anytime. But I must be more careful.*

"So you know why it's imperative to reach Tabor. My people need me."

The orc nodded.

"What about you? You're not a common orc soldier; your manners and speech portend otherwise. Are you nobility?"

Before speaking, the orc paused, his eyes narrowing as he carefully deliberated his response. "That's one way to look at it."

Nathaniel picked up a loose stick and prodded the crackling flames. "Well, you're one of us now. I'd appreciate and expect your discretion."

Before the orc could respond, Nathaniel pulled himself to his feet, ending the discussion. "Get some rest. I'll wake you when it's time for your guard shift."

It had been four hours when Torque jostled Horatio awake, startling him from his sleep. "It's your turn to be on watch," he said, passing over the responsibility. "Wake Blue Ivy in a couple of hours to relieve you."

Horatio pulled himself to his feet, stretched, and yawned, his wide mouth opening like a hungry baby bird. "All right," he said, not fully awake. Torque handed him the group's only weapon; an iron dagger Torque had pocketed during their escape from the Changelings.

Horatio slowly descended the bank to the river's edge, feeling the uneven ground beneath his feet. As he splashed water on his face, he shivered from the sting of the icy water. *That's as frigid as winter's dew.* Shaking the water from his hair, he started marching around the camp, creating a rhythmic thud with each step. The full moon cast a brilliant glow on the forest, illuminating his path as if he had a torch. The Anuran thought of Ruby, the fawn he'd met in the Hope Wood long ago. As he caressed the hidden broach in his pants leg, memories of their farewell echoed in his mind, the girl's whispered words lingering in his heart. "Keep this as a remembrance until I see you again."

Closing his eyes, he almost heard her voice echoing like a dream as she added, "Wake up, Horatio, or it will be your end."

Horatio's eyes snapped open, and he realized he had fallen asleep leaning against the base of a sturdy maple. He gazed around in a panic, realizing a boat was rowing toward the shore fifty feet away. At one end, a lantern pole cast a dim light on the scene, revealing three bandits encircling two captives who were tightly bound and silenced. Horatio carefully slid towards the trunk, his senses heightened as he used his natural color to camouflage himself, allowing him to hide and listen.

"Why are we stopping, Maz?" One bandit said.

"Too far to keep going. The caves another few hours, and I'm tired," hissed a heavyset Lizardman.

"Me too," added the other bandit, a kobold with a red bandana over his head.

"Old Tick won't be happy," argued the first bandit, a skinny, middle-aged goblin with thick brown fur.

"That's his problem. I'm not paid to row all night."

"Well, I ain't taking the blame if he's mad."

"Shut yer yap and tie the prisoners to that tree, Pox, or I'll shut it for ya," Maz spat, climbing out of the boat and splashing to the bank.

Maz maneuvered the boat until it smoothly landed on the tan sand, then confidently made his way up the bank. With a long rope in hand, Pox took charge of the two prisoners, who were both gagged and bound. Making their way together, they finally arrived at the base of a towering willow tree on the riverbank. After tying the beings to the tree trunk, Pox found a spot nearby to rest. The kobold found a comfortable spot along the boat's thwart and dozed off, his snores filling the air.

Horatio tiptoed to the Willow trunk. "Don't make a sound, or we'll all be dead," he whispered, cutting the bonds of the prisoners.

The Anuran signaled for them to come closer, and the three of them crept silently, closing the distance until they were a mere thirty yards away from the snoring bandits. Horatio's shoulders relaxed, thinking they had escaped until a prisoner's misstep shattered the silence with a resounding "crack" as a branch snapped beneath his weight.

The scene became a chaotic flurry as multiple things occurred at once. Horatio's voice, filled with fear, reverberated as he shouted, "Run!" Pox and Maz leaped to their feet, their cutlasses poised and ready for battle. The two prisoners, one elf and one human, stood frozen, their eyes locked on the approaching bandits, until Horatio shoved them toward the safety of the Brotherhood's camp. Whirling around, he found himself face to face with the Lizardman, his cutlass raised to strike. In one swift movement, Horatio evaded the reptile's attack by leaping onto a willow branch, leaving the predator to strike at thin air.

'Whoosh,' the cutlass missed the Anuran by a hair, landing with a thud on the ground.

"By the demons!" the Lizardman said. "Where'd he go? Where'd he go?"

Pox hurried forward, but Horatio camouflaged himself among the dense foliage, rendering him almost invisible to the bandits.

"Forget him. The other two's getting away," Pox said, turning his attention to following the escapees.

An idea crossed the Anuran's mind, and like a rocket, a red streak shot out from the canopy above, wrenching the cutlass from the stunned man. Then Horatio jumped down, flipping the sword from his prehensile tongue to his hand, and attacked. As Maz turned to face the attacker, his shoulder collided with Pox, causing them both to stumble. Pox somersaulted down the bank, landing with a loud splash in the river below. Maz righted just in time to block Horatio's blow, then re-engaged with a thrust of his own. Horatio dodged, then slashed with the dagger as he slid by, opening a gash in the Lizardman's shoulder. The sword dance unfolded for several minutes, the rhythmic sound of strikes and counter-strikes echoing through the night.

Horatio heard a limb snap behind him and realized the Kobold had snuck behind him. He felt a sharp agonizing pain as the beast's short sword stabbed into his right hamstring. Horatio crumpled to the ground on one side, just as the Lizardman struck. A gut-wrenching scream cut through the night as the blow missed Horatio but connected with the unprotected kobold, slicing him from head to chest.

"Damn fool," Maz raged, pulling the blade free and turning to finish Horatio. The frogman closed his eyes, ready for the end. He heard a deep, guttural grunt reverberating through the air, followed by a resounding thud. Opening his eyes, he saw Nathaniel looming over the unconscious bandit, gripping a weighty log in his hand.

"Are you alright?" Nat said, throwing a hand out to pull him to his feet.

"No, my leg." Blood bubbled through Horatio's fingers.

"Hold on," Nat said, then moved toward the willow tree. He grabbed the rope, and skillfully tied the Lizardman's hands and feet. With a strong effort, he lifted the Anuran onto his shoulder and returned to camp.

"Allai'nn, we need your help," Nathaniel whispered, his voice barely audible as he tried not to disturb the slumbering infants. The sounds of the other Brotherhood members filled the air as Jacoby conversed with the captives while Grull, Blue, and Torque headed out to find a hidden location for the skiff.

Rue and Allai'nn knelt next to a pale Horatio, examining his bloody leg wound. "I can't see the bleeding source. Nat, we must carry him to the water to clear the field."

Nathaniel lifted Horatio and brought him to the water's edge, where the two healers worked to clean and bandage the wound.

"How is he?" Cor'in asked, his voice filled with concern.

"I stopped the bleeding, but without my needle and thread, all I can do is apply herbs and cover the wound," Allai'nn said.

Cor'in frowned. "Just like Horatio to get himself nicked while I slept like a corpse." The half-elf cursed, feeling frustrated, as the damnable frog continued to annoy.

"He'll be all right," Nat said, reassuringly touching Cor'in's shoulder.

Nathaniel strode over to the two prisoners, speaking with Jacoby.

"Prince Astor and Colonel Samuel, this is the leader of our band of misfits, my brother Nathaniel."

Samuel smiled and stuck out his hand, while Prince Astor nodded, an air of superiority in his expression.

"Welcome," said Nathaniel, taking Samuel's hand and shaking it warmly, then offering his hand to Astor. Astor hesitated, then took the hand with the grip of a jellyfish.

Just as Nathaniel opened his mouth to speak, Astor took the lead and started talking. "Just like I mentioned to your brother, it is crucial that I reach Clobryn Nyth, the capital of the sylphs, as soon as possible. How soon can we leave?"

"How fortuitous," Nathaniel said, the heat of his rising annoyance coloring his cheeks. "We, too, are traveling to Elyra. We can leave when Allai'nn allows my injured friend to travel."

"What? I demand we make all haste. I am an envoy of the King of Whispering Haven with urgent business," Astor said, his chin elevating. "Where is this Allai'nn? A simple healer must not deter my mission."

Jacoby snickered while Samuel's mouth hung open.

"Please, Your Majesty, follow me," Nathaniel said with a half bow, his arm pointing the way. He led the insufferable royal to the clearing and stopped beside a blond elf hovering over the injured Anuran warrior.

"Ahem," Astor said, clearing his throat. "Are you the healer?"

"Yes," Allai'nn mumbled over her shoulder as she placed an herbal poultice over Horatio's wound.

"Madame, I am Prince Astor of Whispering Haven, and I must insist we leave immediately for the Sylph capital."

"I know who you are," she said, not looking up.

"You know?" Astor said, his brow furrowed, confused. But he continued, undaunted. "As it should be. I expect you to have this man prepared for travel within the hour." He declared with a brusque tone. When Allai'nn did not respond, Astor threw his chin up in the air, a hint of anger flashing in his eyes, and abruptly turned to leave. After just one step, Grull's fist collided with his face, sending him reeling from the impact.

"Don't you ever speak to my wife like that again," he shouted angrily, his voice filled with fury. "Do you know who she is?"

Without warning, Grull delivered a powerful punch to the elf's stomach, leaving him gasping for breath. Astor let out a strained grunt, desperately gasping for air, as Grull approached once more. With a firm grasp on Astor's collar, Grull hoisted him off the ground, his eyes fixed on the river, ready to dispose of the elf. Suddenly, powerful arms wrapped around him from behind, squeezing him in a bear hug and trapping his arms. "Calm yourself," Jacoby whispered in a hushed tone, barely audible. After several heartbeats of resisting, the fire in Grull's eyes receded, and his muscles relaxed.

Astor, his head throbbing with excruciating pain, could only let out a feeble moan. Sprawled on the ground where Grull had dropped him, he winced from the sting of a bleeding lip and clutched his belly. Instead of extending a hand to help the prince stand, Blue and Cor'in gave Grull an affirming slap on the back, their hearty laughter filling the air.

Nathaniel knelt next to Allai'nn, offering her a comforting touch on her shoulder. "If Grull hadn't hit him, I would have," he whispered with a wink.

No one noticed Samuel stood beside Torque, whom he whispered to in hushed tones as if speaking to an old acquaintance. Torque nodded, but his eyes studied the team's dynamics as the melee ended.

Allai'nn stood and knelt by Astor, and the camp fell into an unsettling stillness. Carefully, she dabbed a wet cloth against his chin, gently wiping away the blood, while speaking softly to her patient.

"I am Allai'nn Hýnhasbren-Furr, daughter of the High Regent of the Elven council, King Polaris. The number of royals in this group far exceeds what you would encounter at the Whispering Haven royal court. You just met my husband, a very protective, experienced warrior, as are all in this group. Think twice before speaking or face the consequences."

Astor's eyes bugged from both recognition and fear but remained silent. Thoughts rocketed through his mind. King Polaris' daughter? Other royals? Warriors? This rabble? Could what she says be true?

But he knew well the power and reach of the Elven council. Polaris wielded more power than any other elf in Curth Talem. And his throbbing jaw and belly taught him the invaluable protection that Allai'nn's companions provided.

Astor got to his feet, brushed off, and said, "I apologize to you, Lady Allai'nn, and also to the group. However, my mission remains imperative. I appreciate my rescue and would like help to reach Clobryn Nyth."

Nathaniel gave a sideways glance at Grull and Jacoby, his arms crossed. Then his eyes drifted to Allai'nn, who gave a slight nod. As he deliberated, a thick mist of silence hung in the air, making the atmosphere heavy with anticipation. He shifted his gaze to Torque and Samuel, their expressions filled with curiosity. For the first time, he noticed the uncanny connection between the human and the orc, making a mental note to explore it further later.

"If you feel ready, Horatio, let's get moving."

"I'm ready," the Anuran said weakly.

In a hurried search, the group gathered whatever food they could find and loaded it onto the boat. The limited space became apparent, prompting them to create room for the children and Horatio. Allai'nn, Rue, with Grull at the oars, filled up the limited space on the boat while the rest of the group trudged along the bank.

Nathaniel called for a halt in a small clearing, the weariness of the long day's journey evident on the faces of the troop. Blue Ivy had taken over rowing, allowing Grull to rest. The elf navigated the dory towards the shore, gently grounding it on the soft river sand.

Jacoby sat beside Nathaniel under the broad canopy of a River Birch.

"Long day," he commented.

"Nothing new for us," agreed Nathaniel.

"Any idea how close we may be to the Sylph lands?"

Nathaniel shrugged, sharing his waterskin with his brother.

Jacoby took a long swig, both quiet for several heartbeats, watching the other group members as they rested and shared some of the stored berries. Then Jacoby broke the silence, whispering," Have you noticed Samuel and Torque?"

"They seem familiar, but I haven't spoken to either about it."

"My gut tells me..."

A buzzing sound, similar to the approach of locusts, erupted from the trees behind them, causing Jacoby to halt mid-sentence. Ten winged bowmen, their wings creating a mesmerizing fluttering sound, surrounded the group. The leader, a tall, bronzed elf with iridescent wings, landed in the center of the startled brotherhood, his green military uniform catching their attention. Grull and Cor'in instinctively reached for their weapons, but their hands froze in mid-air as they realized the bowmen had encircled the group. "I am Captain Lynx," he said, his voice filled with a melodic charm. "Who are you, and what brings you to trespass on our sacred Elyran land?"

Nathaniel rose, placing his palms up in a gesture of surrender. "We mean no harm, sir. We are traveling to Clobryn Nyth."

As the officer scanned the group, their eyes lingered on Torque, suspicion in his gaze.

"We don't accept vagabonds or refugees in Elyra." Then, turning toward Torque, added, "And we hang bandits on the spot."

"Please, we are not bandits nor refugees," Nathaniel implored. A heavy silence hung in the air, intensifying the scene as the officer weighed his options.

Allai'nn stepped forward and, head held high, said, "Officer, I am Princess Allai'nn from Serensith Talem. And this is Prince Blue Ivy of the Heart Wood," pointing to Blue. "Bandits attacked us during our travels and wounded our companion. We search for help in the capital."

Astor added, "And I am Prince Astor of the Whispering Haven. I must speak with King Goldbriar."

"Royals, huh?" the officer said, rubbing his chin. "You don't look the part."

The sound of chuckles from the other troopers filled the air. The officer continued, "Until I can be sure of your identity, you're under arrest. Bind their hands, except for the women, so they can care for the infants," the officer commanded. "And seize that skiff."

The elves swiftly landed and bound the brotherhood's hands behind them, securing an additional rope around their waists to keep them connected.

The troop followed seven elves as they walked along the riverbank, pulling the skiff behind them, eventually stopping at a small wooden dock. Meanwhile, three elves flew in wide ellipses from above, watchful for danger or a prisoner escape.

Secured to the pier, a thirty-foot river sloop bobbed up and down with the river current, tapping like a woodpecker against the wooden jetty. The elf guards stowed the prisoners on board, released the bow and stern lines, and pushed the boat away from the dock. As the boat drifted along with the river's powerful current, two elves used the chance to hoist the main sail. With a sudden jolt, the wind filled the sail, catapulting the craft forward as Captain Lynx steered at the tiller. After several hours under the scorching morning sun, Lynx steered the ship around a dogleg turn to the river.

"Coming about," yelled Lynx, tacking the boat across the river to make the curve.

As the ship's boom swung across and the sail filled, Jacoby couldn't help but exclaim, "Look at that!"

All eyes instinctively shifted toward the south, captivated by the first glimpse of Clobryn Nyth. From afar, a grand palace constructed with stained wood emerged, seemingly growing out of a cluster of towering hardwoods. Hundreds of smaller treehouses, connected by rope bridges, surrounded the structure like an intricate web woven by a long-extinct giant spider.

"It's stunning," Rue said with a gasp. "I hear my cousin's voices from those trees."

"As you should," Captain Lynx said. "Several oreads sacrificed their homes for King Goldbriar's great-great-grandfather to build the palace. Many still live within the city's forest."

As the sunlight hit the polished palace walls, a kaleidoscopic rainbow danced before the eyes of the onlookers, leaving them in awe. Nathaniel took notice of the limited number of jetties in the capital as Lynx skillfully maneuvered the ship into the city wharf, realizing they were less than a third of what Mar Napor had. The slips were mostly empty, with only a few sloops and barges docked.

Once the boat secured, the elves led the captives up a long, inclined gangway, ending in the trunk of an enormous tree spanning two hundred paces in width. Carved into the center of the trunk stood a colossal gate and portcullis, bordered by two guardhouses. A muscular sergeant stepped out and saluted Captain Lynx.

"Take the women and children to the nursery under guard. Escort the other prisoners to the palace dungeon for safekeeping until I can report the matter," he commanded after returning the salute.

"Yes, Captain," responded the elf, taking the rope from Lynx. "Follow me. And no acting out, or you'll be sorry."

"Wait! We aren't prisoners. I told you before, I'm Prince Astor," screeched Astor in a panicked voice.

"Right. You can sort that out with Chamberlain Mydir," responded Lynx. "Until then, you'll wait in the dungeon with all the prisoners."

The sergeant yanked hard on the rope, making Astor stumble and fall. He kicked the prince hard in the stomach. "Get up, you oaf!" he chortled with another guard who came to help. Nathaniel, behind him, helped him to his feet and whispered, "It will get sorted, and there will be hell to pay. Until then, keep your mouth shut."

Astor, with tears in his eyes, nodded while hugging his stomach. The elves escorted the prisoners through the gate and up a steep slope, passing through residential areas, shops, and markets until they arrived at a massive iron door at the palace's foundation. The sergeant rapped twice, and the door swung open, revealing a descent into darkness, only lit by sporadic wall torches. Jacoby and Nat, lacking Twilight vision, struggled to stay upright as they descended the barely visible path in semi-darkness. After a quarter hour, they reached a level hallway with two bolted cells on each side. The guards split the group in half, pushing them into large communal cells. Inside, multiple prisoners of all races sat dejectedly along the wall. Nathaniel, Blue, Torque, and a hobbling Horatio stepped into the darkness and found an empty spot along the far wall.

Nathaniel turned to the captive beside him, a middle-aged human with brown, unwashed curls and wearing a tattered uniform.

"What's your name, friend?" Nathaniel asked.

The human looked up and said, "Colonel Devin Ashoke," offering his hand.

Nathaniel took it, "Nathaniel. Where do you hail from?"

Surprise washed over Ashoka's face. "I'm Taborian."

"Good to meet you, Devin. How are things going in Tabor?"

"Honestly? Horrific," Devin said, sadness reflected in his eyes. "We'd need Thor incarnate to turn the tide."

"That serious?"

Devin nodded. "That's why I'm here. To beg King Goldbriar for help. But the outer guard arrested me, and I have yet to speak to the king."

Nathaniel nodded, understanding he was in the same predicament.

"And you?"

"My companions and I were traveling to the City of Spires when we ran afoul of changeling bandits. We escaped, only to be captured by an Elyran patrol."

Devin's face betrayed his confused amazement. "Are you mad? What in Curth Talem could move you to travel to the City of Spires during a war? The Taborian council has voted to evacuate the city except for men 15-70!"

"I have a valid reason which might solve that issue."

Devin's eyes went wide. "What reason?"

But before Nathaniel could answer, the cell door swung open, and Jacoby was pushed into the dim cell, the door locked behind him.

"By the Gods," Devin exclaimed, his eyes widening in disbelief. In the soft light, he squinted, and a smile spread across his face as he recognized the tall human. "Captain Jacoby?"

The tall warrior abruptly halts, his gaze fixed on the man beside Nathaniel. After a few heartbeats, his eyes widen in surprise. "Devin?" Jacoby rushes over excitedly, his hand extending eagerly for a firm shake, a wide grin stretching from one ear to the other. "Devin Ashoke! I can't believe it!"

"Nor I! I thought you'd gone down in the Giant onslaught years ago," Devin said, pumping his hand enthusiastically. "Where have you been?"

Jacoby ignored the question, introducing Nathaniel, Blue Ivy, Cor'in, and Torque.

Devin shook each being's offered hand but eyed Torque suspiciously before tentatively accepting the muscular orc's plate-sized hand. The hesitancy didn't go unnoticed, so Nathaniel said, "Fear not. I vouch for Torque."

Devin turned his gaze back to Jacoby. "What happened to you? You were at our head, leading the first cohort into the enemy line. I could see King Aarmon by your side, his white steed trampling the enemy like ants. I never saw you or the king alive again."

The warmth of Jacoby's smile vanished, replaced by a chilling aura that settled upon his face, foretelling impending danger. "It's a long story, and one I'm not proud to tell."

Sensing the temperature drop suddenly in the room, Devin sat, waiting for the explanation.

"But how have you been? Up in rank since the days I commanded you as a corporal," Jacoby said, deflecting to another subject.

Devin's eyes narrowed, knowing Jacoby hid the truth.

"I'm a colonel now, head of a new division."

"Interesting. What division?"

"The division of Special Affairs, created recently to handle foreign affairs," Devin said robotically as if a trained answer. "So, tell me the truth," he said, his penetrating stare boring into the tall human. "Where have you been?"

Jacoby looked away, but Nathaniel came to his rescue. "Excuse me for butting in, but what does 'Special Affairs' really mean?"

Devin gazed at Nathaniel, concluding the younger man was sharp as a knife's edge. "I'll tell you if you explain your trip to the besieged Taborian capital."

"Fair enough," Nathaniel said. "You start."

Devin frowned, sensing he had somehow lost his advantage. "Special Affairs division is based on espionage."

"That sounds nefarious. Can you break it down?"

Devin sighed. "With comprehensive information on enemies and allies, I can utilize my knowledge to strengthen Tabor's defense. In addition, I serve as a personal emissary for the council, representing them in other lands. In this case, I am sincerely imploring Elyra for her help," Devin said, folding his arms. "Now, your turn."

Jacoby glanced at Nathaniel, giving him a nod to proceed.

"During the last battle against the giant army, Jacoby was called urgently to the palace by a dying Queen Elana. She had just given birth to a son, her birth complicated by relentless hemorrhaging. She implored Jacoby, her closest protector and friend, to take her newborn to safety before the city fell. Despite his duty to the King, he felt a stronger allegiance to the Queen and agreed to raise and protect her son."

Nathaniel paused, allowing the news to soak in. Devin's face became a canvas of emotions as surprise, anger, sadness, and resignation played across his features. The poor man's emotions were like a wild storm, his face transitioning from a flushed pink to a blazing fire red, finally settling into a hauntingly pale gray. He understood the man's turmoil all too well - the heavy weight in his heart and the restless thoughts that plagued his mind. A year ago, he had experienced the same news, and now, the memory would occasionally resurface, stirring up a tornado of pain in his heart.

As Nathaniel spoke, he couldn't help but notice Torque inch closer, his inscrutable face betraying nothing as he leaned forward to catch every word.

"After the city bells tolled, alerting the world to Elana's death," the prince continued. "Pandemonium took over the city. Jacoby used the opportunity, with the child's wet nurse, Maire, to secret the boy away. Seeking a fresh beginning, the young refugee family made their home in the tranquil hamlet of Streamside in the Halfling lands. Jacoby purchased a deserted property and transformed the dilapidated estate into a flourishing inn. He and Maire, until her death, raised the boy in peace and anonymity until last year. That's when Ravenite's army launched a surprise attack on the region, massacring and pillaging. Jacoby and a small group of friends narrowly escaped."

Nathaniel paused, realizing the story had burst out like an internal tsunami.

"And?" Asked Torque's deep, gravelly voice.

"Unbeknownst to the group, the evil sorcerer knew the prince lived, sending wave after wave of assassins to kill him. By Odin's grace, Jacoby's strategic wit, and providence, most survived. But the journey was long and harrowing, leading us across the continent's width, north to Serensith Talem, south to Tajman Sghur, and west across the Bleak Waste; our group survived and even picked up a few fresh faces."

Devin relaxed, sitting back, his eyes closed. "An astounding tale," he murmured. "But why come back now? Tabor is in ruin, and the entire west is under siege."

Jacoby interjected, saying, "We've been trying to return for almost a year. It's time to reunite Tabor with its one true king."

Life sparked behind Devin's eyes, leaning forward again. "You mean the prince lives?"

With a gesture, Jacoby indicated Nathaniel, who then exposed his clover-shaped birthmark by moving his hair aside. Devin's eyes bulged, and he gasped, "I... I can't believe it!"

"I know this whole mess is a shock, Devin," Jacoby said. "But we could use your help."

"Help?" Devin mumbled, still rocked by the revelation.

"Are there any surviving members of the old guard, men who remain loyal to the royal line in Tabor?"

"Some. Despite many deaths, a core still exists," he said cautiously, narrowing his eyes.

"Can you send word to them to meet at the Horn River bridge in the coming days? I think it's wise to garner support after so many years before entering the City of Spires," Jacoby asked.

The tall warrior studied Devin for a long moment, gauging his reaction. He remembered the colonel from years past. He had picked Devin to join his elite troop for his intelligence and cunning strategic mind. And he had not disappointed, rising from private to corporal in the year before Jacoby vanished. If he agrees, he will be an invaluable partner for Nathaniel in the future. He held his breath, waiting for the officer's response.

Rather than answering, Devin shifted his attention to Nathaniel. He studied the young prince intently, as if he had unexpectedly discovered a priceless historical text and understood it completely. Unexpectedly, he knelt and bowed to Nathaniel. "I pledge my loyalty to you, Nathaniel, the one true king of Tabor."

TWENTY

Jacoby's sleep was restless, his guilt haunting his dreams like an evil succubus. The same haunting dream that had tormented him for an entire year since he left Streamside resurfaced once more. The dream always began the same way. Jacoby stood at the door of an ancient log cabin deep in a wood of evergreens heavy with new-fallen snow. He was naked and freezing, his teeth chattering so hard his jaw hurt. He rapped at the door with three heavy knocks and waited. A woman in her twenties normally opened the wooden door and ushered him toward the fire, but not tonight. The cabin door opened to a heavy shadow, split only by the light from a crackling fire.

As he stepped inside, his eyes were drawn to the comforting sight of the old witch in her rocker beside the crackling fire, rocking gently like a pendulum. She wore a heavy shawl, pulled up over her head for added protection from the chilly air.

"Hello, Old One," he said.

"Hello, my warrior."

Jacoby's eyes widened, the greeting triggering a vivid memory from the past. A single thought rocketed through his brain: It can't be her!

Then, the figure lowered her shawl, revealing the decaying features of Queen Elana.

"So good of you to visit Jacoby. How long has it been? Oh, yes, since our rendezvous at the Sleeping Dragon Inn."

Dumbfounded, Jacoby stood frozen in disbelief. Just before an enemy giant attacked the inn, the Queen sent him a warning through a vivid dream.

"Cat got your tongue? No matter. I'm here to remind you of your promise. Until now, you've ensured my son's safety. But danger seems to follow you and your friends like a shadow in high sun," the Queen said, chuckling. "In Tabor, a different threat awaits you."

As the queen pulled Jacoby close, the noxious smell of her breath made him feel sick to his stomach. "Beware, my warrior, of the serpent that hides behind the cloak of friendship."

Then, a slimy black snake's tongue emerged from her decaying teeth and caressed his face. Jacoby screamed and bolted upright, his heart pounding in his chest. In a panic, he jerked his head from side to side, startled by the sensation of Sinbad's wet tongue on his cheek. He sighed deeply, feeling the tension leave his body as he embraced the hound in a tight hug. "Good boy, Sinbad," he whispered as he nuzzled his face into the soft fur of the hellhound, feeling his heart rate gradually slowing with each breath.

Jacoby rose to his feet to find Torque awake, studying the sleeping group.

"Nightmare? I considered waking you, but feared you might think you were being attacked," Torque said.

"No worries," Jacoby responded, bending to stretch the kinks out, then sitting next to the orc. "May I ask you a question?"

The orc gazed at him without expression.

"You've overheard my history, but I know little about yours. Will you tell me more about your background?"

Torque hesitated, his face inscrutable. "My history is unimportant. Returning to my homeland remains my priority."

"Why? What's so urgent?"

"As with you and Nathaniel, Destiny calls," he growled, his voice filled with bitterness, before abruptly walking away without another word.

Not long after, Jacoby's ears picked up the distinct sound of heavy boots echoing on the wooden floor, accompanied by the growing illumination of torchlight. The gate swung open, revealing the same two guards, followed by an older elf with a crown of white hair. Draped in a lengthy blue coat atop a cream-colored tunic and breeches, his flowing snow-white beard reaching his chest sharply contrasted with the coat's dark blue color.

"Where are they?" demanded the graybeard, eyes scanning the cell.

A guard stepped inside and timidly pointed his arm towards Nathaniel and the others.

Graybeard stepped into the gloomy cell, waited a moment for his eyes to adjust, and then directed his attention to the group of captives. He frowned as he noticed Prince Astor, then focused on Blue Ivy.

"Prince Blue Ivy? I apologize for the treatment given to you and your friends. Chamberlain Mydir, at your service," he said in a surprisingly robust tenor voice, giving Blue Ivy a small bow.

Blue rose to his feet and bowed when Astor pushed by, almost knocking Blue to the ground.

"I am Prince Astor of Whispering Haven and demand an audience with King Goldbriar," he insisted in a rushed, breathless tone.

Mydir sighed, his brow crossing in anger. "I know who you are, sir. I will make an exception and forgive your rude interruption this time," the chamberlain barked, his brow furrowed irritably at Astor.

"But I...," Astor started again, before Mydir shut him down with an iron stare. He turned to the guards. "Place Prince Astor in the private holding room where he can await an audience with King Goldbriar."

Then, turning to Astor said, "You may await your audience with the king there."

The two guards rushed in, each taking an arm, and forcefully dragged Astor out and down the hall.

"Wait, wait..." Astor pleaded, but his voice stopped abruptly when one guard stuffed a dirty rag in the prince's mouth. A thud, then a loud slam, followed by the sound of jingling keys, sliced the dungeon air, then boot steps back to the cell entrance.

"Please forgive me," Mydir said apologetically. "I have zero patience for pretentious nags who rudely insert themselves where they don't belong."

"Now," he exclaimed, smiling and rubbing his hands together eagerly. "Will you and your group accompany me?" The chamberlain gestured with one arm toward the cell door. Blue looked at Nathaniel, who shrugged and gestured with a jerk of his head.

Blue led the way, followed by Nathaniel, Jacoby, Torque, Devin, and Cor'in, supporting the injured Horatio. They trudged out, ignoring the guards, down the long hallway and made an abrupt left at the stair bottom. There, Mydir pressed on one of the wooden wall panels, which gave way to open into a torch-lit tunnel.

"This is a shortcut, not meant for everyone, but I'd like to get you to your rooms quickly."

"Rooms?" Blue asked.

"Of course. King Goldbriar insists you stay in the palace as long as you'd like as his special guests."

"What about our other friends?" asked Nathaniel, concerned.

"Princess Allai'nn and the rest of your group await you in your apartments," he said.

As Mydir exerted pressure on one panel, a secret door swung open, unveiling a vast rectangular room. The fragrance of old books permeated the air, as bookcases spanning from floor to ceiling adorned all four walls, displaying an impressive collection of tomes and books.

"This way," he said, gesturing with his hand to follow. "The King's library is quite extensive," he remarked, noting Blue and Nathaniel's greedy eyes lingering on the countless leather-bound volumes, their gold lettering gleaming under the soft lamplight. "Feel free to borrow a book or two if you'd like."

"Thank you," Nathaniel said, running his hand over several of the titles before pulling out, "Ancient Sylph History."

Mydir crossed the library and moved down a wide hallway. Every fifty paces, a polished wooden door gleamed from each side. He stopped at the door at the end of the hall.

"Your apartments, gentlemen," the chamberlain announced, his knuckles rapping loudly on the door three times.

Grullach Fur opened the door, a broad smile blooming on his face.

"Odin's beard!" He rushed over, hugging each member. "I feared you might have been lost in that dark dungeon labyrinth."

"Good to see you too," Jacoby said.

"King Goldbriar wishes to celebrate your visit. I will send an attendant to escort you to the feast this evening. Until then, please enjoy the hot spring baths and rest," Mydir said, bowing and closing the door behind him.

Moments later, Lani and Rue burst into the room, engulfing Nathaniel and Blue in tight hugs and showering them with kisses.

"Hard not to feel left out," Jacoby said to Torque and Devin. Both chuckled.

"Nothing like romance to fill the soul," Devin mumbled, moving into the main common space and retrieving an apple from the copious fruit plate on the center table. Private rooms opened like spokes on a wheel from the shared area, with enough room for the entire group.

After introducing Devin to the Brotherhood members, everyone retired to their rooms for baths and rest.

Allai'nn appeared from her bedroom, her golden locks covered in a towel twist. "There are new clothes in your bedrooms and warm baths, too. I had to estimate your size, Torque, so I hope they fit."

"Thank you, my lady," he said and, with a slight bow, retreated into his bedchamber.

"Doesn't say much, does he?" Grull noted. Jacoby agreed and nodded. Who was this mysterious orc? Had he connected and traveled with the group solely for his gain? Or was there more to this picture? Jacoby wondered, but truth be told, it had nothing to do with his mission to reach and save Tabor.

In the evening, a young page guided Torque, Devin, and the Brotherhood to the king's dining hall, lit by flickering candlelight. The space had elegant furnishings, including a grand mahogany table that extended the entire length, providing ample seating for all, and then some. Moments later, the far-end door opened, and a middle-aged elf escorting a handsome red-haired lady strode in, followed by lovely younger women and several court royals.

Goldbriar halted before the Brotherhood and grinned broadly. "Welcome, friends!" the king said, nodding to each member. "I am honored to welcome you all to Clobryn Nyth, especially Princess Allai'nn, and Prince Blue Ivy; your presence graces our humble halls."

Allai'nn curtsied and said, "Thank you, King Goldbriar. Let me introduce my companions. Cor'in Virdis, Count of Oyster, Lady Rue, daughter of the mother of Oreads, Byrgid, Lady Lani Belial, Horatio of Anura, Jacoby Ironfist, Colonel Devin of Tabor, Nathaniel Aarmon and Torque of the Black Mountains."

Goldbriar extended a welcoming handshake to everyone, pausing briefly to lock eyes with Jacoby and Torque, as if trying to gauge their character.

Goldbriar's voice rang out with joviality as he introduced his family. "My wife, Queen Marian, my daughter, Princess Laurel. I extend a warm welcome to each of you in our humble abode. Please sit and enjoy!"

Jacoby's breath caught in his throat as he locked eyes with Princess Laurel, her fiery red hair framing her stunning features. In my dreams, she appeared as the woman who led me to Mother Norn and became my savior in the barren and lifeless Bleak Waste. I can't believe it! He stood there, dumbfounded, like a schoolboy who had just laid eyes on his first crush, his heart pounding. Cascading waves of auburn hair brushed against Laurel's creamy-white complexion, a button nose, high cheekbones, and cherry-red lips completed the most beautiful face Jacoby had ever seen. A stunning burgundy gown, the color of red wine, hugged her voluptuous figure, its silk whispering against her skin, taking his breath away. However, he found himself mesmerized by her eyes—pools of deep mystery, like the green ocean waves before an impending storm. They possessed a hidden strength beneath their captivating beauty.

Laurel couldn't take her eyes off the warrior's broad shoulders and powerful arms; a blush crept onto her cheeks as a shy smile touched her lips. The room fell into an awkward silence as everyone realized the two were still standing, even after the king and queen had taken their seats. Allai'nn waited for a few heartbeats before reaching out and touching Jacoby's arm, causing him to turn towards her. She spoke softly, "Why don't you sit down and have a chat with her?"

The moment her hand grazed the tall man it felt like a sudden shock of electricity. He dropped into his seat, his face turning as red as a sunburn.

Nathaniel clinked his wineglass and stood. "Thank you, King Goldbriar and Queen Marion, for your gracious hospitality. To the royal couple!" He lifted his glass, followed by the entire company.

The table overflowed with a lavish feast of cooked mutton, roast hog, and various colorful vegetable fruits, each dish bursting with exquisite flavors. Minstrels played a chorus of lovely lute, guitar, and harp tunes, filling the dining hall with soft, relaxing melodies.

Laurel sat across at one end of the table from Jacoby, but the two constantly stole desirous glances at one another. Nathaniel conversed with the royalty while keeping one eye on his brother. The intensity with which Jacoby stared at the woman caught him off guard; he had never seen such longing in his brother's eyes. *Is there a reason for me to feel concerned? Or be ecstatic he found someone who caught his interest?* He felt a storm of emotions in his chest, unable to understand why Jacoby's actions bothered him. He looked at Grull, his halfling eyes reflecting the same emotional tumult Nathaniel felt in his heart. *I will address the issue later in private.*

Following dinner, the king cordially invited the men to the library. The women made their way to the nursery to check on the infants before proceeding to the sewing room for conversation and needlepoint.

Goldbriar sat in his favorite plush, high-backed chair before the enormous fireplace and poured himself a brandy from the snifter on a side table.

"Please, enjoy," he said, motioning with his hand at the spirits. After everyone had a glass, he relaxed and addressed the group.

"So, I've gleaned some bits and pieces of your history from our dinner conversations, but I'd like to hear more."

For the next twenty minutes, Jacoby recounted the adventurous travels of the Brotherhood, occasionally answering Goldbriar's questions. When he finished, the king stroked his beard. "That's quite a tale, Jacoby. And you're telling me Nathaniel here is the heir to the Taborian throne?"

"No, Your Majesty. Nathaniel is the rightful king, and I have proof," he said, motioning for Nathaniel to reveal his birthmark.

King Goldbriar's lips formed a firm line as he surveyed the mark before him. With a heavy sigh, he leaned back in his chair, his eyes fluttering shut as he sought a moment of respite. The king's silence stretched on for what felt like an eternity. Then he rose, pulling Nathaniel into a bear hug. "I must speak with you and Jacoby alone," he whispered.

Then aloud, "Congratulations, my boy!" as tears welled in his eyes.

"Damnable chimney smoke," he muttered, wiping his eyes with his cuff.

Then he turned his attention to Devin, changing course. "But where do you and friend Torque come in?"

"I first met Jacoby in the Taborian army almost twenty years ago, Your Majesty. But we haven't seen each other until today."

"I don't understand," Goldbriar said, confused.

"I came here to speak with you on a mission from the Taborian council."

Goldbriar furrowed his brow. "Under what pretenses?"

"Ravenite has called upon the undead to join his forces. If Tabor doesn't receive aid, it will collapse, exposing the entirety of Curth Talem's west coast," Devin replied.

Goldbriar's face went pale and his eyes bugged. "Impossible. Only a sorcerer of immense power could arrange such an alliance with a demon!" Almost shouting the words, spittle flying.

"I can only relate what I know, Your Majesty. Tabor needs help from their neighbors to survive," Devin implored.

"I will confer with the Elven Council immediately, Devin," the redness in his face receding. "We will talk again soon."

He looked at the orc who observed the group and absorbed the news without expression.

"What is your story, friend Torque?"

"I come from a simple existence in the Black Mountains, Your Majesty. My only goal is to return forthwith."

A hint of intrigue crossed Goldbriar's face when he locked eyes with Torque. A flicker of understanding crossed his face as he nodded, hinting at the untold story lurking beneath his stoic demeanor.

"Well, gentleman, it's grown late, and I tire more easily as I age." He rang a silver bell from his chair, and an attendant entered.

"How may I serve, Your Majesty?" said the butler, a stout elf in a dark green household uniform.

"Rodney, please escort my guests back to their rooms and ask Sergeant Nils to step in," said Goldbriar, "Jacoby, may I have a private word with you and Nathaniel?"

While the others dutifully followed the butler, Torque hesitated, his eyes locked onto the king briefly before he exited. As their eyes met, a silent understanding exchanged before the orc shut the door behind him.

Nathaniel observed the link and inquired, "Have you previously encountered Torque, Your Highness?"

"No, but I know of him. Despite his icy demeanor, he is an important figure in the Black Mountain Orc community," the king said.

"Are the orcs hostile?" Jacoby asked.

"Neutral, although their leadership seems currently under transition."

"Hard to know which side they might support—Tabor or Ravenite," Goldbriar said as if reading the human's mind.

Then he turned his attention to Nathaniel.

"Young man, you may know I raised your mother, Queen Elana. Although my ward, I loved her like my child." Goldbriar paused, searching Nathaniel's eyes for recognition. He grasped Nathaniel's hand, his eyes clouded by wistful sadness. "I adored Elana, and my heart shattered at her passing. I can see much of her spirit in your face and mannerisms," he said, lightly caressing the young man's cheek.

Abruptly, the king's countenance grew serious, his lips forming a grave and somber line. With a fierce glint of iron, Goldbriar fixed his gaze on the prince, erasing all cheerfulness and leaving behind only the stern creases of age, like scars earned from years of combat.

"Nathaniel, I recognize you've been through horrendous trials since leaving your home. But," he cautioned, "the challenges ahead will make your past battles pale in comparison. You will face vipers under every political bush in the Taborian capital, waiting to strike at the first sign of weakness. In addition, the evils pushing south under Ravenite's command will strike like a tidal wave. It is crucial to never underestimate the capabilities and intentions of both acquaintances and foes. That is the hard truth of leadership."

The tension in Goldbriar's hand eased as he let go of the younger man's grip, relaxing as he sat back in his chair and a smile crossed his face. "However, forget these troubles for the next few days and enjoy my humble abode. My home is your home."

As Nathaniel sighed, he could feel the tightness in his neck and back finally easing, like the relaxing of taut lute strings. "Your Majesty, I am immensely grateful," he said, his voice filled with reverence. "I think it's time for me to retreat to my bed for some much-needed rest. Good evening."

When Nathaniel had departed, Goldbriar turned his attention to Jacoby. "So, the once mighty leader of Elana's palace guard transformed overnight into an on-the-run felon, new father, and tavern keeper. I would never have believed such a tale if Friend and Traveler had not revealed the truth," he said, shaking his head in astonishment. "And now? Twenty years later, you arrive with the screwball plan to reinstate that lad as the true king? I wonder if you realize the madness of such a foolhardy endeavor?"

Jacoby stood frozen in place, his mouth hanging open in astonishment. "I..." His throat felt dry, and his mind spun like a cyclone after the king's words hit him like a powerful blow to the jaw. Regaining his bearing, Jacoby said, "If Ravenite hadn't sent an assassin to Streamside, I would have waited to reveal his true identity. But destiny intervened."

Goldbriar's eyes narrowed, a mix of amusement and skepticism, as he observed Jacoby's discomfort. "Destiny?" Goldbriar scoffed, his face twisted in angry frustration. "Tabor's ruling council is in turmoil, with a depleted military and the population facing starvation. Do you think that Nathaniel's ascension to the throne of Tabor will miraculously turn a depleted, ill-equipped army into an unstoppable force that can annihilate Ravenite?"

Jacoby gritted his teeth, his mind no longer reeling but filled with unyielding determination. "Yes, I do. Nathaniel has his father's gift for leadership and his mother's passion for the common people. If anyone can succeed, even in these trying times, it would be him."

Goldbriar frowned, considering his words.

"With Nathaniel at their head, and with the backing of Tabor's allies, their likelihood of triumph grows considerably." Jacoby's voice filled with defiance as he clarified, "By allies, I mean Elyra and the entire Elven Council. Although Nathaniel is too humble to ask, I plead with you to support him."

Goldbriar eyed Jacoby for several long heartbeats, studying the tall human. Then he said, "I can't promise Elven support. But I will personally speak with Polaris and the other council members on your behalf."

Jacoby remained silent. Goldbriar's response was no answer at all. He hated politics and refused to embroil himself in the endeavor. But he knew in his heart that Nathaniel's presence would inject energy into the Taborian defense. Would it be enough? No. Tabor could not stop Ravenite and his minions without silver weapons and reinforcements. Why, in Odin's name, didn't Goldbriar understand the importance of Elven support?

As Jacoby locked eyes with the king, his heart pounded with frustration. "I am completely worn out from my travels," he said through gritted teeth. "Your Majesty, may I be excused?" Ignoring any response, he bowed and left, the door slamming forcefully behind him.

After Jacoby departed, Chamberlain Mydir and Sergeant Nils bowed and entered from a side door.

"Did you catch any of our conversations?" Goldbriar asked.

"One could hardly miss the loud voices, Your Grace," replied Mydir.

Goldbriar had known Mydir since childhood, and they had been lifelong friends. He relied on his wise counsel and his uncanny ability to gather useful information. Nils became captain of his palace guard after saving the king's life several centuries before when a pack of wild boars had attacked their hunting group. Goldbriar leaned on the two elves for their loyalty and sound advice.

"And your thoughts?"

Sergeant Nils interjected before Mydir spoke.

"I hazily recall Jacoby from years ago, during my regiment's visit to Tabor," Nils said. "Queen Elana held him in high esteem."

Elena. The name still pierced the king's heart, even twenty years later.

"And?" Goldbriar said gruffly, his grief turning to irritation.

He knew his ward's death was an inexplicable horror, a premature loss of such a warm and intelligent spirit. But the wound to his heart had never completely healed, leaving him with the unanswerable question—why? Why had she died so young? Why had he been impotent to help?

Now, at the sight of Jacoby and Nathaniel, his loss and anger came rushing back, violent and overwhelming. Whether innocent or guilty, the emotional tornado he felt would engulf anyone connected to her death. Why hadn't Jacoby saved her? Was he complicit in her death? After so much time, how could he bring Elana's son here? The fool human must be either mad or vengeful to perform such a hateful act! Didn't he realize Nathaniel had her piercing gaze, noble spirit, and love of life? Could he be so blind? Everything about the lad reminded him of the cherished child he'd lost. Goldbriar slammed his fist on the table, then kicked it hard, toppling it over.

He caught his reflection in the mirror, his face scarlet, his brow beaded with sweat. One look, and he realized he'd lost control. He slumped back into his chair, taking deep, rapid breaths to slow his pounding heart and refocus on the present.

Nils chose his words carefully, understanding the abrupt change in the king's demeanor.

"His survival over the last years proves his excellence as a warrior and strategist," the officer said. "I can't imagine transversing the continent in the middle of a war and surviving, much less while being chased by assassins. Their group must be unique and fortunate."

"And what about you, Mydir? You've always been a shrewd judge of character."

The chamberlain's voice was a gentle, comforting whisper. "I believe Jacoby flawlessly executed his duty, fully aware that he would have to live a fabricated existence as a Taborian outlaw for the rest of his adulthood. Despite facing immense challenges, he consistently fulfilled his obligation of raising the Queen's son in obscurity, prioritizing his safety above all else."

The king frowned, considering the point for several heartbeats. Then asked, "And the young prince?"

Mydir spoke, his voice laced with sadness. "He has the fire of Queen Elana in his veins; I can see the best of her reflected in his spirit."

"As astute as ever," remarked the king, looking away, his eyes moist with grief.

"As far as the others," Nils added, anticipating the king's next question. "I haven't met a single one who isn't intently loyal and protective of each other, especially Nathaniel. They have forged a rare bond."

Goldbriar mulled over the words of his closest advisors for several moments.

"What is your advice concerning aiding Tabor?"

Nils and Mydir locked eyes briefly, then Mydir said, "His reign will be short-lived without Elven support. I expect Polaris knows this and may have already broached the issue with the council.”

“Perhaps.”

Goldbriar went silent for several minutes until Mydir said, “Sire, there is one other issue?”

“Yes?” Goldbriar asked.

“Prince Astor remains in the solitary holding cell.”

“What? The son of King Topper of Whispering Haven?”

“The same, your grace. He caused a terrible upheaval, and I thought it best to cool his arrogance for a few hours.”

Goldbriar gave Mydir a stern look. “That is not how we treat royalty in Elyra, no matter how ridiculous a pop-in-jay.”

“I apologize, Your Grace. Shall I have him brought in?”

Goldbriar sighed. The last thing he needed was the headache of dealing with a young, arrogant royal, especially the son of a close ally.

“Place him in the executive suite, ply him with wine, and surround him with beautiful attendants. I’m sure that will take the sting from his time in the dungeon. Provide a soothing bath and bring him to me in one hour.”

“Yes, Your Grace.” Mydir and Nils exited, leaving Goldbriar to his memories.

An hour later, a revitalized and tipsy Astor knocked on the library door and then entered. He found King Goldbriar sitting beside the fire, conversing with Mydir in low tones.

Upon seeing Astor, Goldbriar rose, extending his hand to Astor. “Welcome, Prince Astor! And how is my friend, King Topper? Well, I trust?”

“Not well, Your Majesty,” Astor said tartly. “But better than what I’ve experienced. I’ve been waiting for hours!”

“Yes. I must apologize for my over-zealous guardsmen. The war in Tabor has even the most low-ranking soldiers on edge,” Goldbriar said, motioning for Astor to sit. The gangly elf took the chair opposite the king. Mydir hovered quietly behind his king like a life-size Elven vulture studying carrion.

“Mydir, bring Prince Astor a brandy for his frazzled nerves.”

“Immediately, Your Grace.”

With his back facing Astor, Mydir slipped a vial of white powder from his pocket, dumping it into the drink. He swirled the mixture, dissolving the addition, and handed it to the prince.

Astor downed the drink in one gulp, then extended the glass for another. Mydir filled the snifter and waited.

"So, what message are you here to deliver?" Goldbriar asked.

"Sir, my father's dedication to maintaining Whispering Haven as a seaport for elves seeking safety remains unwavering. However, the rumors circulating from the north and south deeply trouble him."

"Rumors?"

"First, that Ravenite has added undead to his army, intent on swarming and destroying the humans in Tabor."

"And the second?"

"Witnesses have observed dark elves in Mar Napor, speculating that they are an advanced force used to disrupt life there. Our intelligence suggests King Gooseberry has died, and his son Caron, a completely inexperienced youth, will take leadership."

"Are you implying that there have been sightings of Svartalfs in Mar Napor?" Mydir asked incredulously.

"Yes. As we speak, some think a horde of black devils is moving north."

"Unbelievable!" Goldbriar blurted, theatrically throwing his hands in the air. "I don't suppose Topper plans to send troops to either site in aid?"

Astor emphatically shook his head. "Never. We aim to remain an unrestricted port solely for the Elven community."

"What does your father need from us?"

"He suggests you evacuate Elyra and bring your troops and citizens to the safety of Whispering Haven."

Goldbriar's eyes went wide. He placed a firm hand on Astor's shoulder. "This news is deeply troubling, and I need to discuss it with my advisors. Thank your father for bringing this horrifying news to light," Goldbriar said seriously. "I will send word on our decision. Until then, please enjoy my hospitality and rest while here in Elyra."

"Thank you, Your Majesty. But..." the elf yawned, his head spinning. "I'm feesing so tired," Astor garbled, stumbling to his feet. He swayed, and his eyes closed, pitching into Captain Nil's waiting arms.

"Take him to the royal guest suite to sleep it off," Mydir ordered.

Nils signaled to two burly guardsmen who carried the prince out.

"That was subtle. Will he remember being drugged?"

"No, Your Majesty. He won't remember anything of his visit here by tomorrow. I suggest encouraging a return to Whispering Harbor forthwith, with our sincere thanks, Your Grace."

"Excellent plan, as always, Mydir," Goldbriar said, not giving Astor another thought. However, his revelation was far more troubling. Naturally, Polaris had informed him of the rumors a week earlier. But could they be true? And if so, how could the Elven council deal with such an enemy?

After several minutes, Mydir broke the silence.

"I wonder where Topper got his information? Is this just a fictitious tale to scare us in an attempt for Whispering Haven to gain recruits?"

"A concerning question. Let's hope for the latter. We have plenty of worries already," the king said seriously. Then he chuckled, shaking his head. "Topper has always been a self-serving prat. Only he would send his pompous son to order me to evacuate my land. Send Prince Astor packing by the fastest horse on the sunrise."

TWENTY-ONE

King Goldbriar sat out on his balcony, feeling the warmth of the first rays of the sun against his tired eyes. Drained from a sleepless night of anxious thoughts, exhaustion settled heavily upon him like a physical weight; his eyelids felt heavy, and his muscles ached. The question of how to assist young Nathaniel had been spinning in his head like a tumbleweed. He was only vaguely aware of a knock at the door. Someone cleared their throat from behind him, and he looked up into Mydir's eyes.

"Morning, Your Majesty," Mydir said, placing a tray with tea, cups, and fresh-baked muffins on the table beside the king. "I thought you might be hungry."

"I'm not hungry."

"Tea, then," Mydir said, his brow furrowed in concern. "Rough night?"

"I couldn't sleep."

"I understand, sire. There is a significant amount of distress in the world right now."

Goldbriar remained silent, looking off at the horizon.

"Sire, Nathaniel Aarmon is outside and would like to speak with you."

Goldbriar's eyes brightened, and he sat up in his chair. "Yes, show him in."

Mydir returned with Nathaniel. The young man bowed and said, "Good morning, Your Majesty. "

"Hello, Nathaniel. Tea or muffins?"

Nathaniel smiled. "No, thank you. However, I have a question I hope you can answer."

"Sit," Goldbriar said, motioning Nathaniel into a chair. "What can I do for you?"

Nathaniel handed the enchanted stone over to the king. "I found this at the bottom of a lake in the Horn Wood," Nathaniel said.

"Interesting," Goldbriar said, studying the stone closely.

"It may sound crazy, but I think it called to me," Nathaniel added hesitantly. "And it has some ancient writing on one side."

Goldbriar gave the younger man a dubious look and studied the stone. Years in the water had smoothed the stone, revealing no engravings or runes. "Are you sure this was the stone?"

"I'm positive I could see writing on the bottom when I held it underwater," Nathaniel said, reaching for the stone.

What happened next took Goldbriar and Mydir by surprise. The stone glowed upon the prince's touch, ancient runes burning into the stone. Staring in disbelief, Goldbriar carefully examined the words, his breath catching in his throat as he gasped. "By the Gods! Can it be?"

"What is it?" Nathaniel and Mydir blurted together.

"These runes are in an ancient tongue," he stated, his fingers brushing lightly across their weathered surface. "Their style suggests an origin in the earliest part of the First Age." The king rubbed his weary eyes and examined the stone again. His voice caught in his throat. "I...I believe this stone could be one of the Founder stones."

"Founder stones?" Nat asked. "I've never heard of them."

Goldbriar sat back, still gazing at the stone as if he'd found a rare insect. "After Odin and his brothers slew the giant Ymir and formed the world, he created the first inhabitants of Curth Talem," the king said. "Do you know the tale?"

"Most," Nathaniel said, struggling to remember the details of the myth. He recited the legend, his voice filled with the wisdom he had gained from years of studying with the Priest Guild. "Using an Elder tree, Odin shaped the first race of elves known as the Lakarians. He carefully mixed the twigs of an Ash tree with the soil, forming humans. Then he forged dwarves from the very rock of the mountains, imbued with strength and resilience, and so the creation continued until all the races and animals came into existence."

"Correct," added Mydir. "But I recollect there was more to the tale."

"Rightly so," said Goldbriar. "According to legend, Odin took the heart of a celestial star, shattered it into fragments, and bestowed each piece with magical powers, gifting one to every major race as a symbol of their bond with him. One gift he gave to the dwarves and another to the humans, but the elves, his cherished and original creation, received two. They became known as the Founder stones."

"Thor's beard!" Exclaimed Nathaniel, letting out a sudden burst of air, realizing he had been holding his breath in anticipation.

Goldbriar's face turned grave. "Odin linked each stone's enchantment to the first royal bloodline of each race, making this item both powerful and priceless. In this case, it belongs to the bloodline of Whitestar, the first human king of Tabor and your ancestor. It carries tremendous power, Nathaniel. Never, ever lose the stone, as your forbearers did." The king hesitated, letting the words soak in. "Regrettably, I can only discern a handful of the runes. This rune here," he said, pointing to the ancient stone writing, "strongly implies that it is a key. But to what? To fully understand the message, you must seek the guidance of someone older and more experienced than me."

He wearily handed the stone back to Nathaniel and sank into his chair, beads of sweat on his brow.

"Who do you recommend?" Nathaniel asked, wondering who could be older than Goldbriar. Although he appeared middle-aged, Nathaniel had learned from Blue Ivy earlier that the king was over a thousand years old.

"Few living might decipher the message. I suggest visiting the Sacred Wood and asking Friend for his help."

Nathaniel nodded, rolling the stone across his palm with his fingers, his thoughts rocketing through his brain like fireworks. What in Thor's name had he found, and why had it picked him? Did the blood of the first human king, Whitestar the Magnificent, flow through his veins? And what of the hidden runes that formed with his touch? Did that suggest some hidden power he had yet to discover? Or had Goldbriar exaggerated the stone's power and importance?

He expressed his appreciation and thanked the king, saying, "Thank you, your Majesty, for your help."

With determined strides, he rushed down the hallway, his heart pounding as he looked for the others to share the news.

Jacoby wandered through the vast gardens, relishing in the peaceful atmosphere that enveloped King Goldbriar's opulent palace of Clobryn Nyth. Throughout the night, he tossed and turned, his dreams haunted by vivid images of Princess Laurel. She had appeared in his dreams even before he reached the Sylph lands. First, she appeared as his guide to meet with Mother Norn. On another occasion, she had appeared again when he was on the brink of death, bitten by a venomous snake man in the scorching heat of the Bleak Waste desert. In the delirium from the poison, he had dreamed she tended to his wounds, soothing his pain with her gentle touch. He hadn't seen her in months, not since her last visit, and now, here she was. Her presence was overwhelming; he could only stare, his mouth dry, captivated like a lovesick teenager. He spent the whole evening tripping over his words, the silence between his fumbled phrases heavy with his embarrassment. *What a complete idiot I've been! I'm acting like a love-struck schoolboy. Pull yourself together, Jacoby!*

But since the feast, he'd not seen her, and each passing moment made his stomach twist. Worried thoughts ran over and over in his mind like a repeating story. *She's ignoring you. She feels nothing for you. To her, you're just another visiting warrior, nothing remarkable or special.* Jacoby's mind was so consumed with self-criticism that he didn't notice the princess until they collided.

"Oh, my!" Laurel said, surprised. The collision knocked her off her feet, and she landed on the soft grass with a thump.

"I'm so sorry, My lady," Jacoby said, his cheeks flushing crimson as he awkwardly offered his hand to the princess. "I can't believe I did that."

Laurel gave him a warm smile. "No harm done. I'm Laurel," she said, squeezing his hand.

"I'm...um...Jacoby," he stammered, his face a fiery red, a nervous tremor in his voice.

"I know you, Jacoby," she breathed. She gazed up at him through emerald green eyes, intelligent and penetrating.

"You know me?" Jacoby whispered, still embarrassed and a little ashamed. He could not admit the truth; she had dominated his thoughts for months.

The sylph tilted her head, her eyes narrowing. "Have you forgotten my visit's already?"

"I wasn't sure," he said, unable to break her gaze. "I'm unaccustomed to dreams of lovely princesses coming to my aid. I thought it might be the venom."

"Humans," she giggled, shaking her head. "Will you sit with me?"

Laurel guided Jacoby to a secluded alcove adorned with vibrant wisteria and pink bougainvillea, concealing a carved stone bench from prying eyes.

Her touch on Jacoby's hand was calming and reassuring as the elf requested, "Jacoby, will you share your history with me? I want to know everything about you."

The warrior's brow raised, and his heart pounded in his chest. *She wants to know about me!*

Normally quiet and reserved, Jacoby spoke freely as he shared his life story, starting from his humble beginnings in Narn. He recounted his time serving in the military in Tabor, the daring escape he made with Nathaniel to Streamside, his days as a tavern keeper and surrogate father, and the thrilling experiences he had with the Brotherhood over the past year and a half. It was as if he and Laurel had been lifelong friends. His story tumbled out, a torrent of words and emotions cascading like a waterfall. The entire time, Laurel's touch was gentle as she caressed his hand, her eyes sparkling and inviting, almost casting a spell that compelled him to share his deepest thoughts. Her thoughtful, insightful questions, delivered with a gentle warmth, showed genuine interest, her soft tone and kind eyes betraying no hint of judgment.

"And then, after escaping the Changelings, your father's outer patrol brought us here," Jacoby said.

A sly, knowing expression danced across Laurel's face, her lips curling into a mysterious smile, leaving Jacoby with a sense of being subtly played.

"What?" he asked before the answer dawned on him. "You knew."

"I know you, Jacoby Ironfist. Our meeting has long been bound by the threads of destiny."

"I don't understand."

"Centuries ago, Mother Norn selected you for this mission, fully aware of its importance."

"Is that so?" He questioned, his tone tinged with doubt. "And our meeting?"

"Let's call it a fortunate gift," Laurel said, smiling.

Jacoby's face squinched in confusion. His mind felt addled around this enchantress, and his heart pounded.

"What's your story?" he asked.

"My story is as dry as boot leather. I've never physically left Elyra."

"Surely a princess's life pales compared to a lowly warrior's."

"I'm not just a princess, but a Dreamwalker."

Jacoby's brows rose. "A Dreamwalker? Is that rare in the Sylphen bloodline?"

"Quite rare, and thus, I am used by the Norns and others as a messenger."

"I stupidly thought maybe you came to my dreams because... well, maybe there was some magical bond between us, not out of compulsion," Jacoby murmured, his voice barely a whisper, his energy draining like water seeping from a cracked pot. Standing with slumped shoulders, his face wore an expression of sad resignation.

"I enjoyed meeting you, Your Highness. But I must attend to other duties. Hopefully, your next visit will be to one more deserving."

After giving a subtle bow, he hurried away.

"Wait. I didn't mean it like that," Laurel said, her outstretched hand grasping at thin air as the human warrior disappeared.

Later that afternoon, Jacoby and Nathaniel stood on the Clobryn Nyth wharf, watching longshoremen loading dry goods aboard a royal catboat.

"We should be ready to leave within the hour," Jacoby said with a hint of sadness.

Nathaniel glanced at his brother. "What Is it?"

"Nothing," Jacoby growled, looking away.

"You mean the 'nothing' walking towards us down the jetty?" Nathaniel said, holding back a grin.

Lady Laurel and Captain Nils approached the two warriors. "Jacoby, Nathaniel, King Goldbriar begs a word before you go. Please follow me," Nils said, motioning for them to walk behind him. Nathaniel followed, with Jacoby trailing behind. Ignoring Laurel, the tall warrior kept walking until he felt a soft touch on his arm, causing him to pause.

"Afternoon," she said, smiling and looping her arm in his. "I wanted to apologize for earlier."

"Nothing to apologize for, Your Highness," Jacoby said stiffly, focusing his eyes straight ahead.

"But there is," she said, tugging on his arm for him to face her. "You misunderstood what I said earlier."

"I don't think so. Your meaning was clear."

Laurel shook her head. "I volunteered to meet with you because I had already envisioned you in my dreams."

Jacoby scowled, his eyes skeptical. "No need to lie, Your Highness."

Anger flashed across the Sylph's face. "I'm not lying, Jacoby."

The tall warrior arched a skeptical brow and remained silent as they continued walking. Laurel's brow furrowed a moment, then she said, "I can prove it."

"How?" Jacoby responded.

"I dreamed of a tall warrior, his mail shirt glistening as he peaked the crest of a hill on which stood an ancient Elder tree. You carried a carved wooden box in your pack," Laurel said, undeterred by Jacoby's doubt.

The tall warrior stopped short and turned to look at the princess in the eye. "If what you say is true, what did I hold in the box?" Jacoby demanded, fully aware that the answer was a closely guarded secret known only to the Brotherhood.

Without hesitating, Laurel said, "A green stone."

Jacoby's heart flipped, and his jaw fell open. Seeking refuge from bandits of the Fossil Wood, the group had climbed the hill months before and discovered solace under the Elder. The Oread's home offered them safety and much-needed respite. But how could she know? The uncertainty clouded his mind like a heavy fog. Was this woman a witch, harnessing ancient magic to shape her destiny? Or an innocent tool used at the whim of the Norns?

Before he could utter a word, Nathaniel's call from the palace entrance, his arms flailing to get their attention, shattered the moment.

"Hurry, Jacoby. The king is waiting," Nat yelled.

"Thank you," Jacoby uttered awkwardly before turning.

"Wait! My gift," Laurel cried, holding him in place. In his hand, she placed a small leather pouch. The warrior opened it, and the contents spilled out - a leather thong necklace in his hand. At the center, a robin's egg-sized stone of marbled blue. "Blue Lapis, the symbol of my house. For protection."

"Princess, thank you," he said, admiring the shimmering iridescent stone in the sunlight. "This is too grand a gift."

"Jacoby!" Nathaniel shouted once more; his voice filled with frustration.

Before Jacoby could continue, Laurel leaned in, rising onto her tiptoes, her wings fluttering. The meeting of their lips sent electrifying sparks through Jacoby's heart, merging them into a flawless union. They embraced for what felt like an eternity before he released her.

"Don't forget me," she asked in a breathless whisper.

"Never," he whispered, tightening his grip on her hand. Then, he quickly jogged to meet Nathaniel, leaving the princess all alone.

As Laurel watched him depart, she murmured a prayer of appreciation to Mother Norn for entrusting her with Jacoby's secret. His role in the upcoming battle for Tabor would be crucial. She vowed to reveal the truth eventually, but for now, she savored the quiet joy of reconnecting with Jacoby, feeling a warmth spread through her. The sight of Jacoby's ruggedly handsome face always made her heart leap; his tousled hair and chiseled features filled her with joy. His gentle and reserved personality amplified his charm. And, her attraction to a Dynol, a forbidden love that went against the traditions of the pure-blood Elves, only fueled her rebellious spirit.

"Logic be damned," Laurel whispered, her words barely audible. "I choose to bind my heart to Jacoby." For a split second, she questioned her choice, wondering why she had chosen him. Or did she? Perhaps the Norns influenced her heart more than she knew.

Shaking her head and murmuring, "My heart is my own," she strolled into the palace, a broad smile illuminating her face.

The two men stood before King Goldbriar, seated on his elevated throne.

"Thank you for coming. We said our goodbyes last night, but I couldn't let you leave without offering each a gift." He motioned to Mydir, who handed the king a jeweled sword. "Nathaniel, as the rightful heir to the kingdom of Tabor, you deserve to wield a weapon of special significance." He handed Nathaniel an elven sword, expertly crafted, with a jewel-embossed handle. "Long ago, I had this blade forged as a wedding gift for your father. The arrogant fool refused the gift, responding with a note saying, "Nothing good ever comes from Elves." I hope you will accept it as a renewed bond between our nations."

Nathaniel reluctantly accepted the blade, mixed emotions swirling inside. None of the stories told by Jacoby and Grullach about his father matched the level of harsh honesty found in this one. His father's action angered and insulted the Sylph king. So why did he feel defensive? A fleeting thought crossed his mind: Is arrogance required to be a triumphant king? No. I will maintain a confident demeanor, never allowing that confidence to transform into arrogance. The greed for power that fed my father's arrogance will never consume me.

He focused on the present and removed the sword from its sheath, sensing its weight in his hand. The jeweled handle momentarily pulsed like an electric shock as he held the perfectly balanced, long, broad blade. He swished the blade in a figure eight, slicing the air like an enemy.

"I am deeply grateful, Your Highness. It feels like this blade was custom made for me."

"Actually, in a way, it was."

"I don't understand," Nathaniel said

"Friend aided me in imbuing the blade with ancient magic that bonds the sword to its owner. I named the blade 'Blueblade' after the magnificent sapphire in the hilt."

"I can never repay you, Your Highness," his eyes reflected his appreciation.

"Tut tut," the king said, waving it off. "My only regret is that your father never used the sword. It could have made a difference in the battle for Tabor."

"Why do you say that?" Nathaniel asked.

"Naturally, I neglected to inform you," he said, chuckling. "Our finest smith constructed the blade using Làdir Ell'yn Elven steel. Even the undead cannot withstand its power."

Nathaniel's face split into a wide grin. "I don't know what to say," the young prince said, his eyes wide.

"Oddly," Goldbriar continued, a strange glint in his eye. "With a forceful insistence, Friend demanded the artisan make the jewel within the pommel easily replaceable. I believe I understand the reason now."

Goldbriar placed a reassuring hand on Nathaniel's shoulder. "This is the best protection I can offer. I loved your mother like a daughter. You are her son, and thus, I will always be here for you."

Nathaniel pulled the king into a fierce embrace for several heartbeats, then let Goldbriar go. The king wiped tears that ran down his cheeks, still smiling.

"Ahem. Now for you, Jacoby." Again, Mydir handed a short sword to the king. Unlike Nathaniel's blade, the short sword carried no adornment, just a common leather sheath below a simple iron hilt. He handed the sword to Jacoby. The tall man wrapped his finger around the handle but felt no magic. He pulled the blade from the sheath, revealing a thin, blood-red blade engraved in an ancient language.

Jacoby gave the king a confused look and said, "Sire?"

"Whitestar, the first King of Tabor, forged this blade during the First Age when he defeated the nefarious necromancer Yex. Legend says he mixed the silver with the blood of a unicorn, making it extraordinarily magical. He referred to it as 'Wizardeath'. These two blades may be the only ones that can defeat Ravenite."

"Thank you, Your Majesty."

The old king pulled Jacoby into an awkward embrace and whispered, "Whatever happens, stay alive, or Laurel will never forgive me."

As the afternoon sun drifted behind the horizon, rays of pink, orange, and gold shrouded the catboat as Horatio guided the ship upriver. The other brotherhood sat about the cockpit talking, eager to be back on the journey. Grullach had been down below in the hold, helping Allai'nn and Rue feed, change, and put the infants to bed. As he climbed aft, he noticed Jacoby sitting cross-legged on the aft thwart, taking in the last glimpses of the palace at Clobryn Nyth.

He stepped up, placing a comforting hand on Jacoby's back.

"When his adventure is over, she'll be waiting for you," Grull said.

Jacoby nodded, but his mind wandered restlessly from one thought to another. What awaits us when we finally arrive in the City of Spires? With a cloud hanging over his departure from Tabor twenty years ago, he now felt an immense sense of dread as they drew closer to the destination. Will Nathaniel face a warm welcome or hostility? Does my presence pose a risk? Will any of my previous allies recall my service and support our cause? How many, if that's the case? If we can rally the Tabor army, what will be the outcome? Are we capable of vanquishing Ravenite and his undead followers? A heavy feeling settled in his stomach as he questioned the significance of the past year and a half, filled with battles, near misses, escapes, and losses. His thoughts had completed a full cycle, grappling with one unsolvable query after another until he arrived at the most heartbreaking one. Would Laurel still be waiting for him if she knew the truth about his sacrifices to keep Nathaniel alive and the lives lost on their journey back to Tabor?

TWENTY-TWO

From the open tower window, thirty stories high, Ravenite could feel the chilling night breeze sweep through the dark woods, sending a shiver down his decaying spine. Centuries had passed since his death and reanimation, rendering him numb to human emotions and devoid of sensory pleasure. Despite still feeling pain, he found that all the positive attributes had vanished, leaving behind a dark cloud of greed, anger, malice, and malevolence. The significant cost of near immortality weighed heavily on him, a consequence of his pact with Asmodeus, the underworld deity. However, everything changed when he encountered Cas, a formidable red witch with a commanding presence, reigniting something deep within him. Their personalities not only seemed perfectly matched, but he also felt a surge of attraction and yearning that he hadn't felt in decades. Do I feel love coursing through my veins? No. Desire? Yes, in every imaginable way, especially our shared craving for power. Luckily, he remained the more powerful of the two, his immense magical ability pulsating through his veins because of selling his soul to the underworld king. Cas found pleasure in assuming a submissive position for the time being, riding his coattails toward a future of world domination.

The wizard's ears perked up at the distinct sound of the vulture's wings flapping in the distance, growing louder with each passing second. Eventually, the bird landed on the tower with a soft thud against the weathered gray stones.

"Awwk. I carry two messages, one from the demon, Sin, and the other from the black witch," the carrion bird squawked, flapping its wings in a flourish.

"Speak," Ravenite growled as Cas rubbed against his legs in her Tabby cat form.

"The army unleashed its destructive power after crossing the Narn River, leaving only charred farms and haunting corpses behind. As agreed, his ravenous undead soldiers devoured every soul upon death."

"Excellent!" Ravenite said, rubbing his skeletal digits together gleefully. "And the other message?"

"Mistress Lazelle has found the prince. He and his group approach the City of Spires via the River Horn."

Ravenite's face grew purple with rage, and he grabbed the enormous bird by the neck, smashing its body over and over against the tower sill like a club. "A pox upon that wretched prince!" he screamed. After several moments, he felt Cas' calming touch again on his back. "Be calm, my heart," she cooed. "There is still hope."

Trying to regain control, Ravenite gulped in quick, shallow breaths. A macabre ensemble of vulture feathers and splattered blood adorned him, covering his arms and chest. With a mix of disgust and regret, he flung the mangled carrion eater's corpse out the window before collapsing into a chair, his head sinking into his hands.

"Why won't he just die?" he muttered, unable to contain his annoyance.

Cas gently stroked his neck and back. "It's not too late to stop the prince from succeeding," she said.

"But how?" he whispered, his voice filled with confusion and desperation. "No matter how hard I hit, I cannot strike a killing blow."

"Perhaps a different approach is in order?" She leaned in and whispered into Ravenite's ear. The mage raised his head, a crooked smile crossing his decaying lips.

"Clever girl," Ravenite said, pulling Cas into an embrace.

Hundreds of leagues to the south, Horatio skillfully maneuvered the catboat along the Horn River, feeling the gentle breeze fill the sails from behind as they glided effortlessly downstream in a broad reach. From the south, a moderate breeze swept through, overpowering the gentle current of the river. Horatio had alternated shifts steering the craft every six hours with Blue Ivy, Nathaniel, and Jacoby as they traveled from Clobryn Nyth north toward Tabor two ago. So far, there had been little excitement as the craft glided over the glacier-blue water, except for the occasional splash when Grullach reeled in a trout while fishing.

Horatio stood in awe as the evening stars emerged, their brilliance captivating his gaze. The frogman's keen ears detected the distant rumble of rapids, prompting him to steer the boat towards the shore for further investigation. Despite his best efforts, the tiller resisted his every attempt to turn towards shore. "What the demons?" Horatio exclaimed, his voice filled with shock and disbelief as he leaned his weight on the sturdy wooden shaft. But the tiller barely budged an inch. Just then, the frogman observed the river current growing stronger, causing vibrations to ripple through the ship.

After captaining the vessel last night, Jacoby slept soundly until he felt the ship jostle, causing him to raise his head.

"What's happening?" he asked Horatio.

"I hear choppy water ahead. I wanted to head towards the shore, but the stubborn rudder wouldn't move."

Jacoby stood up and went to the back of the boat, pulling with all his strength on the tiller shaft, but it made no difference. He tried again, putting all his weight into it, but the movement was minimal.

"I can't budge it."

"It worked fine all day. I don't understand what happened," Horatio lamented, his face a mask of confusion.

The boat rocked again as both the breeze and the current picked up.

"Go forward and see what's ahead while I keep trying," Jacoby ordered.

"Should I wake the others?" Horatio asked over his shoulder, moving toward the bow.

"Not yet. There's a chance I can remove it from its current hold."

Horatio was at the bow in two hops, peering into the night with his Twilight vision. He could hear the water churning ahead but saw no waves or eddies. As the boat sped through the dark river water, he looked down at the swirling wake and realized they were speeding up.

"Jacoby, I think we're gaining speed," the frogman called out, trying to hide the worry he felt. "The rapids are getting louder, but I still can't see them."

"Hurry, wake everyone up," Jacoby replied, still struggling with the tiller shaft.

Horatio hopped aft to the mid beam and climbed into the hold, then returned with Cor'in, Nathaniel, and Torque in a few moments.

"What's going on?" Nathaniel and Cor'in said together.

"The current's strengthened suddenly, and there are rapids ahead."

Cor'in's eyes widened in shock as the realization sank in. Nat swiftly accepted the situation and rushed to Jacoby's side. The three warriors struggled to use their muscles to change the ship's course, but even with the strength of the muscular orc, the result was barely noticeable.

"We can't budge the blooming thing," grunted Cor'in, straining to move the shaft.

"Horatio, can you go underneath the boat and see what's happening?" Jacoby asked.

"Sure," the frogman said, diving into the churning water. Even with his muscular legs, Horatio had trouble keeping up with the boat's speed. He kicked hard and seized the tiller, seeing the problem instantly. A morass of fishing line and lead weights tangled the wooden rudder, freezing it in a neutral position. He tugged with all his strength, but the line wouldn't budge. He sensed increasing turbulence and knew he had to resurface. Pulling himself up over the boat side, he said, "The tiller's tangled with fishing line. Let me have a dagger and I'll cut it free."

"There's no time," Nathaniel urgently exclaimed, pointing ahead to the rushing rapids. "Corin, tell Grull to secure the children and the ladies for a rough ride, and the rest of us should lash ourselves down."

Everyone moved simultaneously to secure the vessel and themselves as the boat's speed accelerated. Grull rushed into the hold while the others sprinted to lash themselves to cleats or the masthead. Nathaniel worked to shorten the mainsail sheet and tie off the boom, preventing it from swinging wildly in the chop. Once accomplished, he sat down low in the cockpit, holding with a firm grasp onto the rope.

As the boat approached the rapid, Nathaniel experienced an unsettling yet tranquil feeling of anticipation. When he looked up, he noticed that the velvety sky, once filled with stars, had vanished, casting an eerie darkness that seemed to swallow everything, even the river's surface. An unsettling stillness enveloped the seconds, only interrupted by his rapid, nervous breaths.

Then it happened.

The ship's bow dipped abruptly, catching Nathaniel off guard, and his terrified scream filled the black abyss. Clinging to the edge of the cockpit, he could feel his stomach lurching towards his throat, bracing himself for the imminent crash. However, the expected impact never occurred. Upon opening one eye, the prince witnessed an unexpected and captivating sight. The ship soared through a water flume, shooting by boulders and rocks on either side. The water's force pushed them forward, scraping and jostling over submerged stones like a toy boat rocked by the sea. Finally, the boat leveled out after several minutes, the river's current expelling the ship free onto a serene lake with a final splash. The boat jolted at the sudden deceleration, slowing to a crawl over the glass-like surface of clear water.

"Everyone okay?" Nathaniel called out, unleashing himself. He ducked into the hold to check on Lani, Allai'nn, Rue, and the children, although Sinbad curled protectively around the four wailing infants. "Okay?" he said, and Lani gave him a thumbs up.

He climbed back to the cockpit where Cor'in stood, rubbing his shoulder. "I lost my footing and slammed into the tiller," Cor'in explained.

"Where are the others?"

Cor'in motioned forward, where Jacoby and Grull stood at the bow while Blue and Horatio busied themselves with checking the sheets and tackle.

"Everyone alright?" Nat asked.

"Only a few bruises from the jostling ride, thank Odin," Grull answered. "There weren't rapids on the map Mydir gave us."

"Hopefully, just a minor hiccup," Nathaniel responded, gazing out at the vast expanse of water. Blue topaz-colored water extended to the horizon in all directions, with only a glimmer of land far ahead. No breeze or bird sounds penetrated the morning air; the water's surface was placid glass twinkling from the morning sunshine.

On the verge of asking Horatio to dive overboard, Jacoby tested the tiller, finding it moved freely. "Hey, look! The rough ride must have freed the rudder, moving the tiller arm back and forth. "Still some minor stiffness, but good enough to sail."

Jacoby guided the ship across the immense lake, immersing himself in the profound stillness of the azure water framed by dense, emerald foliage. The muscular orc leaned out from the cockpit in front of him, gazing at the vast landscape.

"This area is lovely," Torque said, sitting nearby. "It reminds me of my homeland."

"Are the Black Mountains home to such a dense forest?" Jacoby asked, taking in the evergreen scent and thick limbs of the lush wood.

"Yes, except for the summits, which are perpetually snow-covered."

"What's life like there?"

"Clans of different families scattered over the hills, led by one Jarl or chieftain," answered Torque, his eyes fixed on the Western horizon.

"Sounds a lot like where I grew up in Narn," Jacoby said. "Do the clans get along?"

"Not all of them. It's been years since a Jarl has successfully united the clans under one banner."

Jacoby nodded. "You know, you've been a little secretive about your history. What are you afraid to tell us?"

Torque hesitated, picking his words carefully.

"I grew up in a world filled with corruption and political betrayals. Finding trust outside your immediate clan can be an arduous task. Over the years, humans have proven to be the most troublesome beings for my kind. Trusting others, especially humans, is a challenge for me."

"Why humans?" Jacoby questioned innocently.

The orc locked eyes with Jacoby, his fierce gaze cutting through him like butter.

"Let me answer it this way," Torque said, slyly turning the tables on the big human. "During your conquests as a Taborian officer, how many orc villages did you destroy and the inhabitants imprison or kill? Have you ever met an orc you trusted?"

Jacoby looked down, the reality of his own bias clear. In those days, he obeyed the king's orders, suppressing anyone who dared to oppose King Aarmon's quest for more land or resources. Refusing meant a court-martial, followed by exile if lucky or execution if not. So, he did his duty until that fateful day when Queen Elana called him to her room, and his entire world turned upside down.

"Maybe not. I followed orders and did my duty, even when I should have had the courage to voice my disagreement," Jacoby confessed, avoiding the orc's eyes. "I regret many of my past actions, but I always aimed to show respect and dignity to all my opponents."

Torque let out a disgusted chuckle. "Dignity? You and Nathaniel treat others respectfully, but that's not what I've experienced with many men. Most humans fear us and live by the adage: The only good orc is a dead orc."

"I'm sorry for that. I hope things will change if Nathaniel becomes king."

Torque's silence stretched out, making Jacoby realize that pushing further would only lead to more regret for his past mistreatment of non-humans. As an officer, he had lived in a dangerous world, constantly assigned to handle problems he believed deceitful creatures caused, requiring swift elimination to protect innocent Taborians. Were their intentions truly malicious, or were they merely struggling to exist in a world controlled by avaricious humans? He had followed orders obediently, but as time went on, he couldn't ignore the underlying motivation behind his assignments - King Aarmon's unquenchable desire for conquest and power. Over the years since his defection from Tabor, he realized that most species exhibited a mix of positive and negative behaviors, regardless of origin.

"I appreciate your sharing," Jacoby said, genuinely grateful. "Considering your past encounters, I understand why you would be suspicious of humans. But fear and hatred don't fuel all humans, just like orcs or elves; a sense of fairness and empathy guides some."

Torque gazed thoughtfully into the distance. "Like Nathaniel?"

"Yes. Growing up with a human, an elf, a dwarf, and a halfling as his family, Nathaniel's perspective on life was anything but ordinary. He also interacted with a broad spectrum of patrons at the Sleeping Dragon Inn."

Torque let out a deep, rumbling chuckle. "He had quite an upbringing for someone keeping a low profile."

"Luckily, Streamside was a backwater hamlet far from Tabor."

"Thank the Gods," Torque mumbled.

As the afternoon progressed, the wind grew stronger, causing the small boat to skim over the shimmering surface of the pristine lake. Now and then, a majestic moose could be seen taking a dip in the water, and the sound of flapping wings alerted the group to flocks of nesting green-feathered ducks. At the far end, the water slowly tapered into the entrance of a wide river, the current becoming noticeably stronger and creating rougher waves. Jacoby guided the boat across the chop at an angle, hoping to limit the turbulence and keep the infants from panicking. By evening, the boat reached a fork in the channel, split by a thin, forested island. Wooden rope bridges stretched across the cuts, providing a unique and adventurous way to access the island from both sides.

"Let's stop here and camp for the night," Jacoby said, weary from the day's sailing.

"Great idea," Allai'nn said enthusiastically, sticking her head out of the hold to feel the rush of wind against her face. "The children need a wide-open area to crawl freely and release their pent-up energy before bed."

Nathaniel pulled out the deer-hide map given to him by King Goldbriar. "Our route to the Sacred Wood should be that way," he said, gesturing to the right channel with his arm. "We can rest tonight and start again at first light."

Jacoby guided the craft to a notch in the island's shore, where the bank was less steep and the beach sandy. The group piled out, happy to be back on dry land. While Grull and Blue Ivy laid out a blanket for the infants to play on, the others pulled supplies to make camp.

"Lani and I will fetch wood for a fire," he said, winking at Lani.

"Absolutely," she said, smiling, happy to be alone with her love.

"We'll help," said Rue, channeling a message to Blue Ivy with her eyes.

"Oh, right," Blue said, grasping Rue's hand before following Lani and Nathaniel into the thicket.

Once out of earshot, Nathaniel said, "We'll search closer to shore while you check here."

Blue understood the message, and a smile spread across his face. He answered eagerly, his eyes lighting up as he said, "Of course. Come on, my lady." He pulled Rue further into the trees while Nathaniel and Lani scampered closer to the shoreline, laughing and holding hands.

Once Blue and Rue were out of sight, he pulled Lani into a firm embrace, planting a hefty kiss on her lips. "I've wanted to do that all day," he grinned.

"Me too, my heart."

He kissed her again gently, and they strolled together, holding hands, along the island's bank, picking up driftwood and small branches for the fire. They rounded a bend in the shoreline and found a hidden beachhead sheltered by large bushes and scrub trees. "What's this?" Nathaniel asked rhetorically as he crossed the beach to a boat partially covered by tree branches and vegetation.

He and Lani removed the branches, revealing a dory, its hull stuffed with weapons and containers of dry goods.

Nathaniel gazed around, wondering who might have left such a valuable haul.

"We may have stumbled on a bandit stash," Lani said.

Nat nodded, and then an idea struck him. "Get in. I'll row us back to camp."

"What? Are you sure that's safe?"

"I don't see anyone around, and the boat's coverings are old and decaying. The owners appear to be long gone," he reassured Lani.

She hesitated and looked at the surrounding woods, assessing the risk. "Okay."

Nathaniel passed the oars through the locks, and they climbed inside before pushing off. They followed the shoreline, the rhythmic sound of the waves guiding their path. He skillfully maneuvered the boat, gliding it onto the soft sand beside the sleek catboat.

Jacoby and Grull greeted them, pulling the boat higher onto the shore. "Where did you find this?" Grull asked.

"Along the shore. But that's not the best part," he said, motioning to the weapons bundled in the boat's stern after lifting Lani to the sand.

Grull examined the many swords and daggers, picking up a blade and running his thumb along the edge. "Thor's beard! These are part silver!" he exclaimed excitedly. "There must be close to fifty blades here."

A sense of unease washed over Jacoby, causing him to scan the area for any sign of lurking enemies. "Judging by their looks, they are in great condition. Were there any signs pointing to bandits or changelings?" the tall man asked, his voice tinged with concern.

"No. A tangle of old branches and withering shrubs concealed the dory," Nathaniel answered. "I don't think anyone has been near recently."

Torque walked up and examined the blade, its sharp edge glinting in Grull's hand. "These weapons have the mark of the wolverine. I only know one smith who marks their weapons like that: Henry Oakshield."

Nathaniel and Jacoby locked eyes. Had this been a shipment of arms destined for Tabor? Mar Nâpor? One of the Elven lands? How did they end up here? Waylaid by pirates and stored for sale on the black market? The thoughts tumbled through Nathaniel's mind like a tumbleweed in a high wind.

"Doesn't matter where they came from. These will be a useful and needed gift for the Taborian army," Jacoby stated, knowing his brother's mind would dig through an avalanche of questions.

"Help me load them into the catboat," Nathaniel said.

Over the next hour, they transported all the weapons aboard and sat down for their evening meal. Grull broke out a small bottle of Taborian brandy, took a swig, and passed it to the next person.

"What's this?" Cor'in asked, holding the unlabeled silver flask to the firelight but unable to see the contents.

"Tabor's finest," answered Grull with a wry smile.

"What? And you've been hoarding this for how long?" bellowed Cor'in, taking a long draught.

"It made its way into my pocket from Goldbriar's stock," confessed the halfling, feigning embarrassment. "I thought it was only fair that we receive compensation for enduring a night in the Clobrŷn Nŷth prison."

"So fortunate the bottle fell into your coat pocket," rumbled Torque, accepting the bottle.

"Too true, friend Torque," said Grull, looking away. "The gods favor me."

The flask made its rounds around the fire, and everyone's laughter filled the night with joyous echoes.

"Tell us a story, Horatio," Rue said to the bard.

Horatio cleared his throat. "Long ago there lived a fat tinker who traveled from town to town. He made a fair wage, but spent most every night on food and ale, often drinking to oblivion. One night, he woke to the sound of a high-pitched cry. "Help me. Help me".

So, the tinker staggered toward the noise until he found a tiny pixie caught in a large garden spider web.

"Please help me," she pleaded, "and in exchange, I will guarantee generous rewards of gold for all your needs, but there is one condition."

"What condition?" Blue Ivy asked, entranced by the tale.

"The pixie delicately passed a small bluebell to the Tinker," Horatio continued.

"According to the young pixie, King Tybex, the Pixie king, had enchanted the flower. "Ensure its safe keeping," she emphasized, her voice urgent, "and remember to return it to your wagon by midnight without fail or face King Tybex's anger." The tinker placed the flower in his lapel, then released the tiny pixie."

"What happened next?" Cor'in said.

"Each year, the Tinker's business grew more prosperous, his pockets becoming heavy with gleaming gold and silver. He ate and drank recklessly, relishing every bite and sip, but he always returned to his wagon by midnight. However, one night, he encountered a mysterious hooded man who incessantly offered him ale until he eventually succumbed to unconsciousness. The only thing that roused him from his slumber was the resounding chime of the tavern clock at midnight. He rushed back to his wagon, only to find the once vibrant bluebell lifeless and wilted. From that point onward, his business declined, his health deteriorated, and he found himself reduced to a sickly pauper, begging on the street. Some claim he met his demise, while others insist, they witnessed the mysterious hooded man visiting the Tinker on a stormy night, adding to the intrigue. He revealed his true identity as King Tybex when he pulled back his hood. In an act of compassion, he gave a bag of gold to the Tinker, who left with newfound wisdom."

No one spoke as the group sat, lost in their thoughts, contemplating the story's significance.

"Well, with that, I will call it a night," said Grull, stretching and intertwining his fingers with Allai'nn's hand. "Sleep well, all," he said, his warm smile bidding everyone a restful night. As the others followed, Nathaniel and Torque remained, their eyes fixed on the mesmerizing dance of the fire before them.

"I'll be heading home tomorrow," Torque said, breaking the silence.

"What?" Nathaniel said, gazing up at the orc.

"May I see the map King Goldbriar gave you?"

Nathaniel brought out the deer hide and unfurled it, laying it out for Torque to see. The orc carefully examined the map, tracing his finger over the parchment to understand his surroundings.

"This channel leads west," Torque said, gesturing at the map. "And the other cut will take you north to the Sacred Wood. If you don't mind, I'll take the dory."

"No worries," he said with a reassuring smile. "I'll be sorry to see you go, Torque. Thank you for all your help over the past weeks," Nathaniel said, extending his hand out to shake.

The large orc reached out and warmly shook it, his rough hand engulfing it. "Nathaniel, I should thank you. Your unquestioning acceptance of me has profoundly affected me," Torque responded.

Nathaniel smiled, his eyes reflecting the deep respect he had developed with the orc. He'd never known an orc could be anything other than a cutthroat and a robotic minion of evil. He'd learned a lot about trust over their time together.

"Why don't you get some rest? I'll take the first watch," the prince said. The orc nodded and moved to his bedroll.

Rising to his feet, Nathaniel walked a path around the camp, his footsteps creating a soft crunch on the forest floor as he checked the boat's mooring lines. Sparkling stars adorned the evening sky, along with a three-quarters full moon that cast a shimmering reflection on the river. He gazed out at the channel that led north and wondered what might be at the end. His kingdom? Victory in battle? Peace? Or a disastrous defeat? Time will tell.

The following morning, Grull shook Nathaniel awake.

"Ahh. Morning already?" the prince said, the morning sun shining in his eyes. He rubbed sleepy dirt from his eyes and climbed to his feet.

"I'm afraid so. And I have bad news."

Nathaniel sighed, waiting.

"Torque has disappeared with the dory," Grull said as the two walked to the riverside. "But that's not the worst news."

"What happened?" Nathaniel asked, his heart sinking.

"The bloody orc took half the silver weapons."

TWENTY-THREE

Nathaniel slammed his hand against the side of the catboat and cursed.

"What in the demons was he thinking?" he said, his voice laced with anger and betrayal.

"Maybe he needed them more than we did," Grull said, putting a comforting hand on the young man's shoulder.

Nathaniel's face burned red with anger, and he swore. What had happened in the six hours since his watch ended and Torque took over? He gazed down at the thirty swords left in the catboat hull. There were insufficient swords for a platoon, let alone an army. He kicked the boat's hull with his boot and stalked into the woods.

"Wait!" Lani said, jogging after him.

"Let him go, lass," Grull said. "Betrayal can be a hard pill to swallow."

Lani halted, tears forming in her eyes, knowing Grullach was right. Nathaniel would need to resolve this alone.

With an hour gone by, the brotherhood, minus Nathaniel, loaded the catboat with supplies and placed the eager children and their beloved Sinbad in the ship's hold. Excitement filled the air as they gathered their gear and prepared for their journey. The others climbed in, except Jacoby, who waded knee-deep in the river at the boat's bow, ready to push the craft into the current whenever Nathaniel arrived. A quarter-hour later, Nathaniel appeared and climbed into the boat without a word. Jacoby pushed the craft into the deeper water, feeling the resistance against his muscles, then heaved himself onto the deck, taking hold of the tiller.

The gentle breeze rustled through Jacoby's salt and pepper hair as he maneuvered the boat down the narrow cut. The calm waters sparkled and danced under the warm embrace of the morning sun, creating a mesmerizing display of shimmering light. A sense of tranquility and anticipation filled the air as Jacoby navigated the winding path, keeping one hand steady on the tiller while the other rested on the cleated mainsail sheet. The boat glided effortlessly through the glistening water, leaving a soft trail of ripples in its wake. The vibrant colors of the surrounding landscape added to the scene's beauty, with lush greenery and blooming flowers lining the banks. This morning on the water seemed picture-perfect, and Jacoby guided the boat toward their destination, feeling an overwhelming sense of contentment. He had forgotten Tabor's beauty and felt a kernel of longing that he'd not felt for many years.

Yet as soon as his eyes met Nathaniel's gaze, his serene moment shattered into fragments. Despite the surrounding beauty, Nathaniel remained seated next to Lani, his eyes filled with the anguish of betrayal. He had seen that same look before, the mixture of anger and betrayal when he confessed his history to Nathaniel, and the lad had delivered a decisive blow to his jaw. It took him weeks of dedication and remorse to earn back the trust he had lost, and he could still sense the deep scars his lies had left on Nathaniel's heart.

Part of him wondered why the prince seemed so vexed by Torque's act but understood that it had triggered a reminder of previous betrayals. He turned his gaze on Grull and gestured with his head for his friend to console the young man. The halfling crossed the deck and sat next to Nathaniel.

"Nathaniel, I can see the anger in your eyes," he said, trying to console him. "I know you're upset and have every right to be. And it's hard not to take this to heart. But truth be told, the events that unfolded remain a mystery. Most significantly, adding a handful more swords wouldn't have altered the war's outcome. You can accomplish that only with courage and strategy, and I have faith in your intelligence to achieve it."

When Nathaniel gazed into the halfling's eyes, a genuine smile illuminated his face. At that moment, it felt as if the dark cloud hovering over him had finally lifted, allowing a glimmer of sunlight to shine through. "Grull, I appreciate it," he said, grateful for his help.

Grull nodded toward Jacoby; memories flooded Grull's mind, taking him back to the days when he was under his friend's command. His words echoed in his ears, "Every moment presents a chance to push forward," Jacoby had said, instilling a sense of purpose and determination in his soldiers. Those words had become Grull's guiding principle since rejoining Jacoby at the Sleeping Dragon Inn, reminding him to seize every opportunity that came his way; to never back down in the face of adversity, and to always strive for progress.

"Your brother has always had my back, even when I was a lowly soldier in his Taborian platoon. He lifted me out of despair at my worst moment, and I've never forgotten what he told me." Grull hesitated, then continued. "When life knocks you down, dust off and don't waste time complaining. Every moment is a chance to move forward toward something better."

Nathaniel smiled. "That sounds like Jacoby."

Grull's voice, laced with a touch of regret, resonated as he acknowledged, "Those are wise words to live by, but implementing them is no simple task." Grull gave the young man's shoulder a squeeze before returning to the hold to help Allai'nn.

Resting against the hull, Nat felt the coarse texture against his back as he stole a quick glance at Jacoby, Grull's words lingering in his thoughts. He closed his eyes, trying to clear his mind and regain his focus. The events of the past few days had been tumultuous, and his emotions were running high. Torque's betrayal had left him feeling vulnerable and empty, but dwelling on it would only hinder his progress. I must let go of the gnawing sensation in my gut and move forward. Nat reminded himself that he couldn't change the past, but he could control his reaction to it. He had to detach himself from the situation and view it objectively, like a puzzle to solve. Taking another deep breath, he attempted to release the tension in his body, allowing himself to relax against the hull of the ship. In order to achieve my goals, I need to approach them with a clear and rational mind, free from the distractions of anger and resentment. Nat resolved to focus on the present moment, to strategize and plan his next move, leaving behind the suffocating weight of his emotions.

Far to the south of the catboat, Commander Kristopher Hundmeister walked towards the deserted beach, feeling the fine grains of sand beneath his boots. By midmorning, the sun's rays had grown fierce, creating a sweltering atmosphere that clung to him like a weighty shroud. The oppressive humidity made his dark uniform stick to his body, and rivulets of sweat streamed down his face, mirroring the relentless heat. The sound of crashing waves grew louder as he made his way between white-sand dunes and stepped onto the shell-studded beach. Just in time, he arrived to witness the narrow, black-stained long boat being pushed ashore by the relentless ocean current. As the boat drew nearer, Commander Hundmeister noticed the figures in the boat. Their hooded cloaks concealed their identities and created an aura of intrigue. The tension in the air was palpable as the boat inched closer to the shoreline, delivering his king and personal security. Hundmeister's heart raced as he waited, consumed with fear. King Barnabus never personally called a meeting.

The long boat slid to a stop in the soft sand, and two sailors leaped out and pulled the vessel higher onto the beach. Two other figures exited the boat and walked towards Hundmeister, who stood erect at attention. The smaller of the two figures stopped in front of Hundmeister, followed by the other figure who removed his hood and face covering, revealing the face of the Svartalf king.

"Walk with me," Barnabus said and began walking parallel to the surf.

"Good to see you, Your Majesty."

Hundmeister walked beside the king but noticed the other hooded figure following the two elves a respectful two paces behind.

"I received your recognizance message concerning the damage done in Mar Napor. It was a disastrous start," Barnabus said.

"As I reported, no one expected the warriors who saved Prince Caron. But we accomplished our aim of terrorizing the citizens and burning almost a third of the city."

"By not killing the prince, you left the crown in control, despite Crow's assassination of King Gooseberry."

"He's a sixteen-year-old boy, wet behind the ears and scared of his own shadow," Hundmeister retorted.

"You know how I feel about mistakes," Barnabus said, staring at his commander with sad eyes.

Just then, Hundmeister's instincts kicked in as he detected a subtle movement from behind. The other figure had silently and unexpectedly crept closer, his footsteps masked by the stillness of the sand, and launched himself toward the commander, brandishing a dagger in each hand. With a swift spinning motion, Hundmeister unsheathed his own daggers, using his forearms to block both incoming blades. His leg shot out, and as he twisted, the killer's balance faltered, sending them stumbling. Lightning-fast, Hundmeister tackled the assassin, bringing him to the ground and trapping his right arm with his weight. Before Hundmeister could strike, the dark elf drove his knee into the commander's groin, unleashing a surge of agonizing pain through his abdomen. On instinct, Hundmeister rolled to his left, narrowly evading another powerful kick from the assassin. But as Hundmeister rolled, the dark elf shot out his arm, slicing his dagger across Hundmeister's biceps and leaving behind a deep, bleeding gash. As the two warriors squared off, Hundmeister's right arm dripped with a steady flow of blood.

Hundmeister and the assassin circled each other, their eyes locked in a deadly stare. Hundmeister's biceps throbbed with pain, the blood from his fresh wound staining his sleeve, but his determination remained unwavering. Adrenaline coursed through his veins, heightening his senses and sharpening his focus. The sand beneath their feet shifted with each cautious step. Hundmeister's mind raced, analyzing the assassin's every move, searching for any weakness to exploit. His heart pounded in his chest, a steady rhythm matching the steady flow of blood from his arm. With each passing second, the tension in the air grew thicker, as if the world held its breath, waiting for the clash of steel and the resolution of this deadly encounter.

The assassin moved like a viper, deceiving the commander with a feint to the left before ruthlessly striking his right blade towards the ribs, aiming to deliver a fatal blow. However, Hundmeister's honed skills allowed him to evade the blade in the nick of time, though he could feel the knife rake across his armor. However, the failed attempt proved to be the assassin's downfall, as the commander skillfully seized his arm, effortlessly twisting it and hurling the dark elf soaring over his shoulder, landing harshly on the gritty sand. The assassin sprang up like a cat; his blades raised high as he charged forward, striking down with a forceful cleave. Hundmeister parried the blows once more, his wounded arm throbbing with pain. With a swift movement, he seized the assailant's shirt and executed a backward roll, sending the dark elf flying over him, his daggers flying off into the surf.

The moment Hundmeister saw the elf rising, he lunged forward, colliding with him in a powerful tackle that sent them both sprawling to the ground. Rolling over and over into the foamy surf, the two grappled with each other, desperately trying to gain the upper hand. Hundmeister's advantage in size and weight became clear as he descended upon the elf, overpowering him and pushing his head below the surface of the water. The assassin fiercely punched and writhed, his nails digging into the commander's forearms as he desperately fought to break free. The commander's heart pounded in his chest, fueled by adrenaline and determination. He could feel the elf's strength waning, his punches weakening, and the desperation in his eyes fading. Hundmeister's face contorted with a mixture of rage and triumph as he pressed harder, not relenting for a moment.

Finally, the elf's body went still, his eyes vacant and lifeless. Hundmeister tore free the elf's face covering but didn't recognize the face. In some corner of his mind, he had hoped he had ended Crow, the preeminent Svartalf assassin. With a tinge of regret, Hundmeister released his hold, the weight of his victory settling upon him as he stood up, his chest heaving with exertion. The foamy surf washed over him, cleansing away the remnants of the intense struggle. Hundmeister scanned the surroundings; his senses heightened to ensure that the threat was truly eliminated.

As the adrenaline subsided, a mix of emotions flooded Hundmeister's mind. Relief for surviving the encounter. Sorrow for taking another life. But above all, a seething rage consumed him, aimed directly at King Barnabus for masterminding the brutal attack. He turned to the monarch, who stood watching, his arms crossed, his face a stone mask.

"As expected, Commander," the king said flatly as if he'd witnessed a game of tenpins instead of a battle to the death. "I will not accept failure again."

Hundmeister leaned in, his eyes locked with Barnabus', and snarled, "Try that again, and you'll be next."

Barnabus chuckled, but Hundmeister glimpsed anxiety in the king's hollow, coal-like eyes. "Commander, you seem to have forgotten your place," he remarked, then hesitated. "I will disregard it this once," the king said, deciding to attribute it to the intense heat of battle. "Remember this day," he warned with an authoritative voice, "or suffer the consequences from Crow."

"Is it true?" Regent Mossbrook spat, his face betraying his resentment.

Taking a seat at the Taborian Council table, Devin Ashoke calmly replied, "If you're referring to King Goldbriar, yes, he won't send troops without first getting approval from the Elven council."

Only three others were at the table: two older councilmen and General Thorn. Many of the political retinue and lesser ministers had already fled the city, leaving only a handful of loyal or frail individuals behind. The young general had aged a decade in the month Devin had been away, his eyes now hollow and surrounded by dark circles.

"He actually exceeded my expectations," Ashoke continued, a hint of surprise in his voice, "by promising to notify Polaris."

"More than expected?" Roared Mossbrook, the veins in his temple throbbing. "Doesn't he understand what we're up against?"

"To put it simply, the Elven community can be quite capricious. They encircle our country but sadly remain unhelpful," stated Ashoke in a matter-of-fact tone, expressing his unfortunate sentiment. "But I have news," he exclaimed, his eyes sparkling with hope. "That just might change everything."

"News? What news?" asked Mossbrook, rising out of his chair, hope kindled in his eyes.

"Please sit down, Regent. This news…well… it may be hard to swallow."

Mossbrook eased back into his chair. "All right. Don't hold an old man hostage; out with it!" he bellowed.

"I met a young warrior who traveled with two old friends I served with in the regimental corps almost twenty years ago. He told a rather fantastic story about his upbringing and family."

All three councilmen leaned forward; their interest piqued.

Fixing his gaze on each man, Ashoke said, "He told me he hailed from Tabor, but he spent his childhood in the Lea Lands." He hesitated, then added, "He claims to be the lost son of King Aarmon."

The room descended into pandemonium, the news detonating like an explosion. In a state of disbelief, Mossbrook leaped to his feet, his eyes filled with astonishment, while someone else shouted, "Ridiculous!" One alderman leaned back, cackling, while Mossbrook stood there, speechless. Only Ashoke and Thorne remained calm, the young officer holding up his hands for quiet.

As the tension in the room eased, Thorn's voice resonated with a somber tone. "It's my understanding," he said, "that the prince met his demise on the night of the Battle of the Spires. What makes you think he's not some imposter looking for prestige?"

"I believe him for two interesting reasons," Ashoke answered. "First, it's worth mentioning that the boy's caregiver was none other than a celebrated Taborian officer." He paused, contemplating whether to proceed with the truth.

"What officer?" Mossbrook asked, his eyes narrowed with suspicion.

"Captain Jacoby Ironfist," Ashoke said, wincing in preparation for more chaos. But the room remained silent for several heartbeats as the members digested the news.

Mossbrook spat, his voice dripping with contempt, "That despicable coward! I'm surprised he dares to come back to Tabor. Not only did he desert his post in the middle of a battle, but you contend he also committed the unthinkable act of kidnapping the true king and raising him as his own." The Regent rolled his eyes. "You're right. I find it hard to believe such nonsense."

"Hold on, Regent," Thorn said, holding up his hand for quiet. "I've read about Jacoby Ironfist. Before that battle, he held the record for the most commendations of any officer in Taborian history, including four silver spurs and the King's Star."

"The highest honor offered," added Ashoke

"So?" Mossbrook spat, still seething at the news.

"Something must have happened that turned his loyalties," said Thorn evenly.

Ashoke nodded. "That's exactly what I believe happened," his tone leaving no room for doubt. "The Queen summoned him urgently off the battlefield, her dying wish being for him to rescue the child. And that's exactly what he did, without hesitation."

"Nonsense!" Mossbrook yelled, folding his arms, his face purple with rage. "The man's a blatant coward and a traitor."

"It's the truth. I know because I carried the message to him from Queen Elana," Ashoke said definitively. "I don't know what was spoken between them, but events and Ironfist's character lead to one explanation: That he did his duty for the royal family."

The room fell into an abrupt silence, with the council members and Thorn all stunned, mouths hanging open.

They had all heard rumors of the Queen's dying wish, but now, hearing Ashoke's confirmation, the gravity of the situation sank in. Jacoby Ironfist, a renowned warrior and trusted ally of the Queen, had been called away from the battle to fulfill a sacred duty. The child, a symbol of hope for their kingdom, had been in grave danger, and it was Jacoby's responsibility to ensure his safety. Despite his skepticism, Mossbrook couldn't help but feel affected by Jacoby's unwavering conviction. The room fell silent again as each man digested the immense sacrifice Jacoby had made without a moment's hesitation.

Finally, Mossbrook whispered, "What of the boy? Can you confirm he's an Aarmon?"

"I've seen the clover leaf birthmark with my own eyes," Ashoke said. "I hope he is on his way here."

Again, the room fell silent; each member lost in thought. They couldn't help but wonder about the boy's upbringing and the challenges he must have faced growing up as a potential heir to the throne. Mossbrook looked away, considering the burden that rested upon the young man's shoulders, the weight of expectations and responsibilities that would come with his heritage. Ashoke gazed at the councilmen, their faces reflecting a mix of hope and concern as they all pondered the future of their kingdom and the role the prince would play in it. Questions swirled in their minds - would he be ready to take on the mantle of leadership? Would he possess the strength and wisdom required to guide their people out of this crisis? Only time would tell, but for now, they could only hope that the young prince would arrive safely and that Jacoby's mission would be successful. Would the fate of our kingdom rest on the shoulders of an inexperienced noble? Mossbrook wondered. Then, his mind shifted to more prudent thoughts. How can I artfully manipulate the prince, ensuring that I maintain the power I've gained through years of court politics?

Ashoke observed Mossbrook and Thorn exchange a brief, knowing glance, their silent communication speaking volumes. Thorn had risen in rank because of the losses the Taborian army had endured, the weariness of responsibility etched on his face and eyes. Ashoke wondered if, besides Thorn's moderate skills as a warrior, he might have relied on crucial political influence to succeed. The news didn't elicit joyous reactions from the council members. Instead, they maintained a calmness that resembled arachnids lying in wait for their next meal. He would remain vigilant, carefully watching their every move for any suspicious behavior towards Nathaniel.

After several moments, Mossbrook cleared his throat.

"Thank you, Ashoke, for the incredible news. I suggest we all take a few days to adjust and decide on how best to tell the public. For now, I think it best to keep it amongst ourselves."

"I agree," added Thorn, a little too quickly.

"Then if there's nothing further, let's adjourn."

The Brotherhood continued sailing north, and with each passing day, the temperature dropped, and the nights grew longer. Jacoby noticed that Nathaniel's once vibrant energy had faded, replaced by a muted and sober demeanor. His normally bright eyes were dull and tired, and his usual quick wit seemed to have vanished. The weight of coming crucial decisions and Torque's betrayal had taken a toll on Nathaniel's spirit. Despite Jacoby's attempts to offer support and reassurance, Nathaniel remained distant, lost in his own thoughts. Jacoby noticed the growing dark rings under his brother's eyes, further evidence that he carried a heavy burden and had difficulty sleeping. But when he asked about it, Nathaniel just shrugged and walked away. Things came to a head on the night of the fourth day, when the Brotherhood beached the craft on a small outcropping in the river. Nathaniel, as had become his habit, sat alone on the edge of the camp. Lani carried a plate of supper to him as she often did, looking for any way to please the prince. But as she approached, her foot caught on a root, and the plate splattered over the ground. Nathaniel jumped up like he'd been struck, anger exploding inside.

"What in the demons is wrong with you? Can't you carry a simple plate of food?" Nathaniel bellowed. His outburst stopped the others' conversation, and everyone's attention focused on him.

Lani's eyes bugged in surprise, and she said, "I...it was the root," she stammered.

Nathaniel's face turned red; his eyes consumed by rage. "You stupid girl, I should," he screamed, raising his arm.

In an instant, Jacoby stood between Nathaniel and Lani, his eyes as hard as forged iron. "Stop it right now and apologize to Lani. How dare you raise a hand to a woman, especially one who adores you," Jacoby said, his eyes stabbing Nathaniel like two daggers.

"What are you going to do about it? You and the orc know all about betrayal, don't you?" Nathaniel screamed.

In one movement, Jacoby slapped Nathaniel across the face. "Control yourself and stop acting like a baby. We've all dealt with treachery, and endured much greater personal loss than you."

Nathaniel's hand flew to his searing cheek, and his eyes ignited with anger once more. He pulled his arm back with a menacing look, preparing to unleash a powerful strike on Jacoby's jaw, but the blow never materialized. Instead, Grullach's fist collided with Nathaniel's abdomen, forcefully expelling his breath and doubling him over in pain.

"Don't you ever strike your brother, you ungrateful brat! This man has given up everything for you," Grull fumed, his face a mask of fury. "Maybe the chill of the river will cool you off."

Jacoby and Grull grabbed Nathaniel under each arm, dragged him to the river's edge, and tossed him into the icy water. He landed clumsily with a loud splash. The two turned to Lani, tears streaming down her cheeks.

"Are you all right?" Jacoby asked.

She nodded, whimpering as Allai'nn and Rue came to her side. "I...I've never seen him like that," she cried.

Jacoby affectionately rubbed her back. "I doubt you ever will again, gods willing." He paused, then continued. "Since leaving Streamside, we've faced a multitude of difficulties that have tested our resilience. Circumstances forced Nat to mature much faster than anyone should expect. I guess he reached his breaking point."

Lani wiped away her tears, her cheeks glistening with moisture. Memories of her past flooded her mind, reminding her of the dramatic shifts in her life since she departed from her quaint village of Gullyweed. Similar to Nathaniel, she had encountered the full spectrum of emotions - from exhilarating triumphs to crushing defeats, from moments of freedom to periods of confinement, from enduring harsh beatings to tasting the sweetness of true love, and even facing the inevitability of death. Losing her sister Loree, Granny G, and many others weighed heavily on her soul. In the Brotherhood, she not only found a new family, but also discovered a love that surpassed anything she had ever experienced. But never the sting of betrayal. Nathaniel's life was a labyrinth of falsehoods, constantly shifting and unstable, while hers remained steadfast and genuine. Uncertain if things would ever change, she vowed then and there to help him remember to cherish the few who consistently supported him, no matter the obstacles.

Nathaniel dragged himself out of the river, water dripping off his hair and limbs. "I'm so sorry, everyone. I apologize for my stupidity. I have no excuse." Everyone turned their back on him, ignoring him. He frowned and sat by himself, away from the others, shivering in the night air for almost an hour before Allai'nn brought him a towel to dry off and hot coffee.

"Here," she said angrily, thrusting the towel and mug forward. Her anger boiled over as she thought about how he had treated Lani. "After what you did, I should just let you freeze to death," she spat. "How could you act like such a cretin? It seems you fail to remember that she is madly in love with you and deserves your full respect. Witnessing your selfish behavior is frustrating, a stark contrast to the hard work Jacoby, Grull, and I invested in your upbringing. Since the day we departed from Streamside, you have never been alone in your struggles. Each member of our group has been there for you, and that unwavering support will remain constant."

Allai'nn hesitated, the fire in her eyes dimming slightly. "Nathaniel, you need help; you can't handle things alone. We handle problems as a family, just like always," she said sternly, her arms tightly crossed, her piercing gaze fixing on him like drills.

"I know. I guess Torque's actions triggered me," Nathaniel mumbled, feeling ashamed.

"That's no excuse for how you acted," Allai'nn countered.

Nathaniel nodded.

"Now, get off your brain and stop acting the fool. And beg Lani for forgiveness before she's too hurt to give it," she said, stamping her foot for emphasis.

Nathaniel could feel the weight of disappointment in Allai'nn's words. He knew she was right - he had let his anger get the best of him, forgetting all the support and love that his friends had given him throughout their journey. He had acted selfishly, hurting Lani in the process. Torque's actions had sparked a fire within him, but he now understood that it was not a justification for his behavior. He felt a deep sense of shame for his actions, similar to the way he used to feel when Allai'nn would catch him misbehaving as a child. Her stern gaze and crossed arms only reinforced his remorse. Nathaniel knew he had to make things right and beg Lani for forgiveness before it was too late. He took a deep breath, ready to face the consequences of his actions and make amends.

Nathaniel dried off and returned to the campfire, the crackling flames casting a warm glow on his face as he knelt before Lani, who sat alone nearby.

"Hi," he said, his face a mask of shame.

Her voice trembling, she whispered, "Hi." Her face was pale and marked by tear stains. However, her eyes were as cold and unyielding as steel.

"Will you walk with me?" he whispered, his voice filled with longing.

"You can say what you want right here," she said, her tone icy and devoid of warmth.

Nathaniel glanced at the others, their eyes averted, feigning disinterest. "I deeply regret my immature and self-centered behavior. I acted like a spoiled adolescent."

"Go on."

"I promise never to behave like such a jerk again, ever," he vowed, determined to make amends. "And I give you my word that I will never harm you, both now and for the rest of my life."

"That's a start. Why should I believe you?"

The question caught Nathaniel off guard, sending his thoughts into disarray. He furrowed his brow and asked, "What do you mean?"

"You heard me. Why?"

"Because I will never..."

"Why, specifically?" she interrupted.

Her eyes were like vast oceans of blue, and at that moment, he felt a profound sense of understanding wash over him.

"With all my heart, I love you, and I will make it a point to treat the people I love with utmost respect and admiration," he said with sincerity.

She fought to keep a straight face, though her heart pounded with excitement. Despite our deep connection, Nathaniel has never publicly acknowledged his love for me. However, he had done her wrong, and the emotional wound would need time to mend.

As she firmly grasped his hand, she locked eyes with him, her voice filled with conviction as she declared, "I will not accept hearing your voice raised to me, let alone your hand. Swear to me."

"I swear."

Later that evening, Grullach found him and said quietly, "Lad I fear the future may hold greater treachery than Torque's. You must control your emotions with a stronger will. It may save your life someday." He slapped him on the shoulder and walked away as Nathaniel contemplated the lessons of the past few hours.

Finally, after three days, they sailed under the Web Bridge, a remarkable rope structure that arched across the river. Its crisscrossing supports reached from tree to tree, creating an awe-inspiring scene. Just after, the river split, leaving a choice: east or west.

"What does the map indicate, Jacoby?" Nathaniel asked.

Jacoby had watched his brother intently since the incident with Lani and was pleased to see Nathaniel strong in spirit again. He pulled the parchment map from his pack and unfurled it for Nat to see.

"The starboard fork leads further into the wood, ending at Mirror Lake. It should lead us to the doorstep of the Sacred Forest," Jacoby said, pointing his index finger at the map. Nat nodded and steered the small boat east with the current.

As the group sailed further into the Horn Wood, the air grew heavy with the scent of damp earth, and the sounds of chirping birds filled the surrounding trees. The dense foliage of the forest seemed to close in around them, creating a sense of mystery and adventure. Nathaniel maneuvered the vessel through the winding waterways, navigating around fallen logs and overhanging branches. Nathaniel's anticipation grew, eager to discover what secrets and wonders lay hidden within the heart of this enchanted forest.

By afternoon, the once wide cut had dwindled to a stream, abruptly halted by a massive beaver dam that divided the flowing water. The dam, constructed from an intricate arrangement of hundreds of logs, branches, and limbs, stood like a towering wall, reaching a height of over three stories. The dam was a marvel of engineering, showcasing the skill and determination of its creators, who had meticulously woven logs and branches together, forming a resilient structure that stood firm against the powerful current of the river. The sound of water rushing through the narrow channels echoed through the air, adding a sense of power and wildness to the scene. The dam, perhaps the work of several generations, had transformed the once free-flowing river into a series of cascades and swirling eddies, making it nearly impossible for any creature, big or small, to pass.

"Now what?" Cor'in asked, frowning.

Jacoby twisted his mouth, studying the map. "Nothing marks this dam on the map," he said, confused. "I guess we land and continue by foot."

"I'll swim to shore and scout around," Horatio said.

"Interesting structure," Blue Ivy commented. "This must have taken years, even centuries, to build."

"Do you hear that?" Rue asked.

The others shook their heads, but Allai'nn answered. "I hear the Mother's song, vibrant and alive."

"Yes, the trees carry her melody," Rue said, smiling.

"I can't hear a thing," Cor'in said grumpily.

Rue giggled. "Open that curmudgeon's heart, Cor'in, and listen."

"Very funny," he responded with a smirk. But he tried closing his eyes, and his Elven blood carried the softest of sounds to his ear, like a whisper on the wind. He smiled, the faint melody carrying with it a deep feeling of peace.

"I found a game trail," Horatio called out excitedly, his voice echoing along the riverside near the dam. "From the looks of it, it seems to go towards the east. Land here!"

"Okay. Let's get packed up and see where it leads us," Jacoby said.

Grull and Nathaniel gathered branches and rope, working quickly to construct a makeshift litter that would safely transport the children. When they were ready, the group set out down the trail, with Horatio leading the way. As the group passed the dam, Nathaniel marveled at its impressive size, with its solid construction spanning over twenty feet and stretching a hundred feet wide. The trail followed the river's course, revealing glimpses of the shimmering water through breaks in the trees. In less than an hour, the trail abruptly ended at a towering cliff face, where the lazy river cascaded over the edge, transforming into a breathtaking waterfall. The tumultuous crashing water below sent mist rising like a curtain, creating a captivating, arching rainbow that blocked any glimpse of what lay below.

"I think I see a way down," Horatio said, leaning over the cliff face. He dropped his pack and squeezed his way between two boulders before disappearing from view.

After several minutes, Cor'in leaned over the cliff face and yelled, "Can you see anything, Toady?" knowing the remark would ruffle Horatio's feathers. But no response came for another quarter hour when the green frogman reappeared from the mist, his skin dripping river water.

"I found a way down, but it's slippery and dangerous. We'll have to carry the children and watch our step," Horatio said. Addressing Cor'in, he quipped, "I can't believe they didn't teach you at the orphanage that frogs are aquatic creatures, unlike toads, elfie." He moved on before Cor'in responded.

The trail down was treacherous, winding through a series of large rocks and crevasses, their surfaces slick with misty moisture and adorned with damp moss. Horatio took the lead, his tongue darting out occasionally to clutch a stone and maintain his balance as he guided the brotherhood down the cliff face. The base of the waterfall was a dissonant symphony, the water crashing down with a thunderous roar, creating a wide pool that seamlessly blended into the meandering river that wound its way through the forest. At the end of the trail, there was no way forward. The lush understory and towering hardwoods created an impenetrable barrier. A small island, not larger than twenty by twenty feet, sat at the center of the pool, densely populated with spikey, moss-covered willows, bushes, and an assortment of wild weeds.

"What next, professor?" Cor'in asked Horatio, but he just shrugged his shoulders.

With narrowed eyes, Nathaniel pointed at the small land mass, his finger trembling slightly.

"I think that island may be moving toward us," he said, his voice filled with concern.

Everyone fixed their eyes on the tiny island across the pond as it slowly edged its way towards the group.

"I'm not sure. Maybe a trick of the sun on the water," Blue said dubiously.

"So," Jacoby said, capturing the group's attention once again. He turned to Horatio and asked, "Do you think you could slip into the water and scout for another trail, either ahead or across the river?"

"Gladly," the Anuran said and began stripping off his tunic and armor. But he halted and uttered, "Oh, my!"

Jacoby looked up and realized Nathaniel had been correct. The island had moved even closer, and now two enormous black eyes crested the water's surface only fifteen feet away. He eased his hand to his sword pommel, his heart pounding as he prepared for the impending danger. However, Nathaniel drew his blade first, the metal gleaming in the sunlight, and positioned himself between the approaching eyes and the group, Sinbad barking ferociously by his side.

At that precise moment, the tranquil pond water erupted into a frenzy of churning and bubbling, resembling a cauldron about to boil over. Simultaneously, the once-steady island trembled, accompanied by a cacophony of sounds. Above the roaring waterfall, distinct cracking and sucking noises clawed their way into the onlooker's awareness as the two eyes rose above the surface, revealing the head of a gruesome monster. The beast had the head of a monstrous hound with long, jagged teeth and a wide moss-covered snout with flaps covering the nares. A reptilian pink forked tongue slithered between the teeth, the beast's neck extending back under the surface to the island. The monstrous creature's eyes, a fiery shade of crimson with black, empty pupils, glowed with an otherworldly intensity as they fixated on Nathaniel. Dark, slimy fur covered its head, and sharp, curving horns protruded from its skull. The creature's elongated neck, adorned with bony ridges, snaked back towards the island, disappearing into the murky depths below. As it emerged from the depths, the colossal beast sent water cascading off its shaggy, moss-covered body, creating a mesmerizing display. Its hulking upper body revealed itself, a smooth reptilian belly boasting powerful limbs that terminated in sharp, curved claws. Robust plates adorned the broad expanse of its back, serving as a fertile bed for the thriving life of the lake island. The sight of this grotesque monster sent shivers down Nathaniel's spine, its presence emanating an aura of ancient malevolence.

"What on earth is that thing?" Grull shouted, his eyebrows furrowing in confusion. For a heartbeat, the sight left Jacoby and the other brotherhood members frozen stiff before leaping forward to assist Nathaniel.

Lani screamed, "Nathaniel!" who registered her piercing scream, but his unwavering gaze remained fixed on the terrifying beast.

With a menacing roar, the monster opened its mouth wide, revealing its enormous jaws poised for a lethal attack, yet it faltered as it caught sight of the warrior's formidable blade. As Nathaniel faced the creature, his sword emitted a brilliant blue light that steadily intensified. Simultaneously, the Founder's stone in his pocket started vibrating, amplifying the energy of the blade and illuminating the area around the prince in a dazzling, blinding light. The creature covered his eyes with one arm and shrieked in a rumbling ancient voice, "Blue Blade!" With a single, swift movement, it collapsed under the intense light and crashed back into the lake, creating a surge of water. The impact of the lake water hitting Nathaniel was so strong that it swept him off his feet, along with the others who stood behind him. Waves of water flew in all directions, drenching everyone in its path as the splash hit with a powerful force. The sheer force of the impact sent them reeling, knocking the wind out of them, and leaving them wheezing and struggling to find their footing again. Through the chaos, Nathaniel could hear the distant echoes of his companions shouting his name, their voices filled with concern and urgency.

As the water drained away, Nathaniel slowly rose to his feet, his clothes clinging to his body and his hair plastered against his forehead. Despite the creature's appearance, the lake and island were back in their original location once more, offering no hints of the chaos that had ensued.

The Founder's stone, still vibrating in his pocket, emitted a soft hum, its power now subdued after its momentous contribution to the battle. Nathaniel reached into his pocket and retrieved the stone, inspecting it. The ancient runes' molten golden glow was fading, but Nathaniel could still see its faint luminescence, reminding him of the intense energy from the battle. As he held the stone in his hand, Nathaniel felt a surge of gratitude and reverence for those who had come before him, their spirits guiding and empowering him. With a deep breath, Nathaniel turned to his companions, his eyes reflecting both exhaustion and triumph.

Lani sprinted into his arms, wrapping him in a bear hug. "I thought you were dead for sure. Thank you for saving us," she whispered. He hugged her back as if he would never let her go.

"Great job, Nat," Cor'in said, his voice cutting through the reunion. "One look at your ugly mug, and the creature collapsed in fright," he said, amused.

Nathaniel released Lani and rolled his eyes.

"A brave move, lad," Grull said, his hand slapping him on the shoulder, a mix of admiration and concern in his eyes. "Thank you for stepping up and taking charge."

Nathaniel turned to Jacoby. "Did you hear the monster?"

"It definitely said, "Blue Blade," Grull interjected.

"I heard it, too," answered Jacoby. "I guess these swords that Goldbriar gave us have a well-known history. But what was it, and why here, of all places?"

"I could swear that looked like a Dragon Hound," Blue Ivy said, his eyes widening in disbelief. "But I've never heard of them living off land."

"A what?" Horatio asked, his voice filled with confusion.

"To call my sentinel a mere dragon would be an understatement," a voice boomed inside their minds. "It is a formidable being with unmatched power. He's ancient and utterly unique."

Nathaniel, with the others, searched for the source, his heart pounding, but there was no one to be seen. "Who said that?"

"Follow the path behind the waterfall and find out."

As Nathaniel peered at the majestic waterfall, a sudden clarity washed over him, revealing a concealed pathway blending into the rocks. Intrigued by the discovery, Nathaniel couldn't resist the urge to investigate further. The well-hidden pathway, almost invisible against the rugged stone surface, seemed to beckon him toward an unknown adventure. Moss-covered stones lined the footpath, hinting at its age and secretiveness. Nathaniel's heart raced with anticipation as he motioned for the others, then stepped between the rocks onto the pathway, curiosity guiding his every step. He couldn't help but wonder where this hidden passage would lead him and what wonders awaited him on the other side. With each passing moment, his excitement grew, and he found himself consumed by the allure of the unknown. The others followed, their footsteps mirroring Nathaniel's, cautious not to slip into the lake.

The path wound through jagged rocks and dense underbrush, eventually leading Nathaniel to a secret cave hidden behind the thundering waterfall. A stone wall blocked further exploration at the back of the cave. Despite his thorough study of the wall, Nathaniel could not uncover any concealed doors or passages.

"Anyone detect anything?" Jacoby asked.

Nathaniel shook his head, dismayed. "Allai'nn, would you mind looking again? Maybe with your powers, you can detect a magical entrance."

The elf princess walked forward, closed her eyes, and laid hands on the stone. She remained muted for several heartbeats. But then opened her eyes and remarked, "Nothing."

"Maybe we missed the doorway?" offered Grullach.

"Let's split up and search the other walls and the cave mouth, to be sure," said Jacoby.

The group turned to exit, their eyes scanning every rock and cranny. At that moment, the Founder's Stone in Nathaniel's pocket began to vibrate and glow.

Crack!

When he turned around, the sight of the cave's back wall cracking and splitting open startled him. It's stone glowed orange, then bright red, heating as if thrust into an inferno, liquifying into a burning magma, filling the cave with the stench of sulfurous brimstone. In a matter of seconds, the solid stone transformed into a radiant portal, emitting a vibrant red glow. A beaver emerged from the radiant glowing doorway, followed by Friend, the majestic white unicorn.

"Augustus?" Nathaniel said incredulously. He had last seen the talking beaver months before in Hope Wood.

The beaver bowed. "Wonderful to see you again, my prince. Welcome to the Sacred Forest."

TWENTY-FOUR

Augustus beckoned them to follow, disappearing from sight as he stepped through the portal behind Friend. The warm, red glow from the doorway bathed Nathaniel's face, causing him to pause before finally stepping into the light. He heard a loud rush, his body falling like he'd stepped off a cliff. As the wind whistled through his hair, his heart raced and his stomach dropped until he finally felt the solid ground beneath his boots, revealing an expansive iron gate guarded by two enormous Rhinomen right before him. Each guard spanned twice Nathaniel's height and three times his width, with muscular arms and legs the size of tree trunks.

He took a shaky step forward, feeling the ground shift beneath his unsteady feet. As he landed, he could hear the others arriving behind him. Cor'in's voice filled with annoyance as he complained about portals, followed by the unmistakable sound of him retching. Staggering to his feet, Nathaniel scanned the area for Lani. Sitting on the ground, she massaged her foot, her face contorted in agony. As he knelt by her, she winced and confessed, "I twisted my ankle when I landed awkwardly."

"Can you stand?"

He laced an arm under hers and helped her to her feet, but when he released her, she crumpled to the ground, unable to put weight on the ankle.

"Demons!" she cried, clutching her leg.

"I'll carry you. Climb on my back," he said, squatting for her to put her hands around his neck.

"Everyone else, all right?" He asked after picking Lani up piggyback.

"Just fine. Except for Sir Retch-a-lot," Horatio said, patting Cor'in on the pack.

"Hilarious, Toadie," Cor'in exclaimed. "Nobody informed me I would be spun around like a top."

"I told you not to eat that jerky for breakfast," Horatio said.

"If you are quite finished, Friend is waiting," Augustus said at the gate entrance irritably.

"Coming," Jacoby said, and the group passed between the guards and continued down a forest trail.

On each side, mammoth ancient hardwoods sprouted up hundreds of feet above them, their canopy filtering the sun into a spray of sunspots over the path. Elder, maples, redwoods, sequoias, and aspens grew between the largest trees, a variety Nathaniel had never seen. A crisscross pattern of maroon and green bark adorned the massive trunks of the trees while their branches reached high above and spread wide like an umbrella. The tree's compound leaves had an unusual mauve color, resembling five-pointed stars with a delicate light blue central stem. The trees had large, lobular yellow fruits throughout their branches, more prominent than a man's head.

"Augustus, what kind of trees are these?" he asked, pointing at the towering giants. I've seen nothing like them."

"Those trees have grown here since the First Age," the beaver said studiously, adjusting his thick spectacles over his nose. "Although their fruit is delicious, they are best known for the strength of their wood. Most call them ironwood trees."

"Fascinating," Nathaniel said, marveling at the colors and immensity of the forest.

After several minutes, the trail abruptly ended, revealing a vast marsh that stretched as far as the eye could see, covered in lifeless sawgrass and overgrown weeds. The air was thick with the putrid smell of dead wildlife, causing Nathaniel to cover his mouth and nose with his sleeve. The forest at the marsh's edge contorted into gnarled, decaying forms resembling distorted caricatures of the lively forest they had just encountered.

"What's that smell?" the prince asked. "I thought this wood was enchanted."

"I'm not sure I can sleep in such a nasty place," added Cor'in.

"Did we take a wrong turn?" suggested Lani.

"Nasty?" Augustus proclaimed with an air of superiority. "I'll have you know that this is the epitome of serenity in Curth Talem."

"I think he's lost his mind," suggested Grull.

But then the beaver realized the entire group had their noses covered, and for a moment, he couldn't comprehend the reason behind it. "How insulting," he exclaimed, his face contorted with disbelief and offense. "I would have thought better of royalty," he muttered, walking. Augustus took a few steps before realizing that the brotherhood had not followed him; instead, they had turned around and marched back towards the forest path.

"Wait! What on earth is the matter?" he begged.

"All we see is a putrid marsh that smells even worse than it looks," Nathaniel said over his shoulder. "It was a mistake to come here."

Augustus' eyes bugged, unsure of what had just changed. "Please, ladies and gentlemen. I don't understand," he insisted, waddling after the group to catch up. Nathaniel and the others turned, frowning. Suddenly, Augustus understood the mistake had been his.

"Please, let me explain," he gasped, panting to catch his breath. "What you see is another security measure. Please say 'Marigold' to see the true meadow."

As the brotherhood said 'Marigold' in unison, a sudden shift occurred, instantly transforming everything. The meadow transformed into a vibrant tapestry of colors, with the lush green grass blending seamlessly into the vast expanse of the sky. The lea stretched before them, a vast expanse of beauty extending endlessly into the distance. A burst of wildflowers painted the meadow in a patchwork of shapes and colors. The air filled with the intoxicating scent of blooming flowers, their delicate petals swaying gracefully in the breeze. Daisies, sunflowers, and tulips stood tall, coloring the landscape with vibrant yellow, red, and purple hues.

Sprites and dwarves rode on the backs of enormous butterflies that danced among the blossoms, their wings a kaleidoscope of patterns and colors. Bees the size of birds buzzed from flower to flower, collecting nectar in a harmonious symphony of nature. With its vibrant tapestry of life, the meadow was a haven for pollinators and a sanctuary of beauty. The sheer diversity and abundance of wildflowers in the meadow captivated them, creating a fairytale-like scene that was impossible to resist. The entire brotherhood halted, awestruck by the diversity and grandeur.

"Now that's more like it," Cor'in crooned, mesmerized by the sight.

As if summoned from thin air, Nathaniel heard a "pop," and Friend appeared.

"Welcome, my friends," a voice echoed in their heads, "to my mystical home. I apologize for the misunderstanding earlier," as Friend stared sternly down at Augustus, now hanging his head. "However, please enjoy the Sacred Forest as your home and immerse yourself in its peaceful ambiance." The unicorn hesitated a heartbeat as if considering his next word. "Rest, for later, we shall feast in celebration of your arrival. Augustus will escort you to your rooms."

With another 'pop,' the unicorn disappeared.

"How does he do that? Blue Ivy said, amazed.

"Friend's magic is unmatched," Augustus reminded them, his face still blushing with embarrassment. "Teleporting is his favorite way to travel, surreptitiously moving from one place to another. It can be annoying when he unexpectedly shows up next to you, interrupting your thoughts. Just this morning at breakfast, he gave me such a fright I spilled my porridge."

"I don't see any buildings or homes. Where are our rooms?" Cor'in asked.

"And where are the animals?" added Rue, seeing only the open meadow.

"Why, they're everywhere," Augustus answered, gesturing to his surroundings. In frustration, he kicked the dirt with a sudden burst of energy, letting out a string of curses. "Once again, I sincerely apologize to esteemed lords and ladies. Please say 'Pumpkinseed.'

The group all said, "Pumpkinseed," their voices in chorus. The world transformed instantly, awakening with vibrant sights and sounds as if a switch had flipped. Many animals emerged from the shadows, filling the meadow with vibrant energy as they gracefully traversed the grassy expanse. Families played horseshoes or enjoyed picnics while a giraffe teacher with glasses taught a class of young deer and mountain lion cubs nearby. Brilliantly painted treehouses stood proudly at the forest's edge, their colors mirroring the hues of a rainbow soaring above the treetops. In one of the Ironwood trees, they had built a luxurious structure that offered breathtaking views of the surrounding forest.

At the structure's base, Augustus stopped, handing Nathaniel a ring of keys. "Your rooms with warm baths are waiting, each marked with your names. You can find a myriad of snacks and drinks in the common room."

"Thank you, Augustus," Nathaniel said as the beaver bowed and took his leave.

"I'm starving," Horatio said, striding up the bridge.

"Me, too," added Cor'in.

"I'm looking forward to a long, hot bath," Lani said dreamily.

"The kids could use a thorough washing," suggested Grull.

"Right after us," responded Allai'nn, rushing up the rope ladder leading to the first level of rooms.

Finally, after days of hard travel, each member found their room and breathed in relief, grateful for a moment of peace and solitude. Nathaniel discovered his room next to Lani's. Upon stepping inside, he found a generously sized yet elegantly simple bedroom and sitting area. He dropped his pack at the door, feeling the weight lift from his shoulders, and eagerly stripped off his clothes. With a contented sigh, he slipped into the tub, where warm steam enveloped him, inviting him to unwind.

In Tabor, Regent Mossbrook sat across from General Thorne at the tiny cafe table in the city's slums on the city's edge. In contrast to Mossbrook's simple attire as a tinker, Thorne wore the typical artisan outfit, leather apron over heavy wool trousers and smock. Today, I must be both a salesperson and an empath, Mossbrook thought. Thorne's strategic mind may be challenging to manipulate.

Mossbrook began expressing his appreciation. "Thank you for the meeting. Nice disguise. What are your thoughts after digesting the news from Ashoke? Is it possible that King Aarmon's son is alive and returning to Tabor?"

"I can't believe it," Thorne said, his eyes betraying his disbelief.

Mossbrook murmured, "Neither do I," with a hushed tone. "If, and I stress, if he speaks the truth, I wonder what effect it might have?"

"The effect?" Thorne barked, emotion rising in his voice. "Gods know what could happen."

With an inviting gesture, the Regent mused, "It's difficult to know. You may be too young to remember, but the people disliked King Aarmon's incessant need for conquest, their discontent palpable in every conversation toward the end of his reign. Lady Elana was the glue holding the monarch together, and that sentiment died with her."

"I've heard the stories. Aarmon's narcissism and lust for conquest almost destroyed Tabor."

"If the mob did embrace the prince, the atmosphere would shift dramatically," Mossbrook noted.

"This is no time for the mob to decide Tabor's fate," Thorne said, his face scarlet with emotion.

"Of course, unless the mob was on our side," Mossbrook suggested, a sly look on his face. "Still, if the prince appears, our leadership roles would transform. I suspect resistance to the new authority may lead to demotion at best, even possible imprisonment," Mossbrook counseled, looking away.

"Don't forget the executioner's ax," Thorne said seriously. "So, what can we do?"

"He has no reputation to undermine. And the mob could rally to a royal standard. So, that can only mean…" Mossbrook solicited.

Thorne's eyes grew large. "Are you suggesting?"

"I suggest nothing," Mossbrook stated, locking eyes with the general. "I only worry about the future of Tabor, especially at this critical juncture in history. How can our beloved country survive a sniveling, inexperienced teen as our leader?"

Both men remained quiet for several minutes as Thorne rubbed his chin, lost in thought. Through relentless determination and cunning, he had climbed the ranks from a lowly infantryman to the esteemed position of Imperial General, finally attaining the power and prestige he had long desired. Could I allow everything I've accomplished to be stolen by a royal youth? Resentment surged through his mind, clouding everything but the path to keep his position. Conveniently forgetting the imposing army marching toward the city at that very moment, Thorne knew he must act to survive this future coup.

The general's eyes narrowed. "I can find someone who might help resolve the issue before it ever reaches the ears of the citizens."

Mossbrook grinned, relieved and delighted that he had hooked the young general. "Excellent. I will advance you ten thousand gold sentochniks from the public tax revenue to use as an incentive. But one must act urgently before he arrives in Tabor."

"Do you know his location?" Thorne asked.

"I took it upon myself to interrogate Ashoke. He reluctantly offered the prince may travel toward the city through the Horn Wood by the river."

A pained expression came over Thorne as he realized Mossbrook had already crossed the line, his resolve cracking.

"Don't weaken now, my friend. Our survival demands pragmatic action," insisted Mossbrook.

With a nod of resolve, Thorne rose to his feet and walked away briskly, his steps infused with the unwavering determination of his mission.

Mossbrook counted two minutes before leaving the cafe and walked around the next corner into a dark alleyway. As he sidestepped refuse and discarded garbage, kicking a giant rat out of his way, his body morphed into a simple serf wearing ragged clothes. "Better to fit in," he murmured to himself. Nari Mudpucker, Ravenite's doppelgänger extraordinaire, proceeded to a ramshackle doorway, opened it, and entered. The room carried the stench of human excrement and urine, more rats scattering in surprise from his intrusion. He passed through an outer room into a pitch-black inner room. A figure sat tied to a chair in the room's center, his head hung to his chest, covered with unwashed gray hair. Mudpucker stepped in front, lifted the man's head, and said, "I'm afraid your presence is no longer needed, Regent." Mudpucker congratulated himself for having the forethought to capture and interrogate the Regent the day before. He was surprised to learn the that the Regent and his General were so well informed about the prince and his plans.

"Wait," Mossbrook rasped, his throat as dry as dust. "Don't kill me; I can help you."

"I think not," the doppelgänger whispered in his ear.

With the quickness of an asp, Mudpucker sliced his dagger across the semi-conscious Mossbrook's neck, opening a long gash. The man's eyes bugged as he uttered a strangled scream. Scarlet bubbles surged from his mouth as maroon liquid pulsed from his throat.

Mudpucker's face lit up with a satisfied grin as he left the regent, blood gushing from the open wound, and walked out into the warm afternoon air. It will take days to find the body, only when the overwhelming scent of death masks the stench of the alleyway. As he inhaled deeply, a wide grin spread across his face. It's been a successful day, and I can already feel the subtle shifts in the air, signaling the beginning of change. With a chuckle, he reflected on how easily he had manipulated Thorne, amused by his cunning and Thorne's ruthless sense of self-preservation. The master's plan was unshakeable, and nothing could deter him at this point. With a cheerful whistle, his steps became light and bouncy as he descended the dirty street that led to the notorious wharf. As he walked by, he couldn't help but notice the sinister groups of shady sailors and grimy dock men, their dead eyes silently observing him. Ignoring the threat lurking in the shadows, he confidently strode across the harbor, aware of his strength and skill. Feeling carefree, he delighted in the soothing touch of the sun on his skin while making his way up the lengthy stone walkway that led to the city's gate and onto the aviary to message Ravenite about his success.

After hours of feasting, laughter, and lively conversations with animals of all kinds, the welcome celebration had concluded. A harmonious quartet of wildebeests serenaded the crowd with gentle melodies from their harps, lutes, and shawms. The air filled with the delightful aroma of a bountiful feast of fresh fruits, vegetables, and tubers. Everyone had a splendid time, especially Horatio, who couldn't stop smiling after being playfully tackled by Ruby, the faun from the Hope Wood. Horatio sat down, his face transitioning from its usual deep green to a bright shade of red after several minutes of hugs and an overwhelming number of kisses. As the festivities came to a close, Horatio felt overwhelmed with joy. The playful interaction with Ruby had brought out a side of him he rarely showed. His usually reserved demeanor had melted away, replaced by a radiant smile that seemed to light up the entire clearing. The other animals watched, their eyes delighted at seeing this unexpected bond between Horatio and Ruby. A sense of harmony and love filled the air as if the very essence of nature had come alive at that moment. Horatio knew this celebration would always stay in his memory, serving as a cherished reminder of the magic in unexpected connections.

As the other men trailed behind Friend to his chambers, Horatio gallantly offered to escort Ruby back to her house.

"You're here," the Anuran exclaimed, tightening his grip on her hand.

"Did you miss me?" she said playfully.

"Yes, certainly. But how did you find your way here?" Horatio asked, his voice filled with curiosity.

"Can you recall the words I spoke to you before you departed from the Hope Wood?" Ruby inquired.

"You promised you'd see me again."

"And now I'm here, in Tabor, where I need to be."

Horatio chuckled at the faun's confidence. "Thanks for coming. I've really missed you," Horatio said shyly. "But you know Tabor is dangerous, especially with the war."

Ruby turned to face him; her dark eyes locked on his. 'Do you care about me?"

"You know I do."

With a heartfelt declaration, she stated, "I'm glad to hear that because my heart belongs to you." Determined, she added, "I won't leave your side again. The war be damned."

As he enveloped her in a warm embrace, Horatio's heart overflowed with thankfulness to Odin for her. He silently implored for the god's guidance and safeguarding as they moved forward.

Nathaniel sat across from Friend in the smoking room, surrounded by the other Brotherhood. Jacoby and Grull puffed on their pipes, watching Nathaniel pull the founder's stone from his pocket. At his touch, the ancient runes glowed an orange hue, and he held the stone high for Friend to see.

The unicorn's eyes widened, and he spoke telepathically. "You are a blessed human, Nathaniel Aarmon. I have not seen this stone since your ancestor, Whitestar, lost the stone in the first millennia."

"Can you read the words, Friend?" inquired Nathaniel.

"Of course. Thor allowed me to observe when he etched each stone with its specific inscription," the voice in Nathaniel's mind said.

Nathaniel held his breath as Friend read the inscription.

"Created soul of Elder core and soil pitch;
my gifts to men are powers rich:
courage, strength, and grit to aid,
from noble acts, success is made."

A heavy silence enveloped the room, lasting for several heartbeats as each member absorbed the weight of the words. The answer appeared straightforward to Nathaniel, with no complexity or difficulty. Odin had imbued the stone with additional power, courage, and grit. But what power? What is the purpose of including the ending line? Depending on how one perceives it, noble acts can encompass various actions, such as self-sacrifice, assisting others, or even eliminating bandits or enemies to protect the land. What noble deed was called for?

Friend's voice filled his mind as if on cue, enlightening him with an explanation. "Each message carries a subtle variation for every recipient. Nathaniel, this stone and its message are meant specifically for you. Only with the passing of time and the accumulation of experience will its genuine message and powers become apparent."

Nathaniel nodded, rolling the stone over and over in his palm. He sensed the stone spoke to him, but he failed to understand. "Thank you," he said to the unicorn. "I am weary from our travels. I think I'll turn in."

"As you wish," Friend replied.

Nathaniel locked eyes with Jacoby as he said, "Good night, all." Jacoby could read his younger brother's unease but chose not to follow him. He will be king soon and must carve his own path.

Nathaniel never saw the figure waiting in the shadows, his mind preoccupied with the stone.

"Hello, stranger," a sultry voice said.

"Hello," Nathaniel said, his face breaking into a smile. "Waiting for someone?"

"Yes. I'm searching for a handsome, strong, and courageous warrior. Seen any?" said the voice.

Nathaniel rubbed his chin, pretending to consider the words. "No, but will a tavern stable hand do instead?"

"If it's the best I can do," Lani teased, appearing from the shadows and kissing him lightly on the lips. "I've been waiting for you," she added.

"I'm glad you did," he responded.

They walked hand-in-hand out the entrance of Friend's estate, Lani pulling close to Nathaniel. He felt her warmth radiate beside him, comforting his anxiety. Many shining stars blanketed the velvet night sky, casting a silver glow over the sprawling gardens surrounding them. Lani's soft laughter filled the air, echoing through the tranquil atmosphere. Nathaniel couldn't help but smile, captivated by her infectious joy. As they strolled along the well-worn dirt pathway, the scent of blooming flowers enveloped them, adding to the enchanting ambiance. Lani intertwined her fingers with Nathaniel's, perfectly fitting their hands together as if they were made for each other. Moments like these would dissolve Nathaniel's worries, leaving a deep sense of contentment. Lani's presence was like a soothing balm to his restless soul, giving him the reassurance he needed.

"Did Friend decipher the stone's runes?" she asked.

"Yes," he responded and recited the inscription.

"Interesting, but a little vague," Lani said, her brow furrowed. "At least now you know."

"Friend says time will reveal the true meaning," Nathaniel said, stopping at the entrance to Lani's room.

"I trust Friend," she said, her voice low and husky, as she leaned in and kissed him passionately. Nathaniel's chaotic mind cleared, and a serene calmness settled within him.

"Our future is ours to shape," she said, pulling back with a resolute expression. "For one night, sleep in peace."

She pulled him into the room, and he immediately sank into the softness of the bed. She lovingly stroked his hair and gave him a gentle kiss, covering him with a soft blanket before departing.

"Sleep well, my heart," she murmured, closing the door behind her.

Feeling exhaustion's heavy weight, Nathaniel nestled into the bedcovers, his leaden eyelids fluttered closed, and sleep claimed him in seconds.

The prince dreamed of his youth at the Sleeping Dragon Inn, reminiscing about fishing with his friends along the nearby creek and the practice sessions with Jacoby and Grull, who mentored and trained him with the sword and bow in the meadow behind the inn. However, an eerie presence interrupted his dream, hiding in the shadows and eventually revealing itself as a chilling face. The vision, not of monsters or evil wizards, revealed the face of the dark Svartalf, who he had battled in Mar Napor. The elf spoke in a firm tone. "Beware, human. We are coming."

The prince's heart raced as he stared into the piercing eyes of the Svartalf. Memories of their previous encounter flooded his mind - the intense battle, the strength and cunning of the dark elf. The prince had thought he had defeated his foe, but now it seemed the threat was far from over. The chilling voice echoed through his dream, sending shivers down his spine. "You may have defeated me once, human, but the darkness never truly fades. We have regrouped, grown stronger, and now we come for you and everything you hold dear." The prince's dream turned into a nightmare as he felt the weight of impending danger settle upon him.

Then the face changed again, transforming into the gaunt, skeletal visage of the evil wizard, Ravenite. The face of Ravenite twisted and contorted, the gaunt, skeletal visage sending chills down the prince's spine. The decayed flesh on one side of the skull seemed to pulse with a sickening energy, revealing the true extent of the evil that resided within. As the voice of the demon Sin rasped from behind Ravenite, the prince couldn't help but feel a wave of dread wash over him.

"Following your instructions, we have ruthlessly razed every village within a fifty-mile radius of our advance, mercilessly taking the lives of each citizen, their souls eagerly devoured by our undead minions," the demon rasped.

"Wonderful!" A rumbling chuckle erupted from Ravenite, echoing through the surroundings. "Prince, behold the wonders that await you. Your meddlesome Brotherhood will be the last to fall when my army reaches the City of Spires. Once I erase Tabor from existence, I will present you as a gift to the demon lord, Asmodeus, for his unwavering assistance to my conquest."

The prince's heart sank as he realized the extent of the devastation that awaited the City of Spires. With his beloved brotherhood destined to be the last to fall, Ravenite's true intentions became apparent. He planned to erase Tabor from existence and offer the prince as a sacrificial gift to the demon lord, Asmodeus, in exchange for his unwavering help in conquering the world. The prince's mind raced, knowing he had to stop this impending catastrophe and save his Tabor from utter destruction.

Gasping for breath, his heart pounding in his chest, a loud, piercing voice startled him as it shouted, "Begone, wicked one!" The dream's dark corners vanished in a blinding flash of white light, revealing the flowered meadow of the Sacred Forest. The sweet scent of blooming flowers filled the air, and a gentle breeze rustled through the vibrant green leaves of the ancient trees. A crystal-clear stream gurgled nearby, providing a soothing backdrop to the scene. As his eyes adjusted to the sudden change, he saw Friend, his white coat shimmering and eyes glowed with wisdom, standing patiently by the stream. A warm smile graced Friend's face, welcoming him to the tranquil haven of the meadow.

"My prince," Friend's soft voice observed, "it seems you've had a busy night."

Nathaniel said nothing, his heart and breathing finally normalized.

"For enemies to dream walk in the Sacred Forest, they must possess immense power," continued the unicorn.

"Am I still dreaming?" Nathaniel asked, unsure of what reality he was living in.

"Yes, but that does not make what you experienced untrue," Friend stated. "Intimidation is a sign that the enemy recognizes your power and fears you."

"How can I defeat two invaders when I'm not even sure if we can defeat Ravenite?" the prince moaned, dropping his head. The combination of extreme loneliness and an overwhelming burden made him feel as if he were carrying the weight of a mountain on his shoulders, causing him to feel more alone than ever before. He entertained the thought of abandoning his royal birthright and escaping to Streamside, where he could live in seclusion with Lani, ignoring all other responsibilities. However, would that solution resolve the issue at hand? If evil were to prevail, it would mean the slaughter of thousands of innocent people across western Curth Talem. Eventually, at some point in the future, the evil would inevitably make its way back to Streamside, and once again, I would be forced to fight for our survival. No, I believe taking action and potentially sacrificing our lives is preferable to allowing Ravenite's army to continue victimizing and killing innocent people.

In its rational manner, the unicorn proposed, "Sharing the load might solve the difficulty of carrying a heavy burden."

"But won't they consider me a weak leader?"' Nathaniel asked.

"There is strength in knowing when to delegate. More importantly, no one man born has ever defeated an army of undead."

Nathaniel understood. Both he and Tabor would need all the help they could get to reach victory. But from where? Whom outside the brotherhood can I trust?

"You have friends that may help. But for now, be at peace," Friend said, disappearing.

Nathaniel sat by the brook for several minutes, wondering what came next. Over time, his eyelids grew heavy, and he fell fast asleep on the soft meadow grass.

As his eyes slowly fluttered open, the morning light filled the room. But his peace was short-lived, hearing a loud rap sounded at the door. He slipped out of bed and padded to the door. He opened the door a fraction, saying, "Who is it?"

However, at that same moment, something forcefully shoved the door, knocking the unsuspecting prince onto his back. With no warning, a mysterious and shadowy figure pounced on top of Nathaniel. Reacting on pure instinct, the prince defended himself by using his forearms as a shield, effectively blocking the attack. A jaguar man with razor-sharp teeth violently snapped inches from his face, the beast's fetid breath warm on his skin. With a swift movement, it pulled back its enormous paw, equipped with sharp two-inch claws, and raked the prince's side.

Nathaniel's scream echoed through the room as a sharp, shooting pain coursed through his side. Despite his blood-soaked tunic, Nathaniel fought on, his heart pounding with adrenaline as he battled the ferocious creature.

Lani burst into the bedroom, a glinting dagger gripped tightly in her hand, but the beast swatted her aside effortlessly. The monster's supernatural strength sent Lani hurtling across the corridor, crashing into the wall and losing consciousness.

Pinned under the monster's weight, Nathaniel could feel the creature's immense size pressing down on him, making it nearly impossible to break free. Understanding its advantage, the beast unleashed a powerful attack again, effortlessly tearing through Nathaniel's tunic and leather armor on the other side. The prince screamed again, blood pooling from the deep gouges on both flanks. He could feel his strength leaking away as blood saturated his back and pants.

Just when he could hold out no longer, a brown blur shot through the door and, with an unearthly howl, clamped its mighty jaws on the neck of Nathaniel's assailant. In a blink, the battle tide turned as a massive hellhound, twice the size of the jaguar man, lifted the monster by the neck and gave him a vicious shake before tossing him across the room.

Determined and relentless, the jaguar man clawed up the wall before leaping at Sinbad. With one swift motion, Sinbad swatted the cat aside but not before feeling the sharp claws of the feline cut into his side. With the agility of a striking snake, the resolute jaguar man swiftly rolled to his feet and leaped again. Sinbad snarled and growled, prepared to face the charging monster once more. As the monster feline leaped, Sinbad released a fiery plume from his mouth, engulfing the creature in midair. Unable to control his momentum, the jaguar man crashed to the ground, a blazing ball of fire, and rolled like a fiery tumbleweed before it catapulted out the window.

At that moment, Jacoby, Grull, and Cor'in charged into the room, swords ready. Allai'nn arrived just behind and stopped to check Lani, who had just regained consciousness, before leaning over the bloodied Nathaniel.

"Quickly, Grull, get a towel to staunch the bleeding. Jacoby, carry Lani to the bed, and Cor'in, check on Sinbad," the elf princess ordered.

The men scattered in all directions. Jacoby lifted Lani in his arms, carrying the still-dazed woman to the bedroom while Grull appeared with a towel. Allai'nn put pressure over the wound that continued to ooze blood.

"Sinbad will need stitches too," Cor'in exclaimed, frantically tearing off his tunic to staunch the bleeding from the hellhound's wounds.

"How is he?" Jacoby asked, kneeling next to Nathaniel. Allai'nn calmly inspected the wounds, ignoring the prince's moans.

"He's injured badly. What happened?" Allai'nn asked, blood seeping through the makeshift bandage and covering her hands.

"I don't know," he replied, uncertainty in his voice. "When we arrived, I found Lani and Nathaniel injured and a bleeding Sinbad barking at something outside the window."

The unmistakable scent of burned flesh filled Cor'in's nostrils as he cautiously peeked out the open window. A smoldering heap greeted his gaze from three stories below, the smoke curling and twisting into the air.

"Whatever attacked him lies below, reduced to a smoldering mess, thanks to Sinbad," the half-elf remarked.

A sudden popping noise echoed through the room, making everyone jump, and Friend appeared. "What's the meaning of this?" the flustered unicorn demanded.

"Someone attacked Nathaniel and Lani," Jacoby said, unable to hide the anger in his voice.

"I don't understand. I placed the mightiest security hexes and spells on the sanctuary imaginable."

"It was…" Nathaniel rasped, trying to swallow, but his throat was dirt dry. "a black jaguar man," he finished, sweat beading on his brow from the exertion.

"A jaguar man?" Friend said, perplexed. "There are no jaguar men here, no cat men at all."

Horatio's voice carried in through the window from the ground floor. "Cor'in, get the others to come down here," the Anuran yelled.

"Toadie, I've got my hands full, and so do the others," Cor'in bellowed out the window.

"Pop," and Friend disappeared, arriving next to Horatio.

"What did you find?" he demanded.

Horatio knelt over the burned assassin; his finger directed towards the charred feline head of the Jaguar man. The black panther's concha carried a tattoo etched with intricate designs:

Five menacing claws adorned the black skull, circling it like a sinister crown.

As he witnessed the unexpected sight, Friend's reaction was immediate - he sucked in a deep breath and involuntarily recoiled, moving half a step back.

"What is it?" Horatio asked.

"I…I haven't seen that symbol in over a millennium," Friend said, his wide eyes reflecting fear.

"What does it signify?" Horatio asked, feeling anxious at the change in the stoic unicorn.

Friend hesitated, regaining his composure. "It's the symbol of an ancient assassin's guild linked to the underworld."

"The underworld?" Surprise registered on the Anuran's face.

"That's what I said," Friend snapped, anger replacing the shock now draining away. "But how did he get inside?"

"With the sentinel watching the secret portal entrance, I can only think of two ways," Horatio suggested. "One is by magic."

"And the other?" Friend spat, anticipating the answer.

"You have a traitor."

After spending what felt like an eternity meticulously stitching layer upon layer, Allai'nn finally finished tending to Nathaniel's wounds. She gently wrapped bandages around him, administered a few drops of soothing poppy elixir, and carefully laid him beside Lani in bed.

Grullach brought her a water basin, and after cleaning away the prince's blood, she wiped her brow, feeling a mix of relief and exhaustion.

Grullach handed her a simple meal of bread and cheese, a welcome relief after the grueling work of stitching and healing.

"Thanks, but I need to look after Sinbad," she responded, her eyes fixed on the hellhound wrapped in a bloody blanket and nestled in Cor'in's lap.

"Eat first," Cor'in whispered gently to Allai'nn. "His bleeding has finally stopped."

She settled down beside Cor'in with a half-smile and ate her meal. Grull sat beside her, his voice filled with concern, and asked, "Where did Jacoby disappear to?"

"He followed Friend," Cor'in said.

Three stories below, Jacoby, Horatio, and Friend could hear the distant chirping of birds as they strode across the open meadow and onto a narrow path that wound through the dense woods. After navigating through several twists and turns, the path finally led to the base of a small hill where a colossal stone door stood as an imposing barrier. Friend silently mouthed some words in the ancient language of the Elves, and with a soft creak, the door opened. Jacoby strained to slide the door open with all his might, creating a narrow entrance for them. They followed Friend down a dimly lit corridor of sturdy wood and compacted dirt.

"Where are we going?" Horatio asked.

"My special place, full of breathtaking beauty and enchanted magic. You are the rare few I trust to share its location," answered the unicorn.

"Thank you for the honor," mumbled Horatio, his heart pounding as he nervously navigated the cramped tunnel. The Anuran halted, feeling his heart thumping against his ribcage and his breath coming in rapid gasps. With a soothing touch on his shoulder, Jacoby whispered, "Just keep your eyes on me," as if trying to anchor him at the moment. With Horatio holding onto his belt, the tall human stooped and shuffled forward, his steps marked by caution.

Are we passing beneath the hill? Jacoby's curiosity grew as the tunnel sloped downward, wondering what lay ahead in the dark depths. The tunnel gradually sloped upwards after a few hundred yards, and light beams flickered from the end. The lighting in the area seemed peculiar, resembling a dense curtain that Jacoby mistook for the exit. However, upon closer inspection, he noticed a web of woven vines blocking the way out.

Once again, Friend mouthed a phrase, and as if by magic, the vines parted, unveiling a small open arena. In the center, a serene pond reflected the sunlight, its silver surface shimmering. The path led to the pond's edge, revealing a small platform extending into the tranquil water.

"Wait here," Friend's voice echoed in their minds as the majestic unicorn gracefully emerged on the dock.

The unicorn's voice broke the silence, its powerful tones reverberating over the water in an ancient language that Jacoby and Horatio couldn't comprehend. The once serene pond water turned ominously dark, and the surface bubbled as if it boiled. A ghostly gray mist rose from the center, taking the shape of a man.

"Who dares summon Whitestar from the halls of Valhalla?" rasped the specter.

"I, Friend the righteous."

"Pray, what needs thee, favored unicorn?"

"A question, Lord Whitestar. A Kavari has visited us. I humbly ask how and from whom?" asked Friend.

"A Kavari?" the ghost rasped, surprised. "A name not heard since the First Age. Art thou sure?"

"He wore the mark of the beast," admitted sadly.

Whitestar hesitated. "I know of only one demon with the power to assassin-bind. In the evil tongue, he's called Grine, the Soul Stealer."

Friend nodded, his face growing pale. "And the other?"

The ghost stroked his chin and said, "Thou have protected the Sacred Forest well, but not from the tiniest pests. A flyspeck shape-changer, perhaps entering as a tick, a cockroach, or rodent."

Friend shook his head, chastising himself for the foolish mistake. He would never underestimate the enemy again.

"A warning," the specter said to the majestic unicorn. "The presence of an enemy capable of brokering with Grine demands careful consideration and vigilance."

"Thank you for your wisdom, Lord Whitestar," Friend said, bowing his head. The mist vanished, revealing only the serene pond and the vibrant landscape.

Jacoby spoke, "What's a Kavari?"

"The name for an ancient assassin's guild, blood-linked to a demonic presence. The name means "Shifter" in the ancient tongue. I haven't heard of an attack in centuries," Friend said.

"Ravenite has upped the ante. How do we defend against shape-changers?" Jacoby inquired with a rhetorical tone.

"It might be best to leave the sanctuary as soon as Nathaniel and Lani can and make haste for the City of Spires. In the meantime, I'll investigate the Kavari's presence further," suggested Friend.

Jacoby stopped, disbelief washing over him as he strained to comprehend what he had just heard. "Leave? Nathaniel and possibly Lani are both seriously injured. It could take weeks for them to heal," Jacoby responded, his voice tinged with irritation.

"You misunderstand, Jacoby. This attempt on Nathaniel's life suggests Ravenite must know you're almost to Tabor. And he appears to be desperate to halt his arrival."

"How could that be true?" Horatio interjected. "We've seen no sign of animal spies."

"The mage's magic appears to have not only recovered from the event at the Tree of Souls but strengthened. Gods know what devices he can use to find you."

"But Nat and Lani won't be well enough to travel for some time," suggested Jacoby.

"I can help with that," the unicorn said, surprising the tall man again. "My healing magic is slightly rusty, but may help speed their recovery."

"That would be wonderful!" Horatio declared with passion.

"I still don't fully understand why leaving the security of the sanctuary will help," Jacoby questioned.

"Establishing Nathaniel as king in the City of Spires as soon as possible will seriously hinder the mage's twisted plans for domination. He will do anything to avoid a formidable leader in Tabor. Beware the undead lich, Jacoby. His expansive resources will stop at nothing to take Nathaniel off the board."

Jacoby wondered what traps and subterfuge Ravenite had prepared for the Brotherhood. He could kick himself for not expecting the evil mage wouldn't stop his attempts to kill Nathaniel. I've been a fool and underestimated Ravenite's vast resources and power in the dark magic arts. He remembered the battle at the Tree of Souls a year earlier when the Brotherhood had barely survived their first encounter with the wizard. Their victory was solely thanks to Allai'nn's magic, but the entire team suffered severe injuries that took weeks to heal. In the past, the wicked mage sent assassins, but they were fortunate enough to survive by the grace of Odin. Jacoby knew deep in his core that the assaults would continue until the undead wizard triumphed over Tabor or the brotherhood destroyed Ravenite.

Friend assumed the lead and led the group back to the brotherhood's chambers. They discovered Lani and Nathaniel peacefully slumbering side by side in the bed. Friend placed one hoof lightly on each and spoke an incantation in an ancient tongue. He repeated the phrase multiple times, and Jacoby observed how the words affected the couple, causing them to toss and turn as the magic enveloped them.

Friend stepped away, and he whispered to Jacoby, "I've done all I can. The magic should improve their healing by several days. Until then, I will have Augustus and Ruby help Allai'nn with their care."

With a "pop," Friend disappeared, leaving Horatio and Jacoby at the bedside.

"Get some rest, Horatio. I will take the first watch. We will guard Nathaniel like he's a precious gem."

TWENTY-FIVE

Augustus and Ruby led the group through the towering hardwood forest, their footsteps echoing among the ancient trees. The group took refuge in the sanctuary, spending a week healing physically and emotionally after the grueling encounter with the Katavi assassin. Friend's magic had been miraculous and restorative, mending the wounded in no time. Lani had almost no ill effects from her concussion except for occasional short-term memory loss. Nathaniel and Sinbad's wounds had nearly healed, and they were well enough to restart their journey to the City of Spires.

With their gear and supplies replenished, the Brotherhood set off at dawn, their eyes turning to the horizon toward the City of Spires. The quick mending filled everyone with hope as they finally saw the opportunity to reach their goal after months of traveling. Ruby and Horatio whispered in low tones, holding hands and oblivious to their surroundings, while the others chatted lazily about Tabor's capital.

"How big is the city? As big as Tajman Sghur?" Blue Ivy asked.

"No, but bigger than Mar Nâpor. It's shaped differently, too. The city and fortress lie on an island extending into Lake Mor," Grullach revealed.

"How do you reach it?" asked Cor'in.

"An ancient causeway stretches across the lake, connecting the west to the east. And there's the river," Grull explained. "As one of the largest inland ports in Curth Talem, the City of Spires is a bustling hub, rivaling the likes of Tajman Sghur."

"Can you describe the people?" Rue asked, knowing the citizens of Tajman Sghur could be stand-offish.

"Friendly enough, but that was decades ago. I hope it hasn't changed."

Among the group, Jacoby stood out as the only person on edge, insisting on walking just ahead of Nathaniel as his guard. The tall man cautiously scanned the forest, alert to any sound. Despite being attacked, he could feel the others gradually relaxing, although a hint of anxiety and irritation gnawed at him. *How can we protect Nathaniel if others ignore the attack?*

"Stay sharp there," Jacoby barked, giving the others a stern look. "We're about to cross out of the Sacred Forest."

"No worries," Grull said, returning the tall man's gaze, irritation in his voice. "Just making small talk."

Augustus halted the group at the river's edge, next to a tiny jetty. The Brotherhood's catboat, left days ago, was now replaced by a larger boat.

"I'm afraid we've reached the end of our journey, my friends," Augustus said solemnly. "Friend, heartsick over the attack, asked me to beg your forgiveness. Our engineers replaced your craft with this new one to aid you on your way. With any luck, it will ensure your safe arrival in the city."

"Thank you, Augustus, and please thank Friend. No one could have expected the attack," Nathaniel said. "I hope we see each other again, friend Augustus."

The beaver's face colored with scarlet. "You're too kind, my prince."

The assembly stowed their gear, secured the children, and loaded everyone on board except for Jacoby, who was waiting to cast off the dock lines, and Horatio.

The Anuran took Ruby off the trail, away from curious eyes.

With a tight embrace, Horatio held the faun close, relishing the sensation of her heartbeat resonating against his chest. Like a soft melody on the breeze, he whispered, "I'll miss you."

"Will you?" she murmured.

The frogman released his embrace and locked eyes with her, declaring, "You know I will."

Ruby's eyes glistened with teardrops as her heart ached with pain. "I don't want you to go." Her head drooped in despair as she admitted, "I'm afraid of what awaits us."

Horatio smiled and gently lifted her chin, misunderstanding her words. "You know I'll be with you again soon, my love."

While the sunlight danced on her tears, Ruby's face became overshadowed by the clouds of an impending storm. "I have a confession," she admitted. "Last evening, I tried to divine what lies ahead, but our future together remains uncertain."

Horatio reacted as if she'd slapped him, rearing back, eyes wide. "You did what?"

Embarrassment washed over her as she recognized she had employed her seer gift for her divination. Ruby, hailing from a renowned family of visionaries, possessed the ability to foresee the future. Ruth the Magnificent, her namesake and grandmother, was a legendary seer known for her incredible power. Under her guidance, she had trained her granddaughter to harness and strengthen her gift. Through time, she perfected her power and became a trusted guide for those seeking insight. However, in a moment of vulnerability and longing, she succumbed to her desires and attempted to uncover what fate had in store for her and her beloved. The weight of her actions now bore down upon her as she realized the selfishness of using her seer gift for personal gain. The same clouds masking her future with Horatio mirrored the turmoil in her heart, reflecting the storm of uncertainty that now enveloped their relationship. Ruby knew she had made a grave mistake and hoped her confession would bring clarity and forgiveness.

"I'm sorry. I felt so much worry...fear of knowing you were leaving to face the sorcerer Ravenite's undead minions," she explained, shaking her head.

With a deep sigh, Horatio pulled her back into his embrace. He embraced her fiercely, never wishing to let go. The rapid beats of her heart matched his own, deepening their connection. The frogman, refusing to let go, clung tightly to the faun, tenderly caressing her fur as though their connection was indestructible.

"Don't be afraid, Ruby. I'll always be with you," he said with a smile. Then he vanished, leaving a deep longing within her body and mind, craving more.

Once Horatio boarded, Jacoby wasted no time pushing off and smoothly sliding into the cockpit. Adjusting the mainsheet, he steadily brought it in until he sensed the sudden jolt of wind seizing the sail. Then, maneuvering the boat away, the Brotherhood waved goodbye to their cherished friends.

Over the next three days, the group sailed over calm waters, following the lazy river current west. Blue Ivy stretched and shivered at the chill night air; the late summer having given way to the beginning of autumn. At four hours into the night watch, he tiptoed out of the ship's hold and into the cockpit, tapping Nathaniel on the shoulder. The prince had thrown one of the clan's blankets over his shoulders for warmth as he steered the sloop over the dark, motionless water.

"My watch, Nathaniel," the wood elf said.

"Thank the gods," the prince exclaimed with relief. "With Fall's arrival, the night temperatures are cooling down." He shuffled out of the heavy blanket and handed it to Blue. "This will help. Jacoby will relieve you in the morning."

After stepping away, he disappeared into the hold, leaving Blue alone on the deck. Blue took a moment to soak in the serene atmosphere surrounding him. Nature's melodies filled the night air, blending in harmony with the gentle lapping of the river against the ship's hull. The moon's delicate glow highlighted the ripples on the water's surface, creating a mesmerizing light dance. The stars above, scattered across the sky like diamonds, seemed to guide Blue on his solitary journey. He pulled the cover tightly over his shoulders, providing a comforting warmth against the cool night breeze. Blue felt a profound connection with the Mother in moments like these, finding solace and peace in its gentle embrace.

The wood elf's eyes drifted shut, the natural world's rhythm lulling him into a restful sleep. He didn't know how long he had dozed, but his eyes shot open when he heard a noise coming from the shadowed darkness of the dense riverside overgrowth. Inadvertently, he had allowed the ship to drift within ten yards of the shore and quickly righted the course to the river's center. Suddenly, he felt a sharp pain in his left shoulder. He touched the area, thinking a mosquito had stung him, but felt an embedded dart instead. As his vision blurred, dizziness crashed over him like a wave, his hand on the tiller going slack. Blue slumped forward, feeling the weight of darkness trying to consume his entire world.

Three shrouded figures stood motionless, concealed by the long willow tendrils, their eyes fixed on the craft as it drifted closer to the riverbank. The middle figure, tall and muscular, gazed at the shorter, lean figure to his right and nodded. Stepping back a few paces, the smaller man built up momentum before effortlessly leaping onto the boat's deck, his movements as graceful as those of a feline. He hesitated, listening for any sound of movement from the sleeping crew below deck, before cautiously inching towards the bow. As he leaned over to grab the bowline, rustling leaves caught his attention as the other two pirates pushed off the bank in a dory hidden in the brush. They rowed out, the sound of their oars cutting through the water barely filling the air, and caught the bowline tossed to them from the more petite vaulter. He held up one finger, his eyes scanning the surroundings for any sign of danger, then tiptoed in leather moccasins back to the cockpit, careful not to make a sound. Deftly, he slid a thin wire across the hatch door, effectively securing it from the outside. With a burst of latent power, he lifted Blue onto the deck side and gave him a firm shove. With a muted splash, the wood elf tumbled into the water. The cold river water slapped Blue like a hand, pulling him out of his drugged state enough to drag himself to shore. He collapsed on the sandy riverside, his mind still reeling and body shivering from the cold.

As the boat drifted downstream, the pirate made his way back to the bow, descending into the dory with the boat's bowline. He quickly tied the line to the aft cleat and gave the thumbs-up sign. With significant effort, the two robust men strained at the oars; their faces contorted with determination as they navigated the two crafts through the powerful currents of the murky river.

Jacoby opened his eyes, awakened by the splash. He strained his ears for a few moments, then allowed his eyelids to gently shut as he slipped back into a deep slumber with the other Brotherhood, completely unaware of the predicament he and his friends were in.

Darkness shrouded the river, and its waters reflected the pale moonlight that struggled to penetrate the dense canopy of trees. The air was heavy with the scent of damp earth and the distant sound of nocturnal creatures. The three pirates moved with eerie precision, their movements fluid and calculated as they pulled the boat into a narrow estuary three miles upriver. After several switchbacks in the cut, they arrived at a small sandy beach. The riverbank sloped gently upward to a forest clearing where ten more corsairs, clad in identical attire, awaited their arrival.

Sitting in the dory's bow, a tall figure known as Ace scanned the riverbank, the moonlight reflecting off a jagged scar across his cheek, a testament to his countless battles. His eyes, a piercing shade of icy blue, surveyed the surroundings with caution and anticipation. A shorter, lean figure to his right manned the tiller, guiding both crafts to shore. He had a scarred face and a long, thin nose likened to a rodent, his eyes darting from tree to tree, ever vigilant for any potential threats. The third figure, a burly man with a thick beard and robust build, was the group's muscle. His calloused hands and bulging arms showcased his strength as he rowed in.

With a quick gesture, Ace signaled the men on shore to execute the well-rehearsed plan. Tip-toeing onto the deck of the captured boat, each of the ten men held a short sword, ready for whatever lay ahead. Three positioned themselves strategically around the hold door, blow guns poised and ready to strike. The warrior's calloused hand reached for the wire; his grip steady as he removed it from the door. Glancing at the men behind, he mustered strength and crashed through the door, entering the musty darkness. The chaotic scene unfolded before Ace's eyes, with women screaming, babies crying, and jarring crashes resonating from within the hold. One dark pirate's body flew out of the ship's hold, landing with a crash on the deck; another followed, tangled in a dire hand-to-hand battle with Grullach. With no hesitation, two darts struck the halfling in the thigh. His resistance rapidly drained as the poison rushed through his body, and in seconds, they dragged his inert body away. Cor'in and Horatio were next, wrestling against a captor on each arm, until hit by darts and collapsed, groggy and disoriented. Allai'nn, Lani, and Rue climbed out at sword point, carrying wailing children and cursing the dark-clad villains.

More banging and loud thumps erupted as bodies smashed against the inner wall. Two more pirates charged into the hold, with more sounds of grunts and battling. Glass shattered, and the entire boat shook as the battle raged beneath the deck. Then, as if a switch had flipped, complete silence settled over the ship. The warriors on deck didn't move, holding their breath for what seemed like an eternity, waiting for the last prisoners to be escorted out.

Nothing happened for several minutes until one of the dark warriors, his face covered with a balaclava, appeared at the hold door. He nodded and dragged Jacoby's bloodied body, his head down and dark hair hanging over his face. Another pirate followed, dragging the inert body of Nathaniel, his chest and face covered in blood. Allai'nn and Lani screamed at the sight of the bodies, Lani crumpling to the ground in a faint. Horatio and Grullach, both arousing together, eyes bugged and their faces drained of color. What in Odin's name? How is it possible? Both brothers, their two leaders, who'd conquered every foe in every fight this past year. They couldn't be dead!

As Cor'in's eyes opened, what he witnessed caused his world to shift. He felt a wave of dizziness wash over him, leaving him bewildered and unable to make sense of his surroundings. As he pulled himself to one knee, his heart crumbled before his eyes, draining him of all energy and leaving an unsettling void within. What the...?

Suddenly, the cold air seemed to freeze everything, including the surrounding sound. His ears felt muffled as if filled with cotton; his brain fogged and unable to understand what he saw. All he could do was watch in horror as the pirates dragged his friend's dead bodies across the boat's deck, leaving a stark and unsettling trail of crimson. As if hearing a distant rumble growing louder, he heard the anguished cries and gnashing of teeth as Horatio collapsed, pounding the ground with his fists, and Grull charged against his captors.

Unable to move, he watched the two pirates tumble Jacoby and Nathaniel overboard into the ebony river.

Ace crossed his arms, a scowl twisting his lips as he watched the pirates, their dark clothes stained crimson, drag the bodies, his frustration palpable. "What took so long?" he demanded.

"They heard us coming and put up a savage fight. The enemy killed those two, but we lost three of our own," said the larger warrior, blood staining his tunic and arm.

"Bloody hell!" Ace howled, shaking his head in disgust, his fists clenched. Three dead! Losing three warriors in my unit is too high a price to pay for these scoundrels, no matter what General Thorne's orders. The capture was seamless and executed with precision and efficiency. How could this serene night have transformed into a chaotic disaster?

"Bury our men," Ace said, anger coloring his face. "And place the prisoners in shackles."

"Yes, sir."

With tears welling up in his eyes, Cor'in mumbled, "No, no, no," his voice filled with anguish. He fought with all his strength, but the lingering effect of the poison darts and the muscular warriors restraining him was unrelenting, rendering his attempts to break free in vain. Horatio knelt, frozen in shock; his gaze fixated on the balaclava-clad warriors who hadnheartlessly tossed the lifeless bodies of Nathaniel and Jacoby into the depths. The frogman swooned, his body swaying unsteadily as he leaned to one side, and then he emptied the contents of his stomach.

"I'm gonna make you pay for what you've done!" Grull screamed, struggling and writhing to break free. Ace stepped over and delivered a powerful punch to his belly as fast as a striking asp. As the air whooshed out of Grull's lungs, he collapsed onto the ground, desperately gasping for breath.

"Another word from you," Ace sneered, "and you'll be the next gator meal."

As other pirates carried the dead from the hold to shore, their footsteps echoed in the silence, adding a somber tone to the scene. The pirates shackled Cor'in, Horatio, and Grullach's wrists together, and their chains rattled as the pirates attached them around a thick oak trunk. Then two raiders, covered in blood and sweat, leaped down to the shore and shackled Allai'nn and Rue together.

"I'm leaving you untethered to care for the babes," the taller pirate said, his voice a gentle whisper, as he gestured towards the wailing infants. "But you must never, under any circumstances, try to escape," he warned sternly, loud enough for the others to hear. Then the raider did something unexpected. He winked!

The pirate's gentle demeanor and action perplexed the elf princess, but her memory of Nathaniel and Jacoby's ruthless murder rushed into her mind, bringing clarity. Anger surged through her veins; she could no longer hold back her words, and she spat at the monstrous creature, "Leave me and my children alone! Haven't you done enough?"

"Not by half, princess," he growled, a faint chuckle escaping from under his mask.

Blue Ivy emerged from the frigid river water, feeling groggy and shivering from the piercing cold as he pulled himself onto the bank. His mind whirled with thoughts, and a bone-chilling coldness seeped into his body. He collapsed onto the sand; exhaustion washing over him like a comforting embrace, and his eyes shut despite the chill. The sensation of a cool liquid against his cheek startled him, causing him to pause. In his semi-conscious state, he dreamed of the soft touch of Rue's lips brushing against his cheek. As he thought about it, a low moan escaped his lips, and he turned his head to meet her for a passionate kiss. But his eyes shot open, assaulted by the disgusting odor of Rue's breath, reminiscent of old leather shoes and rancid meat. Sinbad sat inches from his face, his haunches resting on the ground. His mouth was open wide, revealing his menacing hellhound teeth, while his pink tongue hung out, panting. As the dog vigorously shook itself, icy water droplets from its rust-colored coat pelted Blue.

"Sinbad," he sighed, the disappointment clear in his voice. Blue, still half-asleep, stroked the hound behind his ears and muttered, "I'm awake, boy." A renewed sense of hope filled the elf's heart at the hellhound's presence.

Maybe I have a chance of finding the others. But where in the world are we? He looked around, trying to identify any familiar landmarks. Holding on to the sturdy hellhound, he staggered to his feet, still feeling dizzy and disoriented. His mind, like a dense fog, could not recall the events that transpired. His last vision before losing consciousness was of Nathaniel maneuvering the tiller.

Next to Sinbad, he knelt and locked eyes with the hellhound, mesmerized by its fiery red gaze. "Boy," he said sternly, "your task is to locate the children."

The hellhound began sniffing in all directions, its nose twitching as it picked up scents along the riverside. The determined hound led Blue through the enchanting scenery, where the starlight reflected off the water and sandy riverbank like countless shimmering diamonds. With each step, they negotiated the tall grass, the damp earth cool beneath their feet, careful not to disturb the serene quiet of the morning. They maneuvered through a maze of trees and bushes, covering what appeared to be an immeasurable distance. Despite still feeling groggy, the refreshing coolness of the night air helped Blue shake off his drowsiness and stay alert. The hound would occasionally come to a halt, his nostrils flaring as he sniffed the air, his triangular-shaped head scanning the surroundings before continuing on his path.

Finally, after entering a narrow opening between a copse of shaggy firs, Sinbad stopped, the silence enveloping him.

"What is it, boy?" Blue whispered, but the hound didn't move. A faint sound that reached his ears caught Blue's attention. Beyond the trees, Blue heard the unmistakable sound of movement and the muffled chatter of men filling the air. He inched closer to witness the somber sight of three dark-clad warriors digging graves for three bodies nearby.

"How'd they get the jump on old Jiles, I wonder? He was a sturdy fighter," a thin pirate digging said.

"I wish someone had warned us about the prisoners' being armed and dangerous," another stout raider said.

"These aren't just bandits, but trained warriors. We're lucky we had numbers to overwhelm them," said the third.

"Captain will take care of them. There's no way they live to see the palace dungeons," said the thin man.

"I hope I get my chance at them. We got three friends to avenge," Stout man retorted.

"Hear, hear!" the others said in unison.

Blue waited until they finished their grim task of covering the bodies and watched the pirates stomp away. Then, he and Sinbad stealthily followed until they were outside the raider's camp.

To his surprise, after a short walk, he found the pirate camp bustling with activity. The marauders had erected tents in a clearing near the water; several fires lapped the sky with orange flames as men lined up for food from a large pot nearby. A tall bearded man watched the proceedings, arms crossed, with a stoic expression. The man's keen eyes missed nothing, scanning the surrounding woods and riverbank for trouble.

Each raider took his plate and sought warmth next to the fire, except for the final two in line, who strolled to a tent on the far side, carrying three plates. Upon passing the tall man, they all made a gesture of respect by lowering their heads.

"Feed the females first, then bring the scraps to the other prisoners," the leader instructed, not looking at the men.

"Yes, sir," the larger of the two said behind his balaclava-covered face as they passed. The leader had a lingering feeling about those men, but it vanished when laughter erupted by the fire. The officer's attention veered towards the rowdy warriors, who were exchanging a flask of wine and laughing in great amusement. "One gulp each," the leader barked in a commanding tone. "This is no picnic."

He then focused his piercing gaze on a robust man standing by the fire, warming his hands. In a gesture of affirmation, the man nodded his head and then swiftly took hold of the bottle from the pirate located nearby.

"Hey, Marx! I ain't had none," the warrior protested.

"You heard Captain Ace," the sturdy man said. "This is not a social gathering; it is a mission," as he stood up and flung the bottle into the nearby river with a single, powerful swing.

Inside the tent, Allai'nn sat stoically beside the sleeping infants. Lani and Rue leaned against each other, weeping softly, their hearts broken by Nathaniel and Blue Ivy's loss. Each carried purple swollen bruises from their initial interrogation with Captain Ace, but none had divulged information.

"We brought food," said the taller pirate, placing a plate in front of each woman while the shorter man leaned behind the women to remove their shackles to eat.

Allai'nn's eyes flared, and spat, "Do you expect a reward for treating us like humans instead of cattle?"

"Nothing could be farther from the truth, Allai'nn," the taller pirate said, removing his face covering.

Allai'nn gasped. "Jacoby!"

Lani twisted to look at Jacoby, then at the other pirate who she instantly recognized as Nathaniel. In a flash, Lani had tackled Nathaniel, tears streaming down her face, smothering him in kisses. "Nathaniel, Nathaniel, Nathaniel," she mewed, holding him tight.

Nathaniel gently lifted her off of him after giving her a deep kiss. "We have little time. We must free the rest and leave," he whispered.

Allai'nn bear-hugged Jacoby. "We thought you were dead," cried between tears.

Before Jacoby could answer, Rue broke in unexpectedly. "Is Blue with you?"

"Blue?" Nathaniel said, realizing in the chaos he'd not seen the elf since relieved from directing the ship hours earlier. "No, I'm sorry, we haven't seen him." Then, hesitating, he added, "But I'm sure he's on his way here as we speak."

The hope in Rue's eyes vanished as she fell back, avoiding eye contact.

"We need to get to the others," Jacoby interjected, changing the subject. "I've loosened the screws on the shackles so you can get free. After a brief wait, cut through the tent back and head north. About a league ahead is a rope bridge to the opposite river bank. We'll meet you there," Jacoby instructed, handing her his knife.

He and Nathaniel replaced their balclava covering their faces, and strode out with the remnants of the food. Moments later, they found the prisoners, with two warriors as their guards.

"Captain says we're to take over guard duty so you can eat," Jacoby said.

"About time," said a thin pirate with a scar running down his cheek. "I'm starving."

"Me too," added the other through his shaggy beard. The two left in a hurry, leaving Jacoby and Nathaniel alone with Cor'in, Horatio, and Grull. As the toxin cleared, Grull's serious expression transformed into fierce anger.

"Is it true?" Grull said, his voice breaking with emotion. "Did you kill our friends, you bloody monsters?"

"They killed three of our men. They deserve what they got," the smaller guard said chuckling, dropping his face mask.

"When I get free, I'll kill...by the gods! Nathaniel!" Grull gasped, his face colored with astonishment. He turned to the other pirate, who removed his disguise, a smile spreading over his face.

"Jacoby!" He grabbed his friend's hand as if it tethered him to reality. "I can't..." But his words failed him as fat tears filled his eyes. Cor'in and Horatio swarmed the two men with pats on the back.

"We can't believe you're alive! Thank Odin!" Cor'in grinned. "How'd you get away?"

Jacoby smiled and placed a reassuring hand on his shoulder. "Time for that later. Are you well enough to fight?"

"Like Thor's hammer," Grull choked.

"Us too," added Horatio and Cor'in.

Nathaniel patted Horatio and Cor'in on the back. "Stouthearted, as always," he said. "And we are glad to be alive."

"Right," Jacoby added, leaning behind the others to open the shackles and free them.

Suddenly, a harsh voice sounded from behind. "Stop right there."

Jacoby and Nathaniel turned to see Ace, his arms crossed, with three warriors behind.

"It took a moment, but I could see it in your eyes - you didn't fit in with the rest of us," the pirate captain said, his voice filled with venom as he unsheathed his short sword. "Now, you'll pay for your trickery."

The scene erupted with a flurry of simultaneous occurrences. Jacoby leaped forward, unsheathing his sword as he charged to engage Ace, while Nathaniel swiftly tossed his knife to Grull before attacking the next pirate. As Grull rose, a wave of dizziness washed over him, causing him to sway and fumble with the blade. In that split second, Cor'in reacted swiftly, snatching the knife from Grull's grasp and flinging the blade at the other pirate charging toward him. Cor'in's throw shot so fast, that the pirate had no time to dodge, the dagger driving deep into the man's chest. As the pirate crumpled in a heap, Horatio, always vigilant, caught Grull just in time, preventing him from hitting the ground.

The clash of steel filled the air as Jacoby and Ace locked blades, their movements a blur of speed and skill. Jacoby's eyes blazed as he parried Ace's strikes, sending sparks flying. During the next attack, Jacoby blocked the pirate's lunge, then he pressed forward, using his superior strength to push the shorter man backward. Ace pretended to trip, landing in a crouched position with his hand touching the earth for balance. With a surge of confidence, Jacoby lunged forward, striking at the pirate captain's chest. However, Ace saw the assault coming and instinctively grabbed a handful of forest debris and dirt. He flung it into Jacoby's face, temporarily blinding him, as he rolled to the side, the blade missing him. Jacoby staggered back, his heart pounding, as Ace counter-attacked, charging with his sword raised. Jacoby swung his blade back and forth, frantically trying to fend off his attacker while trying to clear the debris from his eyes. But Ace pressed his advantage, easily overcoming Jacoby's puny defense, and slashing his sword toward him for a death blow.

Out of nowhere, a brown blur burst forth from the forest, slamming into the man and sending him tumbling into the dirt and knocking his sword free, narrowly missing Jacoby's heart. Sinbad bit and snapped like a rabid wolf, as Ace tried to block the vicious attack with his forearms.

Blue Ivy arrived next, wielding a large stone and slamming the warrior fighting Nathaniel in the back of the head. The raider's eyes rolled back, and he collapsed onto the sandy ground. The last pirate, realizing the odds had shifted, desperately fled to evade capture. But Cor'in lunged forward with the dagger, driving the blade deep into the man's side. The sound of his piercing shriek filled the air as he staggered backward, taking several unsteady steps before collapsing backward off the bank and rolling into the water.

Startled by the piercing scream of the pirate, the rest of the crew leaped into action, their adrenaline pumping, as a wave of five additional pirates charged out of the camp. Filled with a burning desire for vengeance, the Brotherhood picked up the discarded pirate weapons and attacked. The clash of blades created a frenzied whirlwind of action, occasionally interrupted by the sound of a pirate succumbing to one of Sinbad's brutal bites. The clash of steel filled the air as the two groups battled, each determined to survive. Nathaniel dispatched one pirate with a slash over the spine, while Sinbad's relentless assault brought down another. Running in terror, the other three let out a chorus of yelps and screams, their fear palpable as they tried to escape the brutal marks left by Cor'in, Grull, Blue, and Horatio.

"Run, you dirty dogs," Grull's voice echoed through the air as the group erupted in joyous cheers.

Two raiders fled into the woods, vanishing among the thick trees. Tripping as he reached the forest, the last pirate landed hard, his face hitting the ground. He drew himself up, only to be tackled by Horatio, who quickly tied his hands behind him.

"Nice catch, Toadie," Cor'in remarked, patting Horatio on the back.

"Bring him over for questioning," Nathaniel ordered.

But before they could begin the interrogation, Jacoby heard coughing and movement behind him. He whirled, anticipating a wounded enemy sneaking up from behind, but only saw Ace, scratching at the dirt to roll over.

Ace, bloodied by bites and ripped flesh over his chest and arms, coughed violently, rolling to his side. Kneeling by the dying man, Jacoby could see the tears in his flesh, revealing the bone beneath, as blood flowed steadily from the gashes.

"Who sent you?" Jacoby said.

Ace locked eyes with the warrior, a spark of recognition flickering in his eyes. "I know you. Ironfist?"

Jacoby nodded.

"If I had known...." The man rasped through shallow breaths. "Too late." The man coughed again, clotted blood spilling from his purple lips, his eyes closed.

"Who?" Jacoby insisted, shaking him awake.

"General Thorne." Ace rasped, more blood oozing from his mouth. "Capture and execute...outlaw group. But...did not know..." Ace coughed violently, his body convulsing as he desperately fought for air. Suddenly, his unfocused, glassy eyes widened with shock, and he froze in death.

TWENTY-SIX

The young raider fought against the ropes that shackled him to the base of a stout Elm trunk. He cursed as the movement tightened the bonds on his wrists; the ropes cutting into his skin.

Jacoby knelt next to the young warrior, studying him. "Do you know who I am?" he asked.

The young man shook his head.

"At one time, I held the title of captain of the King's guards. Many of the Taborian elite highly respected and coveted my reputation. I know you're Taborian - your accent and the familiarity in your eyes give it away. I want to know about the details of your regiment and the present state of the remaining Taborian army."

The young warrior stared at Jacoby, his mouth tight, then shook his head. "I'm one of the Core, a special unit used by General Thorne to do his bidding. We answer directly to him," the youth hesitated, his brow furrowed. "Regarding the army, we're losing ground daily, even with conscription at sixteen."

Jacoby nodded. He couldn't help but feel sorry for the boy despite being a part of a company ordered to capture and execute the Brotherhood.

"Tabor needs every man at the front. Let General Thorne know we're coming for him," Jacoby said sternly. "Cut him free."

Grull cut the boy's bonds and shoved him toward the forest. "Get moving." The young man ran off into the brush, not looking back.

"Isn't letting our enemy know we're coming a little audacious?" Cor'in said. "Now what?"

"We stirred up a hornet's nest, for sure," Jacoby stated. "Now we find the women and continue to the City of Spires."

"What about this Thorne character?" prodded the half-elf. "Won't he be waiting?"

Jacoby stroked his beard for a heartbeat, considering the question.

"I remember Thorne as a young officer," Grullach interjected, a hint of a smile on his lips. "If my memory serves, I recall that his affluent father paid for his commission. Poor dolt was a few bricks short of a load, killing more men with his mistakes than the enemy. His demeanor was one of a boaster, always tooting his own horn. Like many wealthy officers, he carried himself with an air of haughtiness and arrogance, always quick to shift blame onto others. I honestly don't remember anyone who liked or respected the man. But somehow, he had a cunning ability to curry favor with his superior officers."

"I remember," Jacoby said, a hint of bitterness in his tone. "In addition, he harbored long-lasting resentments. I had a run-in with him that should have led to his dismissal, but it almost got me demoted."

"What happened?" Horatio asked, intrigued.

"He made a foolish error that resulted in the tragic loss of half his company. When our commanders learned of the incident and confronted him, he falsely accused another lieutenant of the mistake. As an adjunct to General Titus, I received the order to investigate the incident. Having spoken with each person involved and piecing together their accounts, I discovered the truth and delivered my report, exonerating the other officer. Thorne faced a possible court-marshal or demotion for lying. But his wealthy father's intervention led to the charges being dropped," Jacoby said, looking away, his lips pinched as if tasting something foul. "Thorne blamed me for his humiliation, and over the next year, he dedicated himself to sabotaging my reputation in any way he could. Lucky for me, I had friends who heard of the plan and let me know to be on guard. General Titus, aware of my skills and past successes, saw through the deception, and his attempts to discredit me failed."

"Sounds like quite a scoundrel," Nathaniel said.

"Right you are, lad," Grull agreed.

"Water under the bridge," Jacoby said, rubbing his chin in thought. "Is it possible the Thorne we knew could plan this attack?"

"What do you mean?" Blue Ivy asked. "Ace told you he did."

"Maybe the order came from Thorne, but someone else encouraged him?" Horatio suggested.

"Once those warriors gossip, the news of Nathaniel's arrival will spread like wildfire," Grull predicted. "The person responsible for the attack should tremble in fear if they have any sense."

"Here, here," echoed the others.

Nathaniel only partially registered the halfling's words, his focus fixed on penetrating Grull's facade of false confidence to uncover the underlying truth. The precision of the attack revealed the mastermind's intricate knowledge of their whereabouts. But how did they figure it out? Nathaniel felt confident that no one could follow them from the Sacred Wood because the boat's swift movement would have been difficult to track. The only logical explanation would be a mystical form of divination. The power required for such a specific divination would require immense magical energy. Nathaniel was unsure if even the ancient Friend, or Traveler, possessed such extraordinary power. Then the truth hit him like a sudden splash of cold water. Ravenite, his lich-mage enemy, had recently forged a sinister alliance with the underworld, augmenting his army with hordes of undead. In addition, could he have requested other abilities? The idea settled in his stomach like a blazing ball of fire, causing a tight, uneasy feeling. The palpable presence of the evil mage's specter filled the air, its dark form seemingly always lingering just out of reach.

Locking eyes with Jacoby, an immediate understanding reflected between them. Confirming Nathaniel's fear, Jacoby glanced downward momentarily, his face filled with worry. Then a half-smile slowly appeared, causing Nathaniel to feel a sense of relief. They were determined to stick together until the very end, no matter what.

"It's almost daybreak. Let's catch up with the ladies and keep going," Nathaniel suggested, underscoring the need to advance. "We'll learn more once we reach the capital." Without a word, each man grabbed his pack and trudged north along the riverbank with Nathaniel in the lead.

After a long hour of trekking, the golden sunlight scattered through the canopy in spots across the forest floor. Finally, the group arrived at the ancient rope bridge. Enormous braided ropes, the thickness of a man's leg, wrapped around four-foot-thick oaks, acted as braces for the pedestrian crossing. The wood and rope structure extended across the entire river's width, leading to a clearing on the other side. The women and children were nowhere to be seen, adding to the current of anxiety in the air.

Nathaniel gestured for the group to stop, and he knelt at the base of the rope bridge. From this elevated position, he had a clear view of both the river below and the far bank, unobstructed by any obstacles on the far side. The eerie melody of the wind echoed through the wooden bridge. Nathaniel felt a faint uneasiness creeping up in the back of his mind. A thick layer of pine straw and decaying leaves had blanketed the forest floor, making it impossible to see any footprints the women might have left. He could only speculate if they had arrived safely. Adding to the disturbing atmosphere, there were no human sounds above the foreboding wind's call, no laughter or children's cries, leaving the prince with a sinking feeling in his gut.

As Grullach knelt next to him, he could see the understanding in the warrior's eyes, reflecting the prince's worry.

"Where are they?" Grull asked, kneeling next to the young prince.

"I can't see them."

"Allai'nn may have hidden in the trees on the far bank, in case of more enemies," Grull said, but his tone lacked confidence.

"Only one way to find out," Nathaniel said. "Wait here and I'll check it out." Nat stood, taking a resigned breath, and stepped onto the bridge, his gut cramping with worry with every step.

"Not without us," Grull declared stubbornly, motioning for the others and following Nathaniel.

As they entered the rope bridge, the group formed a single file line, their hands gripping the weathered rope tightly for stability. The wind howled, and the planks beneath their feet rocked and swayed, making their journey across more challenging. At the midpoint across the river, all Nathaniel could hear were the whispers of the wind and the distant chirping of birds. Continuing their journey, his senses sharpened, and he felt a chill crawl up his back as he caught a fleeting glimpse of movement near the clearing's edge.

"Did you see that?" he called out to Grullach behind him, the urgency in his voice cutting through the wind's howl. He had barely taken a step when his eyes locked onto the sight of a crossbow bolt hurtling towards him, its whistle growing louder by the second. His eyes widened in alarm as he ducked, shouting, "Watch out!" In an instant, he felt a searing heat as the projectile burned past his ear, causing him to drop like a stone. From behind him, he heard a resounding smack, followed by a Grull screaming, "Ahhh!"

Nathaniel turned, just as Grull, windmilled his arms backward, struck the support rope, and flipped backward, followed by the sound of his body hitting the water fifty feet below. Nathaniel screamed, "Grull!!" his eyes wide. Then he saw the crossbow bolt, the tip bent at an angle, apparently striking something metal on the halfling's chest, the force propelling him backward off the bridge.

Chaos reigned as a swarm of thundering marauders dressed in black uniforms and face coverings charged up the bridge from both sides. Powerful hands gripped his arms from behind. Before Nathaniel could resist, he felt white-hot pain explode behind his eyes as something heavy slammed into the back of his head, the impact ringing in his ears. His vision blurred with a rush of dizziness, and as he stumbled forward, his hands scrabbled for purchase against the support rope. But his strength failed, and he collapsed onto the rough-hewn bridge planks, the bright morning light dimming, swallowed by the encroaching shadow.

Nathaniel's eyes fluttered open, and he squinted at the faint rays of light streaming in through a small grate high on the far wall. His blurred vision took several seconds to clear, revealing a cold stone communal cell. The floor resembled a scene from a battlefield, with unconscious bodies scattered and sprawled out like discarded ten pins. He yearned to move and ensure the safety of his friends, but his muscles were rigid and numb, impeding his every effort. The room was so cold that it felt as though his limbs were stuck in glue, and with each exhale, his breath materialized into a frosty mist. As he struggled to his knees, a searing bolt of pain shot through his head, accompanied by an overwhelming wave of nausea, forcing him to double over and empty his stomach. He wiped his mouth, pushed to his knees, and crawled to the first form. Jacoby lay unconscious, his face covered with angry purple bruises, one eye partially swollen shut. He shook his brother, but Jacoby remained out, so he crawled to the next form.

Congealed blood covered the back of Cor'in's head, and he moaned when Nathaniel rolled him over. His eyes opened to slits, his vision clearing to see Nathaniel's smiling face.

"Welcome to our new accommodations," Nat said. "Can you sit up?"

"Ugh. Yeah," Cor'in moaned as Nathaniel lifted him to a sitting position, then moved to the next prone figure.

Several minutes later, Horatio and Blue Ivy, beaten and bruised, crawled to the side with the others. Jacoby, now awake, leaned against the cold stone cell wall as Nathaniel dragged Grullach to lie beside him. Mud covered Grullach's legs and belly, evidence of being dragged up the riverbank, his clothes still cold and damp from his plunge into the river, and a blood-tinged field dressing covering his head. The halfling appeared pale but alive, shivering with shallow breaths. Jacoby leaned in, the sight of his injured friend sobering him, and used his body to warm the halfling.

"You're going to be all right, mate," Jacoby whispered in Grull's ears.

"Where's...All...ai'nn?" Grull asked between shivers.

"I don't know, Grull. But we'll find her and the kids," Jacoby reassured.

The halfling shook his head, sighing.

"Damn pirates! Wait until I get my hands on them," he said before a coughing spell cut him off.

"You don't sound too good," Jacoby said, narrowing his gaze at his friend. "What happened up on the bridge anyway?"

Grull coughed again. "Probably inhaled some of that river water, but I'm okay," he said with a broken smile. "And I don't know what happened. Suddenly, I heard Nat cry out, and a bolt rocketed right at me. I had no time to move and was sure I was a dead man. The bloody missile struck me right in the cloak clasp above my heart, knocking me backward. You know the rest."

"You're one lucky halfling," Cor'in said, shaking his head.

For several moments, no one spoke, each digesting their situation. Finally, Nathaniel said, "Where are we? The capital?"

"I'm guessing the city dungeon," Jacoby said. "But I remember nothing after the ambush."

"I saw Grull tumble off the bridge, and then I got clubbed," Nathaniel added. "Did anyone get a look at the attackers?"

"I did," Horatio said. "Dressed like the others who attacked the boat."

Nathaniel rubbed his chin. "How did they find us so quickly after we'd escaped?"

"Probably had a second group waiting as a contingency," Cor'in suggested.

Nathaniel nodded, his eyes scanning the dimly lit dungeon cell. He stood and walked the perimeter of the prison room, pushing against sections of stone wall to test for weakness. The dank cell filled his nostrils with the musty scent of moss, which covered the ancient stone walls, but found no signs of loose stones. The room measured nearly ten by twenty paces, with a single iron door at one end and a narrow-barred window on the opposite side. Stone ceilings towered above, reaching twice Nathaniel's height. Plenty of room for more prisoners, Nat thought.

Shuffling back toward the others, Nathaniel's ears perked up as he caught the sound of approaching footsteps. Moments later, the heavy iron door let out a squeak, swinging open to reveal two burly guards and a shorter man, elegantly dressed in a blue doublet and pants. With a confident flick of his wrist, the man handed the lead guard a leather pouch, which he skillfully tossed in one palm, the sound of coins jingling faintly.

"Thanks, governor," he said. The guard's grin widened, exposing his toothless mouth, as he issued a warning, "But remember, this only buys you two minutes."

"Excellent, Corporal," the man's voice resonated off the prison walls, the echoing sound amplifying as the guard closed the door with a resounding clang.

The man approached Jacoby and Nathaniel with swift strides, revealing a handkerchief filled with freshly baked biscuits tucked inside his shirt. "I brought some food," the man said, revealing a tantalizing aroma of freshly baked bread.

As Jacoby's brow raised, he recognized his old friend, Devin Ashoke. He spoke, but Devin silenced him with a simple gesture.

"I have little time," he said, his voice rushed and filled with urgency. "How are you faring?"

"A little bruised, but alive," Jacoby said, motioning to his friend. "We could use an exit strategy."

"I'll do what I can to get help," Devin said, his voice determined, but despair lingered in his brown eyes.

"What is it?" Nathaniel inquired, his eyes narrowing with intrigue.

"General Thorne has labeled Jacoby as a traitor and branded your group as outlaws," Devin said, avoiding eye contact.

"And?" Jacoby asked his one good eye narrowing.

With a tone of disgust, Devin stated, "Thorne plans a public execution, with the approval of Regent Mossbrook, for the near future - just two days away."

"And what about the women and children?" Horatio asked, his voice filled with concern.

"They will auction them off like commodities, stripping them of their freedom," Devin said, unable to face the frog man.

Suddenly, a loud knock reverberated through the room, startling everyone. "Times about up, Guv," said the guard with a raspy voice, his laughter echoing in the air.

Devin turned to respond, but Jacoby, his strength fading, desperately clutched onto his shirt and yanked him closer. He whispered into Devin's ear, his words stretching out into several long moments, while the man's eyes widened in surprise. With a squeak, the iron door swung open, and as it did, Jacoby released him. Exhausted, he collapsed against the cold stone wall. Without uttering another word, Devin nodded once and departed.

"What did you say?" asked Nathaniel.

Jacoby opened his one eye. "I reminded him of an old debt."

Hunched over the heavy oak conference table, Nari Mudpucker, disguised as Regent Mossbrook, studied the map of Tabor, analyzing the enemy army's latest maneuvers. Ravenite's undead hoard had emerged victorious in battle after battle, leaving the Taborian forces battered and their spirits crushed. If this continued, his master would claim the coveted pearl throne of Tabor, just in time for the mystical winter solstice.

"Excellent!" he chuckled, a wide smile spreading across his face. My impersonation of Regent Mossbrook for the last week had been a resounding success, and killing him affords me a perfect way to further my master's plan from inside Tabor.

Unfortunately, he realized that the evil army still had many leagues to overcome before reaching their goal of conquering the city of Spires. His face contorted with frustration, revealing his inner turmoil. He loathed the ridiculous politics and responsibilities of being a regent. Days filled with endless paperwork, monotonous meetings with royal sycophants, and tedious peasant court cases threatened to push him to the brink of insanity. Taking some deep breaths, he closed his eyes and felt his anxiety melting away. No, he played a crucial role as an indispensable asset for his master, Ravenite, and must maintain his facade to ensure the success of the plan. *In this critical moment, growing impatient is the last thing I should do. In just a few more weeks, my master's dream of sitting on the pearl throne of Tabor will become a reality. True to his word, the reward he promised me will be beyond measure!*

A loud knock on the sturdy oak door startled him out of his thoughts, and he focused his attention on General Thorne approaching him.

"What's this sudden disruption?" Mossbrook asked, his voice filled with annoyance.

Bursting with joy, Thorne couldn't contain himself as he announced, "I have wonderful news!"

"Pray, tell," Mossbrook invited.

"We have them!" he exclaimed, his voice filled with triumph.

With a doubtful expression, Mossbrook locked eyes with him.

"I have the prince and his rowdy companions confined in the dark confines of the palace dungeon," Thorne said with a wicked grin. "I've arranged a public execution in 48hrs.... with your approval, of course."

Mossbrook's eyes smoldered with angry disappointment. What had the idiot been thinking? A simple implied assignment now ruined by Thorne's typical hubris. A public execution of King

Aarmon's lost son? How did he think the battered, struggling population would react to that? All Thorne craved was recognition instead of sticking to the simple plan.

Mossbrook squinched his eyes shut, hoping the general's presence might be a bad dream. But when he opened them, Thorne remained, an arrogant expression of triumph on his face.

"Didn't we discuss this?" Mossbrook said, voice laced with anger.

"Well, I thought..." Thorne began, his hubris fading.

"You thought?" Mossbrook barked, taking a step toward the general. "I understood, as I thought you did, the importance of eliminating the problem, not bringing it to our doorstep."

Thorne stepped back a pace. The scolding drained the elation from his face, leaving behind a blend of rising anger and embarrassment. "In my opinion," he stated in a petulant tone, "a public execution would give a stronger message, the sight of the condemned person's last moments etched into the memories of the onlookers."

Mossbrook locked eyes with the younger man for several heartbeats, contemplating whether to throttle the officer now or wait. He held the man's gaze for a long moment, then, with a resigned sigh, asked, "Who else knows about this?"

"Only a few of my most loyal Core regiment warriors. But they don't know the prince's true identity," Thorne answered indignantly.

"How do you know he's the prince?"

Thorne's face blanched. "I..uh...the information you gave me. He fit the description and was on the river just like you said," Thorne mumbled, looking down at the floor.

"And the others?" Mossbrook asked, his eyes narrowed.

"One of my men reported he traveled with an older Taborian officer, Jacoby Ironfist, some elves, and a few others," Thorne admitted. "I remember Ironfist. He was captain of the palace guards and disappeared around the same time as the prince."

Mossbrook frowned and reluctantly consented. "Very well. I'll use the time to inform our supporters in the city that the prince is a false usurper." He paused, aware of Thorne's sour expression. "And Thorne, well done. I applaud your ingenuity," he added, squeezing the general's arm. Like water rushing from a shattered dam, the officer's pout disappeared, and his self-importance returned.

"Thank you. It was rather clever," he said haughtily.

Mossbrook ignored the statement and said, "Now, update me on the Taborian army's struggles against the undead hoard."

For the next several minutes, Thorne solemnly recounted the fallen soldiers the army had lost during the intense week of fighting, blaming the losses on his younger officer's poor strategic skills. Mossbrook stifled a laugh at the general's lack of responsibility but refused to show it. How he detested Thorne's undeserved arrogance. Instead, he painted his face with a concerned expression, trying to hide his inward delight at his master's victories. He realized the Taborian army, with its constant conscription of men and even some women, was teetering on the brink of collapse. The time had come for him to execute the last step of his plan, and he felt a mix of excitement and nervousness. Despite his arrogance, General Thorne had developed into a somewhat competent tactician. Above all, his mere presence on the battlefield lifted the spirits of the Taborian army. But that would end soon enough. When the right moment arrives, I must strategically eliminate him from the board, causing the entire army to crumble, and allowing my master to achieve ultimate victory.

"Keep the pressure on the enemy. Once the prince is out of the way," Mossbrook said, tenting his fingers, "we can start negotiating for peace. Ravenite will need crops grown from our rich farmland to feed his army and our ports for commerce and to continue his conquest southward. I'm sure he'd happily have men like us oversee such assets for a minimal fee."

In sheer astonishment, Thorne's eyes bulged, and his mouth hung open. "What are you saying? Our plan was never to surrender but to dig in through the winter and hold until one of our neighbors finally reinforced us."

"What reinforcements?" Mossbrook shot back. "We've contacted everyone we know. Open your eyes! No help is coming to our aid. Our army might delay the inevitable, but without peace, Tabor's finished, and our reign with it."

Thorne's vacant stare lingered, his face a mask of confusion and bewilderment. "I understand," he said, his voice carrying a hollow resonance.

Mossbrook's eyes narrowed suspiciously. "Do you?"

Unable to process Mossbrook's realization, Thorne hesitated, his thoughts racing. Either he met his demise valiantly on the plains of Tabor, fiercely battling to protect a land already conquered, or he aligned himself with the enemy, seeking survival and the potential to maintain his social standing. But at what price did it come? He experienced a swirling sensation as if his body had detached and floated above, observing. A question surfaced from his mind's recesses, inching into his consciousness. What do I do? In a sudden moment of clarity, his self-confidence surged to the surface as if he'd awakened from a haze. His survival instinct took over, and the decision was made. "I said, I understand."

In one motion, he stood and strode from the room.

The shapeshifter's eyes remained fixated on the young general as he exited. The arrogant officer, surprisingly, had reacted to the news with more composure than he had expected. Whether it was the corrupting influence of power or the fear of death that drove him, the consequences were undeniable. Now that he had set the next phase of the plan in motion, only time would uncover the path Thorne would choose. With the next few days at his disposal, he planned to reinforce to Thorne the importance of choosing the path to maintain power and ensure survival. As he contemplated Thorne's actions, he couldn't help but feel a chilling sense of certainty that Thorne would do whatever it took, even the unthinkable, to save himself. Yet a strange sense of disquiet settled in his gut, leaving him with an inexplicable sense of concern. Mudpucker knew he couldn't leave anything to chance. To guarantee the desired outcome, he would make sure that Thorne was being closely monitored. The Master's words echoed in his mind: "Always expect the unexpected."

Mudpucker stepped over to an alcove in the wall behind him, feeling the rough texture of the stone under his fingertips. He looked around to make sure he was alone, then pushed on a loose stone hidden in the wall. As soon as a click resonated through the room, an unseen door revealed itself. With a mighty tug, the door swung open, revealing a dark closet with only a solitary shelf on the opposite wall. Thanks to his Twilight vision, he could see a 1-foot by 1-foot iron box in the dark recess. With surprising difficulty, he strained to raise the heavy box and place it onto the table. Placing his hands on the box, he caressed its smooth, cool surface and began reciting the incantation his master had taught him. The phrase "Shamut te "Rüthi dameo fornik quet, Misdrik lameno gayo pluthak" rolled off his tongue, filling the air with an ancient, enchanting energy.

The iron box emitted a bright, fiery red light, pulsating for a few heartbeats. As the light faded, the iron dissipated, revealing a square wire cage that enclosed a figure in deep sleep. Instantly, the tiny imp, barely the size of a dove, charged toward the cage bars, and pressed its moss-colored green-gray scaled body against the bars of the cage, causing a loud rattling sound and chirping incessantly.

"Calm thyself," Mudpucker barked in the ancient evil tongue, causing the imp to shrink back in fear. With wide red eyes, a sausage-like bulbous nose, and a wide mouth full of needle-sharp teeth, the beast's face had a menacing appearance. Between the cage bars, a long, pink serpent's tongue flicked in and out, searching the air. A hunched back supported immature bat wings that flapped back and forth, while a long, pointed tail with a nasty barb undulated to one side.

With the monster finally subdued, Mudpucker instructed the monster, "Follow General Thorne, Gaft, and bring me regular updates."

"As the master wills," the figure squeaked, its voice dripping with malice. Mudpucker opened the cage door, and the imp vanished in a puff of sulfur-tinged smoke.

Nathaniel awoke, his senses alert, as a barely audible noise reached his ears during the late hours of the night's watch. Unsure of whether he had been dreaming, he listened intently, but there was utter silence. Just as he closed his eyes, he felt a sharp sting on his cheek. As he pulled himself up to his elbows, he felt the stubble on his face and the dirt clinging to his skin. Darkness engulfed the room, leaving him completely blind without Twilight vision to see further than a couple of inches.

At that moment, a sudden ping caught his attention, followed by a sharp pinch on his shoulder. He realized that someone had thrown a pebble through the barred window above him.

He stood and called out, "Who's there?"

"A friend," came a whispered female voice. "I carry a message for the prince."

"I am Nathaniel Aarmon," he returned the whisper.

"My Lord," the woman gasped. "So, the tale is true. Praise Odin!"

Nathaniel waited, hoping for more.

"General Thorne and the High Council have scheduled your execution to take place in two days. They have already made progress on the gallows," the woman whispered sadly, her voice filled with sorrow. "Yet, be aware that you are not alone in this predicament; there are loyal companions spread across the city, actively planning an escape."

Nathaniel's face sank with disappointment, but a glimmer of hope flickered in his eyes. "Thank you," he said, his voice lingering in the air for a moment. Then, breaking the silence, he asked with a hint of uncertainty, "What's your name?"

"Many know me as "the Scarlet Thorn", a title that instills fear in the hearts of the unjust," responded the voice. "But you, My Lord, may use my given name, Esmeralda."

Nathaniel imagined the woman behind the voice was a seasoned adult, melded and hardened over the years on the city streets, fighting to survive. But he sensed a passion for justice in the woman's tone, perhaps using her skills to right wrongs that life doled out to the underprivileged. As a result, she developed a fearsome reputation for dealing with anyone who dared to challenge her or took advantage of the least favored.

"Thank you, Esmeralda, for risking so much for me," Nathaniel said. "May I ask one favor?"

Her silence hung in the air, encouraging him to press on.

"The warriors that attacked us apprehended a group of three women and four infants. Please, I beg those with you to prioritize their survival above mine," Nathaniel said. "It would be a profound source of solace to know they lived freely, regardless of what happens to us."

Esmeralda remained silent for several agonizing minutes and Nathaniel wondered if she heard his plea.

Then from the darkness, she said, "Your reputation has proceeded you, mighty Lord, and now I understand why. I will pass on your message and hope to return soon."

"Thank you," Nathaniel said, but only silence greeted him.

He found a spot to sit, leaning his back against the cold stone wall as the damp darkness closed in around him. The countdown began: 48 hours until the execution. Time loses its grip in the darkness, stretching and warping with each passing moment.

Then, from the darkness, Jacoby's voice emerged, providing his characteristic reassurance. "Brother," he said, his voice filled with conviction, "where there is hope, there is always a way."

TWENTY-SEVEN

Sweat dripped down Jacoby's face as he slid down the stone wall beside the iron door. For what felt like an eternity, he relentlessly pounded on the door with his fist, but there was no response. A high-pitched moan shattered the darkness, echoing through the air like the cry of a wounded deer. He turned toward the noise, his body tensing as a low groan escaped his lips, a painful reminder of the brutal beating he had endured just days earlier. Grullach Furr's uncontrollable shivering reverberated through the cell, filling the air with a chilling tremor as his fever-ravaged body fought against it.

Witnessing his friend's hacking cough and fever unsettled Jacoby. The foul stench of refuse and moldy decay swallowed the entire cell, making it hard to breathe, and even harder for Grull. Overwhelmed by a high fever, the halfling descended into delirium, his moans becoming increasingly incomprehensible. Jacoby had seen enough illness over the years to know Grull's cough had progressed to pneumonia and was a hair's breadth from overcoming his defenses. He needed immediate help, or he wouldn't last a week.

Where in the demons are those guards?

Jacoby's stomach churned and growled, intensifying his discomfort. The lack of food and minimal water over the past day and a half took a toll on the group's morale, and Grull's condition only deteriorated further.

Finally, Jacoby heard footsteps approaching down the corridor, the golden hue of lantern light glowing under the iron door base. The iron door swung open with a loud creak, the silhouette of two guards, one larger than the other, outlined in the bright light.

Jacoby covered his eyes with his forearm, squinting against the light's assault.

"What's causing all this noise, you wretches?" one bulky guard barked, kicking Jacoby in the ribs. Jacoby groaned, the air escaping in a rush and rolling on his side.

"Stop, please," he rasped.

"Stop?" the guard chuckled. "I'm in charge here, scum."

Behind him stood the other guard, a young man with a slender frame. Jacoby hesitated, giving his eyes a moment to adapt to the dim light, and then suddenly, his eyebrows shot up in surprise. Locking eyes with the younger guard, his mouth hung open in sheer surprise. The moment he laid eyes on the younger man, he knew it was the raider he had set free a few days earlier. The young man subtly shook his head, silently signaling Jacoby to keep the secret hidden.

"My friend is sick," Jacoby explained. "He contracted a lung infection. He needs a healer."

The heavyset guard let out a hearty laugh, causing his ample belly to jiggle like a bowl full of jelly. "Oh no, what a disappointment. One less for the executioner tomorrow." Then his face turned serious. "You make another sound, and I'll make sure you regret it," he threatened, jabbing a meaty finger in Jacoby's direction. As he slammed the door, the younger man watched anxiously, his face filled with worry.

With the enveloping darkness came a sense of impending doom, crushing any remaining hope for Grullach's survival. What now?

But an hour later, he received an answer to his question when he heard footsteps again and saw the glow of a lamp. The guard placed the lamp on the floor and pushed open the heavy iron door. The young guard held a brazier in one hand and a bundle of herbs in the other and called out, "Big man? Where are you?"

Jacoby pulled himself to his feet, feeling the soreness in his muscles, but hesitated to approach the guard. He stood at a distance, his senses on high alert, unsure of what might come next.

"A healer friend suggested using an aromatic eucalyptus poultice and lots of hot steam to break up the congestion. They suggested a tea of echinacea, coltsfoot, and astragalus," the guard said, gesturing with the offering.

Jacoby shuffled over to the guard, locking eyes with the younger man. "Why are you helping us?"

The younger man averted his gaze, his face a mask of shame. "Our company had received explicit instructions to locate and eliminate you. But when you captured me," the guard replied, "you surprisingly set me free. I wanted to do whatever I could to show my gratitude."

Jacoby's eyes narrowed with suspicion as he observed the guard. "Where's your companion?" he asked, scanning the area.

"Sleeping like a baby. I added a bit of poppy tincture to his grog," the younger man said with a sly smile.

Jacoby nodded, a relieved expression washing over his face. "Come with me," Jacoby said, his voice carrying a sense of command. He turned from the watchful guard, using the light from the brazer and Grull's moans to guide him through the dark cell. The other Brotherhood watched from the shadows in tense silence, unsure of the guard's intent. If it weren't for the droplets of sweat beading over his face, the halfling's pale, gaunt form would have an almost angelic quality. After placing the brazier and bag to the side, the guard pulled out a clean rag and offered it to Jacoby.

"To catch the steam," the young man said, turning away.

Nathaniel stepped forward and grasped the rag.

The young man studied the prince intently, his eyes searching for any sign of confirmation of the rumors of the man's identity. Finally, he mustered the courage to ask, "Are you really the person who the rumors claim you to be?"

Nathaniel wordlessly revealed the clover birthmark behind his ear as he pushed back his greasy, unwashed hair. The man's eyes widened in astonishment, and his mouth fell agape, yet no words escaped.

"What's your name, friend?" Nathaniel asked, his eyes softening.

The man found his tongue and stammered out his name. "Julius, sir."

"Julius," he said, his voice filled with gratitude, "Thank you for what you did. We could use more help in getting out of here."

Just as the young guard was about to respond, the sound of someone stumbling down the hallway interrupted them.

"Jules," called out the other guard, his words slurred and muffled. "I don't feel well," he said in a weak voice.

Julius' face grew ashen with sheer panic. "I have to go," he whispered urgently, snatching the brazier and darting out the door. He slammed the heavy door shut, the sound echoing through the room.

"Well? What news?" the shapeshifter demanded.

Though seemingly simple, the statement carried heavy suspicion and the risk of punishment if answered wrongly. Nari Mudpucker gazed down at the tiny imp who had abruptly appeared in a puff of foul-smelling sulfurous smoke on his desk.

Gaft hesitated a heartbeat before answering, then said, "The human met with another man before heading to the front."

"Another man?" the doppelgänger asked, one brow elevated in surprise. "Who? Where?"

The imp shook his head. "They met at a bustling cafe near the palace, embracing as if old friends. An older gray-haired human dressed in ordinary clothes and walked with a noticeable limp. Nothing suspicious."

"What did they say?" Mudpucker asked, his gut feeling a tickle of unease.

"It was a time of reflection, mainly focusing on memories from the past." With a weary expression, the imp scoffed at the human's conversation. "Seemed like boring drivel."

Nari rubbed his chin, his brow furrowed in surprise. After Thorne's reaction the night before, he expected some nefarious action. Luckily, it appeared the general understood his role and acted accordingly. But who had been this commoner? Likely a relative or old army buddy. Nothing to worry about.

Mudpucker wrote off the encounter as unimportant. Just another old man, unfit for active service, riding out the war until needed for the last stand on the palace battlements. He would soon learn that they would conscript him to the Taborian front lines within the month. If he were lucky, he might last a week, although Mudpucker guessed he'd fall in the first attack.

"What happened next?"

"Next?" The imp put a gnarled gray finger to his chin and looked away as if thinking. "He said his goodbyes and rode to meet the troops. A contingent of Lord Ravenite's army attacked shortly after his arrival. To boost morale during the brutal skirmish, Thorne foolishly encouraged his troops to counterattack, but his misguided actions only resulted in more lives being lost. He was fortunate to survive, even though he suffered a non-lethal wound," the imp said, chuckling. "The remaining Taborian army retreated, setting up camp and fortifying their position just seventy leagues outside of the city."

With a broad grin, Mudpucker felt a shiver of excitement course through his body for the first time. Surprisingly, he realized he might not have to eliminate Thorne after all. A new opportunity had presented itself, playing right into his hands. Thorne's continuous string of strategic errors gradually weakened Tabor's army, leaving them vulnerable and on the verge of collapse. Mudpucker saw the potential for victory and envisioned a scenario where Tabor's forces would become a feeble group of elderly men and women desperately using pitchforks and sickles to defend their beloved city. This prospect delighted him, as it would finally allow his master, Ravenite, to rejoice after months of grueling battles and tireless efforts to conquer Tabor.

He stood, ready to dismiss the imp to feed, then back to watch Thorne for the evening until bedtime. But an odd feeling of concern shot through his mind, extinguishing his good humor. Mudpucker remembered the old man and realized he needed reassurance he was not a threat. As his eyes narrowed, his heart pounded in his chest like a thunderous drumbeat. Taking a long, deep breath of the frosty evening air, he exhaled slowly, attempting to quiet his racing thoughts. The imp, realizing a change in Mudpucker's demeanor, studied the doppelgänger with intense curiosity, as if it were an unusual insect that had somehow developed wings.

"Yes?" the imp coaxed, wondering what ran through Mudpucker's mind.

After a long moment, the doppelgänger's heart slowed, and he said, "I worry Thorne may have passed this interloper restricted information. Are you sure the conversation was nothing?"

"Trivialities, My Lord," Galt answered, waving a hand dismissively.

"What happened to the old man?"

"The old man, Lord?" the imp choked. Now it was the Galt's turn to panic. He fought to keep his brows from rising and his breathing normal. The imp, conjured by the magic of the demon lord, Asmodeus, had learned to stay alive through obedience and various levels of fabrication. And so, the lie rolled off his tongue as naturally as if he'd spoken his name.

"The old man hobbled with his crutch down the street into the city bazaar after the meeting, Lord. I chose to follow the general, and leave the cripple to his shopping."

Mudpucker's face twisted into a suspicious expression, his eyes narrowing. After several heartbeats, he said, "Keep me updated."

With a nod, the imp vanished in a foul-smelling sulfur cloud.

The older man limped through the bazaar, occasionally glancing behind to ensure no one followed. He rushed past kiosk after kiosk, shoving zealous merchants out of his way despite his infirmity. He took a sharp left at the end of one corridor into a partially shadowed alley filled with stinking human refuse, finally reaching a painted wooden door. With his crutch, the man rapped twice, and the door opened and the older man felt muscular arms grasp his woolen tunic and yank him inside. The door slammed with a bang, and the man stared into the eyes of a large male faun.

"That was uncalled for, Heroclus!" The man said, rising to his feet, and brushing off his costume. In seconds, he tore off his wig and fake eyebrows, dropped his cane, and rose to his full height of six feet and one inch.

"Sorry, Devin. It's better to be safe than sorry. Did anyone follow you?" the faun said in a low, rumbling voice, his arms crossed. The beast had sandy brown hair and a muscular physique covered in shaggy brown fur to the ankle. He tapped a cloven hoof impatiently, worry written in his golden eyes.

"I don't believe so," Devin said, his tone laced with irritation. "But one thing troubles me."

Heroclus waited, his heartbeat speeding up.

"I could have sworn I caught sight of an imp. But after I left Thorne, he disappeared."

"An imp?" Heroclus almost shouted, his eyes wide. "Could he be following Thorne?"

"Perhaps. But why would a creature from the underworld be informing on Thorne?" Devin said, rubbing his chin. "Maybe I imagined it."

A clammy sweat slicked Heroclus' face, and his heart hammered a frantic rhythm against his ribs. If an imp had watched the meeting, then greater forces than we imagined are manipulating events. Our plans have become a matter for urgent action.

"Is everything ready for tonight?" Minister Devin Ashoke asked, changing into his royal tunic and pants.

"Ready. I've had our contacts spread the news throughout the city."

"And Esmeralda?" he asked, his eyes suspicious. "Why isn't she here?"

"I don't know," Heroclus said, looking away. "I'm sure she'll be ready."

"You're sure?" Ashoke said incredulously. Then his expression turned fiery red with anger, and Heroclus swore he saw smoke emanating from his ears. "The timing for tonight's operation is not optional. Everyone must be on the same page!" He demanded, his face flushed.

"Calm down," the faun said. "If she said she'll be there, then she'll be there. She's never lied to us."

"Calm down? General Thorne disclosed the fate awaiting the prince and his cohorts - execution by hanging, with the women and children destined to become indentured servants within two days! I won't be calm until I know the prince is safe," stated Ashoke.

"Nor I," said Heroclus seriously. "But I trust Esmeralda. And I trust you," he said confidently, as he placed a reassuring hand on the minister's shoulder.

Devin's shoulders relaxed. "Thanks, mate."

Jacoby watched as the tiny candle flame flickered weakly, its feeble light struggling against the engulfing darkness. His guard, Julius, had given him a gift - a small nub of a candle. As he watched it burn, the flame inched closer and closer to the end of the wick. Just like our lives, evaporating into the void of blackness. Jacoby had never been morose, always finding the silver lining to every storm cloud in life. But, with less than a day before execution, he could think of nothing else. Have I led a decent life? A life of honor? Have I been a good father?

His attention shifted to the far wall where Nathaniel rested, and his thoughts immediately gravitated towards him. His mind wandered back in time to the night the young man was born. In a rush to obey the Queen's final command, he located and used the concealed passage that led directly to the Queen's study—a clandestine escape route he had frequented in the past. Only a handful of people were aware of the labyrinth of passages and secret paths that King Whitestar had skillfully integrated into the walls. As her guard, he had accompanied Queen Elana on her private walks, where they would venture outside the castle walls. It had been through those same tunnels that he, Mare, and baby Nathaniel had fled on the night of his birth, their footsteps echoing against the damp stone walls. Memories rushed through his mind like a powerful river current, vividly recalling sunny picnics on the bank of the Black Owl River with Mare and toddler Nathaniel, as well as the bleak and lonesome days that followed Mare's passing. Through his grief, he mustered the strength to persuade Grullach, Bluebeard, and Allai'nn to assist him in managing the Sleeping Dragon Inn. Together, they aimed to provide the boy with a secure and nurturing environment.

A warm, genuine smile spread across Jacoby's face. With his friend's help, he had raised a kind, compassionate leader who always prioritized the needs of others over his own. Despite their tireless efforts, they had fought their way across the continent and back again, only to find defeat waiting for them at the last step. Jacoby couldn't believe their misfortune, even though they had endured countless sacrifices, lost dear friends, and narrowly escaped death multiple times. Yet here they were, hours before being executed on bogus political charges. His heart sank at the sight of the young man he cherished peacefully resting across the room. Without warning, the candle flame flickered and went out, casting the room into a suffocating darkness that mirrored his profound hopelessness.

Jacoby leaned back against the uncomfortable stones of the cell wall, the coldness seeping through his clothes as he stared into the unmitigated darkness. The candle had been a godsend, a tiny remembrance of life, and a symbol of hope. But now, the impenetrable gloom enveloped him again, its presence so overwhelming and menacing that it felt like a heavy weight on his chest. The dark encased him like an enormous amoeboid organism, draining away any remnants of time or hope. A profound feeling of loss consumed him, leaving him empty and incapable of providing comfort or reassurance to his friends. His mind drifted, giving into the void.

But in the recesses of his brain, he registered a sound. At first, his mind ignored the noise as insignificant. But as the sound continued, the tone moved to the forefront, and he listened closely. He heard a faint scratching, followed by a sudden crunching sound that echoed from the wall on his right. A line of golden light caught his attention, expanding into a three-foot tall, vertical line of luminosity. The big man rubbed his eyes, unsure if what he saw was real or a figment of his imagination. The crunching noise grew louder, and the golden glow from a candle intensified as a hidden section of the wall swung open. A hooded figure cautiously peered into the cell, its features backlit by the soft, golden light.

In a distant whisper, the form called out, "Jacoby?"

The big man sat motionless, his mind racing to comprehend the disorienting change in the world around him. The form slowly crab-walked towards him, its limbs moving in an eerie and unnatural manner until a face came into view. Devin Ashoke stared directly into his eyes. However, the Devin he knew had transformed into someone entirely different, becoming an older man with sagging eyes, gray hair, and a nose that was bent out of shape.

"Who..." Jacoby whispered, but the figure quickly silenced him by placing a finger over his mouth.

"We're leaving," he said, his voice filled with determination. "Wake the others," Ashoke whispered, offering to assist with their injured companion.

The unexpected turn of events left Jacoby feeling paralyzed, his mind racing as he struggled to find a response. Acting on instinct, he quickly followed their mysterious savior's instructions and, with his help, guided a disoriented Grullach into the hidden tunnel. Jacoby's bulky frame required a forceful push to fit through the compact three-by-three-foot opening, but with the older man's help, he managed to squeeze into the tunnel. Ashoke pulled the secret door closed with a grinding crunch, hoping the flask of wine laced with poppy extract he left for the guards would be enough to keep them occupied. Once inside, the prisoners discovered the tunnel expanded, allowing them to crawl on all fours. With every step they took, the damp earth clung to their clothes, and the aroma of soil permeated the air. After 100 paces, the tunnel abruptly ended, revealing a sturdy wooden door. In the lead, Nathaniel pushed the heavy door open, tumbling into a pitch-black root cellar surrounded by the earthy scent of fresh turnips, cabbage, and carrots. The others followed, and for a moment, nothing happened. Then he heard a match strike, and another candle bloomed to light the room, held by a tall, black, shaggy-haired faun.

"Took you long enough," grumbled the faun, clearly frustrated by the delay. "The guards could wake soon."

"With the wine infused with the fragrance of poppies? They should be out for hours, maybe until the next guard change," responded the older man.

The group found themselves in a spacious underground root cellar, where the rough walls were made of a distinctive blend of dirt and stone. Cool, damp air filled the room, mingling with a faint, musty smell. Wooden shelves adorned the walls, displaying a bountiful supply of canned vegetables and fruits. Baskets filled with onions, chives, potatoes, and radishes were scattered throughout every corner.

Nathaniel stepped up to the man beside the faun and extended his hand, introducing himself with confidence. "I'm Nathaniel. Thank you for rescuing us."

The older man no longer stooped but raised to his full height, tall and regal in appearance, with an aura of authority surrounding him. His eyes widened in surprise at Nathaniel's words, realizing that the young man had unknowingly humbled himself. Beside the man, the faun watched the exchange with curiosity. Both beings stood in stunned silence for a moment, processing the weight of Nathaniel's unintentional revelation. Then, as if a spell had enchanted them, they both kneeled simultaneously, bowing their heads in deep respect.

With a voice filled with reverence, they spoke in unison, "Our honor to serve, your Majesty. Devin Ashoke and Heroclus, at your service."

For a heartbeat, Nathaniel stared at the man, stunned by his disguise, unable to believe this had been the same man they met in the Horn Wood. Then, he stepped forward and motioned for them to rise. "Please, my friends. I am honored by your courage." Glancing over his shoulder at Jacoby holding onto an unsteady Grullach, added, "My friend needs immediate help. Can you lead us out of here to a healer?"

"Of course," said Heroclus. "Follow me."

The far ceiling revealed a wooden ladder with worn rungs, each one bearing the marks of years of use. Instead of using it, he turned to his right, where a long shelf lined the wall, filled with an assortment of preserved fruits, vegetables, and other intriguing items. With a mischievous grin, the faun reached out and grabbed a large container of canned peaches, causing an audible click as it shifted on the shelf. Satisfied with his selection, he leaned against the shelf, revealing a hidden opening. With a grunt of effort, he pushed against it, revealing another secret corridor. The group eagerly followed him down the dimly lit hallway, their footsteps echoing off the stone walls. They maneuvered around one corner after another, their anticipation growing with each step. Finally, they arrived at a massive gate, its iron bars imposing and seemingly impenetrable. Undeterred, Heroclus stepped forward and pushed open the gate with a mighty heave. With a nod of satisfaction, he stepped aside, allowing the rest of the group to pass through and continue into a shadowed alleyway.

"We have a safe house nearby, your Majesty. My apologies for its location being in a less desirable part of the city," said Devin, taking charge. "Stay in the shadows. Royal council spies are everywhere." As if by magic, he stooped and again became a disabled elder leaning on his staff for support.

"This way," he said.

In a matter of minutes, the group traversed through a series of winding alleyways, strewn with litter and permeated with the putrid smell of decay, until they finally arrived at a weathered wooden door. Devin knocked twice, the sound echoing through the silence as he anxiously waited. A strong, responding knock emerged from within, creating a hollow echo that reverberated through the stillness, and when the door swung open, an impenetrable darkness consumed the room. Devin entered, and the others followed, with the door closing and locking behind them.

In the depths of the palace, the three women sat hunched, their heads lowered. They rested on large piles of freshly harvested corn, their hands rough and bound together by a thick rope. Under the command of a merciless head cook, whose wrath was clear from the multiple facial bruises adorning the ladies, their task was to shuck, peel, or harvest food to feed the retreating army and palace staff. Their hands were red and sore, with minor cuts and lacerations from their work, stinging with every move.

"What's to become of us?" Rue cried, wiping tears from her eyes with her forearm.

Her bleeding hands trembled as Allai'nn recalled the vivid image of her husband, Grullach Furr, tumbling into the icy river current after falling off the rope bridge in the Horn Wood. A platoon of the same darkly dressed bandits from which they had just escaped ambushed the three women as they crossed over the river island bridge. In the blink of an eye, they were gagging and restrained, their hands and feet tied with heavy rope. Hidden among the bushes on the island side of the bridge, they could see, but not warn, the Brotherhood as they made their way across the bridge. From her vantage point, Allai'nn observed the attack unfold, each side executing their moves with impressive expertise. She couldn't forget the memory of Grull, her husband, friend, and heart, being ambushed and taken away from her. Her heart shattered; she became an empty vessel drained of all vitality. Her tears flowed for days, her grief consuming her as her world spun in chaos. To make things worse, her vicious guardian had denied her access to visit her children. The decision felt like a dagger to her heart, repeatedly driven in over and over.

But Rue remained optimistic. The dormant ember of hope within Allai'nn, long cold, and lifeless, felt the breath of renewed possibility at Rue's words.

"Jacoby and Nathaniel will come for us. We must focus on staying alive," she whispered to Allai'nn and Lani.

Like candlelight repelling the dark, the elf princess' hope reignited, dispelling her despair. She knew the Brotherhood would stop at nothing to rescue them, not even if it meant sacrificing their own lives.

"Yes," she said, wiping away her tears. "We must lift and lean on each other until they come."

Beside her, Lani lifted her face, swollen and puffy from crying. A profound sense of conviction welled up inside her, affirming the truth of Allai'nn's statement and leaving no doubt that Nathaniel was still breathing.

Her response was concise and self-assured, leaving no room for doubt. "I have faith, Rue," she said, her words carrying a sense of reassurance. "Nothing yet has been written."

Soon after, the storeroom door banged open, and a husky female cook strode in, carrying a heavy wooden spoon the length and thickness of her arm over her shoulder. The cook stood over the three women with a frown, her hands on her hips.

"Is this what you consider work?" she smirked, her face scarlet with rage. With one quick motion, she extended her leg, delivering a powerful kick to Lani's abdomen, causing her to hunch over in pain. She followed the move by driving down the spoon like a makeshift club on the girl's back. Allai'nn leaped to her feet, but her bound state with Rue hindered her from defending against the attack. The heavy club landed on Lani's left shoulder with a resounding thud, causing her to scream out in agonizing pain.

"Stop it, witch," Allai'nn shouted, her voice echoing through the air as she pulled Rue to her feet. With a sadistic grin, the cook swung the club sideways, sending both Allai'nn and Rue crashing to the ground.

"Witch, eh? I'll show you just what an evil witch is capable of!" The beefy cook snarled, raising the spoon high over her head to rain down a death blow on the elf. Unable to block the blow, Allai'nn cringed, closing her eyes to prepare for the end. But the end never came. Instead, the brawny cook dropped the club at its zenith, collapsing in a heap at Allai'nn's feet.

As the elf opened her eyes, she saw a dark-haired woman with a blood-stained blackjack baton in one hand, her intense gaze fixed on the prone form.

"Who...?" she stammered, her eyes widening in fear as she looked around for any sign of the mysterious assailant. A female figure dressed in a black tunic, vest, and leathers, rose behind the fallen cook. Intricate colored tattoos covered her arms, neck, and face, giving her a sinister appearance. But her eyes told the greatest story. A vivid ice blue, they reflected a mixture of bland indifference and weathered street smarts.

Allai'nn asked, "Who are you?"

"Quickly, get up on your feet! We have little time," snapped the woman, ignoring the question. She stepped forward, producing a knife from her boot and cutting through the women's bonds. Then she knelt next to Lani and whispered into the woman's ear.

"Get her up if she's coming. Another servant will come shortly and discover this filth," she ordered.

Allai'nn could hear Lani's soft sobs and feel the trembling of her body. She knelt next to her and gently made contact with the shoulder, exploring its contours from the neck outward.

"No bones broken," she declared, then lifted the girl back onto her feet.

"Hurry," the tattooed woman hissed, listening at the cellar door and sliding the knife back into her boot.

Lani leaned against the two women, feeling the warmth of Rue on one side and the comforting presence of Allai'nn on the other.

On closer observation, the rescuer, in her late teens, had cascading black curls that framed her round face, which was tanned from years spent outdoors. The commanding presence of the woman's intelligent, glacial eyes captivated the prisoners, instilling a spark of fear in their hearts.

Allai'nn's voice was firm as she stated through pressed lips, her arms crossed, "We appreciate your help, but I won't take a step until I know who you are and where we're going."

With a sharp turn, the woman's narrowed eyes locked onto the figure standing behind her. "Call me Esmeralda, elf. I'm a friend, but I can become an enemy in a blink if you wish."

The tension in the air was palpable as the two women locked eyes, neither one willing to break the silence. Several heartbeats passed, and Allai'nn let out a heavy sigh. "Understood," she replied, her tone showing her agreement. "We can leave, but not without my children."

"Follow me," Esmeralda said, her footsteps echoing as she hurried across the room towards a section of wall that was opened to reveal a hidden corridor. The group shuffled down the passage lined with cold stone and dirt. After turning a corner, Esmeralda motioned the others to stop, and she leaned her head against a small door.

"Wait here," she mouthed.

After a moment, she gripped her knife tightly, ready for whatever might come next. As the door swung open, she swiftly entered the room, ensuring she made it inside before the door shut. Muffled words reached Allai'nn's ears, and a loud, anguished moan soon followed them. With a creak, the door opened, revealing Esmeralda, who carefully entrusted four sleepy infants to the women. Over the girl's shoulder, Allai'nn's eyes fell upon two matrons lying motionless on the floor, their bodies drenched in blood.

An hour later, the women stumbled down a shadowed path, their footsteps reverberating through the stillness. In the darkness, Esmeralda reached a dilapidated wooden door and gently rapped her knuckles against it twice. A sharp, reciprocating knock echoed through the air, causing the door to swing open, revealing a wedge of obsidian. In a flurry of movement, she burst into the room, tugging the women along with her. As they entered, the heavy door slammed shut with a loud bang, and a metal bar slid noisily into place as a lock. The room remained pitch black for several seconds until a candle was lit, and a bright orange spark illuminated a short, older brownie. The creature, dressed in a tunic and leather pants covered by a bloodied tanner's apron, held the candle high, its flickering light casting eerie shadows as it studied each woman and child through thick spectacles. Despite being half their height, the brownie stood on tiptoes, carefully examining each eye and prodding ribs with curiosity. After a moment, he turned on his heels and said, "You look only a bit worse for wear. Follow me, My Ladies."

He hurried down a narrow hallway leading to the back of the structure. Allai'nn, Rue, and Lani stumbled after him, with Esmeralda trailing behind.

"I am Doctor Phineus," he said, his voice sounding nasally as he spoke over his shoulder. "Please disrobe the children so I can examine them in more detail," he added matter-of-factly, his words hanging in the air with a clinical detachment. "My assistant, Leyka, will bring a basin to wash up." He stepped away, leaving the four women gawking in stunned silence.

"He can be a little...brusque," Esmeralda said, passing the fourth child to Rue. "But there's no better healer in the entire city."

Within a few minutes, a young woman entered with a warm basin of water, wash clothes, and a satchel of new clothes.

"I'm Leyka, Dr Phineus' aide," the young blond elf said as she cleaned and changed an infant. The girl seemed older than her youthful age, with powder-white skin, golden curls, and a cherubic face.

"Thank you for caring for my babies, Leyka," Allai'nn said, more at ease despite the swirling changes experienced in the last few hours. She considered how to break the ice and asked, "Where do you hail from?"

The girl smiled. "I'm a Waterfall elf from the Rainbow Falls in the Horn Wood, Princess."

"You know me?" Allai'nn said, taken aback.

"Who in the Elven world hasn't heard of Allai'nn Hŷnhasbren? Or Lady Rue?" she answered with a warm grin, her eyes sparkling with pride. "All young Elven women look up to you both as shining examples of courage, resilience, and bold action. It is my utmost honor to serve alongside you."

Allai'nn and Rue exchanged a meaningful glance, their connection palpable even in the silence that hung between them. They had never realized their immense impact on their fellow Elves, unknowingly serving as beacons of inspiration and hope. Despite their doubts and insecurities, they had become symbols of strength within the Brotherhood, even without possessing the typical warrior abilities that others deemed valuable.

"Thank you," Allai'nn murmured, gently touching Leyka's hand. "We are the ones humbled by this great honor."

Leyka blushed, her cheeks turning a rosy shade, and nodded in agreement. At that precise moment, a sudden knock reverberated through the door, signaling the entrance of Dr. Phineus.

Facing Lani, the brownie said, "Let me look at you," his eyes scanned her from head to toe. With a gentle touch, he palpated her orbital region, cheeks, and jaw, assessing for any signs of tenderness or swelling. Moving along her neck, his fingers trailed over the angry, discolored skin of her left shoulder, now swollen and marked with a deep purple hue. Lani winced at the touch, a reflexive reaction to the unpleasant feeling.

Dr. Phineus stepped back, his hand on his chin, brow together in thought. "There is no fracture, thank the Gods. But it will throb like a demon's bite for a few days," he said. "Leyka, apply a poultice of calendula, tea oil, and turmeric to the shoulder three times a day."

"Yes, Healer," she said obediently.

Locking eyes with Rue, he studied her intently for several seconds, trying to read her emotions. "Lady Rue," he whispered, his voice barely audible in the silence. "You favor your mother, Byrgid," the brownie said, his half-smile revealing his observation, "but there's a trace of the mischievous Gruawane in your features, too. Are you in pain other than from the beating?" he asked.

"My back hurts," she whispered, her eyes downcast.

Turning her around, he said, "Let me see," as he examined her. The dark purple and yellow bruises on her back told a story of the violence she had endured. One spot in the lower back appeared red and swollen, a break in the skin oozing green pus. Phineus's sharp intake of breath highlighted the gravity of the situation.

"Quickly, ladies, move the children to the other table," Phinius ordered. "Rue, lie down on your stomach." Then turning to Leyka added, "I need poppy powder and the flask of grain alcohol."

"What's wrong?" Allai'nn said, alarmed, as Leyka rushed out of the room.

"She has a serious festering infection that must be drained immediately," answered Phineus, worry painted on his face.

When Leyka returned, he carefully poured several swallows of poppy elixir into Rue's cup and whispered, "May you drift into a peaceful slumber, little oread."

Rue closed her eyes as Phineus prepared to perform the procedure, feeling the sting of alcohol on her lower back. After heating the blade over a flame, he allowed it to cool down. With no hesitation, he made an incision into the abscess, eager to relieve the pain. Phineus carefully cleared the wound, removing the noxious green ooze that seeped from it. After ensuring that all putrid fluid was gone, he carefully doused the area once more with alcohol, filling the air with its sharp scent, then filled the wound with a combination of healing herbs.

"Same poultice, plus feverfew, honey, and yarrow, as with the other patient, Leyka. Check for fever every two hours," he said, his hands dripping with water as he cleaned them in a basin.

As he turned to Allai'nn, he couldn't help but notice the determination in her eyes. "May I examine you, princess?" the doctor asked, his gentle touch putting her at ease.

"What about Rue?" she asked, her voice filled with concern. "Is there any danger to her well-being?"

Phinius hesitated, his eyes darting back and forth as he weighed his options. "I believe she will heal as expected," he replied, his eyes sparkling with confidence. "I promise to watch her closely."

"But?" Allai'nn said, her heart in her throat.

"But...the future remains unwritten. You of all elves know that, My Lady. Draining the purulence is just the beginning step toward healing," Phineas said, his eyes filled with gentleness. "Now, may I examine you, please?"

"I'm fine," Allai'nn said, her voice filled with worry for the oread. Not a word escaped Rue's lips about the relentless beating she'd endured or the overwhelming discomfort in her back from the infection coursing through her body.

"Please," the healer implored.

Allai'nn sighed and allowed the healer to examine her, but other than a few bruises to her face, she seemed healthy.

"Very well. Leyka will apply a paste of yarrow and calendula to Lady Rue if you approve," the healer said. "Would you mind accompanying me?"

He walked down the hallway and entered the first room to the right. Inside, a figure lay sleeping in a bed by the wall.

"Grull!" she screamed and rushed over to his bedside, showering him with kisses.

"I can't believe you're alive! Is he all right?" she implored.

"He suffers from pneumonia, on top of the beating and neglect. But he's strong and should survive with the proper care," reassured the healer. Silently, Jacoby, Nathaniel, Horatio, Blue Ivy, and Cor'in tiptoed into the room.

"Are these men familiar to you?" he inquired with a rueful smile, his eyes filled with understanding. Sobbing tears of joy, Allai'nn melted into a group hug with the warriors, feeling their warmth and love.

An hour later, Jacoby, Nathaniel, Cor'in, Horatio, Allai'nn, and Lani waited at the long table. The door opened, and Devin, Ashoke, Heroclus, and Esmeralda strode in and stood at one end.

"Ahem," Ashoke said. His voice filled the room, commanding the attention of everyone in the group. "I know you've been through a rough stretch, but it's only two hours before sunrise. Once the guards report your escape, the palace will descend into utter chaos. That is the moment we march boldly to the palace, with the energy of the people propelling us forward," he stated, slamming his fist on the table. "Agreed?"

Ashoke's eyes fixed on each person, and each gave a nod of assent. "Very well," he said, relaxing. "I suggest we all take a brief rest."

He gestured for Heroclus, who approached with a canvas sack, its contents bulging and clinking. As he unraveled the oiled canvas, the glint of polished steel and the earthy scent of leather filled the air, revealing the weaponry and packs of the Brotherhood salvaged from the prison. A palpable sense of danger hung in the air as the men in the room reached for their weapons, altering the jubilant atmosphere that was present.

"Thor, be praised," Cor'in said, rubbing an affectionate hand over his sword, followed by the others.

He turned to leave, but a gesture from Jacoby caught his eye. He met Jacoby in one corner, his brow furrowed. "What is it?"

"Did you complete the task we spoke of?" Jacoby asked in a whisper.

"Of course. But so far, no response."

Frustration washed over Jacoby as he shook his head, trying to decipher the meaning behind Devin's words. Having told Ashoke of the special green communication stone in his pack, Jacoby hoped his friend had used it to contact King Polaris for help. A lack of response from the leader of the Elven Council did not bode well for aid soon, his hopes crashing like shattered glass. Not wanting to dash the other's enthusiasm, he nodded, mouthing the words, "Thank you."

Jacoby's mind turned to the anticipation of what the day held, leaving him both eager and anxious. More chaos? Or finally, some vindication? Only the Gods knew. One thing is certain: we are on our own whatever the outcome.

TWENTY EIGHT

With the sun's golden rays emerging over the eastern horizon, the Brotherhood gathered alongside the citizen leaders, whom Regent Mossbrook condescendingly referred to as "the rabble", in the city of Spires town square.

"I remember you," an older shopkeeper said dismissively, addressing Jacoby. "I waste no time for cowards." Jacoby felt the deep sting of the words, remaining impassive. The elder locked eyes with the young prince, taking in his full measure. "Is this the next majestic ruler?" he said sarcastically.

A warm smile spread across Nathaniel's face as he extended his hand. "I am Nathaniel Aarmon," he said confidently.

The elder warily took the hand, feeling Nathaniel's firm grip. He examined the younger man's face for signs of trickery but saw nothing. Nathaniel revealed the clover birthmark behind his ear, a small red symbol hidden beneath his tousled hair.

With narrowed eyes, the elder stated, "It's possible to create such marks through the power of magic or even a skilled artist. What other proof of your heritage?"

Nathaniel expected the retort and calmly displayed his sword, Blueblade, the Lládir Ellÿn silver blade gleaming in the morning sunlight and adorned with the Founder's stone embedded in the hilt.

The elder studied the sword, running his fingers along the flawless edge and admiring the intricate details of the jeweled hilt. With a furrowed brow, he directed his attention to the ancient, circular stone, studying its intricate details.

"I may not be well-educated, but this blade holds a unique significance. What makes this stone important, and why does such a young warrior like you possess such a magnificent weapon?" the elder asked, his curiosity piqued.

"A gift from King Goldbriar of Elyra," Nathaniel replied, acknowledging the elder's fascination. "But the stone holds its own legendary tale." He felt the same pride and intensity radiating each time he unsheathed the magnificent weapon. "They call it the Founder's Stone," he whispered, his voice full of awe and reverence.

Recognition sparked in the man's face, causing his eyes to widen in astonishment. "Could it truly be the relic from the first age of men? The mythical artifact from our founder, Whitestar?"

"The same," Nathaniel said in a respectful tone.

With solemnity in his eyes, the elder nodded and allowed his grey hair to cascade over his face as he knelt before Nathaniel.

"The blood of Whitestar has returned!" he exclaimed, his voice filled with surprise and joy. "Praise Odin!"

Nathaniel acknowledged the honor, placing a reassuring hand on the elder's head.

The elder stood and spoke to the gathering crowd: farmers, artisans, laborers, and merchants alike, who had mingled to witness the proceedings.

"Here me," he shouted, echoing through the crowded throng. "Our long-awaited prophecy is now fulfilled!" he exclaimed, his voice filled with triumph. "The true king of Tabor has arrived. Spread the joyful news among every neighbor and citizen. We will march to the palace within the hour, determined to reclaim what we have lost for so long."

A forceful kick delivered by their replacement guards to the thigh rudely awakened Julius and the other guard. Startled, Julius attempted to rise, but an intense headache pierced through his skull, accompanied by a wave of nausea rising from his stomach. He fought back the urge to vomit, struggling to maintain his balance as he leaned against the stone wall.

"What the.." his compatriot exclaimed, his voice filled with utter confusion and disbelief. Before he could utter another word, he convulsed, expelling the contents of his stomach against the wall.

"Asleep as usual!" His replacement, with a look of disgust, muttered under his breath. "Adolf, are you not able to handle your drink?" Both guards laughed uproariously at the struggling pair.

"I pray for your sake," chuckled the other guard, "that the sergeant doesn't catch you drinking spirits on duty next time." Then added, "Get up, dog, and sober up. Your shift is over."

Julius and Adolf stumbled away without uttering another word, determined to reach the prison gate before their stomachs emptied again.

The leader of the two guards shook his head, watching the pair weave up the prison stairway to the next level. Then he turned and said, "Time to feed the animals."

The younger of the two uncovered a pail full of foul-smelling mush, unlocked the prison door, and walked inside. It took several moments for his eyes to become accustomed to the utter darkness, as thick as a heavy curtain. He hesitated, unsure of where the prisoners were located.

"Breakfast has arrived, gents. Fresh gruel to warm your bellies! I hope you enjoy this last meal," he said, chuckling at his joke.

At first, he couldn't visualize the prisoners, but his mind had no sense of unease. He assumed the poor wretches had gathered in a corner, their bodies pressed tightly together for warmth. He examined every corner, his heart pounding in his chest until he finally realized they were nowhere to be found. Not being the smartest of the dungeon guards, the man scratched his head in confusion. Then alarm seized him, and he tried to scream, but his tongue twisted. After a heartbeat, he shouted, "Max! Max! The prisoners...they're gone."

Max, the elder guard, entered with a confident stride, expecting to encounter a minor issue. He had dealt with his partner's overreactions before; the other guard often made a big deal out of minor problems. "What's happened, mate? Prisoners kicked over the poop bucket again?" When his partner said nothing, his mind flew to the next obvious issue. Maybe a few had perished during the night, finally giving in to the unforgiving environment, lack of food, or voracious rodents.

With a half-eaten biscuit wedged in his mouth, Max asked, "Whatsa matter," his words muffled and laced with irritation.

"Ah, they're gone," the younger exclaimed, his disbelief evident in his voice.

"Whadya mean, gone? They ain't no way out a here, except in a body bag."

"Look around. They aren't here!" The younger guard said with alarm.

Max followed the same path as the younger guard and discovered an empty room, save for a half-full bucket of human excrement, emitting a nauseating stench.

"By the gods! Run up and alert the sergeant. We got us a jailbreak!" he bellowed, pushing his partner toward the stairs. The younger man sped off, tripping in his haste after two steps, then, regaining his feet, he ran on. All the while, one prominent idea blinked repeatedly in the older guard's mind: Somebody's gonna get blamed, and it ain't gonna be me.

Not long after, the assistant cook, Sarah, entered the storeroom, searching for more carrots to add to the morning meal. The storeroom was dimly lit, with only a flickering candle providing a faint glow. As Sarah stepped into the room, she could feel the chill in the air and the musty smell of old vegetables. She had forgotten her torch, but she was determined to find the carrots without disturbing anything else. Tentatively, she moved forward, her hands outstretched to guide her way. However, in her haste, she failed to notice the object that lay in her path. With a sudden jolt, she stumbled over something cold and hard, losing her balance and landing with a thud on the hard-packed earth floor. "What in the demons was that?" she muttered irritably, rubbing her sore back.

As she regained her composure and slowly got up, Sarah realized that she had tripped over more than just a random object. Her hands, still trembling, extended into the darkness, feeling the obstruction in the center of the floor. Her fingers brushed against a frigid mass, and as she explored further, she could make out the unmistakable features of a human body. A wave of horror washed over her as she realized what she had stumbled upon. Beside the lifeless figure lay a pool of thick, partially dried liquid, adding to the chilling scene before her. Sarah's mind struggled to process the shock, her eyes widening in realization, and her mouth contorting into a horrified scream that echoed through the silent storeroom.

By the time the news of both the prison escape and the murder of the head cook reached Regent Mossbrook, the city was already buzzing with the news of Nathaniel's arrival. A crowd of hundreds filled the town square, their loud jubilations creating a festive atmosphere.

A messenger wasted no time and forcefully knocked on the Regent's door before barging in unannounced. Mossbrook and Thorne leaned over a map of the Taborian plain, their fingers tracing the paths of the advancing troops as they spoke.

"What's the meaning of this?" Mossbrook demanded. His voice dripped with irritation, annoyed by the interruption.

Private Peters had experienced more than once the repercussion of Mossbrook's temper, and this intrusion gave the regent an easy excuse to beat or imprison the man. He rapidly came up with an excuse.

"I'm so sorry, Regent," the Peters said, holding out a communique with a trembling hand. "Sergeant Poss demanded I deliver this immediately on penalty of a severe beating."

With a look of intense anger, the regent's eyes fixed on the man before grabbing the missive from him. In a bid to escape, the terrified messenger cowered, his head down, inching backward towards the door, resembling a mistreated hound creeping across the ground. However, Thorne quickly caught him by the arm, his grip unyielding. "Hold there," he said, his voice firm and commanding.

Mossbrook eagerly tore open the envelope, revealing two dispatches that he promptly read aloud to Thorne.

"The prisoners have escaped after the guards inexplicably received a bottle of drugged Taborian brandy, leaving them incapacitated. The prisoner's whereabouts remain undiscovered," the regent said, feeling a sinking feeling rising in his gut. He opened the second dispatch and read, "Someone has murdered the palace head cook, and the female prisoners have disappeared."

"By the gods!" exclaimed Thorne. "That's impossible!"

"Despite our best efforts, our plan is slowly unraveling before our eyes," Mossbrook said. "Instruct the Core platoon to scour every inch of the palace and surrounding area, ensuring no corner is left unexamined. I doubt they could have gone far." Mossbrook added, his gut twisting with a growing sense of unease.

"I want a thorough interrogation of the two guards who were on duty last night," the general insisted. "Maybe someone bought them off to look the other way," Thorne suggested.

"I'm sure someone paid them to get drunk and sleep," Mossbrook said, his words dripping with sarcasm.

He realized someone had intricately planned and flawlessly coordinated the two escapes. Not one man, but at least two groups of rescuers. But who? No one knew the prince's true identity, or that they planned an execution for later today. Perhaps...

"Did you tell anyone the identity of our prisoners or the planned execution?" he demanded of Thorne, slamming his fist on the table.

"I..." the general swallowed before continuing. "Of course not."

Mossbrook's eyes bored into Thorne's, and he instantly knew the general lied. He frowned and shook his head. Having Thorne as an ally had merits, but his foolish impulsivity outweighed his value.

Once again, the idea of choking the life out of Thorne tickled his mind, but he had his orders. A more insightful general than Thorne could impede his master's army's advance on the capital. So, he said, "Our plan is unraveling, thanks to...leaked information. We must find and remove the prince before he rallies support."

"Don't fret, Regent. I will oversee the investigation," Thorne said confidently, puffing out his chest. "And once apprehended, I'll ensure the prince rots in the dungeon forever."

Mossbrook rolled his eyes, shaking his head, his anger rising inside like a volcano preparing to erupt. How could the general remain so dense? He took in a deep breath, doing his best to calm himself. "No, the prince must disappear. Today," he said, his fury carving into Thorne like a blade.

Thorne's face blanched, and his eyes widened.

"We've come too far to turn back now. Can you get the job done?" Mossbrook demanded, his body shaking in anger.

"I can do it," Thorne said, his entire body shrinking back, his head dropping.

"Thank you, general. May I suggest you start immediately?" Mossbrook said in a mocking tone.

"Of course. I'm on it," he said, rushing out of the room, dragging the messenger with him.

Once Thorne had left, Nari Mudpucker changed back into his natural form, an amorphous humanoid with translucent skin and wide, deep orbits. He hurried over to the secret compartment in the wall behind his desk, opened it, and removed the iron cage containing the sleeping imp.

"Gaft, wake up. I have an urgent assignment," Mudpucker ordered.

Gaft gave an exaggerated stretch and rubbed his eyes free of sleep dirt. Mudpucker chuckled, knowing that these demonic minions never slept or ate.

"What task may I do for my master?" Graft asked in a lazy tone. The beast, loaned to the doppelgänger by the demon Asmodeus, showed little motivation to fulfill the monster's demands promptly.

"Find and report on the movements of Prince Nathaniel Aarmon. He's hiding somewhere in the city," demanded Mudpucker.

"And how do I identify this royal?" he asked petulantly

"Use your magic, you dolt," Mudpucker shouted angrily. "Perhaps a good beating will focus your mind."

Gaft lowered his head in mock submission. He suspected the doppelgänger's threat had little substance, based solely on agitation.

"I am yours to command," said the imp, and in a flash of stinking puff of sulfur, disappeared.

Sitting at the table in his dimly lit chamber, Mudpucker felt a sense of relief wash over him. His furrowed brow relaxed, for he knew he had executed every possible action to salvage his plan to capture and eliminate the prince. A wicked smile danced upon his lips as he pondered the fate that awaited the unsuspecting royal. Would it be a swift execution, right on the spot, extinguishing any hope for rebellion? Or perhaps a more satisfying option - capturing the prince and presenting him as a precious gift to his master, the ruthless Ravenite. Oh, the delight it would bring to see the prince's spirit crushed, his dreams shattered, as he became nothing more than a discarded pawn in Ravenite's twisted game. Mudpucker's anticipation grew, his heart pounding with a mix of excitement and anxiety. Now he waited. The success of his plan hinged on the events of the morning. If all went according to his calculations and the ridiculous general did his job, victory would be within his grasp. If not, he would adapt and improvise, for he was a master of manipulation and deception. As he pondered his next move, a sudden notion struck him like a bolt of lightning.

His master's disdain for failure was clear in the harsh punishments he inflicted on those who failed. "I must report to my master, Ravenite," he muttered to himself, realizing the importance of keeping his superior informed. As he rose from his chair to fetch his scrying bowl, a sudden realization made him freeze. What happens if I cannot eliminate the prince? He eased back into his chair, the uncertainty of the situation sinking in. The fate of Ravenite's forces hinged on the events of the upcoming twenty-four hours. The death of Prince Nathaniel would deal a severe blow to both the morale and potential leadership in Tabor. But, if my plan fails, Ravenite will have to confront an invigorated Taborian army under his leadership. A sliver of self-interest infiltrated his thoughts, worming into his mind. His master despised failure and punished it accordingly. Have I placed my neck on the chopping block? He shook the thought out of his mind, feeling the pressure rise in his chest. He began repeatedly reciting a familiar mantra:

I am Nari Mudpucker, the greatest of the doppelgangers. I do not fail.

Jacoby and Horatio walked on each side of Nathaniel as they pushed closer and closer to the palace steps by the enormous chanting crowd. The throng of several hundred waited at the base of the palace entrance portico, demanding words from the future King Aarmon.

"The King returns! The King returns!" the crowd chanted repeatedly, the voices rising higher to a fever pitch.

"Better get up there before there's a riot," Jacoby whispered in his ear.

Nathaniel took the palace steps by twos until he stood alone at the entrance landing. He smiled, raised his arms, and gestured for quiet.

"My name is Nathaniel Aarmon," he declared confidently. "My proof is in the Aarmon birthmark," pulling back his hair to show the clover scar, "and in the Founder's stone, the one handed down through generations from King Whitestar himself." He raised his sword for all to see the magnificent, multicolored stone.

The crowd of people remained silent, riveted by the young prince.

"Many have asked me, "Where have you been these last twenty years?" Nathaniel continued. "My tale begins with a devoted Taborian officer defying death to rescue me on the day I was born, fulfilling Queen Elana's last wish. Despite the danger to his own life, he cleverly concealed me in plain sight, shielding me from prying eyes and the relentless scrutiny of the enemy. Moving to a tranquil, off-the-beaten-path hamlet, he invested in a shabby tavern and nurtured me as if I were his son. As a tavern rat raised by a surrogate older brother, I had no aspirations beyond leading an unassuming life. As a father figure, he showed me the importance of humility and treating others with equality and respect. I learned the essentials of swordsmanship, hunting, fishing, and survival skills. With the modest earnings from his tavern, Jacoby supported my education under the guidance of the Order of White monks as I came of age, and with the help of friends, he equipped me with everything necessary to shape the person I have become today. To me, Jacoby Ironfist is more than just a name; he is a father, brother, mentor, and hero to whom I owe everything."

Pausing, the prince's gaze swept the massive crowd before resuming. "My upbringing was like many of yours. I toiled in anonymity, ignorant of my lineage, until Ravenite's assassin targeted me two years ago. My friends and I have been fighting across the continent since then to reclaim my destiny as Taborian leader. I am not like other royals; I have a different perspective. I dream of a better Tabor, a place where justice prevails, where the weight of oppression is gone, and where men and women find peace and harmony. A land of opportunity for all, where prosperity is not limited to those born into privilege but is accessible to everyone who works for it."

Captivated by the tale, the crowd cheered enthusiastically until Nathaniel raised his hands as a gesture of silence.

"I have witnessed the destruction and suffering inflicted upon our people, and it has only fueled my determination to bring Tabor back to its former glory. Even without the aid of our allies, we have remained fierce defenders of our nation and the West. As I stand before you today, the enemy horde drives relentlessly toward our city. Stopping and defeating them seems an impossible task. But I believe in the Taborian people. With your indispensable support, we can triumph over the evil sorcerer Ravenite and rid the world of his malevolent presence. Together, we will restore Tabor to its rightful place as the shining gem of the West," he shouted, raising his sword high, his face alive with energy.

The crowd erupted into thunderous applause, their enthusiasm echoing through the city square. People in the crowd carried makeshift weapons like sickles, hammers, and clubs, clanging them together to create an overwhelming noise of determination. As quickly as it had started, the noise gradually died down as the farmers and artisans, one by one, knelt with bowed heads, leaving only Nathaniel and the Brotherhood standing. Nathaniel's arms tingled with excitement, feeling the electric atmosphere of hope and anticipation in the square. The time for action had come, and the fate of Tabor hung in the balance. The young hero knew that the battle ahead would be arduous, but he also knew that with the united strength of the people, they stood a chance to reclaim their homeland and rewrite their destiny.

"Rise, friends. Let us stand together now, ready to confront the enemy and defeat the darkness that looms over us," Nathaniel shouted.

At that moment, a group of black-robed "Core" warriors emerged from the palace, their dark chain mail glinting in the sunlight as they brandished lethal spears and encircled the prince. The panic-stricken crowd screamed. Some hastily retreated, while the majority pressed closer to the portico, as the brotherhood swiftly formed a protective circle around Nathaniel, their backs pressed firmly together, swords gleaming in the sunlight. Jacoby realized in a heartbeat that the Core troops outnumbered the Brotherhood ten to one, making any chance of protecting Nathaniel and surviving the battle seem futile. After several tense heartbeats, the wall closest to the palace door parted, revealing Regent Mossbrook, General Thorne, and the other council members striding onto the landing.

"What is the meaning of this outrage?" Demanded Mossbrook, spittle flying from his mouth in rage. "Arrest this charlatan!"

But Devin Ashoke stepped forward, shouting "Hold! This man is the true Prince Aarmon!"

"Prove it!" Demanded Mossbrook.

Nathaniel pulled back his golden curls, revealing the red clover-shaped birthmark behind his ear. Several of the councilmen gasped, their eyes bugging in astonishment.

Mossbrook's eyes narrowed, his face twisted in a sinister thin smile. "Any decent artist could have made that mark, even a childhood burn. That's no proof at all," Mossbrook stated.

"Perhaps," suggested Ashoke. "But I swear to the gods that is the true sign of the Aarmon family."

Mossbrook hesitated a heartbeat, then said slyly, "I demand more definitive proof."

"As do I," added Thorne for good measure. Mossbrook ignored him, fighting hard not to roll his eyes.

The air was heavy with tension as the crowd held their breath in anticipation, waiting for what would happen next. A few moments passed before Mossbrook burst into laughter. "That's what I thought. Take him into custody."

Nathaniel abruptly cut the words off as he raised his sword pommel high, commanding everyone's attention. "Behold the weathered stone in the hilt of my sword!" he shouted, drawing everyone's attention. "Whitestar himself passed down the stone from generation to generation, dating back to the First Age of men. Legend states that only those with the blood of Whitestar flowing through their veins could wield the legendary Founder's Stone."

The ancient gem held everyone's gaze, captivating all present with its mesmerizing allure. As Nathaniel touched the stone, he could sense its coldness against his skin. The gem on the sword sparkled, shining more intensely with each second until the entire weapon crackled with vibrant green energy. A blinding light filled the air as the blade ignited into green flames, forcing onlookers to avert their gaze or cover their eyes. Nathaniel and Mossbrook stood as the only witnesses, their intense gazes locked in a silent battle of wills until the regent finally succumbed and fell unconscious. The green flames slowly diminished until Nathaniel stood with the sword held high, Mossbrook in a heap at his feet.

Thorne and his troops, with the other ministers, cowered before Nathaniel, bending a knee and dropping their weapons to the ground as the crowd burst into ecstatic cheers. The citizens rushed towards the portico, their cheers echoing as they lifted Nathaniel in their arms and carried him inside the palace. After marching down the marble hallways with him in their arms, they gently placed him on his father's throne, which had been empty for the past 20 years.

After Ashoke and the brotherhood kindly shooed away the crowds, Nathaniel stepped down from the throne and marveled at the beauty of the intricate marble reliefs and the exquisite mosaic arched ceiling. Massive embroidered tapestries depicting the legendary adventures of Taborian heroes and kings adorned the walls.

"This may be the most beautiful palace I've visited," he mused.

"Yes, it's magnificent," Jacoby said with a sad smile. "Your mother worked tirelessly to plan and instill this palace as the premier royal house in the West. Now, it goes back to its rightful owner."

"No, it belongs to the people of Tabor," he clarified. "I will be a grateful tenant."

Ashoke caught the prince's gaze as he shifted his focus towards him. "Devin, please find a scribe and summon Thorne, along with the other ministers, to join us."

"Of course, your Grace," he responded and rapidly exited.

"What's that about?" Grull asked, surprised at the request. "Didn't we just get rid of the varmints?"

A reed-thin scribe, dressed in a lavender suit and bearing ink, quill, and parchment, entered the room and bowed to Nathaniel, who responded with a smile.

"Percival, at your service, Your Grace," he introduced himself with a polite nod. "In what way can I assist you?" the scribe said in an oddly high-pitched voice.

Nathaniel leaned in close and whispered into Scribe's ear, causing Percival to nod in agreement with each sentence. After Nathaniel finished speaking, Percival bowed low and uttered, "Your wish is my command, your Grace. May I be permitted to use this table?"

"Please," Nathaniel said.

Percival sat at the desk; his face focused as he transcribed onto the parchment with the precision of a scholar. At that moment, Ashoke returned with General Thorne and the other five ministers.

"Thank you for coming," Nathaniel said in a steely tone. "I understand my return to Tabor may have come as an unexpected shock. But, like it or not, I am the rightful leader of Tabor." He fixed his eyes on each man, assessing their reaction. Only Thorne frowned at the statement.

"There might have been chaos and political drama before I got here," he continued, "but now it's a thing of the past. I offer a new era in Tabor, and with it, I ask for simple universal values for every citizen, including those who offer me counsel. I not only expect but insist on respect in words and deeds, wisdom used for the progress of all Taborians, and steadfast honesty and integrity in every dimension. Above everything else, I require absolute loyalty to the Taborian realm."

Indicating the parchment extended by Percival, he instructed, "If you agree, pledge your allegiance by signing this paper. If not, I grant you and your family safe passage out of the city with my best wishes. That includes all soldiers belonging to the Core Guard. What do you choose?"

The ministers exchanged glances with each other before taking turns to step forward, bow, leave their mark and exit. Among the group, it was only Thorne who hesitated, a nagging question consuming his thoughts.

"Um, what about my role in the army?" he inquired.

Nathaniel shook his head, a look of sadness clouding his eyes. "Would you not agree that your actions as general of the Taborian forces have been a complete catastrophe? Not to mention trying to first assassinate me, then taking me prisoner. A lesser man would have you executed on the spot."

Thorne stepped back; his hands raised. "No, I would never...I just followed orders," he stammered. "Minister Ashoke, tell him!"

"Your Grace, it was Thorne who met with me about your capture and Tabor surrendering to Ravenite. Although terribly misguided and his actions self-serving, I believe his loyalty ultimately rests with Tabor," Ashoke said.

Nathaniel's eyes bore into Thorne like two spears, and the man took a step back. "You're lucky I lean toward mercy," Nathaniel said through gritted teeth. "But your commanding days are over. You are now Corporal Thorne and reassigned to the front lines as a scout. I expect regular reports as the enemy army approaches."

Tears gathered in the man's eyes, yet his military training kicked in, masking his inner turmoil. Rising to attention, he stood with his back straight, saluted, and then signed the parchment.

"Minister Ashoke, please accompany the corporal to break the news to the Core Guard and have them enter and sign. Count Oyster and Grull will aid you."

Confused and disoriented, Regent Mossbrook awoke in a different wing of the palace. Every joint in his body creaked like an old, rusty door as he forced himself to sit up, feeling as if he had just gone through a brutal prize fight. His head pounded like crashing cymbals, making it hard to focus as his vision blurred. He finally recognized his bedchamber and noticed the familiar scent of lavender in the air. The gentle breeze brought with it the distant sounds of chanting from the street below. Peering out, he witnessed a crowd of ordinary townsfolk singing and parading down the street in merriment, some holding tankards of ale or bottles of brandy. His headache intensified as the abrasive cheers became louder, filling the room, and stirring a feeling of unease inside. What in the demons had happened? Despite his efforts to ignore it, the truth kept scratching at the back of his mind. His unease intensified into a budding fear as the chanting of "Nathaniel Aarmon" echoed through the air, filling him with dread."

It can't be. I had him at my mercy. Trying to remember the sequence of events, he shook his head, the recent past appearing hazy. At the palace portico, he had confronted the prince, surrounded by the intimidating Core Guard, ready to arrest the young man. With a swift motion, the prince raised his sword high, and a dazzling light pierced through the onlookers. The scorching heat from the light was like a bonfire's radiance, consuming him until everything faded into blackness.

"The intense heat must have caused me to blackout," he mumbled under his breath. "What mysterious powers had the young man harnessed? Nothing my master can't match and overcome."

Despite his attempts to reassure himself with words, the nagging fear only intensified as he listened to the growing celebration below. His breaths came in quick gasps, tingles moving down his spine. He covered his ears with his hands, but even that could not drown out the blossoming terror he felt. He sat down on the bed, willing himself to slow his breathing. The noise from the jubilant crowd outside seemed to seep through the walls, fueling his anxiety. Thoughts raced through his mind, searching for a solution to the impending disaster.

"I have to come up with a plan before Ravenite realizes my failure," he muttered to himself, desperation creeping into his voice. "I have to do... something, or he will!"

He clutched his head, feeling the weight of the situation bearing down on him. As he tried to calm his racing thoughts, a spider of an idea crawled tentatively across his mind. The faint glimmer of hope it carried ignited a spark within him, and an alternative plan materialized. With newfound determination, he scribbled down the details of his ploy, mapping out the steps he needed to take to mitigate the impending crisis. As he considered the hasty undertaking, a sense of relief washed over him. What lay ahead would not be easy, but it offered a flicker of hope in an otherwise dire situation. With renewed confidence, he rose from the bed and headed towards the door, ready to face the challenges ahead.

The shapeshifter tiptoed to his room door, opening it just a crack to see the uniformed back of a palace guard. He closed the door silently, and a broad grin curled his lips.

"You are a devious and dangerous being, Nari Mudpucker," he chuckled to himself.

TWENTY NINE

The palace guard strolled along the corridor, relaxed and unhurried, pausing at the heavy wooden door. In the early morning hush, the hallway remained empty, but he took nothing for granted. He looked back to ensure he was the only one there before entering the dark room. A powerful smell of aged books and years of settled dust met the guard upon entering. The Queen's study had remained untouched, a solemn tribute to her memory, ever since her passing two decades ago.

He strode to the far bookcase and scanned the books and parchments for what he needed. With a grin, he found the aged, black tome with silver script on the spine, feeling its weight in his hands as he reached up and pulled it down. He heard an audible click, and the bookcase shifted, a plume of dust billowing from a new crease in the wall. He leaned his weight on the bookcase and pushed. A hidden and forbidding passage, blocked by cobwebs, opened wide enough for him to slip through. The guard brushed away the webs, forcing a palm-sized spider in its center to crawl for cover.

Before entering, he glanced out the window, the glowing half-moon high in the inky sky.

"I must hurry," he murmured to himself as he stepped into the pitch-black tunnel and closed the door behind him. Rushing along the narrow stone corridor, he could feel the coolness of the stones beneath his feet intensifying as the path sloped downward. He walked for several hundred yards until he reached a rusting iron gate positioned at the foot of a short stone stairway. The gate creaked loudly as the guard struggled to unlock it with an oddly shaped key from his pocket. Unperturbed by the noise, he continued with his task, confident in his seclusion from the bustling palace staff. He strode up the stairway and into a small eight-by-eight-foot room. He scanned the walls, feeling for any sign of another hidden exit, but found none.

"I don't have time for this," he said in frustration. He felt in his pockets, his hand resting finally on a thin stick. He pulled the item free, revealing a thin wand with a tiny ruby embedded in the handle.

"Optium," whispered the man, moving the wand across the wall.

The ruby's glow transformed from a muted red to a brilliant brightness as he passed it over the irregular mason's stone.

"There you are," he said triumphantly, pressing on the pitted brick. With a resounding crunch, a section of the wall gave way, and he slipped through into a dark alley.

He hesitated, listening for any movement. He could hear drunken revelers roaring around the corner, but no one nearby.

Best to change your appearance again, Nari old man. In a flash, the palace guard was gone, and an elderly woman with a hunched back appeared. The woman scuttled down the street toward the city gate, her walking cane clicking on the cobblestone road as she walked.

Disregarded by the city guards as nonthreatening, the woman slipped through with ease. The woman hobbled down the road and, once out of the guard's sight, shape-shifted into a wolf and dashed into the nearby wood. After some time, the wolf skidded to a stop in a small clearing, his bushy tail lashing behind him. Waiting only a few yards away, a disfigured woman dressed in black waited, her scarred face twisting into a sneer.

"You're late," she spat, as the doppelgänger changed again to his normal translucent skin.

"Now is a time for caution. It may be my master's last opportunity to kill the Taborian prince," he retorted, irritated by the witch's impatience.

The witch ignored the response, removing a small glass vial from her pocket and extending it to Mudpucker.

"What's in it?" Nari asked, his eyes narrowed. "Potency is essential for my needs."

"Fear not," the witch cackled. "Dog mercury, black locust, and a hefty dose of scorpion venom mixed with blood from the coven. Not even the most magical elf could survive it."

Nari smiled, feeling reassured.

"Did you bring the payment?" the witch asked.

Nari handed her a fist-sized bundle wrapped in bloody rags.

The witch unwrapped the mass, revealing a human heart covered in gelatinous clotted blood. She leaned down and sniffed the organ, and her face twisted into a sly grin.

"Not fresh? I said only a few hours old," she demanded, her fists clenched.

"It's the best I could do on short notice," he said honestly. Killing the guard and taking his identity had been a risky necessity. How to get rid of the body became a more pressing concern. For the moment, a seldom-used broom closet was sufficient. However, he knew someone would start searching soon, so he had to return quickly to continue impersonating him.

For several tense moments, their eyes remained locked in a silent battle of wills. Nari thought about transforming into a troll to confront the witch, but he felt drained and lacked the determination. To center his thoughts on the current mission, he shifted his eyes away, stashed the vial, and morphed into a fierce grizzly bear. He then ambled off without casting another look, abandoning the seething witch.

An hour and a half later, he had returned to his quarters after impersonating the palace guard during shift change, then reanimating into Regent Mossbrook. He walked to a display cabinet and, using the key he took from the guard's keyring, opened the cabinet and removed the large pearl ring from its velvet bedding. He studied the artifact, noticing the ancient mark of the Aarmon house embossment. This will do nicely. How could the future king refuse to wear the symbol of Taborian authority - his father's ring?

Nari chuckled at the ruse. Nothing could be easier than tricking the prince into accepting the weapon of his destruction. He hummed a merry tune as he used gloves to delicately open the vial of poison. Then, using a tiny make-up brush stolen from one of the female royal's rooms, he painted the inside of the ring generously with toxin.

"Death awaits you, Nathaniel Aarmon," he laughed to himself, his face split with a wide grin.

The brotherhood sat at the conference room table, Nathaniel at the head. The group had bathed, rested, and wore new navy blue uniforms. Nathaniel had asked the royal tailor to add a patch on each breast of a rearing unicorn, his realm's new insignia.

To Nathaniel's right stood a portly, graying man in a brown cassock, his pudgy arms hugging several large scrolls to his chest as if holding priceless jewels. To his right stood his trusted scribe, the willow-thin Percival.

"Let me begin the meeting by introducing everyone to Meister Colin, the chief Taborian historian," Nathaniel said, introducing each member of the Brotherhood. Colin gave each a deferential nod.

"First order of business must be the city's defense," Nathaniel continued. "Jacoby, did you have time to assess the frontline troops?"

Jacoby cleared his throat. "Yes, I did, and as expected, the truth isn't pretty. Under Thorne's leadership, our army suffered not only significant losses in numbers but also a noticeable decline in discipline. Desertion has become a widespread issue," he paused for a moment, allowing the gravity of the news to settle in. "I recommend a rotating schedule of retraining, led by us, as soon as possible, besides training new conscripts."

Nathanial rubbed his chin thoughtfully, feeling the rough stubble against his fingertips. "What additional resources do our troops need?"

"Sharpened weapons, repaired uniforms and armor, and, of course, silver weapons," Jacoby replied.

A frown creased Nathaniel's brow. Despite bracing himself for bad news, the true health of the army hit him hard, making his heart sink. The problems seemed more daunting than he had expected.

"Cor'in, Grull, and I may have come up with a hopeful solution," Nathaniel said. "Cor'in, will you explain?"

"Of course. Grull and I have been discussing with Meister Colin whether the previous Taborian rulers had stashed weapons. Could there be a royal armory so far untouched?" questioned Cor'in.

"And? What did you find out?" Blue Ivy asked, leaning forward in interest.

"Let's have Meister Colin explain," suggested Grull.

Colin stepped forward and handed a parchment to each member. "Unfortunately, thieves looted the royal armory many months ago, right under the noses of the Council. Most of the silver and jeweled weapons either disappeared or found their way to the black market for sale. "We worked hard to retrieve the weapons, but honestly, we only recovered a few," he said sadly. "However, with Prince Nathaniel's urging, I scoured the ancient blueprints for any hidden armories, lost and forgotten over the many centuries of palace renovations." He took a deep breath before continuing. "And, as you can see, we've found a possible weapons cache."

Colin stepped back, waiting for the members to analyze the blueprint.

"This room you've marked appears to be walled off and difficult to reach," Horatio said. "How can we access that?"

"Good eye, Toadie," Cor'in said. "Grull came up with a plan."

"As you can see," Grull began, "It's impossible to reach the room from the inside without tearing through several stone walls. But this corridor here," pointing to a narrow path between walls, "leads to an underwater entrance. That's where we need your help, Horatio."

"My help?" the frogman asked, surprised.

"From the last dry level to the storeroom door is at least a hundred-foot swim underwater. And the door will probably need prying open because of rust. No one can do it but you," Grull said expectantly.

"What's the catch? Why not ask me before?" Horatio queried.

"First," Nathaniel interjected, "we just received this information in the last hour. There might be potential risks to consider."

"Danger?" Horatio said nonchalantly, but his heart skipped a beat.

"The inhabitants in the lake are mostly favorable, but over the last year of Ravenite's conquest, citizens have sighted freshwater sahaugin," Nathaniel stated bluntly.

Horatio froze, unable to respond.

"What's a sahaugin?" asked Blue Ivy.

"A predatorial marine humanoid, covered in shell-like scales with a vicious temperament," answered Meister Colin as if reading an encyclopedia. "Like sharks, but less predictable."

Grull's brow furrowed and asked, "How wicked are they?"

"Envision marauding packs of water-living lizard men with nasty dispositions," interpreted Blue Ivy.

"Gotcha," said Grull.

"I've never heard of them except in sea tales," surprised Jacoby. "The lich-mage must be orchestrating this incursion."

The room fell silent for several heartbeats as each member digested the news. Horatio hadn't moved, his face still frozen in shock.

"You okay, Toadie?" Cor'in said, his brow furrowed. His friend's reaction worried the half-elf. He'd never seen the happy-go-lucky Anuran in such a state.

"Mm... my mother died at the hands of a sahaugin," Horatio mumbled, sweat beading on his forehead. His hands clasped to the armrests. "She sacrificed herself so my siblings and I could survive."

"I'm sorry, mate," Cor'in said sympathetically. "I never knew. But maybe the sightings are just exaggeration?"

"Eight children have disappeared in the last six months, all near the lake edge," reported Meister Colin sadly. "I interviewed the families myself and believe the reports."

Horatio remained mute, unable to move. The memory of the encounter remained etched in his mind as vividly as if it had happened yesterday. His mother had taken them to the basin near the Southern border for a day of swimming and relaxation. What began as a pleasant adventure quickly spiraled into a scene of violence and horror. Out of nowhere, the green-scaled lizard men appeared and attacked from below the water, catching everyone off guard. Even though his mother fought with tremendous courage, the overwhelming number of ambushers proved too much for her. His heart was heavy that day as he mourned the loss of two siblings and his dear mother.

"I lost half my family that day," murmured Horatio, his chest tight. "Two younger sisters and my mother."

"I'm so sorry, Horatio," Nathaniel calmly said. "I won't pressure you to go, understanding the trauma of your past. But if this room holds weapons we can use to defeat Ravenite, it might be worth the risk. You know, if I could handle this myself, I'd be the first in line to volunteer."

"Don't do it," Corin warned. "We don't even know if the weapons are in there."

"True," said Grull. "But if you don't try, Tabor's finished. If we had more weapons, we might stand a chance."

"Think it over, Horatio. No hard feeling if you decide not to go," Nathaniel said kindly.

"Now," the prince said, changing the subject. "Blue Ivy and I came up with an idea. Percival, will you escort the smiths into the room?"

"Yes, Your Grace." The thin man strode out in long, determined strides. Nathaniel gestured for Blue to begin.

"Ahem. Our main issue is the apparent scarcity of silver weapons to combat the undead. To address this issue, Nat and I brainstormed an idea that could help, at least to some extent."

At that moment, Percival returned with ten muscular, bearded men wearing leather aprons covered with soot and sweat stains.

Nathaniel stood and rounded the table, welcoming each man and shaking his hand. "Come in, gentleman," Nathaniel beckoned. "We were just discussing our plan." He nodded at Blue, who continued.

"We need silver to kill or wound the enemy," the Timber elf explained, sounding as knowledgeable as a metallurgist. "Keeping this in mind, Prince Nathaniel has depleted the royal coffers of all silver coins and artifacts. Furthermore, we have gathered every silver candlestick and trinket in the palace that is not secured."

Several of the smiths gasped at the prince's sacrifice, anticipating the next statement. No royal had ever given his wealth, much less property, for the defense of the people. Only a unique leader would devote all he had for the good of the people.

Nathaniel's face turned serious, and he interjected in a firm voice, "I need your help, gentlemen. I know I'm asking a lot, but we must have this silver melted down and every weapon in the city dipped for our defense. Time remains short, so it may require running your smithies non-stop over the next several days. Will you help me, men?"

"Indeed!" the smiths said in a chorus of voices.

"Thank you. I will supply any additional help you need," Nathaniel said, smiling. "The fate of Tabor's defense against the oncoming horde is now in your capable hands."

Regent Mossbrook entered the conference room and bowed. "Your Grace, it appears nothing has hindered your assumption of power," said Mossbrook, his words flowing pleasantly, but laced with jealousy.

Nathaniel frowned. He wanted to mend disagreements and unite Tabor. But in his gut, he felt a knot of unease in his stomach every time he conversed with Mossbrook. His sixth sense suggested something odd and distrustful about the man, a feeling that he just couldn't shake. Unfortunately, the man held a respected position with the Taborian elite and would be a perfect friend to help segue his transition to power.

Nathaniel moved around the table and extended his hand to Mossbrook. "Welcome. I hope you're feeling much better after your...ah...illness," Nathaniel said kindly.

Mossbrook hesitated a heartbeat, taking a half-step back, before grasping the hand and shaking. "Much better, Your Grace, despite the magical attack," the older man said irritably. "I apologize for my reaction. Your arrival was...unexpected."

Nathaniel stepped back, locking eyes with the politician. "I understand your reluctance to embrace the change, Mossbrook. But

I hope we can put differences aside and unite Tabor," he said in an iron tone. "However, I will not accept continued resistance."

"Of course," he said with a slight bow of his head. "We all must work for the betterment of Tabor. To that point, the sooner you become king, the better. I instituted a plan for your coronation, scheduled to take place two days from now."

"In two days?" Jacoby and Grull echoed from the table, jaws dropping. "Are you mad?"

"I apologize," said Mossbrook with an exaggerated bow. "I assumed that a speedy coronation would result in faster unification and leadership, particularly with the horde at our back steps. I hope I did not overstep, My Grace."

Nathaniel paused, the uncomfortable knot in his gut twisting. Was this man genuine, or was he trying to create an opportunity for mel to appear power-hungry by rushing to become king? He remained unsure, but from a practical angle, Mossbrook had a point. Accepting the crown would unify both the army and the people behind a single leader, allowing for stability in a time of uncertainty. However, Nathaniel couldn't shake the feeling that the ex-regent's motives were not entirely altruistic. Perhaps Mossbrook saw an opportunity to maintain his influence and power in the new regime. Despite his reservations, Nathaniel knew that for the sake of the kingdom, he had to consider the proposal seriously.

"Very well," Nathaniel finally spoke, his voice filled with a mix of determination and caution. "In just two days, the coronation ceremony will take place." He looked directly at Percival, whose loyalty, intelligence, and resourcefulness were quickly transforming the scribe into a trusted aide, "Percival, will you help Mossbrook with the arrangements?"

Percival's eyes narrowed suspiciously, reflecting the wariness that Nathaniel himself felt. After a momentary pause, Percival nodded, his expression one of unwavering commitment. "Of course, Your Grace," he replied, his voice resolute.

With Percival by his side, Nathaniel hoped to navigate the treacherous waters of power and politics with wisdom and integrity. As the days leading up to the coronation ceremony dwindled, Nathaniel couldn't help but wonder what challenges awaited him on his path to becoming king.

Two days later, Grullach Furr sat quietly in the storeroom's corner, rubbing his hand affectionately over Sinbad's rusty coat. His heart swelled with pride, a surge of excitement coursing through him at the thought of defending the crown, a sense of purpose blooming within him. He remembered the last coronation he'd attended, which turned unexpectedly from celebration to tragedy as a villainous enemy attempted to assassinate Prince Michel of Tajman Sghur by poisoning the crown. The memory of Prince Michel's pallid face, contorted in agony, haunted Grull, fueling a desperate need to shield Nathaniel from such a fate. Michel miraculously weathered the attack, but only after Jacoby and Cor'in faced the dangers of the city's underbelly to find a rare antidote for the poison. So, Grullach calmly protected the crown the entire night, never letting the jewel-encrusted circlet out of his sight. He handed this responsibility to Jacoby at sunrise.

A thrill coursed through Nathaniel as he entered the opulent throne room. The sight of the magnificent crown held aloft by Jacoby ignited a fire of hope within him. A chorus of voices from hundreds of citizens chanting "Long live the king" floated in through the throne room's open windows. Flanked by palace guards, Nathaniel began his walk forward toward the priest from the White Monk order waiting to conduct the ceremony. Several politicians and members of the royal court bowed as Nathaniel passed. Vibrant sound filled the air as trumpets played the majestic coronation anthem. Nathaniel nodded reverently to the section of distinguished guests and royalty directly beside the elevated royal seat. Kings Polaris, Acorn and Goldbriar, Prince Astor of Whispering Harbor, Baldur the bear, Friend the unicorn, and the shape-changing wizard, Traveler, stood next to his family, the Brotherhood. All bowed their heads in respect as Nathaniel passed. The prince climbed to the throne, with Jacoby at his side, and turned to the priest.

"Nathaniel Aarmon, do you solemnly swear, under the all-seeing eye of Odin, that you will faithfully execute the office of King of Tabor and, to the best of your ability, discharge your duty to support, protect, and defend the citizens of Tabor?" asked the priest solemnly.

"I so swear," answered Nathaniel.

The cleric, his voice solemn and resonant, took the circlet, crafted from burnished gold and inlaid with jewels, and placed it upon Nathaniel's head, saying, "Take this crown, a symbol of your sacred bond with the Taborian people, to rule them with wisdom, honor, and equity."

A triumphant grin spread across Nathaniel's face as he felt the heavy circlet placed upon his head, the weight of the jeweled metal a testament to his long journey from tavern rat to king.

The priest pulled a polished silver box with intricate engravings from his inner pocket. The sudden move made Nathaniel's stomach twist with unease. This act was unplanned and not part of the ceremony rehearsed. He shot Jacoby a quick, skeptical look; his eyes narrowed with worry. Jacoby's brow furrowed, a crease forming between his eyes that mirrored his brother's worried expression. But before he could ponder the implications, the elder bishop opened the box, revealing a gleaming pearl ring that bore the intricate Aarmon family crest.

"May you wear this Aarmon family ring with pride, always remembering that kindness and fairness must temper your actions," the priest said as he slipped the weighty ring onto Nathaniel's finger. "Despite your brief reign," he added under his breath. The prince's heart clenched as the priest's eyes changed momentarily into the cold, emotionless eyes of Mossbrook, before returning to brown. Nathaniel shot a hard look at the priest, wondering if his eyes had played a trick on him. However, when he looked again, the clergyman bowed and turned away, his White Monk's robe billowing behind him as he hurried out of the hall.

The disappearance of the priest only deepened Nathaniel's apprehension. Was it a mere illusion, or had he witnessed something otherworldly? With a furrowed brow, the prince vowed to remain vigilant, knowing his reign would hold unknown dangers. As he stared at the ring on his finger, he silently promised to honor the legacy of his ancestors and protect his kingdom with unwavering resolve, no matter what sinister forces may lurk in the shadows.

He vaguely heard Jacoby rise, pulling him from his thoughts. The tall warrior, his blue uniform haloed by the sun's rays, joyfully announced, "Praise be to Odin! Long live Nathaniel Aarmon, King of Tabor!"

Nathaniel stood smiling, his heart pounding with excitement as the wild cheering of the crowd washed over him, momentarily erasing the priest's words. As he and the Brotherhood filed out to the palace portico, a cacophony of bells rang out throughout the city, their resonating tones mixed with the cheers of his supporters, creating an atmosphere of wild jubilation.

Nathaniel held up his hand, a wave of calm spreading through the crowd as they hushed in anticipation.

"Friends and citizens of Tabor," he began, a slight tremor in his voice as he addressed the assembled crowd. A wave of dizziness washed over him, and he felt bile rising in his throat. "Today starts a new era..." Nathaniel stopped abruptly, his head spinning as if the weight of those words was too much to bear. "Today..." he began, but the words died in his throat as dizziness washed over him, sending him staggering. Jacoby scrambled to his side, catching the new king just as his body convulsed violently, sending him crashing to the floor. White foam frothed from his lips in a horrifying sight.

The joyous chatter of the celebration died down in an instant, replaced by an eerie silence as every eye, filled with concern, turned to the ailing monarch. Then a chorus of piercing screams from Allai'nn and Lani, followed by the thunderous pounding of the Brotherhood's boots, shattered the peaceful silence. Wailing and screams pierced the air, creating a scene of utter pandemonium in the crowd as onlookers, unsure of the threat, scattered in all directions.

Jacoby knelt next to his brother, his hands trembling as he gently lifted his head. "Nat, Nat, can you hear me?" Jacoby whispered in a desperate plea.

"What's happened?" Grull exclaimed, his voice tinged with urgency, rushing to help Jacoby lift Nathaniel and bring him inside.

Without turning around, Jacoby barked to Allai'nn, "Get Friend and your father and meet us in his chambers. Quickly!"

Minutes later, Polaris, Traveler, and Friend barged into the king's bedchamber. Nathaniel, his skin as white as the sheets beneath him, lay still and unresponsive. Jacoby, Allai'nn, Grull, and Lani huddled anxiously around him.

"Tell me what happened," demanded Polaris as the three pushed past to examine Nathaniel.

"He seemed fine until after the coronation, then he collapsed," Jacoby said. "Nothing unusual happened."

Friend's voice entered the tall man's mind, "Did anything strange occur during the ceremony?"

"Not that I could see, but I honestly may have missed something in the excitement," Jacoby admitted.

Friend, his nose twitching, sniffed at Nathaniel from head to toe, finally declaring, "Evil lurks here, I can smell it—a sickly sweet stench with a metallic tinge." He sniffed the ring several times. "I believe this is the source," he added, motioning to the ring with his muzzle.

Polaris used his gloved hand to remove the ring, noticing a minute needle on the inner rim. "Look here," the elf said, showing the needle to the others.

"Poison—I suspect dog mercury and black locust, but there is a third scent, something more subtle," the unicorn said after another sniff. He remained still for several heartbeats, then added, "Yes, definitely Devilback scorpion venom."

Polaris and Traveler, their faces etched with concern, exchanged worried glances, their brows furrowed, and muttered curses on their breath.

Grull caught the glance, and a chill went down his spine. "What are you not saying?" he asked, his voice barely above a whisper. "We must know the truth."

Polaris hesitated, then said, "The Devilback scorpion, with its deadly sting and fiery red shell, can only be found in one location in Curth Talem, deep within the fiery Molton Mountains far to the south."

"What does that mean?" Jacoby choked, tears running down his cheeks.

Friend's voice spoke. "That means finding an antidote may be incredibly difficult, if not impossible."

"But we have to do something," Lani begged.

Friend and Polaris locked eyes, and the elf nodded and positioned Nathaniel's sword over his chest.

"I believe our best hope may be in the ancient magic of the Founder's stone," Friend said. "Odin willing, it may empower Nathaniel's immunity and act as a beacon to guide him from the Netherworld."

Lani paled, tears welling in her eyes. "There must be more..." she began, but fear choked off the rest.

"Can we amplify the power by adding our own?" Allai'nn said, her brow furrowed.

Polaris squeezed his daughter's hand. "Odin imbued each stone by race on its creation. As elves, we have no connection."

"Meaning what? We're helpless?" Jacoby asked.

"I'm afraid Nathaniel's fate remains with the Norns," Friend said.

Nathaniel's eyes fluttered open, greeted by the sight of dark gray and purple clouds, heavy with the promise of rain. He could hear the distant rumble of thunder and see the dark clouds gathering, confirming his suspicions of an approaching storm. He pushed himself to his feet, realizing he had landed in the center of a clearing, surrounded by towering ancient evergreens. His mind raced as he looked around, desperately trying to figure out where he was.

The roar of the crowd at his coronation and the weight of the crown on his head all came back to him in a rush, but how he had arrived here remained a mystery. I must find shelter from the storm. He gazed around, not recognizing the wood or knowing in which direction to walk, until his eyes rested on a trail on the far clearing edge. Suddenly, a piercing howl shattered the peace of the forest, a guttural sound that sent a shiver down his spine, heralding a Lupine Ranger Wolfman hunting pack.

Nathaniel felt a jolt of adrenaline and sprinted down the trail, the detritus crunching beneath his feet as he ran. The howls continued every few minutes, the sound coming ever closer. He couldn't tell how many hunted him, but the rustling bushes and echoing growls that echoed through the trees signaled inescapable odds. He knew, with a sickening certainty, that his only options were to hide or outrun them. And even on his best day, he could not outrun a wolf pack.

As he sped down the trail, the trees parted to reveal a narrow clearing, ending in a sheer cliff dropping to a distant valley below. He stepped to the edge, and the sight that met his eyes made his heart plummet. Hundreds of feet below, the rocky cliff dropped sharply into an icy river, its churning current a frothing white against the grey stone. He frantically scanned the cliff face but found no way down, only steep drops and treacherous rock formations.

Fat rain droplets started pelting the ground but quickly escalated into a furious torrent, accompanying the growing, closer howls of the lupines, almost as if the storm was driving them toward him. The air crackled with tension, and Nathaniel's grip tightened around the hilt of his sword as he braced himself for the fight.

At that moment, two things occurred. Three massive lupine Wolfmen crashed through the trees, their black coats dripping with rain and their fangs gleaming in the dim light. The Founder's stone, previously cold and inert, suddenly glowed with green light, its pulse growing stronger and stronger until it erupted into a blinding blaze. The lupine growled and snapped their jaws in defiance, retreating several steps. The stone's light began to dim as a towering warrior, immense and imposing, materialized beside Nathaniel. The giant loomed over Nathaniel, his eight-foot frame clad in heavy plate mail and a surcoat displaying King Whitestar's coat of arms, a snarling lion, which seemed to reflect the man's own imposing presence.

His voice, deep and powerful like a storm cloud, boomed with the words, "Face your demise, wolves!" as he charged, his blade glinting in the sunlight, towards the pack of snarling wolves. Feeding off the giant's courage, Nathaniel ran to his side and attacked.

The air crackled with the energy of battle, the two warriors weaving through the Wolfmen's attacks with effortless grace, their blades cutting through flesh and bone with a sickening crunch. In no time, two lupines lay dead at their feet, and the third scampered away, licking its wounds.

"Take that, you wicked beasts!" the giant roared, his voice echoing through the forest.

"Thank you, friend, for coming to my aid. You fight like a genuine hero," Nathaniel said in sincere appreciation.

The giant let out a chuckle that shook the very air around him, a sound like a distant rumble of thunder. "You're not too bad yourself, pup."

Nathaniel smiled. "What's your name?"

"Do you not know me? I am your forefather, a voice from the distant past," the giant growled, his voice a deep, gravelly rumble, one eyebrow raised in suspicion.

The revelation of his identity hit Nathaniel like a physical blow, leaving him reeling. "King Whitestar!"

"The same, pup," he said, studying the young sovereign. "Nathaniel Aarmon, I am proud to call you a son of my lineage. Your heart is pure, and you have the vision to guide Tabor through these challenging times and restore its former glory."

Nathaniel murmured, "Thank you," his cheeks flushing red as he avoided Whitestar's eyes. The exhilarating cheers and pomp of the coronation had inflated his confidence and pride, making him oblivious to the lurking threats. "I'm not sure I'm worthy of such accolades," he admitted, "but I pledge to do my best for the people of Tabor."

Whitestar nodded. "Spoken like a true king. But never let your pride blind your vision in the future."

"May I ask you a question, Your Grace?"

"Yes?"

"Why am I here?" Nathaniel asked.

"Mmm. You don't remember?" Whitestar questioned.

Nathaniel shook his head.

"Another assassination attempt, this time by a poison-infused ring. The enemy sought to end you in the most agonizing way possible, trapping you in a nightmarish world of dreams. The Founder's stone's power served as a protective barrier, preserving your life," Whitestar said.

"And you?"

"The gods allowed me to come to your aid. Of course, at my urging. I wanted to meet, and warn you, pup," Whitestar said.

Nathaniel looked at him with one eyebrow raised.

"The enemy, with its ties to the underworld, will be difficult to defeat. You will need every ounce of courage and cunning in the coming battle. Never let the Founder's stone leave your grip," he said. "Now, are you ready to return to your world?"

"I'm ready."

Nathaniel felt the gentle pressure of lips against his own, but the tears that followed felt like a cold rain against his skin. As his eyes opened, they met Lani's, her face, puffy and swollen with tears, now crinkled with a broad, radiant smile.

"You're back," she cried, tears streaming down her face as she wrapped her arms tightly around Nathaniel, squeezing him with all her might.

"I didn't intend to leave your side, my love," he whispered, his lips lingering on hers.

Her voice trembled as she pulled back and said, "Don't you ever leave me again. I was so scared you were gone forever."

He smiled, giving her hand a reassuring squeeze, before gazing past her to the others in the room. Jacoby and the other Brotherhood had not left his side, nor had Friend, Baldur, Polaris, or Traveler.

"Thank the gods you're alive!" Jacoby, Grull and Allai'nn said in a chorus of voices, joyous tears running down their cheeks.

"We were sure you wouldn't make it when Friend thought about the magic in the Founders stone," explained Jacoby. "He told us to place it on your chest and let the magic flow through you. It's power is truly amazing!"

Nathaniel replied, "I agree. I saw King Whitestar in my dream state and he told me the Founder's stone would protect me with its power. I am truly grateful and humbled."

"We need to celebrate!" Suggested Cor'in.

"I think he's done enough for one day," Traveler counseled. "Let the lad regain his strength."

"Right," Jacoby said. "We'll leave you to rest." They all nodded, each giving Nathaniel a reassuring word before leaving. Jacoby embraced his brother before leaving him alone with Lani, saying over his shoulder, "I'll be right outside if you need anything."

Lani curled up next to Nathaniel, holding him tight before both drifted off to sleep.

THIRTY

The messenger felt the trickle of sweat trailing down his neck but ignored it as he slapped the horse's flank, coaxing it to gallop faster. He carried an important message from Sergeant Thorne, a trusted officer in the King's army. Written on the outside of the scroll in bold, red letters were the words, "FOR THE KING'S EYES ONLY." The weight of the responsibility pressed heavily on the messenger's shoulders, as he knew that the kingdom's fate hung in the balance. He did not see the message's contents, only that delivering the missive meant life or death for him and countless others. With each powerful stride, his horse snorted white foam, its hooves hammered the dirt road, raising a dust cloud as he rounded the bend. Then, with a sharp tug on the reins, the rider brought the animal to a jarring halt, the dust billowing around them like a thick, swirling fog. A hundred yards ahead, an enormous, moss-covered boulder blocked the road, its presence demanding attention.

I must have been distracted this morning, failing to see this large stone when I rode past. The wind whipped across his face, carrying the scent of dry grass and dust, as he gazed around and realized he was riding on the Taborian plains. With no hills or mountains, only a vast expanse of smooth terrain, the landscape did not explain the massive stone. "Where in the demons did...?" The question died in his throat as he watched, paralyzed with horror, the boulder, inch by agonizing inch unfolding, unveiling a monstrous creature twenty feet tall. His hairless, oval head sported a pair of beady, dark eyes, peering over a carrot-thin nose that drooped over a wide mouth full of sharp, rotting teeth. His hulking, brown body appeared hard and unyielding making it easy to see how the creature could disguise himself as a large rock when hunched over.

"What...are you?" his voice was a shaky rasp, barely audible over the rustling leaves.

The monster's laugh, deep and rough like the growl of a bear filled the air, "Ya never seen a troll before, boy?"

The messenger sat frozen in terror, his heart pounding in his chest. Panic gripped him, and his limbs turned to lead, making it impossible even to rein his horse away from the danger. He felt a gasp catch in his chest as the monster took a step closer, its massive form seeming to devour the distance between them.

"Give me the communique, lad," the troll rumbled, his breath smelling of moss and damp earth, "and I promise to eat your horse first. No messages get through today."

Suddenly, the troll shot forward in long strides, his heavy feet thudding against the ground, long arms reaching out for the young man, his gnarled fingers twitching with anticipation.

The rider jolted into action and yanked on the reins, forcing the horse to rear up in a powerful display of defiance. With a sharp jab of the spurs, he sent the stallion charging away from the danger, its hooves pounding the ground in a thunderous gallop. The messenger felt a sudden jolt as the troll's massive hand clamped onto the horse's hind legs, and he launched forward, tumbling over his startled mount. Pain lanced through his body as he struggled onto all fours, every movement a searing agony. He looked back, and his stomach churned as he saw the Troll lifting the terrified stallion's rump to his mouth, his enormous jaws crunching down on flesh and bone with a sickening, wet crack. The sight ignited a surge of adrenaline through his veins, propelling him forward with instinctual urgency. Instead of sprinting toward the forest, he made a split-second decision to dash to the edge of Spire Lake, the expansive body of water that encircled the Taborian capital on three sides. A deafening thump echoed as the troll let the remains of the horse fall to the ground, followed by the tremors of the troll's heavy footsteps as it stalked closer and closer from behind.

I can make it, he told himself, his heart pounding in his chest as he sprinted toward the lake.

With powerful strides, his legs pumped toward the water, propelling him across fifty yards, then twenty, and finally the last ten. As he neared the edge, the young soldier braced himself for a desperate, all-or-nothing dive, oblivious to the Troll's hand reaching for him just inches away. As his body arced toward the lake, he felt a tug on his uniform leg, almost arresting his momentum. He kicked hard with his boots, striking something firm, freeing his body to plummet in an awkward somersault into the water.

A moment before, the troll, in a moment of sudden realization that his prey might escape, launched himself forward, thrusting out a powerful hand to grab the soldier's legs and stop him from getting away. The young lad racing toward the lake had barely begun his leap when the enormous beast reached its huge mitt out toward him and caught the fabric of the young man's uniform. Gotcha!

For a heartbeat, the messenger hung suspended in mid-air before a searing pain shot through the beast's knuckle from the messenger's boot kick. In a reflexive action, the troll loosened his grip on his prey, allowing the young man to slip through his fingers and crash into the lake with a resounding splash.

The event ended in a calamitous sight as the young man flipped like a rag doll head-over-heels and splashed, back-first, into the blue water. Unchecked momentum carried the troll forward, his considerable girth impacting the bank with the force of a plow, gouging a deep trench into the prairie soil while his body slid to the lake's edge.

The messenger, feeling the icy water against his skin, instantly forgot the dizziness from his fall and swam with renewed determination toward the deeper parts of the lake to escape the troll, who had risen from the bank and was now slowly entering the water. The Troll's long strides were closing the distance, and he realized any escape attempt would be futile. Just as the Troll reached to scoop the young man from the water, the messenger felt an urgent tug on his legs, pulling him under the surface.

Startled by the unexpected attack and his chest burning from lack of air, the young man flailed his arms and kicked in an attempt to reach the surface. But his legs were pinned by what felt like arms. His chest constricted, desperately yearning for breath, panic soaring through his body like an electric current.

"Calm thyself, human. I am friend," came a sing-song, heavily accented voice in his head.

He felt muscular arms climb their way up his body, and panic surged again, but the intruder's grip held fast. As the messenger's blood became depleted of oxygen, his body violently spasmed, his muscles screaming in agony.

As his eyelids fluttered closed, plunging him into darkness, an odd, chilling sensation of something rubbery and clammy made contact with his face. As his world shifted, he gasped, taking in fresh air with a sudden, sharp intake of breath. His vision cleared, except for the blur caused by his life-sustaining air bubble. A beautiful Elf girl, her scales shimmering and hair moss-green, had rescued him; after a moment's study, she smiled radiantly, beckoning him to take her hand. She effortlessly led him through the sun-dappled water.

Navigating submerged stones and schools of fish amidst thick aquatic plants, they arrived at the imposing castle's cobblestone facade.

Moving carefully along the wall, she searched until she discovered a narrow recess, then ducked inside, dragging the messenger with her. The underwater corridor, which wound back and forth, ended with an upward slope that led out of the water. The elf's hand moved towards the surface, a clear indication of the path that lay ahead. With a warm smile and a gentle squeeze of his hand, she disappeared into the darkness of the corridor, leaving him alone.

A sharp wave of regret washed over the young man, his heart heavy with the inability to express his profound gratitude for her brave and heroic rescue. He shook his head and climbed the stone ramp, pulling himself out onto the cold floor and inhaling the dank, moldy air of the chamber. As he collapsed, his bubble device disintegrated, leaving him panting and exhausted by the traumatic events. After several minutes, he remembered the urgent communique and got to his feet, striding up the incline. The faint light from the rare wall sconces guided his steps as he ascended the steep stairway to the upper levels, eventually leading him to a wooden door. Hesitation was not an option as he forcefully pushed the door open, revealing a crescent-shaped opening into a dimly lit scullery pantry. He stepped through the doorway and into a smaller kitchen workroom, where bustling human servants and cooks were preparing the mid-day meal.

"Can you direct me to the King's chambers?" he demanded of a passing cook carrying a vegetable basket.

With a sudden stop, the man stared in shock at the unexpected intruder, his eyes wide with fear and his mouth unable to speak. He pointed towards the main doorway, his only way of communicating his alarm. Exhausted but determined, the messenger used his remaining energy to sprint up a flight of stairs, then down a long hallway, finally reaching the end where two guards stood imposingly before two massive walnut doors that blocked his path.

"A message for the King," the messenger said, pushing past the guards and opening the door. The guards were close behind him.

"Hey, wait a minute," one guard shouted, his hand on the young man's shoulder.

But a voice from the table silenced the guard.

"Who so indelicately has intruded?" asked Nathaniel, stopping his discussion with Blue Ivy and Cor'in.

The lead guard saluted. "I'm sorry, Your Grace," he said, looking down sheepishly. "This courier states he has a message for the King's eyes only."

"Let him pass," Nathaniel said, a flair of heat in his voice. He gestured with one hand for the messenger to wait, then addressed his half-elf friend. "Cor'in, considering your new position as the leader of palace security, how might you ensure that the guards fully understand that an order, like the one prohibiting entry to this room, is not a request but a strict and unwavering expectation?"

"Mmm," Cor'in said cheerfully. "These gentlemen seem to require a duty reminder, Your Majesty, and I'm happy to act as their instructor."

Both guards' eyes grew, and perspiration sprinkled their foreheads. "Please, Your Majesty. We made a simple mistake," the more senior guard pleaded.

Nathaniel frowned and placed a hand on the man's shoulder. "I understand," he said sagely, seizing upon this moment as an opportunity to teach. "The position you hold as a palace guard is one of honor. Those who qualify must possess unwavering dedication and remarkable discipline, setting them apart from the rest. Given that actions require responsibility, additional training is essential to decide your next step."

"Come with me, lads," Cor'in demanded, escorting the guards out the door.

"I apologize," Nathaniel said to the messenger, who stood quietly watching the interaction. "So, the message?"

"Oh, yes," the young man said, snapping to attention and handing Nathaniel the vellum.

Nathaniel read the parchment, his face draining of color.

Blue Ivy noticed the King's change and asked, "What is it?"

"Percival, call the Brotherhood and Devin Ashoke for an immediate meeting. We must prepare for an imminent attack," Nathaniel said.

As the golden hues of the morning sun dispelled the predawn gray, the new commander of Ravenite's army, Sin, prepared to issue the order to attack. He was a skeletal demon, who lead his undead soldiers from the back of a gigantic skeletal hydra. Sin gestured with a scepter adorned with jewels, ordering his army of the undead to advance. General Vulga, Ravenite's former leader, had fallen during the last attack, a lucky Taborian arrow piercing his heart. Ravenite had turned over operational command of the army to the demon. Despite their positions of power, Bloodcoat, leader of the feared Lupine Rangers, and Ice Beard, King of all the giant forces, found the leader to be cold, vengeful, and demanding. With a dismissive tone and a voice laced with disdain, the monster barked orders at the leaders, treating them like lowly recruits. The treatment had been a difficult pill to swallow, for both beings had enormous egos that the demon disregarded, even trampling them without care.

Having refrained from any attack for a week, the enemy used this time to diligently plan their next offensive, aiming to drive the remaining Taborian forces back to the lake, leaving them nowhere else to go. Following the decimation of their remaining forces, Sin predicted that the remnants of the military would concentrate their efforts on one of the two bridges that crossed the lake surrounding the city of Spires. However, his strategic plan involved a force of trolls, ogres, Lupine wolves, and giants marching through the Horn Wood to cut off the Taborian army's retreat, entrapping them in a deadly pincer movement. Unknown to Sin, Thorne and his men had apprehended an orc courier while on patrol, who carried a highly confidential order destined for Bloodcoat. Unable to decipher the written malevolent language, he forwarded the message to the king for his interpretation.

Sin turned to his trusted subordinate, Cajŭn, a rail-thin bone demon, and said, "Is all prepared?"

"Yes. Your undead hunger for new souls."

"Have we heard a response from the warm-bloods?" Sin asked.

"Not yet. Nor any word from the troll patrolling the Lake Road," Cajŭn reported.

"We should have received confirmation of the plan hours ago," Sin said, shaking his skeletal feline head in frustration.

"Despite their arrogance, the warm-bloods can be as vicious and bloodthirsty as are we, sir. The situation might be more complex than it initially appears," suggested the bone demon.

"Send a witch to investigate," ordered Sin. "My attack plan demands precision."

The dark figure, cloaked in the shadows of a vulture spell, vanished on her broom into the predawn sky, becoming a distant speck in the dusky heavens. In a matter of minutes, she had identified the location of the allied encampment and descended in a shot, landing gracefully beside Bloodcoat's tent. Two enormous Gaul

Mantel warriors guarding the tent bounded forward, their ink-black fur ruffling in the wind, blocking her path.

"I have word from Commander Sin," the black witch said by way of explanation.

The wolves sniffed her, their eyes narrowed with mistrust.

"Follow me," growled the larger of the lupine, a herculean specimen.

The lupine lumbered toward the tent opening, stuck his head inside, and barked in the lupine's guttural language. Then, the flap opened, and the witch came inside. Across the tent, the fierce Grau Mantel leader, Bloodcoat, poured over a map of the surrounding Taborian land. The beast, larger and more powerful than any Lupine the witch had witnessed, loomed over her, its massive form dwarfing her small frame, making her appear incredibly tiny. He stared down at her with a twisted smirk, waiting for her to speak. The witch, only a century old, had rarely known fear of any creature short of the powerful lich-mage, Ravenite. But under the scrutiny of the cunning glare of the Pack Leader, her insides turned to jelly, and she hid her shaking hands behind her.

"Lord Bloodcoat," she said, her voice breaking slightly. "Commander Sin asks for your reply to his message this morning."

"I received no orders from the demon," he stated.

She nodded. The news confirmed the undead leader's concern. "Commander Sin intends to attack the Taborian line within the hour and drive them toward the lake. He commands that you and King Icebeard move your troops to the Taborian flank at the bridge, cutting off their retreat to the city."

Bloodcoat looked at the map, studying it, the demon's plan swirling in his mind.

A wide grin stretched across his snout, his long canines shining in the morning light.

"Tell the Commander we will be in place within two hours," he barked.

Hunkered down in a locked section of the royal library, Jacoby watched as Nathaniel scanned through an ancient tome, the Malevolent Underworld Dictionary, to decipher the demon language contained in the captured message. After a long hesitation, the king raised his eyes, an expression of concern on his face.

"Well? How bad is it?" Jacoby asked.

"Sin has ordered an attack to begin this morning, and he's ordered Bloodcoat and Icebeard to institute a flanking maneuver, cracking the army like a nutcracker on a pecan."

Jacoby's jaw dropped. "We need to pull them back!"

"Yes, we need to send the fastest bird to institute an immediate withdrawal of troops to the castle. Second, we will take volunteers armed with the new silver weapons to act as a defensive rear guard to delay the enemy and give our troops time to get over the bridge. Finally, we set fire to the bridges as soon as the army and rear guard have withdrawn," Nathaniel said, standing and calling for Percival. He rapidly scribbled a message on parchment as the brothers rushed out and met Percival and Cor'in, waiting in the hallway.

"Percival, find the fastest falcon we have and send this to our commander in the field. Then have Bullfinch come to the palace as soon as possible." The King's assistant rushed off down the hall, his long legs pistoning his thin frame like a sprinter.

He turned to Cor'in. "I need volunteers to act as a rear guard for the retreating army. Have them wait at the front gate. I'll lead them out within the hour," Nathaniel said.

"The demons you will!" Cor'in and Jacoby said simultaneously.

"'Huh?" Nathaniel said, stunned by the outburst.

"You're too important," Cor'in said. "It will be my honor to lead them."

"I can't ask you to do that, my friend. Survival may be tenuous against such odds."

"Ha!" Cor'in chuckled. "I've faced worse odds without defeat."

"I can't allow you to do that," Nathaniel said, more pleading than an order as tears welled in his eyes.

"I'm volunteering. And honestly, I have more berserker blood in me than you do," Cor'in said cheerfully. "I'm on it." Before Nathaniel could protest more, the half-elf rushed away.

"Why didn't you back me up?" Nathaniel demanded, turning to Jacoby, his anguish turning to heated anger.

"I agree with Cor'in," Jacoby said calmly. "As King, you'll be required to make tough decisions, including sending men into harm's way."

"But... you don't understand," the royal said defiantly. A lie. "How could you?" Another lie. He knew Jacoby had commanded an entire cohort in battle and knew the price of leadership. Guilt hung on him like a smothering weighted cloak, sucking away his breath. His hope.

"Your leadership is in its infancy, and Tabor needs you. Alive," Jacoby said, placing a hand on the brother's shoulder. "You're a symbol of hope. A hope that Tabor desperately hungers for."

Nathaniel's defiance crumbled, and he dropped his head. He took a deep breath, wondering if his guilt would ever disappear. Then, an idea struck him, sparking a sliver of hope in his heart. He turned to Jacoby and, with a half-smile, said, "I think I have a way to help Cor'in."

A half-hour later, as Cor'in assembled seventy-five volunteers to act as the army's rear guard, Grullach stood on the lower bailey, speaking with several burly men led by a lieutenant in charge of the outer guard. The officer scanned the parchment handed to him; one brow elevated with consternation.

"So, the King wants us to angle the ballistae and catapults toward the forest line? I don't understand. What if the enemy attacks from another direction?" the young officer asked, just hitting his late teen years.

"We expect the enemy to come rushing from the wood to flank our troops as they withdraw. When that happens, hit them with everything you have," the halfling instructed.

"But…" the officer stammered, his throat dry as sandpaper, as beads of sweat, like tiny pearls of fear, beaded on the young man's forehead.

"But nothing!" Grull bellowed, his voice rising in frustration. "When the King issues an order, you follow it without question."

But Grull's tone softened when he saw the terror reflected in the young man's eyes.

"What's your name?" he asked, locking eyes with the officer.

"Stylt, sir," the teen croaked, now visibly shaking.

"Stylt," Grull whispered, escorting the teen out of earshot of the other men. "How long have you been commissioned?"

Stylt shook his head, unable to find the words. His wealthy father had paid a lump sum to General Thorne for his commission and to be placed away from the front lines in the safety of guarding the castle. He never expected to face combat.

"Right. I'll be by your side to help," Grull said in a low tone. "Pull yourself together. Courage, even false courage, breeds more courage."

The young man straightened and inhaled a deep breath to calm his nerves. Then he cried, "You heard the order, men. Get moving."

Simultaneously, Jacoby, a skilled tactician and leader, organized a group of townsmen to assist him in a daring plan. Their aim was to secure the area by preventing any potential threats from crossing the two wooden bridges that spanned the tranquil waters of Spire Lake. Jacoby directed two dozen watermen in rowboats to generously slop quick oil onto the underside of the bridge planks and pilings with large mops while other townsmen did the same with large amounts of oil poured onto the bridge's railings. To ensure the army's rapid retreat across the bridge, he left the surface planks dry until the last moment when bottles brimming with oil would be thrown onto them. To ensure the success of their operation, he stationed two men at the entrance of each bridge, each holding an unlit torch. These men eagerly awaited the signal from Jacoby, ready to ignite the incendiary device and set the bridges ablaze, cutting off any further passage.

Jacoby shifted his gaze towards a sizable contingent of archers positioned along the fortified castle walls. The archers, positioned along the battlements at each crenel, stood ready to unleash a devastating barrage of silver-tipped arrows on Jacoby's command; if any hostile forces attempted to breach the castle's defenses.

Now came the waiting game, a part of the battle Jacoby hated. Nathaniel stepped up beside him.

"I've already spoken with Bullfinch and Ashoke, and they've assured me they will have everyone fifteen years of age and older waiting at the palace gate soon. Horatio has resolved to attempt entry into the secret vault within the next sixty minutes. With Odin's blessing, our army will receive many more silver weapons," Nathaniel reported. "Until then, the smiths have dipped every weapon in the city into the vats of liquid silver, coating at least the tip of each." He took a breath and asked, "Are we prepared for the withdrawal?"

"We're as prepared as we can be," Jacoby said, holding a spyglass to his eye. "No sign yet of the army or the enemy."

"Are we sure the falcon got through?"

"Yes, it returned a few minutes ago, flying with an injured wing from an orc arrow. There wasn't any return message."

As Nathaniel rubbed his hands together, a nervous habit he performed without thinking before a battle, he felt a surge of anxiety. For the previous two years, the Brotherhood had been engaged in a multitude of skirmishes, testing their skills and resilience in the face of adversity. Immediate circumstances spurred most of these assassination attempts and involved a limited number of assailants, never exceeding a handful. Now, their foes were many and fearsome, a terrifying legion of undead, giants, trolls, ogres, and lupine rangers. His dwindling army, clearly outmatched in both personnel and weapons, faced certain defeat. The high stone walls of the fortified city and the castle offered the only hope of safety, a last bastion against the encroaching danger. Would it be enough? Despite lacking confidence, he always maintained a public facade of composure. Had they returned to Tabor months or years prior, they might have escaped the gnawing anxiety and perilous circumstances they now faced. However, that opportunity had slipped away long ago.

Jacoby jerked the spyglass down and, interrupting Nathaniel's reverie shouted, "Here they come! Open the gates."

A seemingly endless line of Taborian soldiers charged across the prairie, their eyes fixed on the bridge, their boots pounding against the dense soil in a relentless drive toward the bridge. The soldiers approached at a fast jog across the bridge in a long, flowing line. As more and more troops arrived, a bottleneck formed at the bridge entrance as men fought to reach the safety of the walled city.

Despite the best efforts of Cor'in and his volunteers, the passage across the bridge became a slow shuffle, with the narrow width of the bridge acting as a major constraint. Understanding the potential for the enemy to have expected this hindrance, Jacoby sprinted to prepare his archers for the coming battle.

As the final third of the army retreated, a sudden and unexpected barrage of boulders, launched from deep within the forest, crashed down upon their ranks. Chaos erupted out of nowhere, leading to a flurry of activity. The soldiers, acting as a frenzied mob, stormed across the bridge, many falling over the rails into the water, and crushing anyone who dared stand in their path. Cor'in, caught amid a deafening barrage of missiles and overwhelmed by the terrifying screams of the frightened soldiers, yelled out to his rear guard, "Quickly, men! Form two lines, swords at the ready." The soldiers rushed to form two lines, short spears at the ready.

Emerging from the woods a thousand feet away, Lupine rangers, Hill giants, trolls, ogres, and goblins burst into view.

Grullach signaled Stylt, who screamed, "FIRE!"

A loud creak of shifting wood echoed near Grull as the closest trebuchet's arm swung forward, launching an enormous stone at the charging enemy, followed in succession by another and another until all twenty-five had fired. The whistling of the projectiles sliced through the air for a few short heartbeats before the earth trembled with the impact, followed by a cacophony of screams and roars.

"Reload!" The scene was a chaotic symphony of grunts, creaks, and shouted commands as Grull and Stylt moved between the catapults, soldiers struggling with ropes and others working with furious speed to reload the buckets with heavy stones.

As Cor'in deployed his men in a battle line, the monsters charged across the vast open plain, eager to engage in combat. When the monstrous horde had covered a quarter of the distance across open ground, Jacoby's archers unleashed a devastating volley of arrows from the ramparts in a deadly rain that seemed to engulf the battlefield. Reloading their weapons, his men continued the assault, firing at will. The goblins and lupine fell in large numbers, writhing in agonizing pain, as did several of the larger beasts, but the charge continued undeterred.

Cor'in looked over his shoulder and realized the last of the retreating army had crossed the bridge in a slow dribble. He called out to his platoon, "Regroup on the other side of the bridge and help any stragglers!"

His men sprinted across the bridge, helping the last stragglers across, just as the first lupine reached the bridge approach.

"Get inside the city gates!" Cor'in ordered. With only a few seconds to prepare, the group braced themselves for the onslaught of sprinting canines that were about to descend upon them. The archers stationed atop the battlements, however, continued their assault, inflicting casualties upon those attempting to cross the bridge. The giants and trolls thundered behind the Wolfmen and goblins, their heavy footsteps shaking the very ground beneath them.

Nathaniel and Horatio rushed down to the city gate and prepared to drop the postern and close the massive iron-clad wooden doors to preserve the lowest castle level. The king shouted to the guards, "Ready the portcullis to drop on my command!"

Cor'in, a fearless leader, led his men through the city gate, ensuring that every man had made it safely inside. The Count, with the nearest lupine hot on his heels, found himself in a desperate footrace. Cor'in pushed himself to his absolute limit, sprinting with every ounce of strength he possessed, as he felt the scorching breath of the beast on his neck. As he neared the city gate, just ten feet away, he made a desperate leap for the opening, his attempt coinciding perfectly with Nathaniel's order to drop the portcullis and seal the massive lower bailey gates.

Simultaneously, the lupine also sprang into action, its extended talons raking against Cor'in's legs. As Cor'in plunged through the opening, the portcullis and heavy doors clanged shut, but not before the solitary wolfman squeezed through, too.

As Cor'in rolled to his feet, the wolfman, already on all fours, with its jaws snapping and spittle flying, leaped at the nearest soldier. In a horrifying instant, the beast's sharp, three-inch claws shredded two men who fell screaming where they stood, and its powerful jaws mercilessly crushed another. Time seemed to stop, each soldier paralyzed by stunned terror, until Cor'in and Nathaniel bravely charged toward the beast. The warriors attacked from different sides, slashing and stabbing while avoiding the monster's lightning-quick slashes. For several seconds, the battle was at an impasse, each side causing minor wounds to the other.

A flurry of movement erupted down the avenue as Jacoby and Horatio sprinted to the fight.

"For the King!" Jacoby screamed, slashing at the beast with his sword high.

The soldiers, emboldened by his words, reacted, drawing their swords and launching into a fierce attack. Despite his ferocity, the wolfman was no match for the soldiers, who overwhelmed him with their sheer numbers and cut him down within minutes. The battle left a heavy toll, as four soldiers died and three were wounded. Nathaniel and Cor'in each suffered minor cuts on their forearms, the wounds deep enough to require Allai'nn's stitches but not severe enough to pose any risk to their lives.

A resounding crash shook the portcullis, abruptly overshadowing their victory and replacing it with a sense of dread, marking a sudden and unwelcome change in their fortunes.

"Lower the crossbars!" Nathaniel commanded, and without hesitation, ten men rushed to secure the heavy wooden beams fortifying the gate. Despite that, the assault continued unabated, a relentless barrage of fists from giants, trolls, and ogres hammering against the defenses.

The king turned to Jacoby and said, "How long will it hold? We need time to reassemble the troops to the parapets."

Jacoby stood next to Cor'in and Horatio and rubbed his chin. "Maybe an hour if we're lucky, less if we aren't."

"Less?" Nathaniel froze.

Jacoby gave a wave to the archers, who took rag-tipped arrows, lit them, and then fired them into the bridge planks. With a deafening roar and a flash of flames, a fiery explosion consumed the bridge. The bridge, swarmed by a multitude of monstrous figures, became a scene of bewildered chaos for a fleeting moment. Instinct took over, and most of the monsters either surged back across the bridge or plunged into the lake, seeking safety from whatever had caused their initial confusion.

Jacoby, his breath coming in ragged bursts as he surged uphill towards the middle bailey, shouted over his shoulder, "Come on! That gate won't hold forever!"

With a sharp order, Nathaniel sent his soldiers forward, instructing them to ascend to the next level, where they would encounter the civilian militia under the command of Grullach. As Nathaniel and the last soldier crossed into the middle section, the iron portcullis clanged shut, and the thick iron gate followed, secured by massive crossbars resembling tree trunks in size. He sprinted towards the parapet in a burst of speed, reaching it just beside Jacoby. From his vantage point, he saw an endless line of hundreds of monsters marching across the plain toward the burning bridges and lining up at the lake's edge. Sin rode through the masses of the undead and live monsters with a skeletal hydra as his mount. In a dramatic display of power, he stopped mid-stride, his voice booming with a single, piercing command, "The human meal awaits! Bring forward the boats and ladders."

Towering trolls sprang into action, their lean muscles straining against the weight of the heavy boat hulls. They swiftly secured broad wooden ladders to the back of the transports, ensuring a stable platform for the forthcoming attack. Meanwhile, the undead army, their bodies void of life but filled with an insatiable hunger for destruction, started crowding into the boats, readying themselves to row across the crystal-clear lake toward the distant peninsula. The larger and more imposing beings, such as trolls, ogres, and giants, opted to wade across the lake, their massive frames creating ripples that distorted the otherwise calm surface. Nathaniel watched in abject horror, overwhelmed by the sheer magnitude of the undead horde. The unyielding tide of minions, with their decaying forms and vacant eyes, seemed to multiply exponentially with each passing moment, their swelling numbers instilling a sense of impending doom in Nathaniel's heart. He gazed at the warriors crowding the battlements, preparing to fend off the attack. Lacking true military training, the men and women, simple farmers, merchants, and shopkeepers, prepared for the desperate fight against the monstrous horde with the rudimentary knowledge gleaned from a week of Grull's training and their unwavering bravery.

Dark, ominous storm clouds from the west inched across the sky, slowly covering the afternoon's radiant sun, and the scent of rain permeated the air. The once peaceful City of Spires, a bastion of hope and prosperity, now stood on the precipice of destruction, the fate of the entire population hanging in the balance. The young king felt the weight of responsibility press heavily on his shoulders. Despite the many battles he and the Brotherhood had fought over the last two years, he never imagined being thrust into such a dire situation just after his coronation as sovereign. But the gods had chosen him to rally Tabor's defenders and lead them against the encroaching darkness.

The minions, grotesque creatures born of unholy magic, were unlike anything Nathaniel had ever encountered. Their twisted forms and lifeless eyes seemed to mock the very concept of humanity. And yet, these brave townsfolk were determined to protect their homes and loved ones, even if it meant facing their worst nightmares head-on.

Grull and Jacoby had worked tirelessly with the help of the other warriors in the Brotherhood to impart whatever fighting knowledge they could in the limited time they had. The townspeople did their best to soak up every word, and the two leaders loved their determination and grit.

Now, as they stood side by side on the battlements, Nathaniel surveyed the motley crew of defenders. Farmers armed with pitchforks, merchants wielding swords, and shopkeepers brandishing anything they could find that resembled a weapon. Horatio's daring swim to the underwater armory had turned out to be a wonderful success, yielding another hundred silver swords and daggers, which they distributed throughout the army. That news, in combination with the city's silversmiths working nonstop, had produced enough weapons for most of the regular army and townspeople to have at least one silver-tipped weapon. Against an enormous army of undead and other evil creatures, Nathaniel knew his defenders were woefully under-armed and under-manned. Despair began creeping into his psyche, and he wondered how soon the nightmare would be over and who might survive. I'm glad I gave the order to evacuate most of the women and children from the city. Sadly, many stayed to fight and die by their mate's side.

The first wave of monsters crashed against the walls, their relentless assault testing the resolve of the gate. Jacoby's arm swept through the air, signaling the archers to unleash a barrage of arrows. The archers' arrows thinned the surging enemy ranks, but the enemy seemed inexhaustible as fresh troops rushed forward to fill the gaps left by the fallen.

In a terrifying display of coordinated aggression reminiscent of ants overwhelming a picnic, the enemy warriors massed at the outer gates, their unified force relentlessly pressing to break through and overwhelm the defenders. Again and again, Jacoby watched the chaotic mass slam into the portcullis' outer barrier, each attempt failing. What felt like timeless inertia finally broke as the crowd parted, giving way to a solitary skeletal figure who, riding a venomous, three-necked hydra, waded through the throngs of soldiers. Commander Sin, twenty feet from the barrier, reined in his mount, whose skeletal jaws were hissing and snapping menacingly, before producing a long, gnarled wand from his uniform. As the undead monster mouthed unintelligible words, a vibrant blue stream of elemental fire erupted towards the protective barrier. With a deafening roar and an explosion of blue flames; the portcullis disintegrated, the resulting shockwave sending several undead soldiers sprawling from the bridge. Once the fire had cleared, the defenses, though badly scorched, remained structurally sound, prompting Sin to launch another assault.

Anticipating the unavoidable conclusion, Jacoby shrieked a frantic order to his bowman, bellowing, "Retreat! Withdraw to the middle bailey!"

The bowmen sprinted along the battlements in a flurry of motion, scaling the parapet to the next defensive position above.

A sudden, deafening crash echoed through the bailey, instantly alerting the defenders that the lower gate had been breached. The enemy poured through the opening, fanning out across the green to eliminate any resistance. Fortunately, the defenders had evacuated the area and stood in the more easily defended middle ward.

The attackers regrouped with astonishing speed, filling the entire green within minutes. With ladders brought from outside, they charged forward, and the next assault began. A deafening, rhythmic barrage of ladders hammered against the wall, punctuated by the urgent, determined footfalls of the enemy, their ascent unstoppable.

In a windowless inner room within the fortress's inner keep, Allai'nn, Rue and Lani worked with a dozen other women healers caring for the unremitting onslaught of wounded streaming in from the battle. Two days before, in a miraculous turn of events, Rue's father, the famous brownie healer Gruawane, had arrived unexpectedly at the castle. After escaping Crepitus' orc army near Tajman Sghur and months of searching for their daughter, the brownie and his Oread wife, Byrgid, had settled in the nearby Sacred Wood. Upon his arrival, the unicorn leader, Friend, had related that he had just missed his daughter and recent coronation in the City of Spires. Leaving Byrgid in the safety of her Oread sisters, he had traveled alone, avoiding enemy patrols and bandits, to reunite with Rue. Nothing could have shocked Rue more, but the reuniting was bittersweet.

"I'm so thankful you and Mother are alive and well, but I can't believe you abandoned the protection of the magical wood," she told him, delighted but concerned.

"I had to know you were safe."

"But, the danger."

"I'm craftier than I appear," Gruawane said, patting her arm. "And your mother insisted. She felt I could be of service here."

"I thought I had lost you once, and I refuse to again," she said, her lip quivering. "I won't have it!"

Gruawane sat her down, locking eyes with a steely gaze. "I adore you, daughter, but you have yet to grow out of your petulance," he chided. "I'm here to stay. My skills as a protector and healer are much needed."

And with that, the conversation ended, and the brownie seized leadership of the castle hospital.

The master healer seamlessly returned to his element, giving orders, guiding treatment, and organizing the preparation of bandages, opium elixir, and boiling water for sterilization. He also led the unattached women and children to the Hall of Kings, a protected room surrounded by thick walls. Here, he left Sinbad to guard the few remaining children and older, infirm adults.

Now that the battle had started, litters of wounded soldiers and militia poured inside. Gruawane and the other healers moved from patient-to-patient triaging, then treating the more severely injured. Hour upon hour, they feverishly worked to save lives, doing what they could to relieve their suffering.

In one instance, Allai'nn finished sewing up and bandaging a nasty slice down a teen's leg. The lad, no older than sixteen, appeared anxious, sitting up on his forearms. Her eyes flitted to his face, and she gave him a weary-worn maternal smile. "Wesley, lay back and rest. Do you want to lose your leg?" she asked solicitously.

"But I have to get back, M'Lady. The orcs and goblins were streaming over the wall when one got me. A friend dragged me to safety before he fell to one of the monsters. They need me!"

The elf princess found the boy's courage astonishing. Sixteen, and already had bravely faced the hideous enemy and burned to continue fighting. He was a stable boy, armed with a silver-tipped spear with a thin leather jerkin to protect his upper body. She had met him early on after their arrival, and he was one of her favorite people, kind, polite, and dutiful.

"Didn't I hear you say that someday you aspire to be Stable Master? Can you achieve that with a wooden leg?" she said, patting him on the shoulder.

"But Lady Allai'nn…" he protested, squirming to rise, but the elf pushed him back down firmly.

"Your presence in this battle, Wes, would only serve as a hindrance, and I fear you would put yourself in mortal danger. We will need your strength and courage more than ever for the next battle. Now rest and grow strong," she insisted.

The lad relaxed and turned his head, his eyes filling with tears.

"Having the wisdom to fight another day is not cowardice," she said, giving his arm a squeeze and standing. She wiped the perspiration from her forehead and moved to the next patient.

Nathaniel's heart raced as he urged his comrades to stand strong. He screamed out, "Prepare to repel attackers!"

As though his words had summoned them, a relentless wave of destructive attackers, comprising undead minions, lupine rangers, orcs, and goblins, scrambled over the parapet. Concurrently, a group of Frost giants smashed their mighty, colossal fists against the gatehouse doors, unleashing shockwaves of such intense power that the very ground trembled beneath their force.

"Follow me!" Nathaniel screamed, charging into the approaching mass, the Brotherhood and militia at his heels, swords held high.

Jacoby, Grull, Nathaniel, Cor'in, Blue Ivy, and Horatio formed a destructive wedge, their swords electrified by the humming green glow of Nathaniel's blade. The attackers seemed to be mesmerized by the green glow of the Founder's Stone on the pommel, and some who were within its aura even cowered in fear. Seizing the opportunity, the Brotherhood surged forward, their advantage propelling them into action. Their swords, wielded with deadly precision, created a shimmering, impenetrable barrier of steel, destroying everything that dared to cross their path. Beside them, the militia fought with a ferocity born of desperation, their lack of training compensated by sheer determination. The clash of steel against rotting flesh reverberated through the night, mingling with the agonized cries of both the defenders and the minions. But even as exhaustion threatened to consume them, Nathaniel saw a glimmer of hope in the eyes of his fellow defenders. They were no longer just farmers, merchants, and shopkeepers; they had become warriors, fighting not just for their lives but for the very essence of their town. With each fallen minion, their confidence grew, and their resolve hardened.

Nathaniel initially thought this unwavering bravery might turn the tide of the battle. But the sheer numbers of the enemy, coming wave upon wave over the walls, became overwhelming. Abruptly, the sturdy gates ruptured in a shower of splinters, the blast throwing many defending the gate off their feet. A horde of monstrous creatures flooded in, including ogres, trolls, ettins, and giants, led by Commander Sin riding atop his skeletal hydra and trailed by the lich-mage Ravenite astride a monstrous black-furred beast, the feline Cath Palug. Armed with gigantic clubs and hammers, the monstrous horde unleashed a brutal assault, decimating the Taborian defenses and leaving them in ruins. In a flash, the once stalwart army fractured into pandemonium, the militia, their resolve shattered, abandoning their positions in a chaotic flight, each soldier consumed by the desperate instinct for self-preservation. Faced with an insurmountable obstacle, Nathaniel had no choice but to call for a retreat.

As the horns of retreat blared overhead, he shouted above the chaotic clamor of the battle. "Fall back to the keep!"

Among the last men to retreat, he rushed across the green, cutting down enemies as he ran. Forgetting the other Brotherhood, he focused his attention on getting as many troops to safety as possible. As the king helped drag casualties inside, Cor'in led a small force back through the stragglers to hold off the coming evil horde as a rear guard, allowing the last surviving soldiers to reach safety.

"Cor'in, come back," Nathaniel called, feeling certain the rear guard faced destruction.

He turned to run after him but felt Jacoby's powerful hands hold him back. "Let him go, Nat. You're needed here to shore up the defenses.'"

"The reckless fool's going to get himself killed," Nathaniel snapped, fighting Jacoby's iron grip.

"That's up to the gods. I need you inside," he said, pulling Nathaniel inside the inner gate. He heard Grull order, "Prepare to raise the drawbridge and close the gate on my command."

Cor'in and his twenty-five volunteers made a valiant retreating defense, allowing the last wounded stragglers to reach safety. Fighting bravely at the edge of the moat bridge, the men formed a retreating last line of defense against the horde, managing to cut down a half dozen enemy In a matter of moments, the small band of survivors found themselves overwhelmed by the unrelenting horde of the undead, their resistance crushed under the weight of the monsters' insatiable hunger as many fell where they stood, their souls devoured. The last ten warriors, in a desperate, retreating maneuver, lashed out with their blades, striking at any foe that dared to approach. As Cor'in stepped onto the drawbridge, a mere thirty feet from the gate, he bellowed, "Run for it!"

A giant's club, seemingly out of nowhere, tore through the bridge, sending them plummeting into the inky black depths of the moat.

Horatio, perched precariously on the wall above, let out a terrifying, shrill scream, "No!" as he watched the unfolding scene below, followed by a rumbling, guttural croak. The chilling, dissonant war cry of the Anuran bullfrog, a sound seldom encountered, reverberated through the air, causing the invaders to halt in their tracks, frozen in fear and uncertainty as they tried to decipher the eerie sound. As they looked up, their gaze fell upon Horatio, his form transformed into a monstrous abomination - a grotesquely swollen, green-skinned creature that inspired both fear and revulsion. Then, the Anuran, in one fluid movement, dived head-first from the battlement and disappeared into the black abyss below.

The defenders seized the moment created by the mad outburst, swiftly raising the drawbridge and locking the heavy iron doors, effectively securing the castle keep against any immediate attack.

Nathaniel's eyes filled with tears as he watched the moat, but neither Cor'in nor Horatio returned to the surface. Jacoby, standing rigidly in place, raised his hand in a salute and discreetly wiped away the tears that streamed down his face. He then turned to Nathaniel.

"Brother," he said, "We need an accurate assessment of our losses and must rally the remaining civilians and troops to defend the castle. Hopefully, figuring a way to cross the moat will stymie the devils long enough for us to form a plan."

Grull, with a gentle touch, placed his hand on Nathaniel's shoulder. "We need to honor their memory and make their sacrifice meaningful,' the halfling whispered.

"Help, Help!"

A farmer defending the far battery called out as a green arm appeared over the crenel, followed by a frogman's head, rivulets of water running down his face. Grull and Jacoby took off at a sprint, climbing the battlement stairs three at a time. They pulled Horatio up, Cor'in's unconscious form belted to his back.

"Odin's beard!" cried Grull, lifting the exhausted Anuran behind a merlon. "We thought you were finished."

"Once I found Cor'in, I had to swim underwater as far from the enemy as I could before climbing up," Horatio said between gasps.

"But how?" Grull said, as Jacoby rolled Cor'in's inert form on his belly, and began messaging his back. A stream of water erupted from the half-elf, and his eyes opened, coughing and hacking.

Horatio smiled, showing Grull the suction cups on each finger as an explanation.

"I think I swallowed half the lake," Cor'in said between coughs. Then, abruptly pulled Horatio into a hug. "Thanks, Toadie."

"I couldn't let my checkers rival perish," Horatio said, smiling. "How do you feel, anyway?"

"Like I got hit by one of Grull's catapults, but I'll survive."

"You better," Jacoby said. "We need you." Then the tall human squeezed the Anuran's shoulder. "Great job, Horatio."

"No time for sentiment. Nat needs us," Grull said, taking one of Cor'in's arms and the group descended to find the king.

The drawbridge held firm against the giant's relentless onslaught of hurled stones and hammers, their blows merely rattling the structure, causing no significant damage. Nathaniel, Jacoby, and Grull, the leaders of the Taborian army, stood atop the castle walls, surveying the devastating scene below. The fierce battle had left the once mighty army in ruins, with the losses staggering; a third of their fighting forces and half the civilian militia lay dead, their bodies scattered across the field in a grim testament to the battle's intensity. With a heavy heart, Nathaniel realized his army was no match for the endless waves of enemies that pressed relentlessly against them. Defeating the enemy army and vanquishing the undead lich-mage represented Tabor's only survival path. But how? The most sensible plan of action appeared to be the risky night evacuation of the vulnerable women and children, while he and the remaining soldiers attempted to slow the enemy's forward movement. Understandably, the situation seemed dire, with no response from his urgent pleas for aid coming from Polaris or any of their allies. Like so many times before, the Brotherhood and Tabor stood alone in this fight.

Echoes of the past haunted Nathaniel's mind as he remembered the tales of his father's battles that barely defeated these same adversaries twenty years earlier. The event had unfolded in an ironic twist. After Nathaniel lost his parents, Jacoby bravely whisked him away to Streamside, where the soldier raised him to adulthood. Over the last two years, they had fought for survival, eventually returning to Tabor. It had been a long and arduous journey, but he had finally reclaimed his birthright, only to face the same enemy that had taken everything from him, including his parents. Now, standing on the brink of another devastating defeat, Nathaniel knew that he and his comrades would fight to the last breath for the freedom and survival of the Taborian people.

The king inhaled a deep breath, letting it out slowly. His focus now needed to be on his people and Tabor's survival.

"Jacoby, Grull, what are your thoughts on bolstering our defenses?" Nathaniel asked.

Jacoby and Grull, his most trusted advisors, gazed at the remnants of the army, then at each other. They knew the gravity of the situation and the limited resources they had at their disposal. They had returned to their homeland only to inevitably die here.

"I suggest putting everything we have at the gate. It's the obvious point of attack since I don't think there's any way they could make ladders long enough to span the moat to reach the wall," Grull said, his voice filled with determination.

Jacoby rubbed his beard as he often did when in deep thought, but said nothing.

"The children should immediately evacuate south to Mar Nâpor, led by the women and men too old to fight," Grull continued, his eyes showing concern for the vulnerable members of their community. "The trip will be perilous, but staying here they no chance at all."

Nathaniel nodded, acknowledging the importance of protecting their future generations.

"Jacoby?" Nathaniel queried, his brother still contemplating the situation. Jacoby, a tall and imposing warrior, finally spoke up.

"Maybe there's another way," he said, his voice filled with a hint of excitement. Nathaniel looked at him, confused but intrigued.

"What do you mean?" Nathaniel asked, eager to hear his brother's unexpected idea.

"Grull is spot on with his idea if we had a substantial army to defend the gate. But, gods know, we don't have the personnel to repel another horde attack. So, what if we do the unexpected?" Jacoby suggested, a glimmer of hope in his eyes.

"The unexpected?" Nathaniel repeated, his curiosity piqued. He leaned closer to Jacoby, eager to hear his plan.

"We attack!" Jacoby said with finality.

"Have you lost your marbles?" Grull said, his eyes wide in astonishment. "We can't attack an army twice our size! They would massacre us!"

Jacoby looked up at the waning sunset as it drifted toward a moonless evening.

"Send the most vulnerable south, as planned. The new moon will veil their escape, providing them with the perfect cover," Jacoby asserted. "At dawn, when the undead are most vulnerable, we unleash our full force in a decisive assault. It would be the last thing they would expect."

For the first time, Nathaniel felt a glimmer of hope, gazing at Jacoby with admiration.

"I like it," Nathaniel said.

Grullach pondered the idea, turning it over in his mind. "I suppose it's preferable to just waiting here to meet my end."

THIRTY-ONE

Nathaniel tossed and turned in a fitful sleep, his mind caught in the whirlwind of a dream. In the illusion, he walked along a forest path, lined with twisted, thick trees, and cobbled with roots and stones that bruised his bare feet. The wind, whistling in gusts through the canopy, created eerie, unholy music. Where am I? The path ascended along a deep gorge, forested with thick evergreens on one side, and on the other a cliff dropped a thousand feet to a rocky gulch. He made his way up the steep cut, his breath coming in spurts, his heart racing. With his eyes stinging from sweat, Nathaniel caught his breath by a withered hickory tree, wiping the perspiration from his brow. He walked on, taking measured steps until the forest floor leveled out.

As the trees parted, a small clearing came into view, ending abruptly at the precipice of a cliff. A harsh wind lashed the evergreen branches, causing them to sway and thrash about like children signaling desperately for help. What is this place, and why am I here?

He walked to the cliff's edge and peered down into a rocky abyss, sending an icy shiver down his spine. Sweat bloomed over his back and neck, every nerve on alert. A buzz sounded above the wind's moan, increasing in volume as if Nathaniel had stumbled onto a wasp hive. From above the trees, an odd creature flew into the center of the glade, alighting in front of the king. The winged being, dressed in a black tunic, pants, and a feathered cap, stood three feet tall and had an Elvish, dark complexion. Translucent bee wings fluttered behind him, tucking against his back.

The tiny being bowed, "Hail to you, King Nathaniel Aarmon! Your ascent to the Taborian throne has been remarkable."

Nathaniel recognized the being as a sprite, known for their devious and unpredictable nature. Keeping his eyes locked onto the interloper, his hand slipped to the Founder's stone sword pommel. A mossy green light emanated from the stone, illuminating his palm with an otherworldly radiance.

"Who are you, and what can I do for a dark sprite?"

"Spoken like a true king! My name is Ertis'ah Anadsh, or Crowfeather in the common tongue," answered the sprite, showing no sign of hostility. "I mean you no harm. I am here to offer you aid."

"Aid?" Nathaniel said, raising one brow.

The sprite gestured patience with his hands up.

"First, M'lord, allow me to review your situation. The enemy forces outnumber yours many times over. Worse, you are unaware of the number of their reserves. Another orc-goblin-lupine army is mustering, nearly as large as that which you now face, with more undead soul-eaters. They will take three weeks to muster and arrive here. You will face a tidal wave of enemy troops, overwhelming and unstoppable."

Crowfeather paused a heartbeat and continued. "However, my Master can change all that."

"Nathaniel felt a twist in his stomach, and his eyes narrowed. "Your master? And who might that be?"

"Demon Lord Asmodeus. He is eager to offer you the services of five hundred soldiers, ready to be deployed at your command. By defeating Ravenite and securing Tabor, you would buy yourself three additional weeks to recover and prepare for the next wave of the enemy's attack, assuming they dare to return after such a setback."

"The same Asmodeus who has supported Ravenite with undead minions from the underworld? I think not," Nathaniel said in a disgusted tone, without hesitating. "Why would he offer us help now?"

"My Lord would see them fail."

Nathaniel chuckled. "Why?"

"A realignment of power between the Lords may occur in the ethereal plane," the sprite admitted. "One must do what is necessary."

Nathaniel was seeing the actual picture now. He, the Brotherhood, and Tabor would be chess pieces in a prideful game between competing underworld lords.

Nathaniel knew nothing came free, and he steeled himself before asking, "And what is the price your lord would have me pay?"

Crowfeather's brow creased, his expression sober. "A small matter compared to saving your friends, people, and kingdom. Sign a pact for your soul here, tonight, in blood, and all will be as you wish. You will save your kingdom; when you die, you will have a place of honor ruling under Lord Asmodeus."

Nathaniel chuckled, slicing through the tension on the windy clifftop. "The answer is no."

"You can name your price in treasure as well. Many hidden treasures still lie buried in unknown spots. I will show you where they are. Your power will be immense," the pixie added, greed burning in his eyes.

"No."

"Your Majesty, the enemy has surrounded the city and significantly increased their patrols. You must know any venture to escape will be fruitless," Crowfeather implored. "Everyone in the city will perish."

"I will take that chance. Return to your master with my answer," Nathaniel said. "May luck favor you, Ertis'ah Anadsh."

The sprite bowed and unfolded his wings but before flying away, said, "May you fare well, King Nathaniel Aarmon."

Crowfeather turned away, ashamed, afraid his expression might betray the sadness he felt. *What is wrong with you, Crow? These emotions are unnatural, and if Lord Asmodeus learned of them, you'd face ten thousand years of torture.* But something about this young king intrigued him. *Was it his resemblance to his ancestor, Whitestar, in honor and bearing?* Something in the young king's manner and tone ignited confidence. A long-forgotten sliver of decency inside Crowfeather seemed to grow with each minute in the young man's presence. The pixie felt an urgent tingle in his black heart to follow the king, making him very uneasy. *Have I grown soft over the millennium?*

He took a deep breath, easing it out slowly. All too soon, King Nathaniel would be gone, and more corruptible leaders would take his place. But for today, he brought a long-awaited freshness to Tabor. *Maybe he could survive if given a bit of help.*

With a furtive glance from side to side, as if sharing a closely guarded secret, Crowfeather confided in Nathaniel, "Your enemies, Your Majesty, fear the Founder's stone you possess far more than you can imagine. Like a banshee's cry echoing across the lonely moors, the stone whispers their names among the Lost."

A mischievous glint sparked in Crowfeather's eyes as he offered a sly smile. *That should be vague enough to avoid my Lord's anger.* As he buzzed away, Nathaniel watched the tiny figure disappear on the horizon, left with a burning desire to know more.

Waking with a start, Nathaniel sat up in bed, his sheets soaked with sweat, the dark sprite's words echoing in his mind.

The morning sun cast a golden hue over the horizon, its rays illuminating Nathaniel as he stood before the assembled warriors, a group that comprised men, women, young adults, and members of the Brotherhood. The king, only a few hours prior, had commanded the city's most endangered residents to evacuate, appointing the elder Bullfinch as their leader to guide them to safety. Numerous citizens had ground their teeth, refusing to leave their homes until the King himself begged them to do so. Now, facing the shattered remnants of the Taborian resistance, he must rally the soldiers that were left, inspiring them for the ultimate battle.

"You have poured every drop of your energy into defending our home over these past two days, and because of your valiant efforts, we have inflicted significant casualties upon the enemy. But our costs have been high." Nathaniel's voice faltered momentarily, his words heavy with emotion as he said, "We have lost friends, relatives, land, and homes—all things we held dear."

The king inhaled deeply and released a slow breath, the tension in his neck and shoulders relaxing. "The enemy may believe they've broken us, hungrily waiting outside the gate to finish Tabor. Despite the challenges, we remain unified, unwavering in our commitment, and prepared to fight with everything we have to defeat them."

Nathaniel drew in a full breath, then exhaled with a measured, steady release.

"One hour from now, the gates will open, and I will lead this army into the dark heart of the enemy, striking a final blow for the light of Tabor."

The weight of his next words hung in the air as Nathaniel hesitated. "Who will follow me? We fight not for Tabor's glory, but for our families. Our homes. Our very existence as a people!"

The citizen militia erupted in cheers, and the soldiers, as one, slammed the flat of their swords against their shields in a cacophonous symphony of allegiance.

"Let us prepare and let no obstacles stand in our way. We will only truly eliminate the threat of the undead spawn, giants, and lupine by conquering the lich-mage, Ravenite, and leaving him defeated at our feet."

The evil sorcerer Crepitus, in a secluded part of Curth Talem, chanted the incantation over the scrying pool, waiting with anticipation for the images to manifest. Expecting the usual change in the water's surface from silvery black to a cloudy white, he became concerned when nothing happened. Undeterred, he tried once more, raising his voice as he spoke the words. He held his breath, his heart pounding with anticipation, yet the silence remained unbroken. The sorcerer, bewildered, took a step back, his brow furrowed in a deep frown as he struggled to comprehend what was happening.

He pondered the situation for several minutes, furrowing his brow as he tried to unravel the mystery of what could interfere with the magical communication. The oval, birdbath-like conduit had always been reliable; however, as he stood before it, reciting the incantation again, nothing happened. No response, no spark of energy - his sorcery remained unconnected to the magical plane. It was as if the conduit had become a mere decoration, devoid of its magical purpose. Perplexed, he racked his brain, searching for any reason for the disturbance. Had he missed a step in the incantation? Was there some external force interfering with the flow of magic? He couldn't find any logical explanation for the sudden breakdown in communication.

Determined to sort this out, he took a deep breath and stepped closer to the conduit, examining it for any signs of damage or tampering. But it appeared to be perfectly intact. Gritting his teeth, he rubbed his temples, feeling the weight of the situation pressing upon him.

"Asmodeus' breath!" he swore, sweeping away the scrying tool with his arm and smashing it to the floor. A vine of burning anger snaked up his body, bringing with it scorching heat. He needed an update from Ravenite on his success in the annihilation of Tabor. Having been informed earlier about the catastrophic failure of his eastern army's assault on Tajman Sghur, he craved some positive news. So why couldn't he connect with his subordinate?

An idea struck him, and immediately he seized a knife and walked toward the middle of the room. In a swift movement, he dragged the knife across his palm, creating a deep, gaping wound. As blood gushed from the wound, he collected it, first forming a circle of blood. Standing in the middle of the circle, he drew a pentagram and then carefully stepped away from its center. He let out a low chant, the incantation swirling in the air, and held his breath as he awaited the outcome. Following a moment of silence, a sulfurous cloud exploded from the star's core. As the foul-smelling cloud of rotten eggs cleared, a gray-hued imp, resembling a creature of nightmares, perched in the center of the pentagram, its eyes gleaming with malevolence.

"My Master wishes to know what you require."

"My dark magic fails me. What ails it?" Crepitus said.

Gripped by a sudden, intense pain, the imp squeezed its head with both its tiny, clawed hands as if overcome by a migraine. He convulsed and coughed, then wheezed out, "One uses Luster magic to block your way. Twenty souls as payment for your weakness and twenty more to channel my master's power."

Crepitus' rage erupted, and with a sudden, violent motion, he lashed out, grabbing the imp by the throat. On the verge of squeezing, a bolt of lightning erupted from his hand, sending the sorcerer sprawling. The blast hurled him like a rag doll through the air, and he slammed into the unforgiving stone wall with a bone-jarring thud.

"Be cautious, mortal, about who you choose to offend, for your words may have unintended consequences," the imp hissed, his eyes glowing with malevolent delight. "Your actions now warrant a greater price. One hundred souls will be the cost for your transgression."

Crepitus stood up, his eyes ablaze with fire. Not even a Demigorgon demon known for its cruelty would have treated him with such disrespect. However, he realized he required the help of the malevolent being. Releasing a deep breath, he apologized. "I apologize for my rudeness, Special One. I ask, only because of my urgent need to speak with my lieutenant. How can I overcome this obstacle?"

Silence stretched out, punctuated only by the frantic rhythm of Crepitus' beating heart, before the imp, with a hesitant breath, spoke. Gesturing with his arm, he opened his palm to reveal a small bag. The imp, his voice devoid of humor, squeaked out, "Make your payment," emphasizing the need for immediate action. "Then dissolve the Homonculous blood into the divining pool."

Crepitus bowed and, with a quick movement, took the pouch from the imp. The monster, with a last puff of yellow, acrid smoke, disappeared into the air.

The sorcerer held the pouch in his hand, hating to have groveled to the Demon Lord but also feeling more secure that he could connect with Ravenite. He felt a nagging twist of concern in his gut, his intuition screaming something significant was afoot.

He dismissed the matter as trivial, then approached the door and summoned the castle marshal. The required tribute, a payment of one hundred orc souls, was due without delay.

Yet, the feeling lingered, gradually eating away at his inner peace.

"Have a company of orcs enter the ancient pit outside the castle, by force if needed."

In anticipation of the coming battle, Nathaniel's army of ragtag soldiers and citizen militia was busy sharpening their weapons to prepare for the coming attack. A chilling atmosphere of fear enveloped the group, each member preparing for the worst-case scenario, and a grim expectation hanging heavy in the air. Concurrently, their king was engaged in the solemn task of drafting his last will. In a letter addressed to the remaining citizens of Tabor, he urged them to continue fighting, hoping they could one day return to their home. With a dramatic flourish he penned, You carry the blood of a hundred generations within you, emphasizing the weight of history and ancestry. Even if it requires a century, commit to recolonizing Tabor. When the time is right, the people will choose a new ruler from the Taborian lineage who will listen to their needs.

Nathaniel laid down his quill, satisfied with the letter, signed and sealed it with his signet ring and wax. Nausea churned in his stomach, and a heavy cloak of guilt weighed him down, a constant reminder of the lives that would be lost in the inevitable conflict. He shook the thoughts from his mind, resigned now to whatever fate the Norns weaved. There would be no turning back, whatever the results.

Just as he secured his sword, a faint, almost imperceptible, blare of horns seemed to reach him on the wind, causing a shiver down his spine. With a sense of urgency, Nathaniel dashed to the window, craned his head outward, and inclined one ear to hear the faintest sounds carried on the breeze.

Nothing.

Looking out from his tower room, he saw the enemy; hundreds encamped across the Taborian plain, while others had taken positions in the lower and middle baileys and gathered in large numbers at the castle gate. Was it possible that they were the originators of the horns, or could there have been another source?

From deep within the Horn Wood, he heard the faint, pulsating blast of horns once more, but the source remained hidden from view. Did those horn sounds signal friendship, or did they warn of approaching enemies? He thought he could hear the hollow drumbeats from another area in the wood, as if they were a secret reply to the sharp, commanding sound of the brass. Are two armies joining forces? Could the enemy have divided, one half flanking the castle to cut off any escape?

The king's thoughts wrestled with hope for miraculous intervention, a desperate wish battling the bitter knowledge that no such salvation was coming. He slapped his hand against the cold, damp stone sill, the rough texture jarring against his skin, and shook his head. Please. Please be a sign of help. But he heard nothing more than the wind whistling through the cracks and resigned himself to the truth. No help was coming.

The weight of his despair was a heavy millstone, and as he turned to leave the tower, he cast one last glance westward over the expansive canopy of hardwoods. A sudden, intense glare of reflected sunlight forced him to instantly shield his eyes, the white light nearly painful. What in Odin's name? The mirrored reflection flickered, a distorted image dissolving into a thousand sparkling fragments before vanishing, leaving only the dappled morning sunlight on the dark green trees. For a few moments, the torchlight flickered back to life before its final extinction.

A signal light?

Had he imagined it?

Nathaniel rubbed the weariness from his eyes, but the light never reappeared. He pondered if he had dreamt the vision, then realized the drumbeats had stopped, too. It occurred to him the light flickered in a pattern, long-short-short-long. It's not a random combination, but a clear signal! Considering it further, he realized someone had directed the message toward the king's tower. Toward him. A warning? Or arriving help?

Could it be?

A subtle shift occurred within him; a kernel of hope took root, bringing a warmth he hadn't felt in days. Nathaniel's vision cleared, the path forward illuminated by a sudden rush of clarity and purpose. The seed's growth mirrored his burgeoning optimism, and suddenly, his next steps became clear.

He rushed down to the courtyard where the army and the Brotherhood waited. He reached Jacoby and Grull, explaining what had happened.

"I could have sworn I heard sounds in the distance earlier," Grull remarked.

"I didn't hear them," admitted Jacoby. "Are you sure?"

"Yes. I think it's a signal that help is coming," Nathaniel said confidently.

"Help from whom?" asked Jacoby, one brow raised.

"I don't know, but the flashing lights couldn't be random."

"What flashing lights?"

"I saw a reflection coming from the woods. I went in a pattern."

Jacoby's dubious gaze lingered on Nathaniel for what seemed like an eternity before a long sigh escaped his lips. Lacking any means to confirm the account, he recognized the genuine conviction in Nathaniel's recounting of what he had witnessed.

"We can hope for the best," Jacoby said, his jaw tight, a steely glint in his eyes. "Now it's time to bring the fight to Ravenite. I'll spread the word."

The tall man moved from one group of soldiers to the other, passing on the news and ending with the guards at the gate. To make their attack a surprise, the crossbars would need to be removed as quietly as possible before attacking.

A wave of warmth, like sunlight, spread up Nathaniel's arm as Lani's soft, reassuring hand found his. Her pale and drawn face betrayed the nervousness she felt as their eyes met, and a tremor in her chin amplified her trepidation. Leading her away from the others to a quiet courtyard shaded by ancient trees and fragrant with jasmine, he pulled her into a tender embrace.

Pulling back, her arms outstretched, she lowered her head, unable to meet his gaze. Deep down, she had always known that this moment would arrive. But in her heart, a deep and fervent desire existed to delay this day for eternity, a yearning to escape the approaching moment and its implications. A tornado of emotions ripped through her, a tumultuous force that never ceased its relentless assault, leaving behind only fear, anxiety, and a sense of impending dread. In truth, the reality of their past year had been a relentless series of battles, punctuated by intermittent casualties as they fought to survive. After so many months of endless travel and fighting, she had grown fatigued. She yearned for a peaceful life with Nathaniel, far from this war and the complexities of ruling a power like Tabor. Beneath the mask of exhaustion, a chilling fear surfaced, its icy tendrils wrapping around her heart like a venomous snake. Deep down, she needed to be sure they were safe, far from evil mages, gruesome creatures, and assassins. But a pragmatic assessment of the situation quickly replaced her initial emotional desire; her heart's yearning, she knew, was ultimately just a fantasy. Sadly, certain wishes remain unfulfilled, despite our strongest desires. For her and Nathaniel, the road ahead, fraught with peril and challenge, ultimately led to a decisive confrontation and hopeful victory over the villainous Ravenite and his wicked minions.

Nathaniel lifted her chin, his hand searching her eyes for the hidden thoughts and feelings within.

"Are you ready?" he asked, knowing she wasn't.

"I... I'm afraid." Tears welled in her eyes, and her face paled.

"Me too," Nathaniel said with a smile. "You know our path lies through that gate."

Unable to speak, she emitted a whimpering sound, her throat swollen with emotion. She witnessed the urgency in his eyes, ready to lead the charge against Ravenite. This would be their end.

She cleared her throat enough to croak, "What about us?"

He gazed at her with loving eyes and whispered, "You and I are one, and nothing, not even death, can separate us."

His words ignited a fire of confidence inside her. Whatever happened, they would be together, in life or death.

She pulled his lips to hers and kissed him with all the passion she had inside. Then, she grabbed his hand and led him toward the waiting army.

"Together," she whispered.

THIRTY TWO

Near the imposing castle gates, Jacoby gathered the members of his Brotherhood. He hugged each individual, taking the time to look each one in the eyes and convey his sincerity through this personal connection.

"Our shared history, filled with its fair share of difficulties and successes, culminates in this, our greatest challenge, which we will face united. No matter what twists and turns today may hold, always know that I cherish you, and my appreciation for everything you have done to get us here is eternal and unwavering. Without the support and help of each one of you, Nathaniel and I could never have completed this arduous journey. Thank you."

Grull slapped him on the back. "Don't get all blubbery on us, Jacoby!"

Jacoby grinned, but his face flushed with color.

In a tone thick with emotion, Nathaniel stated, "I want to add my voice to what Jacoby has said. My family, in the truest sense of the word, is the Brotherhood; you are my closest friends and most trusted allies. And as a family, we face this last hurdle together. I would also like to thank Allai'nn, Rue, and Lani for their extraordinary dedication as healers, cooks, caregivers, and steadfast companions. We would not have survived without you."

With a bear hug he enveloped Lani and Jacoby, and then, one by one, each of the other members joined the embrace until every person shared in the group hug. No words passed between them, and none were necessary; silent tears flowed freely down their cheeks, resembling a cascading stream.

"Now to business," Nathaniel said in a lighter tone, pulling away and wiping his eyes with his cuff. "Our best chance of success will be to cut the head off the snake. Stay together. We must destroy both Sin and Ravenite."

Everyone in the group nodded, determination mirrored in their eyes.

Allai'nn pulled Grull aside, as did Rue with Blue Ivy, to offer one last goodbye embrace.

"Come back to me," the elf princess whispered, unsure if either would return. Grull smiled and kissed his wife, mirrored by Blue to Rue.

"We'll be back by suppertime," he said with a wink.

Blue could only nod. Upon his shoulders, he bore the weight of a hollow foreboding, a sense of emptiness and impending doom that clung to him like a heavy blanket. Although he attempted to conceal his emotions, his facial expression reflected Rue's own, betraying his inner feelings. The cruel words that his father, the Regent Green Oak of the Heartwood, had thrown at him during their last heated argument echoed in his mind: "Prove to me you deserve my pride! You're a Timber elf prince, for Odin's sake."

His life, a dramatic arc of daring deeds and reckless mistakes, propelled him toward an ultimate end as either a triumphant hero or a shameful coward. A chilling sense of doom washed over him; sweat, cold and clammy, beaded on his forehead as a rising tide of nausea threatened to overwhelm him. His confidence seemed nonexistent, his eyes betraying a deep-seated fear that went beyond mere battle anxiety.

His hand trembled as he struggled to belt on his sword until he felt the warmth of Rue's hand on his. She finished cinching his belt for him and pulled him into a fierce embrace.

"I love you, Blue Ivy! You will come back to me," she demanded, her tone firm.

"Of course," he said, her words like a tonic for his confidence. He hurried over to the other Brotherhood, who waited by the gate.

The soldiers congregated at the gate, the Brotherhood at their head. Jacoby nervously rechecked his weapons. He had sharpened each to a razor's edge, including the Wizardeath dagger given to him by the Elyran King, Goldbrier. Now he waited.

This was the time he had always disliked, a time he dreaded. In the anticipation of battle, there is always that dull, expectant sliver of time, that space between feeling prepared and when the fighting begins. As he waited, the butterflies in his stomach increased, growing more and more frantic with each passing moment. Throughout his life, the tall warrior had always adhered to a strict code of pragmatism, shaping every decision and action according to its tenets. Of course, that didn't mean he lived free of doubt or dread. Just like every other man, he secretly struggled with several fears. The fear of losing a friend or loved one. The potential for a catastrophic injury. And the chilling fear of one's inevitable demise.

Despite the inherent dangers and uncertainties of war, he approached each battle, understanding that, to a significant degree, his destiny was in his own hands.

The lessons and guidance from his initial drill sergeant, a person who also acted as a mentor, remained vivid in his memory. "Plan meticulously and attack with the aggression of a berserker. That's your best shot at survival."

The words, etched into his memory during his time serving in the Taborian military, had been with him throughout his entire career. During the many brutal battles of the past two years, his powerful will to live and protect the people he cared about allowed him to overcome the challenges they faced.

Today will be one of those days.

He worried not for himself but for Nathaniel.

Whatever happens, I will defend him to my dying breath.

He watched his brother prepare for the coming conflict with pride. He will be a wonderful king. And you, Jacoby, will make sure he survives to live out that destiny.

With a raised arm Nathaniel signaled eight men positioned beside three enormous, brimming copper pots which sat atop the gate wall, where several archers also stood ready near lit braziers. As Nathaniel dropped his arm, two of the men quickly pulled open the coverings to the murder holes, while the remaining six followed suit, all of them efficiently tipping bubbling oil through the narrow slots. The morning air was rent by screams and wails as the boiling oil fell on the enemy below. After another wave from Nathaniel, the bowman lit oil-soaked rags on their arrow tips and shot them down through the holes, causing the entire stoop to ignite.

With a wave of Jacoby's hand, dozens of archers lining the keep's battlements unleashed a volley of arrows into the enemy ranks, aiming at will. The blazing oil and silver arrows raining down created utter pandemonium among the enemy ranks. A multitude of giants and ogres camped at the gate ran about frantically, their skin burning in a futile effort to extinguish the flames. In a scene of immense suffering, the stomping, rolling monsters crushed dozens of the smaller soldiers around them, their agonized writhing a testament to their pain.

"Now is the time to attack," Grull declared.

Jacoby stepped forward and raised his sword in salute. "For King Nathaniel and Tabor!" He shouted.

As one, the soldiers and civilians raised their weapons and shouted, "For King Nathaniel and Tabor!"

The monstrous gates swung open, and the Taborians charged forward, led by King Nathaniel and the Brotherhood. Half-sleeping, the unsuspecting enemy was overwhelmed by the fierce and sudden onslaught of the army, caught in a maelstrom of flashing steel. The attackers cut through waves of undead minions, orcs, goblins, and wolves with brutal efficiency, leaving scores of the enemy slain in their wake. Unprepared for such an effective and ferocious attack, the live enemies' morale crumbled, and many broke and ran, only to be cut down by a group of hobgoblins and hoborcs led by Commander Sin and Ravenite.

The lich-mage sat tall in the saddle of his mount, raised his skeletal arms, and mouthed an incantation. "La minotu te reygalto."

As the air crackled ominously with electricity, the sounds of battle were suddenly and violently interrupted by a series of bloodcurdling howls emanating from beyond the castle walls, immediately followed by a relentlessly rhythmic, bone-jarring thump, thump, thump that echoed through the earth and into the very foundations of the ancient structure. The growing intensity of the sound caused a lull in the fighting as both sides heard what was approaching, listening closely as the sound grew louder and louder. At that precise moment, a catastrophic explosion ripped through the middle bailey wall, resulting in a chaotic shower of stone, bricks, and dust that filled the air, obscuring everything in a thick cloud. Before the dust had even settled, an astonishing sight unfolded as twenty-foot-tall, bizarre creatures, unlike anything ever seen before, burst through a weak point in the wall, charging at full speed into the heart of the battle. With their bodies covered in bushy reddish-brown hair, these titans resembled bears, possessing bloodshot beady eyes and snouts, and they carried enormous clubs that were as large as small trees.

In a flash of recognition, Nathaniel saw at once that these adversaries were not the usual giants or trolls but a different and unexpected foe.

"Odin's beard! They look like Woodwoe," he heard Blue Ivy scream.

Woodwoe? Nathaniel scanned his memory for what he had read about the beasts. Were these the half-wood, half-flesh monsters his ancestor, King Whitestar, had battled? He had no time to consider it, for the beasts had arrived on tree-trunk legs, their massive arms swinging their clubs in wide arcs of destruction.

The enemy warriors, inspired by their leaders and the Woodwoes' arrival, rallied and counter-attacked. Suddenly, the

Brotherhood were again fighting for their lives against overwhelming numbers. Jacoby sensed the tide turning and felt the urge to reach Nathaniel. He cut down a raging orc that charged at him with a slash, then scanned the battlefield for his brother. Jacoby only had a few seconds to gaze about before an undead warrior came at him from the side. He hacked the monster down with a quick stab to the gut, but two more took his place. He had seen that Nathaniel wasn't far away, but unreachable as wave upon wave of enemy warriors attacked.

"Fall back in order!" shouted the king to his troops, knowing that by facing such a massive enemy force, any attempt to flee would have resulted in immediate death. Faced with the danger of being outflanked, his only option was to order a tactical withdrawal. The onslaught continued, many of the enemy destroyed by the silver weapons, but their vast numbers caused the ranks of Taborians to dwindle as more and more of them fell, succumbing to the relentless attack driving them back. Hope appeared lost to the darkness, but then, a sudden and wonderful intervention occurred, changing everything.

From afar, the heartening sounds of pealing Elven bells, powerful blaring horns, and the resonant beat of drums heralded the imminent arrival of a rescuing army. Charging into view, King Polaris led hundreds of elf warriors to storm the bailey, fracturing the enemy lines and causing chaos in their broken formations. Right behind them followed a large and diverse group of animals, including ferocious tawny panthers and savage shaggy bears, as well as swift leopards, bellowing wildebeests, and tusked feral hogs. Augustus fearlessly commanded a contingent of smaller animals — beavers, wolverines, badgers, and even pythons — who together inflicted a devastating mauling upon their enemies. On one flank, a combined force of centaur and faun archers unleashed a barrage of burning arrows at the Woodwoes, setting the monsters afire, complemented by the sporadic attacks of sylph warriors raining down volleys from the sky above.

The unexpected elf attack from behind completely surprised both Ravenite and his minions, leaving them wavering, vulnerable, and unprepared. Though twice as large as the allied forces, the sorcerer's army was experiencing significant fracturing amongst its ranks following the fresh attack.

Sin screamed obscenities at his warriors, cracking a long, barbed whip as encouragement to keep fighting. Ravenite, with his back to Sin, seemed aware but unphased by the attack. Calmly, he closed his eyes, raised his arms to the heavens, and resumed his sinister chanting.

"Sisters of the Seven Covens, come from the four corners of the world to our aid and dispatch our common enemies!" he shrieked loudly.

His eyes opened, his expression reflecting a sudden keen awareness of the battle's trajectory. His arms thrust forward in a sudden movement, vibrant blue spheres of fire erupting from each palm with astonishing speed and power. The unsuspecting animals and sylph archers became victims as a barrage of fireballs unleashed against them, the explosive force of the blasts decimating the bowmen and the smaller animals with fiery destruction.

King Polaris felt a sudden chill, the hairs on the back of his neck standing on end, his jaw clenching in a grimace of concern. The clash of steel and roar of battle drowned out the Lich-mage's words, but he could feel the chilling aura of dark magic radiating from the wizard. He scanned the ravaged landscape, the heavy air thick with smoke and burnt earth, and watched in horror as Ravenite's attack forced the animal line to dive for cover. The chaos allowed several lumbering Woodwoes to strike, their massive clubs and limbs crushing the helpless animals.

I've got to do something!

With his eyes closed, he summoned his magic, a vibrant energy crackling beneath his skin. He wiped the sweat from his brow, and he channeled the surging magical torrent toward the animal line, who were desperately trying to avoid the evil mage's fiery explosions. With a powerful thrust of his arms, he unleashed a vibrant green beam of light, engulfing the group in a shimmering, protective sphere of magic. The Woodwoes within the sphere froze, wailing in agonizing pain as their bark and cambium peeled in layers until nothing but ruined heartwood remained.

With a roar, Ravenite intensified his attacks, his face contorted in a mask of furious rage, but his blows only sparked against the unyielding, imbued shield. Frustrated, he diverts his attention elsewhere, unleashing a barrage that sent Taborian and Elven soldiers sprawling across the battlefield.

Before Polaris could direct more protection, a black-furred lupine crashed into him, the impact sending him sprawling on the ground. The elf king rolled violently to the turf, the impact jarring his senses and sending his sword soaring through the air. Defenseless and with his head swimming, he struggled to his feet.

"How nice, a royal Elven snack," the lupine snarled and charged.

A terrifying panic gripped Polaris, and time seemed to slow as he watched the monster pounce. His attempts to conjure magic failed as the colossal monster thunders toward him. He closes his eyes, a wave of nausea washing over him as he waited for the inevitable death blow. But at that moment, a bloodcurdling howl pierced the air, and he felt the icy rush of air as the lupine's body hurtled past. The beast crashed to the ground, silenced by a sword piercing deep into its side. Grullach stood over the dead beast, his breath ragged, as he pulled his sword free, and turned toward the elf king.

"Polaris, are you alright?"

"By the gods! Your timing saved my life, Grull," Polaris said, catching his breath. "I'm fine."

The halfling winked and sprinted back into the fight.

Simultaneously, like a startled flock of ravens emanating from the direction of the forest, dark shapes materialized in the sky above and swiftly approached the battle. Within minutes, dozens of black-robed witches, their hair blowing wildly in the wind, rocketed from the sky, swooping in to attack the allied forces along the ground. Each witch sat atop a broom and carried a Morningstar mace and light crossbow. Some hovered above the battle, shooting down rival flying sylph warriors. Some fell to Elven arrows, while others landed and, wielding their maces, charged into the fray. The results tipped the scales of the battle, driving the allied attack back after terrible casualties on both sides.

With the Taborians, elves, and animals in slow retreat, maniacal war cries split the air from behind the enemy's position. Hundreds of enormous green-skinned black mountain hoborcs riding quad-horned giant lizards collided with the enemy army from the south. Wearing a long-feathered headdress, Torque, the supposed weapons thief the Brotherhood rescued from the Horn wood, led the attack atop a six-legged lizard wielding a massive war club. Without warning, the orcs slammed into the unprepared enemy, trampling many and slicing through the wizard's forces.

With the numbers on both sides now equal, a barbaric battle of attrition raged for a full hour between the four armies; each side showed equal ferocity and determination to gain victory, resulting in a brutal and prolonged fight.

As the enemy forces surrounding Ravenite dwindled and more of them were cut down, Jacoby caught sight of Nathaniel moving rapidly to engage the lich mage in a surprise attack from behind. He instantly grasped that the tactic, if successful, would eliminate the monstrous lich mage and cripple the enemy's power.

Seizing the opportunity, Jacoby shouted, "Rally to the king!" a call to arms for his fellow Brotherhood. He fought his way forward to reach Nathaniel, cutting down two goblins in his path. As the enemy forces surrounding Sin and Ravenite thinned, Nathaniel and the rest of the Brotherhood confronted the malevolent commanders in a climactic showdown, the fate of the kingdom riding upon their success.

With his blade emitting an ominous, fiery blue-green glow, Nathaniel lunged toward the wizard's back, aiming for a decisive blow. A mere second before impact, Commander Sin jumped in front of Ravenite, deflecting the blow with a spectacular display of sparks erupting as metal clashed against metal. The malevolent warrior, carrying a sword of orange flames, then charged Nathaniel with a storm of lunges and slashes, pressing the young king back. Nathaniel used every skill he had to dodge the flurry of attacks, but the attack was relentless. Keeping Nathaniel on the defensive, the demon hurled a barrage of stabs and hacks until a whipping slash caught the king with a vertical slice along the left forearm. The immense force of the blow caused the young king to lose his balance, nearly dropping his sword as his hand instinctively slid down the pommel, coming to rest upon the Founder's Stone.

Without warning, a potent bolt of energy shot through Nathaniel's body, causing him to feel an electric surge. In a mere instant, his confidence returned, banishing any previous self-doubt. Subsequently, in a display of unforeseen precision, he executed a masterful thrust, transitioning into an aggressive whirlwind of lunges and stabs.

Even with the inherent magical power of his demon blood coursing through him, Commander Sin was no match for Nathaniel's strength; in a moment of astonishing precision, Nathaniel twisted his wrist with impossible force, driving the sword deep into the demon's chest, the weapon sinking to its hilt. The monster shrieked, his voice that of souls enduring inhuman suffering, his essence disappearing in a cloud of sulfurous smoke.

The path to Ravenite proved difficult for Jacoby and Cor'in, as orcs and goblins continuously ambushed them at every turn, delaying their progress. They had struck down three enemies and were about to face the fireball-throwing mage when a Grau Mantel Lupine charged, striking them with such impact that it sent them sprawling. In a ferocious frenzy, Bloodcoat swiped and bit with snarling fangs at the warriors with savage intensity.

"Now you die!" he growled.

With a ferocious roar, the huge lupine charged forward, its claws slashing at both Jacoby and Cor'in simultaneously in a swift, brutal attack. With unearthly dexterity, the beast's three-inch claws raked the air, narrowly missing Jacoby as he dodged but caught Cor'in on the biceps with a swift, slashing movement. The mighty stroke sent the half-elf soaring through the air before he landed hard, a bleeding mess and his sword arm broken. He reached for a dagger with his left hand for defense, but his involvement in the fight had ended.

Bloodcoat's crimson eyes focused on Jacoby, and the monster bared his gleaming fangs, foamy drool dripping from its mouth. The beast feinted left and attacked from the right with a sweeping blow across the tall man's chest. The lightning-fast blow struck Jacoby before he could parry, raking across his chest armor and knocking him backward, his sword and the Wizardeath dagger flying. Pain exploded in his chest, cutting off his breath as he scrambled to reach his fallen weapons. In a single bound, Bloodcoat stood over the wounded human, the beast's predatory jaws snapping.

"Any last words?" the lupine hissed preparing to snap Jacoby's neck.

From nowhere, Lani emerged from the side, plunging her sword into the wolf's flank with all of her considerable strength. A yelp escaped Bloodcoat's lips as he reacted to the pain, launching himself into the air with a pained leap. Having turned to face Lani, the beast was a horrifying sight; its coat was stained with a scarlet liquid that dripped steadily to the ground. Jacoby stood next to her, his wide stance providing some needed stability, his chest armor blossoming crimson.

Badly injured and now confronted by a pair of enemies, the wolf weighed his options, his mind racing to devise a plan of escape or attack. Better to live to fight another day. Bloodcoat, his eyes aflame with frustration, spat blood and, with a sneer, bounded away through the gate.

Weakened and faint from blood loss, Jacoby fell to one knee. With swift movements, Lani tore open her bag, retrieved a handful of bandages, and pressed firmly over the wounds on Jacoby's chest to stem the bleeding.

"We have to help Nathaniel," he grunted, Lani's pressure sending immense pain through his chest..

"Don't move while I make a field dressing. Then we'll help him."

With remarkable speed, she wrapped the tall warrior's torso tightly with a generous amount of cloth. With the task finally finished, she helped him stand, and then they bravely moved forward to fight the sorcerer. At all costs, the monstrous lich had to be destroyed!

"Wait," Jacoby grunted through clenched teeth, his every breath agonizing. "I need to find my short sword King Goldbrier gave me." He scanned the area but couldn't see the sword.

"Forget it," Lani urged, pulling forward. "Nathaniel needs us."

Not far away, a challenging battle was taking place as Blue Ivy and Horatio desperately tried to subdue the unpredictable and dangerous shape-shifting witch Cas. As Ravenite unleashed a furious barrage of lightning bolts and fireballs from his palms, the monstrous Cat, a shapeshifter capable of altering its size at will, stood guard, its form shifting from a towering humanoid figure to a horrifying orange tabby cat of monstrous proportions. As Blue drew her attention with a frontal assault, he signaled Horatio to execute a strategic flanking maneuver. Much to their misfortune, the witch's head, through magical means, completed a 180-degree rotation, blocking any attempts to attack her from the side. The battle raged as the three engaged in a fierce exchange of vicious bites, slashes, and blows, the two Brotherhood warriors hacking and stabbing furiously, their blades flashing but finding little purchase against the feline witch's unnatural agility. Executing a skillful feint to the right, Blue's left jab struck the witch's left shoulder, taking her by surprise. However, in a swift and brutal counterattack, the beast unleashed a devastating blow that tore across Blue's belly. With a shriek of shock and agony, the elf cried out as blood bloomed across the belly of his tunic, a horrifying testament to the four deep wounds inflicted by the cat's claws.

The sight of the brutal attack triggered a violent berserker rage within the Anuran. With two powerful hops, the frogman launched himself onto the back of the feline, quickly securing one arm around its throat and using his other hand to pull his dagger. The

Anuran drove the honed blade deep into the monster's back and neck, black blood soaking his arm and spraying across the surroundings as the mighty beast bucked and rolled in a desperate struggle to throw him off. But no matter how much the monster bucked and squirmed, Horatio refused to let go, tightening his grip with one arm and stabbing with the other. After a frenzied struggle to free herself that seemed to last an eternity, the exhausted witch at last crumpled to the ground. Her final breath triggered a transformation; she reverted to her true self—an aged, withered crone, her garment and hair stained crimson.

Horatio, breathing hard, rushed over to Blue Ivy. The timber elf's eyes were glassy, and his skin pale.

"Help! Help!" Horatio screamed, but with the battle raging all around, no one heard. There's no one to help. What do I do? The frogman pressed his fingers against the elf's belly, feeling the warm, gurgling blood welling up beneath his touch. With no other choice but to save his friend from certain death, Horatio hoisted the elf onto his shoulder and, using his powerful legs, bounded in great leaps across the chaotic, blood-soaked battlefield toward the castle walls.

"Help!" he shouted, pushing his way into the makeshift hospital. Two attendants, followed by a brownie healer, rushed up. Upon seeing Blue Ivy being carried in, Healer Gruawane gasped in recognition.

"Quickly, in here," he ordered, guiding Blue's body into a side room where they laid him on a table. Gruawane pulled back the elf's tunic, blood oozing from four deep gouges from his chest down below his navel.

"By the Gods!" he exclaimed, his eyes flashed in horror. But the brownie returned to all business in a heartbeat, giving quick orders to his helpers.

"I need Taborian Brandy, the brazier, fresh honey and garlic, and needle and thread on the double," the small elf demanded. The brownie leaned in and whispered into Blue's ear, "Hold on, lad, I'll do everything I can."

When the attendant returned, Gruawane said, "Horatio, lift his head." He tilted the brandy, allowing some to dribble into Blue's mouth. The elf, though semi-conscious, swallowed. Gruawane then dowsed the elf's belly, and he screamed, "Argh!" before succumbing to the pain.

Then Gruawane pulled a thin knife from his leather apron, heated it in the orange brazier coals until bright red, then ran the blade gently along the length of each gouge, cauterizing the bleeding and leaving only charred stripes across the elf's belly. Then, he began the arduous work of stitching the wounds, followed by applying the garlic honey paste.

"I need to get back to the fight," Horatio said, his emotions battling over staying to help, or continue fighting.

Gruawane glanced with tired eyes over his half-moon spectacles, sweat beaded on his brow. "You've done all you can here, lad. Thank you for saving Blue," Gruawane said, continuing to stitch the opposing edges of the first laceration. "And may the gods protect you."

Relieved by the healer's words, Horatio bolted out of the room and toward the infirmary door, but after only a few steps plowed into Rue, knocking bandages and herbs in the air.

"Oh, my!" the oread said, regaining her balance. "Why don't you watch where...Horatio, is that you?"

For a heartbeat, the frogman and oread stared at each other, Horatio's words catching in his throat. Rue focused on the fresh maroon stains and dried blood covering Horatio's armor, and her eyes grew large.

"Are you wounded?" she said, reaching out for him, but he stepped back, holding up his hands.

"I'm okay. I just need to get back to the fight."

Rue's features clouded, and her chest tightened. "Is it Blue?" she said, her lips trembling.

Tears welled in the frogman's eyes, his words strangling from the lack of air in his throat. "Uh... ask your father," was all he could muster. "I'm sorry, Rue. They need me..." He wanted to explain but couldn't find the words. Instead, he brushed past her and out of the door.

Once outside, Horatio took long, deep breaths, regaining his composure. "I won't let them get away, Blue," he said to himself and, with a grim determination, charged back into the fray, cris-crossing the battlefield toward the lich-mage.

He reached Lani just as she worked to staunch Jacoby's bleeding wounds. The Anuran grasped the immensity of the situation as the scarlet blossom over Jacoby's chest enlarged.

"I can't stop the bleeding," she said, her eyes imploring. "He needs a healer."

Horatio's gaze hardened; his expression serious.

"I'll take care of him. Help me lift him on my back."

Lani and Horatio each took an arm and hoisted their semi-conscious friend onto his shoulder. The tall human weighed at least forty pounds more than Blue Ivy, and the Anuran struggled under the weight. Lani used Jacoby's belt to secure him, then Horatio pushed off and once more leaped off to deliver his wounded brother to Gruawane. Halfway to the infirmary, Horatio hesitated as he passed Allai'nn, dressed in her armor and carrying a short sword.

"Wait," he called out. "Jacoby's hurt."

Allai'nn stopped and examined Jacoby's wounds and shook her head. "He needs more than I can offer. Quickly, take him to Gruawane."

"What about you?"

"I'm not letting anyone I love die today," she said resolutely, her eyes as hard as stone. With the swiftness of a whisper, she melted into the thick of the fighting, as Horatio hopped on to get Jacoby's aid.

With the other Brotherhood out of the fight, Nathaniel, Grull, and Lani spread out to face the lich mage alone. His decaying face twisted into a crooked sneer. Ravenite glared at his attackers with malevolent hatred. He had seen his lover, Cas, fall, and a boiling rage consumed him. This unworthy king has been a thorn in my side for too long! I owe him a slow, torturous death for taking my beloved Cas. And without the elf princess's magic to aid him, my power will be unmatched.

"I've toyed with you enough, young Aarmon. Time for you and your friends to die!" the mage bellowed.

Unable to control his rage, he gestured with a twist of his wrist, red crackling energy dancing between the fingers. He muttered words under his breath and a barrage of spells shot toward the attackers. Lani, hit by a sleep spell in full swing of her sword, crumpled in a heap. Horatio froze in mid-stride, covered in a sheet of thick ice. Only Nathaniel seemed unharmed. Covered in an orange protective glow from the Founder's stone, the lightning blast the wizard directed at him bounced off. Ravenite's eyes widened, but he gritted his teeth and doubled his effort. More spells struck the protective barrier as Nathaniel charged, his sword back and arm coiled like an asp ready to strike. Balls of fire, crackling lightning bolts, and acid balloons slammed into Nathaniel's barrier but ricocheted off, striking friend and foe alike.

The cacophony of the battle faded, time itself seeming to slow as the two opponents found themselves alone, engaged in a macabre struggle for their very lives. The young king, desperate to strike the wizard, slashed and stabbed with his sword, but to no avail, as the lightning-quick wizard would vanish from one place and reappear in another. With a single word of incantation, a nasty long sword appeared in Ravenite's hand. With magical precision, the wizard attacked, alternating using both swords and spells. The barrage pummeled the king, pushing him back, allowing only the rare opportunity to strike himself. The magical-powered attack took its toll on Nathaniel's defensive shield, slowly draining its power. But Ravenite's magic also waned until finally each adversary faced the other with swords alone.

For what seemed like an eternity, the two opponents engaged in a protracted and brutal fight, each blow met with an equally forceful counter, neither warrior able to secure a significant advantage. In a continuous exchange of attacks and defenses, the battle raged, culminating in a powerful close-quarters engagement, their hilts locked together and the other hand at each other's throat. The sorcerer's eyes burned into Nathaniel's with a menacing intensity, his foul breath a disgusting stench in the air. Ravenite pushed off with a fading movement. Nathaniel, his body exhausted, every muscle aching with the heavy toll of battle, turned toward the lich-mage to refocus his attention.

With a mischievous glint in his eyes, the wizard erupted in a boisterous laugh. "You're weakening, boy. Give up now, and I'll make your death quick."

"Not on your life, lich," retorted the young king, and launched another raking slice, but once again the wizard had vanished.

"Can't find me?" Ravenite mocked, reappearing and stabbing at Nathaniel's side. Summoning every ounce of strength and skill, the king parried with a diagonal movement at the very last moment, preventing the fatal blow from landing. He pivoted left and thrust his sword, catching the wizard with a nick to his forearm before the monster phased away.

"I grow weary of this exercise," the mage grunted, gazing at the tiny trickle of black blood oozing from the cut. "Time to finish this."

In a whirlwind attack, he drove Nathaniel back and, with a final feint, jabbed at the warrior's belly. The king partially deflected the blow, but not before the blade gashed his upper thigh.

"Aargh!" he grunted, his leg buckling to a knee.

Instead of launching the coup-de-gras, the wizard disappeared in a puff of smoke, leaving Nathaniel searching.

Ravenite crept behind him, raising his sword high to end Nathaniel with one powerful blow. At that moment, a shocking white light blinded the wizard, and the ground beside him exploded. The mage staggered backward, his vision blurring.

What in the demons just happened?

As his vision cleared, he saw Allai'nn's form, her hands thrust over her head, her stare as hard as granite. Above the battlefield, the sky had darkened with heavy storm clouds rumbling with thunder and flashes of lightning. Allai'nn's ice-blue eyes locked on Ravenite, and her body glowed with white light. Fear crept into the wizard's mind, his only thought, "YOU!"

As if reading his mind, Allai'nn smiled, her arms dropping, unleashing a furious storm of lightning bolts that crackled and roared from the purple clouds, incinerating enemy soldiers across the battlefield in a blinding flash. The impact was catastrophic, with most undead minions incinerated on the spot, and giants and trolls toppling like felled trees. The raging battle ceased abruptly, all eyes turning to the elf and wizard.

A bone-chilling shriek ripped from Ravenite's throat, his body convulsing as a blinding lightning bolt struck him. The lich-mage dropped his sword, his face contorted in agony, and fell to the ground. Ravenite stared in stunned confusion at the woman, his mind reeling from the unexpected turn of events, unable to process the sight before him.

How could this elf wield the power to defeat me? The thought sent a chill down his spine. "What have you done, girl?" he hissed, his voice laced with a mixture of fury and horror. He closed his eyes, a damaged, empty husk; his magic drained to zero.

But the elf just grinned, her eyes wild with a mixture of joy and madness. She turned and knelt at Nathaniel's side.

"Are you alright?" she asked in a whisper.

"Yes, but..."

At that moment, Nathaniel noticed the stone on the pommel of his sword glowing green. In one move, he shoved Allai'nn aside and drove his sword upward. The evil mage had feigned death, his sword poised to slice Allai'nn in two from behind. Nathaniel's sword, Blueblade, struck Ravenite mid-chest, the wizard's momentum driving the blade to the hilt. Ravenite's eyes bugged, and he staggered back, his sword falling from his hand.

For a heartbeat, Ravenite stared in disbelief, his mouth open in shock. Then he fell backward, his body leaden and unresponsive. A strange hardening spread through his limbs, the chilling feeling of stone replacing flesh as his legs and torso turned to solid rock. A terrible pain radiated through his body, and he took one last gasping breath before his skeletal remains disintegrating into dust.

A heavy silence, like the calm after a fierce storm, settled over the battlefield for a long moment before the situation suddenly shifted. With the mage's death, the remaining undead warriors froze, their magical connection severed. In an instant, the demon lord recalled their life force back to the underworld, and their lifeless husks crumpled into dust. The enemy—orcs, goblins, trolls, witches, and ogres—leaderless and in disarray, fled the bailey, their guttural screams ringing out as they desperately tried to evade Torque's insatiable hoborcs. With the war lost, the lupine rangers scattered in all directions, some scrambling up the walls to escape. Only the giants hesitated, their massive forms silhouetted against the fiery afternoon sun. A desperate scramble ensued as they rallied to their wounded king, Icebeard, before lifting their monarch and retreating. And what of the ancient Woodwoes? Living and dead, the beasts disappeared as if they had never existed.

Grull raced to Allai'nn and enveloped her in a bear hug. Kneeling beside Nathaniel, Lani pressed on his injured thigh to stem the flow of blood, her exhaustion evident. He cupped her face in his hand as tears streamed down her cheeks.

"Is it finally over?" she wept.

"Yes, the war is over. "Now life can really begin," Nathaniel whispered.

Across the continent, Crepitus felt a searing pain, like a bolt of fire, that shot through his chest and radiated across his torso in waves of intense agony. He gasped for air, his breath coming in ragged, short bursts, and the world swam around him, making him feel dizzy and disoriented. Clutching at his chest, he collapsed to the floor. What's happened? A deep, physical ache, living within the very core of his being, served as a poignant reminder of some as yet unknown catastrophe. Only one thing could be so devastating. Ravenite! A horrifying realization struck him; he knew with a sickening certainty that his protégé was gone, and his dreams of conquering the West were finally and irrevocably over.

Hours after the battle, Nathaniel hobbled along the hospital corridor of wounded soldiers, shaking hands, offering encouragement, and thanking them for their service. The king insisted that humans, elves, hoborcs, and talking animals all healed together in the same location, opening up the massive castle banquet hall for this use. After spending time with each warrior, he hobbled into the room at the corridor's end and opened the door to the courtyard leading to the mall. He walked down the path to the middle bailey, following the sound of wails and sobbing mourners. An expansive rectangular trench stretched the length of the field, surrounded by men with lighted torches, mourners, and officials recording the names of the fallen. Lining the grave in long rows were hundreds of different beings who had given their all for Tabor.

Nathaniel waded into the muddy pit, the iron stench of blood heavy in the air, studying the fallen's silent, dirt-caked faces. He recognized many of the Taborians, and some elves and animals, the numbers too high to count. Bowing his head low, the king mumbled a prayer to Odin, beseeching the All-Father to transport their souls to Asgard, where they would await the apocalyptic battle of Ragnarok. With a pang of sadness, he passed the bloodied bodies of Devon Ashoke and his faun companion Heroclus, their forms marred and bloodied, along with the young, kind jailer, Julius, and the grim figure of Ex-general Thorne. He walked past the lifeless bodies of King Goldbriar's bodyguard, Captain Nils, and beside him, Chamberlain Mydir, their eyes vacant and their skin pale in the afternoon light.

So much loss.

Nathaniel felt a constant, dull throbbing pain in his chest, and tears ran down his cheeks. A wave of anger washed over him as he witnessed the needless waste. Odin, please help me make their sacrifice worthy.

Nathaniel wiped away the tears with his hand and continued his somber walk among the fallen. He reached a group of animals and his heart shattered when he saw Augustus, the brave beaver, peacefully lying next to the faun, Cornelius, and two Drashok otter men.

So much loss. Was anything worth such a cost? These warriors believed so.

The months of war against Ravenite had devastated the land, cost hundreds of lives and destroyed innumerable farms, businesses, and homes. At one time, he had thought any price was worth paying to secure victory in this war; however, the sight of the carnage left in the battle's wake caused him to pause. For the past two years, Nathaniel's sole focus and concern had always been the Brotherhood's safety and well-being above all else. But as king, his concern had broadened drastically. He had fought at the side of these valiant warriors, and would carry the burden of their sacrifice with every decision he made from now on. Now, his attention must focus on creating a new Tabor. He would use the pain of his comrade's loss as the catalyst to lift Tabor, like a reborn Phoenix, from the ashes.

At the pit's end, he climbed out and stood next to his loyal assistant, Percival, a pensive look on his face, lost in thought.

"Must we, Your Grace?" the thin aide implored.

"We have no choice. We've allowed time for goodbyes, but if we wait much longer, disease will set in and further devastate the city," the king said.

Percival nodded slightly, his eyes red and puffy. "I knew many of the castle guards, although few recognized my existence," he admitted.

"We will not forget the sacrifice paid today," Nathaniel said, placing a comforting hand on Percival's shoulder. "Tomorrow, we'll start to rebuild what they fought so dearly for."

Nathaniel hesitated another moment, then gestured to the men on the perimeter of the trench. Simultaneously, they threw in bottles of quick oil that smashed among the corpses. Then the torchbearers tossed in their torches, and the trench exploded in flames.

With his head hung low and shoulders slumped, the king, without once glancing back, trudged on the weary path back to his castle. He entered the infirmary, passed down a darkened hallway, and entered a private room. The injured warrior lay in a solitary bed in the center of the room. Several figures hovered around the bed, some seated in chairs positioned close at hand, their presence a silent vigil.

Upon entering, Nathaniel took a deep breath and forced a smile onto his face, a thin mask to hide his profound sorrow.

"How's my favorite patient today?" he inquired, his tone lighthearted.

Allai'nn turned and gave the king a frown, her hands on her hips. "I thought I told you to stay off that leg. So much movement might split the stitches."

Nathaniel held up his hands in surrender. "Allai'nn, you know I need to be with the people, especially as Tabor mourns and heals."

With a sigh of exasperation, the elf princess conceded, "Very well, if you must. But I want that leg elevated later."

"Yes, Mother," Nathaniel teased, then turning to the diminutive brownie healer asked, "May I have an update, Master Gruawane?"

"Holding his own, Your Grace. I'll know more in the next forty-eight hours."

As Nathaniel approached the bedside, the smile on his face vanished, replaced by a look of worry that matched the somber expressions of those already gathered in the room. A worried group—the wounded and survivors Grull, Horatio, the heavily bandaged Jacoby and Cor'in, Lani, Torque, King Polaris, and the unexpected presence of Blue's father, Regent Green Oak—gathered around the bed, their arms crossed, brows furrowed in shared anxiety. Nathaniel felt a surge of dread as he saw a mix of admiration, worry, and unexpected fear in their eyes. He knew that look; it instantly brought back the day they'd tried to save Micah. Even with healers and magic, their dear friend died from similarly grievous wounds.

He grasped the sleeping patient's hand and squeezed it. Blue Ivy's eyes fluttered open.

"Hello," the Timber elf rasped, his throat dry as dust.

"Hello, Blue," Nathaniel said, distressed by his friend's sallow complexion. "How are you feeling?"

"Like a wagon drove over me and dragged me for a league," the elf whispered, but his lids became too heavy, and the dark took him.

The king frowned and, giving Blue Ivy's hand another squeeze, leaned in and whispered, "Heal well, my friend. I need you back, and so does Rue."

He released Blue's hand and turned to Gruawane. "I know you'll do whatever you can, Master Healer. The crown's resources are available for anything you need."

The brownie nodded. "Thank you, Your Grace. I'll do my very best to heal my future son-in-law."

"Son-in-law?" Nathaniel said with one brow raised.

"Despite his injuries, the darn fool had enough courage to pop the question right here in the infirmary," interjected Cor'in, his arm in a sling.

"Better late than never," Nathaniel said with a grin. "Congratulations, Gruawane, and to you, Regent Green Oak. I'm so happy for Rue and Blue Ivy. She will make a stunning bride."

"Rue lit up like a fire, before bursting into tears," added Horatio.

"Thank you, Your Grace. I could not be happier," he responded. And with the first smile Nathaniel had ever seen from the healer, he added, "And she will be a stunning bride!"

"Agreed!" Green Oak added.

"We have a lot to be thankful for," Nathaniel said, then reached out and squeezed Allai'nn's hand.

I never had a chance to thank you properly, Allai'nn. Your bravery saved my life. Maybe all our lives," Nathaniel said honestly. "Thank Odin, the Elven courage and magic runs deep in the Hŷnhasbren bloodline," he added with a grin.

Allai'nn wiped away tears as she pulled the king into an embrace.

"No one messes with Mama Bear's loved ones and lives," laughed Grullach.

At that moment, Rue and her mother, Byrgid, stepped into the room.

Nathaniel greeted the newcomers warmly, and everyone congratulated Rue and Byrgid on the coming nuptials.

"How is Blue?" she asked, worry etched in her expression.

"I can't speak for the healers, but Blue's as tough as they come," Nathaniel said, locking eyes with Green Oak. "I've got a strong feeling nothing would keep a hero like Blue from his mate."

Everyone chuckled, nodding in agreement. And with that, the heavy, worrisome clouds that hung in the room seemed to part. Nathaniel sensed the mood brightening as the group began to converse and jest with one another, their weariness forgotten in the anticipation of the approaching wedding. After a short time, Allai'nn, recognizing her patient's need for restorative rest, began shooing the Brotherhood out of the room.

"It's time to give Blue Ivy time to rest. So, shoo," Allai'nn said, motioning with her arms to leave. "All of you."

"Yes," agreed Nathaniel, squeezing Allai'nn's hand. "Let's celebrate the joyous news!"

The warriors filed out of the room, jubilant they had something wonderful to celebrate, leaving only Regent Green Oak alone with his son. Nathaniel, last to leave, overheard the regent lean over and say, "I love you, son, and am so proud of you. Heal quickly."

Finally! The old man has realized his son is worthy of his respect and admiration, something we've known for months. Nathaniel closed the door behind him, a smile crossing his face.

"Meet me in the library, and I'll have Percival open our best Taborian brandy," Nathaniel said to the group, winking at Jacoby before slipping away from the others. "I have a quick task and will meet you shortly."

The king found an exhausted Lani in the castle garden, enjoying a nap in the afternoon sun. He gently touched her arm, awakening her.

"Hello," Nathaniel said, slipping his hand into hers.

"Hi," she said groggily. "What's happening?"

"Could you come with me? I have a surprise for you."

He took her hand and led her up to the steps to the western battlement. Halfway up, he produced a cloth he promptly tied over her eyes.

"Hey, what are you doing?" she asked, her tone full of eager anticipation.

"It's a secret," Nathaniel chuckled, taking her hand and helping her navigate the stairs. With a gentle hand, he removed the blindfold, and she gasped as her eyes drank in the magnificent panorama of colors displayed by the setting sun.

"What a stunning sight to behold!" she said in awe.

"Indeed, you are!" Nathaniel said from behind her.

She turned to see Jacoby and Allai'nn, both smiling, behind a kneeling Nathaniel.

"Lani Belain, my love for you fills every corner of my heart. In times of hardship and happiness alike, you've been my refuge and my strength. My dearest, will you give me your hand in marriage and reign as my beloved queen by my side?"

Lani's eyes grew wide, and her breath caught in her throat, and for a heartbeat, she couldn't respond. By answer, she leaped into Nathaniel's arms, swarming him with kisses.

"I guess that's a yes," Jacoby said, as he and Allai'nn congratulated the happy couple.

Producing a beautiful ring of garnets and diamonds, Nathaniel placed it on Lani's finger and announced, "Percival found this in my late mother's things. I think she'd be pleased you had it."

As tears flowed freely down her face, Lani spoke, her voice thick with emotion. "I love it!"

Three weeks later, the palace played host to a spectacular triple wedding, a joyous occasion where three couples--Horatio and Ruby, the healing Blue Ivy and Rue, and King Nathaniel and Lady Lani—exchanged vows, sealed their union with a kiss, and then emerged to tumultuous cheers and expressions of jubilation from the myriad of visiting royals, friends, and witnesses. A vibrant and enthusiastic welcome awaited Nathaniel and Lani as they stepped into the palace vestibule; a cheering throng of soldiers and militia filled the space, their excitement palpable. Bowing low, the king then waved to the cheering crowd, bursting with a happiness he had never experienced.

He raised his hands to silence the exuberant citizens and said, "Today marks a new beginning for Tabor." Nathaniel hesitated while a group of palace stewards rolled cask after cask of royal ale down for the populace to enjoy. "Let us celebrate together our rebirth, for tomorrow, we rebuild Tabor into a power never seen since the time Whitestar reigned!" Cheers exploded from the joyous crowd, and they rushed forward to partake of the spirits.

Nathaniel and Lani led their wedding guests into the grand dining hall, revealing breathtaking decorations the palace staff had prepared for the reception. A lavish display of flowers and elaborately tiered candles adorned the walls and tables. An enormous banquet, stacked high with a cornucopia of cured meats, roast hog, vegetables of all sorts, and fruits, crowded two enormous tables at the front. With minstrels playing cheerful festive tunes and wine flowing abundantly, joyous dining and drinking marked the celebrations for the marriages and the survival of Tabor. After the three couples had enjoyed their first dance, Nathaniel broke away from accepting heartfelt congratulations to enjoy the moment. He saw Jacoby to the side, in deep conversation with Princess Laurel, and his mouth curled into a grin. At least for tonight, all is right in the world.

The party raged on for hours, spilling out into the streets. The joyous celebration continued with drunken soldiers and jubilant citizens marching along, singing and cheering as they marched through the city.

As the celebration inside the palace waned, Nathaniel invited the Brotherhood, Friend, Baldur, Kings Polaris and Goldbrier, King Carron of Mar Nâpor, King Acorn of Erewhon, and Traveler to the smoking room for brandy. Although King Tawn of the Meadowland and Prince Michael of Whispering Haven were noticeably missing from the event, they sent written messages of congratulations. As Percival completed pouring brandy for everyone, Jacoby then raised his glass in a celebratory gesture of a toast.

"I want to make a toast," Jacoby said, already tipsy from the evening's celebration. "To my little brother Nathaniel. A valiant warrior, a beloved king, a jubilant husband, and an even better man." The tall warrior hesitated and wiped tears from his eyes. "And in my mind, despite the empty palace coffers, he's the richest man in Tabor!"

"Hear! Hear!" A chorus of agreement arose from the others, accompanied by the delicate clinking of their crystal snifters against one another.

An hour later, Jacoby and Grull walked Nathaniel to the royal bedchamber. They both gave Nathaniel a warm embrace, then gave a playful nudge toward the door. The two friends walked arm in arm down the corridor, tears of joy welling in their eyes.

"I can't believe it," Grull said. "So much has happened since we left Streamside. And our lad has grown into a fine king, and an even better man."

Jacoby smiled wistfully. "He is the best of us

ACKNOWLEDGEMENTS

As always, I have many people to thank for completing and editing this book.

I want to thank Lori for always supporting my efforts, helping to edit, and for being my rock.

In addition, I want to thank my brother Kevin for his editing, idea suggestions, and collaboration from day one.

REMINDER TO READERS

If you enjoyed The King Returns, please take a moment to write an Amazon review!

Dr. W. Penn White is a retired physician and author of the Brotherhood of the Black Arrow trilogy. When not writing, he has worked as a Leadership Coach, podcast researcher, and app content developer. He lives in coastal Alabama with his wife and two miniature schnauzers.

Kevin White, Dr. White's brother, is a linguist, editor, and author of two non-fiction works, and the Dark Elf Summoned series. He lives in Decatur, Ga, with his cat, Myles.

ALSO, BY DR. WHITE

The Prince of Tabor—

Book 1 Brotherhood of the

Black Arrow

Tabor's Savior—Book 2

Brotherhood of the Black Arrow